ENEMY OF

ALLEN A. KNOLL, PUBLISHERS

THE AVERAGE

Margaret Nicol

Allen A. Knoll, Publishers, 200 West Victoria Street, Santa Barbara, CA 93101
© 1998 by Allen A. Knoll, Publishers
All rights reserved. Published 1998
Printed in the United States of America

First Edition

05 04 03 02 01 00 99 98   5 4 3 2 1

Author's Note: This book is based on the life of a woman much like the main character. Though there are many biographical elements in the book, it is a work of fiction, not biography. However, the liberties taken in storytelling did not alter any of the characters' natures as I saw them.
    —M.N.

Library of Congress Cataloging-in-Publication Data

Nicol, Margaret, date.
    Enemy of the average / by Margaret Nicol. – 1st ed.
        p.   cm.
    ISBN 1-888310-60-X (alk. paper)
    I. Title.
PS3564.I333E5   1998
813'.54–dc21   98-13283
                                                         CIP

On the Dust Jacket:
"Le Grand Escalier de L'Opéra"
By LeRoy Neiman
Copyright © 1975 LeRoy Neiman, Inc.
Used by permission. All rights reserved.

CONTENTS

ENEMY OF THE AVERAGE

Mimi: She's certainly
          well dressed.

Rudolfo: It's the angels
          who go nude.

          —*La Bohème*

OVERTURE

Arkel: For since your coming, we have lived here only in whispering around a closed room. And really I pitied you, Mélisande.

I observed you, you were there, careless, perhaps, but with the strange and wild air of someone who awaited always a great misfortune, by sunlight, in a beautiful garden.

—*Pelléas et Mélisande*

McKelsey Mortuary was an upscale undertaker. Two attendants were sent to pick up the body of Hanna Mazurka at her small house in her grand garden now known as Hanna Mazurka Nirvana. They were dressed in striped gray pants and tails, the outfits topped with silk top hats. The young men looked uncomfortable in this attire in the unusual heat of the windy, bright March day, but Hanna would have been pleased; she had loved to dress up in her younger days.

She had not come into this world upscale—she had nothing to do with that—but that's the way she was going out. That she had seen to.

The formal mourning clothes on the attendants were not a perfect fit. They were seldom used at the mortuary, and attendants came and went, and one size, regrettably, did not fit all.

The undertaker's attendants drove through the open verdigris main gate and past many plants they had never seen before—and not just one or two of each, but dozens massed together: palms, ferns, fruit trees, bamboos, agaves, aloes—sometimes hundreds of the smaller cacti and succulents. Madame Mazurka had planted and nurtured them on her forty-acre estate.

It was like moving through a cocoon of your own, the tall, bunched trees shutting out neighbors, cars, and even the sky. The sun was shining, but you didn't know it inside Madame Mazurka's Nirvana.

The hot Santa Anas were blowing, bending the trees to the bellows of those evil winds.

"It's a damn jungle," Alex said. He was the newcomer to the trade. Bert, the driver, had dozens of corpse pickups under his belt.

Bert said the old lady had put almost fifty years in the place. "Spent millions, I hear. A real nut." Bert peered out the window beside him. "Charlie sez she made a personal request. It's in her will, I hear. Monkey suits on the undertakers and nobody looks at her after she's gone."

"How we gonna not look at her?"

"Yeah," Bert said. "She couldn't stop them looking at her when she was alive, how can she stop them dead?"

"Who'd want to look at her dead?"

"Yeah. Geez, it's hot as hell. Stupidest damn thing. I mean, how's she gonna know we got tails on or sweats?"

"No way." Alex shook his head.

"'She's a legend,' Charlie said. Doesn't that frost you? Opera singer or something.'Treat her with respect,' he said, like she wasn't dead or anything. Like we might hurt her feelings—we weren't suitably respectful."

"It's a job," Alex conceded.

"Holeee hell, will you *look* at this place!" Bert groaned. "Need a bolo knife you want to get anywhere in here." Then his back stiffened as he assumed the pose and diction of one of those altruistic motion-picture African tribesmen who spoke perfect English. "Sa-a-ave the white woman, doctor!"

Alex laughed. "Hey, you do that pretty good."

"Yeah," Bert said. "Well, it's too late to save this white woman. I hear she's a hundred years old."

It was a long drive from the gate to the house.

It seemed an eternity before the long black hearse pulled up in front of a two-story house of the Spanish pastiche mode.

"Well, there it is. *Pink*," Bert said, making a face. "Needs a paint job."

"Yeah."

"We go to this small one on the right."

"What's in the big one?"

"Her junk, I hear. I don't think we'll be looking. I don't know about you, but I can't get out of this creepy place fast enough. Let's go."

"Hey," Alex said, "you think the place is haunted?"

Bert considered for a moment, dropping his lower lip. "Sure, why not?"

Alex shuddered.

"What the hell is that stuff?" he asked, pointing to the strange, demented-looking plants that twisted and turned to the second-story windows of the big house, then twisted and turned back to the ground, as though they didn't like what they had seen up there. They were *Euphorbia ingens* in their tortured form—common name candelabra, but they looked like drunken candelabras.

"Dunno," Bert said. "Some kind of crazy cactus, I guess."

Alex and Bert got out of the hearse and opened the back door to remove a collapsible gurney.

The one-story structure had the same faded pink-wash paint as the main structure—separated from it by a patio twenty or so feet wide and stuffed with forty feet's worth of belongings, from outdoor furniture to driftwood, potted plants, cuttings from plants, planter mix, cardboard boxes and trash cans, all in need of emptying. Through an arch out back, they could see a couple acres of grass bordered by large palms, oaks and an enormous cedar tree.

The attendant's tactful knock at the door was answered so quickly by the face and form of the madame's longtime secretary-companion, Phyllis Keck, Bert thought she must have been standing behind the door waiting. She was shrouded in the darkness of the room; she looked like a cadaver herself, and her long-faced, morose

3

expression added to the gloom. The young men thought she was mourning her mistress, but it was the woman's natural expression.

Alex had never smelled anything like the stench that hit them. The closest Bert had come was when he picked up a man who had been dead two weeks without anyone knowing it.

Alex and Bert stepped inside with the folded gurney. The secretary nodded toward the bedroom to their left, where open double doors framed the deceased.

Madame's gray nightgown had once been colorful, as had her hair—now splayed like a harridan's in every direction on her stained pillow. Linen probably hadn't been changed in a year, Alex thought. She was the ugliest person he had ever seen. Bert had seen worse. As if reading their minds, Phyllis Keck said, "She doesn't look it now, but she was the most beautiful woman in the world, in her day."

The men didn't argue. They were eager to get back out into the fresh air, but saw no space to set up the gurney.

"Just clear a place there at the foot of the bed," secretary-companion Phyllis said. "It's all junk anyway." Phyllis was obeying the madame beyond death in her refusal to touch the deceased's belongings. Phyllis's eyes glazed over as she stared at the stash of jewels by the bed. "Avaricious she was," she said, and started to sniffle.

Alex was still. He didn't know what avaricious meant. Bert looked down at piles of what looked like driftwood, dead plants—some in pots, some not.

They unfolded the gurney in the small clearing at the foot of the bed and gingerly lifted the deceased onto it.

The awful smell had commandeered all their senses at first, but now they noticed the woman had lived as the quintessential pack rat, and they soon discovered the smell was uneaten food, as well as a badly soiled, unwashed body. Again, the secretary read their minds. "She wouldn't let me clean up. Her sense of smell was completely gone. She was very bossy that way. I used to argue with her, but I just wore out." She pursed her lips. "I'm surprised she didn't kill me first."

The undertakers saw great piles of jewels, diamonds, glorious settings of every kind of precious stone they could imagine. Both sides of the bed were piled high with her prized possessions mixed with the trash. Parts of the living room were covered in boxes of papers and Oriental-looking artifacts. Jeweled eggs were in another corner, carousel horses (five or six) crammed against the fireplace.

Secretary Phyllis turned her head from the undertakers, and from the dark loneliness of her soul. "Wouldn't let me move anything either. Wanted her belongings close at hand to the end. She got increasingly paranoid—afraid if I touched anything, I would steal it." She shook her head at the woeful injustice. "Feisty to the last, she was."

Alex looked out the window as though hoping he could bring the fresh air inside.

"Some garden she has here," Alex said nervously, causing Bert a touch of indigestion. He wanted to get out of there, not waste time on the secretary.

"Oh, my, yes," she said. "It is world famous. There is just nothing like it. Hundreds of the same plants—all kinds of things. She has the largest cycad collection in the world. People come from all over to see her garden. Over forty years she worked on it. Loved to show it to people while she could still walk. She had groups here all the time—used to flirt with the men up until the last—and no matter how many gardens they had seen, they always went away impressed."

Alex didn't know what cycads were, but he sensed Bert didn't want him to ask.

Alex looked down at his morning's work and didn't see how she could have done anything, let alone build this astonishing garden. But he knew from his vocational experience, life did that to people—ground them down to insignificance at the end, no matter how famous or important they were in their lifetimes. Ashes to ashes for sure.

As Alex and Bert went out the door with the body, Phyllis said, her long, morose face unaltered, "No, she doesn't look like much now, but in her day there was just no one like her; no one at all. Got six handsome husbands," she said. "And rich too…" She got a far-off look in her eyes. "*Very* rich…" And now she is gone, she thought, and I am alone and I don't know whether to laugh or cry.

Outside, the evil Santa Anas were kicking up, and McKelsey's attendants were headed into the wind, their tails standing straight out behind them, like birds poised for flight; one hand holding onto their top hats, the other attending to the business of the gurney.

The sheet covering Madame Mazurka was flapping like the maid was shaking it to get out the dust. Contrary to the wish she expressed in her will, she was visible to all the world.

It was as though the gods were showing her who was boss at last.

After the attendants had loaded the body of Madame Hanna Mazurka and were driving down the long, dark, many-curved driveway out of the garden, Alex said to Bert, "Did you *see* all that stuff?"

Bert drove more carefully with the extra responsibility of the dead woman in back. He nodded.

"Millions of bucks' worth of stuff in that filth," Alex said. The experience had agitated him.

"Yeah."

"Geez, what will they do with all that stuff?"

"That's nothing, I hear the big house is full too," Bert said. "They say that's why she had to live in the little house—the big one was full."

"Geez. She musta been some babe."

"Musta."

ACT I

THE VIRGIN

Julien: Because they gave you birth do they think they possess the right to imprison your golden youth?

♭   ♭   ♭

Your will, from this time forth, is that of a woman, and is as good as theirs. You are a woman; you can, you must act.

—*Louise*

Madame Hanna Mazurka
remembers

THE VIRGIN
Brest Litovsk, Poland

"In Poland there are only two classes: the aristocrats and the peasants. We weren't peasants, so we must have been aristocrats."

Hanna's mother, Novella Winaski, was an only child in the days when only children were looked upon as freaks of nature.

In the case of Novella's parents, Leo and Berthe, Novella's lonely status was not for want of trying. Novella's father was built for constant conception; his wife was not built for childbearing.

One or two stillborns and count-less miscarriages didn't deter Leo, but the sole viable fruit of his loins was Novella. She was a scrawny child and was suc-cored and nurtured accordingly. Some said she was spoiled rotten, but when you have so many misfires, you are bound to coddle the flickering flame.

So Novella grew up pampered, which in her case was not conducive to the development of graciousness. Though there was a spark in her personality, it too easily became incendiary. When she approached marriageable age, there was not a lot of interest in participating in what promised to be a major conflagration.

Novella herself was cool to the idea of marriage, reasoning that anyone who would have her must be deficient in the attributes that might stir her interest.

Her father thought she was cute as a bug in a rug, but worried that her only chance of a union would be a prearranged marriage to someone who had not experienced her rapier tongue.

Though Novella seemed perfectly content to stay at home, her mother was eager to see the last of her. Berthe gave her husband no rest until the matter of Novella's nuptials was settled.

Hanna's grandfather (Novella's father), Leo, considered all the possibilities and decided economic ensnarement was their only salvation. He would have loved to offer a generous dowry, but they were not rich. Yet he had an idea. He invited his neighbor, Walther Oleska, over one blustery, cold winter evening to share the warmth of a schnapps.

Oh, yes, it got cold in Poland. Bone-biting cold. The locals said it was so cold you couldn't talk outdoors because the words froze before they cleared your mouth.

For Leo Winaski, cold was schnapps weather, and he banked on Walther Oleska sharing that feeling.

No human body could have come out alive had it been cut up as often as Poland in the eighteenth century. The nineteenth brought Napoleon and all the financial burdens requisite to keep him and his armies in the style to which they had become accustomed.

When the smoke had cleared, about all the great Bonaparte left the Polish people was one more half-Polish person. The little warrior, with the big libido, had lain with a Polish princess and the little bastard arrived through the courtesy of her womb.

Sooner or later Russia got back in the fray, cementing their dominance of the neighboring Poles with wholesale exportations of this world's goods.

Surprisingly it was a fortuitous time to be a peasant, with the focus of animus on the landed gentry, who, it was felt, were getting too big for their britches. The peasants were adroit at humble pie. It was, you might say, genetically predetermined.

Some of those peasants even found themselves small rural landowners when the government decreed they should become free-holders no matter how long their tenure had been.

The Oleskas and the Winaskis had been the beneficiaries of that startling opportunity. Small parcels, to be sure, but enough, nonetheless, to keep body and soul together.

Leo Winaski's kitchen table was in the dull glow of the kerosene lamp, which was used only in emergencies—homemade candles provided most of the light in the Winaski household. The house was built of rough-sawn timbers, not unlike the Oleska farm-house across the field.

They were both plain-spoken, rugged men with farming bred in their bones. Neither was versed in the niceties of social inter-course so Leo served up the schnapps and took a preparatory slug.

"Walther my man, we see too little of you here. It is good to share a schnapps with you." He tilted his glass to his lips in salute, then drained the remaining contents.

Walther followed suit. He was a reticent man, not given to expansive gestures or extravagant verbosity. He simply nodded.

"You know, just the other day it occurred to me we had something in common." He paused to let his neighbor supply the answer.

"Yes?" was all he said.

"You know what it is—"

"The farms?"

"Yes, and something else."

Walther frowned. He sought, without success, to supply the similarity sought.

Leo helped him. "Come now, Walther, surely you know—our *children*!"

"Our children?" Walther was confused. "You have one daughter; I have three."

"And a son—" Leo quickly supplied.

"Yesss—" Walther said, still perplexed. "And you have no sons."

"Give you any ideas?" Leo asked, bouncing up an eyebrow.

"Noooo," Walther drew it out like the wind howling outside.

"Come, Walther, surely you have thought of marriage for your son."

"Marriage? Augustus? No, I had not," he said, mystified. "He is young yet—and young for his years on top of it. I am more concerned finding husbands for the girls."

"Oh, there it is," Leo said, grandly. "That is my thought exactly!"

"You have someone in mind for my daughters?"

"No—for *my* daughter."

"Yes? For Novella? It is possible? Who?"

"Think, Walther—think."

"I cannot."

"But have we not just discussed your very son?"

"My son? He is far too immature for marriage."

Leo frowned. Surely Walther was being cagey. He couldn't be that obtuse to the obvious suggestion on the floor. "I was thinking, Walther, here we are, side by side—two farms. I have only the one heiress, you have a son roughly her age..." He dangled the thought.

Walther said, "Oh, my dear Leo. They are like oil and water. Your Novella is a bold, outspoken, bright woman. She is older not only in years, but in wisdom and maturity. You are kind, I'm sure, to think of Augustus in this regard..." he paused, putting his teeth to his lower lip, then shaking his head—"but, no, it would be out of the question. There is nothing in common there."

"The land is in common," Leo said, angry that his proposition was not meeting with agreement.

"The land? You are offering your land for my poor Augustus? You can't be serious. How would you live?"

Leo shook his head good-naturedly at the thick skull of his neighbor. More schnapps was poured. Leo set the example by downing his in one draught. Walther had the vague, but uncomfortable, feeling that Leo was trying to snooker him and he should remain sober and on guard. But the schnapps was appealing and it warmed his cold body with heavenly affection.

"Not now, my friend," Leo said, "when I'm dead and gone to my everlasting rest."

"What good will that do me? I will be long gone."

Leo chuckled and filled the glasses. He drank his, Walther did not. "True, I shall outlive you decades. I am strong as an ox and you are a pussycat."

Walther stiffened his back before he realized his neighbor was kidding.

"It is for the children I am thinking."

"Ah, but no," Walther said at last, "it is an impossible match. Your daughter, no offense intended, would eat my poor Augustus alive. He is a sensitive soul—not cut out to run a farm." He threw up his hands. "But what can you do? He is my only son." Walther took his schnapps to his lips and sipped a portion of it. "Sometimes I think I have four daughters."

It was not a question that called for an answer, as surely there was none. Leo sat back and held the bottle of schnapps to his nose. With a deep breath, he drew into his lungs the strong odor of the alcohol, as if to clear his sinuses.

"Sometimes, my dear neighbor, I think we get so caught up in our work we can see nothing but hungry pigs and rocky furrows in the cornfields. In the winter, we freeze to death; in the summer, we burn with sweat and we stink of the manure we must shovel. Not a very pretty picture, eh? But it is our life—our world. To save our sanity, we must sometimes stop to think of the future. We want better for our children while we must fight just to hold our heads above water."

Leo slowly poured another schnapps in his glass and carefully topped off Walther's as though the extra care would expand the diminishing supply.

"Yes, my friend," Leo said, "between us men, I know my daughter's reputation. And I will not pretend it has been easy. And Novella is perfectly willing to go to her grave a maiden lady." Here he bent over to whisper to Walther—"At least that is what she would have us believe. Me, I am skeptical. But her mother won't hear of it. Wants her out of the house in no uncertain terms."

"And this is what you would wish on my poor Augustus?"

"Man to man, Walther, huh—can I speak frankly?" He took a deep breath over the schnapps glass.

"Of course."

"Have you thought what the prospects would be for your son's marriage?"

"Prospects?" He frowned. "Not very great, I'm afraid."

"Yes. With all due respect, I would reluctantly have to agree."

Walther bristled. "You think your daughter's chances are better?"

"No, no, certainly not," Leo hastened to reassure his neighbor. "But that is exactly my point, we kill two birds with one stone. Solve two problem children—and combine the farms in one family"—he paused for dramatic effect, then added—"the combination to be handed down for generations in *your* family name!"

"But, but," Walther protested weakly, "it is *so* impossible."

Leo sighed. "But, Walther, my friend, think of the two farms together. Separate we struggle. Together there is strength. If I may say so, my topsoil is superior—you have the better grazing land. Together, ah, yes, *together* they would make a formidable farm."

Walther studied his neighbor. His proposal *was* intriguing. Walther could not deny the truth of it—if only he were not getting his son in an impossible situation for his later benefit that he would earn in the coin of sorrow. "How old is your Novella?" Walther asked.

"Twenty-seven—soon we will begin shaving that a bit. Now she is twenty-seven."

"My Augustus is not yet twenty-one—"

"So? Am I wrong in saying he could use a steady, mature hand at the helm?"

"You are not wrong. But even if their ages were the same—" he shook his head and clucked his tongue, "Augustus is an innocent—so young for his years."

"Ah, but you cannot tell me the fires don't burn in him—those fires we men understand only too well—the lightning lust of the young man for the woman."

Walther seemed surprised. He lifted his eyebrows. "I honestly don't know—I see no sign of it—"

"He does know what it's all about, doesn't he? The birds and the bees, boys and girls and babies and such?"

"I don't know."

"Because my Berthe will expect a lot of grandbabies in the bargain—to compensate for the difficulty she had."

Walther was uneasy with this personal presumption. He was

a man satisfied to keep his personal thoughts to himself.

Leo tried to understand his neighbor's reticence—he miscalculated: "If you don't want to talk to him about such matters, I'm sure we can count on Novella to show him where it goes!"—and warmed with the alcohol and his unwarranted optimism, Leo pounded the table with his ham hand and roared with laughter so loudly the two women cowering in the next room shuddered, but took it as a sign that all was going well with the negotiations.

Walther drowned his embarrassment in one last schnapps, then said, "I thank you for your proposal and your hospitality. Good schnapps. I will talk it over with Augustus and his mother—" He was on his feet, a bit unsteadily.

Leo smiled and rose also. "My advice would be to think about that nice piece of ground that will come into your family in perpetuity," he said. "I wouldn't ask the boy, I'd tell him. He'll get used to the idea before you know it. If you ask him, he could get negative in his head. Much harder to overcome in the long run—well—good luck!"

Walther went out into the cold night convinced the temperature had dropped at least ten degrees in spite of the schnapps.

It was a quarrelsome marriage, fraught with the inevitable disagreements that two people of such widely disparate natures are bound to have.

And so, it was not unusual that Momma and Poppa were fighting again. And when *they* fought, the sparks that flew blinded them to all else. They didn't even notice their middle child march past them in the parlor straight to the kitchen to pick up the biggest, ugliest knife she could find. It was probably overkill, a lot bigger than she needed to do the job, but it was dramatic. Zdenka Oleska was dramatic.

At thirteen, her face was owl-like, her chin coming to a decided point. The eyes were black and set in milk saucers. Her essence was strongly of the Polish countryside, but her spirit was of the world. Her mother often remarked on Zdenka's spunk, calling it pigheadedness.

Augustus and Novella were dressed up, as for dinner on Sundays and other special occasions—rainy days among them. In their finest clothes they looked out of place—as though constraining circumstances had caused them to be placed in some strangers' garments, and the apparent, sudden elevation of rank embarrassed them. Theirs were skins accustomed to rough wool and muslin, not silks and satins. They looked to Zdenka as nothing so much as pretenders to a throne of plenty on which they would never sit.

All the more strange their argument, Zdenka thought.

"You are spoiling that girl rotten," Novella was shouting. "You treat her like a princess and already she *thinks* she *is* a princess."

"She is to me!" he shouted back.

"Go on! Ruin her life! Fill her with impossible expectations. You'll be sorry when you see the mess you made. When she comes running to you to clean it up, well, I tell you, I will not be here to do the dirty work. That is a job I will leave for you!"

"You will *not!*"

"Yes, I will," Novella fumed. "Brash, know-it-all women are doomed to eternal spinsterhood. You will someday mark my words."

Augustus paused and stared at his wife, reining in his anger for the more effective sotto voce he saved and savored for its explosive effect. "You should know," he said quietly, and she exploded as if on cue.

As Zdenka marched back holding the knife upright in front of her nose like a samurai warrior, the drama was lost on Augustus and Novella Oleska. They were so intent on outshouting one another other, they didn't even notice their thirteen-year-old make that horrid face as only she could—the nose and cheeks scrunched up, and the tip of the tongue showing, ready to burst from Zdenka's twisted mouth. The gestures were acrimonious, outsized on one so young.

Augustus and Novella hadn't the slightest idea Zdenka, princess or not, was on her way to her room to slash her wrists. They hadn't even stopped shouting when she slammed her door.

The small house of Augustus and Novella Oleska and their

19

three children was country Polish—sturdy enough to keep most of
the elements out most of the time and nothing so fancy it would
cause the neighbors to accuse them of putting on airs. It was two
floors, almost square, with two windows top and bottom on each
side. It had been painted white at one time, but time and the elements had turned it gray. The outhouse was reached through the
kitchen in back. It nestled forlornly among intimidating poplar trees
and in the shadows looked like a salt-box that had lost its salt.

The barn was in back, with the pigsty on the side, and
behind that the fields they farmed, beyond which livestock roamed
and foraged.

It was a workingman's farm and the Oleskas were working
people.

Outside, it was raining again, and the gloom cut through the
gray walls of the dark house and right down to the bone. Augustus
couldn't work the farm in the rain, and his wife, Novella, was never
comfortable with him underfoot in the daytime.

Zdenka was a daddy's girl. But when he fought with
Momma, Zdenka hated their fighting so much it made her red in the
face.

The child slid into the straight-back chair at her little desk in
her room, gently setting the knife down on the surface, next to a
well-loved stuffed bear whose amber coat had darkened from
Zdenka's zesty solacing. Zdenka looked at her wrist, so white and
smooth, and suddenly realized she didn't know how to do this. She'd
heard of an old woman in the village who had "slit her wrists," so she
thought it was only a matter of cutting the skin. But what if it didn't
work? Or worse, what if it did?

Why did Momma and Poppa have to fight? Sometimes they
seemed so awkward it was as if they didn't know how to be parents.
Augustus wasn't much taller than his wife and he had hair coming
down the side of his face and pointing toward his mouth, as though
without it he wouldn't know where it was.

Momma looked like a mouse in that silk dress, with her little
head sprouting from yards and yards of black silk. But Novella
Oleska had backbone. Too much, perhaps, for Augustus's liking.
Some of his relatives thought a man who could cry must have something wrong with him. No one could put his finger on why Augustus

hadn't succeeded as a farmer. He was a very nice man, considerate of the feelings of others, generous (within his means) with the workers.

Life in Poland when Zdenka was growing up was fingers-to-the-bone. There was little margin for error in the economic struggle to make ends meet on the farm. The disasters of nature could set you so far back you might never catch up. More than once Augustus doubted the benefits of owning a farm. It was a bucolic existence, but not without tensions. The Poles had been kicked around for centuries by the Prussians, the Russians, the Austrians and even those peace-loving Swedes. It couldn't help but force the character of the Poles into a stance of defensive inferiority.

Zdenka, being the only girl, had a room to herself. She was the only one in her family who didn't give in to feelings of inferiority. Her older brother, Felix—he was fifteen already—and Dimitri, the baby, who was six, had to share a room.

She hated boys, but she tolerated her brothers. Felix didn't seem bothered by the fighting and Dimitri didn't understand it.

Zdenka picked up the knife and tested its sharpness with her thumb, which she quickly retracted. She looked at her wrists again. She decided to experiment first with a gingerly dab of the blade on her pale-white skin. She touched it quickly to her wrist then withdrew it just as quickly.

Nothing happened. Then she drew the blade quickly across the vulnerable skin and saw the blood rise to the surface in rivulets which joined together to form a gently flowing stream.

21

A sinking vision swam in Zdenka's head. It was the color of the rain outside. The walls of her room collapsed on her. She was drowning in death. She screamed a high, shrieking, sustained scream, then dropped the knife, which hit the floor with a resonating thud. The next instant, she swooned and fell on the floor with a heavier, but duller, thud.

The scream pierced the fighting downstairs. There was a sudden silence in the house.

It seemed like an eternity before Augustus called out— "Zdenka? Zdenka! Babushka!"

His feet pounding the stairs sounded like horses on a stampede.

He threw open the door, his eyes riveting in terror on the

lump of daughter on the floor, a modest trickle of blood making a damp red spot on her hooked rug.

Augustus gasped for air and felt suddenly as if he would himself collapse. His wife, Novella, burst through the door and groaned, giving strength to Augustus. Together, they fell to their knees beside Zdenka. The knife lay beside her.

"Lucky she didn't fall on it," Poppa said.

Momma took Zdenka's bleeding wrist in her hand and examined it.

"She's still breathing?" Poppa asked anxiously.

"Oh, yes—" Momma said. "It's a scratch only. She must have fainted at the sight of her own blood." Felix and Dimitri had appeared at the door, and Momma instructed them to fetch some water and clean cloths.

Poppa didn't seem to know what to do. He wanted to cradle Zdenka in his arms, but he feared it might make her bleed more. So he settled for groaning, "Oh, my Babushka, why? Why? Why? Oh..."

When Felix came back with the cloths and the basin full of water, Momma cleaned the wound and put the cold, wet cloth on Zdenka's forehead. She began to stir, and Poppa bent toward Zdenka, then circled her in his arms and rocked her back and forth. The house seemed to exchange its underpinnings for rubber and Zdenka felt like it was rocking back and forth under her.

"What'd she do?" Felix asked.

"An accident," Poppa said.

"What was she doing with that knife up here?" Felix asked.

"Hush," Momma said. "Leave us be, please. Go back to your room."

The boys didn't move.

"Leave us be!" she commanded in that voice mothers save for emergencies.

"Come on, Dimitri," Felix said to his little brother. "We aren't wanted here."

"Is Denky all right?" the six-year-old asked his big brother.

"She's all right. Just got a little scratch on her wrist," Felix said, and the boys went back to their room.

Slowly, like drifting fog, Zdenka's eyes opened. She felt like she was treading water. Poppa hugged her to him. "My baby, my

Babushka," he cried, "what must be going on in that little mind of yours?"

Zdenka's eyes darted about the room, then she closed them again. Her father wailed, "My Princess!" The eyes opened. Mother spoke.

"Are you wanting to play God, child? You don't like the natural course of things—birth, death, not good enough for you? *You* want to decide."

"Novella! So harsh," Augustus said.

"It didn't work," Zdenka said, as though she had been cheated.

"No, it did not. You think God wants a thirteen-year-old? Not you apparently. But God wants to decide, He doesn't want some child interfering with his schedules."

"Oh, my Babushka," Poppa wailed. "You are so young. There is so much to live for."

"I don't want you to fight."

"No," Poppa said, "and that's good. So you don't fight. When we fight it is not you—you make your own life. You are a bright and beautiful child. You are a princess! You can do anything."

Momma talked to the lump of flesh in Augustus's arms. She tried to smooth the voice that was so often rough. "You will find some handsome man, and you will marry him and make him happy."

Zdenka gave her stout response, shaking her head.

"What? Why are you saying no?"

"Why should I make *him* happy? Why not he makes *me* happy?"

Momma shook her head. "Oh, lamb, you just don't understand the way of the world," she sighed. "But you will—I've no doubt of it, someday you will."

It was springtime and the opening buds sat lightly on the trees, like baby butterflies sunning their nascent wings. It was the warmest day since summer in a country famous for too-long winters. The rain had scrubbed the trees and grass clean, and the remaining droplets gleamed like shimmering crystals.

It was almost two miles to the Catholic girls' school. Zdenka usually walked the distance, but after her "incident" Augustus thought it best if he hitch up old Bess to the cart and drive his wounded daughter into town. It would be a good opportunity for an intimate talk.

In the small buggy, alone with her father, Zdenka was in her own pocket of heaven. The cut on her wrist remained unspoken of among them, but it was there in every look, every fragment of conversation. She looked so grown-up in her school uniform—the navy-blue skirt and jacket and the simple white blouse. But she had shown him how vulnerable she was.

"Are you going to be all right, Babushka?" he asked.

"I like when you call me Babushka," she said, pressing closer. He put his arm around his daughter and held her to his side.

Daughters were better than sons, Augustus thought, for fathers anyway. With girls you had more subtlety, more mystery, more devotion. Girls were more giving, more open, more anxious to please—altogether more rewarding, he thought.

He wanted to address Zdenka's dramatic action that caused such an upheaval in the household, but words failed him. He wanted to say, "Look here, Zdenka, one does not commit suicide every time one is unhappy." He might even speak philosophically—but would she understand or would she misconstrue—add a kind of celebrity to her action—would her small mind wrap around the incident as a powerful wedge to get her way in the future? With Zdenka, nothing was straightforward. Yet, he had to say *something*.

"Zdenka," he began with the shyness Zdenka instinctively felt was charming yet somehow a weakness, "we all have our problems. And sometimes they seem like we just can't stand them anymore."

"What are your problems, Poppa?"

He smiled in spite of himself. There she was, so young, and already turning his conversation back on himself. "My problems are not your problems. You can do nothing about them."

She pouted. "How do you know if you don't tell me what they are?"

"Oh, child…"

"Momma is your problem, isn't she?"

He flinched. "Today we are talking about *your* problems. When we get so unhappy with things, it is perhaps best to turn our problems over to the Lord."

"The Lord? What has He done for us so far?"

"He has given us the blessing of life. He has given Momma and me you and your brothers."

"Is He the same one who gave you Momma?"

25

"Child, child, you do not know the strains of being a mother…and wife," he added with a dropped voice. "The farm is a struggle. Sometimes it seems impossible. That is why we turn to the Lord, and that is why you must pray every day for His blessings."

"Pray? I have prayed very hard, Poppa. But my prayers don't work."

"What do you mean, they don't work?"

"I prayed every night for you and Momma to stop fighting, but you still fight."

"You must not lose your belief, child. It is very precious. It is sometimes all we have."

"I don't believe in make-believe." She was being contrary, Augustus thought, she doesn't really mean that.

"We must believe in something," he said.

Her little eyes seemed to throw off flashes of light. "I believe in you, Poppa."

So simple, so direct. It made him swell with pride. He wanted to argue—to set her mind on a higher being, but he had trouble framing the argument. She moved closer to him and he could feel her warm, trembling body beside him.

The clanking of the iron-wrapped wooden wheels on the rutted road gave Zdenka a strange feeling of security. A glow of closeness flowed between her and her poppa.

"Do you fight about me, Poppa?"

"Why do you ask such, child?"

"When you were arguing, I heard Momma call me a princess."

"Ah, yes. She complains I do not make you help her. But you *are* my princess, I argue. It is true I have not raised you to wash dishes and clean house. Someday you will have a maid to do the work. You will be a princess."

Zdenka frowned. "Momma says it is nonsense to want what you can't have."

"Perhaps," Poppa said, leaving no doubt his sympathies lay on the other side. "But we must have our dreams. We cannot survive without them."

"Then what if they don't come true?"

"You *make* them," Poppa said.

"How do you do that?"

"You imagine them in your mind."

Zdenka pondered the idea and decided reality was much better than imagination. But perhaps dreams were a beginning. "Do you dream, Poppa?"

"Ho!" He seemed surprised at the question. How was he to tell her he was a man who lived on his dreams? Should he puncture her innocence with the drudgery of his life? The killing work on the farm; the agony, the acrimony, the animosity of his marriage, they all demanded the salve of his dreams to see him through. But she had asked. He must not belittle her question.

"My dear Zdenka," he said, "how can I explain? When it rains, the mud gets in your shoes; when it's dry, sometimes I can hardly breathe from the dirt blowing in my nose. If I live to be a hundred, I will never get used to the smell of manure. Then I come in the house and Novella is on me about something." He paused and looked at the horse's ears in front of him. "I shouldn't complain—I don't mean to—I'm just trying to explain why you need your dreams. I dream all the time, Denky. It's how I get on."

Zdenka didn't understand how dreams could take the place of reality. "But, Poppa," she said, "don't you have to *have* something? Not just *think?*"

"Farming in Poland is no job for a normal person. It is existence only. There is no reward that makes the heart beat faster in excitement—no thrill of accomplishment, because just as soon as you begin to take some pride in a crop, God sends a drought that kills everything, and you have to eke out an existence on last year's canned food. Yet I must do it. How can I not? In the city, even jobs in the factories are hard to come by. And what is that? Twelve hours a day, seven days a week, rain or sun." He shook his head. "All around life is hard."

Zdenka didn't know what to think. *Her* life wasn't hard—and she didn't want it to be.

They rode for a moment in silence, each savoring the human warmth of the other.

Finally, Zdenka broke the spell. "Poppa?"

"Hm?"

"Momma isn't very nice to you, is she?"

It hit Augustus like a stabbing pain. She was so devastatingly accurate he thought his heart would crack open, pouring out all his resentments. Then he caught himself. Surely he could not expect sophistication from a thirteen-year-old.

He responded carefully, with halting speech. "Momma and I are different people. She is confident of her opinions, I am…less so of mine—as well as of hers. But I am the man of the house and so…though it is not always easy, I must act like it. Sometimes…that means a fight."

Zdenka's ears were perked. She took it in with the seriousness of an equal confidant. She thought about it for a moment, then as Augustus stopped the horse at the church-school grounds, she suddenly said, "If Momma ever goes away I could be the momma."

Before Augustus could catch his breath to disabuse her of that notion, she had given his cheek a quick kiss and jumped down off the cart, clutching her books and paper-sack lunch to her navy-blue jacket, and run into the schoolyard to look for her friend, Katrina.

Poppa watched his Zdenka disappear around the corner and sat there for a long moment staring at that corner, as if he might find there some answer to the riddle of his life.

Zdenka waited behind the corner for the sound of the wheels retreating on the cobblestone road. Then she watched until her father and his poor cart with the swayback mare were out of sight. The aura of poverty it gave off embarrassed her and she was afraid her schoolmates would make fun of her.

The ride home was slow and ponderous. It was as though the old mare sensed her master's mood, and at her age was not in a rush to get *any*where.

When Augustus was over the hill, Zdenka ran back to the street to await the grand arrival of Katrina with her elegant coach with *two* healthy horses.

While she was waiting for Katrina, a pair of girls from town came up the street, swinging their school books in synchronization. "What are you waiting for?" Alma, the leader, asked Zdenka.

"For Katrina. She's coming in her coach. I just love to see it."

"Hah! *Two* horses. She's such a show-off."

"You would be too if you had a coach like that."

"Sister lets her get away with murder," Alma said, "just because she's rich."

"So? Her father gives enough to the school so poor dopes like you can go here."

"And you!"

"So, get rich," Zdenka suggested, shrugging her shoulders.

"Why don't you?"

"I'm going to."

Alma didn't fancy the exchange and, in parting, stuck out her tongue.

There were frogs in Zdenka's stomach kicking up a ruckus when she saw Katrina's coach with two white horses approaching the shadow of the high church steeple. Zdenka loved shadows because shadows meant sunshine, and today the churchyard was taking a bath in gorgeous yellow sunshine.

When the coach came through the sunlight its gold-leaf fili-gree looked like melting butter, and Zdenka thought she would run over and lick it off the coach. When it was parked in the shadow, the gold lost its luster, but Zdenka didn't lose her enthusiasm.

Katrina alighted to the salute of her driver, who was dressed in a gray silk top hat and a greatcoat. She tried to hide the fancy lunch basket Clara the cook had given her. It had a pink ribbon and pale-blue fabric covering the gourmet morsels inside.

Katrina was a chubby girl with pudgy hands and puffy cheeks. Her body was a lightly filled balloon; her hair was severely bolted to her head in two tight pigtails, making it appear Katrina was wearing an uncomfortably tight helmet.

"It's so embarrassing," Katrina muttered as Zdenka fell in step beside her.

"What is?" Zdenka asked. She was holding her arm stiffly, as though it were held by an invisible sling.

"The coach, this basket. Everything! I tell Momma I want to be like everybody else, but it's just no use. She says we are what we are and we aren't going to apologize for it."

"Phew—what's to apologize for?"

"Here,"—Katrina thrust her lunch basket into Zdenka's hands without Zdenka compromising too much the position of her stiff arm. She recovered from the shock in a moment and gladly gave

Katrina her paper sack.

"I want to be rich and you want to be poor," Zdenka said. "I'll change places anytime you want."

"Hah, you wouldn't like it, believe me," Katrina said, pouting. "Most people are poor and I'm tired of being different!"

Why would she think that? Zdenka wondered.

Katrina was in a grumpy mood. "I wish he would let me off down the street," she said. "It's so embarrassing."

"Don't you dare get off down the street. I love to see the carriage. It's the best thing about this school."

Zdenka hoisted her arm a tad, hoping Katrina would ask her what was wrong with it, but Katrina didn't even ask why Zdenka had missed school.

"Don't worry. My poppa won't permit it. He's afraid something might happen to his precious."

"Might it?" Zdenka giggled.

Katrina rolled her eyes.

"Guess what?" Zdenka said.

"What?"

"I did it."

"Did what?"

Zdenka got a gleam in her eye. She was clutching her books to her chest with her right hand, then suddenly twisted her stiff left wrist to show her the long red scar.

Katrina gasped. "Oh, Zdenka, how did you know it wouldn't work?"

"Well, it didn't."

"Did it hurt?"

"Burned a little," she said. "They were fighting again."

"Whee, if I cut my wrists every time Momma and Poppa fought, my hands would have fallen off long ago."

"Maybe you should try it. They stopped fighting when they heard me scream. You should have seen them come running. They haven't had a fight since."

The mother superior came out to the schoolyard and shook her hand bell, calling all the girls to class.

"Gee, Zdenka, I'd try it, but I don't know. I can't *stand* the sight of blood, and I simply can't abide pain."

"Why should you anyway?" Zdenka said as they shuffled like girls that age do into their classroom. "You've everything you want."

"I don't have a boyfriend."

"Neither do I," Zdenka said.

"But you will. You're pretty."

Zdenka didn't know why, but she thought that sounded like an insult when it was meant as a compliment.

"I hate boys," she said.

There were fourteen girls in the classroom, a musty subterranean habitat of rough-wood furniture to match Sister's wood switch, which she flicked at the air to instill the fear of God in her charges. Some light entered the room from the high windows, which were at ground level outside, but it was not enough for Zdenka's taste.

In class, Zdenka and Katrina bantered back and forth, sent notes to each other making fun of their teacher, Sister Marie, and some of their classmates.

"Zdenka! Will you pay attention and stop bothering Katrina."

Zdenka was used to it. But she still made a face as soon as Sister averted her eyes.

Katrina, who usually lay low in these encounters, unaccountably raised her hand. When Sister Marie called on her in that stern, no-nonsense, low voice of hers, Katrina got to her feet and said, "Sister, I was talking too. Do you only pick on Zdenka because my father is rich?"

Sister Marie's face became red as a beet. Some of the girls tittered. Zdenka was terrified to silence.

"We do not show favoritism here," Sister insisted, and a few of the girls could not camouflage their verbal grunts to the contrary.

"Quiet! Girls! I have told you many times how our Lord expressed His fondness for the poor. For example, 'Blessed be ye poor: for yours is the kingdom of God.' And who can tell us what our Lord said about a rich man getting into heaven?"

Zdenka raised her hand. Sister was not pleased. "Anyone?" she said, ignoring Zdenka, who was waving her hand wildly now.

"All right," Sister Marie resigned, "Zdenka?"

"Our Lord Jesus said a rich man has less chance of getting into heaven than a camel has of going through the eye of a needle."

31

"Yes." Many would have been satisfied, but Sister Marie was on a roll, and there was no stopping her. The class all realized she was fishing for support from someone else when she said, "And the parable of the poor widow?" But the girls were not cooperating—except Zdenka, who again raised her hand slowly.

"Anyone else?" Sister asked without subtlety. "Don't any of you know your religious studies? Pauline?"

The young girl shook her head.

"Teresa?"

"No, Sister."

"Janis?"

"I don't remember."

Sister Marie was snorting, but Zdenka, as if in open defiance of her teacher's wishes, kept energetically waving her hand. Finally Sister Marie gave up. "Oh, all right, Zdenka, tell us."

Zdenka stood proudly. "Our Lord Jesus saw rich men giving big gifts to the church, and a poor widow who gave only two mites. And our Lord said the widow gave more than the rich men because she gave all she had. And she would go to heaven."

"Yes," Sister Marie said, as though someone more to her liking had supplied the answer. Then, as an afterthought, she looked back at Zdenka and asked, "Do you want to go to heaven, child?"

A lump came to Zdenka's throat. She knew she should simply say, "Oh, yes, Sister," but something stopped her. Perhaps in her young mind she felt she had overdone the party line and her peers would call her a teacher's pet and it would behoove her to return to her peers' good graces.

"I'm not in a hurry, Sister," she said, and scored big with her fellows.

"That will *do*, Zdenka!" Sister Marie said, slicing the air with her switch to quell the sniveling laughter.

At lunchtime, Zdenka and Katrina ran back outside to sit under the old giant elm tree and opened each other's lunches.

"I *love* crusts," Katrina said. "I wish Clara would leave them on. But she says crusts are for poor people and she doesn't listen when I tell her I want to be like the other girls."

"It's okay. I love sandwiches without crusts."

"Apple butter and bacon, it looks like," Katrina said, inspecting the wrapped sandwich in Zdenka's lunch bag. "Much better than cucumbers and cream cheese."

Though no fan of cucumbers and cream cheese, Zdenka liked the feeling of being rich it gave her to hold and bite into the dainty sandwiches. She ate them with a noble flair, with far greater deliberation than she would have afforded bacon and apple butter.

When she ate the food of the rich, she was rich. She didn't taste cucumbers or cream cheese or bread or butter, she tasted the good life, and she adored the flavor.

"Poppa says I'm going to be a princess," Zdenka tittered, "so I might as well eat like one."

"Cucumbers and cream cheese," Katrina said, making a face. "Dreadful!"

"Apple butter and bacon is barnyard food," Zdenka said.

While they were munching their sandwiches under the old elm, Katrina said, "Zdenka?"

"Hm—"

"Don't you think you must be more careful with Sister?"

"Careful?"

"She doesn't like disrespectful talk, you know."

"I know," she said without any suggestion of defeat.

"Sometimes it's best just not to say anything."

"Yes, but then you make her think you agree with her."

"Sometimes that might be better."

Zdenka wrinkled her nose. "All that nonsense about the poor being so wonderful. Do you believe that?"

Katrina thought. "Well, I don't think they *aren't* wonderful just because they're poor."

"But honestly, the rich aren't going to have to go through needles or anything to get into heaven. They're going to be first in line like they are everywhere else. Don't we both know the poor aren't first anywhere?"

"Well—"

"And that baloney about the poor widow. Maybe they thought that would get the rich man to give all he had. Well, fat chance."

"Zdenka! What makes you so sure you know more than Sister about Jesus and heaven and things?"

33

"All you have to do is be awake. Look around. Suppose, Katrina, you really believed all this about God and Jesus favoring the poor. And if you had a choice about it—which would you want to be; rich now or poor now?"

Katrina chewed the apple butter and bacon in time with her thoughts. In time, she shook her head. "Maybe I'd be poor on earth so I can be rich in heaven."

Zdenka shook her head more vigorously. "Not me. I want to be rich in the here and now. I'll take my chances on that later dream."

"I'm eating your sandwich," Katrina offered lamely in support of her ingratiating humility.

"And I'm eating yours, and I like it better."

The kerosene lights in the school auditorium were hot on Zdenka. Beyond the lights, the small audience of parents disappeared in the darkness. She had just made her entrance from the cold and dark backstage to the hot and bright stage, sashaying the width of that stage and striking a peculiar pose with her knee cocked to one side, her arm jerking to rest on her jutting hip. She was playing the peasant girl as though she were an aristocrat playing a peasant.

Her face was thick with makeup applied by an old nun who had obviously never used it. The greasy substance smelled grown-up to Zdenka. It was, she knew, only worn outside the theater by fancy women who needed to paint their faces for business purposes, but Zdenka liked the grown-up smell and feel of it.

She was fifteen years old and she poured her heart and soul into the role. She thought she heard a gasp of pleasure when she struck her pose—the aristocrat's peasant—and in the play she was to marry a prince! She was to be a princess!

Afterwards, the other performers had gone to meet their families in the audience, but Zdenka remained backstage, still feeling she was a princess. Zdenka took delight in seeing her family fumble around to find her in the semidarkness. Poppa was leading Novella and the boys, and he came thrusting ahead with his arms outstretched, a big smile on his face. "Oh, my Babushka, you are quite a little actress."

"Sister said I was an aristocrat."

Her older brother, Felix, snarled, "That part was a peasant."

"That's why Sister picked me. I said I didn't want to be a peasant. She said it was more challenging for a person to play something they were not—like an aristocrat playing a peasant."

"Isn't that wonderful?" Poppa said. Momma didn't say anything.

"Pooh!" said Felix. "You're not an aristocrat."

His eight-year-old brother hushed him. "She can be if she wants to be."

"I'm going to be," Zdenka announced, "from now on."

There were many more plays, and Zdenka anticipated them with all the bubbling juices in her teenaged body. And she got steadily more important parts as she got older. She even got a singing role, and put her heart and soul into her two songs. She did not have an easy time staying with the pitch of the piano accompaniment, but she had so much enthusiasm no one seemed to notice. Expectations were low, emotions high.

After a particularly spirited performance of a musical play called *The Bird in the Tree*, a puffy-faced man in a shiny suit he had outgrown came backstage seeking out Zdenka.

"Ah, there you are, my cute canary," he said with the flourish of captivation, clapping together his pinky, manicured hands, "you sing like an angel." Zdenka noticed an enormous diamond ring on his little finger. She couldn't take her eyes off it. She thought he must be very rich.

Zdenka was flabbergasted. She had had her share of praise, sure, but mostly from family and friends, and none so extravagant. Her face swelled in instant pride. "Whee," she said. "Thank you."

"Allow me to introduce myself," the man said. "I am Edouard Wallinski from the Aristocrat, a very exclusive club downtown. I would be honored to have you sing for us sometime." He saw Zdenka's jaw drop. "Would you be interested?"

"Oh, my goodness," she said. "Well, whee, wow, would I? Whoosh! Golly, I guess so. What would I have to do?"

"Just be yourself, my dear. You are a very special songbird and my patrons will be most fortunate to have a chance to see...and, of course, hear you." He smacked his glistening lips as though he had just enjoyed a tasty sweet.

She frowned. "Well, gosh, I don't know how my momma and poppa would feel about it. Could they come along?"

"Certainly, why not? I would be happy to meet them."

"Oh, but I'm afraid they wouldn't come—and they wouldn't let me, either."

The puffy-faced man with the showy diamond on the only finger that hadn't outgrown it gave her a conspiratorial wink. "Sometimes what the folks don't know, won't hurt them."

Not much more coaxing was required. Zdenka had visions of being the toast of the town. The fat man told her he knew she would be an instant success and she could just show up at the club on any night and he would let her sing. If she was as well received as he knew she would be, she could sing there on a regular basis.

37

Zdenka could think of nothing else for days. She decided not to tell Momma and Poppa outright. One night at dinner she skirted the subject. "Sister says my singing is coming right along, and someday I could sing outside the school."

Augustus frowned. "Would you sing in church?"

"Well, I could. I think she was thinking of some places outside, though. Like charity meetings and things."

"Really?" His eyebrow cocked. "Sister said that, did she? Well, I'm going to have to talk to her about that."

"Oh, please don't. She'd never forgive me. She'd make it ever so hard on me at school. She knows she shouldn't be talking like that. She's only trying to be friendly—oh, please don't—the mother superior would go *so* hard on her."

Augustus studied his daughter's pretty face with her feverish lies distorting it. "Then we'll hear no more about it," he said.

Zdenka was getting remarkably pretty. Her face was easing into a proportional perfection never seen in the family. Her forehead was broad and strong, her nose finely cut, her lips had just the right fullness to them and her chin seemed to tilt up. The owl about her had flown, and in its place the most delicate swan had landed.

Zdenka's school friend Katrina couldn't hear enough about the singing engagement, as Zdenka called it, and conspired to make Zdenka's dream a reality. To sing in public in front of strangers would be a thrilling, heady experience, and the risk of being caught ignited the adrenaline.

Augustus detected something suspicious in Zdenka's demeanor when she asked to spend the weekend with her friend. She would go home from school in the coach, which she had always wished to do, and go to church on Sunday and back to school on Monday all in the glorious gold-leafed coach with *two* horses.

"Ah, Babushka, you know Momma is very ill. You could be a help to her, you know —"

"Oh, Poppa, I will come right back if you need me. I would do no less for you *any*time." And she pecked him on his cheek.

Augustus wanted to believe his daughter and finally gave in. The overjoyed look on her face, he decided, made it worth the risk.

Dinner at Katrina's town house was an eye-popping experience for Zdenka. Their dining room table was the size of the Oleskas' dining room. There were collections all over the house, groups of porcelain figurines in glass cabinets in the dining room. The parlor contained the bejeweled Easter eggs that sparkled all sorts of ways, depending on where you stood and how you moved your head. And in the hallways were arrayed on the walls the most spectacular crucifixes Zdenka had ever seen. There were so many of so many differing sizes, shapes and materials that Zdenka found it scary. As if she were in the holiest of churches and was being watched by the hidden eyes of Jesus.

Zdenka sat at one end of the enormous dining room table with Katrina. Katrina's momma and poppa were at the other end. Katrina had no brothers or sisters. Servants served the food. How nice it would be to have servants, Zdenka thought. Someday I shall have them.

When Zdenka visited, she pretended she was part of the family. The large rooms, the chandeliers, the opulent art, the fabulous food, the attentive servants were all hers, and the feeling of belonging she took on herself effectively canceled what otherwise would have surfaced as a feeling of inferiority. There's rich and there's poor, she told herself, and I like rich better.

"It was nice you could come to town for the weekend, Zdenka," Katrina's momma said. She was a heavy-busted woman with friendly, crinkly eyes that seemed amused by the visitor.

"It's nice to be here," Zdenka answered as the nuns had taught her. "You have so many pretty things."

"There *are* a lot of things, aren't there?" Katrina's poppa said. "We help a lot of people by buying them." He was older and heavier than Zdenka's father. They had, Zdenka thought, more to eat.

Zdenka loved to look at beautiful things. Somehow it made her feel beautiful. But she had never before thought of collecting expensive things as charity.

"Well, I'm glad you like beautiful things, Zdenka," Katrina's poppa said. "I do too. And you yourself are very beautiful."

Zdenka blushed and dropped her face to her napkin — shouldn't he be including his daughter? "Katrina is very beautiful too," she said brazenly.

"Of course," Poppa said. "Both of you will probably break a lot of hearts in your time." But Katrina was no match for Zdenka. She too showed the effects of a rich, unrestrained diet, which puffed her face a step beyond beauty. Katrina's hair was black and braided, but only to just below her shoulders. She was relieved she no longer had to paste the braids to her head like a helmet. Her skin was creamy, soft and her features dainty; in the heavy, round face her eyes were like young grapes peeking through a cloud. She was more chubby than lean, more gentle than rough.

It was a concept foreign to Zdenka: breaking men's hearts. She hardly knew what Katrina's poppa was talking about. But the idea, foreign as it was to her experience, strangely appealed to her. Having power over a man so you could break his heart titillated her.

The girls at fifteen, going on sixteen, were starting to look

39

grown-up, with still an innocence that would repel a gentleman and excite a roué.

Zdenka had shining, light-chestnut hair all the way down her back. Her eyes had a sparkling gemstone brilliance to them. Zdenka's breasts had developed more than Katrina's. It was, Zdenka's mother said, necessary to cinch them to her chest so as not to attract the wrong sort of attention from the boys. Zdenka didn't like the constriction and decided to dispense with it for her singing engagement. She would wear an undershirt which would obscure the details, but not inhibit the sway. It would make her seem older and, dare she admit it? more desirable.

Her personality was that of an accomplished actress who could play many roles. She was alert and aware and could be flirty or standoffish, friendly or reserved—giving or protective. She was like a magnet pulling everything to its field and immobilizing all. She could use all her wiles to net you, then the systems would shut down and she would become passive.

Katrina was as excited as Zdenka was about her singing engagement. They would go together and walk by the club first and watch the sort of people who went in and out. They wouldn't just go in any dump in Brest Litovsk just to get a chance to sing.

Zdenka was excited because the club was called Aristocrat. "It must be for aristocrats," she told Katrina.

"You think my father might come?" Katrina asked her friend.

"Oh, oh, we better be sure."

When they arrived at the street in the address Edouard Wallinski had given Zdenka, they found low brick buildings that did not put them in mind of the aristocracy.

"Geez," Katrina said, "this is a creepy neighborhood. I've got a creepy feeling—let's go home."

"Oh, Katrina, you don't want to spoil it, do you?"

"I don't see any aristocrats around, do you?"

"It's still early," Zdenka said.

"Where is the place?"

"It should be close-by. Thirty-five—this is eighty-seven."

They kept walking, Zdenka expectantly, Katrina reluctantly. "Zdenka—let's go, we're going to get into trouble down here, I can just feel it."

The street was cold and damp, but Zdenka kept her spirits up. "This is my debut," she said to Katrina, as though that settled it.

They arrived at a place with glass windows in front that were covered with whitewash. "The Aristocrat Club" was painted in an arc on both windows, with the number 35 beneath. In an effort to add cachet to the club, the letters were painted in gold that had long since faded.

A few men came from the other direction, and Zdenka and Katrina crossed to the other side of the street, trying to look as if they belonged there and were just passing through.

The men looked at them, then spoke at once to each other and laughed, a rough, not refined, laugh, Zdenka thought, but she said nothing. Katrina shuddered.

"They look like aristocrats to you?"

"I don't know," Zdenka said. "You're the only aristocrat I know."

"They look like farmers to me. Let's go before we get into trouble."

Zdenka reddened. Her father was a farmer, but she couldn't be bothered to defend him. She was too excited.

"You can go if you want to. I'm going to sing."

"You'd go in there alone?"

"Well...I'd rather go with you, but if I have to, yes, I would go alone."

"Oh, Denky, you're crazy."

"Mr. Wallinski came to our play at the convent school. He can't be a bad man. Besides, he liked my singing. I promised him I'd come sing at his club."

"Does he know you are only fifteen years old?"

"Well, he knows I'm in school. Besides, I'm almost sixteen."

"He could get in trouble."

"How?" Zdenka asked.

"Children aren't supposed to be in places like this."

"Oh, don't be such a stick-in-the-mud," Zdenka said. "You can be a child if you want, I'm going to be a lady. Come on, I'm going in."

"If you go in there a lady, you'll come out something else."

"You aren't coming?"

41

"I can't let you go in there alone."

So with palpable trepidation, the two girls made their way back across the slick, wet street and stood as if paralyzed before the scarred midnight-blue door of the Aristocrat Club.

"Well," Zdenka said. "Shall we knock, or what?"

"Come on, Denky, you're as scared as I am. Let's go home. We'll have some hot chocolate."

"No, I want to sing."

"Then you're going to have to go inside. Unless you want to sing out here."

While they were frozen in procrastination outside the door of the Aristocrat Club, a man in a starched blue work shirt came across the street toward them. Katrina whispered, "Let's go," but was too late. The man, tall and spare, was upon them.

"Looking for something, girls?"

Zdenka spoke. "I'm supposed to sing here," she said. "Could you tell Mr. Wallinski I'm here?"

"Sing here?" The man looked the girls over. He didn't seem to grasp the concept.

He opened the door for them, but they didn't move. The blast of the raucous men's voices pushed against them like a rushing river.

"Well," the man said, "go on."

With the hesitation of a church processional, Zdenka entered the smoke pit, and her eyes stung from it. The smell of beer made her nauseous, and she was afraid she was going to vomit. She felt Katrina gasp beside her.

The two windows in front were the limit of the ventilation opportunities for the Aristocrat Club, but they were closed. The walls of the narrow room were haphazardly arrayed with beer posters, dog-eared and faded, and a few splattered with the products they promoted. Wallinski was not a fastidious housekeeper and if something fell to the floor it, likely as not, found itself a new home.

"Pinky," the tall man called across the bar, where a line of smoking, belching men were shouting in constant competition with the din—"two young ladies to see you."

All eyes turned on the girls, making them both shiver. The looks quickly turned to leers.

The bartender, a fleshy man with a bald head and a bold moustache, leaned over the bar and said, "I'm sorry, girls, children aren't permitted here."

"We're *not* children," Zdenka snapped back at him.

"Oh, well is that so? Well, then, women aren't allowed either."

"I'm here to sing," Zdenka said, holding her ground while Katrina tugged at her sleeve to go. Those men at the bar didn't look anything like aristocrats. Her poppa would never come to a place like this.

The men looked like they never took baths and they were spitting into brass spittoons at their feet. Rows of whiskey bottles were lined up on a shelf behind the bar. Above the bottles was a maroon flannel banner with dirty, gray cut-out letters that said, "Remember, you are an aristocrat." But they didn't *act* like aristocrats. They were whistling and catcalling the girls, saying rude things like, "Come to Poppa, sweetie pie," and "What a pair...," "How about a drink?"

Then Edouard Wallinski presented himself, with his round face and thick wet lips and his enormous diamond on his pinky. Is *that* why they call him Pinky? Zdenka wondered.

"Ah, my beautiful canary, I'm so glad you came—may I get you girls a drink?"

"No, I came to sing. Where shall I go?"

"Go? Why would you go anywhere?" Pinky said. "You sing right here." His clammy claw was on her upper arm. Even though she had a coat for insulation it made her uncomfortable.

"Let me take your coats," he said to the girls. "What are you going to sing for us?"

"I can sing three songs," Zdenka said, and told him what they were. His eyebrows lifted in mock admiration, the mock part lost on the young performer, but not on Katrina.

"Do you have a piano player?" Zdenka asked.

"Of course. Ignance!" he called out, and a white-haired gentleman with a droopy white moustache came slouching in from somewhere in the back. "Ignance," Pinky did the honors, "this is a young lady who is going to grace us with song tonight. Would you be so kind as to tickle the ivories for her?"

Ignance studied the girl and looked as though he were struggling mentally to make sense of it. "Bring music?" he said to Zdenka.

"No, I—"

"That's okay, I know them all. What key do you like?"

"Key?" She didn't know what that meant. She was a singer, she thought, not a locksmith. But she didn't want to appear ignorant.

"You pick," she said.

His eyebrows seemed to cross. "Do you sing high, low, or medium range?" he asked her.

High sounded better than low so she said, "High."

He nodded and Zdenka left her coat with Pinky; Katrina holding on to hers as if to fulfill a primitive protective need. The three of them moved to the piano.

Pinky stood by, Zdenka's coat draped over his arm. The light from the kerosene lamps made his lips and his ring look orange. Her eyes were fixed on his ring. She was quaking with fear.

"I see you looking at my ring." He cocked an eye in amusement. "Do you like it?"

"Oh, I *love* it. So...big, whew!"

"Well, here," he said, caressing the diamond-studded gold metal, "I'll let you wear it."

He set her coat on top of the piano, scarred and scratched from use and abuse, then slipped the ring off his little finger. He took Zdenka's hand in his. She flinched. "I am wearing it on my smallest finger," he said, "but you must wear it on your largest." Still it was too big. "Here, let me have this middle finger." He pried her finger loose from her tense fist. Then he slipped the ring on her middle finger with a deliberate, sensuous motion. Zdenka blushed; then he slid the ring off again, then back on, with slow, liquid motions. "How do you like that?" Pinky asked through his wet lips. "Fine," she said. The ring was loose, but the diamond was enormous. She closed her fist and kept the ring in front of her.

Zdenka felt funny. The fat man seemed too familiar. But she had the ring and that made her feel special. It was a talisman for her—a kind of protection from harm. The men at the bar looked rough to her, but they wouldn't harm Pinky, and perhaps if she had Pinky's ring they wouldn't harm her. There was only the piano between her and the men, but now she had Pinky's ring too.

Zdenka glanced at Katrina, who stood on the backside of the

44

piano shifting her short, thick body with ill ease.

Ignance began to play the piano, and it sounded no better than it looked. Zdenka didn't know what he was playing, it didn't sound like anything she'd ever heard. She looked with an inquisitive blankness at Ignance.

"Just start singing whatever you want," he called out over his fumbling fingers, "I'll pick up the tune."

Zdenka flashed her take-no-prisoners smile and haltingly began to sing. Her hands were crossed in front of her where her dress began to flare out. The gross diamond pointed toward the boys at the bar. As she gained confidence, Zdenka's body movements became innocently sensuous. Not overtly sexy, but the men couldn't tell her movements from slinky, suggestive come-ons. Ignance, true to his word, picked up the tune. He wasn't much of a piano player and she wasn't much of a singer, but it hardly mattered. Most of the men at the bar were talking anyway, as well as coughing roughly and expectorating into the spittoons.

But Zdenka sang away as though the audience was rapt. Occasionally someone shouted something she took for encouragement, like "Atta girl, belt it out," or "Oh, Chickadee, you're gorgeous!"

Pinky kept his position next to the piano, and he didn't take his eyes off Zdenka. Katrina had faded against the wall. Other men were looking at Zdenka now—some of them even stopped talking. She could feel the lascivious eyes burning her young flesh like the tiny hot needles Poppa burned with matches to sterilize so he could take splinters from her skin. The eyes burning her tender skin scared her—but it was a strange and exhilarating power she had never felt before. Though she didn't understand their feelings, these men were admiring her and they clapped lustily after each of her renditions. After the first applause, she loosened her personality, the hands and arms waved in flamboyant gestures and, while her voice got no better, her performance became more suggestive—as though she were struggling to leave behind the innocence of a sheltered youth. But the men clamored for more of Zdenka's particular brand of innocent sensuality: the movement of her hands down the side of her thighs, the swaying of her unharnessed breasts. She was earning the men's blind obeisance to her feminine youth.

No one applauded with more gusto than Pinky. He loved to see the young girl flashing and dashing his ring about. She made him feel young and desirable. His pink tongue roamed his sausage-like lips and wetted them down for another song.

With Zdenka's increasing success, Katrina seemed to shrink more into herself. If the wall hadn't been so strong, she'd have gone through it. As Zdenka became more radiant, Katrina became more subdued. Katrina couldn't wait for the performance to end so they could leave—Zdenka didn't want it ever to end. After all, the eyes were on Zdenka, not Katrina.

After Zdenka had sung her three songs and the first one over again (with more gusto) for an encore, Katrina gathered the courage to come forward and insist Zdenka leave with her. "It's getting late," she said. "We're going to get in a lot of trouble if we get caught."

"Oh, all right," Zdenka said peevishly. She stepped over to Pinky and removed the ring. "I have to go," she said.

"So soon? You're just warming the place up. Well, if you must. Will you come back tomorrow night? I will make you a star. Every club in Poland will be clamoring for you to sing. Come back tomorrow and I will pay you."

"*Pay* me?"

"Why, certainly. When word gets out, it will be standing room only in here. You'll easy earn your money."

She handed him the ring.

"No," he said, putting up his palm to block the ring. "You like it?"

"I *love* it."

"Well, you keep it until tomorrow. Bring it back then."

"But what if I can't come tomorrow?"

"Well," he said with a chuckle, "I think you'll be back—but if you don't come to sing, just bring the ring tomorrow or the next day."

"But..."

"Don't worry," he said with that awful leering wink. "I know where to find you."

On her way out with Katrina, Zdenka felt a hand slide down her back and clutch her behind. Her nervous system wanted to shriek, but her vocal cords were knotted against it.

"I was *scared to death*," Katrina
said when she and Zdenka had found
sanctuary in the dark bedroom they were
sharing at Katrina's town house. "I just
could *not* wait to get out of there. Oh,
Zdenka, why did you do it?"

It was an eerie feeling talking in
the dark. The heavy curtains were drawn
and the girls did not dare light the lamp
for fear someone would notice and question their movements. Zdenka was reticent at first, fearing that someone might
be in the room, unseen in the darkness,
listening to their every word.

"I *liked* it," Zdenka said. "I love to
have people listen to me."

Zdenka found comfort in the
anonymity and the feeling of living in a
world with her eyes closed.

"And watch you, like those animals?"

"Do you think it is wrong to bring people pleasure?"

The bed felt so firm and strong under her and the feather duvet was luxury against her skin.

"Guess it depends how you do it," Katrina said. "Don't you think you were a little, well, provocative? I mean, Holy Mary, that awful man gave you his enormous diamond!"

"He wanted to."

"He's the ugliest man I've ever seen. He gives me the creeps, and you have his ring," she sighed in exasperation. "It's like you were *engaged* to him."

"He wants to *pay* me," Zdenka said. "Did you hear that?"

"Pay you, but for what?"

"To sing, what do you think?"

"For something else maybe."

"Oh, Katrina, how could you be so silly? He could be my grandfather."

"Yes, and if you think that bothers him, you are only five years old."

"Well, at least I have an excuse to go back and sing again."

"Oh, dear, you'd *want* to?"

"Yes, I'd want to," Zdenka said, mimicking Katrina's surprise. "You aren't jealous of me, are you?"

"Jealous?" Katrina smirked. "No, really, you think I'm jealous of your singing in a beer hall?"

"Of the men," she said slowly, as though the thought only occurred while she whispered, "and the way they looked at me."

"And the pawing? I saw that man run his hand down your backside."

Zdenka giggled, but when it had happened it frightened her.

"It's not funny. It gives me the creeps the way they look at you."

"It did feel funny. But, it was strange how it made me feel good too. It's like I was special—important...powerful even." Zdenka closed her eyes in the darkness, as though that would give her extra protection from what she was about to say: "Seductive." It came out, but barely.

"*How* you talk, Zdenka Oleska! I swear I mustn't listen to any more of this."

"Okay," Zdenka said. There was another long silence.

Katrina broke it. "I'm listening," she said.

They laughed so hard they had to smother their faces in their pillows. When they calmed down, Zdenka said, "The Church teaches you mustn't do it unless you want to have a baby."

"I know," Katrina said. "That's why there are so many large families."

"But, you are an only child. Does that mean…?"

"I don't know. Maybe everybody doesn't obey the rules."

"Yeah. I mean, suppose you knew you couldn't have any babies?"

"Well, if I'm going to be a good Catholic…" Katrina trailed off in thought. "I definitely believe you should save it for marriage, and I'm going to do that."

"Felix says that's how a lot of girls *get* married," Zdenka said. "*Not* saving it, I mean."

"Well, I'm not doing *that*. I'm not marrying anyone who doesn't respect me enough to wait."

"So if you never get married, you'll never do it?"

"That's…right," Katrina said, without a lot of conviction. "We must be strong."

"Easier to be strong when you're rich, I bet," Zdenka said, twisting the diamond ring around her finger. "You're rich. I like rich things like you have and I *adore* this diamond ring that man loaned me. It just makes me feel rich to wear it."

"It reminds me of that awful man. It would give me the creeps just to touch it."

"The fat man has nothing to do with it."

"Well, you *will* give it back, won't you?"

"Of course, I will. It's his, not mine. Tomorrow night. We'll go back like I promised."

"I don't want to go back there, Zdenka. I'm scared."

"Then I'll go alone."

"You won't!"

"Nothing will happen to me. Don't worry."

But the next morning, just as the sun was poking up over the horizon, Augustus Oleska's horse and buggy appeared with the urgent message that the Miss must come home at once. Her mother's illness had worsened.

49

"The ring!" Zdenka said to Katrina. "Take the ring back for me, please."

"Oh, no."

"Please."

"I'm not going there alone," Katrina said. "And I can't tell anyone else where we were."

"Can't you get a servant or someone?"

"Oh, no, I'm afraid the ring is yours. You have to get it back. But if I were you I *would* get it back, how ever. I wouldn't trust that man further than I could throw him, and I couldn't even *lift* him."

$$\text{\textphonetic} \qquad \text{\textphonetic} \qquad \text{\textphonetic}$$

The ground was frozen when they buried Novella Oleska on Zdenka's sixteenth birthday. Zdenka stood by her father at the grave site in the churchyard, clutching his hand. She thought she was comforting him. He thought he was comforting her. He was wrong.

Her brothers were crying and so her father. Zdenka would be the strong one, she thought. She just didn't feel that much grief. She couldn't understand why Poppa was so devastated. He and Momma fought so much—and he had his little Babushka to rely on from now on.

It was just the family and a few neighbors at the graveside. The Polanskis were there, surprising Zdenka. They were neighbors with whom they had very little commerce. There were the mother and father and three kids that Zdenka did not want to know. They looked poorer than Zdenka thought her family did, and her aspirations were up, not down.

The priest was more ruddy faced than ever and looked grandfatherly in his fur hat. He seemed intent on stemming Zdenka's father's grief, so she only half heard what he was saying until he said, "The meek shall inherit the earth." Zdenka knew better. If anyone was inheriting anything, it was going to be the rich kids. If the meek saw anything at all, it would be only leftovers.

She wished her father would control his tears. It wasn't manly to cry like that, and that ugly Polanski kid was looking at him funny. Like her heart was breaking just because *he* was crying.

Then the priest was saying something about our Father who art in heaven. Zdenka squeezed her father's hand and whispered in his ear, "I like my real father right here better," and the tears Augustus added to his wellspring were tears of joy.

♪   ♪   ♪

Zdenka didn't have to worry about a ruse to return the ring to Mr. Edouard Wallinski. The next day at school, Zdenka was called out of class by the mother superior, an august-looking woman, stiff of spine and stiff of spirit.

"Zdenka," she began in the hallway on the march to her office, "there is a man here who says you have something for him. Do you know what he means?"

"Who is he?" Zdenka asked cagily.

"Mr. Wallinski, he says."

"Oh, yes, Mother. He lent me something and I couldn't take it back because my mother died."

"Take it back? To this man? Where does a young girl like you meet a man like that?"

"Here at school," she said, proud of playing the card. "He saw me in the play."

"And then he gave you his ring?"

"Loaned. Now he's come for it back." They were outside Mother Superior's office door.

"Have you the ring?"

"Yes, Mother Superior."

"Good. Then give it back and be gone with him. The Lord makes all types of sinners, and He asks us to love our neighbors, but this man could try my obedience."

Zdenka was only a little nervous at what the fat man would say. She followed the mother superior inside the door and curtsied to Wallinski—"Oh, Mr. Wallinski, thank you for loaning me your ring. I enjoyed having it. I'm sorry I didn't get it right back to you, but the day I was to bring it back my mother died and they took me home."

"I'm sorry...I..."

She handed him the ring, which she produced from the

pocket of her uniform skirt.

When the mother superior saw the size of the diamond, she clutched her heart and had to steady herself on the cabinets that held the information on her students.

Mr. Wallinski made a courtly bow to Zdenka, then to the mother superior. "I hope you will grace us with your presence again, soon," he said to Zdenka. "My wife can't stop talking about you. Good day to you both." And he was gone.

Mother Superior watched the fat man with tortured disdain on her lips. Something in the way he looked when he said, "My wife…" didn't ring true. Her imagination stretching over the man and Zdenka together went wild. But, she thought, she had a duty here that went beyond her personal distaste. Surely she did.

"Now, Zdenka," she fixed the still-standing child in her disdainful gaze, "I want to know what that man did to you."

Mother Superior's tone frightened Zdenka. It was the disapproving, suspicious tone of one who thought she had done something terrible and the inference scared Zdenka.

"Nothing," she said, but she was trembling and Mother Superior was convinced of the worst.

"Nothing?" Her eyebrow arched. "You had his ring worth enough to run this school for years. Tell me how you got it."

"He *gave* it to me."

"Yes, for what?"

"For nothing."

"Don't lie to me, child. Liars go to *hell!* Nobody gives a ring like that for nothing. Now tell me from the beginning—if you know what's good for you—*why* did he give you that ring?"

"I don't know."

"You don't know? Come, child, you can do better than that."

"I'm not lying. He just let me hold it."

"I see—and why didn't you give it back then?"

"He told me I could keep it."

"What did you do for him?"

"I just…sang."

"You sang?" One of the mother superior's eyes closed while the other opened wide. "What did you sing?"

"Songs."

"What songs?"

Zdenka's shoulder hiked up an inch. Mother Superior stomped her foot. This gesture was understood at St. Joseph's as the ultimate anger.

"Specifics, child!" she cajoled her. "What songs did you sing?"

Zdenka just looked at the mother superior, meaning to look obstinate, but not even hiding her terror.

"The Ave Maria?"

"Noooo."

"Songs about Jesus?"

"Noooo."

"Then *what* songs?" The foot came down again.

"Just...songs—"

"All right, I warn you fairly, if you are going to be stubborn it will not go easy on you. Shall I ask your father instead?"

Mother Superior hit the mark. Zdenka's eyes fairly exploded out of their sockets.

"He doesn't know about this, does he?"

Zdenka shook her head in fright.

"Then perhaps I should tell him."

"Oh, no—"

"Perhaps he can solve the riddle of what you let that man do to you to get that ring."

"I told you, I just sang."

"From the beginning, child. From the beginning. Where did you meet that...that creature?"

"In church—here—St. Joseph's—after the play he came and said I was a good singer. He invited me to perform at his club."

"Perform? What club?"

"The Aristocrat Club."

"Aristocrat? Some aristocrat. That man wouldn't recognize an aristocrat if he collided with one."

"It's the name of his club, Mother Superior. That's the honest truth."

"So you went to this...club?"

She nodded.

"Without your father or mother knowing?"

Another nod.

"You just snuck out of the house in the middle of the night?"

53

"No—I went to…a friend's house for the weekend."

"Whose house?"

"A friend."

"What's her name?"

Zdenka shook her head and tightened her lips.

"From school?"

"A friend—"

"All right. Did your friend go with you to the club?"

She nodded. Zdenka knew Mother Superior knew who her friend was. Zdenka also knew Mother Superior didn't *want* to know. The rich were always shielded from trouble at St. Joseph's.

"Did she sing too?"

Zdenka shook her head.

"Did she do anything to this man?"

"No."

"Did he do anything to her?"

"No!"

"To you?"

She hesitated a beat. It was too long. "No, I just sang at his club. He gave me the ring to hold while I sang, is all. You can believe anything you want," Zdenka muttered, "but that's the truth."

"Were there any women there?"

"My friend…"

"About your age?"

"Yes."

"I see. Not a lot of protection, was it? A roomful of men and two children."

"I'm not a child!" Zdenka blurted, having had her fill of Mother Superior calling her "child."

"So, you didn't sing holy songs at this club?"

"No."

"Was there a bar?"

"I guess so."

"The men were drinking?"

"I guess."

"Did any of them touch you?"

Zdenka stared blankly in Mother Superior's direction, without seeing her.

"Where did they touch you?"

Unconsciously Zdenka's tongue moistened her lips.

"Child!" The foot hammered the floor. "Tell me what that animal did to you—oh, you may think I don't know what goes on with pigs like that because of my vow of chastity, but I *know*, believe you me, I know. You must not let them defile you with their filthy lust. You must be ever on your guard. You must not enter such dens of iniquity."

Zdenka watched in wide-eyed amazement as the mother superior took on such emotions as she had not seen from her before.

"Now tell me—where did he touch you?"

"He didn't touch me, I swear." Zdenka was starting to feel nauseous.

"Come here, child," Mother Superior commanded her.

"Where?"

"Here—behind the desk."

Unsure, Zdenka started to move to the side of Mother Superior's desk.

"No—here. All the way around."

Zdenka advanced further. When she was close enough, Mother Superior's arm shot out like a striking serpent and snatched child Zdenka by the wrist.

"Now," she said, her hand moving slowly and gently to the young girl's burgeoning bosom, "did he touch you there?" The old veined hand continued to gently rub the buds that pushed through Zdenka's school blouse and the mother superior felt the nipples harden under her hand. She nodded knowingly. "As I feared," she said.

"No, no, *no!*" Zdenka said. "Nobody touched me there."

"Ah—no?" Mother Superior was not convinced. "You seem to me rather..." she searched for the right word—"experienced."

"I'm not!"

"No? Well then, did he touch you here?"—and her hand moved behind the girl to gently caress her bottom.

It wasn't like this at all, Zdenka thought. That awful man grabbed me there and he frightened me to death. This way—it could feel nice—

"Well, child?"

She shook her head.

Mother Superior nodded. "Then—here—in the front—

between your legs?" But Zdenka jerked away and headed for the door.

"You stop this minute," Mother Superior yelled, "or I shall tell your father everything."

Zdenka stopped in her tracks, a wretched feeling of powerlessness sweeping over her.

"Now promise me three things," Mother Superior said, "and you may go."

Zdenka turned to face her, her lungs heaving in her chest as though she had run a long and arduous race.

"Number one—you never see that man again. Promise!"

"I promise," Zdenka mumbled.

"Two—you confess your sins to the priest."

"Yes, Mother Superior."

"Your sin of taunting those animals with your young body."

Zdenka stared at Mother Superior; what did she mean?—it wasn't her fault.

"Promise!"

Zdenka nodded dully, not sure of what she was promising.

"And three—you speak not a word of our ... conversation…here to anyone. That will include the father—or I shall be forced to tell *your* father. Promise!"

Zdenka narrowed her eyes, trying to grasp the meaning of the strange feeling she had. Was Mother Superior afraid? Zdenka closed her eyes, as though that would give her a clearer understanding. Could it be the mother superior *liked* pawing her like that?

"May I go now?"

Mother Superior stood and came toward her. "I didn't hear you promise my third condition."

"I promise," Zdenka said with a slight smile on her thin lips.

"Good. Then we shall go now to Father so he can hear your confession."

"Now?"

"No time like the present." She wanted to make an impression, should the snip of a child ever take it into her head to say she had been fondled by her.

Zdenka looked like a stray dog following behind the imperious mother superior crossing the churchyard to the residence of the priest. They found him at his kitchen table, where Mother Superior knew he would be.

The priest was spreading a thick layer of apricot jelly on a fat piece of bread. The crumbs on his shirt testified this was not his first today. The thickness of his flesh was topped by a ruddy, open face and a bulbous nose red enough to cause speculations about possible abuse of the communion wine. What hair was left to him by what he found to be an increasingly elusive God was slate gray.

On the table Zdenka noticed the half-loaf of bread was surrounded by several jelly jars and a plate of massacred butter.

"Father," Mother Superior began, "would it be presumptuous of me to speak of the sin of gluttony?—no, I shall not speak of it…"

"Very good of you. Nor shall I speak of this interruption of my repast when I see no evidence of dire emergency, lest you would already have spoken of it." His smile was broad and benign.

Mother Superior closed her face down in a disdainful frown. "It is an emergency of this girl's soul, Father. She wants you to hear her confession." The father looked quickly to Zdenka for confirmation, but, as he suspected, found only confusion in her countenance. He picked at a molar with the fingernail of his little finger. "I expect it can wait till Saturday, eh, young lady?"

Zdenka nodded vigorous assent.

"It *cannot* wait until Saturday," Mother Superior said, calling into play her most stentorian voice. "I certainly, you must well know by now, would not *dream* of interrupting your constant intake of food unless the need was dire."

Father grumped, then sighed the sigh of the long-suffering ghosts of the churchyard. The old priest laboriously put on his robe and led the girl to the church confessional box. Mother Superior followed until the father looked back askance at her and said, "We shall do nicely alone, thank you, Mother."

When they were alone in the dark, tiny booth, with the curtain between them, Zdenka heard the priest mumble in Latin then sigh into the silence that followed.

"Have you something to confess, young lady?"

Already she was at ease. He had called her a young lady, not a child. "Mother Superior says I must confess to you."

"Yes?"

Silence.

"But what is it?"

"She says I used my body to taunt men, but I didn't, I didn't, I only sang because I love to sing."

"For the glory of God?"

"Oh, yes, Father, I sing for the glory of God."

"You love God?"

"Oh, yes."

"That is good. God is good and God loves you. You must love Him back in all that you do and all will be well with you. Two Hail Marys before bed until I see you again."

"Yes, Father."

"Oh—and—young lady…"

"Yes, Father?"

"God has made you beautiful. It is His way of keeping the species alive. But it is very easy for a man to misunderstand that beauty. That is, to mistakenly think your young grace and beauty are put on this earth for his pleasure. In God's plan men and women must renew the earth. So, it is your duty as a good Catholic woman to marry someday and to be modest at all times in the eyes of God, and in the eyes of…other men. Do you understand?"

"Yes, Father."

"And you will obey?"

"Yes, Father."

Zdenka wasn't about to tell the priest she didn't think there was a God that looked after her. If He did exist, He was busy with the rich.

And Mother Superior pawing her like that! It was *more* than just asking her where. She could have just pointed. What did it mean? And why was everyone so heated up about the boys and girls? She wasn't going to do anything she didn't want to. And if she *wanted* to, whose business was it but hers anyway?

When Felix came in from feeding the pigs, he found his sister, Zdenka, sitting at her desk absently playing with her hair with one hand and doodling with a pencil with the other. She had drawn a beautiful woman singing on a theater stage to an audience, and now Zdenka was expanding that audience by doodling circles with faces in them.

"Princess!" Felix snarled. The word was pronounced in the opposite sense from her father's rendition.

"Prince!" she answered back.

"Ho, ho, ho," Felix said, "don't I wish. I'm out with the pigs; you're drawing pretty pictures. I'm washing dishes; you're sitting on Poppa's lap like a china doll. It's time you started pulling your own weight around here."

"I do my share," she said with a haughty flip of her hair.

"Hah!" he snorted. "What do you do?"

"I keep Poppa company so he doesn't go to pieces."

"Is that so?" Felix mocked his sister with an exaggerated swiveling of his head, as though he were mightily searching for the absent father. "I don't *see* him," he said with a broad, unnerving grin. "Where *is* he?" Felix was beginning to pride himself on being a person over which nothing could be put.

Zdenka didn't answer. She gave Felix, instead, an indifferent flick of her shoulder to show him just how unimportant that intelligence was to her.

Felix's smile turned from unnerving to taunting—"You don't know, do you? Well, *I* know. He's courtin'."

Perplexity fell in place on her face, as if she couldn't make sense of the word. "Courtin'?" she said. Zdenka looked at him as though she thought he was trying to demean her, using a foreign language she didn't understand. "What're you talking about?"

It was that awful look on her brother's face that told her what he was saying. But she was just as sure as anything that he was making it up to make her mad.

"Where's he doing this courtin'?"

"Down by the Polanskis'." Felix was enjoying knowing more about Poppa than his sister did.

"Polanskis'?" Zdenka said, astonished. "Mrs. Polanski has a husband."

"Uh-huh,"—Felix nodded his ready agreement.

"So what's Poppa doing there?" she demanded angrily.

"More than one female for courtin' down by the Polanskis'."

"The maid? He wouldn't!" Then she realized, "They don't have a maid!"

Felix shook his head.

"Then there is no one else—"

"You don't know Nadia then," he said with finality.

As though struck with a mallet to the skull, Zdenka's mouth dropped as she stared at her eighteen-year-old brother, waiting for him to say he was joking. Hoping.

"You wouldn't believe it," he said, shaking his head at his own amazement, "she comin' 'round here all sparkly sayin' how sorry they all was at the Polanskis', and wouldn't he just enjoy a good home-cooked meal again. Her ma and pa and all the kiddies would be ever so pleased if'n he could."

"But Nadia? She's not older than you are!"

He nodded. "Two years is all. Expect they could have a mess more o' kids."

"Felix!" It was like her brother was torturing her—a Chinese water torture. "I refuse to believe it."

"Laugh all you want to, I haven't seen Poppa this happy in a long time."

"I'm *not* laughing!" Zdenka said.

"'S okay. Way it looks, Poppa won't be needing any cheering up from you. He's full up. You can start pitching in with the chores."

On her next walk in the woods with her father, Zdenka was crying: nonstop. He tried to comfort her but it wasn't working.

"Nadia is a nice girl; you should like her a lot. Can't you grant me some happiness, belated as it is?" Poppa asked his daughter.

"But you're her father's age."

"Can you find me someone older?"

"Why do you need someone? You had Momma."

"Yes, and I was lucky I did, because we got three fine children as a result."

"And that's not enough? You want *more* children?"

"Zdenka, try to understand. Oh, how can I make you see? To understand men and the needs they have?"

"You *don't* mean you are going to marry that child?"

"I don't know yet. We are talking..."

"I'm to have a mother four years older than I am?—like she birthed Felix when she was *two!*"

"Men have needs. It is so difficult for me now. I'm still young. I'm on fire. God made us this way, I can't help it."

"God made the priests too," Zdenka argued.

"But He made them different," Poppa said.

"What about Momma's memory? You were just saying I couldn't spend the weekend at Katrina's because of what people would think. What are they going to think if we all step over to the Polanskis' like we are having a fine old time? Well, I *can't* go to the Polanskis' Sunday, I'm going to be staying over with Katrina."

"No you're not, young lady."

"I am too!"

"Now, we aren't going to fight, because someone is liable to put a light cut on her wrists."

"Oooo!" Zdenka said and ran off, leaving Poppa standing alone in the woods. It would have been a good time for another try at suicide, but Poppa had just trivialized it.

𝄞　　𝄞　　𝄞

When Zdenka came home from school Friday, she threw her books down in her room, then ran back down the stairs and out the door to look for Poppa out back. She was going to convince him there was no need to burden himself with that ugly Polanski girl. She would gladly take her mother's place. Zdenka stopped short at the barn door where she found her Poppa talking inside to Jake, the leader of the small band of workers that kept the place moseying along.

"But I asked you to do that two weeks ago," Augustus said patiently.

"There were so many things," Jake said. "I will go do it right now—"

Zdenka was waiting when he came out of the barn. She didn't want to admit it, but he looked happier than she could remember seeing him in a long time. It couldn't have been the farm work that lifted his spirits.

"Ah, Babushka." He smiled. "Come for a walk."

"Yes, Poppa. I looked forward to it all day."

"Me too."

She led him toward the woods, where they had worn a path between the trees.

Zdenka especially loved walking in the woods with her father when the sun was out because of her beloved shadows. When she was younger, she used to step on Poppa's shadow and he would try to evade her. Now she cherished those memories and strove to keep them alive.

She still hung on him as they crossed the stream in the woods by stepping from stone to stone. It was precarious traveling, but she had him to rely on to keep her balance.

Safe on the other side, Zdenka whispered in confidence, "I love these walks we go on." Her voice was soft and low, as if to keep that confession a secret between them.

They walked in silence up the gentle slope until they came to a small clearing where she bathed in the sunshine and drew in big drafts of the clear air.

"Poppa," she said at last.

"Hm?" He was looking off in the distance as though searching for someone.

"I heard you tell Jake to do something you told him two weeks ago."

"Ah, yes," he said, shaking his head. "It is so hard to get the men to do what I ask."

"That is because you are too easy on them."

"Hm—yes," he said, "I suppose. But they are people, just like we are. We all have our limitations…"

"Oh, pooh, you just go on making excuses for them. You let them get away with murder. You must be strong. You are the boss."

"Yes, I suppose."

"They walk all over you."

"You think it better I should walk all over them?"

"Yes!" She was agitated by his serenity. "At least make them do what you say."

They walked in silence while Augustus seemed to consider his daughter's advice. She couldn't know his mind was elsewhere.

The shadows seemed to float by as they walked and Zdenka loved to see pictures in the shadows—a bear, a fish, a fruit, a tree, even Mother Superior sometimes.

"Poppa," Zdenka said with a sudden directness that startled him, "why can't I be your wife?"

The question was so simple and guileless Augustus was jolted to snort a liter of laughter before he caught himself.

"Oh, Babushka, but you are my daughter."

"I could be both."

Could she be so naive? he wondered. "Had Momma not told

you where babies come from?"

"I didn't need Momma for that," Zdenka said, waving a hand at him. "I'm not a baby." Then she giggled nervously.

Augustus smiled. "You were."

"I'm not talking about babies," she said. "You had enough babies. I could do the rest for you." She paused to consider some details. "The boys would help, of course."

"Ah," he said. "The boys...the rest...I'm sure you could. But you must have a life of your own. A real husband who *you* can have babies with."

"But I don't want babies, I just want to be with you."

"Oh, Babushka, darling, how kind you are. Such nice thoughts. But you will change your mind, believe me. You will meet someone you want to marry."

"No!" she insisted, shaking her head with a vengeance so Poppa thought it would fall off.

"Yes, my Babushka, you are my princess. You will make a big mark in this world—"

"How will I do that?"

"I don't know exactly," he furrowed his brows, "but I know you will. You are special."

"But not special enough for you?"

A slight smile played on Augustus's lips. "*Too* special," he said, and the smile faded. He put his arm around her and hugged her to his bosom while she poured tears down his body.

The Polanski place was even more modest than the Oleskas'. It was the same two-story clapboard house, with smaller rooms, and the farm was about half the size of the Oleskas'. But it was unprotected by trees and sat out on the landscape like a loose button on an old shoe. Zdenka hated the Polanskis' house. It didn't give the feeling of coziness she thought a home should have. The small farm was worked only by the Polanskis— without help. Zdenka couldn't imagine her poppa stooping to a marriage beneath him, because she was perfectly capable of taking her mother's place by his side. At the Polanski place, she felt boxed in, trapped, discarded. She saw her role as the lone wolf on the attack, and she realized how they would all pounce on her if she wasn't careful.

The wine, she noticed, had made her father very happy and Nadia positively giddy. The way her father eyed this girl that was practically *her* age was just sickening. He was like some slobbery lap dog excited to see his master. Nadia was hardly less worshiping with her soupy eyes. The whole mess just made Zdenka sick to her stomach. She hardly ate anything.

Mrs. Polanski was no slouch as a cook. She started them off with a hearty vegetable soup and then produced a fat pot roast with broccoli and potatoes from the garden. Augustus could not stop raving about the food.

"My daughter Nadia is also a good cook," said the mom. Nadia blushed; Zdenka wanted to throw up. Her eyes were on her plate for most of the dinner. She stole quick glances at Nadia and found her not only far too young for a replacement mother, but not very pretty. She was a plain-looking twenty-year-old, with light hair and dimples in her cheeks giving her round face an extra circle. She was a sturdy girl and her mother made some offhand comment about her being built for childbearing.

Zdenka perked up her ears. "Childbearing?" she sneered. "Then Poppa couldn't help. He's already had his children."

"What, only three?" It was giddy Nadia's turn to sneer. "He can have more."

"He doesn't want more," Zdenka reared up on her hind legs. "Grandchildren are next for him, if Felix or Dimitri get married. I'm not getting married."

"Why not?" asked Mr. Polanski, who was a jovial man struggling to return some peace to the proceedings.

"I no longer have any trust in men," she said, and dropped her face.

"Oh, why not?" Nadia asked.

Zdenka brought her head up and fixed Nadia with her most withering stare. Zdenka was denied wine, so she was at an emotional disadvantage. Nadia was giddy, Zdenka was angry. "Because they only care about their animal instincts. My mother is not cold in her grave yet and here is my father panting after a girl who could be his child. It is so *disgusting!*"

Zdenka succeeded in putting a chill on the gathering which

no one was able to warm. Not mother Polanski, with her well-meaning switch of subject to her daughter's sensitivity and sense of propriety, not father Polanski, with his jovial frontal assault, citing the shenanigans of the sexes since Adam and Eve.

Her own father had signaled her with his frowning eyes, in vain. Her outspoken bitterness at what he hoped would have been a joyous occasion cut him lengthwise through the heart.

"Zdenka," he began, "please...Zdenka...please." But she only glared at him. He knew her glare was disapproving his weakness. But surely she was old enough to understand *why* she couldn't take her mother's place. He loved her so much, but it was too unreasonable for her to make him choose between a daughter and a bride.

Zdenka had wet the blanket and smothered them with it. She was already outside the door when she overheard Nadia saying goodbye to Augustus in the parlor.

"You mustn't pay any attention to her, Augustus, she's only a child," Nadia said. "Promise me you won't let her spoil it."

"No, no, I won't. She'll be all right. It goes hard on her. I understand. We all need a little more time."

"Yes, yes," Nadia said, "take your time, if you think time is what you need. I think you need a wife. You need help with Zdenka and Dimitri. And sooner better than later. We should not wait too long for their sake, first and foremost. They must not fall into the neglect of a household without the steady hand of a woman."

Augustus gently closed his eyes and nodded. He opened them and touched Nadia lightly on her arm—"Until next time," he said, and that satisfied her.

After her stoically silent trip home in the buggy, Zdenka focused her thoughts on a return singing engagement and a weekend with Katrina to make it possible. For a moment she feared her father would attempt to punish her for her behavior at the Polanskis' by not permitting her to go to Katrina's—but she figured, correctly as it turned out, that he would rather not have to contend with her contentious presence while he was courting Nadia. The further Zdenka was from him, the better.

Zdenka learned two new songs for her performance, and she turned all her thoughts to this show—her gestures, her costumes, her smiles and winks at the men. Her work was her solace. Without

67

admitting it to herself, she worked on the gestures that got the biggest reaction from the men: the sensual movements of her hands and body. Her school work suffered so much more, Sister Marie kept her after school. She looked down her nose. "What is wrong, Zdenka? Is your mother's death still weighing heavily on you?"

"Yes," Zdenka said, fluttering her eyelashes, then casting down her eyes.

"But she is happy with Jesus now," Sister Marie said. "You must not feel sorry for her."

"Oh, no," Zdenka said astutely. "I feel sorry for myself."

𝄞   𝄞   𝄞

Katrina was adamant about not going back to the Aristocrat Club with Zdenka. So the young girl who had aspirations of being the singing sensation of Poland had to make her own way down the dark and drizzly streets of Brest Litovsk.

For her part, Katrina did assist in the subterfuge required for Zdenka to slip out of the house after dinner and, of course, she couldn't possibly go to sleep until Zdenka had safely returned and told her absolutely *all* about it.

This time Zdenka's entry to the Aristocrat Club was something of a triumph. She was recognized as a celebrity on her return engagement. Her heart skipped to her throat at the cheer that went up when she entered. It was a good thing too, because her transit through these gloomy, dark streets and the depressing drizzle had made her wonder if she was doing a wise thing. But now she felt the reward of adulation, and nothing she'd experienced in her life was anything like it.

She was so elated, she momentarily forgot the beer smell and the dense fog of smoke. Pinky came toward her, his lips glistening, his ring prominent on his little finger. He wore a black suit, with a red carnation in his lapel, and a drooping bow tie. He looked to Zdenka like a peasant pretending to be an aristocrat.

"Ah, my Chickadee," he said, extending his arms as though he wanted to hug her. "You came back. I'm so pleased."

She took hold of his hands with hers, forestalling the hug.

"Let me buy you a drink," he said.

"Oh, no," she responded quickly with a flash of fear on her lips—"I came to sing again."

"Wonderful." Wallinski clapped his hands. Then he frowned. "Oh, but Ignance is not here tonight."

"Oh." Her face fell. "Can no one else play?"

He laughed, that raucous beer-hall laugh. "What do you take them for?" he asked her, waving his arm across the barroom, "aristocrats?" And that amused him more than anything.

"Oh—"

"Do not despair, my Chickadee," Wallinski said, "I will send someone for Ignance. Aronsky!" he called out. A wizened little man appeared as though through the legs of the men at the bar. "Fetch Ignance. Tell him the Chickadee has graced us with a return engagement."

Aronsky disappeared as suddenly as he had appeared.

Tables in the barroom were scarce. There were only three in all, all occupied. Pinky Wallinski tapped a man on the shoulder at the closest table, where two men were contributing to the ambiance with thick, lewd cigars. "What kind of gentlemen are you? Can't you see a lady is standing?—go stand at the bar, it's better for you."

The men got up, grumbling, leaving their empty beer glasses on the table. Pinky called after them. "Hey! What kind of aristocrats are you? Clean up your glasses." The men both returned and picked up their beer glasses and took them to the bar.

"Now, that's better," Pinky said. "Sit down a minute, young lady."

Zdenka appeared uncertain.

"Come, come—only until Ignance comes. You are the guest of honor here anytime you come—I can't have you standing among all these swells. Gives the place a bad name. Now what can I get you to drink?"

"Oh, nothing, thanks." She smiled uncomfortably.

"Hey, what kind of host would I be? You drink beer, don't you?"

"No, I..."

"Aren't too young, are you?"

"No, I—"

"Well, have one then. Time to develop a taste," he said, leering at her. "High time. Here," he said, reaching for her coat. "Let me take your coat. Make yourself comfortable—stay awhile."

Zdenka thought she should keep the coat on until she sang. She had borrowed some clothes from Katrina and had, she thought, made a startling outfit and she didn't want to spoil the effect. She had calculated how she would make the most effective entrance. Taking her coat off without performing for these huddled men would be almost like stripping. But it was so warm with it on that she let him help her out of it. She had a sudden rush when she realized all of the men's eyes were on her, and she felt like Pinky was undressing her for their benefit.

And there were whistles, and there were catcalls, the men were not stingy with their approval—Zdenka tried to block out the suggestive comments.

Zdenka had taken a conservative black silk dress from Katrina's closet then embellished it with two red scarves: one she had tied under her bosom, which served to push it up alluringly, the other she tied around her waist with a big bow in back, the loops provocatively circling and accentuating her buttocks, with the ends hanging limp between the delicately sculpted cheeks.

"Very nice outfit." Pinky beamed his approval amid the cheers from the crowd, while she whispered to him that she just wanted to sing.

"Yes, yes—as soon as Ignance comes." Then he started away from the table and she panicked.

"Where are you going?"

"Just to hang up your coat."

"You can leave it here."

"I'll be right back."

The coat disappeared, and though she craned her neck from her seat to see where he put it, she couldn't. There were just too many men in the way. Pinky reappeared carrying two glasses of beer and sat down across from her, placing one of the tall glasses in front of Zdenka. He hoisted his glass and nodded to her, encouraging her to lift her glass. She let it sit. He took a swallow of his and covered his wet lips with the tiny bubbles of the foam. "Mmm," he said, "*good* for you. Try some." He looked at her glass as though that was all the encouragement she needed. But she stayed still. He resigned for the moment.

"So, how do you like school?" he asked.

She twisted her nose.

"Not too much, eh?" he said. "I never cared for it myself. 'Course, you have all those nuns and no boys. Does that bother you?"

"No."

"Don't you like boys?"

"I don't know."

"Well, I had a girlfriend when I was your age. Don't you want a boyfriend?"

"No."

He noticed she was focusing her attention on his ring. He slipped it off his finger and reached for her hand. She looked at him quickly, then let him take her hand. He did the same gesture he had done before, sliding the ring back and forth on her middle finger, only now it was more prolonged—broader—and he had a lascivious grin on his glistening lips. "You ever feel like doing this?" he asked.

"What?"

"You know—*this*." He kept sliding the ring back and forth.

She blushed. "No," she said. No, she decided, was decidedly the best response. She wasn't sure what he meant, but she had an idea from the look on his face and his tone of voice that it wasn't good.

"You like the ring, don't you?"

She nodded. He didn't have to ask.

"Well, there's a lot more things you could have, you know, if you took it in your mind to be friendly."

"Like what?"

"Oh, money, clothes, other jewels. Whatever you wanted."

"Could you get me other places to sing?"

"Sure. That's easy."

"Maybe...nicer places? Places that have women in them?"

"But you are going to be a *star*, Chickadee. You will have your pick of places. First you get your routines set here—with an audience—then there will be no stopping you."

Zdenka considered her dream. It sounded good to her, but even her young mind was generating doubts.

"And I will even pay you while you learn."

"Pay me?"

"Certainly. You are good for business. The men love you. If they know you are coming, there won't be room to stand here. Think of it—a salary, clothes, jewels..."

"What would I have to do for all those things?" Zdenka asked. "Just sing?"

"Yes, and be friendly."

"Friendly?" She looked at him as though he were speaking riddles.

"Yeah," he said. "Real friendly. *Closer* friends, like...with me." His eye closed in that awful wink. "Intimate," he said.

"Oh—" Her face fell.

"Did you ever think about being with a man?"

"Well, I'm with you now."

Pinky's lascivious mirth returned and he shook with laughter. "Yeah," he said, "that's good. You're with me now—so I got a little room upstairs. Want to be with me there?"

"No, here is fine," she said, understanding too well.

He read her mind. "Listen, Chickadee, you don't have to play dumb with me. I got eyes. I can see how you got yourself up." He waved a stubby finger in her direction. "Now you're a beautiful girl, but the question is, do you want to cash in on your beauty, or do you want to hide it under a rock, spending your life as some farmer's drudge? I'd say from looking at the getup you got on you had a mind to cash in."

Zdenka blushed. How could this creature misunderstand her so? "I'm just wearing a singing costume—that's all it is."

"A singing costume," he repeated, bobbing his head in mockery. "Well, let me tell you something about provoking men. Maybe you are just a peasant and you don't know anything."

"I'm not a peasant!" she said.

"No? Then you know what you're doing."

"What am I doing?"

"You are getting a lot of men worked up for nothing," he shook his disapproving head, "there's no payoff at the end. You're just a tease."

"I'm not anything of the sort," she argued. "You invited me here to sing. Were you lying to me? Did you really invite me here for something else? Because if you did, I can go home right now."

He didn't respond. He just looked deep into her pretty eyes and wondered. Speculated. This was not going to be an easy score, and yet...he couldn't or wouldn't rule it out as a complete impossibility. He tried another tack. He reached over to take her hand in his. She withdrew it to her lap.

"The ring," he said. "Like to have one of your own some-day?"

She looked him in the eye, then dropped her eyes and nod-ded.

"Could, you know. You could own this one. It could be like we were engaged."

"We're not," she said.

"I could give you lots of things."

"The ring?"

He laughed. "Maybe not right away. But you could wear it."

"What would I have to do?"

"Come upstairs," he said, smiling in a manner he thought irresistible, "I'll show you."

"No, thank you," she said, finding his smile revolting. "I'm a good Catholic girl."

"That religion get to you?"

"I don't know what you mean."

"God and Jesus. The stuff the nuns teach you. You go for that, do you?"

"I don't know. I guess some."

"Believe there's a God, do you?"

"Yessss—" She decided under the circumstances to use the religion she scoffed at as a defensive weapon.

"And He watches everything you do?"

"I guess."

"Be a pretty busy fella, wouldn't He?"

"Busy?"

"Yeah, watching everybody—or do you think He only watch-es *you?*"

73

"No, I think He watches you too."

"And everybody?"

"Yes."

"So how could He have time? You know how many people there are? He wouldn't have time to give you a fraction of a second a year. Probably not in your lifetime." He shook his head. "Isn't in the cards, Chickadee. It's all make-believe."

His disbelief got her back up, giving her a blazing, if temporal, faith. "Well, He can *so* do it—He's not a person like us—He's God."

"So you think you do good, God rewards you; you do bad, He punishes you?"

She nodded.

His nod was of weary understanding. "Let me tell you a story. I had the same kind of Jesus stuff drilled into me when I was your age. And I went for it. I come from a poor, big family. City dwellers we was. Went to church every Sunday—the whole shooting match of us. That was eleven, not counting the animals. I was pretty young—seven or eight or so—when my mother took a shine to the priest. Yes, don't look so shocked, he encouraged it. It happens—just people like you and me and the king. My mother was an emotional woman, maybe not as stable as she could be, but that's no cause to do her like they done. I don't know all the details exactly because I was so young—but later I picked up the story. The priest was out for a good time. My mother was more serious about the thing. She thought he was going to throw it all over and marry her." He shook his head dolefully at the memory. "No such luck. I guess she got a little hysterical. So they say anyway. It was in her nature. Wound up in the bottom of the river—nobody saw nothing. Oh, I prayed for revenge like nobody ever prayed before. The same priest had taught me that God listens and the good are rewarded, the bad punished. My prayers were simple—I just wanted that murdering priest struck dead." He shook his head again. "No dice. Never even got a bad cold, far as I could see. Just went on leading other women astray. One after the other—no bolts of lightning to strike him dead. And, as I say, he never even got the sniffles."

"Maybe he'll burn in hell," she said.

"Yeah, that's a good one. This one should have burned *before* hell—because hell is like all the rest of it, a figment of the imagination. No, Chickadee, there are millions of these examples. Your mother—was she a good woman?"

Zdenka's lips tightened. She nodded.

"So why was God so hot to knock her down when all those bad apples are still bobbing about?"

"It must be God's plan."

"Not a very good plan, is it?"

"You mustn't talk blasphemy, Mr. Wallinski. We are not to understand the ways of God. We must have the faith."

"Yeah, that's the best one. Don't try to understand, just believe. Well, I believe—I believe it's all make-believe. And I'm offering you a test."

"What kind of test?"

"Go with me to my room. I'll show you the most beautiful mystery of life. See if God touches either one of us."

She shuddered. "I only came to sing."

"Ah, yes—sing—and sing you shall—just as soon as Ignance shows up. There—I think he's coming in the door now—"

Zdenka smiled tentatively at Ignance when he shuffled to, and sat at, the piano. His familiar shambling presence comforted her momentarily. She wasn't sure he was so happy to be there, but she wouldn't pay any attention. She didn't want to look weak or uncertain. She was the star, after all. He was only the accompaniment. Besides, he didn't *have* to come.

A moment before she started to sing—when she was standing onstage in her provocative outfit, with the red scarf hiking her developing bosom and the circles accenting her haunches—Zdenka felt self-conscious. All the eyes were on her now and those eyes were not aimed at her face. The whistles and rude remarks made her wonder if she had made the right wardrobe decision.

Ignance began playing a few arpeggios and soon Zdenka was in full flower, singing her heart out, flashing Pinky's diamond, strutting the tiny space between the piano and the back wall and singing songs of love that drove the men wild. In the heat of her triumph her fear evaporated.

Pinky had stayed at the table and he couldn't take his eyes off Zdenka. He adored watching her breasts move as she did, following her movements as they did. He thought she was singing words she didn't understand, and some of her gestures made him think of child pornography, an art with which he had been familiar earlier in his career. Her charm was the charm of innocence. It was firing up Pinky's glands.

After her first song ended, she felt the fear return. The men seemed bolder, scarier. Was it because she was alone? Could it be she had overdone the costume?

As soon as she began her second number, the fear retreated again as she concentrated on projecting her cute, coy delivery. During this song a man came up to her, scaring her to death, then passed by her to go out the door on the wall behind her, to the privy outside.

A few minutes later, while she was singing her love song, she heard the door, and suddenly the Aristocrat Club broke into unaristocratic laughter which drowned out her thin voice.

Zdenka turned and saw a scrawny man behind her doing his own dance in mimic of her, only he was doing his dance with the most unflattering gyrations of his pelvis. Her seeing him was cause for extra merriment from the audience; Zdenka was humiliated. She started to move away from him, but his arm shot out and he grabbed her behind.

Zdenka panicked. She wanted to make a run for it, but there were too many men out front and there was this lewd creature behind her. Her terror was cold and complete. Quickly she sidestepped the aggressor, and the red scarf came off her waist in his hand. She got behind him and grabbed his behind and the whole place collapsed in laughter as the pelvic-dancer's jaw dropped and his false teeth hung loose in his mouth.

In the pandemonium, Zdenka got away from her attacker—

who was still holding her scarf as though it were a dead rattlesnake—and shot out the back door. She heard Pinky's voice shout, "Wait!" but she wasn't waiting. In the alley, the rain was falling again, and she ran between two old sheds in the back of the privy. Just as she cleared the second building, the door to the privy shot open and she could see on the wall of the building opposite, a giant, puffy shadow of a man looming in the glow of the single gas lamp lighting the path from the Aristocrat Club to the privy.

"Hey!" the shadow shouted. "Who's there? What...?"

But Zdenka was off and running when she heard the back door of the club open and the laughter spilling out. She was freezing cold and drenched to the bone without her coat, but she had no thought of going back for it.

"Where'd she go?" Pinky asked the shadow. "The bitch got my ring."

"I dunno—I'm just tending to my business and I hear this noise, sounded too big for the usual rats, so I yells and I don't hear nothing more."

"Go after her," Pinky commanded.

"Not me. I got no beef. It's *your* ring. Damn fool thing giving it to her in the first place, you ask me."

"Oh, sweet Jesus," Pinky groaned. "I'll never catch her. Now I got to go back to that prune-faced mother superior on all fours and beg again. Jesus, what if the kid stonewalls me this time—says she dropped it on the way home?"

"So you break her kneecaps—"

Zdenka stopped dead when she heard that. She hid behind a shed waiting to see which way Pinky took. Her heart was pounding, but she was afraid to move. She tried to control her heaving breath, but wasn't doing a very good job of it.

"See which way she went?"

"Didn't see nuthin'."

"Think I'll take a look."

With that tragic news, Zdenka took off running down the alley.

"Hey!" Pinky started after her. "Wait," he shouted, "I'm not going to hurt you. Just give me my ring."

But Zdenka kept on running.

"Take the ring off. Leave it on the street. I won't follow you. The ring! Leave the ring!"

But Zdenka was out of trust, and Pinky was out of breath. Zdenka kept running through the rainy streets, zigzagging in and out of spaces between buildings, and Pinky at last gave up the chase.

When Zdenka reached the back door of Katrina's house—the door left open for her by Katrina—she had to stop and rest for five minutes, she was breathing so hard.

Then she carefully opened the door and took off her wet shoes and tiptoed up the servants' stairs.

Katrina was sitting up in bed waiting in her dark bedroom.

"Oh, Zdenka, I was so worried." Katrina's heart was beating as fast as if she had been party to the escape.

"*You* were worried. I was terrified! Oh, Katrina, you were so right, it was the biggest mistake of my life going back there."

Then Zdenka recapped her nightmare, flopping down on the bed with all her wet clothes on.

"I shouldn't have let you go alone," Katrina said. "They *touched* you again?"

"What could they get out of touching like that? Agh—" Zdenka shuddered. She was so wound up she felt she could never go to sleep. "Oh, Katrina, my heart is still pounding a mile a minute."

"So is mine," Katrina confessed, half embarrassed. "You're sure nobody saw you come here?"

"I'm sure."

"Or even into the neighborhood?"

"He's so fat, he started to chase me, but he didn't get more than a block before he petered out."

Katrina giggled. For a while there was only the sound of Zdenka's breathing and the almost audible sounds of Katrina's curiosity. "Zdenka?" she said.

"Hm?"

"How does it feel...to be touched...like that?"

Zdenka didn't answer right away. She tried to collect her thoughts. "Well, scary," she said at last. "There's all those men and they are all looking at you like hungry animals, so that's scary." Zdenka shook her head. "And it isn't as though they *like* you or anything. It isn't at all personal. I mean, we are all built alike."

"Oh, no, we're not," Katrina insisted. "Sure, there are similarities, but some of us are more...well, touchable than others. I get the creeps when I just think about it."

"Yeah, but did you ever think about it? That this is nature? And this is how we girls get boys to take care of us?" Her voice dropped. "Like Nadia and my father. You know she's only twenty years old?"

"No!"

"And it's so pathetic the way you can see him leering at her. He just wants to grab her like those men grabbed me. And it isn't just one or two men, it's all of them. And you know the really pathetic thing is how defenseless men are. This fat man was offering me the moon to just go to his room with him."

"Well, I'm sure he wanted more than that!"

"Sure he did. But why should he have to offer so much? There are just about as many women as men anyway. Just because our bodies are different than theirs, they go crazy."

"Yeah, pretty stupid, huh?" Katrina said. There was another silence while they considered just *how* stupid.

Katrina spoke first. "But, Zdenka, you wouldn't, you know, you wouldn't *do* anything, would you?"

"*Do?*" Zdenka said, her breathing finally coming under her control. "Lots of women do things or we wouldn't even *be* here. Maybe we don't think about it, but our mothers had to *do* something or we wouldn't be here."

"Oh, but, Zdenka, you don't mean...I mean, what would you do if you had a baby with that ugly man?"

"I won't, don't worry."

"But you still have his big, fat ring."

"All rich men aren't fat and ugly. Some are handsome. They all want the same thing. Women could have anything they want."

"I just want to be taken care of," Katrina said quietly.

"Why would you just want to follow some man around like a faithful dog?"

"It's our place, Zdenka," Katrina said.

"Not *my* place," Zdenka said. "Maybe you have everything you want and you don't need a man."

"I do want to be married. Then I suppose I will do what I

must. But it's sinful to let men touch you before you're married," Katrina said.

"Sinful? Why is it always sinful when someone gets pleasure from something?"

"Would you get pleasure from a man touching you?"

"I don't know. Not that way—at the club. A stranger just grabbing you out of the blue. But there are softer touches I can imagine with someone you care for. And if you can give a man that much pleasure that easily and he'll be so grateful he'll give you the world in return—why not?"

"Would *you* get pleasure from it?" Katrina asked.

"I don't know. Maybe I would. If I wouldn't get some pleasure I wouldn't do it. Maybe it's like trading pleasure for pleasure. You know, like, he gets his animal pleasure and I get the pleasure of nice things, like fine clothes and jewels and stuff."

"And you wouldn't have to be married?"

"I don't know. I guess eventually."

"Eventually!? What if you had a baby before eventually came?"

"Oh, I wouldn't. I'd stop him before it went that far."

"But what if he can't stop?"

"*I* can," Zdenka said, as if she were an old hand at controlling men.

Zdenka had taken to giving her father the silent treatment. She had abruptly cut off their walks in the woods, and much to her disappointment, Poppa didn't seem to miss them. She grudgingly admitted to herself she had been replaced by that repulsive Polanski child.

So, the moment Poppa asked Zdenka to go for another walk in the woods with him, she knew the news was not good.

Here and there little bits of sunshine were breaking through the clouds. The trees were just beginning to leaf out, and the transient sun was making exciting patterns on the ground. But today, those shadowy patterns held no fascination for Zdenka.

She detected a nervousness about

her father that she was unaccustomed to on earlier walks. They weren't very far in the woods when she felt the conversation shifting from small talk about school (fine) and her weekend with her friend Katrina (fine) to more serious matters.

"Look, Zdenka, I'm no good at this," he blurted, "I care for Nadia and I so wish you would try to care for her."

"Care for her? As a school friend? That might be all right—though I would find her rather a silly goose."

"I've been empty since Momma died," Poppa confessed, hoping for sympathy. "Some men do just fine living without women. For me, that is not easy."

"I don't see what's so hard living without Nadia," Zdenka said. "I could live without her just fine."

"But you see," he confessed, "I can't. I have asked her father's permission…and it was granted. I daresay he looks upon the union with favor. I'm rather proud of that." He beamed his pride at Zdenka, who took it as pathetic. "Of course, Nadia has been very happy to accept."

Zdenka's face looked as if she'd had a stroke.

"The boys are taking it in stride," he said, "but, Babushka, you are my favorite, I cannot make a secret of it. I so do need your good wishes to welcome Nadia to our family."

"But…but, you don't mean—you don't mean you are replacing my mother with this child—?"

"Certainly not replacing. No one can replace."

"And so *soon!*"

"A new beginning."

"And you—the one telling me I couldn't go to Katrina's because of appearances."

"Please, Zdenka…"

"How does this appear? What happened to your fine appearances?"

"Zdenka…"

"She is to take my mother's place in your bed and she is *my* age—"

"She is older, Babushka, please—"

"Oh, it's so disgusting—"

"Babushka, please! Someday I hope you will understand.

83

Forgive me—when it comes to love, men are weak. Women definitely have the power," he said with a gesture of hopelessness with his hands and arms.

"And I suppose there will be more babies?"

"Nadia wants children, yes."

"Oh, no." Zdenka began to sob but fought it with all her might. "You're so *disgusting!*" She spat out her assassin's bullets and ran back to the house, across the broken-branch shadows.

Augustus was distraught. He'd wanted to speak of how the first buds of spring symbolized new beginnings. He'd wanted to be so clever, so poetic, but she stopped him cold. The child was headstrong; his late wife said it was because she was born in the middle and had to fight both ends—and boys yet, to toughen her hide. Well, her hide was tough all right. But what good was that going to do her? Women are supposed to be soft, tender, giving, loving. And his beloved Babushka seemed to be just the opposite.

Zdenka did not feel good about calling her Poppa disgusting. She had just coughed it up from the well of her anger. But she wasn't about to apologize. She wasn't talking to him anyway.

In school, Zdenka shut down completely. She refused to participate in class, and on her examinations she didn't answer one question.

Of course that ugly man had come for her ring, without bringing her coat or her scarf. She didn't have the ring at school, and he made a terrible scene in front of the mother superior, insinuating Zdenka had suggested shady things to him for the ring, and she had even taken her coat and scarf off in his room. He, of course, would have none of it. He realized a trap when he saw one. Zdenka was too dumbfounded to argue. Pinky spoke of them drinking beer together, without mentioning that Zdenka hadn't touched hers. It was enough for the mother superior to hear this creature of the nether world tell further tales of consorting with one of her underage students—and whereas she was willing to overlook it before, because the man had seemed earnest, this time she was not.

The mother superior sent a note home with Zdenka for Augustus to come to school in the next few days, at his convenience. There was no response. When she questioned Zdenka, she said simply she had not given him the note, as she was not speaking to him.

The aging nun lectured her on honoring her parents, and Zdenka interrupted.

"I'm going to have a new mother—"

"Yes, I've seen the banns—"

"And she's *my* age."

The mother superior was no more effective placating Zdenka than Augustus had been. "Very well," she said, "do you want to give my note to your father or do you want me to send it by the post, explaining why that was necessary?"

"I lost the note."

"Accidentally?"

Zdenka pressed her lips together in silence.

"Child, you have far departed from the teachings of our Church and the Blessed Mother. To consort with a man like that who now comes here with these unspeakable tales shows a plunging into the sins of hell which I can scarcely imagine. You are no better than a whore!"

Zdenka's head whipped around in fury. She fixed her vengeful eyes on the mother superior. "*What* did you call me?"

"I did not call you anything, don't you accuse me. Know your place, child."

"You did so. You called me a *whore!*"

"I said you were no better than a whore. It is not the same—"

"And you?"

The mother superior cranked her back up until she was sitting at full height, looking down her knife-blade nose as though she wanted to use it to slice the girl in two. "Careful, child."

"I am not a child." Zdenka's anger was building. It was as though "child" was a greater insult than "whore."

"Yes, you seem bent on demonstrating that. Well, let me tell you, you have not the slightest notion about being a grownup. No responsible grownup would have two seconds' worth of society with that cretin. You lack judgment, girl." She shook her head dolefully.

"You have miles to go before you can be called a grownup."

"Oh?" Zdenka stared her undisguised hate at the mother superior. "And what about *you*? I suppose *you* think *you* are a grownup—the disgusting way you pawed me. Is *that* what grownups do? Or are *you* a whore?"

Mother Superior's eyes opened so wide they hurt. "You *disgraceful child!* Your days are numbered here. And God only knows what will become of you. You are headstrong, selfish, mean and thoughtless, and the world is a hard place. Those attributes will not bode you well in life and I strongly recommend you overcome them. I suggest you start with charity toward your father. Now it's back to class for you where you *will* give my words some thought. The Lord knows from your record you aren't giving your schoolwork any thought."

At Augustus's request, the meeting with Mother Superior was without Zdenka. He had tears in his eyes when he told of his dilemma with the girl. Mother Superior was moved by the man's simplicity, his frank admission of being ineffectual with his Zdenka. She said, "I am sorry to have to tell you she is doing nothing in school. We will allow her to finish this term, but if she were to return she would be required to repeat the school year."

When she told him about fat Wallinski and the ring, he was astonished. She suggested he keep a close eye on her. "I will pray for you, Mr. Oleska. The coming weeks which should bring you joy will, I fear, not be easy. Perhaps you want to consider sending her away for a while."

"Oh, no—I couldn't do that."

"Don't you have relatives she could visit?"

He thought before speaking. "I have a sister in St. Petersburg—but her husband is an artist. A free spirit. I don't think that is what Zdenka needs. She needs a strong hand, which I am not. I cannot let my child go. She is so young."

Mother Superior sighed. "Very well, she is your child. I will pray for you both."

Augustus cried all the way home.

Zdenka's father forced her to attend the modest marriage ceremony in their living room, and she saw to it that he'd wished he hadn't. She sat through the nuptials glum and sullen. When spoken to at the reception put on by Mrs. Polanski and Nadia, she answered in monosyllabic grunts, unless addressed by her father or Nadia, in which case she answered not at all.

There had been wine at the party and Augustus and Nadia were quite happy—and the happier they got, the more sullen and withdrawn Zdenka became.

She hadn't wanted to attract the attention of her big brother, Felix, but he couldn't help noticing her behavior.

"Okay, crybaby," he said, "what's

eating you?"

"Nothing!"

"Oh, yah—nothing. You're mad, aren't you? Anyone can tell by looking at you. You *look* mad—so if you aren't mad, you are sure trying to *look* mad."

"I am not!"

Felix looked at Zdenka. She looked away, out the window, to the edge of the woods where she'd gone on so many walks with her father.

"It's time to grow up, Princess. Physically you're almost there. Get the chip off your shoulder. You gotta learn to swim with the tide. You're fighting the current all the time. Look at me, kid. I'm your *brother*. I'm your friend. Poppa is your friend too. This should be a happy day for Poppa. Don't spoil it any more. If you can't be a grownup, go up to your room."

Zdenka was hurt. She thought her big brother, Felix, should be on her side. Now he was siding against her with their new *step-mother*.

Zdenka decided to take Felix's advice about going to her room, instead of about making peace, but on her way, her dreaded Nadia stopped her. Nadia looked so out of place in the white frilly dress she wore. Zdenka thought it was scandalous to dress up like a blushing bride to marry a guy your father's age who had three kids already.

The confrontation took place at the bottom of the stairs. "There is my beautiful Zdenka," she said, smiling so generously, Zdenka thought it was more from the wine than from any genuine feeling. She wanted to tell her she wasn't *hers* and never would be, but that would entail speaking to her, and that she had vowed not to do.

"I want to be your friend, Zdenka," Nadia said. "I'm going to be here morning, noon and night, so shouldn't we try to get along?" She waited for an answer, but none came. Zdenka thought her new stepmother was showing a pathetic weakness when she should seize the position of strength. She feared her household was about to be directed by *two* weaklings. "I will not do you harm," Nadia said. "I love your father and he needs me. I need him. Yes, he's old enough to be my father and I'm not old enough to be your mother. Is that so important? I will take good care of him. He *needs* that."

"I could do that!" Zdenka broke her silence.

"Oh, I'm sure you could. But you are a beautiful, bright girl, and I am plain. You have a wonderful future ahead of you. You won't be satisfied to stay out here in the woods all your life."

"I could now," she offered quietly, chagrined that Nadia seemed to know her inner thoughts.

"Yes, I know you could. And you might even stay long enough so there wouldn't be anyone willing to take care of your father—like a wife would. Or you might feel so tied here—so obligated—that you had to forego your own dreams and never would leave. Would you like that?"

Zdenka seemed to consider that for a moment, but instead of answering her new stepmother, she made a sudden jerking motion, darted beside Nadia and ran up the stairs to her room, passing Felix on the way. He was shaking his head as though he had heard the whole conversation, which he had. He was obviously trying to register his continued disapproval with her, Zdenka thought, but she was, she told herself, beyond caring.

Two hours later, Zdenka was beginning to think she should have brought some food with her. The party was still in full flower and she was beginning to get hungry. The daylight was beginning to fade and, staring out her window, she could no longer see the woods. She was finding her inner resources for self-amusement flagging, when, with a sudden burst of excitement, Felix barged into Zdenka's room.

He startled her at her desk, where she was drawing pictures of her handsome father and an especially ugly, disfigured bride.

"C'mon," Felix commanded, grabbing her wrist so hard it hurt her.

"Stop it!" she cried, tugging her wrist from his grasp, which was too strong for her.

"I'm going to show you something, you brat," he said, yanking her up from her chair and pulling her behind him, down the stairs, through scattered cliques of guests and outside to the barnyard and from there over to the pigpen. They stopped at the three-rail fence that separated the pigs from the people.

Zdenka detested the smell of the barnyard, *especially* the pigpen. The only thing she found more disgusting was the smell of the privy out back. Sometimes she thought that smell clung to her like a leech and she wanted to run to the end of the world and jump off just to get away from it. Katrina didn't smell like a barnyard. Her family had money, they didn't need to have pigs. Dirty, smelly, disgusting creatures. Why couldn't *she* be like Katrina? Someday she would be!

"There," Felix commanded her. "Look!"

At first Zdenka didn't understand. She saw the pigs, there was nothing startling about that, then she looked to where he was pointing—in the far corner. One pig was climbing up the back of another and moving forward unsteadily. But she understood. She blushed, then wondered what reaction she should give her brother: naive, or so what? Felix didn't wait for any signal from Zdenka.

"That's it," he said with a menacing tone Zdenka didn't understand. "The boar and the sow—people're no different. The doing and the done to. Clean sheets don't make no difference. It's all the same. Men gotta have it and women got to take it. Look at this. Who do you think is having the most fun here?"

Zdenka was frightened. She clenched her teeth and tightened her fists.

"You're disgusting!" she shouted, covering her ears with her fists.

"It's the way we're built," Felix protested. "Men are no different 'n pigs. And someday that's gonna be you on the bottom. Look— the things the pigs got are same's people got. The thing goes in—and where it goes—all the same."

"Stop it!"

"Oh, yeah? The princess is too delicate a lady to think of such things? Better start thinking. Now you got yourself some tits, the boys'll be all over you like flies on horse manure. So don't go lah-di-dah on *me. Or* your father. You expect him to go into the priesthood, you're sadly mistaken. Time comes for you I don't expect there'll be any nunnery."

"Oooo!" She broke away from her brother's hold on her and bolted back into the house, darting up the stairway to the sanctuary of her room, where she slammed the door with a resounding wham.

She sat in a huff at her desk and stared at her drawings without seeing them.

Felix had called her a princess. She knew he meant to be disparaging, but she would far rather be a princess, she thought, than a pig farmer for the rest of her life.

But now her anger was being crowded out of her consciousness by her surprisingly uncontrollable hunger.

Finally, people were starting to leave, just as Zdenka was positive she was about to starve to death. She'd had plenty of time to think about what the best way to cope with the new situation would be, and she'd decided flight was the only sure solution. But where would she go? Her father would never allow it, he'd told her as much, and she had nowhere to go by herself. Oh, that ugly fat man at the Aristocrat Club would take her in, but she shuddered at the thought.

When she could simply not hold out another second without food, Zdenka quietly opened her door and tiptoed down the stairs. She almost made it to the kitchen, when her father came out of the parlor to intercept her.

"There's my Babushka," he cried, and put his weightless arm around her and drew her to his chest. He smelled of fruity wine and seemed happier than she had ever seen him. Why should he be so happy while she was so miserable? "Where have you been? I've been looking all over for you."

Well, she knew *that* wasn't true. All he would have had to do was look in her room—the *first* place anyone would look.

"Everyone was asking for you." He smiled and gave her developing body another squeeze. She wiggled free and dashed for the kitchen. Augustus watched her go and felt a sadness squeeze his heart. Why must life present such conflicts? If only he could find a way to make his daughter more accepting.

Then his bride came through the parlor door and put her arm around him and whispered in his ear with her own wine breath, and Augustus giggled and blushed. But he didn't argue.

In the kitchen, Zdenka was revolted at the sound of her father giggling. That was for girls. Men don't giggle like that. With strength enough to sustain her anger, she returned upstairs, without incident this time, and began to wonder what it would be like to be ignored completely. Suppose, she thought, Poppa stops putting his arm around me? Stops talking to me altogether, like I've stopped talking to him? What then? She frowned. After a moment's thought, she dropped the subject. Too unpleasant.

When the last person had finally left the party and Augustus and Nadia had trundled up the stairs to bed, just across the wall from Zdenka's bed, Zdenka decided she had just spent the longest day of her life. And the night was going to be even longer. The giggling, grunting and sundry carrying-on next door turned her stomach. Couldn't they even wait until she went to sleep? Of course, she couldn't *go* to sleep—not with all the turmoil in her life.

The noises became so annoying Zdenka buried her head under her pillow. But even that didn't give her any peace. She got out of bed, moving as noiselessly as she could, opened her door and slid her feet along the wooden hallway floor until she was standing next to her father's bedroom door, the bedroom he now shared with a virtual child.

But, now what? She could knock on the door and ask them to be quiet. She could storm into the room and embarrass them (and probably herself more). She stood facing the door, with her balled fists on her hips, looking like she was about to huff and puff and blow the door open. But she did no such thing, and the frustration exasperated her. In anger, she shook her fist at the air, intending it as a symbolic, yet unseen, warning to the couple. Instead, her fist accidentally bumped the door, which had not been securely latched. The jolt caused it to open partway, enough to show Zdenka much more than she wanted to see of her father and his bride. Startled and paralyzed for only an instant, Zdenka broke and ran back to her room, closing the door carefully then diving onto her bed. She buried her head in the covers in a futile effort to contain her sobbing. It's the pigs, she thought. They are just like pigs.

What had angered and confused Zdenka more than the animal act she had just witnessed was the reality of this girl staying all night in Poppa's bed. Why would he want her to do that? Why would he let her?

Zdenka remembered when she was a little girl going into Poppa's bed after a scary dream. Momma complained at the nuisance, but Poppa was understanding. He liked to have his little girl sleep beside him. He *could* have had her again. It would have been better. Why would her poppa want to sleep with a stranger? She wasn't going to let any man sleep with her all night. Why have someone cramp your space in bed when you could be luxuriously alone. Look at them, she thought, there is not six inches between them. They must bump into each other all night. Disgusting!

In the next room, Nadia sat bolt upright in the nuptial bed, as though the man she had been embracing had not been her husband but raw electricity.

Startled, Augustus said, "What?"

"Did you hear that?"

"I heard nothing, my sweet," he said. "What are you doing?"

"I heard something at the door," she said. "Look, it is open."

"Must have been the wind," Augustus said, peering at the door, which stood a few inches ajar. "I see nobody."

"There is no wind," she muttered, stepping out of bed without covering her nakedness. Nadia went to the door and opened it, peering down the short hallway. She closed the door, carefully latching it this time. She returned to her husband's bed, somewhat sobered.

"Now don't let anything spoil this," Augustus said, reaching for his bride.

"Spying," she said without moving toward her new mate. "I don't want war, Augustus. Talk to her."

"I have," he said. "I'm at my wit's end."

There was a cumbersome silence between them. Augustus was stroking Nadia's bare back. She was biting her lower lip. "Send her away," she said at last.

Augustus snorted at the idea. "Where?"

"Anywhere. Don't you have relatives in Russia? She's sixteen years old. Maybe she'll grow up if she has to take some responsibility somewhere. She could be a governess or a cook or something. She's spoiled, Augustus. Spoiled way beyond your means. Maybe if she has to work for a while she'll come back with a different attitude. I know it's hard on her having me move in, but it's hard on me also."

Augustus seemed to melt into the bedclothes. "I can't do anything with her," he said. "She's so headstrong."

"Then I will," Nadia said, and as though the matter were settled for all time, she sank back down beside her husband, his id instantly wakening, and took him to her.

Act II

THE BARON

Baron: A pretty wench,
egad! She's vastly
pleasing.

—*Der Rosenkavalier*

Madame Hanna Mazurka
remembers:

THE BARON

Saint Petersburg, Russia

"I thought I was marrying a strong man—a member of the aristocracy, who could take care of me like a young woman wants to be taken care of by her husband. Yet I had to make all the decisions, for he turned out to be weak, weak, weak."

The cars of the train to St. Petersburg, Russia, reminded Zdenka of her mother's coffin. There was a whole family's worth of coffins strung together, taking their passengers to the end of their journeys.

Poppa cried when he put Zdenka on the coffin train, just like he had cried beside the coffin at Momma's funeral. It embarrassed Zdenka. People were looking with the long faces of disapproval, she thought, when actually they were preoccupied with thoughts and fears of their own journey.

Standing on that platform in Brest Litovsk, the father and daughter watched as the old steam engine inched the train noisily along to its resting place beside the platform. As they waited for the train to stop, both of them realized this was the end of the journey for their old life as father/daughter. Father had taken a child bride over Zdenka's own offer. Nadia had wanted to come to town to the train to see Zdenka off, but Zdenka had made a scene of protest and Poppa gave in to his child this one last time. So, it was just the two of them, father and daughter, saying their goodbyes.

"You *will* come back to me, Babushka," Poppa wailed.

His despair made Zdenka so uncomfortable. "You made your choice," she said resolutely, without so much as a flinch of her eyes.

"Oh, Zdenka," he said, "you are strong, strong, strong."

Zdenka thought, and you are weak, weak, weak, and I'm not coming back. She got on the train without looking back at Poppa.

The moment the train pulled out of the station, Zdenka felt a chill run through her body, as though the train itself had used her for a tunnel. She began to shiver, though the air inside the train was quite warm. Before the train had left Brest Litovsk, she missed her poppa and wished she had turned to wave. She looked out the window as though he might still be there. He wasn't, and the pain Zdenka felt in the separation cut deep into her. I am on my own, she said to herself, as she watched the city change to country. There will be no Poppa anymore to take my side. He has Nadia. I am alone. The child of yesterday is gone. I am a woman now.

More than one man on the train seemed to share that assessment, and though they made Zdenka feel uncomfortable with their stares, she made believe she didn't see them.

By the time she made it to St. Petersburg, Zdenka felt she had grown two years in stature and savvy.

Zdenka's Aunt Helene and Uncle Vanya Gorky met her at the train.

Uncle Vanya gasped when he saw Zdenka get off the train. He half hoped when he asked her, "Are you Zdenka?" she would say, "No," so he might make a terrible play for her.

But when their eyes met, hers sparkling with joyous anticipation of the unknown mingled with a becoming nervousness, and his in frank admiration, he knew this was his wife's brother's child and he must control his excitement.

Zdenka tilted her head to one side in question, as though she knew what was on his mind and didn't disapprove.

Stop, Vanya shouted to himself. You must get hold of yourself. She is definitely off-limits. But she was *so* incredibly beautiful, he thought it might be worth any consequence.

Zdenka had continued to flower as from an awkward bud that produced a splendid bloom. Uncle Vanya assessed her for the portrait he was already painting in his mind. The chestnut hair flowing down her back had a new luster to it and the humid atmosphere made her clear skin glow. Her wistful eyes might have seemed high and haughty were they not dropped on cue to make her seem blushingly shy. He would paint them haughty. She had a dancer's control of her fine body, and when she came toward her aunt and uncle, she didn't so much walk as lilt. She had a strong chin that seemed to jut out defiantly, masking an inner vulnerability. Above her regal nostrils, her nose flowed into the smooth cheeks, like slowly melting butter. There was, Vanya thought, just enough mystery in her beautiful face to make it interesting, but not so much as to be off-putting. She had an expectant way about her that Uncle Vanya found intriguing. Perhaps most surprising of all to him, she looked intelligent.

Zdenka was surprised to see St. Petersburg was every bit as gloomy as Brest Litovsk. She had expected comparative tropical sunshine.

"Ah, here is my dear Zdenka," Vanya said. Helene had a broad smile on her squarish face. Her dimples were pronounced and friendly. Vanya was a tall, stately man who struck Zdenka instantly as her idea of an aristocrat. Their clothes were relaxed but not informal.

Vanya put his arm around Zdenka and said, "Welcome to Russia, Zdenka. What a beautiful girl you are. I must paint you." Zdenka dropped her eyes modestly.

"Helene," Vanya said, winking at Zdenka, and pointing to his wife, "was my model, but I couldn't afford the modeling fees, so I married her."

Zdenka blushed, and looked at Helene, who smiled and said, "We're so glad you could come." Zdenka was hard-pressed to find a resemblance between her aunt Helene and her father. The eyes maybe—not much else. Helene was a robust spirit with the full figure of memorable time. Peeking from behind Helene's voluminous skirt was a sloe-eyed child with fetching blondish hair and her best Sunday dress. "Here is Carolina, our daughter," Vanya said. He smiled at his daughter. "Say hello to your cousin Zdenka."

Vanya took Zdenka's tattered suitcase, given to her by her father. It had been her mother's. But now she had a new mother, a woman she would never call her mother.

Though Zdenka studied Russian in school and was a good language student, she had to struggle at first to understand her uncle who spoke only Russian. When the going got tough, Helene, who spoke Polish, interpreted for Zdenka.

Vanya put Zdenka's suitcase into the one-horse-drawn coach which made Zdenka think of her school friend, Katrina. It wasn't as grand as Katrina's, but it *was* a coach and it made her feel special to ride in it. She couldn't take her eyes off the passing marvels—the many people dressed up for city living and the elegant, dense architecture. She decided in those few minutes that the big city was for her.

Carolina sat quietly for the trip, but she never took her eyes off her cousin.

The Gorky property had a gate on the front and just enough room for the carriage to move through it and turn in front of the concrete house. It was light beige, like everything else in town. Out back was a barn that housed the horses (two) and upstairs was Vanya's studio, where he did his sturdy painting, portraits mostly.

Inside the house was a testament to Helene's housekeeping skills. Everything was neat and in its place. The walls were adorned with Vanya's paintings, and it put Zdenka in mind of Katrina's house, except it was, naturally, much more modest, with smaller and fewer rooms and lower ceilings.

Zdenka's house had been more casual and she thought nothing of it. She had thought stringent neatness was a function of servants. Perhaps Helene had servants.

"I shall show Zdenka my studio, first off," Vanya said.

"Oh, Vanya," Helene said, "let her rest—she's had a long journey."

"All right, let's leave it up to Zdenka. Do you want to rest or see my studio?"

"Oh, I'm not tired," she said, quickly, her eyes flashing, "I'd *love* to see your studio, Uncle. This is all so very exciting for me, I don't want to miss even one opportunity."

Vanya and Helene exchanged glances. His said, "You see," and hers said, "Why, you old fool, making a play for the child's affection."

Vanya and Zdenka made their way back to the barn and the studio above it. They climbed the steps, Zdenka first so Vanya could admire her figure. She waited for him on the landing. He threw open the door with a flourish and said, "Here I shall paint you." It was a large room with paintings of people: leaning against the walls, on easels and some hanging on the unfinished barn walls.

"What color will you paint me?" she asked.

"Blue," he said—"and some flesh tones as well."

"Will it wash off?" she asked. He looked at her to see if that could be a serious question. When he saw her smile, they both laughed.

"You're all right, Zdenka," he said. "Yes, yes, we shall enjoy having you."

Zdenka looked over the portraits on the walls and decided her uncle was quite a good painter. On an easel in the center of the room was a portrait of a man in uniform, half-finished, that took her breath away.

"Who is this, Uncle?" she asked.

"Ah—the prince. Prince Stephanoff."

"He's very handsome," she said, staring at the unfinished painting.

"*And* very rich," he said.

"Really?" she said. "That's very interesting. I can think of no two finer attributes in a gentleman."

"Did I say he was a gentleman?" Vanya asked.

"Well...no...but."

He laughed at her astonishing frankness. Zdenka had grown up from a petulant child in Brest Litovsk to a graceful young woman in St. Petersburg. And, it seemed to have happened overnight.

"But I wouldn't get my hopes up," Uncle Vanya said. "Every woman on the continent has her eye on him."

Competition, she thought. I must beat the competition. "Tell me, Uncle, are any of these 'competitors' as charming and beautiful as I?"

"Good gracious, child," he exclaimed at her audacity. Then a

103

slow smile curled his lips, and he said softly, "How could they be?"

"When does he come to be painted?"

"When the spirit moves him," he frowned, "which is not very often."

"Do you have warning?"

"Oh, yes. He doesn't just drop in."

"So, what would I have to do to get you to tell me when he is coming?"

"Oh, no! I don't think.... The meeting would surely be disastrous. My brother-in-law, at any rate, would never forgive me."

"Then why tell him?" She seemed to be talking through her eyelashes. What the old man doesn't know won't hurt him, she thought. Pinky Wallinski had taught her that.

"Why, Zdenka, you are a little minx," he said. "Let's see how you do with Carolina for a while, shall we? We certainly don't want to rush things, do we?"

"And why not?" she said.

After Zdenka had been shown her room and "required" to rest, she dropped on the bed with the fluffy dust ruffle and thought that she missed her poppa already. But she realized she had insurmountable competition with someone who could go to bed with him. She thought the whole business disgusting.

Then her thoughts turned to the prince: rich and handsome! The *best* combination. If she looked out her window, she could see the stairs to the studio and she dreamed of spying on the prince as he climbed the stairs. She could follow him with her eyes, as her uncle had watched her, until he disappeared inside. Then she would find a plausible pretense to visit the studio—perhaps to deliver milk and cookies to the artist *and* his model.

$$\oint \qquad \oint \qquad \oint$$

For dinner that night Zdenka put on her best dress, which was not a garment to startle any city folk, but she had an inkling she should put her best foot forward right away.

The meal was prepared by Helene and consisted of roasted

meat, potatoes and some pale-greenish things Zdenka was to learn were brussels sprouts. She didn't like them, so she didn't eat them.

Carolina sat across the table from Zdenka. Vanya and Helene were at either end. Two lighted candles were in the middle of the table and cast a ghostly yellow glow on the white tablecloth and the food.

Carolina continued her furtive staring at Zdenka, which was beginning to make Zdenka feel funny. Her aunt and uncle were nicely dressed, though Aunt Helene seemed a little fleshy in the arms, which extended from the short, puffy sleeves. They made a handsome couple, and Zdenka felt a strange jealousy.

Uncle Vanya speared a chunk of beef. He said, before popping it in his mouth, "Well, Zdenka, how do you like Russia so far?"

"I love it!" she said.

Helene laughed. "Well, dear, she hasn't seen much of it yet."

"We must remedy that, then," Vanya said. "You know what Napoleon said about Russia?"

Zdenka shook her head and felt like an ignoramus. She didn't know anything about the world. So she must learn!

"He said, 'Russia has a great future; and she always will have.'"

Helene smiled, so Zdenka did too. She wasn't sure if that called for argument or agreement, so she took her cue from Aunt Helene. It was a technique she would use until she was more sure of herself with these sophisticated city folk.

Vanya asked, "So, Zdenka, tell me, what are your aspirations in St. Petersburg?"

Helene chided him. "Oh, Vanya, don't be so high sounding, Zdenka is only a child."

Vanya cocked an eyebrow. "Looks like a young lady to me."

That endeared her uncle to Zdenka. She decided he was to be her real friend in this household. Maybe Helene was jealous of her youth.

"Well, you don't ask a young lady that," Helene insisted. "She must take her opportunities where she can find them. And she is not going to appear eager to find a husband, as it is not becoming in a young girl to be too eager."

Zdenka looked from Helene to Vanya. "A husband?" Zdenka

put her napkin to her mouth as if to keep the food from spurting out. "Goodness, I'm not thinking of husbands. Perhaps, I should marry the prince," she said with a twinkle in her eye and laughter on her lips. Everyone laughed except Carolina, who stared at her cousin Zdenka in awe.

Vanya chuckled, while Helene seemed taken back to silence. "Ah," he said, "a lofty ambition, indeed, but don't you think you should know him first?"

"Vanya," Helene said. "Surely you aren't speaking of *biblical* knowing?"

"Heaven forbid!" Vanya said, mocking the sentiment. "All I mean," he said pointedly, "is knowing in the sense you and I knew each other." His smirk told the story, so Zdenka blushed. "Nothing more than that, certainly," he said.

"Well!" Helene exhaled, "since it is the custom for the *bride's* family to pay for the wedding, we better start saving our rubles if we are to keep up with the royals." Then after a moment of silence, she too had a good laugh. "Believe me, you will be a lot happier with someone of your own station than with a no-account count who has never had any responsibility for anything other than his own amusement. And speaking of responsibility, in the morning we shall begin preparing you for the life of a woman as wife and mother."

The announcement startled Zdenka. She feared to address it in the hope that it would go away if she ignored it.

After Carolina was put to bed with a kiss from her cousin Zdenka, Aunt Helene had a heart-to-heart talk with Zdenka in Zdenka's bedroom. Zdenka sat on the edge of her new bed. Helene stood above her.

"So, tomorrow early I'll see you in the kitchen and we begin our lessons, eh?"

"Lessons?" Zdenka was confused. She thought she had escaped that when she put her school behind her.

"Well, yes. We will start with the cooking, then the house-cleaning. These are minimum requirements for the young girl in search of a husband."

"You mean you don't have servants, Aunt Helene?"

Helene was startled. "Why, no, of course not. Where did you get such a thought?"

"Your house…it's so neat."

"Well, yes, as it should be. You can easily learn that."

The prince, Zdenka thought, would not require a scullery slave for a wife.

"I don't want to learn that," Zdenka said.

"Oh, no? What then?" Helene said. "What then did you think you were sent here for?"

"I thought it was for a visit with family," Zdenka said, unconvincingly.

"A visit is it?" Helene nodded. "So you are only here for three days then?"

"No," Zdenka said, dropping her head.

It seemed clear to Zdenka that Helene was not altogether in sympathy with Zdenka's move from her father and stepmother. It put Zdenka on edge. Another challenge from another woman.

"I understood I was to be governess to Carolina," Zdenka said.

"Oh, my, did you now?" Helene responded. "And what kind of work did you expect to do as a 'governess'?"

"Well, be a companion to the child."

"Oh? And then what should I do?" Helene asked. When Zdenka looked perplexed, she said, "If you do the fun part of raising the child—should I be the cook and the scrubwoman?"

Zdenka had no argument with the logic. Her argument was with the messenger, who was her father, and who she suspected had seriously garbled the message. Zdenka shrugged her insouciant shoulders and mumbled, "Poppa didn't tell me that."

"Well, now, I expect he did," Helene said. "But we girls sometimes have a way of hearing things the way we want. It was my understanding that you were so anxious to leave home you would have gladly signed on as a lion tamer to get out. Well, in this life, if you sign on you have to follow through."

Zdenka appeared to consider the wisdom of that, then decided she wasn't convinced. She had little experience with anyone trying to teach her life-lessons. "You mean, if you find you have made a bad bargain, you have to stick to it for the rest of your life?"

"If you make lifetime bargains," Helene said. "This is not one of those. It is only a bargain as long as you are under our roof."

"But—I don't know *how* to cook."

"Really—sixteen years old—the only girl in your family—how could you not?"

Up went the shoulders again.

"You never helped your ma in the kitchen?"

Zdenka shook her head.

"My goodness, you are *already* a princess," Helene said. "What about *after* Momma died?"

"We didn't have much."

Helene nodded, seeing this unlikely past parade before her in the guise of this beautiful, but spoiled-beyond-her-station, child.

"Let me ask you a question, Zdenka. What are your plans for your future? Do you not plan on marrying?"

"Perhaps."

"And who will keep house for your husband and children?"

"I will not marry anyone if I have to keep house."

"Oh?" Helene raised her eyebrows. "That may not be so easily accomplished. Do you understand about classes? About social standing?"

"No, and I don't want to. People who put limits on themselves are doomed to stay in their own limits. I've no intention of limiting myself."

A touch of admiration crept into Helene's skeptical glance. "Well," Helene said, "in the meantime, I see it as my duty to expose you to some domestic skills, in the unlikely event that you should someday need them to fall back on. Now, you present yourself in the kitchen at five-thirty in the morning and we shall begin."

"Five-thirty?" Zdenka wailed.

"Yes, your uncle likes to start work at first light, and we must give him a substantial breakfast to see him through to the noonhour. After breakfast, we shall go shopping and then prepare lunch. Then you have some time off and then you may work with little Carolina on her reading and sums. Then we do the dinner preparations. The next day, we will start the housecleaning."

Zdenka opened her mouth to argue. Aunt Helene put her hand up to forestall her. "No, child. You are part of a disciplined household now. I have instructions from your father to send you home anytime your situation here is not to your liking."

And that was that. Helene was off to bed but Zdenka was not off to sleep. Zdenka felt trapped. She certainly hadn't left home to become a scullery maid. Now it appeared that Helene and Vanya had no maid and Zdenka was to be it!

Her first taste of independence was bitter indeed.

After two weeks in St. Petersburg, Zdenka had gotten out of her aunt and uncle's house only once for a drive in the country. To Zdenka, it looked very much like Poland and the woods she walked with her father. Just another gloomy day, but her spirits were lifted just being out in the air. At home she was beginning to experience cabin fever.

Though she tried to concentrate on learning her duties, her mind was restless and unsatisfied. She wondered if she might find a place in St. Petersburg to sing. She would soon have to find some diversion, she thought, or she would go *crazy!*

During her third week with her uncle and aunt, Zdenka was dusting the dining room when she overheard her uncle and aunt talking in the kitchen:

"Helene, sweet, do you think you might be working the girl too hard?"

"What? Do you?" Helene seemed surprised. "It will be the making of her."

"Or the unmaking," Vanya said. "She's our niece, not a servant."

In the dining room, Zdenka stopped her feather duster midair and let out a silent cheer.

"Nonsense," Helene said. "Hard work never hurt anyone. I think her attitude has improved already, don't you?"

Vanya considered his wife's theory. "I think the old attitude is just waiting to burst back out. You don't find a spirit like hers that easily vanquished."

"Fair enough. We'll just put it in hiding then."

Vanya looked at his wife, inspecting her face as if for some secret. "Helene," he said, "it's just occurred to me, could you be a little jealous of your niece?"

"What? Me jealous of an absolutely gorgeous seventeen-year-old? Where would you ever get such a foolish idea?" And with that, she threw her arms around her husband and gave him a huge, wet, resounding kiss on the lips.

In the dining room, the feather duster moved slower. Zdenka had the feeling her uncle was on her side, and for some reason her aunt thought it her mission to instruct her in the ways of being a wife to some butcher—a prospect that did not warm the cockles of her heart.

That night at dinner, Vanya asked Zdenka, "Are you ready?"

"Ready?" Zdenka said. "Excuse me, Uncle, ready for what?"

"To have your portrait painted."

She glanced at her aunt Helene, as though she might need her permission. "I'd like that very much," she said softly.

After dinner, Vanya and Helene went to a performance of the opera, and Zdenka was left to put Carolina to bed. Once the child was in her nightgown, with the covers of the fourposter bed pulled to her chin, Zdenka read her a story while Carolina stared at her beautiful cousin with worshipful eyes.

"I want to marry the prince too," Carolina said to Zdenka.

How foolish it sounded coming from a five-year-old child.

"Well, it's a long time till you have to think about marrying."

"But you can think about it right now!" she said. "And you will marry a prince, I know you will."

Zdenka gave the child a sudden, tight hug. Then a pesky logic sobered her and she sat back up. "How can you be so sure?"

"Because you are very beautiful."

Zdenka giggled. "That's nice of you to say so."

"It's true," Carolina said, then pouted. "I'm not beautiful," she said.

"Why, that's nonsense. Of course you're beautiful."

Carolina seemed intent on considering that opinion, then shook her head resolutely. "No. Not as beautiful as you."

"Oh, but when I was your age, I was an ugly duckling," Zdenka said.

"Really?"

Zdenka's nod was terse and immutable. "My face was all pushed in like someone had closed a door on it. Sometimes," she said, "we girls get better looking with time."

Carolina giggled gleefully and clapped her hands. "Oh, I hope so," she said.

"Tell me something, will you, Carolina?"

"What?"

"Do your momma and poppa go often out to this opera?"

"Sometimes."

"What do they do there?"

"I don't know."

"Well. What *is* this opera they go to?"

The child shrugged her thin shoulders. "I don't know, a bunch of singing, I guess."

"Singing?" Zdenka smiled. "I can sing."

"Can you? *Really?* Sing something for me."

"Oh, well, I will not—"

"Oh, *please.*"

"No, I will not. I don't want you making fun of me."

Carolina pouted. "But I want to hear you sing. I won't make fun, honest—even if you sing terrible, I won't say so."

"Maybe another time," Zdenka said. "Now you must go to

sleep. You mustn't stall anymore."

"Zdenka!"

"Besides, young girls don't grow up pretty unless they get their beauty sleep."

The next morning, after doing the breakfast dishes, she met her uncle Vanya in his studio over the barn. There he was experimenting with the colors he had mixed. He was painting the colors on paper and turning the paper in the light, then adding other colors next to each on the paper.

"Ah," he said on seeing her come through the doorway, "here is my most beautiful model."

Zdenka blushed, and immediately thought he was comparing her to Aunt Helene.

"Is my dress all right?" she asked him.

"Yes, yes, everything is fine. I will paint you a dress fit for a queen. Now sit here," he said, pointing to the simple straight-back chair that she looked at with a question on her face.

"Oh, don't worry," he laughed when he saw her reaction. "I'll paint you one of those too. A queen's throne. This is what we will do. We will make you a princess and your portrait will be here for the prince to see. He will not be able to resist." He noted the delighted smile on her face and wanted to remember it and capture it for the portrait. "Now we begin, no?"

The sunlight was beginning to fight its way into the room when Zdenka sat on the simple chair. She had a lot of time to think as her uncle worked—sketching her quickly with a soft pencil, then going back more carefully before he took up the brush and began applying the paints. One thing she thought about was how, when she married the prince, she would *never* get up at such an ungodly hour. Let that God the nuns were always talking about set the stage, turn on all the sunshine before the people come onstage. She was sure that was how it was meant to be. Nighttime and darkness were for bats and owls.

Vanya worked in silence for a while, then stood back a step to look at what he had done, as if seeing it for the first time. "You know," he said, "you are uniquely beautiful—like a mythical goddess. It is almost frightening. I really have a hard decision to make: do I try to capture you as you are, or do I try to tone it down somewhat in the hope of making a more believable portrait?"

"Oh, Uncle," she blushed, "I bet you tell all the girls that."

"Oh, no..." He went back to work. "So what's your preference?" he asked her.

"What's so wonderful about believable?" she said, and they both laughed.

As he worked on her portrait in silence, Vanya thought his niece had a special quality about her that he knew men would find irresistible. She gave the impression she had a sophistication Vanya knew she didn't possess. She had a delightful pixyish sense of humor, she was poised and alert and seemed to understand your every thought. He knew this couldn't be, and yet the way she looked at you was so penetrating, Vanya felt embarrassed by it, as though she were contemplating some untoward sexual intimacy. And yet he was strangely drawn to her, even though she was his niece and the sense of taboo was strong in him, she had that kind of androgynous magnetism. He thought it would be a challenge to his artistry to capture on the canvas these unique bits of her character.

He considered discussing it with her, but he couldn't think of a way to say it that didn't sound silly. Instead he said, "You have such perfect features, I could never make a face so perfect if I had only my imagination to go on."

Funny, he thought, the prince too has this classical beauty. The ears protrude from his temples a trifle much, but the face itself is pure boyishness. The nose, lips, cheeks, eyes were those of a very young boy—the kind of unsullied looks one grows out of in puberty—only the prince had not outgrown his childish perfection. If anything, he was even younger featured than he was in childhood.

Vanya tried to imagine the two of them, the prince and Zdenka, together. He couldn't quite see it. The prince, for all his boyish looks, was a roué, and Vanya thought he would be less than responsible if he allowed the two to be together. And yet, with the determination Zdenka exhibited about everything, he didn't see how he could keep them apart. No, he must be more clever. He must not introduce them, for that he could be held accountable by his brother-in-law. And yet, would Augustus really mind if his daughter had a liaison with a Russian prince? Knowing his brother-in-law, he probably *would* mind. Not that he would at all object to a marriage of

Zdenka to a prince, but realistically, a marriage was not in the offing. The prince was, like most royalty, status conscious, and magnetic as Zdenka might be, it wasn't in the stars.

No, he thought as he was rounding out Zdenka's lips, his approach would be oblique.

"Zdenka?" Vanya said softly from behind the easel, almost as though he had not intended her to hear. The subject he was bringing up was embarrassing.

"Yes, Uncle?" she said without compromising her pose. She was, he thought, born to pose for artists.

"Please don't be embarrassed by this, Zdenka."

"Oh, Uncle," she tittered without moving a muscle. "How could you embarrass me?"

"And please don't think I am being too forward, but I am...I find myself in a most difficult position."

"How is that, Uncle?"

"I find myself, in Helene's brother's behalf, indeed at his behest, as a guardian of perhaps the most beautiful girl in all of Russia."

"Oh, Uncle, how you *do* exaggerate. I shall *not* be able to avoid embarrassment if you keep this up."

"It is not a task I shall find easy. I see now your aunt's method, in keeping you close to the kitchen—funny," he mused, "I didn't see it myself until I started painting you." He stood back and examined the portrait from three steps extra distance. "The thing is, I feel bound to protect you, and I don't fancy you are going to like that."

"Why, Uncle, how old-fashioned chivalrous of you. I would indeed be delighted at your 'protection,'" she said with a slight cock of her head, returning instantly to the pose. "As long as," she added with a twinkle in her voice, "that doesn't mean interference."

He smiled. She would be a hard one to keep down. "I don't know what your plans are for your stay with us in Russia," he said. "I don't suppose you know yourself just yet. I would feel a lot differently if you were three or four years older. But you are only seventeen."

"*Only!*" she mocked him.

"Yes, yes, only, from my vantage point. I am more than twice your age."

"You are not so old you forgot what it is like to be seventeen, surely," Zdenka teased him.

"That's exactly the problem. I remember all too well what it was like for a hot-blooded boy in passionate pursuit of pretty young girls." Vanya paused to add a touch of black to the eyelashes. "Have you been the object of pursuit of lusty boys?"

"Uncle!" she scolded him, "I went to a school for sheltered Catholic girls. I am just as innocent as the first rose of summer."

"Hm..." Vanya pondered, doubtful of her veracity. "Is that so?" The question did not call for an answer. "Hm," he said. "Hm. So, then, did your mother ever talk to you about the great mysteries of life?"

"Oh, dear, Uncle, I fear my mother was not one for mysteries."

"Yes—I'm talking about the facts of life. I suppose you pick that sort of thing up in school nowadays."

"I didn't know there were any *facts* of life," she said. "I thought it was all pretty much made up as you go along."

Vanya stopped painting to stare at her. She said the most remarkable things, but he wondered if she was that clever or did she just say whatever popped into her mind?

"I am talking about boys and girls," Vanya said. "Men and women—and intimacy. Do you understand about men?"

She laughed, engaging, guileless laughter, so innocent, yet so somehow sophisticated. Like a woman much older and more experienced in the ways of the world. "Does anybody?" she said.

"Well, you must if you are to survive in this cruel world. Men will take full advantage of you anytime you let them."

"And shouldn't I let them?" she asked him with a grin sweeping her lips.

Oh, God, he thought. Why must I do this? Surely this is not a job for an uncle who has only laid eyes on the child for less than a month. It was completely unfair of my brother-in-law to turn this responsibility over to me. And Zdenka is not making it easy.

"You do know how babies are made," he spilled out at last, and it came as though it were more an accusation than a question.

"Made? I thought they were conceived, then gestated, then born," she said, that grin coming back to her face that Vanya decided was the expression he wished to capture for his portrait of her.

"Yes, very good," he said. "It is the *conceived* part I'm talking about."

"You mean like the Immaculate Conception?" she asked.

"No, not immaculate."

"Oh," she said. "No, Uncle, will you tell me how it's done?"

She was playing with him, he was sure of it. God, he thought, what now? The trick was not how it was done, but how to *not* do it. Any fool could conceive, and he didn't want her doing any conceiving while he was in charge—not without some clerical dispensation. Preferably not at all. But here he was, stuck with the responsibility for the well-being of this gorgeous creature who as soon as she saw the light of day outside the house was going to attract lusty males like flies to honey.

And why, he asked himself angrily, am I having so much trouble remembering she is a *relative?* If I didn't know better, I'd swear she was flirting with me. Would I still be constrained in my passions if she were not my brother-in-law's daughter? Would I still have the obligation? The conflict was tearing at his soul, the brush was trembling in his hand. What am I to make of her making so light of procreation? he thought. It's as if she's taunting me!

"Men, you know," he studied the floor, "have these base instincts, about women. They are always looking for an opportunity to act on them. The challenge for young girls is to keep them from acting until there is a marriage. If a girl gives too easily her most prized possession, she may find herself unmarketable."

Poor Uncle, Zdenka thought. I know what he's trying to say, but he's having such a hard time of it.

"Men, you know," he said sheepishly, "are animals, pure and simple."

Ah, yes, Zdenka thought, remembering the pigs.

"Just tell me, Zdenka," Uncle Vanya said, "tell me you understand what I'm saying and that you will be careful."

"I can take care of myself, Uncle," she said.

My God! he thought. Did she actually wink at me? Oh, God, he groaned inwardly—I wonder if she would pose nude for me?

Vanya worked desultorily on the oil painting, with conflicting feelings. He knew any permanent liaison between the prince and Zdenka was impossible. Yet she had her young, naive heart set on it, and to Vanya (a practicing libertarian) it was a fun idea. Yet, he felt it his duty to keep her unsullied as long as possible. But that thought led him to opposite ideas.

The conflict tormented him. He thrashed in his sleep. His wife commented on the sudden increase in his amorousness, but kept to herself the reason she suspected. Better he takes it out on me than on her, she thought.

Somehow Vanya got through two more sessions with his beguiling niece.

At the end of the second session,

when Vanya had brought the painting far enough along to trust his voice, he said as casually as he could, "Zdenka, would you ever consider posing in the nude—?"

She looked at him with startled eyes. "Why, Uncle! What an idea—"

"You are very beautiful. A portrait of you in the nude would bring large sums. I would, of course, share with you."

"Is that customary, Uncle? To share with a model—?"

"Not customary, no."

"Did you share with Aunt Helene?"

"Nooo, I married her instead," he said. "Now we share."

"Did she do nudes?"

"Yes."

"May I see one?"

"They're all sold."

"So," she said, looking at him sideways across the bridge of her straight nose, "you would exploit your seventeen-year-old niece in this way?"

"Exploit?" He frowned and fumbled his words. "No, dear, you would, of course, have to cooperate. I would not think of it otherwise."

"How much money would it bring?"

"Each? Many rubles—perhaps five times what the prince is paying me."

"Each, you say? You would do more than one?"

He shrugged. "If they sell, why not?"

Her brow furrowed in deep thought. There was a cash register in her head filling up. It would free her from this indentured servitude, make her an independent woman, get her some respect. She could make the rules. "Tell me, Uncle," she said at last, "what is thought of a woman who models in the nude?"

"Thought?" he asked, stalling for time to formulate an answer to a question that had never been asked of him. "Why, I can't say—I certainly think the best..."

"The prince, for example," she prodded him. "What would he think?"

"He would think that you are very beautiful, I'm sure."

"Do you think he would ask a nude model to marry him?"

"Well, I…" Vanya faltered.

"I didn't think so," Zdenka said, stiffening her spine. "I shall only take off my clothes for the man I marry. No one else."

It was clear to Helene that her determined niece had no aptitude for housework. She did what she was told, but not an ounce more. She had no talent for the mundane. She cooked what she was told to cook as she was told to cook it. Food seemed unimportant to her.

Helene mused to Vanya one night in bed that the girl's attitudes were those of royalty.

"So maybe she *will* marry royally," Vanya commented.

"Oh, you dreamer," Helene said, "I guess all artists are dreamers. Well, I'm the practical one, thank goodness. Every family needs a practical one so just in case her royal ship doesn't come in, I'm preparing her for the real world. I have a suspicion she won't regret it."

Vanya was silent a few minutes, then he said, "She *is* a startlingly beautiful girl; I don't think there are many men who could resist her charms."

"Well, she's not much in the kitchen," Helene said. "You know the quickest way to a man's heart is through his stomach."

"It is not," he said.

"What? Then what is?"

"The quickest way to a man's heart is a bullet."

"Oh, you clown," she said, laughing.

"And besides, the kitchen isn't the most important room in the house," he said, "not to a man."

"What is then?"

"We're in it," he said, and rolled over and took her in his arms and proved it.

In a few more days, Prince Stephanoff sent word he would come for a further sitting.

The day dawned as a precious omen, the sun conquering the gray clouds for the first time in weeks.

Zdenka was surprised at how much the sunshine lifted her spirits. She found herself humming a folk tune while she was working.

The morning of the prince's visit, Vanya took Helene aside

and asked her to keep Zdenka occupied in a part of the house where she couldn't see the prince come in.

"Well," she said, "I'm glad to see you've come to your senses about her foolish notions of attracting the prince."

"Hm—ah, yes," he said, as though distracted by profounder thoughts. "But, you do know we mere mortals need our dreams to sustain us."

"Dreams?" she said. "Ha! I wonder what my last dream was?"

"Why, to marry a handsome prince, of course—and you did."

"Hah!" she said. "I got *you* instead."

And with that he laughed, "Lucky you," and slapped her on her broadening bottom.

Zdenka heard the commotion of horses at the front gate, and every time she heard horses, she imagined it was the prince. But this time, she felt in her bones the hoofbeats on the cobblestones could only have been made by royal Thoroughbreds.

The first thing she did was bolt from the inside bedroom where she was cleaning, down to the kitchen, where she could get a glimpse of the prince, only to be blocked by Helene at the foot of the steps.

"Where do you think you're going?"

"Oh, Aunt Helene, it's the prince, isn't it? Tell me, please, oh, please!"

"What difference does it make if it's a prince or milkman? You have work to do, so you shouldn't worry your pretty head about who comes and goes."

"Oooo, it *is* the prince. I knew it was. I just *knew* it!" She threw her arms around her aunt's neck, causing her aunt to slip backwards and catch herself from falling by shifting a foot. "Child!" she started, but Zdenka was already out of the hallway at the foot of the stairs before Helene realized she was gone, flying out the door, blindly, as a bat in the attic, and tearing up the barn stairs, pausing only on the landing at the top to wonder what she was doing.

She burst in the door as though she were a tornado. Then, seeing the prince sitting where she had sat, she stopped dead in her tracks. Her jaw dropped, then, catching herself, she clamped her mouth closed. Were those sparks flying from the prince's startled eyes?

121

"Oh, Uncle, I'm sorry," she said, regaining a regal pose, "I didn't know you had company."

His tacit smile said, "Yes, and butterflies give milk."

"Prince Stephanoff," Uncle Vanya said, "allow me to present to you my niece, Zdenka."

The prince rose from his chair, took a step toward Zdenka and bowed from the waist for so many seconds, Zdenka felt she had been frozen in time.

Her heart stopped dead—as she would write to Katrina in the letter she tore up and replaced with a more reserved recounting of the meeting.

Now he had straightened and was looking so deep into her eyes Zdenka feared they would both drown in unshed tears of joy.

"I am charmed to make your acquaintance," Prince Stephanoff said in a voice trembling with sincerity, his gaze unflinching. "I don't believe I have ever laid eyes on a more beautiful young woman."

"Oh, my dear prince," Zdenka said, dropping her eyelashes. "I'll bet you say that to all the girls."

Vanya was impressed. Zdenka seemed to know how to handle herself after all. She was obviously in awe of the prince, but she wasn't obsequious.

But now Zdenka wondered what she should do next. Her hands began to flutter, as though from them would come magic words to convince the prince that she was not only beautiful, but engaging, charming and witty as well.

She locked her eyes on his again. He was standing over her, staring at those deep, dark eyes highlighting her lovely face, and she suddenly felt naked, as if he had undressed her in his mind. He wasn't speaking either, he was just looking. He was so tall and even more handsome than Uncle's painting of him. He looked stronger than he did in the portrait; his features were boyish, but in a strong, almost seductive, way. The lips were so thin and bloodless Zdenka despaired of imagining him being able to kiss at all. One thing, she thought, his nose wouldn't get in the way—it was so small and delicate, like a china doll's. And his skin was so baby smooth, she wondered if he had ever grown any whiskers—or did he pluck them out with tweezers?

Of course, it was the eyes that were his crowning glory—ice blue they were, and so penetrating it was scary. When he looked at you it was as though he had never looked at another living soul—as if *you* were the *only* creature in his universe; and that was just the way Zdenka felt standing there, her heart pounding like it was about to burst out between her breasts and kiss the prince.

Uncle Vanya was watching the silent ballet with wry amusement. There was his niece, smitten, her facile hands drawing nondescript shapes on the air while the city's leading roué was staring wordlessly, motionlessly at her. It would, he thought, make a marvelous painting. Of course, he could never recapture those priceless expressions.

"So," the prince said at last, "are you here for a visit?" An audible sigh of relief swept over Zdenka, as well as Vanya.

"No, I am here to stay," she said, and Uncle Vanya raised an eyebrow.

"Have you had time to explore our fair city?"

"Oh, no, not at all." She glanced at Vanya. "I've been so busy just getting acquainted with my uncle, aunt and cousin that I really haven't had the time to see the city." She looked at her uncle, in her glance the hope he would not betray her.

"You must allow me then to make you acquainted with St. Petersburg and," the prince added with a twinkle in his eye, as though offering the *pièce de résistance,* "the palace."

"Oh," she said, "I would just adore to see the palace."

"It is easily arranged," he said, waving his wrist in dismissal of all thought to the contrary. "Tell me, do you like opera?"

"Oh, I *adore* opera," she said, then hoped he wouldn't ask her anything about it—like what were her favorites.

"What are your favorite operas?"

"Oh, gee, there are so many great ones, I don't know what to say."

"Do you like Puccini?"

"Oh, yes, that is one of my favorite operas."

The prince broke into laughter—it sounded almost lascivious to Zdenka. She glanced at her uncle, who was shaking his head, as though instructing her to keep quiet about things she didn't understand.

"Did I say something funny?"

"Puccini is a *composer*, not an opera."

"Well, of course," she said, and joined his laughter.

"How about Verdi—do you like that opera?"

She pursed her lips, then shook her head. "No more traps," she said. "If you like so much the opera, I must admit there's much you could teach me. And if you so desired, I can assure you, you will find in me the most willing of pupils."

Uncle Vanya rolled his eyes.

Prince Stephanoff clapped his hands once.

"Capital!" he said. "It is settled then. Tomorrow night we shall attend *La Bohème* and we shall begin our...instruction?"

"Oh, good," she fairly cheered the news. "How shall I get there?"

"Well, I shall call for you in my carriage, of course."

Zdenka glanced at her uncle. He was smiling the smile of astonishment. But, she thought, the opera with the prince and I have not a thing good enough to wear! Zdenka took a deep breath. She thought it would prevent her from fainting.

Zdenka was so excited at the offer of a date with the prince, she disappeared from the studio almost as suddenly as she entered it, and it wasn't until she got in the house that she realized she had neglected to find out what time to expect him. She would die of embarrassment if she had to go back there and admit to him how foolish she had been—how, after all, could he *ever* respect her?

Her aunt met her in the kitchen and gave her the quizzical look. "Well," she said, "so you met the prince?"

"Oh," she swooned, "he is *so* handsome."

"Yes, he *is* that," Aunt said, as though she were withholding the really bad news.

"And, Aunt Helene, he's asked me

to go with him to the opera—and like a goose I forgot to ask him what time he would call. Would you be just a dear and ask him for me? I'd be embarrassed to death if I had to look like a goose to him."

"Wait, hold on just a minute," Aunt Helene said, "what did you tell this forward young man?"

"*Tell* him?" Zdenka scrunched her cheeks at the question.

"Yes—how did you answer his invitation?"

"I said yes, of course."

"You didn't think to ask my permission, Zdenka?"

"Oh, Aunt—the *prince!* Uncle was right there all the time. He gave *his* permission."

"He did?"

She nodded, but she didn't fool Helene.

"But I'll feel such the fool. I have nothing to wear."

"I'll take care of that…"

"I don't know anything about the opera. Could you be just a dear and tell me *all* about it?"

Helene laughed in spite of herself. "*All* about opera might take a lifetime—and, besides, I don't know that much. But I suppose I could tell you some."

"Oh, Aunt Helene, would you? I'd work extra hard if you would."

And, again in spite of herself, Helene got caught up in her niece's girlish enthusiasm, and soon the impracticality, the sheer remoteness of anything good coming of the meeting faded from her thoughts. She became a staunch partisan in Zdenka's unlikely quest for the hand of a prince she had barely spoken to.

After dinner that night, seated in the seldom-used parlor with Zdenka, and Carolina in tow ("Come, child, this talk of opera will not hurt you," Helene had said), the opera lessons began.

"It is said opera is the most complete, the most varied of all art, because it employs all the other arts, like music, drama, dance, art in the stage sets, and spectacle. Everything happens onstage on such a large scale. Spectacular."

Zdenka was rapt in her attention and Carolina wanted so to be like Zdenka that she was just as focused on her mother's words, though she didn't understand all of them.

"In this country, and I guess in all the world," Helene continued, "our opera stars are like gods and goddesses with the adulation they get from the audience. And many people are so wrapped up in opera, they know every nuance of every performance, and can tell you anytime about any single aspect of any of the hundreds of performances they have heard."

"Really?" Zdenka was swept up in the idea.

"Yes," Helene said. "One singer will be judged to have better high notes, perhaps the end-all high C. Another, more stage presence, more verve. Another performance has better third-act scenery. In another, the orchestra is overbearing, and I understand the prince is such a man," she said, not emphasizing her double entendre.

"But..." Zdenka's eyes were large with rapture, "but isn't he rather young to have seen hundreds of performances?"

"Well, he is young, yes, but he is also rich, and he can go to virtually every performance in St. Petersburg, as well as travel to Moscow, and even Paris and Berlin when something that catches his fancy is offered. It is a passion for him. It is why his portrait is so often interrupted," Helene said. "But it is genuine with the prince. A lot of people are only interested in opera for the social connections it offers. Not so the prince."

"Well, naturally not," Zdenka said, "a prince doesn't need to climb up in society, he is already at the top."

"Yes," Helene said, "but even those at the top look to keeping their society constantly in the public eye, lest they be forgotten about. I don't know but that some part of the audience goes to the opera to be seen rather than to see."

"I shall not be one of those," Zdenka vowed.

"Me either," Carolina chimed in.

Helene spoke further about the simple love and tragic stories of operas, and both Zdenka and Carolina were so entranced, Carolina said, "I want to go to the opera."

"Well, certainly you will be able to go someday," Helene said.

"Someday? Why is it always someday? I want to go now."

Zdenka patted her cousin on her head. She understood. The child was not unlike herself in her enthusiasms and ambitions, not to say impatience.

"Tomorrow you shall see one of the great operas of Puccini,"

Aunt Helene said. "It is *La Bohème*, another tragic love story about two women and two men. The women love the men, but the men are poor, so the women are kept by rich men. One of the women says her friend is so luxuriously dressed now she no longer thinks of her poor lover," Helene said lightly. "Then the forgotten lover sings, 'It's the angels who go nude.'"

Zdenka couldn't wait to see and hear the performance. She wondered how she would fare in the same situation as *La Bohème*, then decided she would not ever be in that predicament because she would not fall in love with anyone who was poor.

After Carolina was put to bed amid bleating protests that she wasn't a bit tired, Helene asked Zdenka if she had ever been out with a man alone before. After some foot-shuffling evasions, Zdenka admitted she had not.

The air left Helene's lungs as from a punctured balloon. "Then we'd better talk," Helene said, and they sat back down in the parlor.

For a moment there was nothing but silence between them. Zdenka felt a chill in the air. She was poised to protest the expected admonishments. She could take care of herself, she would argue. She even thought of arguing that she would leave their house if Aunt Helene tried to forbid her to go out with the prince.

But her aunt surprised her. "Zdenka, child," she said, "there is so much to know about being with men. So much, and no one knows it all." She spoke as if she were weary of the world and the crumbs it left for women. She wanted to alert her niece without discouraging her. She thought there must be some magic formula, she just didn't have any idea what it was.

"Men, you know…" she began, then restarted. "It falls to the weaker sex to be the stronger. Sometimes our relationships with men before marriage are little more than resistance. Trying to keep their interest up and their hands down. Prince Stephanoff has a reputation, well-deserved, I'm sure, as a rake. Do you know what that is, my dear?"

"Something you gather leaves with?"

Helene laughed. "Yes, that's good, only this kind of rake gathers women. Lots of them. Just like leaves."

Zdenka laughed now. "Oh, Aunt Helene, I…I mean, I don't…"

"And since Stephanoff is royalty in the bargain, many women throw themselves at him, not knowing he really wouldn't consider them marriageable, so he just takes his fun and is on his way." She paused and frowned. "Do you know what I mean by taking his fun, child?"

"Well, have a good time, I guess."

"Yes, indeed. At the girl's expense. And if he makes a baby in the process, he throws at them a few rubles and that's the end of it as far as he is concerned."

"No, Aunt! Does that really happen?"

"More times than we will ever know about."

"Then how do you know?"

"People talk." She shrugged. "This is not such a big city as you think. Everything is known. That is why we must be so careful how we behave. A girl can have her reputation ruined for life in a few minutes of breathless excitement."

"But, Aunt," Zdenka asked, perplexed at the sound of it all, "how is a girl to go about protecting herself from these terrible men? Should I take along a gun?"

"Well, no... You must just always be on your toes. You must be on guard at all times, watch him closely, don't go to any private places with him alone. Be circumspect. If he tries to touch you, you just tell him very politely you are a nice girl and mean no offense, but you must look out for your virtue and reputation, or no one will ever look out for you."

"Oh, Aunt Helene, you make it sound like such a fright when it should be such fun." Zdenka leaned over and patted Helene on the knee, a gesture that did not bolster confidence in her niece's judgment.

"Just don't ever do that to a man," Helene said, looking askance at Zdenka's hand on her knee.

"Why not?"

"Oh, child, you are so innocent," Helene said, as though she had been thoroughly demoralized.

"Cheer up, Aunt," Zdenka said, "I can take care of myself."

Helene stared at her for an eternity, then muttered, "Oh, I so hope you can."

Zdenka could not get her mind off her date for the opera. Just thinking of the prince was like taking a drug to lift her spirits. And he looked so *nice,* she was *sure* Aunt Helene got some very wrong information. Well, tomorrow night she could set her straight from experience. Now she had more important things on her mind, like making a good impression on the prince. She wished she'd had more experience, but it was too late to stew about that. Your first time with a man should not be a prince, she thought. You should be able to work up. But she couldn't have said no and thrown away the golden opportunity. Her immediate goal on her first date, she decided, was that there should be a second. How was she to stand out from all the other girls of his experience without tarnishing her reputation?

"But what about my dress? You said you'd take care of it," she lamented to Aunt Helene.

Helene smiled. "I will see to it, child," she said.

Zdenka's chores were performed mechanically the next morning. Aunt Helene could tell her niece's mind was elsewhere, so at noon she told her to lie down and rest so she would be fresh as a daisy for her big night out.

Zdenka didn't argue, though she knew she was much too excited to sleep. In a moment, her door opened and her aunt stood in the doorway, holding up the most beautiful gown.

"Here, try this," she said. "It is from my thin period and it might fit you."

Zdenka leaped out of bed as though someone had set fire to it. She took the dress from her aunt and held it up in front of her.

"Oh, Aunt Helene, it is *beautiful*. Oh, you are such a love. Oh, I do hope it fits. If it doesn't I will just die."

"Now, now, before you die, try it on. We can always add a little cotton here and there to fill it out."

Zdenka was already throwing off her dress and stepping into the satin gown of golden threads on which her long, chestnut hair bounced playfully like shimmering sunbeams.

Zdenka looked down at the dress in awe, then looked over at the light reflecting off the moisture gathering around her aunt's delft-blue eyes. "Oh, Zdenka," Helene said so softly Zdenka thought she was talking to herself, "you are so beautiful." It came out like a flat statement of irrefutable fact, not opinion, tinged with as much appreciation as envy.

"Oh, I love it, Aunt Helene, I just *love* it." She twirled around, letting the cool air lift the skirt and tickle her bare legs. "When did you wear this, Aunt?"

"Oh, a long time ago," she said, wistfully. "When I met your uncle."

"When you posed nude for him?"

Helene gasped. Zdenka suddenly realized that may have sounded more sinister than she meant. "Oh, Aunt, I'm sorry—wasn't I supposed to know?"

"Who told you that?"

Zdenka was blushing.

"Oh, who else could have?" she said, resigning in disgust.

"I won't tell anyone, Aunt. I promise."

Aunt Helene nodded very slowly. "Yes," she said into the deadened air, but she knew if it ever served her purposes, the child would use it. "Tell me, Zdenka, did Uncle ask you to take off your clothes so he could paint you?"

Zdenka had settled into a motionless silence, like a flower after a windstorm. "Well…"

"Oh, I don't need to ask," she said with a disgusted snap of her head. "Don't you ever do that, child—"

"But why not?" she asked, responding to the challenge. "You did it."

"Yes, I was a lot older. And he was my lover, not my uncle."

"So?"

"It is not seemly, child." Aunt Helene seemed revived by a revelation. "Surely you don't *want* to do it?"

"I don't…think so," she said, looking at the floor. "But…he said I could have a lot of money…"

"Oh, my God! You take off my dress this minute. You aren't going anywhere tonight!"

"Aunt!"

"I mean it. *Now!* We'll see if a seventeen-year-old charge of mine is going to go nude. I never heard of such a thing. Your father would just die! I'm afraid you'll need a lot better judgment than that before I can allow you to go out alone with a man."

"Oh—Aunt Helene—no—no, no, no," Zdenka started to cry. "I didn't *do* it. I'm not going to—"

"I never heard of such a thing!"

"Oh, Aunt, please! I won't do it, I *won't.*"

"Promise?" She was already weakening.

"I promise! I told Uncle I wouldn't take off my clothes for anyone but the man I marry. I didn't mean—"

"Well, you gave me heart failure, Niece. Talk about money and undressing—I never…"

"Oh, please let me go to the opera. I'd die if I had to tell the prince I couldn't go!"

Helene knew there would be no rest until she relented. The

girl was simply intractable.

The time passed so quickly for Zdenka and so slowly for Helene. Zdenka's mind was buzzing in anticipation of her night at the opera with the handsome prince—a fairy tale come true—and Helene was intent on seeing her out the door without either of them having a nervous breakdown. Vanya kept his distance, working an extra long day in his studio above the barn.

The truth was he was just as nervous as Zdenka was, but for different reasons. She was nervous about not knowing what to do, while he was nervous about what she might do without knowing what she was doing.

Helene tried to get her to eat something. "It will be a long opera," she said. "So the supper will be a long time from now."

"Oh, Aunt Helene, I couldn't possibly eat. I'm much too excited."

"Well, have *something*. Just a piece of bread. It won't do to have you fall over in a faint at the opera."

Zdenka took the bread reluctantly and chewed on it without tasting anything.

"Oh, Auntie, what shall I say to him?" she asked. "I won't know what to say. I'm afraid I won't know the proper way to act. What is the way to act with a prince, and at the opera? Oh, Aunt Helene, what shall I do?"

"Child, child," Helene said, taking her hands in her own, "just you be yourself. You are a beautiful and charming young woman. Nothing else is necessary. If the prince wanted an opera encyclopedia for an escort, he would have gotten one from the faculty of the university. It is important you remember, Zdenka, that the prince could take *anyone* to the opera, but he chose you, for yourself. So just *be* yourself."

Little Carolina lived vicariously her cousin's excitement. She dogged her every step, and Zdenka feared it would take a team of wild horses to keep the child from climbing in the coach with her when the prince came.

Helene found her daughter's unbridled enthusiasm charming. Zdenka worried that the child would somehow spoil her date by blurting something stupid to the prince.

But when the big moment arrived and the prince came to

pick up his date, little Carolina was hiding behind the skirts of her mother, clutching the fabric for dear life and peeking sheepishly around at the most handsome prince she would ever see in her life. The moment would provide her an unforgettable memory for the rest of her life.

Vanya was on hand to see his stunning niece go on her first date. And he was choked up, giving her a strong, silent hug when the prince called. Screwing up courage somewhat above his station, he shook the prince's hand, looking him hard in the eye. "Take care of my girl," he said as though he were commanding an errant child.

"Put your mind at rest," the prince said. Vanya was comforted by the words, until he thought about it and realized they could mean anything—most notably: "Don't get worked up, there's nothing you can do about anything anyway."

The prince's coat was blue velvet with gold buttons, and Vanya thought the prince might have stepped out of some eighteenth-century court.

Then they were gone. No sooner had the door closed behind the opera-bound couple than Helene turned her back to the door and fell against it, as though in added insurance that they would not soon return.

Her bodice was heaving in utter exhaustion.

"Now, Helene," Vanya said. "Calm down. What will it be like when it's your own daughter?" Helene smiled at Carolina, who clapped her hands and squealed in delight.

The back of Helene's hand was touching her brow. "I don't expect I will be turning her loose on a man with the reputation of the prince."

Carolina pouted. "Why can't I have a prince if Denky can?"

"Oh, hush, Carolina," her mother said.

"Well, don't fret, my dear Helene," Vanya said, "sometimes reputations are undeserved. I certainly don't get the impression he is a rake—seems rather gentle and a bit unsure of himself to me."

"Oh, but how would you know? You are a man. It is so different."

"Not so different," he said, wondrously.

"Oh, no?"

He did not seem to be listening. Helene studied him and

tried to read his mind. "What are you thinking, Vanya?"

"What? Oh, nothing."

"Well…" she said, "*some*thing, surely."

"I was just trying to remember what it was like to be so young and full of life."

"Thinking *you* could be in the prince's place?"

"Well—perhaps—do you think that awful?"

She paused as if to consider, but her mind spun on to another concern. "Vanya," she said, "I must know. Did you ask Zdenka to take off her clothes for you?"

"Well…no…I…"

"To paint her? *Nude?*"

"I…it was more…a…a hypothetical question."

"Hypothetical, huh? With your seventeen-year-old niece? What a nice hypothetical question to broach to a young, tender, inexperienced girl. You should be ashamed of yourself."

"Well…I…I suppose I am."

"Surely you didn't have in mind to *do* anything to that child?"

"I didn't…? I didn't. Oh, well, no, not *do* anything. No, no, never—no, no, not me. I wouldn't! No—"

She eyed him suspiciously—ruefully—and nodded curtly. "If I ever hear the *slightest* suggestion that you became a dirty old man with my brother's blushing child niece, I will be out of here so fast you won't know what happened—"

"Oh, Helene—so dour—so extreme. Try to understand men—your husband—"

She nodded a long time, up and down bobbed her head—rhythmically. Fatalistically. "I understand," she said, then added, "too well."

Prince Stephanoff's coach was even grander than Katrina's. The horses were sleek and shining Thoroughbreds. The coach had so much highly polished gold; it had a driver *and* a footman, both dressed in the fanciest red brocade long jackets and silk knickers. And they were handsome men. She thought she could easily flirt with either of them, had they only been as rich as the prince.

Inside, the fabrics were like the finest French tapestries. Zdenka settled back in the seat facing Prince Stephanoff and ran her hands on the silky-smooth threads beside her, feeling the subtle rise and fall of the meticulous patterns, and she had to catch her breath so she wouldn't scream with delight. She, after all, did not care to appear unaccustomed to luxury, for she made up her mind then and there that there would be no butcher's son for her. It was luxe or it was nothing.

Staring boldly across at the prince and his baby-blue eyes, she saw in him freedom and luxury, and she liked what she saw.

Conversation did not come easily to either one of the young suitors inside the coach, and the clanking of the carriage wheels and the clicking sound of the horses' hooves on the cobblestones carrying them to the opera house provided the background music for their silent thoughts. And their silent stares, as though each were taking measure of the other—inventorying their unspoken and unseen charms.

"You are a very beautiful woman," the prince said so softly she barely heard him above the turning of the wheels on the pavement. She dropped her eyes, displaying becoming and appropriate modesty.

But, she told herself, beauty is not enough. You must be charming and engaging as well. But how? She looked at him again—his eyes were fixed on her as though she had hypnotized him. She dropped her eyes again.

This is silly, she thought. He must think I'm the biggest goose. Auntie said I must be myself.

"So, how is it being a prince?" she blurted out.

He smiled. "Lonely," he said.

"Lonely?" she said. "Why? You must have nothing but people around all the time."

"Oh? What makes you think so?"

"Well, I don't know. Aren't palaces full of people—servants and such?"

"I suppose," he said. "But you can be surrounded by armies of people and still be lonely."

She wrinkled her nose. He found it captivating.

"Loneliness," he said, "is within. Like happiness."

She considered that. "Well," she said, "I hope you aren't lonely with me."

"Oh, no," he quickly assured her.

They rode in silence for a while while Zdenka tried to think of something witty to say.

"I do hope you will like the opera," he said, "as much as I do. I just adore opera."

She smiled demurely. "Your enthusiasm is sure to be contagious."

And it was. Zdenka loved every aspect of the evening, from seeing the prince, riding in this splendiferous coach with him, stepping out on the hand of the footman, to a sudden gasping silence of the large crowd, and the prince looking at her with such admiration! As the prince and Zdenka made their way to the entrance, he could tell by the sudden, excited, higher-level-than-usual buzz that Zdenka was a huge success.

Inside the opulent opera house, all bedecked with gold and crystal chandeliers, Zdenka asked her prince, "Why was everyone so quiet when we got out of the coach? Is that some kind of reverence for royalty?"

He laughed softly. "No, my dear, they had never been silent like that before. They are there to speculate on my escort. They even wager, I'm told. Well, when you stepped out they were simply awestruck by your beauty. They had frankly never seen anyone as beautiful as you."

"Oh, hardly," she said. She didn't believe him. Thought he was engaging in outrageous flattery. "That's sweet of you," she said, being herself, "but I'm afraid I can't believe it."

"Modesty becomes a young woman," he said. "I heartily agree with them. You are the most beautiful girl I have ever seen."

They were seated in his box, just to the right of the stage. Zdenka was thoroughly confused by the prince's comment. She didn't see any way in the world that it could be true. Did her aunt's dress deceive them? Could it possibly have made her look that good? But surely there have been other girls...? She was feeling her head swell and was sure all this talk would make her careless. She mustn't get careless.

The house was buzzing, then came to a hush as the conductor made his way to his podium in the orchestra pit. There was applause and Zdenka kept her eye on the prince as the music began.

She decided the best thing for her to do in this strange circumstance was to watch him and do what he did.

The overture ended to enthusiastic applause, and she was already caught up in the excitement of *La Bohème*.

From the moment the curtain rose on the first act of *La Bohème*, Zdenka was enchanted. The music exhilarated her, the spectacle excited her, the story enraptured her. Though she didn't understand Italian, she followed the story from the program notes and from her memory of her aunt's explanation.

Her escort was aglow, hanging on every note and syllable of the arias and recitatives. She could see his body swaying, eyes closed, with the music. It was as though he were in a trance.

Zdenka closed her eyes and imitated his movements and found her hearing was more acute with the curtailing of her vision, but she missed seeing the splendor onstage. She felt a tingle of excitement just thinking about sitting next to the handsome prince.

It was at the intermission that she first noticed the strangeness of the audience. As soon as the gas lamps were lighted by the boys in livery uniforms, she had the feeling everyone was looking up at the box, at first she thought at the prince, but then it became apparent they were looking at her.

She caught her breath and wondered how she was supposed to react: should she wave a glove at them as though she were some kind of royal herself? Should she ignore them? Her aunt's words came back to her—"Be yourself." So she flashed a quick smile, then turned to the prince and said, "Oh, I just loved it."

"I was hoping you would," he said. "Opera is practically my whole life. Now let's go out—a lot of people are dying to meet you."

"Oh, I don't think so."

Zdenka glowed in the orange light from the gas lamps like a marigold in the sun. They had gone to the royal chambers, a large room set aside for the private amusements of the royal family.

Zdenka was introduced to Baron this and Countess that—princesses and counts, earls and dukes. The hum of excitement was so much more genteel than the raucous din of the Aristocrat Club, Zdenka's last musical experience. This was, unarguably, class. It was all head-spinning. She smiled politely and bowed with her eyes at each introduction, until a handsome young man with slightly receding reddish hair barged through the crowd and presented himself to the celebrated couple. "Steph, my boy, introduce me to this gorgeous woman—you cannot possibly keep her all to yourself, she's far too beautiful to be anywhere but in the public domain."

"Baron Chotznic, may I present Zdenka Oleska."

The baron took her hand in both of his—"You certainly may," he said, not taking his eyes off Zdenka. Then he bowed and kissed her hand, which she found titillating and repulsive at the same time. The baron was an acceptable man, but he couldn't hold a candle to Prince Stephanoff. She inched closer to the prince.

"My dear," said the baron, "keep your wits about you with this Don Juan. And should you ever aspire to legitimate companionship, please do me the honor of remembering me."

"That will do, Alexi," Prince Stephanoff said, pulling rank to dismiss him.

Alexi bowed and backed away and was soon swallowed up by the crowd.

"He's a strange one," Zdenka said.

"Watch out for him," the prince said, "he's trouble."

She tittered. "Why, I believe that's what he said about you."

"Yes, but I tell the truth."

The second act was even more delightful to Zdenka. The exhilarating music worked its way into her bones. I must make a study of opera, she told herself, without wondering how a girl who was employed as a virtual house helper could manage that.

During the second act, Zdenka began to notice the prince seemed to be especially enraptured when the soprano sang. Zdenka was surprised, for the soprano was not beautiful—but her voice was sublime. She found herself looking more and more at the mesmerized prince while the soprano sang, and Zdenka felt an odd twinge of jealousy that the sturdy soprano was able to monopolize his attention—Zdenka *was* his date after all. And everyone *had* been staring at her.

By the time the opera houselights went up again, her escort had been drained of his life force, and moved listlessly with her to the waiting carriage which would spirit them back to the royal palace for the post-opera supper.

Zdenka swam through an envious sea of staring faces, and she tried her best to give them in return smiles that were harmlessly, yet endearingly, shy.

In the carriage, the prince sank back in his seat, exhausted. "What a performance!"

"Yes," she said, in enthusiastic agreement.

"A performance like that takes a lot out of me," he said.

"I could tell," she said.

He stiffened slightly. "How could you tell?"

"I could see you were completely wrapped up in it."

"You were watching me, not the opera?"

"Only for a second," she said, and he seemed satisfied.

The palace was a sprawling compound of buildings that looked adequate to house the entire Russian Army.

Entering the palace, Zdenka felt a sudden lift. It felt to her like she belonged there—she *was* a part of the royal family. The high-ceilinged room with the beautiful candle chandeliers took her breath away. She could hardly imagine ever having to walk in a room with low, confining ceilings again. Here was a room for people who were fifteen feet tall, and she *felt* fifteen feet tall. She stared at the rich fabrics on the walls in muted shades of burgundy and gold, the tiny threads set in place by hundreds of servant girls.

And the waiters! There was a regiment of them, and they brought the most magnificently beautiful food and silver trays that shined to the high ceilings and back again.

Stephanoff introduced Zdenka to his mother. A pretty woman, dressed to the teeth, she seemed only half-engaged, as though this were just another of Stephan's inconsequential "companions," to put a nice word on it. Stephan's father was another matter. Zdenka had a far more profound effect on men than she did on women. Some inner voice tried to tell her she need not reason why, but should ride the wave of glory until it led on to fortune.

Count Stephanoff was a broad-shouldered, deep-chested man who put Zdenka in mind of a stalwart oak tree. He had a dramatic moustache which led far into his cheeks and curled up just below his eyes to make him look like he was perpetually smiling.

Zdenka thought it strange that the venerable count took both her hands in his, seriously examined her eyes and said, "Ah, my son, my son." She wondered if the old man was blind or just silly. He shook his head and repeated—"My son, my son," and Zdenka suppressed the titters that were bubbling inside her. "This time," the count said, "he has outdone himself. You are *so* lovely. Promise you will come back—"

"I promise," she said, too eagerly.

"Not many of them do," he muttered to himself, releasing her.

The party sat at a long banquet table, elevated to look down on the royal guests. Zdenka thought she had never seen so much food in her entire life. Some might scoff at people having so much while others had so little, but for Zdenka's part she wanted to be with those who had too much.

Beside her, the prince was almost morosely silent and she asked him if he were still under the spell of the opera, and he professed not to know. He was not, however, communicative.

Zdenka looked out at the hall full of fashionable people and wondered how all of these well-dressed and painstakingly coiffed rich could have fit in the opera house. Then she noticed the man off to her right who seemed unable to take his eyes off her. She frowned at the unsought attention, then suddenly realized the eyes were those of the baron she'd met at the intermission at the opera house, the one who had disappeared into the crowd.

Her face flushed with embarrassment. She dropped her eyes to avoid his gaze. He seemed to be the only one staring—the others having apparently turned their attention to the sumptuous repast before them.

Zdenka tried to engage the prince in conversation, but he appeared hopelessly preoccupied and answered her feeble queries with monosyllabic abstractions.

At the intermission of the royal feast, Zdenka, in an attempt to improve Prince Stephanoff's mood, invited him to go for a stroll with her.

He looked at her curiously, as though that were unheard of. "All right," he said.

Outside, in the vast acreage of the royal gardens, she asked him, "Is something wrong, Prince?"

"Wrong, why?" he said, leaving no room for doubt that something was wrong.

"Because you are so quiet. I'm afraid I don't seem very interesting to you."

"Whatever gave you that idea? You are fascinating to me."

"But you've hardly spoken to me since the opera. Have I done something wrong?"

"Of course not. How could you think...?" he said, then stopped.

They crossed the parterre then slipped behind a tall hedge as Zdenka's heart raced with the anticipation that the prince was going to take her in his arms and kiss her.

Instead, he plunged his hands in his pockets and kicked a few stones in his path.

"What is bothering you, my prince? Perhaps I can help..."

"No, you cannot help. There is no help for my misery."

"But how can you have misery? You have *everything*."

"Everything?" the prince said. "I think not. I do not have a wife, for instance."

"But why not?" Zdenka asked. "You could surely have any woman you wanted."

"Ah, but no," he said. "That is the common misconception. The prince cannot have anyone..."

"But why can't you?"

"First, because we must marry royals. Second, our marriages are arranged and if not arranged, closely supervised. Political considerations...no, I long to be a free spirit—loved not for my money and position, but for myself."

"But why are you talking of this now?" Zdenka asked.

He looked surprised, as though she were asking a stupid question. "Why," he said, "the opera, of course. Didn't you see? The girls in the story were in love with poor men, but they had rich men to marry and to leech on to survive. It is just so with me. No one would ever love me for anything but my money."

Zdenka gasped. "But how dare you say such a...?"

"No, no, it is true. I am not naive. I have eyes to see—I have a heart and it feels, just like yours. Yes, my family is rich, but I have known nothing else. I should like to be rich in love."

The dull glow from the candlelight in the palace was for the most part blocked by the hedge so only speckles of light fell on the couple.

Zdenka was confounded. She searched for something to break the awkward silence. She wanted to throw herself at his feet, but said instead, "Does opera always move you so much?"

"Oh, yes—well, sometimes more, sometimes less. But this diva. She was so superior." He rolled his eyes as if in a swoon.

"What is a diva?"

"A woman who sings like an angel. An opera star who steals my heart." Prince Stephanoff had personalized the word, so Zdenka thought a diva was his special possession. Then and there she made up her mind she must be a diva and win his heart.

"Tell me why you don't marry a diva then," she asked.

"Oh, it would not be proper. I must marry of our own blood. But in my dreams my true love is always a diva."

Zdenka wanted in the worst way to kiss him. She knew that

would be a breach of royal etiquette, but she hoped that he would try to kiss her. But if he did, what would be expected of her? Must she resist or respond? Should she exhibit enjoyment or reserve? Why was there no one to teach her such things? Could she talk to her aunt? She might know—but her aunt was not here and she wanted the information *now*.

She started to lean toward the prince so their faces almost touched, but the prince stayed still, gazing into her eyes. She gazed back, her lips parting slightly. The prince shuddered.

"No," he said. "I must not take advantage of you."

"Why not?" she murmured.

He laughed at her frankness. She was insulted.

"But, my dear, you are only seventeen years old. You are still only a child."

"I want to be a woman," she said hoarsely with a seductive timbre the prince apparently found amusing, if she was to judge by his smile.

"And someday you will be," he said. "You saw all the men gaping at you. You shall have almost any man you want."

"Almost?" she asked.

"Almost," he said.

The prince did not escort Zdenka home that night, but sent her in his coach, saying goodbye with disappointing circumspection as the footman helped her into the lonely carriage. Prince Stephanoff's mind, she surmised, was still on that infernal diva.

The coach stopped in front of her gate. The footman opened the door and helped her down. He whispered to her almost without moving his lips. "The prince is strange sometimes."

Zdenka lifted her eyes to the fancily dressed servant. Then she gave his hand a squeeze before she let go and scurried into her uncle's house.

Though it was an eon past their bedtime, both Uncle Vanya and Aunt Helene were awaiting Zdenka when she came in the house, their sense of excited anticipation unhidden.

"Oh, Denky," her aunt spoke first. "How was it?"

"Yes…" Uncle Vanya chimed in. "Tell us all about it."

"Well…it…was……nice."

"Nice?" Uncle Vanya said. "Nice? That's it? Your old uncle and aunt, who these days can only live vicariously, you understand, two foolish old people who could never go in the palace through the front door—you must throw us a bigger crumb than that."

Zdenka looked at her uncle, then her aunt, and saw the expectation on their faces, then, she didn't know why, she broke into tears.

"Now, now," Uncle Vanya comforted her, putting his arm around her shoulders, and led her to the couch, where he sat beside her. "What's the matter?"

After a few diminishing sniffles, she said, "Oh, Uncle, Auntie—I think I must have been just terrible."

"Impossible!" Vanya said.

"How do you mean—terrible?" Aunt Helene said, settling in on the chair opposite Vanya and Zdenka.

"He didn't even bring me home."

"He didn't?" Vanya was shocked. "Why, the *scoundrel!* But, how was it before that?" he asked. "How was the opera?"

"Fine," Zdenka said, pushing the back of her hand up to staunch a sniffle. "I don't know anything about opera, but it was fine."

"Did you remember what I told you?" Helene asked. "About *La Bohème.*"

"Yesss. But it's hard—so much is going on. The prince was in a trance. I think he's in love with the dreever."

"Dreever?" Aunt Helene asked. "What's a dreever?"

"You know—an important female singer."

"Diva!" Uncle Vanya supplied, and they all chuckled carefully.

Zdenka did her best to slake Vanya and Helene's appetites for stories of the palace, but it was difficult for her. Every time she recalled a happy memory, her thoughts suddenly shifted to the prince's disinterest in kissing her—or even bringing her home—and she sobbed again.

"Child," Helene said, "don't cry. It is such a sadness, yes, but it is also the way of the world, and we can do nothing to change it."

"What am I to do then? Be a maid for the rest of my life?"

"Someday that nice butcher might come along," her aunt said.

"I will not marry a butcher," Zdenka said, startling them with her vehemence. "I shall marry the *prince!*"

Helene shook her head slowly. "Not unless things change drastically."

"Things *will* change!" Zdenka predicted from the vantage point of her seventeen-year-old experience.

"Perhaps," her uncle had said, "maybe not soon enough."

That night in bed, unable to fall asleep, Zdenka set her priorities. She would not give up on the prince. He seemed to like her. Perhaps he was simply distracted by something. But if he was, it must have been by the diva. He seemed so possessed by opera that Zdenka knew she would have to find a way through opera to attract his attention.

She knew she would write him a letter to keep her alive in his thoughts. It couldn't be just any old letter, because he must get lots of them. No, she would have to write a letter so unusual—so unexpected—that the prince would have no choice but to see her again.

And was there any reason she herself should not become a famous diva?

No—a resounding "no" reverberated in her restless brain. She would take singing lessons. Had she not already sung on stage? She would be a great star: the prince would *have* to notice.

Then she began composing in her head letters she would send. She went through many versions until she settled on a final one.

She got out of bed, lit the oil lamp and began to write.

Dear Prince Stephanoff:

I must first and foremost thank you for the very lovely evening you showed me last night. I have many fond memories, which I shall cherish forever. I was most flattered to be in the company of such an important gentleman, and I hope my poor companionship was not too dull for him.

In reference to your comment that girls could only like you for your money, I should be pleased to disagree with you, but I cannot. Not only am I in no position to contradict a royal personage, but I could not honestly disagree. Our class system being as rigid as it is would not permit a non-royal such as myself to form a union with a royal personage such as yourself.

Someday love, such as I have to offer, will be more important than wealth, which I do not have to offer and which I do not consider a just reason for marriage.

I will pray that your heart will be ruled by love and not tradition.

Your faithful subject,
Zdenka Oleska

She filled the remainder of the page with her signature, which she made with large, round letters and bold, sweeping lines, with perhaps more curlicues than might have been considered tasteful at the time—the whole thing giving an air of studied flamboyance, which it was.

"That ought to attract his attention," she muttered.

She sealed the letter in an envelope lest she lose heart in the morning. Then she went back to bed and to sleep thinking she had written a very clever letter indeed.

The letter was posted first thing in the morning and Zdenka settled into an anxious-waiting mode, calculating down to the half-hour when his reply would come to her.

She even imagined what his response would be. He would either summon her to court or even come himself to call on her. She could see him, unable to contain himself any longer, take her up in his arms. "My darling," he would say, "your letter was a stroke of genius. You have shown me how foolish I was, how blind to the truth that was under my very nose. I love you for it and I want you to be my wife, and I don't care a fig for the traditions of royalty. I have finally found a woman who can love me for myself."

When the prince didn't arrive at Zdenka's appointed time, and no message was delivered, Zdenka thought there had to be some extraneous reason. Royal duties had called him elsewhere. Perhaps (heaven forbid) he was sick, or at the bedside of an infirmed relative. Then, she thought he was simply being politic and not sending the answer immediately so as not to appear overly anxious. Zdenka could understand that—and forgive it.

The next day, the smallest doubt was setting in, but she was still what she would characterize as supremely confident.

By the third day, she was telling herself something must be seriously amiss with the prince, for certainly his breeding would forestall him from ignoring her thoughtful and (if she could allow herself some self-congratulation) brilliant letter.

On day four, she told herself that the constraints suggested by the phrase "noblesse oblige" would require a written response at the very least. And if the prince was not the writing sort—she understood that some men were not—he could easily send a verbal message with a footman.

Her hope slipped to optimism, then descended to doubt before plunging to despair.

Then, some weeks after she had given up all hope and had taken to chastising herself for writing a stupid letter that anyone in his right mind would ignore, Baron Chotznic showed up at her house. Her heart shot to the heavens and she ran to greet him. "Oh, Baron, you've come, how grand. You must tell me straight away. What is the message?"

When he looked at her, she could tell he had no idea what she was talking about. "I beg your pardon?" he said.

"Come on now," she teased him. "Don't keep me in suspense. What's the message?"

"Message?"

"From the prince?"

"Oh." He broke into the most disconcerting laughter. "The prince? Well, no, I'm afraid not. I haven't seen His Highness in some days now, but I can assure you I have no message from him."

Everything sank within Zdenka. "Then why are you here?

You've come to tease me—to make me think the prince had answered me. How *could* you *be* so *cruel?*"

"No, indeed, miss," he said. "I've simply come to speak to your uncle about having my portrait painted."

Zdenka felt doubly foolish, and dissolved back into the house to perform her household chores with increasing listlessness, leaving the baron to make his way around the house to the studio in back.

It was inevitable that Aunt Helene should begin to notice and then to complain about Zdenka's lackadaisical performance.

"What is bothering you, child?" Aunt Helene asked Zdenka when she caught her sitting in a chair in the parlor, looking dejected, with the feather duster on her lap.

"Nothing."

Aunt Helene eyed her with the obloquy of doubt. "Has it to do with the prince?"

"It has to do with nothing," Zdenka said, without looking up.

"You must do better, child, or we must send you back home."

"I will try to do better," Zdenka said, but if there was any improvement, Aunt Helene didn't see it. She spoke to her husband about it and he said Zdenka was probably just experiencing the pangs of growth. But he agreed to speak to her. He asked her to come to his studio that afternoon, and immediately he noticed how glum she looked.

The smell of turpentine stung her nostrils, but Zdenka always felt more secure in the company of her uncle than in that of her aunt. He seemed to understand her better—or more to her liking—than her aunt did.

She sat on the stool where the models sat. Vanya sat on the stool he sometimes sat on for painting a portrait. It was as if they were in an artist-model mode.

"It's the prince, isn't it?" Uncle Vanya asked in a way that put his niece more at ease than when her aunt spoke to her.

Zdenka gulped. She felt on the verge of tears, but she fought them back. "Oh, Uncle," she pleaded, but then stopped. She had come to the fork in the road. Admission on the right, denial on the left. She didn't know which way to turn. Then, suddenly, she realized she just couldn't keep it in any longer. "Oh, Uncle," she blurted, "I am *so* keen on him."

Vanya shook his head. Not in disapproval, but in sadness. "Oh, Denky, Denky, you are seventeen years old…and you don't understand our Russian ways."

"Well," she said, "I am not Russian."

"Yes, nor is your aunt, but when in Russia do as the Russians do. The classes here are so rigid. The prince took you to the opera because you are very beautiful, and the prince has an eye for beauty."

"Oh, Uncle, how did I displease him? Aunt said to be myself and I was, but…but…it was not enough. What should I have done?"

"I am sure you were just fine."

"But why have I no word from him?"

"Denky, baby, what do you expect? We are of the common class. Do you expect the prince to propose marriage to a seventeen-year-old commoner?"

"But, why did he take me to the opera? I thought he liked me."

"Well, I am sure he did like you. Denky, please, look at it this way: perhaps he liked you *too* much. He knows he could not pursue the friendship to marriage, and perhaps that saddens him. And to minimize his disappointment, he has decided not to torture himself by pursuing someone he can't have."

"Do you think that is it?"

"It certainly is possible."

"It's a stupid system," she said.

"Perhaps."

"It should be changed."

"Perhaps it will be. But it could be changed in a manner not to our liking."

"How is that, Uncle?"

"The peasants could revolt. They could overthrow the royal family. Then the prince would most likely be penniless."

"Then I could have him," she said bravely.

"I would not get high hopes, dear. If we have a revolution, who knows what will happen to *any* of us? It is especially dangerous for royalty."

"You don't mean…he might be killed?"

"It has happened," Vanya said, "or he could be driven into hiding."

"I would go with him."

Uncle Vanya shook his head, wearily, in sympathy. "It would be best for you not to think anymore about the prince," he said. "You will surely find someone else. Baron Chotznic was in here this morning. He is asking about a portrait. He wants to know if we would permit him your company while he is sitting for the painting. I said it was not a good idea, but he was adamant."

Zdenka made a sour face. "The baron! I do not care for him."

"Yes, I understand. Would you object to spending some time during his sessions? I frankly could use the commission—the market for portraits being down just now…"

Zdenka dropped her eyes. "I cannot deny you, Uncle. You have been good to me. But why is the baron asking for me? Does he not know about our class system?"

Vanya studied his niece, also wondering how much he should tell her. Could she be trusted in her judgments? Probably not, he thought—an impressionable teenage girl with stars in her eyes. But she did say she *wasn't* interested in the baron. "It is not quite the same with a baron," he said. "He is not directly of the royal family. There is more freedom."

"Oh," was all she said.

"Very well," Uncle Vanya said, "I will schedule his first sitting and give you plenty of notice."

She nodded. "Uncle?" she asked.

"Yes?"

"Do you think I could get a job somewhere where I could earn money?"

"Money? What for?"

"I want to take singing lessons."

"Singing lessons?" he said. "What a strange idea."

"Not so strange," she said. "I have already been singing in performances in Brest Litovsk."

"Really?"

"Oh, yes."

"But work is scarce. We thought we were being helpful to you having you here."

"Oh, yes, Uncle. You are very helpful, I just thought if there were some way to earn a little money. Just enough for the singing lessons. Perhaps I could do something for the singing teacher."

He frowned. "I do not know," he said. "We will see. I have an idea."

"Oh, Uncle," she clapped her hands, "what is it?"

"I must talk it over with some people first. I will let you know. But, Denky?"

"Yes, Uncle."

"It seems you have been, well, perhaps not as conscientious about your duties here as you might be. I suppose you were a little unhappy about...the prince."

Her eyes cast down again.

"Well, will you be able to get back up with your duties as you have in the past?"

"Yes, Uncle."

"Good. Then, I shall see what I can do about the singing lessons."

The following day a letter came for Zdenka. In spite of her first excited thought that it was from the prince, it was from her friend Katrina. It was all full of girl news and it picked up Zdenka's spirits.

That night, after adding zest to her chores in the hope Uncle Vanya would find a way to get her singing lessons, Zdenka, bone weary, sat down to respond to Katrina's letter. But her thoughts turned to the prince and the baron. Why was it the wrong man had to be interested in her? It was so unfair! She put off responding to Katrina for several weeks as time weighed heavily on her and her frustration in the prince's non-response built to the breaking point.

Dear Katrina,

I was so happy to get your letter. You will always be my best friend, no matter how far apart we are, no matter who else I meet along the way. And speaking of that, my big news is I have just met my handsome prince. He is Prince Stephanoff of the Russian Royal Family. He has taken me to the opera and on long walks. I find I just adore the opera, and since I have been singing more or less professionally (as you know!!), I am going to be pursuing a career in the opera. It will not hurt any that the prince also adores the opera!!!

In Russia, they take very seriously the distinctions in the classes, so it is like walking on a tightrope with me and the prince. But you know me, Katrina, I am not a quitter and there is more than one trick up my sleeve to achieve my goal. I often think how much easier it would be for me with the prince if I had your family background! There would be no obstacles to a perfect union.

Anyway, I do long to see you. Wouldn't it be grand if you could somehow make a trip to St. Petersburg? I would adore to introduce you to the prince! Then you could see firsthand what I am talking about!!! Not that I could promise St. Petersburg as anything more than the gloomy place it is. I have been here some months already, and believe me, seeing the sunshine is a moment for celebration. Everything is gray and before we know it we shall be going into winter again when the nights are so long, if you blink, you miss the daytime.

Well, enough doom and gloom, I must be off to get my beauty sleep. If I am to be a diva, I can't be looking like a scrubwoman.

All my love,
Zdenka

Before going to bed, Zdenka reread the letter. Perhaps, she thought, she had made her situation with the prince sound a bit on the optimistic side. But, then, Zdenka fully intended to *make* it a reality—by hook or by crook.

It was visions of the prince, constant in Zdenka's conscience, that kept her nose to the drudge-work grindstone. There was still no word from him, but a few weeks after mailing her letter to her friend Katrina, her uncle told her the baron was coming for a sitting on the morrow. She would be relieved of her housekeeping duties for a few hours to keep the baron company.

She spent the remainder of the day focusing her thoughts on how to utilize the baron to come to the attention of her prince.

At the appointed time, Zdenka presented herself in her uncle's studio. She wore her best dress, though she had no thought whatever, she told herself, of attracting the baron. She found him unappealing.

When she arrived at the top of the stairs, she saw the baron seated on the stool she had sat on for her tête-à-tête with her uncle. The baron was wearing a navy-blue uniform with a grand collection of medals over his left breast. These men and their uniforms seemed to Zdenka the ultimate silliness, like little girls playing dress-up.

Zdenka could tell the baron thought he was quite dashing in his appearance, but to Zdenka he merely looked funny. His posture was straighter, his expression more resolute, but he still had that air of self-importance about him that grated on her. His face was so square it reminded her of a child's building block.

The baron smiled when he saw her enter. She did her best to return it, but it was rather tepid. Her uncle tried via his frown to convey to Zdenka his wish that she be civil to his commission.

"So, my beautiful," the baron said. "I am honored here by your presence. Would you do me the further honor of telling me what events have taken place in your life since we last met?"

Zdenka's face was acidic. The baron spoke so stiffly all of a sudden. It must have been the uniform that did it to him, she thought. "Events?" she said. "Scrubbing floors, mostly," she pouted.

Her uncle frowned again. She was going out of her way to make herself unattractive to the baron, but he laughed heartily.

Uncle Vanya was sketching the baron as the first step to the oil painting. "Please, Excellency, could you not move—it is more difficult."

"Yes, yes, sorry. Your niece makes me laugh."

"If you would rather I leave…" Zdenka offered.

"Under no circumstances," said the baron.

Zdenka found it boring keeping the baron company and trying to keep up her end of the small talk. When her uncle called him

Excellency again, Zdenka naively asked, "Why are you called Excellency?" The baron laughed again at her naiveté, while Uncle Vanya shifted his feet and cleared his throat.

"What, you do not think I am excellent?" asked the baron, pushing out his chest.

"I did not mean…I just wondered what it referred to—"

"Oh—what am I excellent at? you mean—"

"Well…"

He laughed again. Zdenka didn't like his laugh. It was too boisterous—like she remembered that awful man laughing back in that Brest Litovsk saloon. "I will tell you what I am excellent at, my little flower—I am excellent at my birth. You see, that is all it takes to be excellent—to have an excellent mother and father and grandfather on back to the apes."

"I see," she stumbled. "And the prince is the same?"

A sly, knowing grin crossed the baron's face. "Ah, yes, the prince. Excellent birth, yes—the best there is. But it does have its drawbacks."

"Yes? What are they?" Zdenka asked. She came alive at the mention of the prince.

The baron winked at Vanya. "Well, he cannot marry whom he chooses," he said pointedly.

"Oh…"

When the session was over for the day, Baron Chotznic asked Zdenka if she would "grace me with your presence on Saturday next at a family picnic."

"Family?" she said. "What family?"

"Why, mine, of course."

"Who will be there?"

When the baron finished cataloging his sisters and baby brothers, aunts and uncles, parents and cousins, and the prince was not mentioned, Zdenka said, "Oh, no thank you. I think I have other plans for the day."

Both the baron and Zdenka's uncle felt their eyebrows raise in unison. "Oh, what might those plans be?" the baron asked boldly. Vanya winced.

"I expect to be practicing for my singing lessons," she said.

157

"Well," the baron said, "perhaps another time I shall succeed in enticing you to go out with me…" When he checked her face for a commitment, and found none, he added—"To the opera."

Zdenka's eyes sparkled. "Perhaps," she said.

At the baron's next portrait sitting he asked Zdenka out to the opera. She accepted instantly, gleefully. His Excellence was so pleased with himself.

It was lucky, Zdenka thought, Aunt Helene had another dress for Zdenka to borrow for the opera. She wouldn't have dreamed of going in the same one she'd worn with the prince.

Aunt Helene did not hide her disdain for Zdenka reaching beyond her status. And she blamed her husband for aiding and abetting these wild fantasies. Whoever heard of a young housekeeper cavorting with princes and barons? "Mark my words, nothing will come of it but heartbreak."

Preparations for going to the opera could take as long as the opera itself—with the fussing and primping and adjusting to one's natural person to make it seemingly as unnatural as possible. Aunt Helene helped and didn't admit the enjoyment it gave her.

The baron called for Zdenka in a splendid coach. When he saw the impression this ordinary display of wealth made on her, he said, "And I promise you, I will see you home."

That failed to please her as much as he thought it would, for she harbored a fantasy of the prince seeing her and being swept off his feet—moved to atone for his gauche faux pas in not accompanying her home from *La Bohème*. He would, in her fantasy, simply insist on taking her home. The baron would bow to her preference and she and the prince would create a lifetime alliance which would surmount convention.

Zdenka was buoyant and the baron was pleased. He misunderstood her mood—ascribing it to her change of heart about *him*. "You're not wearing your uniform," she said.

"No."

"Why not?"

"Well, I don't really like it," he said. "It's so showy."

"But, why are you being painted in it then?"

"Oh, Mother wanted it." He shrugged his broad shoulders. "Tradition," he said.

Zdenka felt her blood racing as the coach pulled in front of the opera house and she alighted with the aid of a footman. She was immediately struck by the lesser attention she received than when she had arrived at the same place with the prince. And she could not restrain herself from looking for him. That was, after all, the unspoken reason for her being here. She knew there would be a gaggle of oglers where he went, but she saw none here. Either he had already arrived and was seated in his box, or he was coming later.

Zdenka really wanted to stay outside to witness His Royal Highness's arrival herself, but she didn't want to miss being in his presence (and line of vision) if he was already inside. So she just went along with the baron to his box, which was across the theater from the prince's.

As soon as Zdenka entered the baron's box, she noticed the prince's was empty.

But once again Zdenka was enthralled with the sight of the

women in their finery and the great quantities of jewels that seemed to weight them down. There was a buzz of excitement that made *her* excited. And every time she heard a sound across the way, she looked to see if the prince had arrived.

The baron noticed her eagerness and at first found it charming. He thought it was a harmless infatuation. Nothing could come of it. Zdenka and he were alone in the box. The baron had arranged it that way—inviting her on a night his relatives who shared the box were not in a sharing mood.

"You look quite ravishing," the baron said, nodding at her attire—a black flowing dress with a lace bodice. "All eyes are enviously on you."

She dropped her eyelashes modestly. Not as they were when I was with the prince, she told herself. She didn't share that thought with the baron.

"Have you been to many operas?" he asked her.

"Only the one with the prince, where I met you."

"Really? I got the impression you were quite the opera buff—only one—?"

"Yes."

"*La Bohème,* was it?"

"Yes."

"Like it?"

"Oh, yes. I love opera."

"So you said. You saw that one with the prince," he said, then let the sentence hang like a taunt.

"Yes," she said, grateful for the opening. "Where is Prince Stephanoff tonight?"

"I don't know."

"You brought me to this opera knowing the prince wouldn't be here?" she said, as though accusing him of a deliberate snub.

"I thought you liked opera."

"I do, but…"

"But? You don't really like opera, you just want to see the prince?"

"Well…I…"

"Well, then, shall I take you home straight away?"

"No. No, thank you. I shall enjoy the opera…"

"But not my company?"

"I don't mean that."

"What do you mean?"

"I just love opera," she said, lamely.

"Good," he said. "*The Marriage of Figaro* is one of my favorites. We've a good cast tonight. The prince shall be sorry he missed it."

"What kind of girls does he go out with?"

"Pretty ones," the baron answered glumly.

"Do you know him well?"

"As well as anyone will ever know him," he said, "and that isn't saying much."

The challenge titillated Zdenka. Her eyes narrowed in a you-don't-know-what-I-can-do expression.

The baron laughed. "I see you think otherwise," he said. "Well, get it out of your bonnet. The prince will not marry a commoner."

The word stung Zdenka, the cold sound of it, the way the baron said it—it was an extra challenge. Her mind was turning. She realized she often said things on the spur of the moment she would not have said if she had thought about it. She knew she should be careful this time too, but somehow it slipped. "You," she said. "You too are of the royal blood. You too could not stoop to marry a commoner."

The baron laughed. "Is this a proposal?"

Zdenka blushed. "Well, certainly it is *not*."

"Thank goodness," he said, his hand resting on his heart. "I am too young to marry."

"Oh, fiddlesticks," she said. "How old are you?"

"I am not yet thirty."

"Pshaw! That's not too young," she said. "Not if you find the right woman."

"You think not?" His eyebrows raised in interest. "But you must also find the right woman who will have you," he said.

"But why would that be difficult? You are a baron, after all."

"So I am."

"Could you marry anyone you wanted?" she asked with a shy nod of her head.

"I suppose."

"Even me?"

He laughed again, then looked deeply into her eyes, and suddenly he was longing for her. "*Especially* you," he said.

Uh-oh, Zdenka thought, perhaps I have pushed him too far. It would not be fair to the baron to lead him to think I would marry him. I don't love him. I love the prince. It would not be right.

When the music began with the overture to *The Marriage of Figaro*, Zdenka stole one more glance at the prince's box. It had filled with people she didn't recognize—but no prince. She didn't stop looking, hoping against hope that he would suddenly appear, but he did not.

In his stiff and wooden way, the baron tried to amuse his escort, but she was not easily amused. Were it anyone else, he would have given up the pursuit long ago, he thought, but she was so ravishingly beautiful, he couldn't help himself.

He had invited Zdenka for the opera and supper afterward, just as the prince had. Now, on seeing the prince had not come and suspecting the baron had deliberately tricked her, Zdenka refused to go to supper. The baron tried to convince her to go with him, then he gave up in a huff.

On the way home in the carriage, he tried to kiss her. She was delighted at the attention, but rebuffed him lest she seem too easy. Besides, she had no desire to kiss him. She just wasn't attracted to the square-faced monkey.

"I don't know why I like you," he said as they neared her door. "I take you to the opera and all you talk about is the prince."

"Yes," she said. "I am sorry. It is only that he fascinates me. No more."

"Do you mean you are no longer fascinated, or you are simply fascinated and not romantically interested?"

"Something like that," she said, without telling him what she meant. His further efforts to understand her feelings went unrequited. Her mysterious way infuriated him. But it intrigued him at the same time—and made him want her all the more.

"Would you consider going with me again?" he asked as the coach stopped at her door.

"To the opera?"

"Yes."

"Will the prince be there?"

"He usually is."

"Then, I will go."

He took her hand and pressed it to his lips, then accompanied her to her uncle's door.

Zdenka got a letter from her father.

Dear Babushka:

I have wonderful news. Nadia has had a baby brother for you. We are naming him Peter. He was just born on the third of this month. Nadia is fine, and Peter is just as cute as you could ever imagine.

I am sorry, my dearest, you have not found it in your heart to forgive me my marriage. Every day I hope for word from you, and every day I am disappointed. But I will not give up hoping to hear from you as that would be the same as giving up life itself.

All my love to my Babushka,
Your loving Poppa

Well, Zdenka thought, he brought it on himself. Now he has *another* boy baby. Quickly she did the math. Nine months and ten minutes was what it came out to. Disgusting! Zdenka was in on the conception, and that made it all the worse. It was a last straw. She no longer had a father. He was already the father of a new baby. God knows how many more there would be. How could he have time to even *think* about Zdenka? She would show him. Once she was a famous opera star, he would be sorry for casting her out of his life.

"How is your father?" Uncle Vanya asked Zdenka when he saw her stewing over the letter in the kitchen.

"You are an uncle again," she said, without any show of emotion. "It's another boy."

"Well, well, isn't that wonderful news?" Vanya said.

"What is wonderful? Another mouth for him to feed. Another person for his thin attentions. I don't think it is so wonderful. He has never had so much time for my brothers."

Uncle Vanya nodded. "He had so little time for your brothers because whatever time he could spare he spent on you. He loves you, Zdenka—do you think it is right to treat him so?"

Zdenka fingered the edges of the letter. "I cannot look back," she said, staring blankly at the page. It was easy enough not to look back, she thought, but how much harder to look forward with any sense of reality.

Vanya sat at the simple table, across from his frowning niece. "Cheer up, Zdenka, I have good news for you."

"The prince is coming?" she asked, her eyes lighting like a woman whose dream has come true.

"No, not that," he said. "Sorry," he mumbled. "But through a colleague of mine—a painter at the university—I was able to make my proposal to Professor Sergi Menkoff at the conservatory. He will give you singing lessons in exchange for having his portrait painted."

"Oh, Uncle," she exclaimed, "that's so nice. When can I start, how many can I take, does he know I only want to sing opera?"

Vanya laughed a good-natured, loving laugh. "Oh, Niece, how many questions and qualifications you have. Since you will be starting with Professor Menkoff, perhaps you should let him decide what path to take. He suggests twenty-five lessons to start—twice a week. If he likes the portrait, or he thinks you have exceptional promise, he will give more. You can start Tuesday."

"Oh, Uncle." She jumped up and threw her arms around him and kissed him warmly on his cheek. "I'm going to be the most famous diva," she said. "Everyone will notice me. Everyone will love me. Oh, won't that be grand, Uncle?"

"Grand indeed," he said. "Now don't neglect your chores. Aunt Helene will not be happy about our arrangement if it means you don't accomplish your tasks for her."

Zdenka was so excited for her first lesson with Professor Menkoff. He answered the knock on his studio door in a black silk cape. Zdenka had to get control of the laugh that was aching to escape her. He had thick, fleshy lips that he continually moistened with his pink tongue. In this way he reminded her of Pinky Wallinski, the tavern owner in Brest Litovsk. His eyebrows were black, white and bushy and all his emotions were telegraphed in those eyebrows. When he opened the door and set his eyes on his new pupil, the eyebrows took flight like the wings of a dove.

The small room at the university had a piano and two chairs and piles of music on a table. When Zdenka sang her first scales for him, the eyebrows contracted like the feet of a pigeon. As the lessons wore on (and wearing was the way the professor characterized them), the eyebrows were mostly in the pigeon-toed position.

The first day, he had Zdenka sing nothing but vowels. When the session was over, she asked him, "Can I sing real arias?"

The moist lips seemed to turn up. The eyebrows stayed put. "My dear girl," he said. "I am the professor here, I have trained many stars of the opera stage. We will get on much better if you do not try to tell me how to teach you to sing. For if you knew better than I, there would be no need of you to come here."

Zdenka frowned. "I know, but—"

He cut her off. "Patience, my dear. This is an enterprise that requires patience from *both* of us."

Professor Menkoff came to his first sitting for his portrait with his silk cape and a jewel-topped walking stick. He wanted to pose standing with the walking stick in one hand like a marching-band drum major, the other hand resting on the back of an empty chair.

Uncle Vanya smiled. He would oblige, but he understood that where singing lessons were concerned, the professor took no suggestions. "So you are willing to instruct me in the best portrait pose?"

"I will certainly not tell you how to paint, what colors to mix, what brushes to use. That will be entirely up to you."

Thank you for that, Uncle Vanya thought, but he was too deferential to say anything. When both principals were in position, Uncle Vanya began drawing the outlines, and gently inquired about his niece's progress.

"Progress? That might be an optimistic characterization at this juncture," the professor said. "She is a young girl who is very beautiful, but as yet I do not see a glimmer of promise in the vocal department. Her voice is sweet, but thin. I am trying to develop some resonance there, but she seems to resist the rudiments. Wants to sing arias right away, and the poor girl simply hasn't the equipment for it."

"Can it be developed?"

"Well, it can be improved, certainly that is my goal. But the idea of her singing on an opera stage—even in the chorus—may well be an unattainable goal."

"She doesn't have it?"

"Well, you tell me. You've heard her sing around here, you say. How does she sound to you?"

"I am no music expert, of course…"

"Yes, yes, I know that. How does she sound to you as an amateur?"

"Well, I would hope she could learn certain things that would make her better…"

"Better? Yes. But she is no diva. Never will be."

"Have you told her that?"

"Of course not. She can derive much pleasure from singing. If she will only be more realistic with her expectations."

Realism, Vanya realized, was not one of Zdenka's fortes. Too great a dose of realism could stifle the stoutest heart.

After eleven weeks of lessons—eleven weeks of ah, aye, eee, eye, oh, ooo, and la, la, la, la, la, la, la, la, and the same thing in reverse—Professor Menkoff gave Zdenka a treat and let her sing an aria by Mozart. His eyebrows were in the crash-landing position as he accompanied her on the piano. He made no comment when it ended, so she prodded him, "What did you think?"

"Well, I am glad it is over," he said.

"You don't think I'm very good, do you?"

"I think you may expect too much improvement, too quickly," he said, tactfully.

She nodded sheepishly—a little flirty, he thought.

He eyed her appreciatively, now. He was looking at her youthful beauty—at the perfect, soft lines of her face and body. The pink tongue circumnavigated his lips. "Would you like more lessons?" he asked.

"Oh, yes," she said. She thought perhaps from another teacher, but that was an impossible dream at this point. Professor Menkoff was certainly better than nothing. And he had let her sing an aria. Perhaps there would be more.

The eyes of this man—three times her age—perked up like a racehorse at the starting gate. Those narrow, grating eyes never left her. It made Zdenka uncomfortable. "There are things…" he began slowly "…a young, pretty girl can do to earn singing lessons…"

"Things?" she said, though she had a good idea of what he meant. Pinky Wallinski had seen to that. "What *kind* of *things?*"

"If you will do me the honor of accompanying me to my apartment, I will be pleased to give you a drink, and we can discuss it."

She closed one eye and asked, "Can't we discuss it here?"

"Nooo…I don't think that would be appropriate."

"Your apartment would be *more* appropriate?"

"Yes."

Zdenka frowned. There was no sense leading on this ugly man whom she found repulsive. How transparent men are, she thought. What prepares a young girl to raise a shield against this kind of behavior? Nothing. It was pure instinct on her part. But if the kind of familiarity the professor was offering was proffered by someone less revolting, would she take such a moral stand? she wondered.

"I'll ask my uncle about coming to your apartment," she said.

"Oh, there is no need to do that," he said, quickly. "This must be just between us."

"Just between us?"

"Yes."

"But I am young—and inexperienced," she said.

"I will…we will change that together."

There were three more lessons, then she could decide. She *had* to take lessons—but where else would she get them? Zdenka thought, I may have to string along the professor until I can make other arrangements.

She tried to think what the professor's proposal would be like, but she couldn't imagine it. One thing she was sure of—if she did anything with the professor, the prince would shun her completely.

She was on her way to her final lesson when the note came from the baron, inviting her to the opera.

Suddenly, the baron did not seem so terrible.

She was all atwitter at another chance to see, and be seen by, the prince. Aunt Helene was helping her dress while Uncle Vanya talked.

"The winds of war are blowing across the country," he said. "The Huns are elbowing their way where they aren't wanted. I tell you, it does not bode well for Mother Russia. Its young men will be gobbled up like guppies in the path of a whale."

"Would *you* have to go to war, Uncle?"

"Heaven forbid!" Helene said.

"I may be too old. Not that I'd do any good at home. Nobody will want a portrait with a war going on."

"But, what about all the heroes with their uniforms and medals?" Aunt

Helene asked.

"I would expect that *after* the war," he said. "During the war, they are too busy fighting to earn those medals—or they don't want it to appear they have time to luxuriously sit for a portrait. I might as well go to war."

"No!" Aunt Helene uttered her command with a shudder.

Suddenly everything seemed dark to Zdenka. A war would stop everything cold. There would be no opera, and no young men. And what of her singing lessons—and the plan she had schemed to get them?

By the time the baron came to pick her up, she was in a state of utter agitation.

The moment the coach door was closed and they were settled inside, Baron Chotznic asked, "What is wrong?"

"*Every*thing is wrong," she said. "My singing lessons are about to end, with no means in sight to continue them."

"Surely there is some way…"

She shook her head vigorously. "No, the teacher has propositioned me, but that is out of the question, of course."

The baron frowned. "Was he a good teacher otherwise?"

"No, he taught me nothing. I must have a teacher who understands my voice, who can bring my talents to the fore."

"Professor Menkoff is considered the best in St. Petersburg."

"I must have second best then."

He smiled at her resolution. "You are a very determined young lady," he said.

"Is that a compliment?" she asked.

He looked out of the window so she wouldn't think he was smiling derisively. "I expect it is," he said.

"And now all this war talk," she lamented. "I expect all the singing teachers will be gobbled up by the war."

He looked back at her. She seemed to him so grown-up for someone in her teens. "Oh, Zdenka, I think the singing teachers are too old to be of much interest to the war."

"What about you?" she asked. "Are you going to the war?"

The baron was secretly pleased that she cared about that. "But there is no war yet," he said. "Perhaps we should save our worry so we don't waste it on something that never happens."

"It will happen," she said, "I know it will. Anything that can happen bad to me will happen."

"Bad to you?" he said. "You won't have to go to war."

"But it will be war at home. Everyone will be gone. There will be no food…"

"Where do you get these ideas?"

"I went to school, after all," she said. Then she thought a moment. "Will the prince go to war?"

"Oh, I don't see why not. But I wouldn't expect him to be crawling on his stomach in some mudhole in the rain. They would find a comfortable job for him, I'm certain."

"Would they find you a comfortable job?"

He shook his head. "I want to be an officer in the field."

"Oh, so you *have* already thought about it, and you said to save our worry until it happens!"

"Thinking is not worry. I am not worried. If it comes, it comes."

"And you would offer yourself to be shot at and killed?"

"The idea would be to shoot at and kill the enemy."

As the carriage stopped, she leaned over and touched his forearm. "Don't go to war," she said hoarsely.

The baron's eyes widened. He was very pleased.

Inside the opera house, Zdenka immediately saw the prince had not yet arrived.

Again, she gloried at the jewels and finery adorning the women. They were walking works of art, Zdenka thought. She also thought you could strip away the diamonds and pearls, the rubies and sapphires, and the velvet and satin, and be left with ordinary-looking women. But the stylish, expensive clothes and the lavish jewelry made them seem royal.

Someday she would have such finery.

As the overture began, a circumspect glance at his box told her her prince was missing this one too. Now Zdenka was convinced the baron had deliberately invited her only when he was sure the prince wouldn't be there. She was furious, but her fury simmered within while she concentrated—or appeared to—on the opera at hand.

By the time the intermission arrived, Zdenka had formulated

173

her plan. She had the sense to realize it would serve no further purpose to berate the baron for bringing her to the opera when the prince wasn't there. She would have to get noticed by the prince some other way. In the meantime, there was her immediate future to consider. War would mean less commissions for her uncle, and it could mean, by extension, that Uncle Vanya and Aunt Helene could no longer afford to keep her. She would die before she went home again.

So she was looking at the baron in a new light. A means to an end, but not the end itself. So when he invited her home for supper, she dropped her eyelashes and said, "It won't be too late, will it?"

"No, no," he assured her.

"All right then," she said, as though bestowing on him a rare favor.

The baron's apartment was large and lavish. Zdenka had to hold back her awe. She thought she should be playing blasé. Not far from the palace itself, it looked like a castle in its own right. Zdenka had not imagined such opulence existed outside the palace. Indeed the name "apartment" did not fit it at all. First of all, it was enormous. She estimated it was five or six times the size of her uncle's house. The ceilings were twice the height of a regular house, and the doors and windows were much larger than any she'd ever seen. The windows were draped floor to ceiling in brocade fabric of deep burgundy with white roses. The baron lived alone — but there were quarters below for his servants: a maid, cook, butler and his coach crew. His family were landowners and sublet miles and miles of farmland to tenant farmers. They also owned and leased living quarters throughout Russia, but principally in St. Petersburg. Their wealth was beyond calculation. Baron Chotznic participated in some superficial way in the management of these landholdings — but his time was more often occupied in sport, hunting, fishing, and the pursuit of attractive females. His appearance was dark and brooding, but he was a prime catch because he was the heir to one of Russia's great fortunes. Many observers had difficulty understanding why no young beauty had yet ensnared him. He was thirty years old and still footloose.

The table was set in the upstairs living quarters. The downstairs was devoted to public rooms for large and formal gatherings.

And for the machinations of business. Tonight it was just the two of them. But the finest white linens and the shiniest sterling silver and gleaming china were on the table.

The butler stood over them and poured the wines, then served the feast—beginning with smoked sturgeon, followed by a creamy borscht, then roast pheasant under glass, fruit and cheese and a rich berry compote. Each course was punctuated by the serving of an appropriate wine, and Zdenka soon felt lightheaded. After the third wine offering, the conversation took on a genial tone. The baron was expansive and forthcoming about his wealth.

"Who marries me will be a lucky woman indeed," he bragged.

"Oh, how so?" Zdenka asked, purposely playing into his hands.

The baron extended his hand to indicate encompassing his vast holdings—his beautiful home and the promise of unseen riches.

"Do you mean she would be able to afford unlimited voice lessons?"

"Oh my, my dear, at the very least."

"Yes? What else?"

"The prestige. She will be, by virtue of the marriage, a baroness, with all the rights and privileges that entails."

Zdenka didn't think she should ask what that was. She was leery about showing her ignorance.

"And what kind of girl does the baron hope to marry?" She was pleased with her choice of the word "hope." She thought first to say "plan," then thought "hope" would make him seem less certain to get what he wanted.

"The baron *hopes* to marry a compatible young woman who can bear him some little barons."

"And baronesses?" she asked.

"Oh, well, that too, I suppose," he said, leaving no doubt the males were preferred. "I would also expect she would not be too hard on the eyes, as I have always put a great stock in beauty."

"Like the prince," she said.

"I suppose," he said, taken slightly aback.

When the berries were consumed, the baron called the butler to ask for a bottle of champagne to be chilled in the silver table-

175

side bucket. "When that is completed, you may retire for the night. Tell the others also."

"Yes, Excellency," the butler said, bowed and departed. When he returned with the champagne, he poured the last of the dessert wine in the two glasses. The baron drank his and his face flushed with a crimson glow. Zdenka let her drink stand.

"Goodness," she said, "I've never had so much food and drink. I swear I am about to burst."

"Perhaps then, I should not dismiss the butler," he said. "We should have an awful mess."

She laughed a musical laugh, and it came easily. She saw he was pleased.

"And what kind of man will Zdenka hope to marry?"

"Oh, goodness," she said, "I am much too young to consider such a thing."

"Oh my, many women are married at your age. It is not at all unusual."

"Peasants," she said.

"No, not only peasants. But you are avoiding the question."

So, she thought, he wants me to tell him I expect to marry the prince? He wants to have a good laugh at my expense. Well, I won't fall into that trap. "I suppose a man who will care for me—love me."

"Ah—what does the young lady know about love? Hm?"

"I know nothing, as no one *knows* about love—love is a *feeling* from inside. I don't think it is rational. It is like a feeling you have for another person, so strong you cannot let go. And I think if you are not certain you are in love, you certainly are not."

"But if you were in love, would you know how to express that love to a man?"

"Maybe I wouldn't express it, as you say. There would be no need to brag about it. It would just be *there*."

"Have you ever been in love with a man?"

She wrinkled her nose. "What if I have?"

"A man that returned that love?"

"Are we talking something here that is any of your business?"

"I am just asking. You do not have to respond."

"I'll bet you've been in love with girls many times."

"Oh, no," he said, "not me." Then he looked deep into her eyes. "Not until now."

The wine was rushing to her brain and playing tricks with her equilibrium. "Now?" it was as though she hadn't heard him correctly. The baron reached over and laid his hand gently upon her bare arm. She looked down at it as though looking at a strange insect that had alighted there, trying to discern whether it was harmless or dangerous. But she didn't move her arm. Her pulse had quickened, and maybe his hand on her arm would return her heartbeat to normal.

When he lifted her hand to his lips and kissed its back, she did not withdraw, and when he stood and said, "Come, let us sit on the couch; it will be more comfortable," she didn't argue, but got up at his gentle urging and followed him to the crushed-velvet couch and sank into the luxurious goose-down pillows with lightheaded abandon.

He turned her head toward his and kissed her. She made no move, either to assist or resist. She was trying to understand if she liked it. She felt a surging of blood to her head, and her heart seemed to be pumping harder than usual, but this was far from the man of her dreams. It was an experience all girls must have, she told herself, but she feared she had drunk too much wine to make any sense of what was happening. His lips were wet and insistent and his arms seemed almost unbearably strong around her.

177

Now his hands seemed to be straying in a peculiar, intimate way and she realized in her hazy state that an action on her part might be called for. She tried to free herself from his grip, but he only became stronger—finally, she turned her head. "Wait," she croaked, "what are you doing?"

"Don't you like what I am doing?"

"I don't know. This is pretty fast. I am not experienced."

There was another clash of male and female hormones— nature's true primordial brew.

Her flesh was so warm and sensitive to his touch, her skin slick in its smoothness. He expected more formalistic resistance to his easing her over on her back on the couch.

She went back easily, the wine had made her sleepy. Perhaps he would let her go to sleep.

Dammit! he thought, she's going to sleep. Yet he'd never felt anything like her in his life. She wasn't bony or fatty, just soft flesh and gently yielding muscles.

She was pinned between the baron and the couch, and she yearned to be more comfortable. His hands felt nice, they made strange stirrings within her, but her movements were uncomfortably restricted. His hand was burrowing under her skirts. She alerted herself, though his hands felt nice making lazy circles on her lower legs, to remain in control of herself. Nice.

Control of himself was far from the baron's mind. Pleasure was his quest—the fulfilling of a strong need. He slid his hand up her legs where no hand had been before.

Zdenka squeezed her legs together so tightly she thought they would burst. Yet, she was embarrassed to admit to herself, his actions excited her.

The baron thought her sudden movement was an erotic reaction and he was satisfied to kiss her sumptuous mouth with his hand held captive so close to her gateway to paradise.

As suddenly as Zdenka had clamped her legs shut, when she could no longer hold his hand captive, or no longer wanted to, she surrendered the pressure and her modesty.

He gloried in her engaging innocence and in engaging that innocence. She had a youthful vigor that was beyond his varied and harried adventures.

Zdenka realized she was losing control of herself. But she realized also she was unwittingly positioning herself for ultimate control of him. He was such an eager lover! Phew! She made feeble gestures of restraint and guttural sounds which she meant to be understood as barriers to fulfillment but which he heard as the excitement of complicity.

She thought of the pigs. The pageant of the mating pigs her brother Felix was kind enough to show her so roughly. The doing and the done to; the giver and the taker. The pigs! she thought, then she groaned an audible murmur.

The pigs, she thought again, and then she was one of them.

Zdenka got home after four the next morning. Her aunt got up to let her in. She could smell the alcohol on her niece's breath, and she looked her over from head to toe. Neither the girl nor the dress looked as if it had remained upright. Helene feared the worst.

"Do you have anything you want to tell me, child?" she said.

"No," Zdenka said, "only I'm not a child anymore."

"I see that," said her aunt, and they went to their separate rooms for what was left of the night.

Zdenka had every intention of rising at six to fulfill her breakfast obligation, but she just couldn't wake up. Her aunt did not call her, but told Vanya what she surmised.

Zdenka awoke just before lunch. Helene was at the kitchen table, peeling potatoes for the lunch—a job that Zdenka would have done had she been up.

"Come here, Denky," she said kindly. "Sit here."

Zdenka's head was pounding as she sat. Helene divined her discomfort and set before her a cup of coffee. "Drink that for now," she said.

After Zdenka had drunk a few swallows of the hot brown liquid, Aunt Helene began: "Zdenka, I must talk to you about last night."

Zdenka was relieved she had the coffee cup to stare at. She wasn't about to meet her aunt's eyes.

"I don't need you to tell us what happened. Vanya and I are adults and we know what goes on between men and women when they stay out until four in the morning." Helene paused to think back. Did she remember what it was like? The exciting, blood-charging thrills? "What I must tell you is this. With the war seeming more and more likely to include Mother Russia, your uncle and I will be in no position to raise a child."

"Aunt—nothing happened," Zdenka broke in.

Her aunt nodded skeptically. "You *do* know how babies are made?"

"Aunt!"

"Aunt what? Yes or no?"

"Of course I do." Her aunt was becoming a nuisance. Zdenka wondered briefly if Aunt Helene had ever given Uncle Vanya such ecstasy. Did she have "the touch"?

"And having a baby without a husband is a disgrace in our class. The aristocrats don't mind at all using poor young women for their pleasure, then deserting them before the baby comes. Young girls can easily have their heads turned by the royals—the barons and such." Then she wondered, *was* she jealous of her startlingly beautiful niece? Would she have yearned to change places with her? Helene would insist not. Yet....

"I would not have my head turned," Zdenka said proudly. She was not one to let her emotions sway her self-interest.

"Well, that may be, but your coming home at four in the morning, smelling like a winery is no indication of chastity in my book."

"Aunt! *Nothing* happened." Why should older people always be such wet dishrags? Zdenka thought.

It was a curious claim on Zdenka's part and somewhat of an enigma as to her own interpretation of "nothing." She had bestowed on the baron the most exquisite pleasure he had ever experienced, and he admitted as much. She had, he said, "an incredible touch." So much so that he half accused her of being a professional, rather than the virgin she professed. She feigned insult, but deep down she was pleased. By "nothing," she meant she had not herself become personally involved, not made herself vulnerable, but rather had weakened her partner. No, she probably would not have done it without the liquor, but that was a convenient excuse.

The whole experience had been a triumph. The baron was eating out of her hand, and she had felt in those moments the invincibility of her sex. Even at her tender age, she had an intuition about it—about how most women become submissive and let males dominate them because it is so much easier to be led than to lead. Perhaps some women could afford that luxury. At this crossroads in her life, Zdenka certainly could not. Zdenka would have to take matters into her own hands. And last night she learned what putty men were. You just had to knead that putty to your will.

The baron had initially suggested—due to the state of his physical exhaustion—that Zdenka let the coachman take her home, but Zdenka used her first, newfound power to insist that would not be appropriate after all she had done…and the baron readily agreed. He then proceeded to beg her for a return engagement, though, of course, he did not put it that way. Zdenka played a little hard to get initially, but she had made up her mind and would reluctantly accept an invitation to another opera performance. This intelligence was not disclosed to her aunt in her present state of anxiety.

"Perhaps I should be blaming myself," Aunt Helene was saying. "I have not made enough attempt to introduce you to young people. The trouble is, I don't know many. I will try to remedy that."

"It is not necessary," Zdenka said.

Her aunt raised her eyebrow. "Not necessary? You are already engaged?"

"No, Aunt, I am not. But I can look out for myself."

"Nonsense. Baron Chotznic is already thirty years old. He

could be your father."

"Aunt! I am almost eighteen."

"Well, perhaps I exaggerate. Still, I must introduce you to people your age. In the meantime, I would suggest you not see the baron."

Zdenka shot a stare of unveiled resentment at her aunt.

"Because any man who will take advantage of a seventeen-year-old girl, who will ply her with wine and God knows what else, and will keep her out until four in the morning, is not a man to be trusted."

"Oh, Aunt!"

"Don't 'Oh, Aunt' me. While you are in my care, I am responsible for you. Letting you see the baron again would be irresponsible." That edict had the effect Helene should have known it would. It made the baron the forbidden fruit.

Though Zdenka was not one to apologize, she did manage to say, "Yes, Aunt," with downcast eyes.

Aunt Helene was as good as her word, and in the ensuing days she arranged a sleigh ride with some young people she had scared up among her friends and acquaintances. Zdenka was to be accompanied by a young boy named Georgi. It was an event to which she was not looking forward.

The boy was a lumpy, awkward lad with a bumpy complexion and Zdenka was so insulted at the match, she barely spoke to him.

The sleigh ride was horrible. It was freezing cold and no amount of bundling up in layers of heavy fabrics did much good. And the ride over rutted country roads was a jolting, bruising journey. She couldn't help but contrast it to the smooth ride of the baron's coach, and the prince's super coach before it. Her aunt was sadly mistaken if she thought Zdenka would settle for plebeian pleasures after she had tasted the nectar of the royals. In her quiet introspection, Zdenka pictured riding with the baron in his coach. In her mind's memory, he had a thinner, less round face, his hair hardly receded, his voice was smooth and soothing, devoid of his male roughness. He was starting to look better to Zdenka, who was thinking about the relativity of life. Next to the prince, the baron was wanting. Next to pimply Georgi, the baron *was* the prince.

Then she realized that her silence was being returned in kind by the lad seated next to her on the straw. Did that mean that Georgi took no interest in her? That would never do. She had an obligation to her sex to be irresistible to men, regardless of their appeal. Zdenka turned to him and flashed him her magnetic smile. "Well, Georgi," she said. "Are you going to school?"

He was, he allowed. It was his last year.

"And next year?"

He expected to be in the war.

"How terrible!" Zdenka said. "War can never do anyone any good. Aren't you afraid of being killed?"

"Sure," he said, shuffling his feet in the straw.

"Then why would you go?"

"All the men will go. It is nothing you have any say over. Only the aristocrats can get out of it."

"They can?"

"Sure—but they want to be considered *real* men, so they go and make their pretenses at fighting—usually from a very safe distance."

"You mean like Prince Stephanoff?"

"Oh, yes, the prince. He has already gone to Moscow to pave a cushiony way, I'm sure."

"Moscow?"

"Yes. He is there to assist in the preparations. That is the official stance, at any rate."

"You think it could be otherwise?"

"Oh, the royals will see to it that they get the maximum credit without ever having to risk a scratch."

"You don't like them very much, do you?"

"People should be equal," he said. "I detest the class system."

I must go to Moscow, she thought. But how? Zdenka spent the following days plotting her strategy. But each idea required the expenditure of sums of money she did not have. Could she get money from the baron? She was sure she could work it, but wouldn't he suspect her motive—and wouldn't that be against his self-interest? Besides, Aunt Helene had made it clear she would do everything she could to block her access to the baron.

Just as Zdenka was despairing of a solution, the baron sent

word of his imminent return for another portrait sitting. On learning of this, Aunt Helene made a strong case to her husband for disallowing Zdenka from seeing the baron. Vanya listened patiently and occasionally nodded. When she ran down, he said, "Yes, yes, but do you know what this war scare has done to my business?"

"Must the girl be sacrificed to your business then?"

His eyes showed the pain of her accusation. "Helene, where is the sacrifice? I will be there with them—"

"Like you were before?"

"It did not happen in my presence."

"I suppose we should be grateful for small favors."

"Helene!"

"I can't help it if I feel responsible. Her father is *my* brother after all. Highly irregular for a portrait sitting to use your pretty, young niece as bait."

"Helene! It was no such thing," he protested. "It was merely company for the baron, to put him at ease. It also helps me—I don't have to concentrate so much on amusing the subjects myself. Look, Helene, everyone is talking war. I have no new commissions in the hopper. Can we afford to alienate the baron now of all times?"

"Can we afford the consequences of not?"

"What consequences?"

"A bastard child!" Aunt Helene shot the words with a stinging vehemence. "Do you want to take care of it? For I do not!"

Vanya was silent. He did not want to believe that, but…. A young, inexperienced girl from the country, a worldly, grown aristocrat. Pursing his lips in preparation, Vanya said, "I have agreed to let her keep him company…"

Helene shot back, "Coming home from this man at four in the morning smelling like a distillery is not behavior that is acceptable to us. Not if he is the czar himself!"

"Yes…well…Helene, I don't disagree. But it is now not a question of staying out with him. Now it is more a question of my fee."

"And what will be the result except to further inflame his lust?"

"The result will be food on our table. Starvation to me is not an appealing prospect."

"Appalling!" she said.

"Exactly!" he said.

When the baron arrived and Zdenka came up to the studio, Vanya felt the electricity in the air, and he was immediately shocked by it. All doubts were erased in his mind before a word was spoken by either of them.

As the baron took his seat on the stool to resume his portrait pose, he said, "You should really be painting your beautiful niece. She is a much more appealing subject than I."

Vanya laughed as he was mixing paints on his palette. He threw a conspiratorial glance at Zdenka. "Ah, Excellency, but she cannot afford my prices."

"If it is merely a matter of money, I would be honored to supply that frivolous commodity and consider it a worthy utility indeed."

Zdenka blushed at the flattery. She only wished the baron had been less stiff and mechanical. Vanya saw another commission flash before his eyes. And he had already started her portrait.

"Why should not the most beautiful girl in all of Russia have a portrait?" His eyes met Vanya's in a conspiracy of intimacy. Without changing his pose, he said, "I should also like to return the favor Zdenka is doing me, by being present to keep her company for your sittings. Would that be a possibility, Vanya?"

Vanya was ambivalent. Of course, he would have to start a *new* painting, but rubles were rubles. "We will see," Vanya said, vaguely, angry that he was nervous that Zdenka might reveal he had already done her portrait. But she was too smart for that.

"And how is my own portrait coming, Vanya—when do I get to see it?"

"Soon, Excellency. I am trying to capture your very strong jaw at the moment, so please do not weaken it by moving. Then your bold and masculine coloring. I must darken a bit and we will be almost home."

"Well," the baron huffed, "I'm glad I'm not paying by the hour."

Zdenka got through the bulk of the sitting relying on her modest, downcast eyes to see her through it. She had wanted to make sure the baron was still interested in her and she wasn't just some plaything to be cast aside after it served its brief but glorious purpose. Now, satisfied the baron was still smitten, she could afford to relax her vigilance and play the demure, somewhat aloof, damsel who had perfected the art of indifference.

"And so, my dear," the baron said, holding his pose, "are you in the mood for another opera?"

Zdenka cast an inquiring glance at Vanya. The artist narrowed his eyes in disapproval.

"I am afraid I have nothing else to wear," she said.

"Wear? What is to wear? You were the loveliest of all the ladies. What you wore was perfect."

"Ah, but I could not repeat."

"Why not? No one is caring what you wear. You are so beautiful you could come in a potato sack and none would be the wiser."

"Oh, Baron, you flatter me," she said with fluttering eyes.

"If it is mere apparel that holds you, I would be honored to send the family seamstress to do you the honors. I am sure she could satisfy your every wish."

"But I have no jewels," she purred. "I am naked next to all those others."

The baron smiled tightly. "It will be seen to," he said.

Another glance at her uncle, and another frown from him held her from immediate acceptance. "Well, I'll have to ask my aunt," she said weakly.

"By all means," said the baron, "and while our seamstress is at it, I'm sure she could make your aunt a fetching costume. Say, why don't we all go? We have ample seats in the box. Yes, yes, we'll make it a family affair."

"Oh, Excellency," Vanya demurred. "You don't want to be troubled with all of us."

"But it is not trouble. It would be my pleasure, I assure you."

When the session was over for the day, the baron asked Zdenka to accompany him to his coach. Vanya was uneasy, but he saw no harm in those few moments alone.

The moment they were out of Vanya's hearing, the baron burst forth, "Zdenka, my darling, nothing in my life has been like those moments with you. I would give anything to see you again."

"Oh, you flatter."

"When can I see you?"

"Aunt Helene has forbidden it. She was not happy when I came home so late. She feels you are using me for your pleasure," Zdenka said, with an endearing roll to her eyes. "She says there is too much distance in our class. You would never marry me."

The broad jaw set, the baron said, "She does, does she? We will see about that."

When he climbed into the coach and waved good-bye, Zdenka saw the resolution in his eyes. It made her very happy, momentarily.

And then, just as quickly, her heart sank in sadness. That seventeen-year-old heart of hearts was in Moscow, with the prince.

"Anything," he had said. "Anything." She'd heard it with her own ears.

"He is turning our heads," Aunt Helene said at dinner. "It can come to no good."

"Don't be so negative, Helene," Vanya said.

Carolina, eyes big as the plates on the table, watched with rapt fascination the conversation at the table.

"But what would I wear?" she asked. "Already Zdenka has shown at the opera the only dressy dresses I have."

"Ah, my dumpling, the baron is sending his family's seamstress to make you both brand-new dresses." Vanya sat back, proud of bringing this news to his dumpling.

Her eyes narrowed as if looking

for the fly in this elixir. "For *both* of us?"

"Yes!" he exclaimed, leaving no doubts where his sentiment lay. "Tell her, Zdenka."

"Yes, Aunt, oh yes!"

"But this is completely foolish," Aunt Helene said, and then as the idea sunk in, a smile crept stealthily across her face. "I cannot believe…"

"Believe," he said.

"My dear Denky," Helene said, examining Zdenka's face with careful curiosity, "you must have cast quite a spell on this poor man."

"Can I go to the opera and get a new dress too?" Carolina asked.

"My dear child," her mother said, "it is bad enough to spoil your cousin at *her* age without reaching so far down the age ladder to corrupt *your* sense of modesty."

"I don't want to be modest," Carolina said. "I want to go to the opera too."

"Oh, cousin," Zdenka said. "Someday you will. You will be the most beautiful girl anywhere, and everyone will want to take you to the opera. You will be the belle of the ball, I *know* you will!"

The child was pleased by Zdenka's high opinion of her prospects and the praise went a long way toward satisfying her, but did fall somewhat short of the mark.

In the ensuring days, Carolina clung to her elder cousin as though her life depended on scrutinizing Zdenka's every movement. In her heart, she knew that Zdenka was the prettiest girl in the world. And Carolina knew, at the same time, she would never match that beauty.

Early the next morning, the seamstress appeared at the Gorkys' with an assistant and gave them a selection of fabrics. "You pick first," Zdenka said to her aunt.

Aunt Helene was as excited as a schoolgirl, and though she felt it incumbent on her to play the skeptic, she said little after the dress was fitted.

"You look ten years younger, dumpling," Vanya said when he saw her in the dress.

When he saw Zdenka, he knew this was the dress he had to

paint her portrait in. It was white satin, close to her hourglass body, with sparkling blue velvet puffed up from the shoulders. Gold buttons graced the blue velvet band that coursed down the front of the white dress. To Uncle Vanya, she looked like an angel. He was so proud of her it took his breath away.

The opera, a performance of Beethoven's *Fidelio*, was an exciting experience for Vanya and Helene, as well as Zdenka. The baron was in the coach to pick them up and he was joined in the box at the opera house by his mother, father and sister: Count and Countess Chotznic (stolid if humorless) and Countessa Riasa, an introspective wisp of a young woman, old for her twenty-six years. The count bowed lowest on being introduced to Zdenka, his eyes popping in admiration. "You are a very lovely young woman," he said, as he stood back upright and the medals bounced against his chest. "I can certainly see why Alexi is so smitten."

At the intermission, in the grand royal hall, with endless tables laden with food and drink, the countess confided in Aunt Helene. "Your niece is certainly beautiful."

"Thank you."

"As you are yourself, of course."

"Oh, that is too kind of you really," Aunt Helene said, "and not necessary. I am no longer seventeen years old."

"Ah, who among us is? I only wish my son would find someone marriageable. You understand, I mean, no offense—but society is so rigid," she said as though it bothered her.

"Oh, I understand perfectly," Helene said, and she *had* understood, but now that she heard it from an aristocrat, it didn't set as well with her.

"I must say I am also taken with her. The girl has a lot of spunk, but I understand her parents are Polish peasants."

"Oh, no, not peasants," Helene jumped to her defense. "My brother and his wife are landowners."

"Really? Extensive holdings?"

"Well, no—a nice farm."

"I see." And what the countess saw disappointed her.

The supper after the opera was at the opulent home of the count and countess. It was many times the size of their son's apartment and was surrounded by untold acres of land. The crystal chandeliers in the entry hall rivaled those in the opera house, and the servant staff could have comprised the population of a small town. There were hundreds of guests, what the Countess Chotznic referred to as "a small party."

At the long and heavily laden table, Zdenka was seated between the count and the baron. How in the world did the table support the heavy silver and gold and crystal, let alone the sumptuous (and heavy) food? she wondered. Helene was to the baron's right. Across the table sat the countess, next to Uncle Vanya, with the baron's sister on Uncle Vanya's left.

The silver candelabra in the center of the table held eighteen candles—burning brightly.

The count carried the lion's share of the conversation—most of it addressed directly to Zdenka. "I fear for what this world holds for its deserving young," he said. "This war will be here before we know it. It may be the end of life, as we know it."

"But surely not," Helene said bravely. "Our institutions and royalty are cherished in the hearts of the Russian people."

The count shook his head with resignation. "In the hearts of the privileged classes, yes. But we are many millions of unprivileged. You will not find them as eager to maintain the status quo."

"You mean, you think we could become a classless society?" Vanya asked across the table.

The count laughed, a robust, humorless laugh that shook the table. "Ah, the dream. But when you wake up from that dream you find a nightmare. There is no such thing as a classless society anywhere in the world. Only pretension to it. Instead of aristocrats born to rule, you trade them for uneducated and uncouth bullies. You take the wealth from the wealthy and pass it out in the name of egalitarianism. But the bullies don't realize that there is not enough of that wealth to go around. They claim to desire everyone should be equally rich, but they are all equally poor instead. An inordinate amount of wealth winds up in the hands of the bullies. Then they begin their executions of anyone who doesn't see it their way, and that, of course, includes anyone with any shred of intelligence—the university faculties will be decimated, we will get run off our land, intellectuals everywhere will be exterminated as enemies of the state. The government, if you can call it that, will be run by the peasants, who have no more idea how to govern than to fly to the moon."

"But surely," Vanya said, "this is a very pessimistic prediction."

"Indeed it is," the count agreed. "And I pray for the sake of the young people here that I am wrong. But there are rumblings already. If the world goes to war, which I fear we must, it will open the floodgates for the Bolsheviks."

"What would you do?" Helene asked.

"Run for our lives. But *where* is another matter. I've no idea where the safe ports will be in the storm of war. And will we be able to go with any of our wealth intact? I'm not optimistic."

The countess waved her hand at her husband. "Enough, sir," she said. "I'm so weary of his doom and gloom," she said to her guests.

"Oh?" said the count in mock alarm. "If you think so, why did you acquiesce to my farewell-to-the-social-graces party? Our last before the war?"

"Oh, well," she said. "A party. I will throw a party anytime. And," looking at Vanya and Helene said, "I hope you all will come to it—Saturday next. We would be pleased to send the coach."

There was a murmur of reluctance from Vanya and Helene. Zdenka was ecstatic. Nothing pleased her more than being among fashionable finery; the tables of silver, gold, and priceless china; the display of rare jewels on the women.

The count's monologue bored Zdenka. Which way would Russia turn? Which way would be to Zdenka's own benefit? Of course, the way the count told it, the country would be run by stupid bullies, and that certainly didn't sound appealing. On the other hand, if the prince were a commoner—on *her* level—there would be nothing in the way of their courtship and marriage.

She didn't know how to take the count's suggestion the royals might be shot. Surely the people were not so barbaric as that! But if they were, wasn't the prince in more danger in Moscow than he would be here at home?

The baron asked to be excused so he might walk for a few moments with Zdenka. The count waved them on—as Aunt Helene's eyes narrowed watching the young couple walk out of the room.

The house was large enough for them to walk a nice distance through the ballroom and gymnasium, even through the stables, which were attached via the servants' quarters. Both the stables and the servants' quarters were much larger than Zdenka's aunt and uncle's house.

"Oh, my dear," the baron began when they were clear of the dining room, where the count was still holding forth, "I can think of nothing but you. I am beside myself when we are apart. We must do something about this forced separation. Come away with me."

"Where?"

"Anywhere."

"Moscow?" she asked, with a coy tentativeness, as though she had picked a location from the air to test him.

"Moscow?" he said, startled. "Why Moscow?"

"I hear the Moscow opera is more professional than the one here. Have you been?"

"Yes."

"Well, *is* it better?"

"My dear, how would I know? I have heard the opposite. But, I go to opera to see and be seen. To the performance, I am indifferent."

Was he really only thirty years old? Sometimes he seemed to Zdenka much older—forty, even. "But...but surely you like music?" she said.

"Well, I suppose I don't mind it. But if there is a difference between opera in St. Petersburg and opera in Moscow, I'm not aware of it."

"Oh, Baron, wouldn't you go—for me?"

"To Moscow? That is a very long journey," he said. "To hear just another opera, that would be an excessively long journey."

Zdenka took the rejection personally.

"Why are you pouting?"

"Because," Zdenka said, "you said you'd take me anywhere and the first place I suggest, you reject."

"You are right. You want Moscow, I should give you Moscow. But I would be remiss if I did not tell you with the war so likely, Moscow could be the most dangerous place in Russia."

"I don't care," she said.

193

"If that is your wish, I can do no less. I must have you."

"*Have* me?" Her eyes shrank in skepticism. "*How* have me? Are you looking then for a wife—or a courtesan?"

The baron was astonished at her boldness. "And what is it *you* want to be?"

"I will not be anyone's whore," she said.

He looked her in the eye. She didn't know what he was saying with that look.

"Will you marry me, Zdenka?" he blurted out. "I am so crazy for you, I will die if you say no."

Zdenka stared blankly at him, as though she were trying to transform him into the prince.

When Zdenka and the baron sat down again at the table, the count was still declaiming on the war, but the guests couldn't help notice the young couple was flushed with excitement.

"What would be the baron's position in the war?" Aunt Helene asked.

"He would go, of course," his father answered for him, "like anyone else. War is a great democratizer."

The countess contradicted. "Nonsense," she said. "If he went, he would *not* be like everyone else. He would be an officer first of all, and there would be no need to have him on the battlefield. There are lots of other positions for men of intelligence and breeding where they are not simply cannon fodder."

The baron was finally heard from. "I will not ask any special treatment," he said. "I will take my chances with the rest of the men."

"Hear! Hear!" his father said.

"Don't be silly," his mother said.

No one noticed how aghast Zdenka was. Her mind was a muddle. Did he expect her to be a war widow? That was not a role she would consent to play.

Baron Chotznic accompanied the Gorky family home in the coach. Casually he mentioned the portrait of Zdenka in her stunning dress, and how he would be so pleased if it could begin that week.

Neither Helene nor Vanya could deny him. Zdenka made an ineffectual stab at reluctance. "Pooh! Who could possibly want a portrait of poor me?"

The laughter was good natured.

To the first portrait sitting, the baron brought a box covered in maroon satin for Zdenka. When she opened it she gasped. It was a string of pearls that could have spanned the Volga River.

"Wear them for the portrait, please," the baron said.

"Oh, thank goodness," she said. "I thought they were a *gift*."

"But they are."

"Oh, no," she said, looking at her uncle. "I couldn't accept." Her protest was half-hearted.

"Nonsense," said the baron. "It is but a bauble next to my esteem."

Now Zdenka blushed as she heard her uncle clear his throat. The baron put the pearls around her neck. "The roles are reversed," he said. "Now you are in the hot seat."

The sessions were daily—the baron was in a hurry. The only privacy the baron and Zdenka had was when she walked him to his waiting carriage. The gray twilight air didn't deaden their high spirits. They were slow, moseying walks, but the baron filled them with eager salesmanship. "You must let me take you out alone," he pleaded.

"My aunt forbids it," she said.

"Then I must speak to her."

"It will do more harm than good," she said.

But he did speak to Aunt Helene the next day and made an eloquent plea to take Zdenka out for a ride. He offered to have his sister chaperone.

Aunt Helene made the expected arguments about needing Zdenka at home for her work, and the baron countered with an offer to send a replacement, which, of course, Aunt Helene could not accept.

Finally, with his assurance that his sister would accompany them, and he would return Zdenka by suppertime, and he would produce a note from the countess saying she did not disapprove the venture, Aunt Helene acquiesced.

It was another overcast day (Zdenka was beginning to think she would never see the sun again), and the temperature was cool in Northern Russia—as the coach rolled along the country road. The baron, his sister and Zdenka felt a warm camaraderie in the coach. Riasa went the extra mile to be unobtrusive, speaking only when spoken to, and then with a sheltered friendliness. The remainder of the time she spent looking out the window, as if to leave her brother and his companion to their privacy.

On the outskirts of town, the coach stopped at a dacha. All the shutters were closed. The baron announced to his sister that Zdenka and he would walk the grounds, then added, "You may join us if you like"—in such a way as to beg a negative response.

"Oh, I think I'll check on the house—I'll catch up with you later."

The house towered above a stream that cut through a skeletal woods with budding trees and rocks that seemed aloof to the meanderings of temporal beings.

"At last!" the baron exclaimed. "We are alone." They walked along the stream like lovers: slowly, thoughtfully, both with their hands plunged in their coat pockets, heads bowed, with shuffling feet. "Have you thought of my proposal?"

"Well, of course I have."

"And?"

"You know I don't know you that well…"

"How can you *say* that after that beautiful episode at my apartment?"

Episode? She thought that a peculiar choice of terms. "That

'episode,' as you call it, almost ruined our friendship."

"Ruined? But how so?"

"My aunt was scandalized."

"You *told* her?"

"Of course not. I kept saying nothing happened. Like I had a speech problem. But she is not stupid."

"But if she knew the true nature of our love, surely she would be pleased?"

"No. She thinks you are taking advantage of me—using me, then going to discard me."

"That is not true," he wailed.

"But your mother said as much. The class differences are too great a hurdle. You must do as you are expected."

"What do you care what my mother thinks? I don't."

"She called us peasants."

"Ah, yes, that did lack a certain tact, did it not? Oh, well, that's *her* problem. I am free to marry whom I choose."

"But how hard that would be for someone your mother doesn't approve of."

"Nonsense—you would be a baroness!"

Zdenka tittered. "Why, I wouldn't know the first thing about how to act as a baroness!"

"It's simple, really," he said. "Just be demanding."

He put his arm around her. She leaned into him. Demanding was something she thought she could be. She sighed. "There is too much to think of for my poor little brain. Aunt says you will abandon me. Then what will become of me? I shall be a pariah is what."

"Where do you get these funny notions?"

Zdenka pouted. "Are you making fun of me?"

"Never! But you worry so much about the most remote things."

"Remote? You think girls of my class are not used and abandoned by men of your class?"

"I don't know any," he said. "Those are scary tales that are made up to keep us apart."

Zdenka was not convinced. It would be, if she let it, so easy for him to take his pleasure—then skip off to war, never to be heard from again.

"Please," he said. "Let us run off to be together as we were before. We don't have to be married if you don't want. I will compensate you well. Buy you dresses, jewelry, fine furs, anything you want. I will give you an allowance."

"And then go to war and never come back!"

"Then marry me and if I don't come back, inherit my property."

"Your family would let you make me your heiress? I don't think so."

"Zdenka, Zdenka, you are *such* a skeptic."

"For good reason!"

"What good reason?"

"Here is a man I have barely known. He gets me drunk and takes advantage of my good nature, and now he wants to do it again."

"Zdenka!"

"He is a baron, I am a nobody."

"Zdenka! You are *not* a nobody. You are the most beautiful girl in the world."

"Pooh!"

"You *must* know it's true. If you don't, it's only because you have not been exposed to men. Anybody who *saw* you would be crazy for you."

"The prince?" she said, challenging him.

"Ah, the prince," he said. "Yes, we are to hear again of the prince. The prince, the prince—always the prince. Well, I have told you the prince is fatally inhibited by his class. I am certain he is crazy about you, but he will not violate what is expected of him. You may pursue him for the rest of your life and you will never change him."

"What if there *is* a revolution—and they are all dethroned?"

The baron shook his head. "Wouldn't matter to him. It's ingrained. He would never accept that he was a mere citizen and not a prince. He will always look on you as a peasant, however beautiful."

Zdenka stared at him as though she could break him to say something more friendly to her ears.

"No, my dear," the baron said. "I am as close to the royal

family as you will ever come. Now, I say we run away together and get married—or not, as you choose—before the war tears us apart."

"So, maybe we'd be married one week? Two weeks?"

"No!" He sounded angry now. "For *all* our lives!"

Zdenka looked into his eyes. The couple had stopped at a bend in the stream where the trees had grown thick. He was keeping her warm on this cool, crisp spring day by hugging her to his broad chest. "Tell me what you want," he pleaded.

"I want? What *could* I want? Security? Freedom from worry, from want. I want a man who is not going to go to the war and be killed."

"Zdenka!"

"You asked me. So that is what I want. What do *you* want?"

"You, Zdenka, all I want is you."

"Then don't go to war."

"Don't...but...how can I not? Am I to be branded as a coward and ostracized from society for ever after?"

"Then we must find some way for you to get out of it that will not brand you as a coward."

"And how will *that* be?"

"Could you have some kind of illness or disability?"

"But I am neither sick *nor* disabled."

"*Could* you be?"

"You mean, could I put my eyes out to avoid the war? No, thank you."

"Of course not. Then you could not see me. But would you sacrifice a finger—or a toe or two?"

Baron Chotznic looked down at Zdenka Oleska, nestled against his coat. Then he turned and seemed to look far upstream. Zdenka shuddered. Had she gone too far? Was chopping off a finger or shooting his toes too much to ask?

"Zdenka," he said at last. "I would gladly disfigure myself to please you. But I don't think it would serve the purpose. When Mother Russia needs men, she will take them without arms and legs."

"Who doesn't she take?" she asked.

He hoisted a shoulder. "Those with communicable diseases," he said, "like TB."

Zdenka's eyes sparkled in the shining air by the stream. She hugged him tighter. "What a wonderful idea!" she said.

Baron Chotznic found himself shocked speechless. Did she take him for a coward? How could one so young and inexperienced in the world have such a talent for conniving? He had thought he would do anything to get Zdenka for his wife, but now she was putting him sorely to the test.

One thing he was sure of, he was not going to dodge his obligation to serve his country. If the enemy were successful, there would be no telling what might happen to his privileged way of life.

But he made no comment to Zdenka's suggestion. He thought if he ignored it, she might see from his somber expression that discussion of such dishonest chicanery was far beneath him. He took her hand and led her back to the house.

Zdenka had no thought of letting the subject drop. "Do you know any doctors well?"

"One of my best friends is a doctor. Why?"

"Because you will need a doctor's validation for your tuberculosis."

"But I don't *have* TB."

"It will be easy to recite the symptoms. You will want to get a place in the best sanitarium—as soon as the war engages Mother Russia. Switzerland would probably be the safest."

"Why, you little minx. What a conniver you are!" he said. But at least, he thought, she is no longer talking of Moscow and the prince. Progress has been made.

"Yes, and I must be. If I were not, I would risk receiving my hero husband at home in a box. You must know, Alexi, I would not be strong enough for such a shock. I would be destitute and friendless in a strange land."

"Nonsense, Zdenka, you are being overly dramatic. I will not leave you destitute. You would get, in the lugubrious scene you have drawn, a handsome settlement."

"If I agree to marry you," she spoke with more conviction than she felt, "I will want to have handsome you—not a handsome settlement."

The baron understood. "Would you like to see the inside?" he asked when they returned to the two-story stone dacha.

"I would."

They went in and found Sis, Riasa, looking out of the living room window. "Such a nice view," she said. The furniture was covered with white sheets and the chandeliers were wrapped in some dusty material. The baron took Zdenka upstairs; his sister remained in the living room, staring out the window.

Upstairs in his bedroom, he tried to kiss Zdenka again. She gave him a perfunctory kiss as he was eying the bed. "Don't be ridiculous," she said. "Your sister could come in anytime."

"No, she won't," he said. "Please!"

"Alexi!" she said. "You must not take advantage. You want to announce the marriage Saturday, at the ball, I will love you with all my heart. You only have to get the certificate from the doctor first. Then we shall make inquiries into Swiss sanitariums and a place for me nearby. I am sure it would also be best to move your money there. They are a neutral country, and I could not have as much confidence in France."

Some peasant, the baron muttered to himself.

It was an agonizing decision for the baron. He had very little illusion that his father could condone any evasion of what he saw as his son's sacred duty, not only to Mother Russia, but to his class as well.

All well and good, Baron Alexi thought, but it doesn't take into account the one incontrovertible fact, that I must have the girl, for she is the most beautiful girl in all the world, and her personality, that engaging balance between earthiness of the peasant and the sophistication of an aristocrat, is simply irresistible. If feigning tuberculosis is her price, how can I afford to do less? And yet…I only wish it weren't so cowardly.

Then, too, there is the persuasive appeal of being with her in Switzerland instead of dodging bullets in the front line: the mud, the cold, the rain, soaked to the bone, thinking about Zdenka every minute…

And by the day of Zdenka's final portrait sitting, Baron Alexi Chotznic was able to show her the certificate from his doctor attesting to Alexi's ineligibility for military service due to an acute case of tuberculosis.

Zdenka was excited, perhaps more at her victory than the

prize itself.

Alexi rationalized that just because he had the certificate didn't mean he had to use it.

Russia had entered the war—and everyone was making the most of this last party.

The count and countess outdid themselves with their final Saturday ball. "Well, for the duration at least," the countess said, then added the dreaded qualifier: "if we win." Zdenka wore a new dress, provided by the baron's seamstress, with the ten miles of pearls the baron had given her. And she felt underdressed.

A diamond tiara on loan from the baron's mother sat atop a head that looked like whipped threads.

The grand ballroom was lined with long tables on all four sides, leaving ample dancing area in between. Behind the head table was a thirty-five-piece string orchestra which played constantly, waltzes, mazurkas, polkas, minuets and two-steps. But the conversation was so animated and jolly that it was difficult to hear much of the music. There were over a thousand people in attendance.

The count joked that they were using up all their larder and wine cellar before Mother Russia confiscated the food to fortify the troops and the wine to make them forget why they were being fortified. Then he raised his glass to toast, "To the brave young men who are going to risk their lives for the salvation of Mother Russia, not the least of which is my son, Baron Alexi."

203

The baron's face reddened and he dropped his eyes after meeting his father's penetrating stare. Zdenka was working a penetrating stare of her own on Alexi. He glanced only furtively at her. The cheers for Alexi's impending service to his country were a welcome diversion.

The count concluded his toast with, "My only regret is that I have but one son to give the cause."

A cheer of greater magnitude filled the ballroom and the orchestra broke into the national anthem. People were raising their glasses to Alexi, whose eyes were downcast. Uncle Vanya and Aunt Helene were among the celebrants Zdenka saw when her eyes swept the room. They were seated at a far table, while Zdenka sat with the baron at the head table. Zdenka had not raised her glass to join the toast. Was it not implicit that when you gave a son to a cause, you did not expect him to be returned? she wondered.

When the patriotic pandemonium died down, and the sumptuous feast (Zdenka counted eleven courses, each with a different wine) ended, Zdenka led the baron to the dance floor. They clung to each other as though it were their last chance before the baron was spirited off to war.

She squeezed his hand, and whispered in his ear—"You must be strong, my baron."

"No," he contradicted her. "You do not want me to be strong. If I were, I would unstintingly and unhesitatingly do my duty for my country."

"Don't be silly," she purred into his ear, sending shivers down his faltering backbone, "you will do your duty to me. It is duty enough."

He whispered in her ear. "I am *so* embarrassed. Everyone is expecting me to be a war hero."

"You'll get over it when we're alone. Perhaps you should counter that mistake with an announcement of your own."

He tightened his lips and shook his head. "That would not go down well when they found out I was eloping with you and avoiding my duty."

"Duty? I am getting fatigued with all this silly talk of duty. It is no one's duty to get killed." She cocked an eye at him. "You aren't getting weak in the knees, are you? You aren't going back on our plan?"

"Let's go upstairs for a minute," he said, "and…"

"To do what?"

"Talk it over."

"We can't talk here—the parlor perhaps?"

"No, no. Privacy. We need privacy!"

She went with him up the grand staircase, down the hall, into the large bedchamber at the end.

When they were inside the ornate room with the large puffed-up bed, Alexi closed the door and threw the bolt home.

"Privacy," he explained, taking Zdenka in his arms. She squirmed loose. "Zdenka!" he exclaimed. "Come here."

"Now, Alexi, we have an understanding, do we not?"

"Yes, yes, but is it cold water that runs in your pretty veins?"

"You are the one with the cold water in your feet."

"Zdenka," he pleaded. "You heard my father, you saw how excited the guests were when he toasted his son going to war. I can't let them down."

"But you can let *me* down?"

"Zdenka—be understanding."

"I *am* understanding. That is the whole trouble, I understand you *too* well. War heroes are stupid. If you want to risk your life for some misplaced glory, it must be your decision, not mine. I will not marry anyone so foolish. We have an agreement. I will keep my end of the bargain—the rest is up to you. Thursday night was our plan. By then you will have had time to submit your doctor's excuse and withdraw the funds. I shall be waiting as agreed. If you do not come, I will understand you have decided on the life of a bachelor hero, however short-lived that might be."

"Zdenka," he pleaded and turned to kiss her lips and she let him. In a few seconds she turned away. "There is plenty of time for that," she said. "We will be lovers like none others in the history of the world." Her eyes held his: tenaciously, lovingly. "First, we must talk…"

The baron smiled at his beauty. "So, what do you want to talk about?"

"What kind of allowance had you planned to give me?" she asked directly.

"Allowance?" The baron was startled. "You shall, of course, have anything you want."

"That's all well and good, but how would I get it? Come running to you every time I needed a voice lesson?"

"It is usual for wives to have their own funds." He frowned. "The husband provides."

"What if he stops providing?"

"Zdenka—why are you so suspicious?"

"I just want to settle a few things. Like my singing lessons. I must have my singing lessons."

"Fine."

"And someday I want to sing in the opera. You wouldn't think that was not acceptable behavior for a baroness?"

He smiled.

"Are you laughing at me?"

"I was just thinking," he said. "All the trouble you have had with your singing teacher. Well, when you are a baroness, you tell the teacher what you want and it is done. If you want to sing opera from beginning to end of your lesson, you do it."

Zdenka looked at Alexi. That she had not considered. She would sing opera and only opera and before you knew it, she would be on the stage. A diva. A command performance for the prince and the entire royal family. They would be carried away with her astonishing artistry and he would come backstage to tell her he couldn't live a moment longer without her.

"Then you must agree to check into that Swiss sanitarium until the war is over."

The baron stared at her. "Look, Zdenka," he made one more attempt, "we can have a very nice life. The wife of an officer of the Russian Army has not only comfort, but respect and prestige."

"I will not be a widow before I am twenty."

"But you would be a *rich* widow. And a *baroness*."

"Oh, my baron," she said, taking hold of his arm and putting her face to it. "I am such a muddlehead. My brain is so soft as my heart. Here I am, carrying on like a businessman when we are talking of love and a lifelong marriage of two people. Will you ever forgive me for being so bold and so stupid?"

"You are not stupid," he said.

"But I am acting stupid," she insisted. "It is all from ignorance, Alexi, pure ignorance. I do not know about these things. Perhaps I am too young to marry a strong and handsome man such as yourself." With that, she turned to face him, then presented her lips for a kiss. The baron took her in his arms and they kissed longingly. The baron's hands began to roam; she let them. In his ecstasy, he eased her over on the overstuffed bed. His hands began making excited movements and soon hers were helping. He was on top of her, then she was on top.

With his heart rate sky-high, the climax of his euphoria settled over the baron like a blanket of eternal contentment.

"I'm convinced," he said.

"Of what?" she breathed heavily.

"You are the most wonderful woman in the world."

She raised her upper body and supported it on her elbow. "How wonderful?" she asked him.

"Argh, grrr, bwuh." He brought her to him, pressing her pretty head to his dark hairy chest. "Most wonderful," he repeated. "For you, I would do anything."

"Anything?" she said. "You mean *any*thing?"

"Argh, ahhh, mmm." He nuzzled her ear—she turned to look at him through neutral space—"Well?" she demanded.

"*Any*thing," he said, reaching out. And she came to him with the enthusiasm of conquest.

Oh, how easy it was, Zdenka thought, like taking candy from a baby. Then giggled to herself—but first you must give him candy.

Zdenka finally roused herself and replaced her clothing. "Thursday," she said. "I'll be waiting," and she left the room and went directly back to the ball, where she told her aunt and uncle she had a splitting headache and wanted to go home.

Zdenka was as nervous as a hen and affright with worry that her carefully crafted plan would fall on the weakness of her intended. She had thought the mechanical process of packing would take her mind off the uncertainty that was building pressure in her brain. But it was not to be. Evasion of service was not a weakness, she assured herself. Conformity was the weakness.

But what would become of her if the baron stupidly decided to join the Russian Army? She thought if all the carefully laid plans she had made came to naught, she just could not go on. Now that she had seen the world from an aristocrat's eyes, Zdenka would never be able to scrub floors again. But what would she do? Her options were thin. He *had to come.*

There had been so many plans to make. So many considerations. So many…conditions. It was a delicate negotiation and Zdenka had planned and executed her strategy with consummate care. There was no use plunging headlong into an unknown abyss. If she were to gain any advantage, it would certainly be *before* the wedding, not after.

She had tried to think of everything. "It's so unfair," she cried to herself. "I have so little experience. If only I'd been married before, I'd know what to expect."

As Zdenka packed the meager belongings she brought from Poland, she was suddenly embarrassed by the poor condition of her suitcase. She should have told the baron to bring her a new one. One befitting a baroness. Her whole life depended on this one move—and that was in the hands of a man she felt now was a weakling who gave in to her too easily. A man who could even consider the glories of war over her love.

Love? Did she love him? She had tried to care about him. It wasn't like the feeling she got when she thought about the prince. Thinking about the prince made her all tingly and it seemed the blood ran faster through her body. Her thoughts about the baron centered on personal survival. She realized she could do a lot worse, and she realized why he seemed to like her. It was the animal nature of men. There were her looks, which she thought left something to be desired—but so many people had told her she was pretty, she was starting to believe it. "Pretty is as pretty does," her mother used to say, and apparently Zdenka had *done* prettily for the baron. She was sorry she didn't have the opportunity to do prettily for a prince, but becoming a baroness would be giant steps up from her present station. Being a baroness would make her more eligible for the prince. Perhaps the war, or even a revolution, would change things with the prince. Class lines would be unimportant.

Her old bag was packed. Then she turned to packing her new acquisitions. Zdenka was surprised at how much more she would take away from Uncle Vanya's than she brought. The baron had given her so many dresses and jewelry. The peasant clothes would stay behind. She didn't have room for all the new clothes in the one suitcase, and had to carry a paper sack with the overflow. Her portrait was rolled into a cylinder, also in a sack. That embarrassed her—to think a baroness should go to her wedding with her belongings in a paper sack, like a peasant. Well, it would be peasant no more if the baron kept his promise.

Every few minutes she looked out her side window. At a sharp angle, she could see the small portion of the street where the baron would park. With each passing minute, she came that much closer to convincing herself the baron wasn't coming. Then, after her twentieth look, she heard a rustling below. It was after midnight, and Zdenka sprang to the window to see a coach parked across the street and one house down. In a moment, the coach door opened and the baron stepped down and came toward her window. In great excitement, Zdenka tied a rope to her suitcase and opened the window, then lowered the luggage to the driveway below, where Baron Alexi Chotznic retrieved it.

At the last moment, Zdenka felt she must leave a note for her aunt and uncle—and even for Carolina. Quickly she found paper she used to write to Katrina. On it she scrawled:

Dear Aunt and Uncle—and Carolina too,

The baron is taking me away
to marry me.
I shall be a baroness!

Love,
Zdenka

She laid it on her pillow, and looked around the room to see if she'd forgotten anything. Satisfied she hadn't, she took off her shoes and held them in one hand and the paper bags with her surplus goods in the other, and she tiptoed down the stairs and out the front door.

The baron had called for her in the everyday coach, not the grand ceremonial coach Zdenka had set her heart on for the elopement. There was only one driver and no footman. They were traveling as poor people, Zdenka thought.

It had been decided between them that the train in Russia would be too risky. Discovery and conscription, in spite of the doctor's certification that the baron had TB, was, they thought, a real danger. A few automobiles were available, but they were so unreliable and Alexi didn't want to risk a potentially disastrous breakdown and exposure.

As the coach moved out of town, the roads were rough and the ride bumpy. "Alexi, my love, I am so excited. Are you?"

"Yes—oh yes," he said, reaching out for her. He put his arm around her shoulder and drew her to him. She nestled into the crook of his arm and shoulder.

"But, Alexi, lover, if you are as excited as I, why are we traveling in this coach?"

"*This* coach? Why? Is there something wrong with it?"

"I should have thought for such a *special* occasion we could have had the ceremonial coach, with the gold and the tassels and the burlwood decor—not to mention the luxurious insides, with the velvet and soft headrests."

"Yes, Denka, if we were having a proper wedding at the palace we would surely have the fancy coach and four horses, two drivers, two footmen. The czar's hussars would be plodding ahead of us, behind us the royal band. But, Denka dear, how could I abscond with the special coach if I am enraging my mother by eloping? Not to mention Father, who is being robbed of familial military glory." Baron Alexi shook his head. "Mother *lives* for these ceremonial events—to rob her of the happiness she so looked forward to for so many years—I speak of the elegant wedding she had planned in her mind over and over for years—" He shook his head. "No, it would be insult on top of injury to her if I stole away with the fancy coach. Mother is going to be mad enough when she wakes up." He rolled his eyes. "To say nothing of the target that gold leaf would present for the revolutionaries. No, I'm afraid we must lay low—until we are out of the country, at least."

"But," she said, timidly, for he had made her feel ashamed, "we are to have a long journey…"

"Yes, *very* long."

"And I was only thinking of your comfort."

"Mine?" He seemed surprised. "Well, that is indeed thoughtful of you. It is I who should be solicitous of your comfort. This coach is perfectly fine for me. When we reach Warsaw, we will board the train for the rest of the journey."

Alexi turned to kiss her; she turned her head slightly away. The kiss landed on the corner of her mouth.

Before the baron went too far, Zdenka inhaled and asked him, "Is everything going as planned?"

"Yes," he said, even more breathless. "By morning we will arrive at the judge's country house, where he will meet us."

"And marry us?"

"Of course," he said, trying again to kiss her straight on. She yielded long enough to get him excited, then intercepted his pair of agitated hands.

"Oh, Alexi, the excitement has made me so tired, I cannot keep my eyes open. Besides, I wish to have a real wedding night, and not before the wedding."

"My Zdenka, you are so charmingly old fashioned." He tweaked her nose. "But is your memory so short? The 'wedding night,' as you put it, has already taken place, has it not? More than once."

She turned up her nose. "Those were indiscretions. Now we are so close, I must have a night like any bride should expect. So now, just hold me, please—I am so sleepy."

Alexi pressed his arm around her and plotted subtle strategies to weaken her resolve. First with his hand.

"No, Alexi," she protested, pushing the invader to defend her privacy. "We must have our little celebration in a nice bed that we share. In this coach it is impossible."

"Not impossible!" he insisted. "A great adventure."

Her tired mind jostled with that, but she came short of a convincing riposte, so she went limp and began pretending the breath of sleep. When he addressed her again, she didn't answer.

He stroked her hair tenderly and anticipated the happy times ahead.

Shortly after the sun came up, they arrived at the judge's house, a lone stone building that looked more like a mill than a house. It was sorely in need of repair, and Zdenka wondered how anyone could live there.

"Oh, he doesn't live here," the baron said. "He's just meeting us here as a favor." But a search of the premises failed to yield any sign of the judge. The baron frowned. "Not here yet," he said. "I expect he'll be along soon. It is early yet."

Almost three hours later, after an idyllic walk in the woods, they returned to the house, where the driver told them there was still no sign of the judge.

"How long will we wait?" Zdenka asked.

"He'll be here," the baron said. "He may have had some trouble along the way."

Shortly before noon, Zdenka began mentioning practical considerations, like food. She was getting hungry. "Perhaps we can find another judge or a priest if we go on."

"He'll be here, I promise you."

"How long to the next town?"

"Not three hours."

"Then I say we go if he isn't here in an hour."

The baron didn't comment, and in another forty minutes a man came riding up the lane on horseback. The man was so old and disheveled, the horse so disreputable that Zdenka's heart sank. This man was no judge.

But the baron quickly hailed him. "Judge," he said. "Good of you to come."

The judge indicated no disagreement and dismounted his nag and almost fell to the ground in the process.

"Shall we begin?" the baron asked.

The judge squinted at the baron as though he did not recognize him. Then he looked at Zdenka, his eyes still half shut. He wore a long, thick, moth-eaten overcoat that seemed to have become black over the years.

"Yes," Zdenka said. "Let us get started."

The judge cleared his throat. Unsuccessfully, for he cleared it again. And again. He looked at the baron inquiringly. The baron nodded, then reached into his coat pocket and produced an envelope. The judge opened it with some difficulty and peered at its contents for a long time, as though he were carefully counting the bills by looking at the edges. Then he finally put it in his coat pocket and took out a tattered book from the other pocket.

He cleared his throat again. Zdenka looked at the baron. "Can we go inside?" she asked. The baron looked at the judge. The judge shrugged. "It's colder in there," he said in his high-pitched, scratchy voice. "I won't take long." He coughed again, then took a handkerchief out of his pants pocket and spit into it. He folded the cloth handkerchief carefully over his sputum and caressed it slowly between his thumb and forefinger. Then he put it away in his pants pocket and opened the book.

He began reading so rapidly in the Russian dialect that Zdenka understood very little of what he was saying. She was almost overcome with the alcoholic vapors that emanated from his mouth. She had struggled with the Russian language ever since she set foot on Russian soil, and here she was, being married without understanding what was being said.

The couple suddenly realized they were not even standing side by side. Hastily they stood beside each other and the baron took Zdenka's hand in his. When the judge stopped reading, the baron turned toward Zdenka and kissed her. Releasing her, he said, "My baroness." Zdenka loved the sound of it. The first thing she whispered to her husband was, "Is this legal?"

"Yes, yes, do not worry, my baroness," the baron said, turning to the judge, who was coughing. "You will see to the necessary filings?"

The judge nodded and coughed again, this time without ceasing.

The newlyweds scrambled back into the coach. Settled inside, the baron embraced his bride and smothered her with kisses. "I'm so happy," he said.

She looked into his eyes and smiled. "Are you sure that was legal?" she said.

"Guaranteed," he said.

Zdenka was skeptical. "You are trusting that old drunk to get the papers to the proper authorities?"

"He's an old friend of the family."

"With the emphasis on *old*. I'd be surprised if he could even *find* the city hall." Zdenka stopped kissing her bridegroom. "I'm hungry," she said.

"At the next opportunity," the baron said, "we will eat."

That opportunity came in two and a half hours, when they tumbled out, dusty and exhausted, at a small way station outside

Kingisepp, where they partook of a heavy meal provided by the wife of the master. They were given an old wooden bed when the wife heard they were newlyweds on their way to Switzerland.

Though the baron had other ideas once the door to the room was closed, Zdenka fell immediately to sleep. The coach driver slept in the barn, with the horses.

Before the sun was up, the groom was up in anticipation of claiming his conjugal rights. Zdenka was asleep and he restrained himself from waking her. But he was too excited to sleep.

Suddenly, Zdenka jumped from the bed as though she were about to embark on a marathon sleepwalk. She rummaged in her suitcase, then threw on her wrap and went out the door to the privy in back.

Baron Alexi was aglow when she returned. "Ah, my beautiful bride," he said, putting his arms out to her. "At last we can consummate our marriage. Come here."

Zdenka frowned. "Oh, Alexi, I have bad news. My monthlies are upon me."

"What?"

"I'm so sorry, I didn't keep track."

"Oh no," he groaned. "Well, I don't care. I must have you, no matter what."

"Oh, Alexi, I can't. It is especially heavy. We would leave blood all over. How could we do that to these nice people?"

"Nonsense," Alexi said. "It will wash off. Come here."

"No, Alexi, afterwards—after it is over, then we can have our wedding night."

"How long?"

"I don't…perhaps a week."

"A week!"

"Yes, it is very heavy."

"Come, then, we will compromise. Come, let me hold you."

"But I have awakened the driver. We must not lose time. We can hug in the coach on our way."

"Oh, Zdenka, what is your hurry?"

"I don't want us stopped in Russia by the wrong sort of person. You could be conscripted for the Army. We could be robbed. It is best to move out early. The sooner we start, the sooner we are safe."

"You worry too much," the baron said.

But by sunup, they were on their way.

Days later, Zdenka gave Alexi a breathy kiss when they finally left Russia. "I am so relieved we are out of Russia," she said.

The baron was glum. "I am not so sure," he said. "In Russia, I was a baron. In Switzerland, I will be a nobody with TB, locked up in a sanitarium."

"Nonsense," she said. "You don't have TB."

"I have a certificate that swears I do."

"Cheer up, my husband," she said. "We are together, married at last. We have a wonderful future ahead of us."

The baron nodded, solemnly.

The honeymoon couple boarded a train in Warsaw. The driver and coach returned to St. Petersburg with only the news that Baron Alexi and Zdenka Oleska were married and boarded a train in Warsaw.

Each mode of travel had its characteristic smells and bounces. Their nostrils adjusted from the dust of the ground and the manure and urine of horses to coal dust and the manure and urine of humans. The clanking of metal wheels on rails made the train noisier than the wooden wheels on the dirt of the earth, but the ride was somewhat smoother in the exchange of rails for rutted roads.

They rode the train through Southern Poland, Slovakia, and Austria—Vienna, Salzburg and Innsbruck.

The closer to Switzerland they came, the more morose the baron became. When they were a day's journey from their destination, a remote village in the Engadine named Ftan, Baron Alexi said, "My dear, why don't we go to St. Moritz for a few days before we check in. It is almost on the way."

"No," she said. "I would be too nervous. Let us check you in first, then we will go touring."

"Why the rush?"

"What if they have no place for you when we get there? Then we must find another. We must make sure you don't get drawn into the war because we were too casual."

The baron was beginning to chafe under what he felt were untoward restraints of his young wife, a woman of limited education and no discernible background. He would have to take matters in his own hands.

When the newlyweds arrived in Ftan, it was early evening. The sun was just about to disappear over the breathtaking mountains. Emerald grasses gleamed in the setting sun. The sanitarium stood on the top of the mountain overlooking the picture-book, tiny town below. It was a full-blown, if overgrown, Swiss chalet, yellowish tan in color and grand in stature. The pitch of the roof was steep to hasten the heavy winter snowfalls to the ground. The long climb in a private coach from the valley below had virtually exhausted the horses. Their rapid breath snorted semaphore messages in liquid vapors. Inside, the sterilized corridors did not seem real to Zdenka. It was as if they were in an unoccupied mausoleum. There they waited at the front desk for the admissions clerk.

When the overfed man in his thirties arrived, in a white uniform, with a nametag labeling him "Hans," the baron could tell they were in for trouble. To Zdenka he was just an unfortunate man who had never learned to smile, perhaps because he never experienced anything to smile about.

Zdenka flashed her broadest smile at him. "Hello, Hans," she said in her halting high-school German. "We are here to check in. Baron Chotznic is the name."

The smile did nothing for Hans. "Sit down here," he said. He produced some papers for the baron to fill in and sign. The baron scowled at all the things they wanted to know. He was unused to doing this kind of clerical work, as well as to having perfect strangers invade his privacy, but he did his cursory best at the task and handed the forms back to Hans, who read quickly over them, as though he were looking for some mistake which he could lord over the baron. When that venture proved disappointing, Hans stood and said, "Follow me, I will show you to your room." The baron and baroness followed Hans down the hall a long way—around several corners— until they came to a cell-sized room with a narrow metal bed, a chair, table and nightstand.

"No place like home," Hans said, with a grim grin.

The baron's jaw dropped. "But...I am a baron," he muttered involuntarily.

Hans shook his head severely. "Here that makes no difference."

217

The baron stared at the bed as though he were realizing his worst nightmare. Zdenka broke the spell. "Hans, where would you recommend we go for a nice dinner? We have traveled long and the journey has been arduous."

Hans looked at her as though she had asked the impossible. "I am afraid Alexi will be going nowhere. He is an inmate of this sanitarium and as such he is not to leave the premises without the doctor's permission."

"What? Well, then let us see the doctor," Zdenka said.

Hans tightened his lips and shook his head. "He will not be back until the morning. In any case, no passes are granted for at least a month—until we are able to evaluate your condition thoroughly. Tuberculosis is a communicable disease. That is why we must be so cautious."

"But—I may stay with him then?" Zdenka said, eying the narrow bed.

"Visitation is by the doctor's permission only," Hans said. Zdenka thought he seemed to enjoy disseminating bad news. Could he be especially pleased to be dashing the hopes of aristocrats? She was already considering herself an aristocrat. "After he evaluates your condition tomorrow, we will be in a better position to speculate on visitations."

Zdenka could see her bridegroom was seething, but she denied herself the luxury of feeling sorry for him. Instead, she thought of all the things she had to do.

Back at the front desk, Hans gave her some suggestions for local overnight lodging. The baron didn't like the way Hans looked at his wife. Zdenka and Alexi kissed goodbye under Hans's disapproving gaze.

"Tuberculosis is contagious," he said.

Alexi was about to protest, "I am a baron," again, but the words stuck in his throat.

That first night, Zdenka found a room in the Scuol Inn, at the foot of the hill where Alexi remained in the sanitarium. She took a simple supper in her quaintly rustic room.

In the morning, she was at the bank when it opened.

"I am Baroness Zdenka Chotznic," she said, and the banker bowed low with great respect. Zdenka liked the feeling very much. "I have come to open two bank accounts."

"Two?" He may have been the manager of a small-town bank, but his class consciousness was big city.

"Yes. Your bank is safe?"

"Perfectly, Madame," he said. She liked the way that sounded. Madame. The respect it embodied had a delightful ring to it.

"Please sit here, Baroness. I shall assist you." They sat across a desk that had been fashioned in the seventeenth century, when the bank opened. Heinrich Zvol, the banker, though gray-haired, was still a man with an eye for beauty, and his eye was captivated throughout his meeting with the baroness. "Now, Madame, how much did you wish to deposit initially, and in what name?"

"First, I want an account for myself and my husband. The names Baron and Baroness Alexi Chotznic." When she told him the amount, his eyebrows registered his respect. It was more than he would earn in his lifetime. "And an equal amount in my name alone."

Now the banker's eyebrows twisted doubtfully.

"My husband wishes it that way," she hastened to assure him. "He is up the hill in the sanitarium, and I must be assured of access to his funds."

The banker nodded. "If you like, we can get the account so only one signature is necessary to withdraw funds."

"That would be helpful," she said. "I don't know what kind of access the sanitarium authorities will allow me."

"Very good, Madame. Do you still want one account in your name only?"

"Yes, please."

When she handed over the Russian bank drafts, the banker was lavish with his gratitude. What he did not tell Zdenka was she had just become the bank's largest depositor. The next morning, she would take the train to St. Moritz and repeat the procedure in the largest bank there.

"You must excuse my clothes," she said. "We have just come from an arduous trip from Russia and the war has made it advisable for us to disguise. Could you recommend a good seamstress?"

"Oh, Baroness, this is a small village. There are women who sew, of course, but you would be better served in St. Moritz. It is perhaps an hour by train. Ask at the Grand Hotel, I am sure they will be able to please you there."

When she completed her business in Scuol, she returned to Ftan to visit her husband. She found him in his room looking pale and shaken. He jumped up from his bed—where he had been lying, staring at the ceiling—and embraced her. "Oh, Zdenka," he said, trembling, "I missed you so—what took you so long?"

"I put money in the bank. I am not comfortable carrying so much around."

"Good, good."

"And I will put the rest in St. Moritz tomorrow."

"Tomorrow? Oh, don't leave me."

"But I cannot stay with you all the time. There will surely be routines for a cure."

"I don't want to be alone, Zdenka."

She looked into his sunken eyes and wondered at his fear. Why should an aristocrat cower like a frightened peasant?

"You will soon settle into the routine here," she said.

He stared straight ahead like a frightened child. "I am not accustomed to this. They speak to me as though I were a peasant. Every time I ask anyone to call me Baron, they snicker and say, 'There are no barons in here,' or 'We are all barons here.'" He shook his head. "It is so *demeaning!*"

"Have you met the doctor yet?"

"No—only disrespectful orderlies."

"I will see to it. They must treat you with proper respect or you will go somewhere else."

"Oh, Zdenka, I want to go home."

"And get killed in a foolish war? The Krauts want more land, so what? Is that worth dying for?"

"But I have been lying here thinking how I am dishonoring my family and my country."

"Nonsense. You have TB. You must be cured. Then we can talk heroics."

"I *don't* have TB," he said.

"Sh!" she said. "As far as they are concerned, you *have* it. Don't spoil it. Now I must go and find a place to live so I might be near you. Last night I was in this small inn, it was most uncomfortable. The mattress was not fit for a peasant, let alone a baroness."

"I am sorry, my Zdenka." He held on to her with desperation. "But don't leave me, please."

"You *are* a baron," she said. "Remember when I said I wouldn't know how to act as a baroness and you said it was simple, just be demanding? Well, that's good advice for you too. This place doesn't come cheap. You are entitled to respect here."

Weak as he seemed, the baron almost crushed Zdenka in his arms. "Let's close the door," he whispered, "and lie down."

"We can't do that."

"Why not?"

"Someone will surely come in. That Hans person would just love to catch you at something like that."

"What? Are we to have no love while I am in this jail?"

"It's not a jail," she said. "As for the other, I will see to it. I will make some arrangements that will be suitable for us."

He kissed her passionately. "*Now*," he said.

"*Soon*—I must go now. I have much to do."

"Don't leave me!" he pleaded.

"I will be back."

"Promise?"

"Well, of course, I promise. What do you think?"

"Come to me every day."

"Certainly I will. I have come a far way from home to be with you. My family I left behind—for *you!* It is *your* welfare I am obsessed with. That is why I must complete these plans," she said. "That reminds me, shouldn't you send a note back to tell *your* family where you are?"

"I don't know what I could say to them."

"Do you want me to compose the note for you?"

"That would be nice," he said.

Zdenka tore herself away from her husband amid his protestations and her promises to return on the morrow.

On her way out, she asked to see the doctor. He was not yet in, she was told by an orderly who seemed to have been cloned from Hans.

"I am Baroness Chotznic. My husband is in delicate condition. He is Baron Chotznic, are you aware?"

The orderly gave a halfhearted smile of quasi-contempt. She thought he must be one of those dreadful Bolsheviks. The whole place, she decided, was a hive of Bolsheviks.

"Please call him Baron," she said weakly. "It is important to him. Because he is sick should not be a reason to be disrespectful to him."

She left without getting a commitment from the orderly. Outside, the coach was waiting for her.

In the late morning, she found an agent who told her rental housing was scarce in the sparsely populated region, but offered to show her what he had. In less than an hour, they had exhausted the inventory and Zdenka was mighty depressed. She told the agent to keep looking; in the meantime she would check into the St. Moritz market.

That afternoon, she boarded the train for St. Moritz.

On the train, Zdenka couldn't take her eyes off the passing scenery. It was so majestic. The mountains so sharp and bold; and she had to admire the Swiss and the way they could live from day to day without entering into this silly war.

St. Moritz was bustling with important people. The kind of people she wanted to be at home with. She went directly to the Grand Hotel to inquire about a seamstress and was put in touch with a woman who worked at the hotel, Hazel Lindt by name. Zdenka liked her immediately and measurements were taken and fabrics were selected from the samples Hazel had on hand. She said it would be several weeks to complete the copious order, and Zdenka asked if she couldn't make one or two overnight. The woman said she had work ahead of her.

"What would it take to put mine ahead?"

"Oh, Madame, that would be…difficult."

223

Zdenka took the signal. She hadn't said "impossible." Maybe she would stay up all night. Zdenka liked the grand feeling the hotel gave her—so much more appropriate to a baroness than the modest lodgings in Scuol. "I would be prepared to pay you double if you could have two dresses for me tomorrow—morning."

"But I must get the fabric. It is already late. It would not be possible before five tomorrow."

Zdenka thought of the baron—he was expecting her back. The train would not get her there before nightfall—but it would be silly to return for the dresses.

"All right," she said.

Then she searched out a voice teacher. She called on Mme. Clara Bruno in one of those houses built right to the sidewalk, before sidewalks were contemplated.

Mme. Bruno was an august, ample woman, dressed in black, with a string of beads that hung to her thighs.

"Sing something for me, darling," she said when Zdenka inquired about lessons. Zdenka was embarrassed and asked if she had any opera arias.

"Certainly. Anything you want."

"You pick something," Zdenka said.

"What are you?"

"Am I? I am a baroness."

"That is indeed wonderful," Clara Bruno said. "What is your voice?"

"Soprano," she said.

"Coloratura? Lyric? Bel canto?"

"Lyric," she said, and hoped it was a good choice.

Madame Bruno opened a book of arias and put them on her grand piano, which was laden with silver-framed pictures. She sat and began to play. Zdenka cleared her throat and began to sing. The aria was not so much finished as it was abandoned, and Mme. Bruno frowned. "Are you sure singing lessons are what you want?"

Zdenka was astonished at the reaction. "Why, yes—why?"

"Well, there is certainly much work to do," the teacher said.

"I'm not afraid of work," Zdenka said.

Mme. Bruno nodded. Obviously the young beauty could pay, which was a not inconsiderable consideration. "How many lessons would you like?"

"Every day," Zdenka answered.

"Well, perhaps that is too many for now. But if you will return tomorrow morning at nine, we will see what the possibilities are."

Zdenka was excited. Her visit to St. Moritz had been successful. The next morning, Zdenka was at the bank when it opened.

As she sat facing her new banker in a reassuringly commodious bank, she began to wonder if she had done the right thing in Scuol. The baron had showed himself to be a weak character. He was unused to doing anything for himself. Why, she was even writing a note for him to his own parents. So when the banker asked Zdenka what name she wanted on the account, she said, "Mine."

Zdenka checked the train schedules. She couldn't get back

to Scuol and the sanitarium and return in time for her lesson, so she checked into the Grand Hotel for the night. She was gratified at the obeisance the staff paid her when she told them she was a baroness.

When Zdenka returned in the morning to Mme. Bruno for her lesson, she told her she wanted only to sing opera.

"But, my dear, you must build a foundation. Your voice has no resonance. If you only want to sing, you do not need a voice teacher, you can hire an accompanist to play for you."

"What is your usual fee?" Zdenka asked—and when Mme. Bruno told her, she said, "I'll double it if you let me sing arias as the basis for my lessons."

"What about warmups?" Clara Bruno was not proud that she was compromising her integrity for a few pieces of silver—but those few pieces would add up from a person who wanted daily lessons.

"I will warm up on my way here."

Carla Bruno nodded, skeptically. "As you wish. Let us begin then with some Mozart." As the lesson wore on, Mme. Bruno felt herself aging in sympathy for poor Mozart. He should be glad he's dead, she said to herself.

Zdenka picked up her two dresses promptly at five and put one of them on. On her way to the train station, Zdenka passed a house with a "TO LET" sign in the window. It was a modest, but picturesque place, only two blocks from the train station. She knocked on the door. An elderly man answered and explained he and his missis had family duties to attend to in Zurich for at least a year. It was a cozy two-bedroom, gingerbread cottage and so much nicer than anything in Scuol. So, though it was an hour train ride from her husband's sanitarium, she rented it on the spot. But by the time she had transacted all her business, she had missed the last train to Scuol. So she returned to the Grand Hotel for another night.

Back at the hotel, with the agreement signed for the house, she wrote and posted a letter to her friend Katrina in Brest Litovsk.

Dearest Katrina:

You'll never guess what happened to me!! I met and married Baron Alexi Chotznic. We are visiting in Switzerland for our extended honeymoon. I am anxious to hear all the news from home.

I have begun with a new voice teacher in St. Moritz, not far from my home. She is much better than that old prune in St. Petersburg. I am taking training daily in anticipation of a career on the opera stage.

I have to run now, I have to attend to my new husband, but I did want you to have my new address. It is 14 Alpine St., St. Moritz, Suisse.

Oh, by the way, if you happen to run into my father or brothers anywhere, tell them I am now a baroness!!!! People everywhere call me Madame!!!

All my love,
Baroness Zdenka Chotznic

She was glad to be in St. Moritz. It was alive with society. Surely Alexi would understand and approve.

Of course, she was dead wrong about that. When she finally showed up at the sanitarium, midmorning, the baron was beside himself with worry and fear. When she came into his room he was lying on his bed. He turned his head toward her and stared blankly, as though at a slightly menacing stranger. "Where have you been?" he muttered, like a frightened adolescent.

"Oh, Alexi, I am so sorry. All my business took me longer than I ever dreamed. Do you like my new dress?" She whirled around in front of his face. He didn't comment. "I got a dozen of them made," she said.

"You promised to come every day," he bleated.

"Yes, I know, and I will. But I had to find a place, and get some decent clothes, and a singing teacher. There is hardly anything in Scuol, nothing in Ftan."

"So where?"

"St. Moritz," she enthused. "Oh, Alexi, you must come. It is the most wonderful town. I just adore it."

"So, you will be in St. Moritz while I am in this prison?"

"It's only temporary, Alexi, you know that," she said. "Did you see the doctor?"

He nodded, with dull, rheumy eyes.

"What did he say?"

"I got the introductory lecture. Very impersonal."

"Did he call you Baron?"

Alexi bowed his head in the affirmative.

"Well, at least they recognize your importance."

"But he told me they *didn't* recognize my importance. Here we all were alike in that we all had TB," he lamented. "I almost told him I did not have it."

"Alexi! Don't ever even think of doing that! You will find yourself in the Russian Army before you know what hit you."

"But why? The Swiss aren't going to send me to Russia."

"They will come and get you. And even if they don't, your shame would overcome you. You would be an outcast—a deserter."

"And what am I now?"

"You are recuperating from tuberculosis."

"Fake tuberculosis. Oh, Zdenka, I am not happy in this prison. Please do something to get me out of here."

"You would not be happy in an army barracks either—trust me."

"But I am a bridegroom and I am separated from my bride. It's not fair! I want to love you forever, and I am locked up."

Now Zdenka was staring. So that was it. Carnality was being denied him and he was acting as though he were a newborn deprived of mother's milk. That had not occurred to Zdenka. She was so busy tending to her business, she had completely overlooked her bridegroom's needs. She looked back at the open door of the room. "Does it lock?" she asked.

"No, but it closes," he said, with a feeble hope.

Without taking her eyes off him, she closed the door with her hands behind her, then sank down on the narrow bed with her husband and cheered him up.

Temporarily.

227

Sometimes Zdenka felt the burden of responsibility the baron shifted to her shoulders would make her humpbacked. He quickly became obsessed with getting out of the sanitarium, or prison, as he called it, and begged her to do something about it.

It was as if she had an invalid child who relied on her strength and succor to see him through. When Zdenka thought about it, she realized it was an inevitable result of being coddled as royalty. How could she expect him to take responsibility when he'd never had to? She herself had not often been responsible for herself, but she thought she had adapted to it much better than her husband had. If you wanted to get anywhere in this life, she told herself, you had to do things yourself!

So, after a nagging, whining session with Baron Alexi in his room, where he claimed he would not move from there until she did something about getting him out, she said, "I will talk to the doctor about taking you out for a few days."

Dr. Mellenburg was a fleshy, unruffled man whose mission in life was to be on the receiving end of a paycheck. Ergo, he had a penchant for following procedures.

He didn't often get the chance to speak to beautiful teenaged baronesses—or any beautiful women, for that matter. Not in the shop, as he called it. When he asked her to sit down, he actually had a courtly smile on his face.

"Baroness," he said, "it is good to meet you at last."

Zdenka wondered if that were a slight for her not coming to see him earlier, but when she flashed her smile and crossed her legs, she could see the pompous doctor sink within himself. Crossing her legs in her new dress, Zdenka noted, was a highly effective procedure—if done correctly. It could not seem overt or calculated, but must be tossed off as though no thought had been given to this seductive act.

Unfortunately, excited as she made him, the doctor was not to be seduced. He went patiently over the rules of the institution, about the dangers of tuberculosis to the person and public if not treated.

"Is there any way you can make him feel like he is not in prison?" she asked.

"All the patients feel that way initially, especially as we get closer to winter," he said. "But he'll get used to it. Many look on our sanitarium as their home."

"Doctor," she said, recrossing her legs, "would you consent to letting the baron go home with me for a day or so, every so often? It would pick up his spirits considerably."

The doctor turned somber. "Ah, Baroness, many people do not understand or appreciate the seriousness of this disease. These institutions exist for the protection and care of the patient, as well as the public. If we felt it was perfectly safe for the patients to be in public, sanitariums would not exist." He peered at her over the top of his glasses. "I take it you have the best interests of your husband at heart?"

"Yes," she said, "and his spirits as well."

"Ah, yes, we will certainly look to that. Perhaps he needs more attention from us. I will see to it, you may be assured."

"Doctor," she said, with a smile, "what would happen if you discovered a person didn't really have TB?"

"We would release him, of course."

"How do you tell?"

"Well, there are the symptoms, of course. In your husband's case, we have the word of a widely respected physician, Dr. Scriabin, who apparently did extensive tests on the baron."

Zdenka hoped her smile was not fading. She thought better of pushing the matter further, since she feared Alexi's release would spur him to return home and enlist in the Russian Army, and she had no desire to return to Russia, where she was known as a poor housekeeper. In foreign lands, the mystique of the gentry was accepted without question.

"One more question, please, Doctor, then I will get out of your hair."

He waved his hand. "You are no bother, I assure you."

"Are there levels of TB that are not so dangerous to the public?"

"Like a little bit of TB, or a little bit of pregnancy?"

She blushed. "I was only thinking Alexi did not seem so seriously ill to me, and perhaps there would be less danger in his going out for a few days?"

Dr. Mellenburg brought up his arms in a gesture of hopelessness. "Dr. Scriabin in St. Petersburg is not a man to trifle with in his opinions. If *he* says your husband needs institutionalization, I, for one, would not argue."

Sometimes Zdenka felt inadequate. Her worldly experience had not prepared her for such eventualities. How was she to know her husband was to be treated as a prisoner? How was she to know what a threat it would be if he joined the army? Maybe he wouldn't be killed. How was she to know how pathologically unhappy he would be in the sanitarium? She herself was adjusting quite well to her new surroundings. Why couldn't he?

But the larger question was, should she confide in the doctor that his admission to the sanitarium was a setup—a fraud even? That might get Alexi released, but it might get them both, as well as Dr. Scriabin, in worse trouble.

Before leaving the sanitarium, she walked down the long, antiseptic, impersonal corridor to check on her husband. He was on his bed. "Alexi," she said, "shouldn't you snap out of this? Get to meet some other patients, and take part in the activities around here?"

"Stay with me," he pleaded.

He was so pathetic—like a big baby. "I will be back," she said, reining in her temper.

"Stay!"

"I would miss my singing lesson," she said. "I must go. I will come tomorrow."

Zdenka took a cab down the mountain and boarded the train for St. Moritz.

She was enjoying her daily singing lessons. She sang to her heart's content arias from operas of her choosing. She would often visualize the prince in the audience in rapture at her voice. Clara Bruno, for her part, made suggestions from time to time, but most of the time her mind was elsewhere. She considered Zdenka a foolish, self-indulged child, but she accepted the inflated fee for her services, five days of the week.

Zdenka thought she was making real progress. To Mme. Bruno, that notion was completely silly. So on the day that Zdenka announced at her lesson she had met a woman while lunching at the Grand Hotel who asked her to sing at some meeting of a women's group—and she had accepted, Mme. Bruno was aghast. "Did you tell her you were studying with me?"

"Certainly," she said. "She was most impressed. Perhaps that was what prompted her to invite me."

"Perhaps..." Mme. Bruno dropped her head to her hands. When she looked up, she said, "I would very much appreciate if you didn't tell anyone I was your teacher."

"But why?" Zdenka asked, startled.

"Because I am not teaching. You made it clear in the beginning you did not want my teaching, you wanted only to sing opera, and so you are doing. I am your listener, not your teacher."

"But, but you make suggestions."

"Suggestions, yes, teaching, no."

Zdenka repressed her hurt feelings. "I wonder, Mme. Bruno, could you help me with another matter?"

"And what is that?"

"A stage name."

"What?" The Mme. could not hide her incredulity.

"Yes. I do not feel comfortable using my own name or my husband's name. Aristocrats don't pursue careers."

For good reason, Mme. Bruno thought. The gall of this young girl is astonishing. Just the mere thought of her singing in public sends shivers down my spine. "Did you have a name in mind?"

"Well, I thought it should be something musical. A dance perhaps. I thought of Tanz in German or Valse in French, but I am Polish, so what do you think of Mazurka? Madame Mazurka?"

Valse Tristesse would be more appropriate, the teacher thought, but Madame Mazurka does have a suitably comic ring to it.

"If you feel you really *need* to change your name," Clara Bruno said. "It is a big step, with many ramifications—and it may not be necessary. Why not sing the engagement and see what the reaction is? Perhaps you won't have the need for such a drastic step."

"No, it is the first step in my career. I cannot go onstage as Baroness Chotznic."

"Baroness Mazurka is better?"

"No, no. No Baroness. I am thinking Hanna Mazurka. It means divine dance. What do you think?"

Mercifully, Mme. Clara Bruno did not tell her what she thought. "Fine," she said. "Now, shall we sing?"

The baroness rarely missed a day visiting her baron. He was getting out of his room more. He'd met some of his fellow patients, or inmates, as he called them, but his spirits did not seem to pick up.

On the day of her performance for the St. Moritz Women's Cultural Club, Zdenka was too nervous to make the trip into the sanitarium. She knew Alexi wouldn't like it, but he would just have to grow up and become self-sufficient. When she finally made her career in the opera, he would have to be able to amuse himself over long stretches.

Before she was to leave for her performance in the public

room in the Grand Hotel, she got a letter from Katrina. She tore it open excitedly and devoured it.

Dear Baroness:

I am impressed! Congratulations to you both. Your letter was forwarded to us here in Moscow, where we have moved for the duration of the war. Daddy is doing something secret. He is working with Prince Stephanoff, who I believe you mentioned in a letter. He is a nice person and we are about to have our third date. Do you remember how we used to talk of boys and things? Tell me, did we think it was all right to kiss on the third date?

I mentioned to him I thought he took you to the opera, and that you were my friend, but he seemed a little hazy about it. He said he took a lot of girls to the opera and he would probably recognize you if he saw you again.

But golly, you're in *Switzerland* and a baroness! I can't get over it! Am I impressed!!! I do hope the Fates will put us together again sometime. Mum and Dad are fine. I didn't get to see your father or brothers after I got your letter as we are in Moscow and they are still, I suppose, in Brest Litovsk.

Write soon—

With love,
Katrina

Zdenka took the news like a blow to the solar plexus. She had to force herself to go to her performance. When she arrived at the hotel, she was greeted by the chairwoman so effusively that she felt like a star. Suddenly the letter was behind her.

"I've taken a new name for my career," she announced.

"Oh, good," the chairwoman said. "What is it?"

"Hanna Mazurka."

"How delightful," the woman said, clapping her hands.

233

Zdenka sat patiently through the reading of the minutes of the previous meeting, and the treasurer's report, and then she was introduced as Hanna Mazurka and a lump of pride jumped in her throat.

She had dressed rather lavishly for the performance, with one of her new dresses of burgundy satin, and the long string of pearls knotted and draped over her bosom.

The club provided the pianist. There were about a dozen women in the audience, and as soon as the music started, Zdenka felt the butterflies in her stomach, dozens of them, but she toyed with the pearls and smiled so beguilingly, the women were enchanted before Hanna Mazurka opened her mouth. And by the time she did, they so wanted her to be a success that she was. None of the women knew too much about singing, so afterwards they characterized it as a "sweet" voice, which, in a way, it was.

Hanna Mazurka felt she had triumphed at what she would consider for years to come as her "professional debut." She was bursting to share it with Alexi. She realized he would pout because she hadn't gone to see him on the day of her debut, but she was not prepared for his explosive reaction.

On her way to see her husband
the next day, the new Hanna Mazurka
was stopped at the front desk by Hans, or
the other Hans-lookalike orderly. She was
having trouble telling them apart.

"The doctor would like to have a
word with you," he said.

"May I look in on my husband
first?"

"He wants a word with you *before*
you look in on your husband," he said
sternly. Hanna was put out that she was
being treated with so little respect.

She flashed her friendliest smile
at the doctor, who this time did not seem
as receptive to it.

"Please sit down, Madame."

His tone was so grim she sat and
folded her hands in her lap without crossing her legs.

"You must speak to your husband," he said directly. "He left the premises last evening and returned drunk in the early hours this morning. He is not only indulging in unacceptable behavior, he is corrupting others. He took three other patients with him. I must impress on you how seriously we view this lapse."

"I will speak to him, Doctor. I know it is hard for him at first, and I do appreciate your concern."

When she got to her husband's room, she found him asleep. She returned to the front desk and asked for some stationery and an envelope. After much commotion ("This is not a stationery store *or* a hotel," Hans emphasized), they were produced. But it had on it a letterhead with the name of the institution. Hardly suitable, Mme. Mazurka thought, to send to her friend. With a little more fuss and bother, second, plain, sheets were produced. She would purchase plain envelopes later.

Back in Alexi's room, she sat at the small table and wrote:

Dear Katrina:

What a coincidence you met the prince! I was trying myself to make arrangements for you to do so. Nothing would have given me more pleasure than to introduce you two. The prince certainly has a wonderful sense of humor when he says he doesn't remember me. I can *assure* you that is not true.

Well, I have had my singing debut, and it went quite well. You may tell the prince I intend to have a career in the opera and look forward to performing for him someday, to repay his many kindnesses to me.

And, oh, I changed my name to make it more suitable to the stage. You know how sensitive these aristocrats can be about bantering their names about the theater world, so henceforth I am to be known as Hanna Mazurka. I haven't told Alexi yet. I bet he'll be surprised!

As ever, I am eager for your news. My very best regards to your mum and dad, and to the prince!!!

All my love to *all* of you,
Hanna Mazurka!

Not long after Hanna Mazurka lay down her pen, Alexi stirred. He groaned and turned his head from side to side. Hanna didn't want to wake him, but she didn't want to have to sit there all day either. So she said, "Alexi—darling? Are you all right?"

His left eye opened halfway, then closed again.

"Are you awake?"

Both eyes opened, then closed again.

"Alexi?"

"Hm?"

"Can you hear me?"

"Umhum."

"The doctor is quite angry. He says you went out last night. Did you?" She was talking to him like a patient mother.

There was no answer.

"He said you took others and you came back drunk."

The baron opened his eyes and fixed them on his wife, who now stood over him. "Where *were* you?" he asked accusingly.

"Yesterday? Why, you know I had my singing debut."

"So, you couldn't even come to see your husband?"

"I was too nervous," she confessed.

"About seeing me?"

"Of course not. About the singing."

"Which is more important?"

"Oh, Alexi. Am I not to have a life of my own? Must I sit in the room all day with you and knit sweaters for soldiers?"

"I should *be* a soldier. Instead, thanks to you, I am a prisoner of a disease I don't have. And you don't care enough about me to visit."

"Alexi! That is *not* true."

"You are my *wife!* It is because of that you can afford to live so far away, because of that you can *take* singing lessons every day of the week. Why should I let you use my money to separate yourself from me?"

"You are being childish," she said, and then he exploded.

"Don't you tell *me* I am being childish! You are the child in this marriage. Not nineteen years old yet, and you continually treat *me* like a child. I am the husband here—you are the *wife*. All the money you are spending is *mine!* Yet you show not the smallest gratitude. You can't even be bothered to come and see me every day." Alexi seemed bent on saying more, but he was seized with a sudden coughing attack. The coughs were like shots jolting his body.

The new Hanna Mazurka stepped back. She put her fist to her eyes to staunch the tears she was projecting, but not experiencing. "How can you be so cruel to me? I have always your best interests in my heart. I was going to tell you my secret, but now I think you don't want to hear it."

"What secret?"

"I'm not telling."

"Tell me!" he demanded, swallowing a cough.

"No!"

"Your secret is you are going away so I shall be alone in this prison for the rest of my life. You know what I think, Zdenka? I think you have had me locked up here on purpose so you would not have to bother with me. Look at this! They feed me, they change my bedding, do the washing. You do not have to see to anything. You were a scrubwoman, now you are a baroness. You do not have to lift a lily-white finger. In the meantime, I am locked up with sick people. Oh, why did I let this happen?"

She fixed him with a withering stare. "Because you are weak, Alexi. You have had life too easy. You never had to do anything for yourself. Me, I have always had to do *everything* for myself. Now you have a little hardship and you complain like a small child."

"Stop calling me a child! *You* are the child!"

"You just called me a scrubwoman. Now you say child. Well, make up your mind. I can't be both."

"Scrubchild," he said angrily.

"Alexi!"

"Zdenka!"

"Hanna," she corrected him.

He jerked his head. "What?" He looked around the room, startled. "Who is Hanna?"

"I am," she said defiantly. It came out as a challenge more than the pleasant surprise she had intended. "Hanna Mazurka. It's my new stage name."

"Stage name? One performance for a half-dozen old biddies and you need a stage name? Are you crazy?"

"We'll see who is crazy," she said. "When I am a famous opera singer—"

"Your name is not good enough? Now you need an alias. Like you were a criminal hiding out. You are *ashamed* to be my wife."

"That is not true—"

"A scrubwoman is ashamed to be a baroness?"

"Don't you understand, Alexi? I am proud to be a baroness, proud to be your wife. I did not think you would like me trading on your name. Singing in public is not considered suitable for the aristocracy."

"Aristocracy! Hah! You are no more an aristocrat than the man in the moon. You *married* an aristocrat, that is all. It will make our children aristocrats. You, *never!*"

"You may be an aristocrat by birth," she said, fixing him in her icy sights, "but you act like a selfish peasant. I miss one day here because I pursue a little pleasure of my own and what happens? You jeopardize not only your safety and well-being, but my future as well."

"Zdenka! Let us not fight. We are newlyweds. We should be loving from morning to night—come here, Zdenka—shut the door." He reached his arms up to her.

She looked down in disdain. "Love must be earned," she said. "It is not a birthright as your title is. So, if I am a peasant, I must act like one. It is the aristocrats who have nothing to do but go to bed all the time. Peasants must work constantly. I am working for my opera career. Hanna Mazurka will be a famous name—not because I was born an aristocrat, but because I *made* it so."

"And you are trying to make it so with my money. See how far you would have gotten on your knees as a scrubwoman."

"Stop saying that. I was a governess for my cousin. I was *never* a scrubwoman."

"Call it anything you like. It doesn't change anything. You are taking advantage of me and you have put me in a position where I can do nothing about it."

Hanna Mazurka held her tongue. She was about to say, "If you were a stronger person you could do something about it." Instead she said goodbye as befitting the new Hanna Mazurka. Besides, she certainly didn't want to catch his cold. A diva, a star of the opera stage was not one to be walked on.

In the ensuing weeks, the baron and baroness had a testy relationship. Sometimes cold, other times semi-cordial, but the early warmth had not returned. She praised him (as any conscientious mother would have) for not running away from the sanitarium again. But she did not share the narrow bed, nor make a further effort to have him visit her. She was, she said, waiting to see a general improvement in his attitude, not to mention his annoying cough.

Back in her cottage in St. Moritz, Hanna Mazurka was practicing the soprano role of Mimi from *La Bohème*:

> *I pity that unhappy girl!*
> *Ungenerous love is unhappy love!*

And as her mind translated the Italian to her native Polish, her voice trailed off and came to a thudding halt, like a derailed train.

Was she, she wondered, being ungenerous to her husband? Should she spend more time with him—give in to his insatiable lust? If only she'd had more experience. But as it was, she was living by her instincts and those were no different from anyone else's: survival and self-interest. There was an extra burden in being a teenaged baroness. People expected royal decisiveness and she was doing her best to give it to them. It would be so easy to make a fool of myself, she thought. That's why I must be extra careful.

That afternoon, while Hanna Mazurka was stewing about her lot in life, the postman brought a letter from Katrina:

Dear Hanna Mazurka, née Zdenka Oleska (it began),

I haven't yet gotten used to your new name, but I think it is very glamorous. I hope this finds you well and happy. I myself am very happy because of my big news: The prince has asked me to marry him and I could hardly wait to accept. We have not set a date yet because of the uncertain conditions here. If things get too bad (all this unrest among the people), we will be leaving Russia. Probably for Paris. Aren't you the clever one moving from Russia when you did?!?

Well, that's all for now, except to say you sure were right about the prince. I can hardly wait to be a princess!!!

All my love,
Katrina

The letter went limp in Hanna's hands. Her mood moved from brooding to injured to anger. How could Katrina?! "I had practically introduced the prince to her," Hanna said aloud. Hanna knew she had to write back, and she would try to be cheerful, but how *could* she?

Hanna thought back on how Katrina had offered her a haven from her poor, struggling family—had given her a taste of the upper class, a taste which developed into an insatiable hunger to be one of them. Hanna's ticket was supposed to be with the prince, but she compromised with a baron.

Suddenly she felt alone. Her father had betrayed her, now her best friend betrayed her with her prince, who also betrayed her. All this betrayal put a heavy weight on her spirits.

Hanna's mind buzzed with images of the past, featuring a much-embellished vision of her date with the prince. Then she thought how odd it was Katrina hadn't said anything about Hanna being in the wedding party. They *were* best friends after all, and she had *practically introduced* the couple.

She sent off her reply, asking to be kept informed and trying

241

to enthuse about Katrina's news. She ended the letter as before, "...my best to the prince," and hoped the message would be conveyed.

Hanna could not get over the prince preferring Katrina to her. Katrina was nice enough, but she wasn't pretty. She was kind of awkward at school and next to vivacious Hanna she could almost be considered a dullard. As Hanna remembered it, she was a lot more popular than Katrina. It must have all been their station from birth, a complete accident that neither had any control over.

After that dreadful news, Hanna Mazurka redoubled her efforts to shape her voice into operatic-star quality. She practiced every free moment she had and sang for Mme. Bruno with more verve and enthusiasm than ever. Hanna felt she was making great strides. But when she tried to get her teacher to validate her claim, Mme. Bruno said, "I am sorry, I do not see improvement in the vocal quality. But that is your choice. You refuse to let me teach you, you would rather have an audience than a teacher, and I have acquiesced largely in deference to the extra stipend you are paying me. But please don't ask me to deceive you about your progress. With no teaching, there can *be* no progress."

But Hanna was adamant. She knew what was better for her than an old voice teacher stuck in the hinterlands of tiny Switzerland did. You couldn't learn to sing opera without singing it, and the more you sang it, the more familiar and hence comfortable you were with the repertoire. The voice would mature with this familiarity. Her teacher, she decided, was just a stubborn provincial. So often people got into ruts and couldn't see that reality was at odds with their prejudices.

So Hanna persevered in her pursuit of learning as she saw it. She persevered in the pursuit of a validation of her preconceptions. And always in the forefront of her thoughts, spurring her on, was her vision of the prince. And always in that vision, she swept him off his feet with a mesmerizing performance of some opera—his favorite, probably *La Bohème*—the one she saw with him.

On the train returning home to St. Moritz from her latest visit to bucolic Ftan, she realized she could never again be happy in such a place where there was no opera, no glitter and no culture. She may have had her beginnings on a farm, but she had quickly grown beyond that. She was a baroness now, and how she would love to go to Paris or London or New York. Certainly she would in the course of her opera career.

When Hanna returned home, bone weary from another unhappy day of arguing with her husband, she found a blue envelope in her mail. It was another letter from her friend Katrina. As always, she could hardly contain herself until she tore it open and read its contents. And those contents rocked her off her feet. She staggered back and sank into the parlor chair to weep openly.

Dear Hanna Mazurka:

I am the happiest girl alive. My prince and I have been married in a hasty ceremony as we are moving to Paris to get away from what my dear prince says is a volatile situation in Moscow. By the time you get this, we will be on our way.

I am so sorry we did not have time to invite you to the ceremony—it was a very simple one, and I couldn't help but feel it presumptuous to expect you to travel all that way for a one-hour ceremony. In truth, I would have loved to have you stand with me as my matron of honor, but I had to make do with my new sister-in-law. She is only fifteen and it pleased her so much. But I thought of you often. Well, if circumstances ever take you to Paris, do look us up. We will be living quite a different life there, I suppose, as his royal standing will not mean so much to the French; and so it is with some trepidation that we make this move.

At any rate, we will be closer than we are now. I will send you our address as soon as we have one.

Love to you both,
Katrina

Clutching the letter, then inadvertently bunching it in her

243

hand while tears cascaded down her cheeks, Hanna Mazurka felt the stinging blow of defeat. Defeat without her having a fair opportunity to present her case through an irresistible opera performance. Without her meeting the prince as an aristocratic widow. Surely if the footing had been equal, the prince would have preferred her over that simp, Katrina.

The next morning, she went by Mme. Bruno's house to tell her she would not take her lesson that day. Then she boarded the early train from Scoul, took a cab up to the top of the mountain in Ftan, where the air was supposed to be so salubrious for victims of tuberculosis.

It was a trip she had made countless times, but today there was more resolution in her step. It was not, as it was on so many previous occasions, the step of dread, but now the step of hopeful resolve.

The baron was asleep when she arrived, but she shook him awake. "Alexi," she said. "Wake up. I have important news."

Alexi did not seem to share her enthusiasm, for he mumbled, then rolled over.

"Alexi!" she insisted. "Have you been out again? Is that why you are sleeping so late?" She turned him back over and now noticed how pale he looked. His eye sockets were dark and sunken and his breathing seemed rattling and labored. She thought he must have a wicked hangover.

After more shaking, he opened his eyes and focused with some difficulty on his wife's face. "What?"

"Alexi, wake up, I must talk to you. I have a plan for getting you out of here."

His eyes seemed to pop forward in their sockets. "Getting me out?"

"Yes, listen," she said eagerly. "I need your approval. I want to tell the doctor the truth. That you don't belong here—that we convinced the doctor to write a false report to save you from being killed in the war. Switzerland is a neutral country, I'm sure they will understand."

Alexi's mind had survived his heart and spirit. He was thinking too rationally for Hanna's taste. "But...but won't we get in trouble? Falsifying documents is a serious business."

"Yes, in Russia," she said. "But we aren't *in* Russia."

He fixed her in his gaze. "Do you have any idea of the concept of loyalty? A man does you a favor—and God knows how wrong I was about *this* favor—and then if it doesn't work out to your liking, you turn on him? I'm so sorry, I can't go along with it. I'd rather wither and die right here than betray a friend. It's a concept we call honor."

"Well, you may want to rot and die here, but I do *not!*" With that, she turned on her heels and stomped out of her husband's room.

She stormed to the front desk and demanded, "I want to see the doctor." She was a baroness, after all.

Hans looked her over and said, "What if the doctor doesn't want to see you?"

"I am sure you find that very clever. Just tell him Baroness Chotznic wishes a few minutes of his time." She gave him what she thought was a withering stare. Slowly, deliberately, with what she was sure was a deliberate slight, Hans disappeared into the doctor's office. In what she thought was a lifetime, he returned to tell her the doctor would see her now.

She went into his spartan office and sat without being bidden. She was a baroness, after all.

"Doctor," she began, adjusting her mood from frustrated anger to seductive reasoning. "My husband has been bitterly unhappy here. I have tried in every way I know to placate him, but I have continually and completely failed. So, with your permission, I would like to withdraw him from your care."

The doctor seemed surprised. "But, Baroness, your husband is a very sick man."

"Oh," she said, "no, no, he isn't sick at all. That was all a mistake." She smiled girlishly at the doctor. "We got that letter, you see, as a, well, a, that is, we were looking for a way to get him out of the country so he wouldn't have to go to war. I'm sure you as a pacifist will understand that. And sympathize with a man who is in a TB sanitarium who doesn't have TB."

Now the doctor was startled. "Doesn't have TB?"

"No, as I said," she said with engaging self-effacement, "we made that up."

"Made that up? Do you *know* what you are saying? You exposed a healthy man to a deadly disease to avoid serving in the army?"

"I'm afraid that is what we did."

"Surely you could have found a simpler, safer solution?"

"No, he insisted on his honor. Fleeing the country would not have been honorable to him. I don't mind telling you I did not agree with his assessment of the situation, but what could I do?"

"My dear madame. You are a very strong young woman. Perhaps I could say headstrong. I am certain you could have convinced him of the danger of living with tuberculosis, if he was not tubercular himself."

"Danger?" She seemed confused, as though she had never considered it. "No, I…"

"Well, I am very sorry to tell you, I do not know if your husband had TB or not when he came here, but it is my sad duty to inform you that he most certainly has it now, and a very serious case. If he survives, I am bound to tell you, it will be a miracle."

Hanna Mazurka found the train ride home conducive to clear thought. The clackety-clack of the wheels on the tracks had an energizing effect on her mental processes.

By the time the train reached St. Moritz, Hanna's mind was made up. So she stayed on the train to return to Scuol, then up the mountain again to the sanitarium and directly to her husband's room. Her mind blocked out everything except her plan.

There she looked at Alexi in a new light, that thrown on him by the doctor, who said he really had TB. She had seen him daily and so the changes had been gradual, but she looked at him now as though seeing him for the first time since they had been married, and he

looked ghastly. Pale, sallow, and given to annoying coughing that rattled his whole body, like the baron's coach going over rutted roads.

"Well, Zdenka," he said. "Two visits in one day. This is
unprecedented. To what do I owe this happy occurrence?"

"My abiding concern for your well-being."

"That's a good one," he said, and closed his eyes, as if that
would make it true.

"Tell me, Alexi, how are you feeling?"

"Feeling?" he said, surprised. "That's the first time you asked
me that question."

"Oh, yes, well, for good reason. The doctor now tells me you
are really sick. Do you feel sick?"

"I don't feel well," he said, coughing.

"But, why didn't you tell me?"

"Tell you? What's to tell you? You are only fighting with me
when you are here for a few minutes a day."

"You should have told me," she said.

"What would you have done?"

"I'd have gotten you out of here."

He gave a dry laugh, then let loose a bone-rattling cough that
slammed against her body. "Get me out? Now that I really need this
place, you want to get me out?"

"They are too restrictive here. This is no way to live," she
said, "even if you are sick."

"So where do you want to take me?"

"To Paris."

"Paris?" He looked at her as if to understand her self-interest.
"What is in Paris?"

"Another clinic. The French are not so strict as the Swiss. It
was a mistake to bring you here. I did not know how it would be."

His eye arched in suspicion. "What about the war? Is not the
war in France?"

"Not in Paris. But we must be sure of that before we move
you. I will go ahead and check, then I will return for you."

"Do not go to Paris, Zdenka. It is a long, dangerous trip. If I
am to be cured, it can happen here as well as Paris or London or
Delhi."

"I want you to have the best medical attention. I don't think you are getting that here. Why, look at you! We brought you in here well and now you are sick."

"So you will take me to Paris sick and they will reverse the process?" He spit blood into the basin on the floor beside him. He shook his head, and the coughing rattled his body again. "I am dying, Zdenka."

"Don't *say* that!"

"Why not? I should hide the truth?"

"I *know* if I can get you out of here I can cure you."

"You? How would that be, Zdenka?"

"Hanna," she corrected him. "I am going by Hanna now."

"Oh, yes, how negligent of me. Of course, it is Hanna Gavotte or something, isn't it?"

"Mazurka," she made another correction.

"As you wish. To me you will always be Zdenka as long as I live. And I should not be a burden to you much longer." Another dry chuckle escaped his emaciated body. "Isn't it ironic, Zdenka, that we came here so I wouldn't die in the war? If I had gone to the war, I would be as strong as an ox. Instead, I am a mere shadow of myself. One foot in the grave, the other on thin ice."

"We will see to that in Paris."

"What is this obsession with Paris, Zdenka? Frying pan to fire, as far as I am concerned. *You* want to go to Paris. The question is why? Are there no more dresses to buy here? Are you in want of bigger and better jewels than are available in the Swiss countryside? Why go so far? A few hours on the train, you can be in Zurich. There is plenty to buy there, I am sure."

"We should have made this move sooner," she said. "I do not wish to buy a lot of dresses and jewels as you suggest. Though I know the reputation of Paris for its haute couture and as a capital of fine things. That doesn't interest me. I have progressed beyond my voice teacher in St. Moritz. I should like to have a teacher worthy of my goals, and I am told Paris is the place. There is also fine opera in Paris; here there is none. Opera is my life's blood, as you know…"

He closed his eyes, then spoke. "The prince is in Paris!"

"Nonsense. I did have a crush on the prince, but now I am married."

"Ah, yes, but soon to be a widow. Tell me the truth—the

prince *is* in Paris?"

"Are you being fair? You knew when we married I was inter-ested in pursuing a career in opera."

"Zdenka, really! You know I would never survive the trip. Please stay with me and love me the few days that I have left. Then you can go to Paris or America or anyplace your heart desires."

"I have interests and I must pursue them," she said, bending to kiss him lightly on the forehead. "If you don't feel up to making the trip just now, perhaps you will when I return."

The baron sat up with great effort and reached his arms out to her. "Please don't go," he begged her. "If you go, I won't be alive when you come back." He paused as if gasping for his last breath. "*If you come back.*" Then he dissolved into a paroxysm of coughing that shook his tiny room.

Hanna looked at the basin of blood again, then swirled with the precision of a mechanical soldier, and left abruptly. She certainly didn't want to contract TB herself.

The new Hanna Mazurka felt an uneasy sense of liberation as she strolled down the cold corridor of the sanitarium. Her body still felt the jolts of Alexi's coughing, the bucket of blood fixed in her mind. Coming upon Hans at the desk, she indulged herself in the luxury of a smirk, pointedly directed at him. In that smirk, she wished to convey the ever-widening gap between them.

Traveling was a great adventure for Hanna Mazurka, whose background included only trips from the farm to town. Now she was able to go anywhere she chose and she intended to take full advan-tage of it. Why, she might even go to America someday, she thought.

She was not afraid to observe others and ask questions, which went over well when she employed her smile and called herself Baroness Mazurka. And so she embarked on another journey across the face of Europe, by train, coach and horseless carriages, which became more prevalent as she approached the city of Paris.

It was an arduous journey from the mountains of the Engadine in Switzerland to Paris, France. The war caused Hanna Mazurka many inconveniences and delays, but she didn't give up.

The tenor of life in Paris was subdued because of the war. Hanna went first to the Ritz Hotel, where she had been told royalty stayed. Hanna asked for a front-facing room so she might be in a position to see the prince on his arrival. None was available. She had to settle for a dark back room for three days before one opened to her liking.

Once settled, she sought advice on banking and made her deposits, again in two banks. Then she called the music academy to inquire about their best voice teacher. When the rundown on the teacher ended with, "But he's very expensive," Hanna Mazurka knew she had found her man.

Her first interview with the voice teacher was at his studio in the Paris Academy of Music, a short walk from her hotel. Baroness Hanna Mazurka took a cab, lest it should appear she was forced to walk by poverty or penury.

Professor Ballenger was a severe man in a black suit, black tie and white shirt, and Hanna considered him the quintessential undertaker: dour and solicitous, rubbing his hands in an off-putting manner, which Hanna saw as symbolic of his repressed sexual appetites. It made her uncomfortable to think she might be the object of his attentions. He asked her to sing, and she obliged. When she finished, he said, "You have a nice stage manner, flirty and seductive, yet not blatantly solicitous,"—and she was embarrassed. The blood flushed to her face, but she quickly forgot her embarrassment when he said, "But your voice needs a tremendous amount of work."

She turned defensive. "Well, it's no wonder," she said. "I have not had very good teachers."

"Oh?"

"Yes. I'm afraid my first teacher had amorous designs on me and he helped me very little as a result. It seemed I was always dodging some advance. My second teacher was the laziest thing I ever saw—why, all she did was listen to me sing opera arias. She never did teach me anything."

"I can see that," Professor Ballenger said. "Well, if you want me to teach you, we are going to have to start at the beginning—and you are going to have to work hard."

"Oh, I'm a hard worker. I'll practice all day long."

The professor did not understand his student. She had a lot of drive and desire, but scant talent. Why she wanted so badly to do something so foreign to her capabilities was not clear to him. The dark war clouds were not raining vocal students. Had his studio been

251

anywhere near capacity, he would not have touched this Hanna Mazurka.

She spent the greater portion of her days singing in her hotel room, looking out the window to check the arrivals for the prince and Katrina.

While she focused on the street below, she thought of ways to attract the prince's attention without being obvious. She rehearsed in her mind, then aloud in her room their first meeting, where she could chide him, "You naughty boy, saying you forgot one of the most glorious nights of our *life!*"

Perhaps she could make Katrina jealous, drive the wedge of suspicion into their relationship. Perhaps the prince would fall in love with her simply at this reminder. She wouldn't recall the letter she sent unless he mentioned it. Then she would titter and say, "Such a bit of childish foolishness. I hope you can find it in your heart to forgive my immature enthusiasm. But I *know* we felt simpatico." If only she could get him to admit it.

If that became too depressing, she went shopping and bought some "darling dresses." And dazzling jewelry. She didn't want to appear before the prince as a peasant. She was pleased with herself and the way she had commandeered the money and put it to good use. She fully intended to make inquiries into a better TB sanitarium for the poor baron, now that she was settled.

Finally, she forced herself to sit down and write her husband a note.

Dearest Alexi,

I do hope this finds you well and in good spirits. I am staying at the Ritz Hotel in Paris and may be reached here should you need anything.

Due to this inconvenient war, the scouting of a more commodious sanitarium for you is proceeding at a slower pace than I might wish, but rest assured you and your welfare are uppermost in my thoughts.

You may have the sanitarium send their charges for your care to me here and I shall pay them with dispatch. And if you need anything, just write me here and it will be taken care of.

> With my love and deep affection,
> Hanna Mazurka

She felt good being the one to offer the largesse, as though the money was hers. And she was developing a fondness for ornate closings to her letters. It gave her a feeling of flamboyance, and anytime she could be dramatic, she felt good.

In the Ftan, Switzerland, sanitarium, Baron Alexi Chotznic waited in increasing despair for Hanna to return to him and tell him she had reconsidered her foolish notion to go to Paris at such a critical time for her husband. With each passing day, the baron's strength deteriorated in concert with his hopes for his young wife's return. He waited a full six months before he called in a solicitor and made a will leaving his entire estate to his siblings. But the cash portion of his estate had mysteriously disappeared into the anonymity of the Swiss banking system, and Hanna Mazurka had no interest in horses and her husband's clothing and furnishings.

When the prince had not appeared at Hanna's Paris hotel after she had been at the front window a fortnight, Hanna began to make inquiries at the other luxury hotels in town, but all to no avail. She began to worry that he had been taken prisoner en route.

As bleak months passed, Hanna threw herself into her vocal studies. Though her spirits seemed on hold, she was optimistic that good times were just ahead.   253

Then one night at dinner in the opulent dining room of the hotel with the exotic potted palms all around and the warm feeling of luxury, Hanna was deep in thought over what might have become of the prince. Hanna dropped her eyelids modestly as she picked the embossed card off the tray and read, in French:

> Please pardon the intrusion, but you
> are a very beautiful young lady and I
> am an American alone in Paris. I
> should be honored if you would grant
> me a few moments of your time.
>
> Your servant,
> Royce Saxon

Hanna looked up at the waiter. "Where is this man?" she asked.

"By the door, Madame."

She looked over and saw a rather good-looking man who wore an expensive dark-gray suit with a red paisley tie. He looked more an English gentleman than an American. She guessed he was in his thirties.

"Do you know him?" she asked the waiter.

"No, Madame."

She smiled an all-knowing smile, though she knew nothing. "Tell the gentleman he may join me for a few moments."

She watched as the stranger marched eagerly toward her table. She now saw he wore shiny black shoes topped with gray spats. So delightfully British! The closer he got, the better he looked, and Hanna was finding herself excited at meeting a new man.

"Ah, Madame," the strange man said, "you honor me. May I sit down?" He spoke in French, and Hanna was relieved. Her French from school was rudimentary, but her English was poorer.

"For a few minutes," she said, flashing her devastating smile at his handsome face. His hair, she now noticed, was dusty blond and not that well combed. It gave him a rakish look, which Hanna found intriguing.

254

Royce sat and repeated his name.

"Yes," she said, "it was on your note."

"Of course, how foolish of me. And may I have the pleasure of learning your name?"

She smiled coyly, as though not certain she would part with that information. "Hanna Mazurka," she said at last, toying with the strange words, as if she were still unsure how to pronounce them. Hah-nah Mat-zoorka is how it came out.

"What an enchanting name," he said. "You are on the stage, of course."

She felt her muscles tighten. She gave him a stern, withering look. "*Baroness* Hanna Mazurka."

"Well, of course," he recovered. "I could see you were royalty. An aristocrat to the core."

She relaxed and returned him her friendly smile.

"Ah, you are thinking only the lower classes would be actresses. That is not as true in America. We are much more relaxed about class restrictions."

"I would like sometime to go to America," she said, "but my English is so poor."

"I would be honored to help you learn my language."

"Why, Mr. Saxon," she said, flashing her flirty eyebrows, "what could you possibly gain from that?"

"A feeling of international goodwill," he said, smiling.

"And where would I take these 'lessons'?"

He smiled at her, and an unnerving smile it was, with a lot of teeth that he played like a piano. "Wherever you choose," he said, then added slyly, "there is my room, of course, or…yours."

"But appearances, Mr. Saxon," she said. "Aren't you worried about appearances?"

"I am afraid not."

"But, I am a married woman you know," she said.

"Forgive me if I have offended," he said like nothing could be further from his thoughts. "Where is your husband?" he asked, making a show of looking around the room as if there could be another single gentleman at one of the tables.

"He is in Switzerland."

"Ah—Zurich? Geneva? St. Moritz?"

"The Engadine—"

"The Engadine? What is he doing there—he isn't a shepherd, is he?"

"That is not funny," she snapped. "He is in a tuberculosis sanitarium." She dropped her eyelids. "He is *very* sick."

"I am sorry," Royce Saxon said, dropping his head in an apologetic nod. "So, if I may be so bold, may I inquire what you are doing in Paris?"

"I am here to locate a more agreeable facility for him."

"He is not happy in the Engadine?"

"No."

"Have you found any sanitariums more to your liking here?"

"Not yet."

"Do you have a car?"

"No."

"Might I then offer you the services of my car and driver to ease your pursuit?"

"I can hire a car," she said.

"Yes, I am sure you can," he said. "You are staying at the Ritz after all. You obviously have considerable financial resources at your disposal. I did not mean to belittle that admirable capacity, I just sought to ease your burden—be neighborly. I could go along and teach you some English, or you could go alone, as you choose."

"That is certainly kind of you, Mr. Saxon. But why should you be so generous? You hardly know me."

"Ah, Baroness, that is certainly true. You are very perceptive. But could you understand that I might want to get to know you better?"

"But, I am married."

"Yes, so you said. But can you not imagine a man and woman could be friends without being married?"

Hanna thought that over and wondered if she had grasped all the implications and nuances of it. Was it just the tone of his voice that bespoke the innuendo? Or was the innuendo intended?

"I find it is good to have as many friends as possible in a foreign country, don't you?" Royce Saxon said. It was the way he said it that gave her pause. It seemed somehow so suggestive.

Hanna stopped to analyze how her befriending this American stranger would benefit her. First, she would welcome help with English. Then there was the use of his car and driver. "A penny saved is a penny earned," her mother used to say. He could also give tips about America, should she ever have the opportunity to go there.

But then there were the appearances to consider. She *was* a married woman after all. She could just not be seen with young men. What if the prince saw her? He would certainly get the wrong idea.

The smile she gave Royce Saxon encouraged him. Her words did not.

"It was most kind of you to introduce yourself," she said, holding out her hand for his attention. "And I do appreciate your many generous offers. Unfortunately, I am not at liberty to accept them at the moment. If you will leave me a card, I shall promise to call on you should my situation change. Now if you will leave me to my dinner, I would be most pleased." She realized her French came out formal sounding, but it was the best she could do.

Mr. Saxon was startled. He really thought he had made a conquest—the woman seemed to have a talent in that direction: making you feel you had conquered her. But now he saw unequivocally, conquest would take more time—and cleverness.

Royce Saxon brought Hanna Mazurka's hand to his lips. "I am staying in the hotel," he said, and bowed. "If your situation changes…" he parodied her with the most enigmatic smile on his face.

Was he, she wondered, mocking her?

The next morning, a dozen long-stemmed red roses were delivered to her room. Hanna had never seen such beautiful flowers. They stopped her breath. The card read simply:

No match for your beauty

and was unsigned.

She took breakfast in her room, but returned to the dining room for lunch. She did not see Royce Saxon at lunch, but had the strange feeling she was being constantly watched. But whenever she turned her eyes in the direction of her suspicion, there was no one there.

In truth, people were always watching her wherever she went. She wore attractive clothes that were a little daring, and she wore showy jewelry that seldom failed to attract attention. She had milk-smooth skin and the high cheekbones of the aristocracy, and she gave no reason to doubt she was a baroness.

While taking a cab to her singing lesson, she thought how much more convenient it would be to have a car at her disposal. Mr. Saxon had offered his. Perhaps she should not have been so quick to reject it.

Her new singing teacher had a talent for making the lessons tedious. Scales and more scales—exercises for abdominal muscle control. Breathing routines. When she asked meekly if she couldn't sing a song now and then, he said, "Yes, once you learn to sing."

Alone in her suite, she practiced arias. From her side of the voice box, she thought she was quite good. She couldn't understand why she received no praise from her teacher. His expectations must have been unreasonably high.

Royce Saxon didn't press his luck with Hanna Mazurka. He had a feeling lying low would work more to his advantage.

That night, he watched the dining room until Hanna appeared. After she was seated, he asked to be seated at a table beyond her, so he would have to be led past her table. When Hanna saw him coming, her face turned to glowing, but he was looking the other way. Her smile fell like a disappointed soufflé.

He sat alone and began studying his menu. Hanna kept trying to catch his attention without being too awfully forward, but had no success. Finally she gave up, deciding it would be improper for her to be aggressive. He might think she wanted him to pay for her dinner. But the offer was not made. When she finished, she thought of going to his table to thank him for the roses, but he seemed so intent on a book he was reading, she decided against it.

She went back to her room, looked in the mirror and wondered if she had lost her appeal.

For two or three hours, before the bellman brought the note on the silver tray, Hanna was unable to practice for her voice lesson. Those bah, bah, bahs and duh, duh, duhs held little fascination for her anyway.

She took the note quickly and closed the door without tipping the messenger. She tore the envelope open and read:

I would be honored to escort
you to dinner tomorrow evening
should your sense of propriety not be
offended. Regrets only. Otherwise I
shall call for you at seven.

With admiration,
Royce Saxon

Hanna had to sit down to recoup her breath. She didn't know
what he meant by "regrets only," but in the context, she speculated it
meant unless he heard from her, he would be at her door at seven.
But how would he know which door was hers? She hadn't told him.

She needed time to think. She *was* married, and to a
baron—there was such a thing as propriety after all, no matter how
lightly Mr. Saxon wished to take it.

Hanna sat mulling over that thought, then from some recess
of her subconscious (she was sure) came the small voice of hedonism
whispering softly to her: "When you got married, you didn't take a
vow to crawl in a hole and extinguish your personal life. What is the
harm of having dinner with the man in a public dining room?
Certainly there will be no one there who knows you *or* the baron."

She spent the next afternoon trying on outfits from her
wardrobe. This skirt with that top, this brooch with that blouse, until
she was satisfied she had the perfect ensemble. She was so preoccupied with how she would look she forgot about the prince.

When she opened the door to Mr. Royce Saxon of the
United States of America, she was a vision of loveliness. She had a
sixth sense about making herself breathtakingly attractive, and as
soon as Mr. Saxon laid eyes on her, he gasped. "You are *so* lovely," he
managed.

"Thank you," she said demurely.

He put out his arm, and she took it.

On the way downstairs to their scheduled table in the far corner of the dining room—arranged in advance by Royce Saxon with a
manageable tip to the maître d'hôtel—he said, "Thank you for consenting to accompany me to dinner."

"And thank you for accompanying *me*."

"It is my pleasure, I assure you."

"And thank you for the roses, they are lovely. That wasn't necessary."

"Oh—*au contraire, très nécessaire.*"

When they were settled at their table, she said, "You must tell me about yourself, Mr. Saxon."

"Well, as they say here, I'm an American from the U.S.A.—Chicago, actually. I work for the great Ken Maxwell. Have you heard of him?"

She shook her head.

"Tanks and cannons is our line here—or anything else you might need to blow up your neighbor. Trucks. The Maxwells started three generations back making wagons."

"Wagons? What is this wagons?"

"Horse-drawn wagons. Simple, rustic things. Then they grew into horse-drawn coaches, much more luxurious. Now we're making auto bodies and trucks, and when the war came along, old Maxwell saw an opportunity to turn a quick dollar supplying the war machine."

"And where do you come in?"

"I'm here selling the good guys tanks and cannons—as well as incidentals."

"Is this a good living for you?"

"I have a nice expense account." He smiled. "Maxwell treats me well—he's richer than God—but I'm still an employee."

"But he is paying for my dinner, yes?"

"Yes. And the roses. They went on the account as a gift to a general's wife. Generals like to have a lot of tanks," he said, smiling conspiratorially. "Now it's your turn."

"My turn?"

"To tell me about yourself."

"Yes, well, you know I am a baroness."

"Yes. How did you meet your baron?"

"I was with Prince Stephanoff at the opera in St. Petersburg. He was introduced."

"Prince Stephanoff? The Russian prince?"

"Yes, you know him?"

"Of course. He was to be a customer. But I think Russia has lost interest in the war—seven or eight million casualties and all

261

those internal problems—no wonder."

"When did you see him last?" she asked too eagerly.

"The prince? I never saw him. We corresponded. But we never made the sale. My last inquiry, they told me he left the country."

"Yes, he was on his way to Paris."

"Really? Well, maybe we'll run into him. I'd love to meet him."

Yes, she thought. So would I.

"Where is your family?"

"In Poland," she said, "we are landowners."

"Aristocrats?"

She let out a small, involuntary laugh. "They say there are only two classes in Poland, aristocrats and peasants. We weren't peasants, so…" she shrugged.

"So you must have been aristocrats," he said with a smile. "Well, I suppose we should order. May I order the wine?"

"Oh, yes. I am not much of a drinker."

He scanned the wine list while she looked at her menu. There were no prices on it. She smiled to herself. When she dined alone, there were prices. "Would you like me to order dinner for you, also?"

"Yes, that would be nice."

The waiter presented himself and Royce ordered a nice wine from the South and the rack of lamb for two.

"Have you had any luck finding a sanitarium for the baron?"

"The baron does not want to come to Paris. He says it is too dangerous."

"I could send a tank for him," Royce said with a smile.

"He is not well," she said, stifling a sniffle. "I don't know if he could make the trip."

"That's too bad," Saxon said, "So what do you want for yourself while you are here?"

"I am wanting a career."

"Oh?"

"On the opera stage."

"So how are you going about getting on the opera stage?"

"Well, I am taking lessons."

"And what else?"

"What else? I will find singing engagements, and when I am ready I will audition for the major opera companies."

"Ever think of starting in the minor leagues?"

"What is this minor league?"

"Smaller companies—and work up?"

"How would I do that?"

"Buy your way in."

"Buy?" She was shocked.

"Certainly. Money not only *talks*, it *sings!* There are opera companies all over the world where you can sing if you pay."

"Really? Where?"

"*Every*where. Cuba, for instance. In Havana, you establish your reputation offshore then return to the mainland with glowing notices from some Havana newspaper—also bought."

"Oh, dear," she said. "You make it sound so mercenary."

He laughed, a hearty, booming laugh she would have associated with someone much older. "But it *is* mercenary," he said. "Look here. You want me to get you the particulars? I know a guy who sells this kind of thing."

"What kind of thing?"

"Opera spots abroad."

"What does he get out of it?"

"A commission, of course. It's a business, like selling magazines or real estate."

"But…but, is that legitimate?"

"Why not?"

"Well, I don't know. It seems so, so…deceptive."

"Lot of deception in the world, I suppose," he said, nodding. "This is one of the more harmless forms."

She did not seem convinced.

"Look at it this way. You are paying for training. You pay your voice teacher, don't you?"

"Yes—"

"So, you pay an opera company for opera training."

"But then you pay for a good review?"

"Well, that's optional, of course. You can just put on your résumé that you were a member of this opera company or that, you don't have to say they raved about you."

"But do all divas begin that way?"

"Perhaps not," he said. "It is just an option if you are having trouble getting started."

"How do you know so much about opera?"

He laughed. "I don't know anything about opera. My boss, Mr. Maxwell, is the opera buff. He practically runs the Chicago Opera single-handedly."

"Really? Where is this Chicago?"

"In the middle of the country. North. Lot of lakes around there. We call them the Great Lakes."

"I would like to meet this Mr. Maxwell."

"Come over to America and I'll introduce you."

She gave him a conspiratorial eye. "I just might do that," she said.

The salad came. She took a few bites, then said, "I will succeed in opera on my own merits. I will not have to buy my way in."

"Of course, it can be done on merit. There are a handful of women in the world with voices so good a team of horses could not keep them from operatic fame—"

"That's what I shall be."

He raised an eyebrow. "The best of luck to you," he said. "But even that handful need exposure. They must find a way to be heard."

"How do they do it?"

"Through a major opera company. Like New York or my hometown, Chicago."

"Chic-kah-go," she said in her halting English. "Yes, I must meet this Mr. Maxwell, no? He must love opera."

"Oh, I don't know if he'd know a good singer if one fell on him (—or her, of course). I think it gives him something to do, a way to funnel some of his enormous wealth back to the community painlessly; and get public recognition for it at the same time. His wife, whom rumor has it he has tired of, is an heiress in her own right. The Crenshaw family. Oil and everything else. She is off somewhere with some kind of guru, I hear. Looking for some meaning of it all." He laughed. "As though there *were* any meaning."

"Why, Mr. Saxon, you *are* a cynic."

"Thank you," he said. "In the meantime, I would be honored if you would accompany me to the opera on Saturday. They aren't giving many performances because of the war, as you know, but this one is to benefit the boys in uniform — so you see, we have an opportunity not only to enjoy ourselves, but to be patriotic as well."

Well, she thought, after she'd accepted a little too enthusiastically, what if I am married? My husband hasn't even responded to my letter. I don't even know if he is still alive. I could grow old wondering what some other man would be like — and I do *like* this Royce Saxon a lot. He is a handsome devil and such a kind, generous, gentle man.

For Royce's part, Hanna Mazurka was the most dazzling woman he had ever seen. Including his wife.

Then just as suddenly as Royce Saxon had appeared in Hanna Mazurka's life, he disappeared without a trace. When it was time to go to the opera, he was nowhere in sight. She made inquiries, but was told at the hotel desk he had checked out suddenly with no advance notice.

She went to the opera alone.

Royce Saxon, who had been what she had seen as a pleasant but inconsequential interlude in her life, now loomed as a pesty, pervasive entity. The more time passed, the more she missed him. It wasn't logical, she thought, but she couldn't help it.

Her vocal activities provided her with an alternate channel for her thoughts about the baron, who, she realized, was still languishing in Switzerland.

The seasons changed twice before she was to see Mr. Saxon again. As suddenly as he appeared and disappeared before, he appeared again with an armload of silk and an invitation to the opera.

Hanna tried to appear angry but the dear man seemed so happy to see her, standing at her door with the overgrown smile on his face and his arms circling a bolt of silk.

Silk had been impossible to come by in war-torn Paris, but Royce Saxon had worked a miracle and produced a fine piece of goods. Hanna was afraid to ask him how. If he had to sell his soul to the devil to do it, she didn't care to know.

When he invited her to the opera, she said, "But, you silly boy," she scolded him with too much good nature to make an impression, "the last time I accepted an opera invitation from you, you disappeared without a word! I was *quite* angry, I don't mind telling you."

He cocked an eyebrow as though she were being unreasonable. "My dear woman," he said, with a patient benevolence Hanna Mazurka thought might have been a putdown, "there is a war going on. I am involved. For my safety, as well as others, many of my movements are by stealth and in secret. I can only apologize and hope you understand. We want to win, you know. I must do my bit."

When he called for her, he saw what an uncanny knack she had for doing wondrous things to yard goods. The color of the silk was champagne, and the creative dressmaker had followed her instructions and draped the goods diagonally from one shoulder to make her look like a Roman goddess. The color brought the fine features of her face to the fore. She surpassed pictures in fashion magazines not only because she was alive, but because she was real. And she moved with a particular ease that set off whatever she was wearing as a necessary ingredient of the whole picture. The dress not only made her attractive, she made the dress gorgeous. And, of course, she had a sense of what worked on her and what did not. She could *feel* that certain dresses off the rack would not be right for her—would cramp her style, would make her look ordinary. And she didn't want ordinary. She wanted unique. You weren't noticed if you were ordinary. To turn the head of a prince, you had to be unique. And perhaps, the unique thing in one so young was she knew the difference.

Royce Saxon felt he looked better in her company. Her beauty had a spill-over effect and at the opera all heads turned in their direction. When they settled in their seats, Royce turned to Hanna and whispered, "You are the most beautiful woman I have ever seen."

She ducked her head in the gesture of appreciative modesty she was perfecting. It was a challenge to appear blasé in the face of all the heads turned toward her. She could tell they were buzzing about who she was. It made her smile to think no one had an answer to the question. When she finally made her opera debut, they would know.

After the performance of *La Traviata*, which she thought was wonderful, and was in fact passable for wartime, she and Royce were on their way out of the theater when her heart stopped dead and she had to gasp for breath to stay alive. She was sure she had seen the unmistakable, incomparable profile of Prince Stephanoff. There was simply no mistaking it. But there was a woman with him she did not recognize. Did she dare to hope that meant Katrina had not married him after all? Divorce? Could he be "available"? She thought in that instant that he felt as she did and was here looking for her. She knew they were destined to meet at the opera — she had always pictured it with her singing a lead role on the stage, but fate had put them together in this way and it was just as well.

From nowhere, she heard a strange voice. "What's the matter?" It was almost gruff, she thought, and that was why she hadn't recognized Royce's voice. Next she realized he was standing her upright. She had collapsed against him without knowing it.

"Oh, I'm sorry, I must have stumbled." She released herself from her escort and, as though he were a stranger, she made her way hastily down the steps of the opera house, in wordless pursuit of the prince.

But the steps were jammed with exiting operagoers and though Hanna got free of Royce and fought her way through the crowd, the going was maddeningly slow.

Frustrated on the street amid a platoon of carriages and automobiles, Hanna went from one to the other, peering inside in search of her prince. Her efforts were repaid in the coin of offended glares. Hopelessly she looked both ways on the street, her head turning rhythmically back and forth numerous times until she felt the hand on her arm.

"Hanna! What's gotten into you?" he asked. "You seem possessed."

"What? Oh, no, I—" She took a deep breath and without looking at him said, "I just imagined I saw an old friend—"

"An old friend?"

"Yes, from Russia," she said. "Her name is Katrina. I should have called out to her."

"Then why do you look like you've seen a ghost?"

"A...ghost? Why, no..."

"Well, come along, we must get one of these cabs. I want to take you for supper," he said.

"Oh, please, oh, could we not tonight?" she said; she feared she would run into the prince and he might not like seeing her with another man. Besides, she had to find him—if it meant she had to visit every hotel in town personally.

Royce was obviously disappointed. He had gone to a good deal of trouble to get her the material for the dress, and he thought she was not showing proper appreciation. But after a weak argument, he honored her wishes.

At the door to her room, he asked meekly, "I don't suppose you would let me come in for a minute?"

269

"Oh, no. Sorry. Not tonight, please. I'm very tired."

He leaned forward to kiss her, but she put out her hand to shake his. He smiled ruefully, and shook her hand. "May I call on you tomorrow?" he asked. When she didn't answer, he added, "Perhaps for lunch?"

"I don't know what I'll be doing yet."

"May I stop by to check?"

"What? Oh, check—for lunch?" She smiled. "Yes—stop by. I'll know better tomorrow where I'm at."

As soon as she closed the door, she went to the telephone and asked the desk if the prince were registered. When they told her he was not, she began calling the grand hotels in town. When that yielded her no pleasing result, she worked down the hierarchy of lodging on the off chance that the prince had fallen on hard times, had his money confiscated when he left Russia or just wanted to lie low. She pressed each desk with descriptions of the prince—the most handsome man, with tousled blond hair and the most sublime face in civilization.

The more calls she made, the more convinced she was that she had seen him. And the more exciting the prospect, since he was apparently not with her friend.

But the calls were unproductive. No one would admit to housing the prince, in spite of her skeptical cajoling.

She could barely go to sleep. Oh, she knew people would make fun of her obsession. She could just hear her aunt telling her to mind her own class. But Hanna knew better. When you shared the kind of feeling she shared with Prince Stephanoff, you didn't need to talk about it. It was just *there!*

Because it was so late when she finally went to sleep, Hanna slept in. She was barely out of her bed when the knock came on her door.

"Just a minute," she called out, and went to her closet to throw on a robe. When she opened the door, she saw Royce's face fall. "Oh," he said. "I'm sorry, were you asleep?"

"No, no, it's all right."

"Shall I come back?"

"Back?"

"Yes—for lunch?"

"Oh, that would be fine, yes, fine," she said.

He thought she still seemed distracted.

"Twenty minutes then?"

"Yes, fine." She closed the door and rummaged around for something to wear. Something simple, not flashy, yet not plebeian. She thought of the possibility of the prince lunching here and thought briefly she would be better positioned if she were alone. But then she told herself she was being silly. She could spend the rest of her life alone—waiting. Better to wait in good company, and Royce was that.

At lunch, in her flouncy lime-green crinoline dress, Hanna said, "I'm sorry about last night. I wasn't myself."

He laughed softly and said, "Or maybe you *were* yourself."

She didn't like that. She was not so secure he could make fun of her. He tried to cover his faux pas. "What was wrong?" he asked her.

"Oh, nothing. I was just tired."

"You *weren't* yourself."

"I told you, I thought I saw my old friend."

He shook his head. "*That* kind of reaction for an old friend, I don't see it."

"Well, you wouldn't understand," she said. "You're *only* a man after all. You probably didn't have the same kind of attachment."

"No, that's a fair statement. I can't think of anyone I'd swoon over like that."

"Oh, I'm sure I looked foolish. I'm so far from home—and so is she—if it was she. I couldn't catch her before she disappeared." Hanna thought a moment, her brow furrowing in her deepest concentration. "Oh, Royce," she said, coming out of it, "would you do me a big favor?"

"My dear, I would *love* to do you any favor. Big *or* little."

"You're sweet," she said, wrinkling her nose and chucking his chin with her fingers.

"What do you want me to do?"

She looked at him longingly, as though her fondest thought, her *only* thought, was to love him. "Find my friend," she said.

"And who *is* your friend?"

"Her name is Katrina," she said. "She's Polish too and just my age. Gosh, am I twenty already?"

How much older she had seemed to Royce.

"And, oh," she said casually, but her heart was pounding, "she's married to Prince Stephanoff of Russia. So if you find him, you'll find her."

Hanna spent an anxious week awaiting news of the prince. Early in the week, she wrote again to the baron, who had still not responded to her first letter. She gave him news of spotting the prince but not making contact. She did not mention looking for an alternate sanitarium, for she had not yet done so, she was so busy, but she did ask him how he was and managed a few pouty phrases about him not caring for her or else he would have written.

She had expected Royce would unearth the prince in a day or two, but as the week dragged on she harbored thoughts that Royce was dragging the process out to appear more heroic, and also to guarantee her attention. She had, she told Royce, half a mind to pursue him herself.

"By all means," Royce encouraged her. "If you have any bright ideas where to look, let me know and I will pursue them."

"Well," she said, "how many places are there where a prince could be?" She knew she was sounding too intent, but she was put out by his inference that she wasn't bright, and told him so.

"What are you talking about?"

"You said I was too dumb to have any bright ideas."

"I said no such thing."

"Well, that's what you meant."

"It is not. I merely said, if you aren't satisfied, maybe you have some better ideas. First of all, we are acting on a large supposition. You *think* you saw your friend, the prince's wife. Maybe you didn't. And if you did, that's not proof *he* lives here. If he *does* live around here, he isn't making it known to anyone. Perhaps he is hiding out."

Hanna forbade Royce to come in her room, but teased him that it might be possible "when you produce something."

The next night at dinner, Royce broke the news to Hanna that he would have to go back to the United States soon. "I would be honored if you would join me," he said.

She was shocked. "But I am *married*," she said.

"So you have said."

"What? You don't believe me?"

The face he showed told her he was doubtful.

"What would I do in America?" she said.

"Get on the opera stage!" he said, enthusiastically. His salesmanship struck an instant chord.

"Oh?" she said. "How so?"

"There are many opera companies in the U.S. They are springing up all over. America has no war at home to slow things down. A woman of your beauty and accomplishment would shoot right to the top, unless I miss my guess."

"You are trying to flatter me," she said, with a coy glance at him.

"If by flattery, you mean insincerity, I do not flatter—I compliment. New York also has the best voice teachers in the world."

"Who is best?"

He laughed. "It's not my line, but it won't be hard to find out."

273

"Do you have any connections?"

"I told you, my boss is the angel of the Chicago Opera."

"Angel?"

"Yes—means big, *big* contributor."

"And he would get me onstage?"

"Well, Chicago—that is starting pretty high up. I'd suggest you get your feet wet in Havana or someplace—then when you get some experience and notices, maybe then you'll be ready for Chicago or even New York."

"New York is better?"

"Oh, most people think so, one of the best opera companies in the world—the Metropolitan. New York is our biggest city. There are other companies there too."

"How do you go to America?"

"By steamer," he said. "Not that easy to come by in wartime," he paused, "but I have connections." He winked at her in a fashion she thought was too familiar.

She let him think she was interested. "I will think about it," she said.

"Good."

"One thing is certain," she said, holding his eye to emphasize her sincerity, "I will not leave here until I meet up with my friend Katrina—and the prince."

"Are you sure you don't have a case on the prince?"

She flushed with anger. "How could I have a case on my best friend's husband? Your suggestion insults me."

"Sorry," he said, nodding to make her believe she had convinced him.

Two days later, Royce Saxon had located Prince Stephanoff in a villa outside of Paris. At Hanna's urging, he delivered an invitation for both of them to join her for dinner at the Ritz.

A hastily scrawled note came back.

Denky (Hanna)!

What exciting news. I
would love to come in for lunch on

Thursday, the enemy willing. Lord,
we have so much to catch up on!

Love,
Katrina

There was no mention of the prince. Hanna was disappointed, but resigned herself. One step at a time, she told herself.

It took Hanna all morning on Thursday to get ready. The
dress was selected with great care, as were the jeweled embellish-
ments. She wanted to make an impression—she was sure word of her
appearance would get back to the prince.

Hanna went to the lobby to meet her friend. Her first
thought on arriving in the lobby was that Katrina had hidden somewhere and was going to jump out and say "Boo!" as they had done
when they were in school together. Then she saw a young woman
coming toward her with a huge smile on her face. Hanna frowned,
trying to understand who this was and why she was smiling so broadly at her. Then it hit her a split second before she said, "Denky!" and
she recognized the voice and they embraced in happy tears. Finally
they stood back and looked at each other.

"Katrina—you look *so* different. What have you done to yourself?"

"Got rid of some baby fat," she giggled, "and grew up, I
guess."

"Boy, did you ever! Katrina, you're gorgeous." It was an
appraisal not happily made.

"Well, I don't know about that. You always *were* gorgeous.
And, I guess I'm just so happy!"

Hanna swallowed and tried not to show her friend how poorly she received *that* news.

They went into the dining room, where the maître d' led
them to a table by the window. Katrina ordered a salad and Hanna
said, "Oh, hah—so you starve yourself to death."

"Oh, no. But I am more careful. But tell me, what brings you
to Paris? This is just *so* exciting."

"I have become quite serious about my music. There are
many fine opportunities here—teachers and the like," she said.

"And is the baron with you?"

"Alas, no," she said. "He is in the sanitarium in the Engadine. I *begged* him to come, of course, but he wouldn't hear of it."

"Oh, dear," Katrina frowned, "and you left him?"

"Well, just temporarily, of course. I will look for a place for him here." She took a handkerchief from her pocket and sniffled into it. "The poor dear is not well."

"So you *left* him?" Katrina was astonished.

"Do you think a woman should not have a life of her own?"

"Well, I think if she is married," she said carefully, "she has her husband to consider."

"Yes, how is your husband?" Hanna deftly shifted the focus.

"Oh, he's so *wonderful*, Denky—oh, you don't mind me calling you Denky, do you? I know you're Hanna now. Hanna Mazurka. It's a *wonderful* stage name, Denky. I just love it, but old habits die hard. Is it all right?—oh, tell me it's all right or I shall be miserable. I so want to call you what you want."

"Oh, it's fine—it doesn't matter," Hanna Mazurka said, trying to be magnanimous, a role that did not suit her. Then, more in surprise than question, she added, "So, you really did marry my prince."

"*Your* prince?" Katrina asked, slightly abashed. "He was *yours?*"

"Well, I told you about my dating him, remember?"

"Oh, yes—I did ask him, but he didn't remember—"

"Why, that's preposterous," she said. "We were very close," she said.

"How close?" Katrina's eyes narrowed.

"*Very*," Hanna said resolutely.

"You don't mean...?"

Hanna waved a hand. "Oh, Katrina, it's no use going over that now. I just can't believe he told you he didn't remember me—not after what *we* had."

Katrina was blushing at her friend. She saw Hanna was out of sorts and instinctively wanted to assuage her sorrow.

"Oh, pooh, Denky. You know how men are. They're so self-absorbed it's surprising they can remember *any*thing. But, gosh, you're making me feel like I took him from you."

"Oh, he wouldn't have married me. That much was clear. I was not of his class. I understand those things, Katrina, believe me I do. Especially now that I am a baroness." She laughed and touched her friend's arm. "Imagine me, a *baroness!*"

"I think it's wonderful," Katrina said. "I'd like to meet the baron—will you be able to get him to Paris, do you think?"

Hanna cocked an eyebrow—"I could ask you the same."

"What do you mean?"

"I'd love to see the prince. Do you think you'd be able to get him to Paris?"

"Oh, he doesn't go out that much."

"Didn't I see him at the opera?"

"Well, of course, he adores the opera, but there are so few with the war. Oh, Denky, he's such an introspective man, and I do love him dearly. But, I wouldn't think of pushing him. If he wants to be a recluse, I will be as accommodating as I can."

Hanna frowned. "Are you sure you aren't just keeping him from me?"

"Why, Denky, why would I do such a thing?"

"Jealousy?"

"Jealousy? Really? Well, I suppose that is not that far-fetched—I always was a little jealous of you. Men were always clamoring around you and I was an awful wallflower. But, Denky, I don't feel even a tiny bit of jealousy anymore."

"I guess you have no reason to," Hanna mused, but not without pain. "You're gorgeous *and* you have the prince."

Gently, but firmly, Katrina changed the subject and got them to reminisce about old times—their school days and Denky's singing adventure on the seamy side of downtown Brest Litovsk, Poland. They both had many laughs.

"That's when you should have been Hanna Mazurka," Katrina said.

"Oh, my," Hanna said, rolling her eyes.

"Oh, Denky, do you know what's going on in Russia? Oh, it's so terrible—"

"What?"

"Everybody was expecting a revolution, and it's started. Lots

277

of people blamed Rasputin for his hold over the czarina, but I'm sure it's more than that."

"What does the prince think?"

"He thinks it's a lot deeper. He talks about history and how the rich must be careful how they treat the poor—there are so many more of them, they could rise up and kill the rich at any moment."

"Oh, no—"

"Well, he thinks so. Noblesse oblige is his byword. He's just so glad we got out of there when we did. You were lucky too."

"It wasn't luck," Hanna said coolly.

"No, I didn't mean to take anything from you: you certainly were in the *avant-garde*, as we say in Paris."

"Yes."

"Everyone is leaving! Can you imagine? And they are bringing all their jewels because Russian currency isn't much good anywhere now—not even in Russia."

"But how will they *spend* their jewels?"

"They'll have to change them into money, somehow."

"Where will they all go?"

"A lot of them are coming here, I hear. Lord knows where we will put them."

When they parted, they vowed to do this again. "I'd love to see where you live," Hanna said hinting without subtlety.

"I'd love you to, too," Katrina said. "If I can work it out, I'll send word. How long will you be at the hotel?"

Hanna considered her reply carefully. "I'm not sure," she said. "I might be leaving in a week."

"Oh, gosh, really? I guess you *should* check on the baron—"

"My opera career may take me to America," she said.

"Why, Denky, how impressive. You've a career already!" She clapped her hands once.

"Yes, I haven't been idle," she said.

"Well, gosh, I knew you'd never be idle—but how you can work it all in with a marriage and all; I mean, you are just a wonder."

"Well," she explained. "I just caught the opera bug." Then she added with just the slightest edge, "From the prince...."

News from Russia was not good. The casualties the Mother Country had suffered were high in the millions. Hanna congratulated herself that she had kept the baron out of it. Over seventy-five percent of the Russian soldiers were dead, wounded, or missing, and Hanna was sure Alexi would have been one of them.

There was still no response to her letters to the baron. Royce was pressing her for a decision. "We'd have to book your passage, and in wartime you never know what to expect. The whole ship could be commandeered for something," he said. "Or it could leave with only twenty-four hour's notice."

But Hanna couldn't make up her mind. She kept hoping the prince would come to see her. She was not happy with

Katrina's ecstasy. Hanna couldn't understand what the prince saw in Katrina. She knew nothing about opera. What, besides class, did they have in common?

Hanna was plagued with doubts. She was doubtful about her responsibility to a husband who did not respond to her letters. She was doubtful about Royce Saxon's intentions—would she be sending him the wrong signal? What signal did she want to send him? But most of all, she was doubtful about leaving the prince. What if he decided to see her the day she sailed?

She thought of the letter she had written him agreeing with him that a woman could only love him for his money. It was a stupid, impetuous thing to do, she thought now, but it had been a gamble for attention—for further discussion. She had presented herself as brazen, a girl with spunk and verve, but apparently he hadn't seen it that way. She would have liked to send some note of apology, of reconciliation, but it was so impossible now with her friend Katrina inconveniently married to him.

If only she could see him now. Alone. She could explain everything. Now that she was an "experienced" married lady, she had overcome the class difference. She was, after all, a baroness. She thought she probably shouldn't have intimated to Katrina that she had been intimate with the prince. Perhaps Katrina would confront him. Of course, he would deny it. Would Katrina believe him or her lifelong friend? It would be natural for a husband to deny an infidelity, she thought, even if it *was* before he was married. But if Katrina did tell him what Hanna said, it would not make him want Hanna any more. But then again, it might. You never knew for certain about men, but she was beginning to understand where *that* is concerned, men were pretty irrational. Look at the baron. Look at Royce. It was obvious to her what he wanted, but she continued to hold him off with her sundry techniques—ignoring his hints, making fun, playing the shocked, married maiden.

But now she had to decide if she wanted to go to America with him. Of course, she *wanted* to go to America. It was frightening being in Europe with the war going on. And America had the opera companies—and the voice teachers she needed to advance her career. She could save years of her training period. Accelerate everything—daily lessons with a teacher who could help her—practical experience with an opera company. *Then* she could return triumphant to Paris and take the Paris Opera and the prince by storm. She could sing, she *knew* she could. It was just a matter of experience—and that she could get in America.

When Royce proposed the trip, Hanna had insisted on a separate cabin, though it was obvious the war-goods salesman had something else in mind. "Cost a lot more money," he said.

"Can you afford it?" she asked, startling him.

"Me?"

"Well, yes, wasn't it *your* idea?"

"My?…but, Baroness…"

She turned down her lips. "I am sorry if I misunderstood. But I would not be able to afford such a trip. And the idea of me, a married woman, sharing your cabin is beyond my imagination. Imagine the scandal!"

"Oh, who would know?"

"I would know," she said.

"But, I am not a rich man…"

"Then I guess it is settled. I stay."

"Hanna—please don't be difficult."

"Who is difficult? You invite me to go to America and then it turns out you expect *me* to pay—or to go as your courtesan."

"If you want, I will swear not to touch you."

"Hah! And what if you did? What do I do then? Jump overboard and swim back? No, thank you. I require a cabin of my own with a lock on the door."

Royce wondered why he put up with this impossible woman. But deep down, he knew. She was so infuriatingly beautiful—body and soul—that he was powerless to resist her devastating charms. He felt weak in her presence and he knew at once that if she asked him to buy her the ship, he would do so if he had to rob every bank in the world to please her.

"Don't you have an expense account?" she teased him, but he had already thought of that. How he could camouflage such a large expense, he couldn't imagine.

But even when he agreed to pay for her cabin, Hanna was not sure she would go. "I have a very sick husband," she said. But Royce didn't bother to argue that. He realized that sick husband, if he existed at all, was not in the forefront of Hanna's thoughts.

Hanna wondered if she should tell Royce she didn't want to go all the way to Chicago. New York was the opera capital of the country, he said so himself, so why should she go another thousand miles? He had enticed her with his boss who supported the Chicago Opera Company, but how hard would it be to find the man or men who supported the New York Opera? A man is a man, she thought, and she was discovering how easy it was to get them to dance when she whistled.

The key with the male sex was to ration her favors. It was easy to get carried away emotionally in the presence of a man—and she did like men—but it was far more astute to keep a lid on her emotions. The one who wants it less, she reasoned, controls the relationship.

Hanna thought about writing again to her husband. The doctor had said he was dying, she remembered, and as was said at home, never murder a dying man. Perhaps he was already dead. No answers to *two* letters. Anyway, just to be safe, she should write to tell him she was going to America to study. He wouldn't be able to protest the trip—by the time he got the letter, she'd be in New York.

So she wrote the letter. Even holding out hope that after the war was over she would return to him—though she knew she wouldn't. She mailed the letter before she told Royce she had decided to go to America.

When Royce inquired about an additional cabin, he was told all the first-class cabins were booked. There were only a few second-class cabins left, and they were, naturally, the least desirable of the class. He reserved one, then went back to the hotel to tell Hanna. He took her to lunch to ease into the news. When she heard it, she said, "Then I cannot possibly go. I shall take a later ship."

"But you can spend your time on deck, or in the public rooms."

"In second class," she said. "I'm sorry, but I do not consider myself a second-class person. Baronesses do not travel steerage."

"It's not steerage," he protested. "Only second class. It is not so bad, believe me. Besides, you can come to my cabin anytime you want."

She gave him a hard stare, and spoke slowly. "If it is not so bad, then you take second class. I will take the first."

"But I'm paying…" he started to protest.

She stopped him with her hand. "Then I pay—on the next ship."

Royce told her she was being unreasonable, but she wouldn't change her mind.

So, he changed cabins with her, saying, "I hope you will extend me the courtesy of allowing me to spend some time in your cabin," he said.

"But I am *married*," she said.

The next day, when Royce brought her first-class-cabin tickets to her room, she let him come in. "I hope you aren't mad at me," she said. She was wearing her most becoming daytime dress, a classic pink, open at the neck, with straight sleeves and ruffled cuffs.

"No," he said, but she wasn't convinced.

"It is up to you," she said. "I can take the next boat."

"No, it's all arranged," he said. "I don't need first class. I'm not a baroness."

She turned sullen. "You make fun of me."

"No, really. If I weren't on an expense account, I wouldn't be anywhere near first class."

With sudden impetuosity, she threw her arms around him and gave him a quick kiss.

Startled, he barely participated until she began to pull away. Then he intensified his grip and pressed her lips to his, his hands moving down her body. She broke loose. "Naughty boy," she said.

"Hanna! I am crazy about you."

"You're crazy," she said. "That is, sure. Now you must go. I have much to do."

"Let me stay and watch you."

"No—it would be too distracting. Now go, or I won't have time for dinner!"

He went. Like a lamb. She loved it.

In the afternoon mail, she got a letter that startled her. It was from the sanitarium in Switzerland and in her husband's handwriting. She didn't want to open it, and almost decided to wait until she was on the ship. But then she realized she could *say* she hadn't gotten it until she was on her way—or even in New York. Besides, she was too anxious to see what it said. She tore it open.

My dearest Zdenka:

I love you from the bottom of my heart. I miss you so. Please come back. I *need* you. I am nothing here without your daily visits.

I was so thrilled to get your letter. I can't tell you what it means to me. I have read it a hundred times. I am just so excited to know you cared enough to write me. It took a long time to get here, but that is the war and we can't do anything about that.

My health is much the same. I tell the doctor the only thing I live for is your return. And if you won't come back, I must resign myself to come to you, though it won't be easy. The doctor says I would be risking my life to make such a trip, but, of course, he can't forbid it. I tell him that I cannot live without you, so I might just as well risk my life as be without you.

A man without a woman's touch is a beast. I am weak, but I would spend my last breath to touch you one more time. If I don't hear that you are coming back to me, I shall make the arduous trip to you in Paris. If you cannot come back, could you send me enough money to make the trip? I do forgive you for taking the money. I understand how hard it is for a woman alone. They tell me the sanitarium bill has not been paid. I told them it must have slipped your mind. They say if it isn't paid soon they will have no choice but to turn me out. No matter, I will come to you in Paris then.

Zdenka, I do apologize for getting angry. I see now how foolish it was. Please try to forgive me. Maybe it is because I am sick that I do not always act as I should with you. But I promise you on the holy book that I will never do another thing to upset you as long as I live.

You see, I never realized I couldn't live without you until you left. My days are agony—the nights are worse.

Please give me something to live for!
Come back!
PLEASE!!!

With all my love forever,
Alexi

Hanna couldn't leave her room for dinner that night. She didn't open the door for Royce when he came for her. He knocked four times before she answered him with a low moan, telling him she wouldn't be going to dinner.

"Is something wrong?" he asked through the door.

She didn't answer.

"Do you need a doctor?"

"No."

"Shall I have some food sent up?"

"No."

He went away and Hanna spent the rest of the evening justifying to herself the decision she had made.

She tried to obliterate her dilemma with sleep, but it would not come. Around midnight, she stopped fighting it and arose to write Alexi a letter. It was not a missive she tossed off without thinking. She had composed it a dozen times in her head waiting for sleep to alleviate her agony.

Dear Husband:

I received your letter some fourteen months after I arrived in Paris, on the day I had completed my plans for a trip to America. I am shocked to hear you talking about taking a trip to Paris to see me. The world has gone crazy with this war, and if I was foolish to travel across Europe when I did, it is ten times as crazy now.

Your enthusiastic pleas for my return would be flattering to any woman. My memory is not so poor that I have forgotten our time together was not idyllic. Have *you* forgotten our terrible arguments?

I am sorry, but I need this time alone to think about my future, and to plan and work toward my career. You could help me with my goal and put my mind at ease by getting out of your head these silly notions about risking your life to come to Paris.

The best thing you could do for all concerned is stay where you are and try to get well. I am happy you understand I had no choice about the money. I will see to the bill when I get settled in America. Things are too hectic just now to muddle my mind with mundane accounts. They certainly wouldn't dare put you out on the street. You are a *baron!*

Living in Paris does not come cheap. I was astonished to see how much my account had dwindled in six short months. I am going to have to search out some way to make money because what I have will not last forever. I suggest you ask your family for money to pay your bills. Surely they would not begrudge you your hospital costs, in spite of what they feel about your marriage to me.

As you know, I haven't been that good for you. If it were not for me you would probably be a corpse in an unmarked grave on some insignificant and forgotten battlefield. But your mother and father would be able to hold their royal heads up. They should be thanking me for keeping you alive!

So stay where you are, Husband, and get better. A top opera diva can earn an astounding amount of money, and when I do, I shall see to it first thing that your needs are taken care of.

Get well soon,
Hanna Mazurka

She thought about adding her former name—Zdenka Oleska Chotznic or Baroness Chotznic—but rejected the idea. Past is past, she reasoned. And she saw no reason to encourage him.

After the letter was sealed, she managed a few hours of sleep. In the morning, Royce returned to tell her, through the unopened door, that the sailing was postponed indefinitely due to the war.

Hanna left the hotel furtively to go to her scheduled voice lesson. She thought it might take her mind off the baron. It didn't.

It was overcast in Paris and the trees on the boulevard looked more gray than green. Hanna had decided to walk back to her hotel from her lesson. More automobiles were crowding the streets and newsboys seemed to be everywhere, shouting at the top of their lungs:

"Czar abdicates Russia! Read all about it."

Hanna was not thinking in French so she didn't grasp the message. Her mind was elsewhere, still stewing over the letter from her husband and his plea that she come back to him. It was just *too* unreasonable. The war was everywhere now and the only thing to do was to get as far from it as you could—like America. She should offer to take Alexi with her, but the journey to Paris would be out of the question. Did he, she wondered, want to give her TB?

Suddenly she was stopped by a newsboy in her path, holding a newspaper in front of her—she read and translated the headline before she tuned into the boy's slurred French exclamations:

Czar abdicates!

Quickly she bought a paper and tucked it under her arm as though she might be in danger if anyone saw her reading it. She hurried her steps back to her hotel room, where she found a message from Royce which she didn't take time to read. She sat on the couch and devoured the news story. "Thank God the prince got out of there," she muttered, then added, "and the baron, of course."

When she finished the page-one story that spilled over to the back pages, Hanna noticed her hands were trembling. The peasants were revolting in Russia and demanding their own land and all kinds of unreasonable, revolutionary things. Hanna forgot her beginnings and sided with the aristocrats.

The news story said that the aristocrats and moneyed classes were escaping Russia as fast as they could. Sometimes with only the clothes on their backs.

Hanna knew that their most portable wealth was their jewels. Katrina had told her about the aristocrats on the run with their jewels.

As a baroness, Hanna felt a personal danger. What if those idiots showed up in Paris and started killing everyone with a title? She must go to America, and she was suddenly put out that the transatlantic trip had been delayed. For the first time, she began to think about actually being in America, and what it would be like. She thought first of money. How much did she have left, and how far would it go in America?

She took her account books from the desk drawer in the sitting room of her suite. She sat and opened the accounts on the desk, and added and subtracted, and she was glad she did. She had certainly spent a lot of money in Paris. The idea of adding to her bank account crowded its way into her thoughts. But how? She was not quite ready to take the opera world by storm and she couldn't think of another way of earning money compatible with her training and expertise.

She thought again of Katrina and what she said about the women leaving Russia with their jewels. It would be a service to help them out, and some profit could surely be made in the meanwhile.

She took a sheet of stationery from the drawer and dipped the quill pen into the inkstand and made notes.

> Train schedules
> Russian Embassy
> Peasant costume
> Cash (method of concealment)

The phone rang on the desk in front of her.

She didn't answer it. She knew it must be Royce. As a compromise, she picked up his note and opened it.

> I am distressed at your apparent unhappiness. Did *I* do something? Tell me how I can cheer you up. Lunch? Dinner? Both? You are such a beautiful woman, your glow and sparkle light the world. When you hide in your room there is only darkness.
>
> Please call me—number 412.
>
> Love,
> Royce

She tossed the note aside and headed out for the Russian Embassy to make inquiries about when and where the Russian émigrés would appear. They had sketchy information, but were not guarded about sharing it with her—she was so disarming in the way she went about things.

Hanna went to her banks and took most of her money in bank notes of various manageable denominations. It was a gamble, and she was nervous, but she decided it was the sensible thing to do.

She didn't tell Royce about her trip. She knew he would worry and try to stop her—or, worse still, insist on going along with her.

"Nice outfit," the cabdriver said to Hanna as she stepped into his car.

"Train station," she said. Hanna had mixed feelings about the driver's familiarity. She was being spoken to as a peasant again, which was, in a way, her goal, dressing up as a peasant and carrying an enormous black bag with sturdy straps so she could carry a generous load over her shoulder. All in all, she thought, she preferred the deference she got as a baroness.

She had fretted about what size bag would be most appropriate for her mission. She didn't want it to be awkward. On the other hand, if it were too large, it would be an embarrassment if it weren't filled. Hanna just had no idea how she would do it. Finally she opted for a large one. At the bottom of the bag she stashed a butcher knife—for "emergencies."

As usual, she got a lot of glances getting on the train, but she was used to that by now. The train would take her to intercept the train from Tallinn, Estonia, to meet the fleeing aristocrats and their astonishing jewels.

Going out of Paris, the train was sparsely populated. There was a war, as Hanna noted in her letter to her husband, and travel was dangerous.

Hanna had stewed over many possibilities. First, she thought someone might get to the expatriates before she did. Or she might be successful and have her stash confiscated at some border or other. Or she could simply be robbed. She was counting on her peasant dress to protect her.

The train from Tallinn, Estonia, was crowded. It was cold and clammy—there was some rain. Hanna was on board early to choose her seatmate, a nervous-looking old woman whose eyes kept darting about, and who clutched a large, expensive-looking bag on her lap. Hanna guessed, correctly, that the bag was bulging with jewels.

Hanna smiled at the woman, shyly, and looked away, as though she were shy herself. "Hello," she said with a broadening smile. "I am Denky Oleska from St. Petersburg. Where do you come from?"

The woman looked at the peasant costume in a way that told Hanna she didn't know whether to be frightened or disdainful. After all, the reason these aristocrats were on the run was the peasants were taking over—killing the czar and his family. Was this young, pretty thing one of them?

Hanna hastened to set the record straight.

"Are you going to Paris?"

"Yes-s-s—"

"Is nice. You will like," Hanna said. "I am representing a Paris jewelry company. If you have any jewels you might consider selling, I can give you best prices of anywhere, so you will not be cheated in the big, strange city, where no one speaks your language."

The peasant was starting to make some sense to the aristocrat. But she was still wary. She cocked a suspicious eye at Hanna. "How much money?"

"Well, that, of course, depends on the jewels. If I could see them."

The woman thought she was going to be robbed and was therefore reluctant to take out her jewelry.

Hanna read her mind. She laughed easily. "You think I would steal? I am from the most reputable shop in Paris—"

"Which one?"

"I am sorry, I am not at liberty to give that information. But if I did rob you with all these people around, where could I go with your jewels? Jump off the train?"

The woman nodded at the wisdom. "You must excuse me," she said. "Everything is turmoil at home. I got out with all I could carry, that is all. My husband is in the army—or was—I don't know, I haven't heard. But our people are finished in Mother Russia." She shook her head. "It is a dark time for the aristocracy. The peasants have revolted," she said, looking at Hanna with a questioning eye.

Hanna hastily shook her head. "I am Polish, we don't revolt. You see how poor my Russian is."

"It is very good—for a Polish girl."

"I am living in Russia with my aunt and uncle for a short time. I learn what I can, is not enough."

Now the aristocrat could feel her noblesse oblige, and her confidence grew accordingly. One by one she withdrew her jewels to show Hanna, protecting as best she could the stash from her fellow passengers.

For her part, Hanna tried to contain her glee for the spectacular stones and settings paraded before her eyes. "You have very good collection."

"Thank you. What can I get?"

"Ah, yes, that is always the question," Hanna said, as though this was not her first transaction. "I can tell you I always give best prices. When you are in Paris, no one speaks your language. Do you speak French?"

"Some," she said shyly—"from school."

"Uh, yes. I too have French in school, but I can tell you, I live there and the French when they talk, you cannot understand. Is very fast, is different accents, inflections are strange." She shook her head sympathetically. "I have been two years already and I still have trouble." By now the woman was nodding her agreement.

"Is much better for you, you have French money in your purse when you get to Paris. If you don't, you will be taken advantage of. I know," Hanna dropped her head demurely, "because I was."

"Oh, dear—no."

She nodded. "And I am just lucky to work for such a wonderful, fair man, who gives the best prices to the unfortunate royal personages who come to Paris seeking refuge from the savages."

The woman looked longingly at her lifetime accumulation of precious jewels, as though parting from them would be the end of her life.

"Oh, Denky," she said, suddenly gripped by her horrible memories, "it is terrible, terrible, terrible. Our peasants have become savages—they are murdering people in their homes, on the streets. They are animals. Our Russia is finished." There were tears in her voice—not the tears of self-pity, the tears of eternal hopelessness.

Hanna put her arm around the woman's shoulder. "There, there, you got away from all that misery. Paris will be a good home for you, if you have the cash your jewels can bring. I will help you, my dear; I will help you."

And soon the woman was eating out of Hanna's hand. And as Hanna named her prices for each piece, the woman felt she was being generously treated, though she didn't have a strong grasp of what the many thousands of French francs would buy compared to Russian rubles. Hanna could honestly tell her the relative rate, but

293

she didn't bother to explain how expensive things were in Paris.

Up and down the aisles she plied her trade, and it wasn't long before people were seeking her out, competing for her attention, "*s'il vous plaît.*" The feeling she was giving good prices abounded (actually around twenty to thirty percent of their retail value. And Hanna, being an inveterate jewelry shopper herself, had a nose for value). Hanna was a good saleswoman. She had the smile of honesty—open, unassuming and the appearance of a waif, only concerned with their welfare. By the time the train reached Paris, she had had to buy (from an expatriate) another bag to hold her acquisitions. It was, she told herself, like taking candy from babies.

She made quite a haul. It was amazing how much fine jewelry the Russian aristocrats owned. She soon had invested her ready cash in an astonishing cache of jewels. As she rode the train home to Paris, she decided to ask more than double what she paid. Some of the pieces were nothing short of startling, and given the right contacts, she might do the retailing herself.

And her plan worked beyond her wildest dreams. She doubled her cash very quickly, and had tons of jewels left over to store in the hotel safe. She smiled to herself. If her customers only knew she stayed at the Ritz! But she put on the peasant costume and this time made it easier on herself by meeting the train as it entered France. She had worried needlessly about someone else beating her to the punch. People actually said to her, "I had heard about you. You are a godsend. We wouldn't know where to turn in Paris, and likely as not would be taken advantage of by someone who doesn't speak our language and is only out for personal gain. We didn't see you in Estonia. We were worried we'd miss you."

Hanna smiled her most modest smile—she told them her name was Denky Oleska from St. Petersburg, as she had the first time. She knew the streets, and customs of the people. She could talk to them of things they knew.

She had been so busy with her jewelry transactions, she had completely forgotten about Alexi's sanitarium bill. Oh, well, if they wanted her to pay, they could send her a bill. She had left him *some* money in the one joint account. What had he done with it?

When Royce asked her where she had been, she said she had been intensely studying opera in the country, and had gone to visit her friend Katrina.

"And the prince?" Royce pressed.

"No, he wasn't there," she said.

He didn't believe her.

While she waited for news of the ship's sailing, Hanna became more excited at the prospect of going to America. There was nothing like forbidden travel to make one more eager for the trip.

When the news came that the ship was ready to sail, she was almost beside herself with joy.

She had had to buy a steamer trunk just to transport the jewelry she had bought from the expatriates and not sold. She would be able to command even higher prices in America, she thought—but her goal was to always have enough money so she wouldn't have to sell *any* of the priceless gems.

On their way to the ship, in two cabs—one for them, one for the luggage—Royce was already talking about what she could expect in Chicago. He was animated, he was excited. He leaned over and kissed her on the cheek. She didn't recoil. This was the man who had given up his first-class cabin for her. Some reciprocity was called for.

Especially in light of the fact that she had no intention of going to Chicago.

ACT III

THE DOCTOR

Iago: While you are feeling
       Raptures unceasing,
       Firmly she holds you
       Never releasing.
       This is a spider's web
       Where your poor heart
       Is caught and languishes,
       Never to part.

                    — *Otello*

Madame Hanna Mazurka
remembers:

THE DOCTOR
New York, New York

"When I married Dr. Weidner I
lost my personality. His death
was the end of everything.
There was no God!"

Hanna loved the ocean voyage. She loved the rocking motion of the ship, the *Arabic*, on the swells. She loved the first-class feeling of luxury. She loved the solitude of her cabin. She especially loved being the toast of a table of eight in the first-class dining room. The four men at the table made terrible plays for her, and she adored flirting outrageously with them. She loved the food and the attentive service. Once or twice she had a twinge of regret that Royce Saxon could not eat with her, but that passed after the second day. He was a good sport about it, and she told him she liked good sports.

"How much do you like them?" he asked when they met on the deck of second class.

"A whole lot," she said, then saw

in his Grecian-god-perfect features what he meant. "Oh, silly," she said, tweaking his nose.

"Why silly?"

"Oh, we've talked about it so often," she said. "I'm a married lady. I must watch my behavior."

"There's no one here either of us knows," he argued. "Besides, aren't we being hypocritical?"

"What is this 'hypocritical'? It is a word I do not know."

She was taking English lessons aboard and Royce was so patient about helping her.

"Simply put," he said, "hypocritical means saying or implying one thing while doing the opposite. One who makes believe he has purer thoughts than he does."

She bristled, her posture stiffening. "But my thoughts *are* pure."

"Well, mine aren't," he muttered.

"That is your problem," she said.

"It sure is," he lamented. "What can we do about it?"

"What we can do is I can stay in first class and not see you at all if that's the way you want to be about it."

Royce thought he should have sealed the bargain before he gave her his first-class cabin. He chided himself for stupidly thinking Hanna's gratitude would spill over on him.

"Are we to have separate rooms all the way to Chicago?" he asked. "And while we are in Chicago?"

"Certainly," she said, seeing no reason to tell him yet she had no plans to *go* to Chicago.

"Who is going to pay for it?"

"Who enticed me to America?" she asked, turning on the flirty machinery.

"Oh, no," he said. "I told you, I'm not a rich man."

She waved a pretty pink hand at him. On her fingers she wore enormous diamonds. "You have an expense account," she said.

He shook his head resolutely. "Only while I'm away from home."

"Oh, pooh," she said.

"Well, pooh yourself," he said. "What is it about you that should make me want to keep, but not touch, you?"

She looked out from under blinking eyes. "Let us see when we get to New York. Maybe if we stay one night there in a fabulous hotel, maybe then there will be some touching."

"I told you, we can't stop in New York. I have to get right to Chicago—business. My boss demands it—and since I *have* to work, *I* don't tell *him*."

"Well, that is up to you," she said. "I myself can only stand so much travel. I will stay at least one night in New York. I *might* invite you to stay with me. That is," (twinkle, twinkle), "if you are nice to me. If you don't want to stay, I will come later."

"Out of the question," he insisted.

Her eyes sparkled, the devastating smile crept to her full, maddening lips. She leaned over and planted a quick kiss on his neck. He reached for her too late. She was gone. She called back over her shoulder, "I'm off to my English class. Think about it," and blew him a kiss.

Think about it? he thought. I don't want to lose my job. But as soon as she was out of sight, he began considering what angles he might work... She certainly was a stunning woman. But she was an unmerciful tease.

To no one's surprise, Royce saw his way clear to the night at the Plaza Hotel. All that was left to argue about was the suite. She insisted on it. "A baroness cannot stay in a mere hotel room."

"We don't have to tell them you are a baroness."

"You think they can't tell by looking at me?" and she passed her bejeweled fingers by his nose.

They took the suite. It was her idea to leave most of the luggage downstairs in the storeroom. "What do we need the luggage for?—with what we're going to be doing?"

The anticipation of his night with Hanna Mazurka nearly killed him. The night itself did kill him—in a manner of speaking. After she plied her consummate skills on him, he was dead to the world. But he had lived as he never imagined he could in his most generous fantasy. And if he did die, he would die a very happy man.

The skill Mr. Saxon felt was Hanna's inborn acting instinct. For her it was a simple matter of trying something until he groaned with pleasure, then doing more of it as though she were experiencing the most exciting time of her life. If that idiot Nadia, her father's child bride, could bring pleasure, Hanna could bring exponentially more.

For her part, Hanna wondered if she would ever be able to do this without thinking of the pigs on the farm, or her father and Nadia in the room next to hers. If she could ever rid her mind of those apparitions, she thought, with the right person, it could be a pleasant experience.

With the prince... Ah, the prince. That would be *paradise*.

Hanna looked at Royce Saxon in the bed beside her. He had on his face a contented grin as big as all outdoors.

"You are the most astonishing lover," he said.

"Thank you kindly, kind sir," she said, and planted a kiss on his forehead.

She waited patiently until he was snoring gently. Hanna prided herself on her patience. Then she slipped quietly and so gently out of the bed, dressed in the sitting room, with the door to the bedroom closed, left her note on the table in the sitting room, and slipped out of the door. Early in the morning, Royce would find the note.

Dearest Royce:

New York has hooked me.
Chicago later. Thanks for everything.

Hanna

Downstairs, she told her premeditated tale about how the gentleman she was with had broken his solemn word and tried to defile her, so she simply must leave the hotel at once. That hotel on Fifth Avenue, just across the corner of Central Park, would suit her, she thought. So she told them at the desk she was going to the Waldorf-Astoria, but to please not tell that awful man.

Her baggage was delivered to a cab at the curb, and she had him drive to the Waldorf, on Park Avenue. There she dismissed him with her bags on the curb—it was now half past two in the morning. When he was out of sight, she hired another cab and took it to the Pierre Hotel, on Fifth Avenue, where a sleepy porter agreed to stash her for the night. She registered under the name Zdenka Oleska, just in case. The dazed porter asked for some identification, but Hanna said it was buried in her luggage and she was dead tired and could bring it in the morning. The way she looked at him, the porter knew he would be unable to deny her anything.

She slept soundly and could only imagine Royce's shock when he found the note. He might well turn the town upside down for her, but it would be tough sledding, she thought. She felt she was being considerate of him not to force a confrontation where she would have to dig in her heels and say "I'm *not* leaving!" No, this way was much more considerate. Men did not like to lose arguments.

The next day, she moved to a suite with a view of Central Park—and the Plaza Hotel, across the corner of the park. She watched out the window, half expecting Royce to come out, balled fists on his hips, looking every which way for her. But it was not to be. Two days later, she called the Plaza, just to be sure, and was told there was no Royce Saxon registered.

The first thing on her agenda was to have a piano installed in her suite so she might practice her singing. The staff treated her with all the deference she had come to expect.

She liked New York. It seemed so vibrant to her. Like she was. The streets were boiling with activity, thick with cabs and pedestrians, and she liked to walk in Central Park and make believe it was her own garden.

The second item on her agenda was hooking up with a theater group. Opera required some acting, so she thought she better get some experience along that line. She auditioned for many groups, but her English was so poor it was difficult to understand her. So she enrolled in a course to improve her English.

And she found a voice teacher. A Mr. Morton, who immediately proclaimed she had ruined her throat with too much singing with faulty technique. She should not be straining her delicate vocal apparatus with demanding opera arias. She should be practicing breathing with proper support for her tones. He recommended she see a doctor—a well-known pathologist by the name of Erik Weidner.

Dr. Weidner's office was on Fifth Avenue, facing Central

Park. She could walk there from her hotel.

The doctor's receptionist was an old crone who passed judgment on Hanna at the instant she opened the door. She found her too pretty to be substantive. There was too much sparkle in the personality for her to be taken seriously.

Nevertheless, Miss Emerson vetted Hanna and her complaint to pass the information on to the doctor. She let her know Dr. Weidner was one of the best known and respected physicians in town, and the visit would not come cheap. She also had the grace to add there were many less respected doctors that might be adequate to Hanna's cause, and she should feel free to consult them if money were an object.

Hanna leveled the crone in her sights. "No, madam," she said, with a chill in her hoarse tone, "I am a baroness. I can pay."

Miss Emerson seemed disappointed.

The waiting room was dark. When she was shown into the doctor's office, that was even darker. The doctor himself seemed dark and brooding, with successful black eyebrows which appeared to cover half his eyes. He wore a black suit, with a white shirt and solid-black tie. Hanna wondered if he was trying to look like a mortician, in a profession that should call for the opposite.

Hanna was disappointed that there seemed no recognition of her as an attractive member of a desirable sex. The doctor barely looked at her. She sat in the chair facing him, though he had not asked her to.

Finally, he glanced at her through his eyebrow thicket, and said, "What seems to be the trouble, young lady?"

She stared at him as though she had expected more. Then she cleared her throat and said, "It's my throat."

He looked at her as though she had said something meaningless. He looked to her as though he was a hundred years old. "What's wrong with it?"

"I'm hoarse. I can't sing right. My teacher said you could help me." But she was beginning to wonder.

He got a thin, wry smile on his face. Hanna was encouraged. "I'm not a singing teacher," he said, and he seemed to think that was funny. Hanna wasn't so sure.

"*Can* you help me?" she asked. "With my throat?" she added.

He opened the middle drawer of his desk and extracted a flat wooden stick. He stood and took a thin flashlight from his pocket. She was surprised at how tall, thin and gaunt he looked—perhaps a hundred was too young.

He stood over her and said, "Open up." She opened her mouth, he laid the stick on her tongue and flashed the light down her throat.

"Hurts, does it?" he asked.

"Argh—" She couldn't speak with the stick on her tongue. He seemed to find that amusing also.

He was taking so long she wondered if he was looking for gold in her throat. Finally, he withdrew the stick and disposed of it in the wastebasket beside his desk. "So?" he said.

"So, what?" she asked.

"Does it hurt?"

"Well, yes, it hurts. Why do you think I'm here?"

He stared at her so hard she began to feel uncomfortable. She shifted her weight in her chair. "Can you help me?" she asked.

"Help you?" He smiled, that thin, enigmatic, maddening smile. "Why do you think I'm here?" he said. He returned to sit at his desk. "How does it feel?"

"My throat? It hurts."

"Scratchy, like a pin is pricking it, hot, raw? What would you say?"

"All of those."

He kept staring at her.

"Well?" she prodded.

"Yes," he said. "I will give you some medicine." And he went off to another room, leaving her alone in the gloom of the interior office. Her eyes roamed the room. There were no personal pictures anywhere. On the wall were his diplomas and awards. He had graduated from a medical school in Vienna in 1889—so if he had been in his twenties, he wasn't a hundred at all. More like fifty. But he looked much older. Maybe he was fifty when he got his medical degree.

The doctor returned with a small bottle in his hand. "Here," he said, handing it to her, "four times a day—I've written it on the label." She looked on the bottle and couldn't read his writing. "And come back a week from today," he said. "I want to check your progress."

What a strange man, she thought as she left his depressing office.

In the week that followed, she couldn't get that gloomy man out of her mind. The way he looked at her was creepy, no other word would describe it. But, she took her medicine and supposed she had to go back. She was not looking forward to it.

That week, she practiced muscular control of her diaphragm to minimize the passage of air through her throat.

When she presented herself at Dr. Weidner's office, she felt much better. Miss Emerson showed no sign of recognition.

That was not the case with Dr. Weidner. His suit had changed to light gray and the tie seemed to have some color in it. The room was still too dark to tell for sure. And the doctor was definitely smiling and not like an undertaker either.

"Sit down, sit down," he said, affably, and she sat, remembering his lack of that courtesy on the first visit. "I have something to show you," he said. She was taken aback, as she expected some question about how her throat was. Instead, he reached into a side drawer in his desk and took out a silver-framed picture of a woman some years older than Hanna. He turned it to face her. "Look at this," he said.

She looked at the picture, not understanding his motive.

"Do you know her?" he asked.

"No," she said.

"Look like anyone you know?" He seemed inordinately pleased with himself.

Hanna frowned. "No," she said, "should it?"

He withdrew the picture from her sight and gazed longingly at it himself. "You don't think she looks like you?"

"Me?" She didn't know if she should be insulted or not. The doctor obviously liked the woman in the picture so Hanna decided not to take offense. "Who is she?" Hanna asked, trying to be a good sport.

"Alma Werfel," he said, "Gustav Mahler's widow."

"Mahler," she said, not wanting to let on she didn't know who he was.

"The symphony conductor," he said, "and composer. But you aren't a New Yorker—I was to marry her," he said, staring at the picture.

"Why didn't you?" she asked.

He looked up from the silver-framed picture, into the eyes of Hanna Mazurka. The longing look on his face made her squirm. "Because, I met you," he said. "Will you marry me?"

"Me?" She was astonished. "*Marry* you?"

"Yes."

"But I don't *know* you."

"Well, we can take care of that. We can start with dinner tonight."

She was about to tell him she was already married, but the idea was so preposterous, why waste her breath? If he had known a symphony conductor, it might not hurt her to get to know him. She laughed easily. "Do you propose to all your patients?" she asked, a twinkle in her slanting eye.

"Just the girls," he said, returning the twinkle with one of his own, which she was surprised to find rather engaging.

She agreed to the dinner and he promised to call at her hotel for her.

She left feeling rather surprisingly buoyant. It wasn't until she was outside that she realized he had not asked about her throat.

On the short walk from the Pierre Hotel across the corner of Central Park to the Plaza Hotel, Dr. Weidner complimented Hanna on her dress and on her English.

Out of the dark and foreboding environment of his office, Dr. Weidner looked surprisingly younger. His step was sprightly, his manner courtly. A smile of appreciation found a home on his face. There was no mistaking him for anything but a happy man.

The mere thought of being in the Plaza Hotel excited Hanna. She'd heard about all the rich people who owned corner suites where they could see the length of Central Park and over to the East River. It was the closest thing she had seen in America to an overblown Russian castle, and any suggestion of royalty reminded her of the prince.

Inside the Plaza Hotel, Hanna was haunted by the fear that her one-time lover, Royce Saxon, would appear and blab the whole story. Once in the Fifty-eighth Street dining room, with a quick inventory of the room, she relaxed a bit. Her eyes swept over the opulence of their surroundings.

Carved, ornate ceilings, teardrop crystal chandeliers, brocade chairs, and enough fabric in the draperies to clothe a small European nation. Dr. Weidner watched her surprise with a satisfied smile. "You approve of my choice of restaurants?"

"Oh, yes."

"You have not been here before?"

"Oh, no," she said, quickly. Well, it *was* true, she thought. By *here* he surely meant the restaurant, not the hotel.

All the waiters were dressed alike. The lines of their black vests and white shirts made Hanna titter.

"What's funny?" her companion asked.

"I was just thinking how the waiters look like penguins."

"Yes, yes," he agreed, looking at their waiter advancing toward them. "How very observant of you."

She smiled. Observant was not yet in her vocabulary, but she would let it pass. It didn't do to make a man think you were too stupid.

The waiter handed her a menu with a flourish. She was surprised at how expensive everything seemed. Littleneck clams were thirty cents, ribs of beef were seventy-five cents, and vegetables were extra, fifty cents for brussels sprouts! She should have known. The suite had cost Royce Saxon fifteen dollars for just the one night. Her head was swimming at the thought of making the right choices from the two pages of finely typed items. She leaned over and put her hand on the doctor's arm.

"Would you be a dear and order for me?"

"It would be a pleasure," he said, flattered. "Is there anything you don't like?"

"Well, if you see anything on there a pig wouldn't eat, I probably wouldn't either." They shared a good laugh.

"You certainly are no pig," he said softly.

"Oh, no? Well, I eat like one."

311

"Then why aren't you fat?" the doctor asked her.

"Oh, but I am. The clothes cover it up."

"I don't believe it."

She smiled and looked at him on a slant. "Perhaps someday you will see for yourself. Hmm?"

"Oh." He held his hand over his heart as though that might slow the pounding. "If I thought I could ever aspire to that ecstasy, I should die a happy man."

"Die? Not you."

"Yes, all of us."

"Oh, well, that. But didn't you propose marriage?"

"I did indeed. The offer will be good in perpetuity."

"Then I should expect you would have an opportunity or two to see the real me."

"Ah—"

"Fat."

"I *refuse* to believe it."

The doctor ordered with magisterial care. When the courses began arriving, Hanna said, "I'm so glad I let you order, everything is delicious. Why, I do believe it's almost worth the money."

"The money?" He waved a hand. "I have more than I can spend. If you would allow me to bestow a little on you, it would give me a great pleasure."

Hanna smiled like a bashful pixie. The pleasure would be mine, she thought.

He felt warm in her presence. Warm and secure. He thought she would be surprised to hear that: a fifty-year-old doctor in a practice that included all the financial and social titans of New York could be insecure. He could look in their eyes, ears, noses and throats, thump their bellies with his fingers, even examine them naked, but to him it felt no more important than had he been an automobile mechanic ministering to worn-out engines.

He had made a lot of money. People, he discovered, would pay anything in the pursuit of health. He had made so much money he often didn't send bills to his wealthiest patients, and that not only astonished them, it endeared him to them, and he knew if he ever needed anything, he could call upon an Astor, a Vanderbilt, a Harriman anytime and not be turned away. It gave him a secure feeling—as Hanna did tonight.

And he told her as much. Hanna was always careful to make it appear she was blasé about money.

Dr. Weidner was staring in frank admiration at his dinner guest. "She lived across the street here," he said mysteriously, waving his hand in the direction of Fifth Avenue.

"Who?"

"Alma Mahler—the woman you remind me of so much."

"Oh, the woman you want to marry," she teased him.

He tightened his lips and shook his head. "No more," he said, looking as deep into her eyes as he did with his ophthalmoscope. "Tell me all about yourself," he said with a soft, seductive voice.

"There is so little to tell," she said, dropping her eyes in abject modesty. "I am a simple Polish girl from the town of Brest Litovsk. I went to a stern Catholic girls' school, met a handsome prince, married a baron, and have come to New York to pursue my opera career."

"Opera? Well, my goodness, I must take you to the Met. My patients are always foisting tickets off on me. It would give me pleasure to take someone who actually enjoys opera. I myself fall asleep."

"Shame on you," she said.

"If you will go with me, you can keep me awake." Then, as though the fact that she was married just registered, he said, "So where is this baron?"

She sniffled and looked away, then, as if overcoming a strong emotion, said, "He is in a TB sanitarium in Switzerland."

"Ah, is he very ill?"

She nodded. "I don't know if he is alive or not. He was very weak the last I saw him."

Dr. Weidner shook his head. "Too bad," he said in a tone he hoped did not belie his hope for the poor man's speedy demise. He slid quickly off the subject. "It was uncanny, you coming in like that. I was stunned," he explained. "I wasn't myself. I must have seemed odd to you."

She smiled and cocked her head. "I like odd," she said.

"It must have been fate," he said. "Do you believe in fate?"

"I don't know."

"In karma?"

"What is karma?"

"A Buddhist belief that your soul is destined for a certain something. That's your karma—fate, destiny—you can't escape it."

"Buddhism, that is a religion I do not understand. I do not believe that we have no control over our fate."

"No?" he asked earnestly. "I used to think we controlled our destiny—until you came into my office when you did."

"Why is that?"

"My wife is gone. She died just five months now. I thought I could get over it. But I am a lonely old man."

"You aren't old."

"No? Fifty—look at me. Don't I look seventy?"

"No."

"Well, you flatter me, and I appreciate it. But I must tell you I am not a well man. If you marry me, you won't have to put up with me long. Five years at the most."

"Doctor!"

"No, it is my field. I am good at my field. I know, and there is nothing so terrible as a doctor kidding himself. I have two children, who ignore me, and I go home every night to an empty apartment."

Hanna was chewing a piece of lamb chop while he spoke. But she didn't take her eyes off him. Rapt attention was one of her endearing traits.

"I would just love to have someone worthy to leave my money and my property to. Will you give at least some thought to making this old man happy in his last days?"

"But that is nonsense. You do not look like a dying man."

"No? But then you aren't a doctor, are you? If you were, I could show you my x-rays. But enough gloom. I find you irresistibly enchanting. How could I hope to enchant you—however slightly?"

"But you do enchant me."

He looked at her through half-closed, skeptical eyes. "Your singing," he said. "How can I help you with that?"

"But you already have," she said. "You cured my throat without even looking at it a second time."

He smiled and bobbed his head. "You could talk," he said. "It is very common. Time heals all."

"Ah, so it will heal you also."

"You are wonderful," he said. "You must sing for me."

"Oh, no," she said, blushing. "I couldn't do that."

"Why not? You are going to sing before huge audiences, why not me?"

"That is different," she said. "That is impersonal. If I sang alone for a friend, I would be frightened to death."

"Well, then, if I can't hear you sing, what can I do for you?"

"But why would you want to do anything? I am a stranger to you."

"No, I am getting to know you. I fell in love with you the moment I met you. I said to myself, there is the woman I shall marry. You have already brought sunshine to the twilight of my life."

"How sweet you are."

"No, it is all thanks to your beauty. You cannot fail on any stage. People will come just to feast their eyes on your incredible beauty."

"My, but you are a flatterer."

"You shall see, I have a patient who is a professional photographer. Tomorrow I shall make an appointment for you. He will take many pictures. We will circulate them. You will see what effect your beauty has. I expect you will be onstage before the pictures are dry. Then we will get the best teacher in town."

"I have a teacher."

"No, no, not a teacher, the *best* teacher. Whoever teaches the stars, that is who you must have. It will give some purpose to my life," he said, "seeing your career blossom."

"But," she said, with a wide-eyed innocence., "why would you do this for me?"

"Because," he said, "I am going to marry you."

For the moment, Hanna could not think of a convincing rebuttal.

When Hanna got back to her room, she wrote to Alexi to ask for a divorce. They had grown apart, she said, it was no one's fault, but she was becoming settled in America and she didn't see how she could interrupt the great strides she was making in her career to return anytime soon to Switzerland. Then, too, the war and the revolution in Russia had made things so difficult, and she just couldn't imagine what his prospects might be without his barony to fall back on. She would be a burden. He needed a wife with money, she said, without mentioning she had the same requirements for a spouse, or that she now had *his* money.

The doctor had been a perfect gentleman when he saw her to her door.

He proffered her a sedate good-night and overflowing gratitude, and a promise to get in touch with her tomorrow about the photographer.

After sealing the letter to Alexi in Switzerland (she didn't want to risk changing her mind), she thought about how kind and gentle Dr. Weidner was and how comfortable she felt in his undemanding company. And what girl wouldn't be flattered by all his attention, compliments, and marriage proposal? True, he was over twice her age, but age to her was wisdom and experience—and financial stability and career contacts. She thought she was lucky to have found such an obliging man so soon after she landed.

And marriage, so unthinkable at its first mention, now seemed less impossible. There would be virtually automatic citizenship, of course, not to be taken lightly in this day and age. A lot of girls had to do a lot more for a lot less.

And Dr. Weidner was as good as his word. He not only set up (and paid for) the mega-photography session, he got her the best voice coach in New York.

The proofs arrived from her photo session, and though Dr. Weidner thought they were dazzling, Hanna wasn't satisfied. They didn't do her justice, she said, and she asked for another session.

The photographer, who thought he had worked miracles, was temperamentally unwilling to repeat the artistic process, and another photographer was found (presumably the *second*-best man in town). There, with Hanna selecting her own outfits and jewels, the session yielded results more to her liking, though Dr. Weidner could not discern any difference.

"I hope you'll hang on to the first batch too," he said. "You might change your mind in years to come. They could come in handy, if only for variety."

"But they are so unflattering," she said, but kept them anyway.

In the following days there was no flagging in Dr. Weidner's assiduous attention and genteel courtship. And he asked for nothing in return other than to be in her company—and for her to consider marriage. And with each passing day—and dazzling evening at the finest restaurants, the opera, the theater—her resistance wore away. When she asked herself the question, what's in it for me? the answers flooded so thick and fast she thought she would drown. He was a generous man, rich, well-thought-of by the best people, so well-connected, and if what he said were true, she would be a widow before she was thirty—a *rich* widow. (Heaven forbid, she was gracious enough to tell herself, but the thought stayed with her.) A girl had to consider what kind of life she would have, married to an older man who lived forever. Bedridden, reducing his wife to a bedpan slave. No thank you, she thought, I'm too young. But five years, maybe less, she thought she could take. He really *was* a dear man. None of the abrasiveness of her baron. Not as handsome as the prince, but handsome enough. There were no butterflies in her heart like there still were when she thought of the prince—it wasn't a romantic thing, but Dr. Weidner so transparently adored her, she couldn't help feeling good in his presence.

It was after one of those tragic operas that ends with dead lovers all over the stage, *Carmen* maybe or *Romeo and Juliet*, she couldn't remember which, that she began to think about the tragedy of death when it separated two lovers. She was actually thinking about Erik—Dr. Weidner had long since insisted she call him Erik—"Makes me feel young—in your league, rather than like the grandfather figure I am."

She gave him a hug and called him Erik henceforth. And she could see the transformation in him from that simple act. It made him young again, almost giddy. And from that day on, she began to picture herself as Mrs. Erik Weidner, and though at first it seemed awkward, in time she grew to accept and occasionally *like* the idea.

Erik often spoke of their marriage as a foregone conclusion, but he never pressured her. She would smile and make some endearing retort that let him know what a foolish idea it was and yet not slam the door on the concept.

"What would a rich and famous doctor like you want with a plain, poor Polish girl like me?" she would ask, and that would send him into a rhapsody on how his world revolved around her sun and how, without her, he would be in complete darkness—like the backside of the moon.

And she would laugh at that backside vision. "Sometimes," she said, crinkling her nose, "your English is as funny as mine."

"Ah, yes, but my German is better. *Besser*," he said.

"Yes, I have almost no German. Thanks to goodness they didn't win the war. I couldn't learn another language. Already I have so many my head is spinning."

In the cab on the way home from the weekend performance of *Tosca*, Hanna said to Erik, "Phew, so much dying for love. I think it is better to live for love than to die. Don't you?"

"Amen," he said. Then his eyes got that rheumy look they did when he was going to say something syrupy. "I live for your love," he said in a trance.

He was obviously thinking of a different definition of love than she was. In all this time, he had been a perfect gentleman. *Too* perfect. She wondered if there were something wrong with him—or *her*.

He paid the cab and walked her to her door as he always did—and he always saw her inside, but never asked to come in.

Tonight, she surprised him. "Come in for a minute—will you?"

His heart jumped up in his throat and pounded so hard a dozen symptoms of diseases ran through his head.

"Well," she said, examining his dumbstruck face, "cat got your tongue?"

"What? Oh, yes, yes, he does. Cat, yes. *Yes!* I will come in," he said. "Thank you for asking."

She smiled and unlocked the door. "You must pardon the mess, please," she said, sweeping into the parlor of her suite.

"Very nice," Erik said, his eyes traveling around the room full of flower patterns.

"Yes, I just love flowers, don't you?"

"Flowers?" He had never given them any thought. "Oh, yes, flowers. Lovely."

"Well, sit down, won't you? Can I get you anything?"

"Oh, no thank you—I mean, yes, I will sit with pleasure. I don't need anything else."

"Sure? A nice glass of water perhaps?"

"Oh, no. My goodness, you have a suite. I had no idea."

"Well, of course, what do you think? You wouldn't expect me to invite a gentleman into my bedroom, would you?" She looked at him through a cocked eye he didn't understand. Was she toying with

319

him? Was she in fact inviting him into her bedroom? He was very uncomfortable.

He sat on the couch covered with cabbage roses. She sat beside him and patted his knee. "You know, you have the most beautiful eyes I have ever seen," she said. "Really! I would not lie to you."

"Why, thank you." He was pleased, but he wished his heart would slow down.

They sat in silence for some moments, each waiting for the other to say something. Finally Erik seemed to realize there was an emptiness about the room that needed filling. "And you are the most beautiful woman I have ever seen."

"Oh, pooh," she said. "You flatterer."

"No, I'm not," he insisted. "I am such a lucky man. I don't know how I could be any luckier."

"You don't?" she teased him, but he didn't understand. She crossed her legs and the swish of material kept his heart pounding. She began swinging her foot back and forth.

He looked longingly into her bright eyes, and reached over for her hand. She gave it to him. They held hands in silence.

"Did you like the opera?" she asked.

"Oh, I suppose. I am not such a big opera fan. I go for you."

"You're so sweet. But do you think people would actually die for love that way?"

"The way I feel now, I could die for your love. But for me, that is not so much. I am dying for your love in any case."

"Oh, pooh, there you go again. How long has it been since you spoke of marriage?"

It was as though he didn't hear her at first. Then he seemed to have trouble understanding what she was saying, then what she meant, then how to take it. "Marriage?" he sputtered. "But I have made you a standing offer. You aren't telling me that you would accept my humble proposal?"

In response, she squeezed his hand.

"Dare I to *dream* that you would accept me? My life would finally take on a real meaning. I would devote myself to your happiness."

"Oh, pooh—your life has abundant meaning." She paused, lifting his hand to her lips and kissing it lightly. "I love you," she murmured.

"Oh," he trembled, putting his arm around her shoulder. "I promise you, I will do anything in my power to make you happy. Will you—would you marry me?"

She leaned into him, feeling the pounding of his heart and trying to understand how she could excite him so. Then she wondered if it were good for him to be so excited. She backed off. "I don't know how any girl could think she could be so fortunate to get you for her husband."

"Now, now," he said, "you are far too extravagant in your thoughts of me. And too modest. For an old man like me to have a young and vital, beautiful wife like you—it would be a dream come true."

"For me too," she said, and leaned back into his chest.

He stroked her hair and said, "The finest silk in the world would never feel anything like this."

"You say the nicest things," she purred.

He seemed to wake from his dream. He straightened on the couch. "Do you mean you accept my proposal? Oh, could I dare to hope...?"

"Yes," she said, "dare to hope. But, I would only ask a few questions?"

"Anything!"

"Well," she said, taking his hand and drawing circles on the back of it with her finger, "what about your children—won't they be angry?"

"Angry? Why should they be? They pay me no attention."

"But won't they be afraid I will take their inheritance?"

"And I expect you shall. Of course, I would leave them something—a token—I wouldn't feel right cutting them out altogether, and the lawyers would no doubt advise against it."

"Do you have a lawyer?"

"Of course."

"I don't have a lawyer."

He laughed. "Why would you want a lawyer?"

"Well, there is the small matter of my divorce."

"Oh, yes, well, certainly my lawyer will handle that for you. Have you heard from the baron?"

"Not yet. Transatlantic mail can be painfully slow."

"Yes. You wouldn't expect him to contest the divorce, would you?"

"Nnnooo."

"You mean he might?"

"Anything is possible."

"But you don't still love him?"

"Oh, no. That is over. I never loved him like I love you."

He hugged her close to him. "You make an old man feel young again."

"While we are speaking of a lawyer, I am so dumb about these things, but I should feel so much better if you would allow me to speak to a lawyer about marriage in the United States."

He chuckled. "Well, if you want, but it's pretty straightforward—much like a marriage anywhere else."

"Yes, I imagine. But—forgive me for bringing it up—you are talking about dying—and heaven forbid that should happen before your time. But if it did, I would have to be thoughtful about what would happen to me. I am just a poor Polish girl who will have been already twice married, and I have no idea what would become of me if I were left penniless." This last she pronounced with a Dickensian tug at the heartstrings while she looked worshipfully into his big, dark eyes.

He smiled—then chuckled again.

"What are you laughing at?" she asked in mock pain.

"Poor Polish girl," he said, nodding. "Staying at a suite in the Pierre. A baroness! I do notice you aren't at the YWCA, where the poor American girls are."

"Are you making fun of me?"

"Oh, no—no, no, dearest. I could never do that."

"Because if you are, we should stop discussing marriage."

"No, please."

"I only have these questions. You must take me seriously or I can't take you seriously.

"No, no—please. What else?"

"I would have to have an understanding about my career. I will not give it up. If you are the jealous type who expects his wife to sit at his feet all day—and look up worshipfully into his eyes all the time—that is not me."

"No, dear, of course not. I might have liked that when I was your age, but I am mellower now. I don't need constant excitement and stimulation. It wouldn't be good for me anyway."

"I might have to leave for a time to tour with an opera company. I don't know if that will happen, but I am investigating some possibilities. I would have to have freedom to take my opportunities as they arise."

"Of course," he said.

She stopped. "It sounds like I ask too much," she said.

"No, no," he argued. "I understand."

"No, I am finally listening to myself babble on here. Before, I am talking but not listening. Now I listen and I sound like an awful child. Telling you I want this, and I must have that, and never stopping to ask what you want."

His eyes swelled up like full moons, his lips trembled.

"You," he said. "All I want is you."

The smile of unconditional victory broke out on her face and she kissed him like he had never been kissed in his life—and he knew at that moment he would agree to anything she asked.

And she knew it too.

The bargain was made and sealed, but only with a kiss. Dr. Weidner explained, to Hanna's disappointment, that he wouldn't seek any intimate favors until the wedding ring was firmly on her finger.

Now that the engagement was official, Hanna found she had much to do. She had briefly questioned if she could be engaged to one man while still married to another, but Erik had told her that was what lawyers were for, and had arranged for her to see attorney Felix Barton in his office a few blocks down on Fifth Avenue.

Attorney Barton was a crusty old gentleman who catered to the carriage trade and was frank to tell you he didn't know what this modern world was coming to. To Felix Barton, Hanna Mazurka *was* the modern world. A young woman changing her name to be on the stage was still unthinkable to him. He couldn't get over his suspicion that she must be hiding something.

She sat in his office, which she found stuffy and not at all imposing. The man himself did not impress her either. He had a belly that no amount of tailor's art could hide, but even worse, no attempt was made to hide it. He wore a brown suit and vest and the bottom buttons on the vest were unbuttoned to make room for the belly. He had some gray hairs left, but not enough to completely cover a dandruff-flaky head.

He started out lecturing her. "Now, young lady, I want you to know Dr. Weidner is one of my dearest friends. He is widely known and respected in these parts. He has asked me to represent you in your divorce, as well as to satisfy any of your needs and desires before your marriage to him." He looked down his nose at Hanna and she was beginning to resent his tone.

"I'll say this for you, young lady, you have a colossal nerve— but Dr. Weidner is so smitten with you he told me to give you anything you want. I argued, of course; he has children who will scream bloody murder and drag us through the courts when the time comes, but the doctor turns a deaf ear. You must be *some* sorceress! So let's get right to it. What *do* you want?"

Hanna shifted her body from his accusative stare. She took out a handkerchief from her purse and used it to buy time, pretending to wipe some tears that weren't there. She wondered if old Barton were jealous of her fiancé.

"I...I don't know," she said. "I'm here for advice—for help with my divorce, for some understanding of how I am to live if anything should happen to Erik—God forbid!"

Barton nodded with his own brand of understanding.

"I'm afraid you are treating me like I was some heartless gold digger. Perhaps if you are not happy about my engagement, I should ask Erik for another lawyer."

"You may suit yourself on that score," he said. "Though by your presence here you must know I am willing to work with you at his behest. Many, I daresay, would not."

"It's not what you think," she said, sniffling into her handkerchief.

"Oh, put that thing away," he said, waving at her in a manner she thought was decidedly contemptuous. "Be all that as it may, what do you want?"

"Advice—help."

"I'm talking money," he said.

"What would you suggest?"

"Me? I would suggest you don't marry him. Where is the call for such audacity? A girl like you—he could be your grandfather! Keep him company if you like—but why marriage? I'm sure he would make the same financial arrangement."

"Mr. Barton!" she snapped, "*he* wants to marry me. I have been very reluctant for all the reasons you harbor and more! Now, I come here because he suggested I should." She laid an accusative stare on him. "Now either we understand each other, or I call the whole thing off."

Attorney Barton looked at her with newfound admiration. "Very impressive, Madame Mazurka, very impressive indeed. I think I can fairly say we certainly *do* understand each other. Now then, here is what I am prepared to offer you. The house on Fifth Avenue is worth perhaps four hundred thousand. On top of that, you may choose any of his personal belongings and one hundred thousand in cash. They would be willed to you—in case you are still his wife when he dies."

She looked blankly at him.

"Understand, Dr. Weidner is not a wealthy man. He is well-off, yes, but he is too modest about charging for his services—as I, by the way, am not—to have any real money. This bequest will leave around one hundred thousand for each of his children." He paused for a reaction. It was still blank. "What do you say?" he asked.

"Make it two hundred thousand cash," she said without blinking.

He smiled and nodded. "Yes, sir," he said. "You are *really* something."

She gave him the particulars about her marriage and added that she often wondered if it was really legal—from the look of the judge who performed it, she wouldn't be surprised if he had taken the money, without bothering to record the marriage papers.

Felix Barton said he would look into it. "But this will take some time," he said. "Dealing with foreign countries is slow." He shook his head. "With Russia, after a revolution, it could be forever. I suggest you try to work through your husband, get a consent decree from him. It would make it a lot simpler."

"I've tried. I haven't heard from him."

"Well, try again," he said.

Within the next week, she got her response from the Swiss sanitarium.

Dear Baroness Chotznic:

> I am saddened to tell you of the passing of Baron Chotznic on Tuesday last. He received your letter the Friday before, and thenceforth refused all sustenance. Death was recorded at 4:18 a.m.

> I have taken the liberty of enclosing your seriously overdue statement, in the hopes we may look for some payment from you. Unfortunately, this is a private institution and we are dependent on the goodwill and integrity of our patients' families. Would you be so kind?

She folded the letter and let it sit on her lap while she replayed in her mind memories of her courtship and marriage to the baron. She tried to think of happy moments, but had trouble recalling any. Most of her thoughts of the baron had a way of leading to longing thoughts of the prince. How, she wondered, would the prince take her second marriage? Certainly he would understand she had to do *something*. She couldn't live indefinitely on her jewels.

The wedding of the doctor and the baroness took place in his living room, with a New York jurist who took his responsibility more seriously than the clown in rural Russia. Lawyer Barton stood in as the witness, at Dr. Weidner's urging, and against his wishes. Neither of Weidner's children attended, though both were invited. Lawyer Barton was right, they were both aghast.

On their wedding night, in his bed, Hanna discovered why her doctor had been so "considerate" of her virtue and reticent about lovemaking. The poor man was close to impotent, and her magical powers did not avail her.

He apologized. "You are just too much for me. My wife didn't care about it. I don't even remember how we were able to conceive children—perhaps she did it without me."

"Erik! You don't think…?"

"Oh, no, she had no interest in those things. You are a godsend. I must regain my virility. I see if anyone can ever make me do it, you can. I love you. Hanna, please be patient."

"Oh pooh," she said. "You're fine. Don't worry—it will come."

"I am *so* lucky," he said, then seemed to fall off to sleep, only to be jolted by a racking cough. It seemed interminable, and Hanna was alarmed. When it finally subsided, he said, "I'm sorry. Too much excitement for this decrepit body. Can you forgive me?"

"Yes," she could forgive him, but she was unable to sleep because of the raucous, bombarding coughing.

In the morning the maid brought the morning newspapers to the honeymoon couple's bedchamber. Hanna was shocked and distraught to read what she considered several unflattering accounts of her marriage. There were snide comments about their age difference, her national origin, they even found fun in the Russian Baron as though he were somehow an impostor or worse, that she had made up the whole thing.

"Why do they *do* this?" she fumed. "What business of theirs is our life?"

"Oh, darling," he said, soothingly, "don't pay any attention to them. They are poor souls writing for poor souls with nothing better to do."

"But, it's so *unfair!*"

He nodded sympathetically, then shrugged.

That night Dr. Weidner's cough seemed to worsen. At his suggestion on the third night, she moved into another room. But sleep there did not come much easier. Soon she began to shiver at the first fusillade, which tore through her like machine-gun bullets. Then she could hear him moaning in agony and she thought she would have to do something to preserve her sanity.

Fortuitously for Hanna, at that time her voice coach was at the end of his rope with her. He too was a fan and friend of Dr.

Weidner's and wanted to do nothing to upset that icon. The doctor had saved the teacher's fiancée's life and he was unable to say no to the doctor. But he had found Hanna virtually unteachable and it was frustrating for him to battle her thick head every day. Besides, he never knew what to say to the doctor when he asked how she was progressing. He spoke of her beauty, her iron will, her perseverance, anything but her vocal ability. Cuba seemed the perfect solution, he told the doctor. "She will gain much-needed experience and it will be fun for her too. Who knows, it might even get it out of her system."

"Oh, I doubt that," the doctor said.

I'm afraid you're right, the teacher thought.

Hanna had mentioned the possibility of her "getting my feet wet in opera." She told her teacher of Royce Saxon's mentioning a company in Havana, and he seized the idea like a lifesaver. "It would be so good for you," he agreed (and me too, he thought), "but it costs money—and is so far from home."

"Oh, I can get a ship and be there in no time. I love to sail."

She was so happy at the prospect, Dr. Weidner couldn't say no. All he could hope was that she wouldn't like Cuba or the director or something and would come home and be content to be by his side.

But it was not to be. She *loved* Cuba and working with a real company—learning the business from the ground up. She adored her director and he seemed keen on offering her ever increasing responsibilities with the company.

For his part, Dr. Weidner kept sending cash to keep his wife happy and living in the style to which she had become accustomed (no small thanks to him) as well as ample infusions of cash to keep the company afloat. All this arrived with poetic letters about Hanna being his star, moon, sun and galaxy.

> When I look to the heavens, I see only you—I
> live for the day you come back to me—
> I long for your embrace. I cannot look at a
> tree without thinking of the unadulterated joy you
> have brought to my bleak life.

329

Each letter seemed to top the last in flights of poetic fancy. His confessions of loneliness were heartrending in the extreme.

Hanna was having such a good time and was so busy, she was unable to answer all his letters—but she wrote when she could. And she never asked for money without sending along a brief, but newsy, note of her activities.

Opera was such fun.

Hanna spent Christmas and the New Year in Havana. The weather was so much better than New York, she told Erik in a letter asking for another fifteen hundred dollars, which he sent with his love.

She worked as a stagehand, super, chorister, stage manager, prompter; as promised, from the ground up. And she had never been happier. After eight months, she was given a small role and she played it to the hilt. And she was a hit with the small audience, the way she strutted onstage as though the whole company belonged to her (which in a way it did). She wore her most striking, some thought outlandish, jewels, a necklace so heavy with gems more than one spectator wondered on how she could keep her head up. But her engaging personality flew over the footlights, and her dramatic exit following her brief stint on the boards brought down the house. Stardom, she felt, was in her blood, and no amount of transfusions would take it out. She got so many raves, her feet didn't return to the ground for several days.

Her future was unalterably set; her career was on the path to fame and fortune. She had never been so excited in her life. All through her brief performance, she had imagined she was playing to the prince.

After the performance, she could not sleep in the suite her dear husband had hired for her at Havana's dearest hotel. She decided to share her excitement—with Katrina and, she hoped, the prince.

Dear Katrina:

> I am *so* excited. I have just performed my first large role with the Havana Opera Company and I must say (modestly!!!) I was a sensation. I think of you and the prince often, and he, being such an opera lover, I thought would be interested in my news. Of course, my goal is to return to Paris and perform there. I am working toward that goal daily with every fiber of my being.
>
> Please write me c/o Havana Opera Company, The Grand Hotel, Havana, Cuba. I'd love to hear the latest news from you and the prince.
>
> With warm affection for you both,
> Hanna Mazurka

The next day at rehearsal, the entire company applauded her when she arrived. She acknowledged the plaudits with an exaggerated curtsy, and after the rehearsal the director asked her for more money.

"Already? It seems yesterday I wrote for fifteen hundred."

"That was a month ago. Opera companies are expensive business. You see the size of the audience. Ticket sales barely pay for the costumes and props. We can save by cutting back, of course, but that would first affect our wonderful trainees, and that would be, in my mind, a tragedy—especially in light of your absolute triumph last night."

"Yes," she agreed. "They *did* seem to like me." She paused and tried to search for the most effective words. "I wonder, do you see any singing parts for me in the near future?"

The opera managing director was nothing if not a pragmatist. He knew about butter and bread, and which side had the fat. "You have developed so nicely," he said, "I would not be surprised to find you in a small singing role in the not-too-distant future—assuming we are still solvent."

"*How* distant a future?" she pressed.

"Not too long—"

"Specifically," she said. "If I have to ask my dear husband for more money, I have to tell him something about what his investment is buying. He is such a dear man, I cannot keep asking for thousands if I am to stay in bit parts."

The director sighed. He was buying time.

Hanna understood. "My husband is not a well man. Perhaps someday I shall inherit. Then I shall be in the market for a company that is able to give me parts. You understand."

He nodded gravely, but not without a certain salivation at the thought of that much gold coming their way. "How sick is he?"

"Sick," she said. "Every day I am myself in agony because I should be by his bedside. I must return to him soon. How much more money would be required for me to sing a part in the next production?"

The director smacked his lips. Hanna thought that uncouth, but she wanted an answer.

"Two thousand," he said.

"I'll see what I can do."

That night, she wrote to her beloved husband to share her triumph with him and explain that the two thousand she was requesting was her last request before she came home to be with her true love. This would guarantee her the singing part she had always aspired to, and if the audience reaction to her walk-on was any indication, she might just break into the New York companies, and be closer to her beloved.

The two thousand came by return mail, with a note.

My dearest jewel:

The news of your coming home has glad-
dened my heart beyond my soul's comprehension. I
knew you would be a star on the opera stage because
you are the only star in my heavens.

I am so lonely without you. I live for the day I
may embrace you once again.

Sleep well, my sweet.

He rarely signed his letters, feeling that was somehow
immodest.

When Hanna delivered the money to the director, she said,
"Here it is. Where is my music?" He looked longingly at the check,
kissed it, then kissed her on the cheek and took his briefcase from
the seat beside him in the theater and handed her a score. "Here,"
he said. "It's going to take some work, but—" he shrugged his shoulders, "you brought home the bacon."

She didn't like the sound of that—it seemed to her to lack
refinement, but she soon buried herself in the score and began working feverishly on the part.

During her first run-through with the accompanist, Hanna
seemed frightened, hoarse and without confidence. She managed to
sing the words, but the notes were only approximated, without clarity
and resonance. She had the vocal prowess of an infirm robin.

Hanna struggled to improve her singing, fought valiantly,
practiced diligently. The dress rehearsal was a fiasco. Afterwards, the
director spoke to her like a Dutch uncle. "Hanna, you have a stout
heart," he said. "The whole troupe is pulling for you when you sing,
you can just feel it. But putting you on the spot like this in your first
singing part may be premature. Hilda has sung this role many times.
She could step in if you want to give it more time—develop your
voice a little more—make it stronger."

Hanna was staring at the director while he spoke—in a barely
suppressed rage. When he ended, almost apologetically, she gave

him a stare that would have melted a lesser man.

"No," she said, with an admirable finality. "I got you the two thousand, now you keep your end of the bargain."

"Yes," he sighed, exasperated, "I am not asking you to relinquish the part for all time, I only thought to give you the opportunity to buy some time."

"I have already bought all the time I plan to," Hanna said. "You say Hilda can sing it—but Hilda is a cow. She has no stage presence. When she gets on the stage, you can't wait for her to get off. When I am on the stage, it is a triumph."

"Yes, yes, I agree," the director replied hastily. "For stage presence, you can't be beat. Nobody, *anybody* in the company. But the singing voice…" he held out his hands in hopelessness, "it needs work. I only sought to save you from embarrassment."

"I will not take any more of these insults!" she screeched, turned on her heels and stormed out of the auditorium.

Good, the director thought. Perhaps she is angry enough to keep her from coming tonight and ruining the performance.

Wrong. Hanna was there on time in costume and makeup, ready, yea, raring to go, as though there had been no discussion. She was bedecked in jewels again, but this time the director spoke to her. "Hanna, you are playing a peasant girl. Do you think she would have all these jewels?"

"I am not playing a peasant girl," she said. "This is Madame *Hanna Mazurka* playing a peasant girl. My audience has certain expectations from me which I must fulfill."

And when her time came, she went on stage with the look of a world-renowned diva in yet another triumphal role. There was a gasp from the audience when she appeared, then applause, for even the newcomers had the sense that they were in the presence of a great star.

Until she began to sing. Or tried to. She planted her feet, center stage, and opened her mouth wide, but nothing came out. The orchestra played on as though nothing were amiss. The audience began to titter, then laugh. The director signaled for more volume from the orchestra to drown out the laughter.

Two days later, Hanna Mazurka was on a ship back to New York. Her husband would be glad to see her. *He* appreciated her.

335

Erik Weidner was as happy as he could ever remember being at the prospect of seeing his wife again. He was in a dramatically weakened condition, but he would not hear of staying home and letting James pick her up at the dock alone. The doctor wore a tattered Oxford-gray overcoat that had seen better decades. It had about it the faint but annoying odor of mothballs. He walked slowly, with the aid of a cane, was noticeably thinner (he had lost over thirty pounds), and breathed with greater difficulty—still, he would not miss her homecoming for anything in the world. Hanna had been gone almost a year of their year-and-a-half marriage, and her husband was eager to get to know her all over again.

When she came down the gangplank, in her derby hat, with her mink coat open just enough to show a silken green dress, and the dim sunlight caught the prisms of her diamonds, Erik felt again the pounding heart he always did when she was close to him. She smiled and waved when she saw him, and he raised his hand in a powerless gesture. The smile on his face, she thought, was heartfelt but wan. When they met they hugged, and the doctor tried for a few moments to choke back his sobs of happiness, but was finally unable to do so. He held on to her to keep from drowning in his tears.

"Oh, my baby," he said over and over.

"Oh, darling, it is good to see you," she said. "Are you feeling well?"

"Now that I am holding you, I could lift this ship out of the water."

"Oh, you flatterer."

"But when you are gone..." He shook his head, without completing the thought.

Finally, when she thought she was about to suffocate, Hanna freed herself from his bear hug and from the unsavory smell of his breath. It was, she told herself, the smell of death.

He held her hand tightly in the car and did not let go until they were inside his Fifth Avenue house. He asked her softly if she would come to bed with him, "And just hold me. I don't know if I can offer you anything more, but I have thought of almost nothing these many months but what it feels like to have you hold me."

His fervid attentions, which she had found so charming initially, were getting on her nerves. There was no doubt he had become frailer, but his spirit of ardor had not faded, and that seemed annoyingly contradictory. Did he actually think she could find him attractive in his condition?

"It's the least I can do," she said, and they lay down on the bed, in their clothes. "Can we take these things off?" he asked meekly.

"It is so cold," she said, and he was hit with a coughing attack that sent a shiver down her spine.

"You need a doctor," she said, releasing her arm from his shoulder.

"I *am* a doctor," he reminded her.

337

"Yes, but someone to tell you what to do."

He shook his head sadly. "There is *nothing* to do. My condition is irreversible. You will soon be a rich widow."

"I don't want to be a widow, poor or rich," she snapped. "Do not talk so."

"But, baby, I told you I had at most five years. Almost two are already gone. You are not surprised?"

She put her finger on his lips. "No more of that," she said, and they lay there entwined—amid Erik's sporadic bouts of coughing.

She turned her head away. "Are you sure that is not contagious?"

He nooded his head. "Let me undress you," he pleaded.

"But, Erik." She intercepted his hands with hers. "In your condition, this could not be good for you."

He grinned at the ineffectual rebuff. "Nothing better," he said with grim determination as he lifted her dress and gazed at her naked perfection. "Just what the doctor ordered."

It was the least she could do.

On subsequent nights, Hanna's husband deteriorated before her eyes. Not only did his coughing increase in volume and intensity, but he groaned in agony, and one time Hanna went into his room in response to an animalistic shriek, only to find him face down on the floor, clawing at the Oriental rug like a demented cat. She sank to her knees and held him. She was startled at the gaunt, desperate look on his face, as though he were a man who had seen death.

Then, just as suddenly, his condition would seem to improve—which gave her an uneasy sense of calm.

Then one morning, a month or so after her arrival, she read a notice in the paper that Ken Maxwell was in town, staying at the Plaza Hotel. The idea of the Chicago Opera angel stimulated her imagination to a full gallop. This was the man Royce Saxon had told her about. The man of enormous wealth who was single-handedly keeping afloat the Chicago Opera Company, much as *she* (and her doctor husband, of course) had supported the Havana Opera. She and Maxwell would have much in common. But how to gain entrée would not be as simple. After much agonizing, Hanna decided the frontal approach would be best. It was the quickest and she would have an early answer, but also time to work around a negative response. She called the hotel and asked for him. And to her surprise, he answered the phone himself and said, "Maxwell here."

Hanna swallowed, then unleashed her feminine charms. "Hello, Mr. Maxwell. You do not know me and more's the pity I don't know you, but I would like to. I am Hanna Mazurka, an opera singer, and I call you to get into your Chicago Opera Company. I hear many good things about it, and I would like to be part of it."

"Well, thank you," he said, as though he were so glad she had called. "I'm sorry, but I am on my way back to Chicago. Otherwise I would like to meet you."

His surprising graciousness encouraged her. "When are you leaving for Chicago?"

"In about an hour—"

"Well, I could come to your hotel right now," she said, not disguising her eagerness. "I don't need much time—just a minute to introduce myself."

"Look, I'll give you my Chicago address. You can write me. I will be back in town sometime. Perhaps we can meet then. What is your background with opera?"

"Well, I am Polish. As you can tell, my English is not so wonderful. I have training in Europe—in Russia—as well as Paris and now in New York. I have recently been performing with the Havana Opera Company."

"Havana?" he asked. "In Cuba?"

"Yes."

"I'm not familiar."

"Look, I come over to your hotel and tell you about it."

"I'm leaving—"

"I am only across the street. I come right now. You sound like very sexy man—am I saying that right?"

There was a pause. Maxwell was astonished, albeit happily so.

"Because my English is not good. Maybe sexy is not right. Maybe interesting is better word."

"Sexy is just fine," he laughed.

"I see you in a few minutes." And she dropped the phone and ran out of the house. In five minutes, she was in the hotel lobby, calling his room. "I'll be right down," he said.

Ken Maxwell was a man of fifty, about the same age as her husband, but plumper and more healthy. He had an engaging smile that he used generously on her. And she could tell instantly he liked what he saw. She fixed her sparkling eyes on him and they stared deeply into one another's eyes.

"I must not make you late," she said, softly. "I was so attracted to your voice, I had to see you, if only for this minute. And now that I see you, I am especially glad I came. You are a big, handsome man…phew!"

"The pleasure is mine," he said. "You know how we picture people we only hear, and how when we see them they never live up to our picture?"

She nodded enthusiastically.

"You are the exception. You are even *more* beautiful than I pictured you."

She dropped her head and smiled, receiving the compliment in encompassing modesty. But her eyes never left him, and they never lost their sparkle of anticipation. "Oh," she said, with a tinkling laughter that rang bells of their own in his heart. "Oh…"

"May I speak frankly, Miss Mazurka?"

"Madame Mazurka," she said, "excuse me, but I have been a baroness in Europe, and there I was called Madame."

"Yes, with pleasure—Madame!"

"Oh, is not important, but, please," she encouraged him, "please speak freely."

"I wish I had more time to spend with you, but I must go or I will miss my train. I suppose there is no chance you could accompany me to Chicago?"

"Oh, Chicago. How I would *love* to go to Chicago. But my husband is very sick."

"I'm sorry to hear that," he said. "Not critically, I hope."

She dropped her eyelids. "I'm afraid so. I must stand by him, I can do no less."

"That is very noble of you."

"It is my duty. Were it not, I assure you I should take you up on your offer in a minute. I should love nothing better than to perform on your Chicago Opera stage. For," she said, with a becoming, halting hoarseness of voice—deep, throaty, sexy, "I should not admit this, but you are a man who is taking my breath away." She put her hand flat and high on her chest and gasped for air as literal evidence of her plight.

"My breath was gone for good the moment I laid eyes on you," he said, and they stared away another minute of their private eternity.

"Will you promise to write to me?"

"Certainly," she said.

"And tell me how your husband is getting along."

"Yes…" She hung her head to show her great concern for the health and well-being of her revered husband. "And you will write me back?"

"Of course."

They hastily exchanged addresses, she of her Fifth Avenue home, and he of his workplace in Chicago.

He thought it best that any letters he might receive from this beautiful young woman, not be seen by his wife.

Erik Weidner's condition continued to worsen. Before long, Hanna could hardly bear to be in the house with him.

The only thing that saw her through the shoals was her lively correspondence with Ken Maxwell. Each letter was answered the day he received hers. She sometimes held on to hers for a day or so, so as not to appear too eager.

She decided to keep her first letter short. Whet his appetite.

I hope I have not been too forward in coming to see you, but as for myself, I am so glad I did. You seem to me the most impressive man I have ever met. If I never see you again, I should not trade the experience of meeting you for anything in the world.

> With warmest memories,
> Hanna Mazurka

Mr. Maxwell wrote back immediately.

Dear Madame:

On my lonely trip home on the train, I could not get you out of my mind. I was struggling to understand what it was about you that made you so unique, so special—what set you apart from the millions of your fair sex. Your beauty, of course, but it was much deeper than that. You have a personality like no other I have encountered in this vale of tears. You are warmly friendly without being too forward. You express an engaging interest with your eyes alone—as though I were the only man in your universe.

Since we are both married, I hope I am not out of line in telling you this. But I would not be honest if I suppressed it. Yours is a translucent beauty, as the purity of your soul illuminates the sublime stature of your being.

> Sincerely,
> Ken Maxwell

343

In the adverse circumstances of her husband's suffering, Hanna felt her role was to give succor as expeditiously as she could. She felt her emphasis should be on the quality of the time spent with her suffering husband rather than the quantity. To console him in his present worsening condition, she felt she had to conserve her strength by spending as much time outside the home as she could. It was absolutely essential to rejuvenate her soul for the agony she suffered from Erik's agony.

Her old voice teacher was not subtle when she asked for additional lessons. He said, "I do not think, at this stage, they would help you. What you need is patient practice to build your breathing apparatus—the muscle of your diaphragm. You must learn to relax your throat, to send the tones from deep in your chest to resonate in your head, to support your tone with your whole body. This takes practice, not many expensive lessons."

"But that is what you said before I went to Cuba. I have had all that experience since."

"Perhaps so, but there has been no improvement."

If Hanna had been a crier, she would have broken down on the spot. Instead, she employed her signature displeasure: she pouted. "But there *must* have been *some* improvement," she insisted.

"Alas, no, my dear. If anything, you have lost ground. Did you have instruction in Cuba?"

"Every day I was involved with the opera," she said. "I learned so much—"

"Ah, but not about *singing*," he said. "It seems you have no patience for fundamentals. You want to be a star without laying any foundation. Well, a house with no foundation soon crumbles."

"Would you rather I get another teacher?" she asked.

"Certainly, if you find someone more to your liking—someone who knows shortcuts I do not—be my guest. You just tell me— anytime—I will not be…offended."

Perhaps the teacher's hormones had congealed, because he didn't seem affected by Hanna's flirtations. She was accustomed to such success through the force of her personality and shimmering looks that she was at a loss to cope with the man's indifference.

She began to sniffle. She hung her head and let it bob from side to side desolately. "I…" she began, haltingly, "…I am…only looking for some…some relief from the agony of my husband… It is so…so…unbearable."

"Now, now," Hanna's teacher said, putting a warm hand on her shoulder. "We will try again. What would you say if I added a few lessons in exchange for concentration on fundamentals?"

And for a time, Hanna worked hard on her breathing exercises. But she wanted to *sing*—to *perform*—not do calisthenics. She felt she was already a stage personality who only needed to smooth out some rough spots in her voice before her opera career burgeoned.

Hanna became a slave to the mail delivery. Trying to be at home for both daily deliveries, she was frequently rewarded with generous handwritten letters from her chief correspondent, Ken Maxwell. They were full of praise for her and understatements of his ardor:

> I don't know how old you are or how old I looked, but being with you those few moments I certainly felt a lot younger than my fifty years.
>
> How is your husband? I trust with your expert care he is improving.
>
> To answer your question, no, I do not think you have only befriended me to gain entrée to my opera company.

Hanna's "expert care" amounted to brief and controlled visits to her husband's sickroom, as though she were visiting an amiable uncle. "Uncle" Erik, for his part, was solicitous of her comfort and well-being, and usually said, "You are my angel—coming to see your sick old husband can hardly be enjoyable for a pretty young wife. If you knew how I looked forward to your visits, you would probably pity me more. I *live* to see you. I am so grateful you are spending this time at home with me. I know you would rather be somewhere else, pursuing your career. To me, you are a vision of loveliness—you are my sunshine and the moon and stars all rolled into one—my universe." He couldn't complete that sentiment without breaking into a hacking cough which grated on her nerves.

He had surrendered to her insistence he hire another doctor to look after him. Dr. Bonner was a kindly old gentleman who looked like he had been painted by John Singer Sargent.

Hanna thought he came not so much to cure as to chat with his colleague of many decades' standing. They were old friends and Erik winked at him on his first visit and said, "Charlie, you don't have any miracles up your sleeve, do you? I may be dying, but I can still diagnose. My beautiful wife has insisted on outside care and opinion. So, I thought if I were going to enrich any sawbones, it might as well be you."

Charlie Bonner served his friend from decline to extinction, but never sent a bill. While New York's elite would insist on paying their favorite doctor, Erik Weidner, and send him money and gifts unbidden, Hanna Mazurka never mentioned her gratitude to Dr. Bonner for attending to her husband. She thought it was between the men, and Erik had a tacit way of expressing his appreciation without talking about it.

Erik held his wife's hand, between coughs, on a cool and overcast morning which, even with the drapes open, cast a pall of gloom on the room. "I'm afraid I'm going to leave you, dearest Hanna. I know you think you have done little for your old husband, but just your presence has made my life at this ending unalterable joy. I love you, Hanna, more than anything in the world."

Hanna patted his hand maternally and kissed him on his forehead. The words were always sweet, of course, but her romantic yearnings had been transferred to her Chicago correspondent, who could make her the star of the Chicago Opera Company. She wrote him that afternoon:

> Phew! Fifty years. You certainly don't look anything like fifty years. I would have said forty at the most.
>
> My husband is not doing well, I am sorry to report. It takes constant care and supervision of the staff to keep him in small amount of comfort. My entire time and energy is absorbed by his illness, but I am content to do my part. He has always been good to me.

Neither she nor Ken Maxwell could honestly say they were sorry Erik was not doing well, for by now each saw the other as his romantic attachment. Ken Maxwell still had a wife, of course, but she had gone to India to be in the company of a guru who would infuse her life with meaning. A divorce was never mentioned—it was more or less understood.

Dr. Erik Weidner, physician to the sick and famous, died while Hanna was at a singing lesson. He went a happy man in spite of his pain. Happy to have had such a young, vital and beautiful wife.

The funeral overwhelmed Hanna. All the social lions of New York society attended and offered her their kind condolences. There were glorious flowers everywhere. The best money could buy in the New York winter. At first, Hanna was awed by the finery these people displayed and at the thought of their enormous wealth. The Park Avenue mortuary, in a dark and brooding demi-mansion, was brimming with American aristocrats. There was such a show of wealth, and such an outpouring of sympathy, Hanna was able to concentrate on extraneous things rather than the open coffin of her waxen, embalmed, husband.

Gustav and Irma Weidner, the doctor's children, seemed to have joined forces against her and seemed bent on upstaging her as grieving survivors. Gustav was tall and gangling and he looked unsure of himself. Irma was a beady-eyed little creature whose eyes shot arrows of animosity at Hanna. Irma expended impressive tears, and every time Hanna glanced at them, she saw them as a united army defending the family fortress. Obviously, Hanna thought, they were trying to make a case for the inheritance her beloved Erik had seen fit to bestow on her.

Hanna managed to get through the funeral and interment without speaking to Gustav or Irma. The doctor's children did not seem disposed to speak to her, why should she make any overtures in their direction?

No sooner was her beloved husband, Erik, in the ground than Hanna took lawyer Felix Barton aside at the funeral and asked when she would be getting her money.

"These things take some time," he said, glancing furtively over at Dr. Weidner's children.

"How much time?" she asked.

"Months," he said, then added, "unless the will is contested."

"Is that possible?" she said.

He glanced at Gustav and Irma again. "Not only possible," he said, "but likely."

"Why is that?" she asked. She seemed shocked.

"He was so generous with you," Felix said, "he left little for his two children."

"And why not? They spent no time with him."

"They are saying the same about you," he said.

"Why, that's nonsense," she said. "How can you *say* that? Whose side are you *on* anyway?"

"Side?" He bristled. "I was on Erik's side. I did his bidding. That's what lawyers do. I certainly felt no affinity for you. His children have already been to me with their hands out. I have told them the situation. They feel they have been left the crumbs. They are hiring an attorney of their own who will undoubtedly cite fraud and undue influence as part of their claim."

"Can they *do* that?"

"Certainly. It is not uncommon when a young woman marries a dying man with children."

"I didn't *know* he was dying," she said.

Attorney Barton looked askance at her. He knew it wasn't true, but he didn't argue.

"I need money to live," she said. "I am not a rich woman. I can't wait months to fight about what is rightfully mine!"

"Do you wish me to attempt a settlement of the case?"

"Settlement?"

"Yes—a compromise."

"You mean giving them some of my money?"

"It is not yours until you get it. Irma and Gustav can make that a long and difficult process. The settlement would involve a redistribution of the bequests."

"You mean giving his children a bigger share than he wanted to?"

"Yes," he said.

"Never!"

Attorney Barton sighed. "Very well," he conceded. "I will try to get you a small stipend to live on."

"Small? I am not a woman who lives on *small* stipends."

"I'm aware of that," he grumbled. "We are, however, going to have to cope with reality as best we can. Erik's last few years were costly, not only his illness and the fact that he could no longer work, but also your extravagant jewelry and clothing purchases, as well as that nonsense in Cuba."

"How dare you! I'm wondering if you have my best interests at heart."

"The simple, honest answer to that is, of course, no. But I will fight tooth and nail to get all parties to abide by the terms of the will as Erik wished it. He was my client—now *you* are my client. I don't have to like you, I don't even have to sympathize with you, but I will fight for you and your cause until the bitter end. That is what lawyers do. Is that what you want?"

"That is what I want," she said. "But I will also need something to live on."

"I will see you do not starve. The house is paid for. You can stay there. I'm sure his children will not contest that."

Hanna put her hand on the lawyer's arm. "Mr. Barton, you don't understand. I cannot stay in the house. It has too many sad memories of Erik's struggle. I must go away, at least temporarily. I need a change. For this, I must have some money. Erik knew I was not a rich woman. That is why he provided for me as he did. And he trusted you to see that I was taken care of. Am I to starve to death waiting for those cannibals to devour me?" She shifted her glance to Gustav and Irma.

Attorney Barton followed her eyes with his. "I'll see what I can do," he sighed.

Lawyer Barton managed to squeeze from the estate funds, a three-thousand-dollar advance for Hanna's living and travel expenses, which she felt woefully inadequate to her needs.

Her note to Maxwell on the day of Erik's death was simple.

> Dear Ken,
>   My dear Erik has passed this life at 10:44 this morning. It is comforting to my grief to know that he will suffer no more.

The reply was a more effusive.

> My Dear Hanna:
> Your sad news has reached

me and I can only feel a sense of relief in the easing of your burden.

I plan to be in New York within the week. I would be pleased to call upon you to express my condolences in person. I shall be staying at the Plaza.

When Maxwell arrived in New York on the train from Chicago, Hanna was on the platform to meet him. She had chosen her outfit carefully so as to be stylishly attractive without being too disrespectful of the dead. Black was a color that flattered her. It was a simple dress, open at the neck, showing off her long strand of simple white pearls. On one finger, she settled for a lone diamond the size of a quail egg.

There was a modest majesty about Ken Maxwell as he stepped off his private car at the end of the train. It was a pleasant change to see him come toward her, confident yet diffident and expectant. Her Erik, at his last, exuded pain in every step, and had become painful for her just to watch him.

It made her feel strong to meet this important man. She wondered briefly if any of her brothers or even her father could ever break out of his simple cocoon and take advantage of American high society as she had. She doubted it. She alone had made the great strides in her family. It was she who was destined for great things.

Maxwell's face was round and ruddy, with enough innocence to belie his wealth and success. Hanna thought he looked a little weak. Not nearly so strong as his employee, Royce Saxon. But was it a weakness she could benefit from? She was a young woman, alone in the world again, and that made her uncomfortable. How was she to live in this foreign country?

Perhaps she had been too lenient when she had agreed to marry Erik. She should have gotten the cash up front. He could have deeded her the house in the beginning; it would have spared her all this unpleasantness with his children.

When she saw Ken approach her, she smiled without breaching her mourning duty—it was a reserved smile, the one she might have saved for funeral guests, if she had found anyone at Erik's funeral to smile at.

Hanna took a step toward Ken Maxwell, then stopped. She

351

didn't want to seem too forward.

He embraced her warmly, as though they were already very close friends.

Ken stood back and looked longingly at Hanna. He hoped he had been careful enough, with his frank stare, not to compromise her bereavement—but there was no mistaking the love in his eyes.

He wanted to hold her longer—forever—but thought he should be circumspect. He waited for a signal from her, but she was uncertain.

Her beauty and beguiling smile blinded him. He was bright enough to realize the relationship was outrageous. They had virtually nothing in common, but he was drawn to her with a magnetic force he was powerless to resist. He knew it might be at his peril if he chose to ignore the dangers lurking behind her dazzling smile. But ignore them he did. He was bewitched and he loved it.

They had lunch in the dining room of the Plaza. Hanna was still excited to be in the grandiose Plaza, which dominated its corner of Central Park. Hanna thought of her dinners there with Erik and her rendezvous with Royce Saxon.

She admired Ken Maxwell, who took luxury in his stride.

Maxwell had never mentioned Royce Saxon to her, which made her even more curious about Saxon. As a conversation starter, she asked, "Do you have a man working for you by the name of Royce Saxon?"

He seemed startled. "Yes, I did, have you heard from him?"

"No, I met him aboard ship."

"You did? Did he have a girlfriend with him?"

"Oh," she answered casually, "I wouldn't know about that. I think I spoke to him only once, and he mentioned he worked for you."

"Is that so? What did he say?"

"Spoke very highly of you, as I recall. Funny, I can't think why I would remember that now."

"Strange," Maxwell said.

"Why strange?"

"He was one of my best—no, I'll correct that—he *was* my best salesman. Sent him to Paris and he got orders like there was no tomorrow. Then after he'd done better than anyone dared to dream,

we called him home. He didn't want to come back, can you imagine? Rather stay in Paris with a war going on than return home to his
sweet wife and two kids."

Hanna froze inside. Royce had deceived her, but she
couldn't tell Ken that.

"Then there were the strange charges on his expense
accounts. An extra cabin on the ship. Bizarre expenses in Paris. He
never gave anyone a satisfactory explanation. That's why I asked if
you saw any evidence of a girlfriend. When a man that solid starts
acting so completely out of character, it usually can be laid at the
feet of some female."

Hanna looked deep in his eyes, cocked an eyebrow and said,
"Oh?"

He blushed. "I'm afraid I can't exempt myself from that judgment."

"So what happened to Mr. Saxon?"

"He disappeared, no trace. Just up and left his family and the
Maxwell Company without so much as a fare-thee-well."

"That *is* strange," she said, and changed the subject. "How
was your trip?"

"I spent all of it thinking of you," he said.

"Oh, pooh!" she said. "Why would you do that?"

"I wonder."

"But you are still a married man, are you not?"

"In a manner of speaking, I suppose I am. And you are a
widow—"

"Yes—do you think I should be mourning?"

"You are a young and beautiful woman. It would be a tragedy
for you to throw yourself on a funeral pyre."

They smiled smiles of understanding. Of kindred souls. Just
how kindred did he see her? Hanna wondered. She sensed already,
between the salad and the roast chicken, that she would have to
make a decision on the intimacy she was willing to share. How much
was he willing to promise her: marriage? A starring role in the
Chicago Opera? Both? With both, there would be no question. She
would have a sacred duty to him. Conversely, with neither, he certainly could not expect any favors. But he was undeniably a handsome man, rich as Croesus and the mainstay of an opera company.

353

She could not think of a better combination.

She had finished the chicken, and she had not even mentioned his opera company. In her gut, she felt it was time to broach the subject. "How is your opera company?"

"Oh, Chicago?" he said, as though he made no connection between Hanna and his opera. "Struggling along. It is not a profit-making enterprise, and that is how I fit in. I am a make-up angel."

"I am sorry, I don't know that term."

He laughed. "Not many people do. What they lose, I make up. Ella Jardin pretty much runs it now."

"Oh? Is she a...a lady friend?"

"Heavens no. She's a prima donna, and you know what they are like."

"No," she said, with a sudden chill in her voice, "what are they like?"

"Temperamental," he said. "High strung."

Her eyes narrowed. "Like me?" she asked.

He stopped short. He obviously didn't know what she was talking about. "You?" he chuckled. "No, I don't see you like that."

"Perhaps you do not know me."

"I would very much like to remedy that." He reached over and placed his hand on hers. She did not move her hand, but smiled into his eyes. "That would be nice," she purred. "But there is still the matter of your wife." It came out a little colder than she had intended. "And my career."

He didn't show any hurt feelings. "She's in India, you know, finding herself and how she fits into the universe."

"So you are not contemplating divorce." It was a flat, if disappointed, statement, not a question.

He answered anyway. "I contemplate nothing else."

She looked at him through a long silence. "So?"

He took a deep breath as his large frame swelled up, then sighed. "It is hard. Well-known, socially prominent families like we both are—in the public eye." He shrugged, hopelessly. "Noblesse oblige."

"You are *nobility*?"

"No, no, not in the European sense. Some think we are the American equivalent."

"And so it is noble to stay in a bad marriage?"

"Many men do. But they also have close women friends."

"Are you suggesting?"

He could tell she was not enthralled with that idea. "No, certainly not in your case. No, no, you deserve the best."

"I had thought you were the best," she said, coyly.

"Oh?" He seemed surprised at her good opinion. She was his children's age, after all, and none of them seemed to hold him in high esteem. When the dinner was over, he asked her, "Would you be willing to continue our conversation in my suite?"

She feigned shock. "But, Mr. Maxwell, you are a married man, and I am a new widow. What about this noblesse oblige? Young women do not visit married men in their bedrooms."

"I have a suite—a living room—and *two* bedrooms. We would talk in the living room. I hope you haven't made assumptions about my presumptions." He frowned. "I think we should explore this opera thing...a little deeper. The more I think of it, the more I see you taking a prominent role there."

It was an offer she felt she could just not refuse.

On the way to the ornate elevator, he slipped his key into her hand. "Room seventeen-eleven," he whispered. "I will come from the floor above."

She got off on seventeen; he rode to eighteen on a different elevator. When she opened the door to the suite, she was overcome. It was not just a larger version of the suite she had shared with Royce Saxon. This had to be the grandest suite in the hotel. Reserved for the handful of movers and shakers of the world. The furniture, in muted golds, could have been from any number of European palaces. The view of Central Park was straight on the horse-drawn carriages waiting to take lovers on rides through the park. She looked out from one of the corners not owned by permanent guests. There was even a grand piano, painted to match the furniture. Hanna ran her fingers over the keys and imagined practicing her singing here. The doors to the bedrooms were closed, as though he had sensitively planned the events. Well, she thought, why not?—so have I. But, I must get him back on the subject of his opera company. One can afford to be more blunt when visiting a gentleman in his rooms. His wealth came home to her as never before. Now that she thought of it, she saw no one get off the same train car as he did.

When he came in the door, after a gentle knock, he interrupted that thought. "Do you have your own railroad car?" she asked.

"Why, yes," he said. "What makes you ask?"

"I was just wondering."

"I'd be pleased to show it to you anytime," he said. "But sit down, by all means. You haven't been standing all this time?"

"It wasn't long." But she sat on the couch as she had with Dr. Weidner. She could have chosen a single chair. He sat on the couch with her. "May I ask you a question?"

"Certainly, my dear. *Anything.*"

"Did you make any inquiries about a place in your opera company?"

"I asked Ella Jardin—mentioned it only in passing. She had not heard of you—which I suppose is her loss."

"That's *all?*"

"Well, yes," he said, sensing her disappointment. "Perhaps I was remiss—but I think of you as too fine a person for the stage. You know there is this old, odd prejudice against theater people."

"But we are talking about *opera!*"

"Yes, a cut above the stage, surely, but still..."

"That is cruelly unfair. One kind of a person is no better than another—especially not because of their chosen pursuit."

"I agree—it's just..."

"What?"

"Society. People—strata of civilization. Classes—wrong, perhaps, but with us from the beginning of time."

"Yes? Well, does it bother you?"

He knew what she wanted to hear, but his true feelings belied his answer:—"N-o-o-o—"

"It doesn't bother me in the least," she said. "My career is very important to me." She paused, searching for an appropriate and convincing follow-up. "I would not marry a man who would not support my career."

There was another stunning silence. "I would support you," he said softly, trying to infuse his tones with a quiet conviction. To Hanna, it only sounded quiet.

"You?" she said, pursing her lips in a mock pout. "But you

have not. You are Mr. Opera in Chicago—I thought I was your friend, and yet nothing has happened in Chicago to help my career."

"Well, perhaps I can get you an audition."

"Audition? Did Ella Jardin audition?"

"She was a star."

"I am a star."

"Yes, I'm sure—but perhaps not known…to the same degree as Miss Jardin."

"Not totally unknown to you."

"What do I know? I have not heard you sing, but even if I had, I wouldn't know what I'd heard. They try to observe certain formalities in Chicago. I try not to meddle in the artistic side of it. Ella Jardin is well-qualified in that aspect. I just give money."

Hanna moved closer to him on the couch—until their bodies touched. "Would you not use your influence," she asked, "even for me?" She reached out to him with her arms, he did the same and they touched their cheeks together. Then she kissed him with a tornado of passion, dead on his lips. When she finally released him and looked deep into his eyes inquisitively, he said—

"I'll see what I can do."

The torrid kiss in Maxwell's hotel suite ignited his passions like a brush fire sweeping all before it. Hanna put up what she felt was a ladylike resistance—token, really, but not so forceful that he might stop. She made him lead her to the fussy bedroom.

And for Ken Maxwell, too long celibate, she was a godsend. While she was loving him, she was thinking how she could parlay his obvious ecstasy into something concrete for her future, but he was so far gone, she decided, communication would be useless.

"You are a phenomenon," he said. "I've never been touched like that in my life."

She smiled and touched his nose with the tip of her finger. "Just a sample," she said. "When we are married…phew, the sparks will fly then!" His muscles tightened. She drew back, and carefully covered herself with the sheet. "What is the matter, my lover?"

"Nothing," he protested too much. "I've never been happier." Suddenly he said, "Will you come to Chicago with me?"

She snuggled up to him. "When we are married, certainly."

"Yes, yes," he said. "I will ask Elizabeth for a divorce. It is time. In the meantime, we can be together," he added in a hopeful tone.

"Together?" she said. "You mean a *mistress?*"

"Darling…a woman of your rare gifts—and character— could never be a mistress."

"That is correct! You were thinking more of a courtesan?"

"No, dearest. I am thinking of the time it takes to get a divorce. I can't be without you all that time. I will do whatever you want."

"Marry me."

"As soon as I can."

"That is when we will live together."

"Oh, please don't be so difficult. I love you. I need you. I will divorce for you. But there is a lot of wealth involved—on both sides. I don't expect Elizabeth to object to anything. The marriage has defi-nitely gone stale—but it's been twenty-nine years. That's a lot of time to unravel."

"And the opera?"

"I will ask Ella."

"*Ask?* You must not ask, you must tell. Where would they be without your money?"

"According to them, nowhere. There would *be* no company."

"You see—"

He shrugged. "But I expect they would find someone else."

Hanna was disappointed. This great captain of industry who wrote her such strong and endearing letters seemed to be a pussycat when she made a few simple requests. "It takes time," he said, "twen-ty-nine years, blah, blah, I will *ask* Ella…" She had the uncomfort-able impression she was being taken for granted, and nothing irked her more—unless, perhaps, and *only* perhaps, it was being ignored altogether.

She rose from the bed, pulling off the sheet to wrap around her naked body. Maxwell thought she was going to the bathroom, but she went to the parlor, where she had left her clothes.

She dressed before Maxwell realized what was happening. When he did, he presented himself, naked, in the parlor as she had her hand on the door to leave.

"Where are you going?"

"Home."

"It's three in the morning."

"I'm not afraid of the dark."

"Stay here—please."

"Not tonight, thanks," she said. "It's been fun."

"Fun? That's what you call it, fun?"

"What do you call it, infidelity?"

"Hanna! Please!"

"Call up Ella. Perhaps she will spend the night with you."

"Ella Jardin? Ella is much older and not half so pretty as you."

"Has she auditioned for you in bed?"

"What does that mean?"

"If you audition for the owner, it is not necessary to pander to an underling." She opened the door. He reached out a hand to stop her.

The last words she heard before the door closed on the naked tycoon were, "Don't go, Hanna, I love you!"

She walked across Fifth Avenue and did not pass a single person. She opened the door to the house the doctor had willed to her. As soon as she was inside, she wondered if she had pushed Maxwell too far. He *was* a rich and important man, unaccustomed to having anyone contradict him.

When she got upstairs to her bedroom, the telephone rang. She didn't answer it. She knew who it was. Perhaps she hadn't taken it too far after all.

She left a note for the maid to disturb her under no circumstances. "Open the door to no one."

Maxwell was at her door at seven, again at eight, eight-thirty, nine and every half-hour after that. Hanna awoke at ten and when she heard the news of Maxwell's visits from her maid, she left through the rear servant's door and made her way along back streets to the steamship office, where she booked passage for the next Atlantic crossing.

That afternoon, after she had made her reservation to sail on the *Aquitania*, Hanna Mazurka received Ken Maxwell in her living room. As soon as he entered, she knew she had a distraught man on her hands. Her first instinct was the feminine one of consoling the poor man. Then she thought better of that. Let him stew, she thought. He richly deserved it.

She let him pour out his agony, replete with protestations of his undying love for her. Had Hanna not been so strong and resolute, she could easily have had her head turned by all the extravagant flattery. It was clear he had no intention of forgetting her, even though she suggested that as a simple, effective option. So she pressed the basics:

"Have you spoken to Elizabeth about the divorce?"

"Yes, yes. I was up all night writing her a letter."

"A letter?"

"She's in some godforsaken spot in India with her guru. There is no way to reach her by phone or I'd call her right now."

"What did you say in the letter?"

"I told her I wanted a divorce. Something had come up that made it imperative. I said I'd agree to any financial settlement she wanted in order to expedite it."

Hanna frowned. "Did you want to be so…generous?"

"She is a millionaire many times over. Money is nothing to her—look where she is—in India, for God's sakes. Her money won't do a thing for her there. That's why she does it. Thinks money is the root of all evil. Wants to get as far from its influences as she can. And I'll say she's gotten pretty far."

"So why even mention it? She could just take you at your word and make you penniless, give it all to her guru or something."

"I wouldn't care—as long as I had you."

Hanna parted with one of her famous musical laughs. "Two poor church mice happy as clams? It is a charming idea, Ken, but I'm afraid I am much too practical a girl for that. I have tasted the good life and it tastes good. I have also had struggles and I don't want to struggle anymore. If you give her all your money, you might as well stay with her, because I'm sure even you need money to live."

"I'm exaggerating and so are you. But I would be happy just to live on modest funds with you as my wife."

Hanna wondered if he had not heard what she said. The idea of a man that rich losing or giving away all his money had to be fantasy. He was grasping at straws to win her approval.

"Well," she said at last, "let me know when you hear from her."

"In the meantime, what about us?" He was a man beside himself with distress.

"I guess we'll wait to hear from Elizabeth—and Ella Jardin."

"Oh, Ella. I called her this morning. She says this season is already set—they plan so far in advance these days. But she certainly will consider you for next year."

"Consider? *Consider!* That is all you are getting for your millions—this woman says she will *consider* your suggestion?"

"Please, Hanna—go easy on me. I have never had anything to do with the production part of it. For me to suddenly throw a tantrum and tell her she had to use you right away,"—he threw out hopeless hands—"well, surely you realize how untoward that would be."

Hanna exploded, and gave him an earful of Polish curses, followed by a few choice entries from the Russian. She stood up, caught her breath, and said, "The interview is over, Mr. Maxwell."

His mouth opened, but he quickly closed it.

"Sarah will see you out," she said, and she marched out of the room and up the stairs without looking back.

Maxwell called Hanna three times a day, and it wasn't until the third day that she took his call. He was the beggar; she the reluctant debutante. Finally she agreed to dine with him at a French restaurant on Sixtieth Street.

It was an unseasonably cold night, with fine flurries of snowflakes. Hanna inspected her wardrobe and passed over the mink coat Dr. Weidner had bought her, choosing a simple black cloth coat instead.

When Maxwell called for her, he raised an eyebrow. "Hanna," he said, "are you going to be warm enough in that coat?"

"Oh, I shall be all right."

"Don't you have a fur?"

She tittered. "Me? I am simple Polish girl. Where should I get a fur coat?"

The restaurant was cozy, long and narrow with low lighting and attentive, but not intrusive, waiters who unbeknownst to Hanna had been well tipped in advance. The couple retired to a private table in the back.

It was there she told him she would be leaving the following day for Paris. He was devastated and pleaded with her to stay home—to no avail. Then he insisted on coming to the ship to see her off. She insisted he should not.

Hanna felt the only way she could get away from him was to agree to cable him when she planned to return. With his own cabin—and him offering to pay her way, first class, the circumstances seemed amenable for him to join her for her return.

Aboard ship the next day, she half expected to find Ken Maxwell lurking in the shadows somewhere. Instead, she found her cabin crammed with flowers from him. Six bouquets, each too large for the space.

On the dining table in the living portion of her suite was a large white box with a gold ribbon lounging indolently on top. A small envelope enclosed the engraved card of Kenneth Maxwell.

She opened the envelope. In his handwriting, he had crossed out his engraved name with a simple, clean, black ink line and written—

> For when I'm not there
> to keep you warm.
> Love, Ken

She tore open the box, the golden ribbon coming sprightly to life in its resistance. Inside was the most gorgeous deep-chestnut mink coat she had ever seen.

Her cloth-coat experiment had produced greater (and quicker) dividends than she had imagined. Her control over him excited her.

But she was equally excited by another prospect. This time she vowed to see the prince—she was again marriageable and certainly by now His Highness must have tired of Katrina. How she would get him to see her was not clear, but she would have the luxury of planning her strategy during the voyage.

In her cabin on the first-class deck, she chose her dress and accessories carefully. With her astonishing cache of jewels, it was always a fine line between being garish and simply tastefully attractive. But with whatever she adorned herself she had the uncanny ability to carry off wearing perhaps fifty thousand dollars' worth of gold and silver and diamonds as though it were the most natural thing in the world.

And she timed her entrance into the dining room for just the moment when everyone else was already seated. She adored the attention of all eyes aboard as she swept to her table like the diva she aspired to be. Her byword was, "You'll never make it if you don't look the part." And she rarely let down—she was "onstage" all the time, carrying her body just so and tilting her head with the *joie de vivre* of a gorgeous ingénue.

She got a thrill out of hearing a room suddenly go silent as she entered. The wave of hushed gasps came as she passed by, starting at one end of the room and following as she moved. It wasn't until she was out of sight that conversation resumed, the subject centering around who that beautiful woman with the extraordinary jewelry was.

Hanna was disappointed to see there were only three men at her table, and none of them under sixty-five, as far as she could tell. And they all seemed to have their decrepit wives with them. So she could settle down to an uneventful trip, or request a table change. Hanna looked around the dining room to see if there were any tables that looked more likely to produce stimulating companionship. Most of the tables seemed to have been cloned from hers. She did spy an oddity: a man seated alone at a table by a porthole. He was tall and thin, with a pleasant-enough face and the expression of one who had just wandered into the wrong room and was searching for the closest exit. When she looked in his direction, she was surprised to see that confused face already looking at her.

She didn't know exactly how old he was, his age was not tattooed on his forehead, but he did seem younger than Ken Maxwell and Erik Weidner, though a good deal older than the baron. She herself was on her way out of her twenties and could, she thought, seem beyond marriage in the heart and eyes of the prince. Her eyes made the circle again, only to be arrested by the same gentleman alone, who now had a startled look. Hanna smiled at him briefly, then, as though no longer interested, turned to her table companions and said, "So! What is looking good tonight?" She had meant on the menu, but the women seemed to think she was comparing her youth and vitality to their staid age.

It was not long before the wine steward appeared with a bottle of the rarest vintage. One of the men frowned, perhaps thinking of the exorbitant expense, and said, "I think you have the wrong table."

"Not at all." The steward smiled. "This rare claret is the gift of Mr. Ned Sharkey Butterworth—the gentleman seated alone by the porthole. He wishes me to impart this message—'A rare vintage requires rare beauty to complement it.'"

Hanna turned to the benefactor and flashed her sparkling eyes and straight teeth at him. Then she took the testing glass from the sommelier, made a show of smelling it, then carefully, slowly tasted a small amount, taking her time to form an opinion. All eyes were on her when she gave the wine her blessing with a brief nod. In truth, she didn't know wine from salad dressing, but she knew what was expected and she played the part. From the raves for the libation at her table, she thought she must have made the correct decision.

Nobody seemed to notice she drank very little of the wine. She knew one rarely had the advantage by compromising one's sobriety.

By the time the dessert had been consumed, the noise level at her table had risen to the point that made her think she should have drunk more to insulate her brain. She was the first to leave the table of new friends; most of whom could have been the grandparents she never knew.

Hanna passed by the wine donor's table and stopped to thank

him for the gift of the wine, "and the poetry that went with it."

"Poetry?" He laughed. His laugh, she noticed, was more of a snort. "I'm a poet, am I?"

"Well, yes," she said uncertainly. "I thought it was poetic."

"Well, well, good for you," he said, and his voice, part bluster, part introverted shyness, perplexed her. She thought he might be drunk, but then she thought he might be making fun of her. He had still not risen, and she thought if he were a gentleman, he would have done so the moment she appeared at his table. She decided the best move for her was away from him.

"Well, good night," she said.

"Just a minute," he said, stopping her mid-turn.

"Yes?" She had had, by now, her fill of him—having decided he was something of a bore.

"Young lady, I don't know who you are or where you come from, but I am certain of one thing." He stopped short, but his narrow, close-set eyes were boring into her in an intense manner that made her uncomfortable.

"Oh?" She tried to treat his pious pronouncement lightly. "What's that?"

"I'm going to marry you."

She let out a startled laugh. "In your dreams!" she said, then turned and walked away before he could see her blushing.

ACT IV

THE PLAYBOY

Marina: No! Even if you gave
your life for me, heedless
my heart shall be!

— *Boris Godunov*

Madame Hanna Mazurka
remembers:
THE PLAYBOY
Paris, France

"A million francs' worth of sable coat that I found in my room, Ned's invitation to go with carte blanche to Cartier and choose anything I desired as a wedding gift, and his businesslike announcement that my bank account would receive $100,000 yearly for my 'pin money'—all that went by me without actually touching my inner being."

Back in her cabin, Hanna threw the extra bolt to double-lock her door. She was trembling. What incredible nerve that man had. Maybe he was God and thought he could have anything he wanted. Simply by buying a bottle of wine for her table.

She took off her jewels, always a careful routine, and placed them in her leather jewelry box. It was a rote action, for her mind was on that aggravating man and his audacious pronouncement. Hanna was agitated; she was annoyed. Men were self-centered creatures who thought they could get away with anything with a young woman. She was feeling vulnerable, and she didn't like it. She found herself searching for some way to get back at him, but she couldn't think of anything. She could lead him on, then at the height of his passion reject him cold. But with a man like that, it could be dangerous.

Sailing, she thought, had many advantages, but one of the *dis*advantages was her universe was restricted to the length and breadth of the ship, and, in those confines, it was difficult to avoid a fellow passenger should that become necessary, as she felt it was in this case.

After an uneasy night, Hanna opted for breakfast in her cabin. She sat staring at the whitecaps perpetually undulating on the dark-blue surface of the Atlantic and wished she could emulate the perpetual motion of those low waves. But she couldn't stay in her cabin alone for the entire voyage. She would develop cabin fever in short order. Besides, one of the things she enjoyed about ships was meeting people. You never knew when someone could give you a boost in your career—like Ken Maxwell. Oh, how much more desirable that man was than this crude bully who had told her—he didn't even have the courtesy to *ask*—he was going to marry her—as though she were some chattel available to the highest or most persistent bidder. Oooo, she got shivers just thinking about it.

Then she had an inspiration. How nice it would be if Ken Maxwell came over to Paris to insulate her from her nemesis. The prince, of course, would be the ideal insulator, but she knew she couldn't count on him so soon. It would take some time to rework her magic on *him*. Katrina had not answered her letter, so she wasn't even sure they were still in Paris. In the meantime, this rude man could dog her steps and make her life miserable. It was the disadvantage of being young and beautiful on an ocean full of lonely old men. Well, perhaps that was an exaggeration, she thought, but it certainly fit *him*.

She was so agitated, she decided she would write a telegram to Ken Maxwell and send it from the ship. She took the telegram pad provided in her desk drawer and wrote:

KEN MAXWELL
MAXWELL CO.
CHICAGO, ILL.
VOYAGE UNDERWAY TO PARIS
STOP ACCOMPANY ME HOME

END OF SPRING STOP
HANNA MAZURKA

She took it forthwith to the telegraph office, not trusting it to anyone else. She felt a flood of relief after she handed it in. But walking back to her cabin, her anxiety level shot up when she thought of the next week on the ship, without Ken Maxwell to protect her.

At lunchtime, she decided to check the dining room. If the Mr. Rude was there, she would take the lighter fare offered on deck. She strolled as nonchalantly as she could on the deck. She glanced in the porthole and saw the back of his neck. And she turned quickly on her heels and retreated to the deck buffet and wolfed down a semblance of lunch before returning to her cabin for a nap. She counted each meal she passed without bumping into the bully as a victory.

As she lay on her bed, she had second thoughts about her telegram. What if she were successful in locating the prince, and rekindling his interest? Maxwell would be like a squeaky fifth wheel. Well, she would have to cross that bridge when she came to it. Better to have too many options than too few.

She decided she could not avoid the dining room for dinner. Mr. Rude might read too much into it. He might think she was avoiding him deliberately, and that was bound to make him feel over-important. The best tack was to ignore him. If he pressed her, she should smile and look away like he bored her, but she wouldn't make a scene. She also decided to sit with her back to him, so she had to arrive earlier for dinner. She was at the dining room door when the gong sounded. She took her place at their table for eight, with her back to Ned Butterworth's table. He had not come in yet. She could watch the door out of the corner of her eye without being too obvious, she thought. When she saw him move toward his table, she turned away to make sure there was no eye contact.

Her table was full, and the small expected pleasantries had been exchanged when the maître d' approached. He leaned over and said softly into Hanna's ear, "The gentleman who sent the wine last night bid me to ask if you would consider joining him for dinner."

Her body turned rigid, but the smile stayed on her face.

"Oh, tell him that is a very kind offer, but I do not feel disposed to leave my friends." Her tablemates were impressed and flat-

373

tered. The maître d' nodded and withdrew with this sad message to deliver it back to the bachelor. Hanna's tablemates began buzzing.

"Are you so sure you want to turn him down?" one of the dowagers said.

"Yes." Hanna's eyes sparkled, and the light was making the rows of diamonds around her throat dance.

"Do you know who that is?" asked another.

"No...I..."

"That happens to be Ned Sharkey Butterworth, heir to the Sharkey fortune. Pharmaceuticals. They say he's richer than God."

"Never been married," another woman chimed in. "Said to be extremely fussy abut his women."

"Is that so?" Hanna said.

"You can always change your mind," the gentleman to her left contributed. "We would miss you, but we would understand."

Understand? she thought. What is he talking about? They act like I am a gold digger. The man really is insufferable, even if he is the richest bachelor...

She passed the mealtime uneasily. Well, she told herself, he may have more money than anyone, I am definitely *not* interested in him. Never could be.

Someone else mentioned the maître d' had gotten a hundred-dollar tip to ask the question, with another hundred offered if he succeeded. She didn't think to ask how they knew that, but later she realized what a small world the first-class section of a ship was.

She took her time with dinner, and dawdled over the dessert. She was knocking herself out entertaining the table to keep an insulation of safe people around her. She never turned around to see if Ned Sharkey Butterworth was watching her. When the last couple said good night, she quickly rose to go out with them. To her surprise, Mr. Butterworth was nowhere to be seen. She asked her tablemates to walk her to her door, and they scoffed at the thought some outlaw would accost her in the passageway, but she begged, and they obliged.

They made it without seeing her nemesis. The couple turned to leave her. "Oh, wait," she said. "May I check the cabin?"

They smiled and indulged her. She checked but found no one. She was slightly embarrassed when she said good night to her escorts. When she was alone in her room, she got over her embarrassment but then felt a different twinge of emptiness. Regret. Could it be that she was feeling ignored, shunned? There was really no man in her life, and it did make her feel somehow incomplete. But the man said he was going to marry her, and she had wasted all that time stewing about his audacity only to find now he was ignoring her. Had he found someone else to "marry"? Did he lose interest that quickly? Her interest had been piqued on hearing he was the richest bachelor in the world *and* that he was extremely fussy about his women. Even though she was not attracted to him, she thought it couldn't hurt to get to know him. Maybe have a meal with him.

Next morning, she went to breakfast. He was not there.

At lunch, she sat facing his table. She was almost finished when he came in. She smiled at him and gave a slight wave of her hand. He ignored her. She spent the afternoon on deck, watching the now-monotonous whitecaps, wondering if he would come by.

He didn't.

That night at dinner, she told herself she should take the bull by the horns. She hung back from entering the dining room until she saw he was seated at his table alone. She had put on her most startling jewels and her most daring dress—a shiny bright-green silk that showed a maximum amount of flesh without scandalizing the National Legion of Decency. Hanna strutted to his table as though she were on a fashion-show runway. The room predictably hushed while she was en route. She stopped at his table, leaned over and extended her hand. He pretended not to notice her by concentrating on the menu in his hands.

"I'm Hanna Mazurka," she said. "I thought we should be formally introduced if we are to be married."

He looked up in shock, then burst out in one of his snorting laughing fits, which traveled throughout the low-ceilinged dining room, then bounced off the walls and returned with hurricane force.

"May I join you?" she said, pulling out the chair and seating herself with a studied adjustment of her skirts before he could say no. He seemed highly amused, but he brought his snorting under control.

"So," she said to the richest bachelor in the world, "about this marriage—" She waved a hand heavy with diamond rings before

375

his nose. "What are your prospects?"

Ned Sharkey Butterworth trembled with his own brand of raucous laughter. "Oh," he said, catching his breath, "oh, *prospects!* Oh, that's a good one." The table between them shook with him.

She laughed with him. She'd gotten the reaction she'd hoped for, and she felt this turn of affairs was much more desirable than them ignoring each other. After all, for him to marry her required *her* consent. And it certainly was not a foregone conclusion, and she would let him know that at the very first opportunity.

"My prospects, eh?" he said. "Well, for starters, I have a trust fund that would run several mid-sized European nations. I have more money than you and I could spend if we went at it twenty-four hours a day, seven days a week. It just keeps compounding faster than I know what to do with it."

She giggled and showed him her rings again. "I could help you with that."

He snorted his approval. She didn't think much of his snorting laughter, but she couldn't deny she felt intoxicated in his presence—just the idea of that much money…

"And what are *your* prospects, Miss Mazurka?" he asked.

"I am an opera singer."

"Really?"

"Yes, really."

"Where are you appearing?"

"I am beginning an engagement at the Chicago Opera Company."

"Ken Maxwell's place?" He raised an eyebrow.

"Do you know him?" Had she gone too far? Would Ken Maxwell back her up?

"Of him," he said.

She was relieved.

"When do you sing?"

"As soon as I return."

"And why are you going to the Continent?"

"I am from Europe. I am Polish."

"How charming," he said. "Are you visiting family?"

"No," she said, "friends."

"Good for you. I have nothing to do with my family either.

Bores, every last one. Killing themselves day in and day out to make even more money for me to spend. Sometimes it's a real burden, this spending. Looking for something new to blow it on. That's one reason I decided to marry you," he said. "I saw you coming with enough jewels to choke a show horse and dressed to kill the same horse. Here, I said, is a woman who knows how to spend money."

"Is that a compliment?" she asked, with her curious head cocked.

"To me it is," he said. "Spending's a burden, I tell you."

"And you want me to share it?"

He snorted again. "Well, perhaps you should give it serious thought. I mean, you have to weigh the pros and cons. The spending on the one hand." He raised his right hand. "And the burden of it on the other." Up went the left hand.

They were silent a moment.

"Think you're up to it?" he asked.

She smiled gently, her eyes boring into his. "I could give it a try," she said, then added quickly, "once I get to know you," lest he think the money was all that was important.

He waved a hand of nonchalance at her. "Fair enough," he said.

"My career is very important to me," she said, examining his impassive face for a reaction—finding none—it was almost as though he had not heard her. She added, "Would that be all right with you?"

"Oh, opera? Sure, what do I care? I have my polo ponies and my yachts; you want to warble like a songbird, more power to you. Say—maybe I could buy you an opera company, would you like that?"

Feeling he was making light of her abilities and suggesting she had no talent, but needed to *buy* an opera company to perform, she said, "Oh, that is not necessary. I am already set in that regard." And no sooner were the words out of her mouth than she regretted it.

"Oh, yes," he said. "Chicago."

They ordered their meal, then ate in silence for a while. Whenever she glanced at her table, she found some of her tablemates looking her way. She smiled, they waved. Some of the men raised their thumbs to her.

"Say," Ned said, as the dessert was being served him—she had declined it, "what do you say we go dancing? I checked out the band and they're okay."

Hanna got the feeling it was too much, too fast and begged off. "I'm a little tired," she said.

"Tires you out being swept off your feet?" he said with enough of a question in his voice to reassure her.

"No doubt," she said with a hint of sarcasm. "Maybe tomorrow. I'll rest up."

He did not push, in fact certain times he seemed downright disinterested. It threw her off.

He saw her to her cabin and gallantly kissed her hand before departing without a fuss.

When she opened her door, she saw the telegram under her feet. She picked it up and tore it open.

> HANNA
> WONDERFUL NEWS STOP
> ARRANGEMENTS ALREADY
> MADE STOP RETURN TO-
> GETHER FIRST WEEK OF JULY
> STOP EXCITED STOP

She was of two minds after she read Maxwell's telegram: first, he had done her bidding, quickly and efficiently. And he was coming as she had wanted him to—originally. But now he could be in the way. He had not mentioned her opera debut, and she was skeptical that it had come to fruition. She decided she had to press him harder. She took out the telegram tablet and wrote:

> KEN
> RECEIVED YOURS STOP MAY
> BE CHANGE HERE STOP HAVE
> OFFER TO DO OPERA IN
> EUROPE STOP IF NOTHING IN
> CHICAGO WILL STAY HERE
> STOP
> HANNA

She was pleased with her work and took it right to the telegraph room. Back in her cabin, she thought about Ned Butterworth and his enormous wealth. Ken Maxwell was also quite wealthy, but he had a wife. That was certainly a limiting factor. The two rich men were so different. *All* her men were different. Whoever said you marry the same man every time didn't know what he was talking about. Though she knew very little about him, this rich bachelor seemed the strangest of the lot. He could be attentive and gallant one minute, and distracted to boredom the next. From time to time he vacillated from rapt attention to what she was saying, to the blank stare of one whose mind was not in the same room as his body. He was a guy she could not get a good focus on. His character seemed elusive. Like mercury in your hands.

The snorting laughter could get on her nerves, she could see that. But she liked his talking about them spending money. What was a poor Polish girl expected to do when a man told her he liked her and wanted to marry her because he thought she would be able to help him spend some of his money?

Perhaps she should be insulted. But she wasn't. Over the years, she had developed a fondness for buying things: clothing, hats, jewels. She was unable to explain the exhilaration she felt when she stepped up to a counter in some exclusive store and announced she wished to examine closely some priceless jewel. Or the same feeling trying on a dress that cost as much as an automobile. But she was always careful not to buy apparel she might see someone else in. She didn't want to be off-the-rack. So, she hired dressmakers and was quite demanding of them. She was known for her eclectic style, and sometimes felt it was a burden keeping up her reputation. But then when she walked into a room to gasps of delight or admiration, even envy—it was all worth it.

And the conversations she generated! There was something about being the center of attention that was inexplicable. It sometimes strained her acting capabilities not to show just how thrilled she was to be the person in the room who was noticed. This, admittedly, was easier to bring off when you were a generation (or two) younger than everybody else, as she was in first class aboard ship. It could have been, she admitted, one of the reasons she liked being on a ship.

She began taking all her meals with Ned. By dinner the second day of their companionship, she was telling him about avoiding him that day after he had shocked her with his pronouncement he would marry her.

"Marriage shocks you?" he asked.

"Well," she said, "the way it was put."

"Too direct for you?"

"Well...a little."

"That's the way I am," he said. "To the point. Waste a lot of time shilly-shallying about. If I am going to marry you, why keep it a secret?"

Her eyes opened wide. "And do you not think I should be consulted on the matter?"

"Ultimately," he said, "of course. But I was just stating a fact."

"Doesn't it take two...?"

"To tango, yes," he said. "But I've been called the world's most eligible bachelor for so long I am just assuming any girl would be only too happy to tame me."

"What makes you more eligible than anyone else?"

"Money," he snorted. "Lots of it. It is the main interest of most women," he said.

"Well!" she protested. "Not of *this* woman!"

"What about all those diamonds?" he said, pointing to her dramatic jewelry. "This dress didn't come from a five-and-dime."

"I am more interested in the soul of a man than in his bank account."

"Yes? Lot of beautiful souls on skid row, I imagine," he said.

She didn't know how to take him. He seemed so unconventional at times, she thought it was a ruse. But she also claimed to admire the unconventional. After all, wasn't she unconventional herself? Yet he seemed so hard to reach—aloof in a way—that it posed a challenge for her.

At dinner the next night, he seemed distant. He did not invite her to go dancing, but she had dressed for it and was looking forward to it. She had worn her apricot chiffon creation, with the swirling skirts. Around her neck was a special crucifix, studded with diamonds, rubies and sapphires. It was her favorite of all her purchases from the Russian émigrés.

After dessert, he said, "I will see you to your cabin."

Her eyes turned wounded, then flirty. "But aren't you going to invite me to dance tonight? Last night, I was tired."

"Maybe tonight, I am tired," he said.

"Oh, are you?"

"Never too tired to dance with you," he said, and they made their way to the room where a ten-piece orchestra was playing. "May I have this dance?" he asked, bowing as an earnest young boy at dance class might.

"It would be my pleasure," she said, curtsying.

They danced for hours. He drew her close to him and moved with his leg between hers, her chest pressed to his. She felt him hardening and closed her eyes and muttered, "Oh dear."

When the music ended, he asked, "Do you want to see my cabin?"

"Oh, I have one too," she said. "They are all alike."

"No," he said. "Mine is bigger."

"Oh," she said. "Bigger—well, perhaps—just for a minute."

They strolled, hand in hand, passing a few smiling couples on the way.

Hanna was astonished to see the size of Ned's cabin. "Owner's suite, I call it," he said.

"Do you own the ship?" she asked.

"Could," he snorted. "Too much trouble; make my money easier."

He wasted no time in taking her in his arms and kissing her. She was reluctant at first, then felt a wave of pleasure infuse her body. She didn't resist until he started to move her toward the bed behind a wall of drawers. "No," she muttered. "Please."

"No?" he said, looking at her in a confusion. "Why 'No' all of a sudden?"

"Too far," she murmured into his shoulder. "Going too far. I am in mourning—I can't."

"But you are also a young, vibrant, beautiful woman and you don't have to get a wrinkled face before tasting pleasure again. By then it may be too late."

"It's too soon," she protested. He was now tugging her intermittently, then stopping to examine her face for explanation of what he thought was highly peculiar behavior. "Hey," he said, "it's the twenties. Speakeasies and bathtub gin."

"There is still original sin," she said, batting her eyelashes again and toying as if unconsciously with the jewel-encrusted crucifix around her neck.

"Yes," he snorted, "and I always say, original sin is better than unoriginal sin."

It had been a struggle, but she had not given in to him. She decided he was the kind of man who if he got it for nothing would quickly forget about marriage. She had gotten more suspicious of his pose that marriage to her was a foregone conclusion. He seemed like the least likely man she knew to *ever* get married.

Hanna was too agitated to sleep. Ned was a wild man, she decided, willful, self-possessed, boorish, but also enchanting, funny—and different. So different from any other man she knew. The depth and breadth of his wealth was unimaginable. She was still knocked out by the size of his cabin. She had no idea one could get one that size. It was twice hers, easily, and she thought she had the largest. She wondered if Ken Maxwell traveled in such luxurious quarters when he crossed the ocean.

Next morning, Hanna received another telegram from Ken:

> HANNA
> OPERA ARRANGED STOP
> PASSAGE SET FOR JULY 1 STOP
> MISS YOU STOP

At first blush, Hanna was ecstatic. She had won a place in the Chicago Opera. Her career would zoom from there. Then she began to think. What would be expected of her? Maxwell was still married. And Butterworth was single and wanted to marry her. Maxwell had done half his job. He had gotten her in the opera. But he hadn't said anything about divorce. It hadn't been that long, but certainly he'd asked Elizabeth to phone him with her response. Did he expect her to be his mistress? A ruined reputation could not be repaired. Not in the circles she wished to inhabit.

She had vocalized daily, practiced some scales and breathing exercises. Now she doubled her efforts. She must be in shape for stardom. She was being given the opportunity; she must not disappoint.

Her jumbled thinking smoothed out enough for her to send another telegram:

> KEN
> GOOD NEWS STOP
> GRATEFUL STOP
> ANY NEWS FROM
> ELIZABETH STOP
> HANNA

These telegrams cost over a hundred dollars each to send and Hanna agonized over each word. But she thought she could get Ken to pay for them—in the right circumstances, of course. If not Ken, Ned. She had two options for marriage. Neither, at the moment, was the prince, but she had to live. What were a few hundred-dollar telegrams when her future was at stake?

Waiting for a reply from Ken, Hanna spent her time with

Ned Butterworth. She thought she was beginning to like him. His funny, devil-may-care attitude she found endearing.

On the second to last day of the cruise, they were dancing after dinner, their lithe bodies feeling in each other a sensuality that precluded conversation. That night, while Ned was rubbing Hanna's bare back with his hand and pressing her breast into his so close he could feel her heart beat, he said, "When we get to Paris, where will you stay?"

"I usually stay at the Ritz."

"You could stay with me. Cost you a lot less."

"Might cost me more in the long run," she murmured.

"Just an idea."

"I don't live with men I'm not married to. No." She pulled away. She was already concerned about the wagging tongues. Their relationship was the sensation of the ship. When she had mentioned to Ned they should be more reserved in public, he'd said, "The hell with them. I don't care what anybody thinks. I can buy and sell the lot of them." It was a concept Hanna liked. She always aspired to live without regard for the opinions of others. But with her, it was an aspiration that had its limits.

He held her hand as they floated back to their small table beside the dance floor.

"So," he said, "why don't we get married? Solve all the domestic problems."

"Oh? What's in it for me?" she teased, as they sat down.

"Carte blanche," he said.

"No, really..." It was an admonition for him to speak seriously.

"I mean it. It is a challenge to spend this damn money. I don't have anyone I want to leave it to, and I can't begin to spend it myself—I doubt that both of us could, but it might make a dent in the pile."

"Ooo, why are you always talking about money?"

"Because that's all I have. If I were handsome or charming, I would be selling that. As it is, I am trying to tempt you with dollars and francs."

Hanna Mazurka frowned. She was in a crazy dilemma. Would there be an advantage to telling Ned? There was no sense pretending she had no interest in money and what it would buy. She had spoken to him about her fondness for the purity of soul, but she was crossing the Atlantic in a first-class suite, and Ned was too cynical to understand anyway. Yet her unusual position might offer her some unexpected leverage.

"My dear Ned," she began. "You have certainly made my head spin these last few days."

"Getting dizzy?" he snorted.

"Am I!" she laughed. "But I am in a bit of a predicament—" She stopped suddenly and blinked her sensuous eyelashes at him. He said nothing.

"Do you want to hear about it?"

"If you want to tell me," he said, disappointing her with his tepid response.

"Yes, well, there is another suitor for my hand."

"Oh, well," Ned said, "I'm not surprised. There might be a hundred of them—you are so damn beautiful."

"You are very kind."

"Is he rich?" Ned played his trump card up front. He always did.

"Yes," she said.

Ned raised an eyebrow. "Do I know him?"

She bowed her head modestly. "Ken Maxwell," she murmured, as if in strictest confidence.

"Oh, yeah," he said, "we had a lot of his stock." Ned smiled like a Cheshire cat. "Oh—yes, he's rich, but he is also married. Or doesn't that bother you?"

"He will get a divorce."

"That's an old song, my girl. Tell him to come 'round *after* he has the divorce."

"He's working on it," she bristled.

"A bird in the hand is worth two in the bush," he said. "What has he offered you?"

"Offered me?"

"Yes, in the way of…material inducements."

"Why, nothing. What have *you* offered?"

"A house in Paris, a sable coat, bigger diamonds than anything you have—a hundred thousand in a bank account in your name for pin money. Carte blanche at Cartier—Tiffany—anywhere you like. A Rolls-Royce or two."

Though she had every intention of keeping cool, her dazzled eyes betrayed her interest. Perhaps she had overdone that talk about soul being far more important than money. After all, she had certainly observed that those with money were better off than those without. And the way Ned presented it, he would be an endless fount of the world's goods. An undeniably fascinating thought.

Hanna tried to weigh the advantages of both men—as well as their drawbacks. Neither, she thought, could hold a candle to the prince in personality, charm, looks, character. What was left, she told herself, was material security. She leaned toward Ken Maxwell, thinking he was the better person. And he had gotten her an opera role! But she couldn't hide her disturbance at his not answering her cable questioning him about his divorce. In this case, no news was *not* good news.

"Ned," she said, "you don't happen to know a Prince Stephanoff, do you?"

"A prince...? Is he *another* sweetie?"

"Well..." She hesitated. "We were very close."

"*Close!* Yeah, a lot closer than you came to me, I'll bet."

"Well..."

"Prince of what?"

"Russia." She sipped her ginger ale.

"Oh, pooffff," Ned said, letting the air escape his concave lungs. He was drinking something stronger. "Those Russians have all been shot."

"Shot? No—"

"Well, they shot the czar and his family."

"Yes, I know, but Stephanoff was in Paris. You have a home in Paris; I thought you might have run into him."

"No, no, can't say I have. But those boys are out of business—those Russian royals. I hope he took a lot of rubles with him when he left and converted to francs straightaway, because those rubles aren't worth the paper they're printed on now. He's probably working as a waiter somewhere."

"No!"

"Really. You see a lot of those Russian former hotshots driving cabs, waiting tables. I can't imagine him having any money left.

Russia is in ruins. Lost millions of men and rubles in the war. It's staggering."

"Were you in the war, Ned?"

"Too old. Rarin' to go, however—I covet a chestful of medals and topics of conversation that never end. But they wouldn't have me. Just as well, I'd probably be fertilizer now. Say, your friend Maxwell made a tidy fortune off the war, didn't he?"

"I wouldn't know."

"Think about it. Blood money. Is that what you want to spend? My money's untainted. You could hold your head up when you go to the bank."

Ned gave Hanna pause to consider her options. Did it always have to come down to money? Fortunately, both her leading suitors were well stocked with that commodity.

Hanna didn't intend to end up like the prince and Katrina, if Ned was to be believed. And she had no desire to ruin her reputation by being the consort of a married man. Secretly, she hoped Maxwell would have his divorce—or at least news that it was coming. Ned said Maxwell didn't want a divorce. "Why should he? He's married to a Crenshaw, for God's sake. They are rolling in it—and now that the war's over, they may have to tighten their belts at that factory. I've sold my stock in Maxwell," he said. "It's peaked, for sure."

Hanna had not gotten the telegram she'd hoped for by the ship's farewell dinner.

Ned and Hanna sat uneasily at his dining room table. He was tapping his fingers on the table, she was reading the menu for the seventh time and chattering nervously about the dishes.

"You must have that menu memorized by now," he said.

She put it down abruptly. "I'll have the salmon," she said with studied finality.

"And will you have me with it?"

"You?" She chortled low in her throat. "Think you're good enough to eat, do you?"

"I suppose that too," he said. "What I had in mind was good enough to marry."

"Oh, Ned," she said, expressing a gentle frustration. "I *told* you. I've promised Mr. Maxwell…"

"But you haven't heard from him—"

"N-o-o-o."

"I can buy anything I want," he said, looking unhappily at his drumming fingers. "Why, I've bought more women than you could shake a stick at."

"I don't want to be bought, Ned—"

"Why not?"

"Oh," she sighed her exasperation, "I told you. My soul is pure. I am interested in spiritual things…"

He interrupted her with his annoying laugh.

"Makes a nice speech," he said, looking aslant at her, "but all the evidence is to the contrary."

"Oh, Ned," she said, "that's just not true."

He wasn't convinced. "Tell you what," he said. "I'll bet you anything I can pile enough material stuff on your bed to make you marry me."

"No you can't," she said.

Hanna checked into a suite at the Ritz. As soon as they quoted the price to her, she realized her funds from Dr. Weidner's lawyer, Barton, would not last long. She would have to sell more jewelry or plead with Barton for another draw or take charity from one of her admirers — or get married.

She told Ned she didn't want to see him for a day. She wanted to get her land legs back. What she wanted was to look for the prince and give Ken Maxwell another day to tell her he had managed the divorce.

The prince seemed to have dropped out of sight. She hired a driver and traveled to the villa the prince had shared with her friend Katrina, but the villa was empty, and no one seemed willing or able to tell her where the royal couple had gone. The Russian Embassy was no help at all, and there was no word from Maxwell. She could not bring herself to ask him again.

She went to lunch alone on what she considered her day off (from Ned). When she returned, there was a sable coat, full length on the bed, along with a large box from Cartier and an envelope.

She opened the box first. It was the most stunning diamond necklace she had ever seen. "It must have cost him a *fortune!*" she exclaimed aloud. There was a note with the necklace:

> The wedding ring will put this neck-
> lace to shame.
>
> Love,
> Ned

She opened the envelope. It contained a check made out to her for a hundred thousand dollars, unsigned. There was another note:

> Here is a token to open a bank
> account for your pin money. It's just a
> start. Carte blanche charge accounts
> whever you want them also come
> with my best wishes. The accounts
> will be activated and the check signed
> when you sign the marriage license.
>
> Love,
> Ned

Hanna sat at her desk and took a pencil and wrote some numbers on the hotel stationery. When she saw how much cash she had left and figured it would take her about five or six weeks to go through it, she was beside herself. She hadn't planned on anyone contesting the doctor's will. To be safe—and to save her from a precipitous marriage—she wrote out a cable:

ATTORNEY BARTON
FUNDS DEPLETED STOP
REQUIRE ANOTHER ADVANCE
STOP
    HANNA
    RITZ
    PARIS

That night, she tried to think of some way to have both the Chicago Opera and the generous wealth of Ned Butterworth.

But what of the prince? Even if he was penniless, wouldn't she rather have him? Yes—a resounding yes. She could live in a barn with that handsome, sweet, sensitive man. The man with a passion for opera. But where would she find him? And what of Katrina? They would have to get a divorce, of course. But she realized she needed some currency herself to win her true love—her first love! Could Ned provide that? All this money he was willing to give her—she could share it with Prince Stephanoff. She would have to be married to Ned, of course, but she would be in a position to save the prince from destitution.

The following day, the bad news arrived via telegraph.

HANNA
ERIK'S CHILDREN CONTEST-
ING WILL STOP ANY ADVANCE
MINIMAL STOP ECONOMIZE
STOP
    BARTON

She devoted the rest of the day to her search for the prince. Then she launched one last telegram to Ken Maxwell.

KEN
MARRYING JUNE 27TH STOP
WILL FULFILL OPERA CON-
TRACT STOP
    HANNA

The date of the "marriage" was the day before Ken was scheduled to arrive at the dock. He would be powerless to stop her. Perhaps Ned was right and Ken had no intention of going through with his divorce. The fact that he had secured the opera spot for her when he said he had nothing to do with it proved he could do anything he wanted. With his money, he could have sent a battalion of lawyers to India with papers for his wife to sign. She had probably run off with the guru already anyway.

Ned was strangely incommunicado. He was staying in his villa outside of Paris, and he had said he would call after her self-imposed twenty-four-hour exile. But he had not called.

She began to worry: she had set the date of the wedding without consulting the bridegroom. Would he want to invite his family? There wouldn't be time. Well, she had taken a chance. Considering all the stash he had put on her bed, Ned seemed to be amenable to her wishes. And if he didn't marry her on the twenty-seventh, he could still be used as a bargaining chip.

Ned showed up at her door, without calling as he promised, only an hour and a half after Hanna thought she would die from hunger. She had about given him up, and decided she should try on the gifts—the sable coat and the jewelry—if he didn't ever return, she thought, she would not be obligated to return anything.

She opened the door without thinking.

"Oh, it's you," she said, startled.

He laughed, baring a maximum of teeth. "You were expecting Ken Maxwell?"

"No, I... You said you'd call."

"Well, here I am. I saved the call. All the more diamonds for you. By the way, you look smashing."

"Thank you." She blushed. "Oh, this is just an old rag I threw on," she said, twirling around so the sable flew from her sides like wings.

He advanced and put his arms around her, caressing the fur. "Umm, nice," he said. "Wouldn't you like to lie down on this fur?"

"Well," she said, "I might surprise you..."

"Good," he said, maneuvering her toward the bedroom.

She stopped him—"If I wasn't so darn hungry," she said. "I waited so long for you, I almost passed out."

"Mmm, then I'd just have to revive you." He reached for her again—she straight-armed his chest.

"Now, you behave," she said. "Where were you?"

"You told me you needed a day." He shrugged. "I gave you a day."

"You gave me *more* than a day."

"Isn't that better than less?"

"No!" she said. "Not when I'm so hungry."

"Well, let's eat right here so you won't faint going somewhere. Shall we have it in the room?"

"Oh, no—I can make the dining room. Besides, I want to show off my new diamonds."

"So you accept!" he said, obviously pleased.

She floated one of her enigmatic smiles in his direction. "*If*…if we can agree on conditions," she said.

He laughed—a sound that now reminded her of some animal—there was the snort of the pig, of course, that was always there. This was more like a coyote or perhaps a hyena. It made her wonder if he were laughing at her.

She started to take off the sable coat.

"What are you doing?" he said. "Leave it on."

"But we aren't even leaving the hotel," she protested.

"I want to see you in it—see you move, watch it sway on you. They were animals, you know," he said, stroking the furs. "We can be animals too…" He left the suggestion hang on his smile.

In the dining room, they checked her sable coat. Hanna liked the look of admiration she got from the coat-check girl. After Hanna attacked a hearty meal, she eased into a discussion of her career. "I must have it, you know."

"If you say so," he said, not showing much interest.

"I do."

"Well, you might change your mind," he said offhandedly. "After you have everything money can buy, what's the point?"

"The point is it's my art. My lifeblood is singing opera. Large opportunities are presenting themselves. It is my lifelong ambition. Your financial support would ease my burden."

He laughed. "I'll say," he said.

"I may have to travel," she said quietly.

He shrugged his shoulders. "I can travel too."

"Yes-s-s," she said, drawing it out uncertainly.

"We'll see if you still want to."

"Oh, I'll want to."

"We'll see…"

Then she told him she wanted to get married soon — not drag it out.

He leered at her and said, "Fine with me."

"You aren't planning to invite some family members from overseas, are you?"

He laughed. "I have nothing to do with them, and vice versa. Just the money," he snorted, "that's my only connection."

"So does the twenty-seventh of this month sound all right?"

"So long?" he said.

She chuckled — "Two weeks?"

"I don't know if I can wait that long."

She fixed him with her best come-on look. "Maybe you won't have to," she said.

He stared at her lasciviously and hoisted his wineglass. As always, he had drunk the lion's share of the wine and the result had been an artificial inflation of macho; and she was playing to it shamelessly.

"How about some dessert, doll?"

"No thank you."

"Why not?"

"Dessert goes right to my thighs."

"I don't believe it."

"But you haven't seen them."

"Ah, yes." His cunning smile lifted his features like a predator. "And that is a void I must fill."

She giggled. He did too. "Oh, Mr. Butterworth," she said, "your choice of words…really…"

"Why really?" he said, raising an eyebrow. "Don't you like to have your void filled?"

"Oh, Mr. Butterworth." She energized an eyelash modestly.

"Because I like nothing better. I just better tell you that right now."

"Oh, Ned…"

He showed her his straight white teeth in a lusty grin.

Ned had the chocolate cake with vanilla ice cream for dessert. He chewed every mouthful deliberately, not taking his expectant eyes from his companion.

They retrieved the sable from the coat-check girl and Ned gave her an extravagant tip. "Here, buy one yourself," he said and sniggered.

"Shall I put it back on?" Hanna asked him.

"Yes—I want to see my animal in her animals."

He helped her with the coat and when she had it on, he buttoned it for her, brushing his hands against her, here and there. Then he took a handful of the fur at her buttocks and said, "Take me to your lair," and he held onto the coat there through the lobby to the elevator, on the elevator to her room. Hanna was embarrassed at the spectacle he was causing, but as she reminded herself, she was almost broke.

Inside the door of her room, Ned began kissing her, slobbering his tongue all over her mouth.

"Wait," she gasped.

"What for?"

She stepped back. "Don't rush. It's better slower," she said, as though she meant to teach him a thing or two.

He snorted.

Hanna pulled her arms from the large sleeves of the sable coat. With strange, unknown contortions, she unbuttoned and wiggled out of her silk blouse, which she threw at his face.

Startled, he caught the garment, then pressed it to his cheek. Her skirt followed.

Then, with a sharp twist of her body, a satiny, lacy camisole dropped to her feet. Ned was breathing hard now, wordlessly staring at this lovely young woman who knew how to please a man more than any professional of his acquaintance.

When her panties came at him, Ned lost all control—he grabbed Hanna by the shoulders and threw her to the floor.

"Oh!" she said, "not so rough—"

"Oh, my animal." He breathed hot breath at her neck.

"Don't you want to go to the bed?" she said.

"No time," he said.

As he fumbled with his pants, she whispered hoarsely, "Fill my void…"

He tore at the buttons of his coat and lay flat on top of her. His dead weight knocked the breath out of her. She was pinned between the unyielding floor and his full body. She tried to move to make it easier on herself, but he didn't understand. His hands groped and squeezed where Hanna had expected caresses. He was so intent on his pleasure, he had little thought of hers.

He was a performer, proud of his acrobatic ability, without the least understanding of a woman's feelings.

He wanted the lights on; she wanted them off.

"It is a matter of feeling," she said — "not seeing."

"I like to see what I feel," he said, snorting that annoying, incongruous sound.

Afterwards, she lay still, and he fell immediately asleep. There was no tenderness, no thoughtfulness, no endearing sweet nothing in her ear. He was a rather clumsy lover, she thought. When you get right down to it, she told herself, all he was was rich.

But she had no other choice — for now.

Hanna was disappointed. She had tried her best, but he had treated her like an object. But when she considered the financial benefit that would accrue to her from the union, any complaint seemed petty.

The next morning they went to the city clerk's office to get the marriage license.

It was a gray, drizzly day and Ned was in a grumpy mood.

When they stood facing the bored clerk in the old, dark building, answering his monotone questions, Ned said, "Why am I doing this?"

"Because you want to," Hanna said. "You are filling a void, remember?"

"Ah, yes." He softened. "Yes, yes, yes! Where do I sign?"

On their way back, they stopped at Paris's most exclusive jewelry store, where Ned told her to pick an engagement and wedding ring.

"Oh, dear," she said, trying to blush, "I don't know if I can —"

"Of course you can —"

"But…but, do I have a budget?"

397

"Carte blanche!" he exclaimed with a snort.

"Oh, Ned," she said. "I'm embarrassed. I'd like you to pick something—"

"Oh, if that's the way you feel about it, okay. I'll get a little something." And he left the store without further word to the clerk. Hanna smiled across the counter and nodded her apology, then followed Ned out the door.

They made arrangements to be married in a civil ceremony June twenty-seventh. Hanna still had visions of finding the prince or hearing from Ken Maxwell that his divorce had come through. Though she had not settled in her mind exactly what she would do if she found the prince, she had fantasized numerous scenarios—he was broke, so Katrina left him; he had saved enough of his fortune to live comfortably and when he saw her, he fell in love all over again, divorced Katrina (amicably), and married her.

As for Ken Maxwell, every day she did not hear from him was another rung on the ladder of pessimism. Though she had not yet found a new voice teacher, she still practiced her singing daily. But as she practiced and visualized herself on the Chicago Opera stage, she realized that Mr. Maxwell could easily have lost interest in her after getting the telegram telling him of her marriage, and he probably canceled her engagement with the opera company. She would fight him, of course, breach of contract, all that, but she realized he could just deny it. All she had was a telegram, and she might look rather foolish if she made an issue of a married lover's promise.

After all the preparations were made for the wedding, Ned suggested they celebrate with a session of lovemaking.

"Oh, dear," she said, "let us wait it for our wedding night. It will be *so* much more exciting."

He laughed and said, "Think so?"

"Oh, yes, it will give us something to build to."

"Ha, ha," he said. But he was beginning to wonder just why he was so obsessed with this woman. She was extraordinarily beautiful. Her face was simple, smooth loveliness and her figure was perfection. The way she wore clothes, not tight, but not loose either, with just enough spur to the imagination, fueled Ned's fantasies. But the personality—so effusive at first—was beginning to trouble him. She seemed so self-absorbed, he thought he should be annoyed, but, for some inexplicable reason, he was charmed. He loved the way she reacted to his outrageous behavior—with a mixture of cowering and bravado that ill suited such a feminine thing.

Chemistry, he decided. It must have been chemistry.

But if she were bent on keeping him at a chaste distance in the meantime, he would obtain his affection like he did everything else; he would buy it.

Next day, he showed up at her hotel with the engagement ring. "Sorry it took so long," he said. "I had it made specially. You like the design?"

Hanna's eyes almost popped out of her head. Diamonds seemed piled on top of diamonds, like a pyramid. A platinum band circled them and was intertwined with the platinum that went around her finger.

"Oh, Ned, it's *gorgeous*. But how could you have it made so quickly?"

He rubbed his fingers together. "Money," he said. "Money talks." Then he snorted.

Oh, dear, she thought. I'm going to have to break him of that awful sound.

"Here, try it on," he said, and she did. "You can have it adjusted if it doesn't fit."

"Oh, no! It fits *perfectly!*" she said, admiring it, first close to her eye, then at arm's length.

"Most expensive ring Cartier ever sold," he said, proudly. "An expensive jewel for my expensive jewel," he said, and gave her a kiss, which she didn't deny him.

He looked peculiar when he picked her up for their trip to City Hall for the marriage ceremony. Peculiar but dapper. He wore his yachting blue blazer, gray flannel pants and had his yachting cap with him. She wore a light-pink chemise dress and a pink hat to match with a face-length veil.

The formalities took only a few minutes, and they were man and wife. She signed the marriage certificate, then he signed the hundred-thousand-dollar check before he signed the marriage register.

"Good as my word," he said, laughing.

Oh, that laugh, she thought. It could be the death of me.

Then he surprised her. "Why don't you run to the bank. I'll meet you at the hotel later."

"But...you don't want to come to the bank with me?"

"Nah, you've seen one bank, you've seen them all. I'll see you tonight," he said, then embarrassed her by patting her on her fanny, lightly but repetitively, and before she could couch her protest in adequate terms, he was gone.

When she deposited the hundred-thousand-dollar check in her bank account, they treated her like royalty. A little girl from the backwoods of Poland, she thought, but she didn't think often of her past. Past was prelude, after all. The overture to the opera, to be enjoyed while it was being played, to be considered as a sampling of what the real thing will be like, but generally forgotten when one is caught up in the real thing.

She had to wait for Ned again. What was he doing? She became more curious now that she was his wife. It was not fair for her to sit around waiting on his every whim.

She had half a mind to teach him a lesson—go out herself and not be in when he got back. But since she was leaving him for Chicago in a few days, and she hadn't told him that in so many words, she thought now was not the time to make a stand about being left alone.

Hanna tried to practice her singing, as she did every day. Why, she thought, should my wedding day be an exception? Especially without a new husband to compete for my attention.

When Ned finally returned, Hanna was tired and hungry again, and she wondered if this was going to be a pattern.

"Where were you?" she asked.

"Having a drink with some of my pals," he said, in a manner that made her think he'd had more than one.

"On your wedding day?"

"That's what we were celebrating."

"Wouldn't you think to include your new wife in a celebration of your wedding?"

"What? With the *boys?* Why would you want to do that, you have your boy—you don't want to still play the field, do you?"

"Of course not," she answered petulantly. "But couldn't you and I celebrate?"

"Of course, that's what we are about to do." He put his arms around her and kissed her hard on the mouth.

"Nnnn—o—not now." She pushed him away. "I'm starving to death."

"Me too," he said, and kissed her again, attempting to maneuver her toward the bed. She balked and put both her hands between them and pushed his chest. He looked at her curiously. "Well, all right," he said. "Eat first, then celebrate."

In the dining room, he stared at her with bleary eyes that made her curiously uncomfortable. "Well," he said, after the menus were delivered, "are you ready to move to my villa?"

"Tonight?" she said. "You don't mean tonight?"

"Well, why not? You don't have that much to move, do you?"

She could only think of her meeting with Ken Maxwell, which was scheduled for the morning, when his ship would come in. She was sure her opera contract was on shaky ground as it was. It would certainly be aggravated if she was not there when Ken came. "Oh, I'm so tired," she said.

"We'll have the bellboy do it all. You don't have to lift a finger, now that you are mine."

She didn't like the possessive sound of that. But instead of pointing that out, she decided to store it up with her other resentments. "But it's spread all over the suite—couldn't we do it later—tomorrow—the next day? Is there any hurry?"

He looked at her as at a stranger. He cocked an eyebrow. "We're husband and wife. We should at least live under the same roof."

"They have a lot of rooms under this roof."

He stared blankly at her. "You mean you don't plan to share a room with me?"

"Goodness," she said, "why would we do that? Surely you are rich enough that we can each have our own room."

He stared again, this time with blinking eyes, as though trying to focus on her pretty face. Her words seemed to blur with her face.

The waiter took the order without Ned removing his gaze from her face.

"What are you looking at? I never agreed to share a room like some peasant. I have never shared a room." She leaned over and touched his nose playfully with her finger. "That doesn't mean you can't come to visit," she said. "But sleeping, that is different. I always sleep alone."

"Alone?"

She nodded.

He mimicked her nod and seemed unable to stop nodding.

"What's the matter with you?" she wanted to know.

"With *me?* I suppose I must be horribly old fashioned—expecting to sleep with my wife."

"Is that why you got married? Well, you should have asked me first."

He looked at her with homicide in his heart. "Yes, I daresay."

The first course was served and they ate in silence. "Why did you get married?" she asked.

"Well, I needed a wife," he said. "I didn't have one. I had my polo ponies and my yacht, my fast cars. All that was missing was a wife."

"You make it sound like a wife is on par with a trophy for polo playing."

"Oh, not *that* good," he said unsteadily.

"But that's *terrible!*" she exclaimed.

He laughed so heartily, she was annoyed. "Every bit as good as your motive, wouldn't you say?"

"Oh!" she sputtered in anger. "I...love...I married for love," she insisted. "I'm an incurable romantic."

He nodded, signaling his insight. "Sure you are," he said. "And I'm Teddy Roosevelt."

After dinner, Ned told her he would see her in her room and sent her up alone. From there he roamed the streets of Paris, saying goodbye to as many of his ladies of the evening as he could find.

When she arrived in the room, Hanna quickly slipped into a seductive black silk negligee and covered it with a creamy satin short robe, which hung open invitingly.

Then she propped herself suggestively on a pile of pillows on the bed, hastily arranging them in the most arresting manner. She had no desire to be crushed on the floor again. Then she waited. And waited. The time dragged by and still no husband.

Hanna was furious. Did he actually

think it was all right with her for him to always keep her waiting?

After an hour of anxiety, Hanna got up from the bed and put on the clothes she had worn for dinner.

To take her mind off the grievous slight of her bridegroom, she did some singing exercises. It was more imperative than ever, with this treatment at the hands of her new husband, that she get the place with the Chicago Opera. But it was going to take some doing to convince Maxwell of that, she was sure.

Agitated as she was, she had fallen asleep before Ned came to her door. And she saw to it that he had a lot of trouble waking her up.

She half opened one eye. "Hmm?"

"Hanna, wake up. It's your husband, coming to collect his conjugal due."

"Umm."

"Hanna! That's a good girl. Open both eyes—well, heh, heh," he said, unbuckling his belt, "maybe you don't *have* to open both eyes."

He got into bed with her, and she decided to open both eyes. "Ned!" she said.

"I hope so," he chuckled.

"Where have you been?"

"You're sounding like a wife already," he said, reaching out for her.

"I *am* a wife," she said, trying to fend him off. "But you don't seem to realize that. You just go blithely off on our *wedding* night…"

He nuzzled his nose in her armpit. She pushed him away. "Talk to me," she demanded. "I want to know where you were."

His alcoholic breath, wafting across her face when he snorted, did not appease her. "I was out on the street," he chuckled. "I'm always on the streets when I'm in Paris. Had a lot of friends on the streets. Had to say good-bye."

"Female friends?"

"Certainly, you don't think I'm one of those queer fellows, do you?" And he thought that was quite funny and added a raucous laugh to it.

"You don't mean you were visiting prostitutes?" She was alarmed, and let him know it.

"Well, I never call them that. Seems so...low class somehow. But you understand I was single a long time..."

"But on your *wedding* night!"

"Well, yeah, I was out there saying goodbye. You know we didn't have any guests at the wedding. Maybe I should have invited them."

"Over my dead body."

He laughed. It irked her. "I was wandering around out there, checking out all my old honeys, when all of a sudden I realized, by God, I was a married man, and I had a *wife* to go home to—who would be needing some attention. So what do you know? Here I am!"

"Ooo!" she snapped. "How can you be so uncouth?"

"Uncouth?" He was perplexed. "Why? I'm here, aren't I?"

"But, you were out with *whores*! On your *wedding* night. Despicable!"

Ned Sharkey Butterworth did not argue. Instead, he reached for her again, and as it developed, had to fight for his prerogatives. She resisted, of course. He was an animal if he thought he could have his way with her without considering her feelings. But he was much the stronger of the two. Hanna didn't give up; she struggled so long and hard that when it was over, she considered she had lost the battle but won a moral victory—in spite of the inherent immorality of the conflict.

Hanna was humiliated. But she was not vanquished. If her new husband thought he could behave like a savage with impunity, he would learn a powerful lesson from her. And the next morning, she would put her revenge in motion.

It was only seconds after his assault of his new wife that Ned fell into a sound sleep. Repulsed by the idea of sleeping with this animal, Hanna arose and went into the parlor of the hotel suite and slept fitfully on the couch. The following morning, she was awakened by a knock on the door.

Groggily, she stood up and straightened her clothes, looked hastily into the mirror and was chagrined that she looked exactly like a woman who had been raped. Her hair was scraggly, her face blotchy and her clothes disheveled. It was impossible for her to face a visitor.

"Who's there?" she said hoarsely into the door, but she knew the answer even before it came.

"It's Ken," came the answer, with a combination of hope and despair.

"Oh, Ken, I'm so glad you came," she whispered through the door. "I'll see you in the lobby in a few minutes."

"Can't I just come in?"

"I'm not presentable," she said, apologetically. "It will only take a minute."

"Hanna," he pleaded. "I've had a long trip—"

"Only a minute," she said, scurrying around for her toilet articles to repair the damage as well as possible. Ken Maxwell still called from the other side of the door, but she didn't answer. She was afraid he would knock so loudly her husband would awake, but he finally subsided.

Hanna tiptoed into the bath, afraid she would awaken Ned, who was snoring soundly. She did what repair work she could, hastily, and was dissatisfied with the results. Then she thought better of her efforts and decided to change her approach. Quickly, she reached into her accessory drawer and withdrew a bandanna, which she placed on her head, covering her hair. She took a towel and blotted off her makeup. A few of the skin blotches still showed. She put on no jewelry, took off her enormous wedding diamonds and left the room, closing the door quietly behind her.

She felt she couldn't trust her legs as they carried her downstairs. She had so carefully planned her handling of Ken Maxwell, but now she found she was nervously questioning all of her imagined ploys. As she approached the lobby, she saw Ken pacing the large room as if he were completely out of sorts. She went over and gave him a perfunctory hug. "Don't look at me," she said, "I'm a sight!"

"You'll always look good to me," he said.

"No, no. Not today." She sat on a brocade couch. "Not after what I've been through."

"What have you been through?" He sat next to her.

"Oh, I don't want to talk about it," she said, hanging her head and sniffling. "It's too terrible."

"What is?"

"Oh, nothing."

"Hanna! Are you all right?"

She looked at her hands twisting in her lap. "I'm married," she muttered.

"And he has done *this* to you?"

"Oh, Ken," she said, breaking down and laying her head on his shoulder. "I've been so foolish. But, I was almost broke—I pictured myself out on the street...without a franc."

"Nonsense," he said. "I wouldn't let you go hungry."

"Oh, but I've become used to so much more than mere food."

"I'd give you whatever you wanted."

"Oh, how could I accept that, after the way I behaved—?"

"Why didn't you just *ask* me?"

"But I did. I cabled you. You never answered."

"I *did* answer your cables. As soon as I got them."

"Not this one. Not about your divorce. You ignored it. I thought you wouldn't get a divorce, and so I married a man who offered me the moon."

"I offered you the moon."

"You were married. Bigamy is still a crime."

"Well, I don't know what cable you are talking about. I never got one about a divorce, but maybe I left home before it came. I've been over to India to see if I could scare up Elizabeth to talk some sense to her."

407

"And?"

"I found her. It's so pathetic. Here she is, this rich, successful, socially prominent mother of five grown children, throwing herself at the feet of some bogus guru with bedroom eyes and an oily way of talking, as though this charlatan had in his power the complete universe."

"What did she say about the divorce?"

"That was just it. She had to talk to her oily guru about it. It sounded like she couldn't make a move without his say-so."

"How did *she* feel about it?"

"She wasn't opposed. I might even say she was amenable. It's just...she's so damn dependent on this fake messiah—can't make a move without him."

"Did she ask him?"

He nodded.

"And?" she prodded.

"He has to meditate on it."

"How long?"

He threw up his hands. "I'll get the divorce. I've no doubt. I realize now if I had only made the offer of a substantial contribution to His Holiness, I would probably have permission to proceed. Sooner or later, it is going to occur to him that he can milk us for his approval. But," he said, with a hopeless shake of his head, "you got married!"

"I hadn't heard from you…"

"You got the cable about the opera?"

"Yes," she said, leaning over to kiss him on his cheek. "I am so excited. I love you for it. I promise, I'll make you proud."

"You know I have tickets for us to return in a week."

"I know," she said.

"Does your husband know?"

"He will," she said. "I've laid the groundwork."

"This is *terrible!*" he said, hanging his head. "How could you do this, when I've been devoting my life to your wishes?"

"But you are *married*, Ken."

"Why couldn't you wait?"

"I told you. I was almost destitute."

"Can you divorce him?"

"But I just got married," she protested.

"Apparently not too happily," he said, studying her studiously unkempt face.

"Perhaps I owe it to him to make it work."

"Do you?"

"He has been very generous."

"How generous?"

"A sable coat, diamonds and jewels. Carte blanche at Cartier, a hundred thousand dollars pin money. Anything I want."

"I'll double it," Ken said.

"Oh, dear," she said. "If I had only known you were working on the divorce. With you, it is not the money. You are a pure soul, and I always loved your soul. My husband, he is perhaps not so pure in his soul, but he is so much generous, I cannot tell you. And *so* much money, *phew!*"

"I can match him, dollar for dollar," Ken boasted. "And he is living on a trust fund, while I am continuing to create wealth—Oh, Hanna, I implore you. Leave him."

She bit her lip. "Do you think I could?"

"Of course. I'll take care of everything."

"And what of me? What becomes of me then? I am without a husband."

"I will be your husband."

"In the meantime, I will be your mistress? A woman married one day decides to give up who was the richest bachelor to be the mistress of the married man." She shook her head. "The newspapers are already making a circus out of me. Can you imagine what they would say if I left Ned now and ran off with you?"

"Why would you care what they say?"

"I have my career to consider. My public. I must not disappoint them."

"But," he asked cannily, "what career will you have without Chicago?"

She sat bolt upright. "What? Are you threatening me?" This was not how she'd planned it.

"No," he said gently. "It is not a threat. But I had to offer big money to them to get a place for an unknown quantity. Apparently, they checked with Havana and some of your teachers, and the feeling was you might not be quite ready."

"Oh? Is that so? Well, they have never heard me sing."

"That's true. That contributed to the reluctance."

"They have never seen me onstage. I have magnetic stage presence!"

"I'm sure you do. But, I had to tell them you were going to be my wife and they had to accommodate you. They agreed reluctantly. But you can surely see the embarrassment it would cause me if I took you back to my opera and told them you were instead someone else's wife but I wanted them to take you anyway."

Hanna's eyes narrowed, more in concentration than in anger. Don't ruin it, she told herself. "You have to save the Chicago Opera. Perhaps," she said, "perhaps you have found the solution—"

"What solution?"

"To the opera. Your wife, they *must* take. Someone else's wife could only be hired on her merits."

"Yes, but that's just the problem—as *they* see it, of course."

"No, no, let me finish. Hiring me as your wife is pandering to you, patronizing to me. The word will be out I was some kind of legacy. Now, you will reverse that. You will say that I have married someone else, but that is no matter to you because I am a large talent that Chicago should have."

"And," he said, looking away from her haunting eyes, "why should I do this?"

There was the inevitable question. She had tried out several answers and variations of ideas on herself. But in her heart, she knew she had one, and only one, possibility.

"Because," she said, looking with a deep longing into his eyes, "when I am in Chicago, I shall *be* your wife."

Hanna's suggestion of illicit love made Ken Maxwell's scalp tingle. His heart was so warm, he saw no reason to cancel her Chicago Opera debut.

Ken Maxwell took a suite at the Ritz, and asked Hanna to come with him, but she said, "No—in *Chicago*, not in Paris. In Paris, I have another husband." He thought she was speaking of Ned—but in her heart and mind, Prince Stephanoff would always be her rightful mate.

When she passed the desk to return to her suite to break the news to Ned about her Chicago debut, she saw a pile of newspapers. Then a headline caught her eye:

PLAYBOY WEDS
POLISH SINGER

She snatched up the paper and hurried to her room with it. There she fell into a stuffed chair and read the piece, to the accompaniment of Ned's snoring in the other room.

Ned Sharkey Butterworth, heir to the Sharkey pharmaceutical fortune, married Polish songbird Hanna Mazurka, née Zdenka Oleska, in a civil ceremony yesterday at City Hall with no guests in attendance.

This is the first marriage for Mr. Butterworth, a yachtsman and polo fancier. He is 47, Miss Mazurka is 28. She was formerly married to Baron Alexi Chotznic of Russia and Dr. Erik Weidner of New York.

Considered the most eligible bachelor in the world, it took the practiced hand of twice-married Mazurka to saddle Mr. Ned Sharkey Butterworth.

The couple plan to make their home at Mr. Butterworth's villa outside Paris, where Mrs. Butterworth will pursue her opera career.

Hanna was angry at first. Then she thought the prince or Katrina might see the notice and contact her. And it might bring her to the attention of the local musical world.

She dreaded further confrontation with her new husband, Ned, but her situation demanded it.

She considered waking him, then thought better of the idea. She didn't have long to wait until he began stirring like a man much troubled by unsettling dreams. He grumbled himself awake, opening one eye at a time. "Where am I?" he asked aloud. Hanna came into the room. "Oh," he said, "you must be my bride. Where were you last night?"

"Ha! As though *I* was the one roaming the streets of Paris."

"I opened my eyes and you weren't in bed."

"I was on the couch. I don't want to sleep with a man who rapes me."

"Rapes you?" He was perplexed. "What are you talking about?"

"You forced yourself on me last night."

"Why would I have to do that?"

"Because I didn't want you."

"You didn't want your husband on your wedding night? Whoever heard of such a thing?"

"I waited for you for two hours, then you came in smelling of whiskey and told me you were out with your whores. Would you want me if the roles were reversed?"

"I'll always want you," he said, reaching out his arms. She jumped back as though she was revolted at his touch.

"Ned! Stop it," she cried out. "We have to talk. Now get your clothes on so I can talk to you seriously."

His mouth dropped. He scratched his head, pondering what seemed to him foreign sounds. "Excuse me, Hanna, but are you speaking in Polish?"

"I am *not!*"

"Well, in English it sounded like you were ordering me around. Like I was your servant."

"Oh, don't be so literal. Would you *please* get your clothes on so I can talk to you?"

"You don't seem to be doing badly with my clothes off. If it's parity you're after, I have a better idea. Why don't you take *your* clothes off?"

She glared at him. "Ooo! You think that's funny?"

"I think it's funnier you want me to dress before you can talk to me, and yet you are talking to me all this time."

She turned and went out of the bedroom to the parlor, slamming the door behind her. She paced the room and fumed, and she was still fuming when her husband came out dressed in his blue blazer—and nothing else.

She looked at him, her face startled, then she broke out laughing. "So, you don't have to see anything you don't want to see," he said, then pointed to her fully clothed body, "and I can't see anything I want to see." He snorted a few laughs.

Hanna collapsed into the single stuffed chair and brought her laughter under control. "Ned," she said, beseechingly, "you can be a dear boy." She waved at his blazer. "But you can be an awful bore also. Like last night."

"You know, I'm afraid I can't remember last night. You say I forced myself on you—are you sure it wasn't just the normal exercise of the groom's prerogative?"

"There is no prerogative if the woman does not wish it."

"No? Where did you come up with that one? I'm to support you and give you a sable coat, a hundred thousand dollars, a Rolls-Royce, and a diamond ring large enough to choke the entire cavalry, and I have no rights?"

"I didn't get a Rolls-Royce," she corrected him.

"Yes, you did. It's outside. I was picking it up last night. Get a chauffeur too if you want."

"Why, Ned, I…" She stopped short. "You are a most generous man."

"Wouldn't you say *the most* generous?"

"Why, yes, yes I would."

"Well, you're Mrs. Ned Butterworth. I couldn't have you driving in some diddly little Ford, could I?"

"Do you have garages at your place?"

He laughed. "More garages than bedrooms."

"Well, that's very good. Could I leave it there then?"

"Sure. We'll move out there today. A home for you, a home for the Rolls."

"First we must talk," she said.

"Well, talk," he said.

"About last night," she began. "A woman must not have intentions forced on her she does not welcome."

"I agree," he said. "And no wife should unwelcome her husband."

"There are times when a woman must be able to say no."

"Oh? The Bible is all full of admonitions for the wife to obey her husband. What have you got to go against that?"

"Common sense," she said. "I didn't know you were a religious man."

"We can all be religious when it suits us."

"Ned," she said. "I don't want to argue. Not on our first day of married life."

"Save it for tomorrow?"

"No, listen. I told you I couldn't share a bedroom with anybody. Never have. That doesn't mean we can't have our little visits when we both feel like it, but I just can't sleep with another person. That's definite. You said you had plenty of rooms."

"But you're my wife. Husbands and wives share rooms. They share everything."

She shook her head. "Not me. Not bedrooms."

"Isn't that the beauty of marriage—it's there when you want it? You don't have to get up and stumble down the hall in the cold."

"No."

"But this is a business transaction. Men pay for what they get. My whores got cash; you get jewels and furs and cars *and* cash. For that, I am entitled to some return, am I not?"

She glared at him, wondering how she could have married such an insensitive man.

"Perhaps," he went on, moving his eyebrows in a skeptical arc, "you just need a little education about men. Though since I'm your third husband, I wonder why it should be necessary."

"My other husbands were not so crude."

"Crude, is it, darling?" he said. "I thought it rather honest. I believe you don't understand men, or a woman's place, for that matter."

"Oh? And you are going to enlighten me?"

"Do my best," he said, marshaling his thoughts for what he considered his facts-of-life talk. "It all comes down to how we're built. You have an opening, I fill it. Men see women in terms of that opening. That void between your legs. Everything else—face, figure, jewels, hair styles, makeup—just frosting on the cake."

She shook her head in open disgust. "You can't speak for *all* men."

"Why not? I'm a man. That is the way I see women. I can't imagine a higher calling than gynecology. But I'm not a doctor, so I must largely make do with my imagination. When I look at a woman, that is what I imagine. Make all the clucking sounds you want, that is the nature of the beast. Our thing is out, yours is in. Out goes in, it couldn't be any other way."

Hanna glared at her husband, trying to reconcile his expressed heresies with her former husbands. Ned was, she decided, a man she could not fathom.

"If you don't want to recognize my needs, we can divorce," she said. "I'll give you your things back. I won't need them. There are plenty of rich men who are anxious to marry me, on *my* terms. I leave it up to you. And you can have a few months to think, because I am going to sing in the opera in Chicago."

"Chicago!?" Ned took the announcement like an uppercut to his jaw, not having paid much attention to Hanna's prior warnings.

"Yes. Mr. Maxwell has arranged a place for me in his opera."

"Maxwell? Are you flirting with old Maxwell?"

"Certainly *not*, he is a married man. He happens to think highly of my singing abilities and he has obtained a position for me in Chicago."

"Horizontal?"

"Excuse me?"

"Is the position he has obtained for you horizontal?"

"Oooo! You are certainly uncouth."

"Well, was that what turned you so cold on our wedding night?"

"It was *not*! I told you, it was you coming in late and smelling of whiskey without telling me where you were going."

"I told you, I went to pick up your Rolls."

"But I knew nothing. I am alone in a hotel on my wedding night. I am worried about you."

He laughed again, and it annoyed her. He was always laughing at inappropriate times. "Are you worried that I won't come home?" he asked, his eyebrows shooting up again, "or that I *will?*"

"Oh, Ned. That's not funny!"

"So, you are going to leave me on our honeymoon," he said. "Can't you at least put it off a few months?"

"No, the season is now. The opportunity is now."

"There will be other opportunities."

"I told you, I must have my career."

"You didn't tell me you had to have it during our honeymoon."

"So come along. We'll have our honeymoon in Chicago."

He grimaced. "I can't think of a worse place to go than that windy slaughterhouse. Unless you happen to be a pig on your last legs."

"Ned!"

"How are you getting to Chicago?"

"On the *Mauretania*."

"You have already booked passage?"

"Yes, Mr. Maxwell has arranged it for me."

Ned cocked an eye at her. "Mr. Maxwell again. How thoughtful he is."

"He has booked a cabin for himself also."

"So he is here? In Paris?"

"Yes."

"Don't tell me—I can guess—he's in the hotel. And you snuck out to see him last night. That was why you weren't in my bed. That was why you were so cold to me."

"No! I was right here in the parlor. Mr. Maxwell did not arrive until this morning. I tried to wake you to tell you I was going to talk to him. I couldn't wake you, so I went downstairs."

"To his room?"

"No. I saw him in the *lobby!* He just arrived. He is a married man. I am a married lady. I had arranged all of this debut before I even met you. Now, will you stop this insane jealousy or I will leave you instantly."

"For Maxwell?"

"He's *married!*" she shouted.

He looked at her with one of his maddeningly penetrating looks. "For how long?" he said.

417

At the last minute, Ned decided he would join his bride and Ken Maxwell on the Atlantic crossing. When the chips were down, he couldn't see abandoning his new bride to the American industrialist.

Hanna would not hear of him sharing her cabin, even though he offered to sleep on the couch. But all the first-class cabins were taken, and he was given the choice of a second-class cabin or staying behind. He accepted second class.

It was Royce Saxon all over again. She ate her meals with Mr. Maxwell, who had paid for her first-class passage; and visited her husband on his deck whenever she felt she could spare some time from her arduous schedule of vocal preparations.

As the time drew closer, Hanna became nervous and highly strung—the anxiety of anticipation built in her.

Maxwell invited them both to share his railroad car to Chicago, but there were only two sleeping compartments and Hanna would not bend her rule about not sharing a bedroom. So Ned was obliged to take a compartment in an adjoining car. When he suggested, for the sake of propriety, Hanna do the same, she said she didn't want to hurt their host's feelings. He was a married man, after all, and Ned had no need to worry.

Ken Maxwell made suggestions of his own to Hanna, but she responded she was a married woman. It was a tribute to his perseverance and her magnetic pull that he continued to pursue her. Other men might have turned elsewhere, but Hanna Mazurka was Ken's life's dream, and he could not imagine being interested in someone else. For Hanna Mazurka had about her an inexplicable spark—an X-plus, he called it—that no other woman in his long acquaintance with women had. The chemistry was sizzling.

But it was not an easy situation for Hanna, balancing her would-be husband with her de facto husband. One was giving her a living with his generous purchases and bank deposits; the other was giving her life with his Chicago Opera Company.

Mr. and Mrs. Ned S. Butterworth took a two-bedroom suite in the Palmer House in Chicago. If the desk clerk found that arrangement peculiar for notorious newlyweds, he didn't let on.

The day she landed in Chicago, Hanna contacted a celebrated voice teacher. The next day, she began her lessons in preparation for her first day at the Chicago Opera. She concentrated with all her powers and practiced until she was blue in the face. This was a most important milestone in her career, and she planned to make the most of it. And when Hanna put her mind to something, nothing stood in her way. Hanna was a lot happier in Chicago than Ned was. He was at loose ends on strange terrain. His home was now in Paris, and though he'd heard the cliché, "Home is where the heart is," his heart was in Paris where his home was. His yacht was anchored in the Mediterranean, his polo ponies stabled near his villa outside Paris, and all his social contacts and friends were there. He had in Chicago only his new wife, and she was so preoccupied with her preparations for her opera debut there that she had scant time for him.

Ned thought he would go mad if he heard Hanna sing another note. He knew nothing about singing, but he could tell she had a squeaky-meek voice that wouldn't make it to the footlights. When she began to practice, he fled to the hotel bar, where he soon became a familiar face with his illicit silver flask. "My prohibition buster," he called it. He never left home without it. Ned's threshold of tolerance was soon exceeded. Having dinner with a distracted wife who was "too exhausted" to do anything else tried his patience far beyond its breaking point. After only a week into Hanna's arduous routine, Ned threw down the gauntlet:

"Hanna, let's cut this nonsense," he said, at dinner. "I've heard you practice." He shook his head. "You're no singer."

She put down her fork and turned her head slowly to focus her quiet wrath on her husband. "And just *what* do you know about singing?"

"You don't have to know much. Now, I'm going stir-crazy here. I want you to go back to Paris with me. You can take lessons there." He shrugged. "Who knows, someday you might be good enough to sing opera."

"But you don't know *any*thing about opera!"

"True," he readily admitted. "So let me ask you, who knows so much more about opera, do *you* think you can sing?"

"Yes!" she spat out, like the word, thought and implications had been giving her indigestion.

Ned tried to turn tender—no mean feat for him. "Hanna, let's face it. You don't want to be embarrassed, do you? You will be swimming with real big fish here. I guess you have a sweet-enough voice, but in opera you need power. Maybe you'll develop that, but you know you don't have it yet."

"I've been told I have a beautiful voice," she argued.

"I'm not trying to fight you," he said, "I'm just giving you an excuse to escape. Tell them your husband is tired of Chicago and insists you come home with him."

"But you can't insist," she said. "You knew before we were married how important my career was. I told you."

"Career," he said, shaking his head. "Has anyone ever wanted such a career with less to go on? And less need? You are a very rich woman, Hanna. What can you gain if you were the most famous opera singer in the world?"

"I do not do it for money."

"What *do* you do it for? Fame? Adulation?"

"Because I love to sing on the stage. It is my lifeblood."

"But it makes you anemic."

"Oooo, you are too cruel. It is better you go back to Paris. When I am established here as a prima donna, perhaps you will change your mind."

He shook his head. "How do you get so much confidence on so little talent?"

"Oooo!" She threw her napkin on the table, "Go back to Paris, see if I care!" And she stormed out of the dining room.

With studied calm, Ned Sharkey Butterworth finished his meal and even decided on dessert. He then retired to his bedroom in their shared suite. Hanna was already in hers, with the door locked.

The next morning, while Hanna was at her lesson, Ned left for Paris, via New York. He left no note.

Hanna hardly missed him, so intent was she in proving his judgment of her singing wrong. What *did* he know about music or singing or stage presence? Nothing!

Ken Maxwell was happy to pick up the slack. His soothing encouragement got her spirits up for her debut.

Hanna was always excited just to be *in* an opera house. The prospect of performing in one lifted her to the heavens. At her request, Ken Maxwell had gone along to introduce her to the director, Gunther Bergstresse, and the artistic director, Ella Jardin. Gunther was a heavy, hearty German whose touch was not soft. Ella was a thin woman deep into her seventies whose days of diva glory were behind her, to the loss of an adoring public. On being introduced, Gunther was gruff but endearing and Ella was sweetness and light, but suspicious.

"Have you brought something to sing for us, my dear?" Ella asked.

Hanna nodded with a self-effacing ducking of the top half of the body.

"Good. Give the music to Gunther. He will play for you."

Hanna handed Gunther the score and took her place on center stage front, looking out into the dark seats where Ella Jardin, artistic director, and Ken Maxwell, artistic provider, sat watching. It was a small audience, but a nerve-racking one. Hanna wished the entire company could have been there. There was a comfort in numbers. More of a chance of pleasing someone. Here, now, it was all or nothing. The butterflies were fluttering wildly in her stomach.

She had a rose over her ear, and she had worn her most startling jewels—the pyramid-diamond engagement-ring gift from Ned, a diamond-studded necklace that seemed too heavy for a slight woman to carry. Her dress was a flamboyant mélange of fabrics of primary colors which she had especially made in the Spanish mode for the role in *Carmen* she sought. When Gunther began the opening strains of the *Habañera*, Hanna came alive and strutted the stage as if she were in a Madrid bullring, caution to the winds, her feet exaggerating the tempo. There was something in her mere presence that lit up the stage. Her persona was larger than life. There was a magnetism that was virtually irresistible.

The shining light of her personality carried far over the footlights. The sound of her small voice hardly made it beyond the orchestra pit. Her powerful personality carried her through two or three bars of the music and then seemed to collapse around her feet. Valiantly she kept up the good front of her stage presence, but the effect was like a dramatic performance in a silent movie. Instinctively Gunther pressed the piano's soft pedal, but dimming the sound of the accompaniment didn't help matters; rather it made more painfully obvious the inadequacies of Hanna's voice.

The performance became increasingly more painful to endure as it slugged on to the end. It was only the benefactor's presence beside her that kept Ella Jardin from shouting out, "Thank you, that will be enough," as she would have to some unconnected aspirant. But it was not all altruism that held her tongue in that dark Chicago theater, the scene of so many of her personal triumphs. No, it was rather the nefarious thought that Ken Maxwell would, as the song wore on, become more aware of the hopelessness of the situation. His protégé child simply could not sing. It would have been so much more difficult to impart that wisdom to Mr. Maxwell had he not been in the theater to hear her singing firsthand. So Ella let Hanna go—gave her sufficient rope to hang herself.

If Ella had bothered to glance over at Maxwell, however, she would have seen him beaming proudly.

The sounds mercifully ended, not any too soon for Ella Jardin's taste, to a startling silence. Ken, still beaming, looked over at Ella. She was staring at the stage to ascertain if Hanna Mazurka had the slightest notion of her lack of vocal ability. Nothing discernible.

Suddenly Ken Maxwell began clapping and lifted Ella from her reverie. "Yes," she said, "well, yes…thank you, Hanna. Yes—thank you—yes."

"Isn't she something?" Maxwell exclaimed into Ella's ear.

"Yes, she is that," Ella conceded. "Yes…"

There ensued a hushed conference in which Gunther joined, leaving Hanna alone on the stage, her arms rigid at her sides to cover the perspiration she felt chilling her armpits. She heard only snatches of the conversation in the dark audience.

"…Impossible…" from Gunther.

"…a chance…" from Ken.

"Seriously, Ken…" from Ella.

Then a garbled exchange between Ken and Ella. Ella: "You must talk to her."

Hanna wasn't sure, but she thought this was said at a deliberately greater volume than what went before.

When the voices stopped and there was only the darkness, Hanna ventured down to the seats, where she came upon Ken alone.

"Phew!" she said, sinking into the seat next to him. "Where did everybody go?"

"Out," he said vaguely. "They wanted me to talk to you alone."

"Oh? Were they pleased?"

"I was pleased," he said. "I think you are simply wonderful. Nobody looks as good as you do on the stage. Not Ella Jardin in her prime, not anybody." Ken Maxwell was a tactful man, and he chose his words carefully. After all, he didn't want to discourage her so she would return to her husband in Paris. He had her to himself here, and he was sure time would wear down her resistance to once again blessing him with her incomparable charms.

"Looks, yes," she said, waving her bejeweled fingers, "but what about my voice?"

"I love your voice," he said. "I love everything about you."

"And Miss Jardin?"

"Perhaps Miss Jardin is a little jealous of your beauty," he said.

"And Gunther too?"

"Gunther will agree with Ella. If she tells him to jump in a lake, he will be all wet in no time."

"So, what did they say about my singing?"

"I think they feel it could use some work."

"Yes, who could not? But the part, it is mine?"

"They may not feel you are quite ready. They don't want you to embarrass yourself—or—"

"The opera? Is that what they said?" She was getting angry now. "They are afraid I would embarrass *them?*"

"Well, there is certainly no chance of that," Ken said. He felt he had to calm her with a strong approval. "They only asked me to talk to you about maybe putting off your appearance for a little while. You could try again in the next season perhaps."

"Ah! They are too lazy to work with me *this* season, is that it? You saw me up there. You think I am a star onstage, and I can tell you the audience agrees with you. I have experienced this in Havana. I am not an untested beginner, you know. Ella Jardin is a singer, period. She has *no* stage presence. She might as well be singing with the curtain down. In opera, you are *seen*, as well as heard. Doesn't she understand that? I have a star quality she could only dream about. Singers are a dime a dozen. I am a *star!* There are not so many stars. A handful!"

"Yes, my dear. I only thought I'd mention it. I leave it entirely to you. If you feel ready and want to go through with it, just say so."

"I will never be more ready," she said, without realizing the awkward truth of that statement.

424

After the poor reception Hanna got at the Chicago Opera Company, she fell out of love with the city which had held so much promise for her. She was, however, not a quitter. She kept her head up and returned to rehearsals, where she was given a small part with one song. And it was without much grace that Ella gave her the part. Hanna could tell the old woman was jealous of Hanna's youth and beauty.

Madame Mazurka had not been in rehearsals more than a few minutes when she felt the resentment of those who thought the part had been bought for her, and those who thought they had earned the right to it, whereas she had not. She would just show them. She remembered her triumph in Havana when she came onstage. She had a spark and she knew it. Men were crazy about her. She would just be patient and persistent and win them over.

Her adrenaline was pumping anyway. It always did when she was on a stage—rehearsal, performance, it didn't matter.

Hanna's first day was especially trying. She returned to her hotel room, exhausted by the mental anguish of coping with pettiness. The first thing she saw when she opened the door was a letter that had been put there by a bellman. Hoping it would lift her spirits, she tore it open and read it immediately.

Dear Hanna Mazurka Butterworth:

We are Erik Weidner's children. We are in desperate need of funds to help alleviate serious health problems of our own and my child who was born with serious deformities which can only be corrected by expensive surgery. I hesitated to burden you with our problems, but I see by the papers you married the richest man in the world. So, I was hoping you would forego the relatively little (to you) money my father left you so that we might save our child.

I have spoken to Mr. Barton on the subject and he is more than amenable to our cause and will prepare the documents at no charge to you—should you be so kind to help.

Irma Weidner Graul

Hanna was so angry at the letter she sat right down and penned one of her own on hotel stationery to her attorney.

Dear Mr. Barton:

This is the most obnoxious letter I have ever received. Are you really in collusion with this grasping woman? She makes it sound that way.

Erik wanted me to have that money for reasons Mrs. Graul could never understand. I didn't care about it, but I would never dream of going against his wishes. Fight her to the bitter end.

With warmest affection,
Hanna

Almost before the ink was dry, Hanna marched her response to the desk for mailing. She was not a woman to hoard her white-hot anger. No letting an angry letter cool off overnight for a fresh, more objective reading in the morning. And though she had not heard from her prince after she'd sent him the ill-fated letter, it did not occur to her to give her subsequent communicative efforts second thoughts.

During the ensuing months, Hanna studied voice assiduously with two new vocal coaches provided for her by Ken Maxwell, who, she said, couldn't have been nicer, really. Ella Jardin was less patient, but Hanna tried to ignore her. She couldn't wait for the dress rehearsal, when she would lay on her most spectacular jewels and wow them with her astonishing stage personality.

She had dinner with Ken Maxwell virtually every night. He was constantly encouraging.

Ned cabled and wrote letters of endearment that she thought he must have paid someone else to write. The letters unfailingly included checks in the precise amounts Hanna had asked for.

Hanna had found it convenient to ask both her husband *and* Ken Maxwell for amounts covering the same expenditures, and was thus able to double her money, so to speak, because neither man could deny her anything. As her bank account grew, so did her confidence. The men in her life were generous not only with their money, but also with their praise. And it often seemed each was trying to outdo the other with his adoration. Would they have been so steadfast if one or the other of them did not exist? She thought it unlikely. She saw it in her interest to keep them both dancing. It was impossible, she decided, for a woman to have too much attention.

Ken Maxwell told her he was working night and day on his divorce. They were eating at a fancy French place with red-velvet wallpaper and overpriced, overly rich food. But the ambiance was to their liking—dark and romantic.

Hanna allowed as how that was nice for him. "There is nothing worse than a bad marriage. You should have gotten out of it long ago."

He looked at her with those sheepdog, longing eyes. "Don't I know it," he groaned. "And how is your marriage? Dare I ask?"

"Well, as you see, my husband has gone back to Paris. That is, perhaps, an indication of how well he cares for me."

"Why do you stay with him?"

"For the same reason I married him."

"What is that?"

"Because you are married."

Ken Maxwell put his hand on his heart. "Oh, dear," he exclaimed, "you couldn't have made me happier."

"That is good, because you have made me very happy here in Chicago."

"But it is my pleasure, I can assure you," he said. "I'm so glad you're here."

"I am too. For you," she said, wrinkling her nose. "The opera—I am not so sure."

"You have the sweetest accent. Did I ever tell you?"

"No, you mustn't make fun, my English is so poor."

"I never have the slightest trouble understanding you. And I *love* hearing you talk. But are you not happy with the opera?"

"I must not burden you," she said, turning her face away as though that would *un*burden him.

"No, tell me. I want to know how you feel about *everything*."

"About the opera, not so good. Miss Jardin, I am feeling, has no good feeling for me."

"Oh, don't worry about her. She is old—past her prime. She is very hard on the young girls. Don't pay any attention to her."

"How can I not? She is there every day, looking down her nose at everything I do."

"You'll be fine."

"If I stay."

"*If?* Why would you not?"

"Sometimes I think it is hopeless and I should just go back to Paris."

He reached for her hand, and held it in his. "Hanna—don't leave me, please. I love you."

"You don't forget you're married?"

"The divorce will be settled soon. This is one time I regret being so rich. There are too many considerations for the divorce. It is costing me a lot of money, but it will be worth it if you will marry me."

"But *I* am married."

"And now I can nag *you* for a divorce."

"Nag? Is that what you think I do?"

"No, no, just a way of speaking. But would you consider a divorce to marry me?"

"I don't know," she hedged.

"Don't you love me?"

"I don't love my husband, that is sure."

"And me?"

She smiled and gave his hand a squeeze. "I've known worse." He took it as a huge compliment.

"So, you don't love your husband, and you've known worse than me—will you marry me when my divorce is final?"

"I don't know," she said with an enigmatic tone and a distant look in her eyes.

"Why? You said yourself there is nothing worse than a bad marriage."

"I know—but maybe it isn't so bad. For instance, Ned is very generous with me. He gives me anything I want."

"And so would I."

"And he lets me sing. I am across the world from him, but he is letting me have my career."

"And so would I."

"Ah, but would you? I wonder. If you were in Chicago, for instance, and I was in Paris, would that be all right with you?"

"I'd rather be with you, of course, but if that is what you want."

"But he is giving me a hundred thousand dollars a year *and* letting me have my career."

"I will match it."

She wrinkled her nose again. Her sign she was not convinced. "But we are getting older. You are older than Ned. I could go to you and pfft, no more Ken, and I would be poor Polish girl again."

"Then I'll give you a hundred thousand dollars a year as long as you live."

"Pooh, how can you do that?"

"I can, believe me. Lawyers can write anything."

"But suppose you lose your money?"

"We'll set up a trust, so no matter what happens to me *or* my company, the money will be there for you."

She considered the offer, searching her mind for loopholes. "But, what if I agree, and you marry me and change your mind?"

"Wow," he said, "you are quite a financial talent—how do you know these things?"

"I don't know, I am only asking. I always feel I should protect myself. I don't want to end up poor like I started out."

"I will be happy to put it in writing," he said. "Right now."

"Really?"

"Yes, really, I love you. I am unable to say no to you."

"You're sweet," she said, and paused thoughtfully. "Would you start the payments now?"

"Yes."

"Before I was divorced?"

"If that's what you want."

It was an offer she could hardly refuse. She liked him better than Ned anyway. He had more opera connections, and would be more supportive of her career.

The closer the company came to the performance date, the more nervous Hanna became. Consequently, the entire creative staff of the Chicago Opera also became more nervous. It was, by this time, painfully evident that Hanna Mazurka was not a singer.

An emissary was sent to Ken Maxwell, in the form of the august and celebrated Ella Jardin, who was said to be the backbone of rejuvenating the company.

She was ushered into his office without any undue subterfuge, and she sat facing Ken Maxwell, who appeared stronger in his own environment than he did out of it. He was the third generation Maxwell to hold the reins of his company and he often seemed an unlikely industrial baron. His features were soft, his manner gentle. But he loved women with a passion that had to belie his benign countenance.

"Good to see you, Ella," he said.

Ella was breathing heavily, with such gusto, Ken expected, at any moment, to see fire flare from her nostrils. "Well, it is *always* nice to see you, Ken, but under these circumstances it is perhaps less nice."

He knew what was coming, he'd known it the moment she called for an appointment, but he let her put it in her own words—get it off her chest.

"Your...how shall I say, protégé—that is a good word under the circumstances, no?"

He nodded, his lips puckered with grudging acceptance.

"She is giving me...ah, she is very beautiful. I can fully understand your great admiration. But she is giving me fits. I am responsible for the quality of the operas we produce. You have been very generous to us. It is no secret we would not be performing these great works today were it not for you. And for this we give you full credit in the program. And I must tell you, I fully understand this business with Miss Mazurka," she pronounced the word with a mixture of distaste and wonder at the bizarreness of it all. "But, Ken, she is no singer."

"She has wonderful presence, doesn't she?"

"I suppose that may be true," she admitted with reluctance. "And if we could have her make a brief entrance and flash her smile and wave her jewelry, it could be a very nice vignette addition to our performance. Unfortunately, you have insisted that she *sing*, and that will be, I promise you, a complete disaster. It will embarrass the company, it will embarrass her and it will embarrass you."

"Oh, come now, Ella, you exaggerate."

"Do I? Please come to rehearsal and you decide."

He waved her off as though her complaint were insignificant in the grand scheme of things. "You know I don't know much about those things."

"Yes, but you can tell the good from the bad, surely."

He shrugged. "What is the solution?"

"The solution is to remove her from the part. As fast and painlessly as possible."

"And how would that be?"

"That is why I am here," she said, drilling her fabled eyes into his. "You must do it."

"I?" He didn't like the idea.

"You got her in, you must get her out."

"But *I* don't want her out. You do."

"Fine. Blame it on me—only *you* talk to her."

"But why me?"

"I told you. Besides, she is so headstrong and so secure, thanks to you, that she wouldn't take anything from me. She would invoke your name and run to you anyway. Look, Ken, it is not new that rich men want to find a spot onstage for their pretty young things—and I'd be happy to oblige you—anytime. But a talent of this minuscule magnitude must surely be restricted to a walk-on—a part in the chorus, perhaps, as long as she didn't sing with them."

Ken watched Ella in silence for a long moment while her emotions subsided. He took her pronouncement with equanimity. Not much riled him except the intimate presence of a young woman. Ella was no longer young. "Hanna has a good heart," he said.

"Hah!" He had pushed her beyond her breaking point. "That woman is a viper! She has twisted you, and God knows how many other men, around her little finger. Three husbands already! And everyone predicting you will be number four. She is out for herself and no one better get in her way."

"That's not fair, Ella," he said, frowning at her exuberance. "Audiences love her."

Ella threw up her hands in exasperation. "All right," she said, "if you must persist, I will add a line to the program notes that Miss Mazurka appears under the auspices of Ken Maxwell."

He looked her in the eye. His face was so impassive, so smooth and young looking, but his eyes burned right through hers. It was Mr. Money against Miss Talent and it was no contest. "No!" he said, "I don't think you will do that."

And she didn't.

He had never asked for anything before. How much could Hanna hurt the opera anyway? She had one song—would it be missed if it was not sung at all? Only by the serious aficionados. So what if Hanna did not sing perfectly? Where was the need to make an opera out of it? He smiled at his pun. Yet he had given Ella carte blanche before and she was understandably disturbed by his uncharacteristic meddling. And in a way, he was sorry about it. It diminished his donation by wanting (now demanding) something in return.

That night at dinner, he sought to speak philosophically to

Hanna. She seemed tired.

"How's the opera coming?" he asked her.

"Oh, fine," she said. "It's a lot of work."

Ken Maxwell jumped at the opportunity. "Yes, I know it is. Maybe you should put your debut off a couple months or so."

"Has Ella put you up to this?" When he didn't answer, she said, "I see the fine hand of Ella here. She's been working against me from the very beginning. It is so difficult to accomplish something while I have to fight her. But I am finally sick of this. If you like, I will return tomorrow to Paris. Let Ella Jardin have her way. Let her walk all over you. You're the person who makes all their jobs possible. When you ask one itty-bitty thing, you'd think you had robbed them of their livelihood."

"Can you see their view, Hanna? Ella has devoted years to the company. She is a perfectionist. She feels your performance is not yet up to her standard. She comes to me to beg me to take you out of the show. What do I do?"

"You tell her in no uncertain terms you have the money; you are the boss. If they want to operate on toothpicks, you will ask nothing! Zero! This is so unfair! They have not seen me. Tell them to wait to the dress rehearsal. If they are not absolutely pleased with my performance there, they may throw me out. Until then, it is all idle speculation anyway."

"Do you feel you are ready?"

"Yes, I do—I've no doubt of my abilities."

"And your *singing* ability? You are ready to *sing?*"

"Oooo!" she trembled, and stood abruptly up and threw her napkin down on the table, as though it were a gauntlet. Then she turned and stormed out of the restaurant. Ken thought he should attempt to stop her, but he did not want to make a scene, and he knew she would be only too happy to make such a commotion everybody in the place would be aware of their differences.

But he had no more appetite—so when the food came, he asked for the check, paid it and left the food untouched on both plates. Then he took a cab to her hotel. He knocked on the door of her room, but she refused to answer. Finally, after many quiet entreaties, he went away, greatly saddened.

Hanna was inside, speechless. Her world was collapsing around her. Not only was she on thin ice with the opera company, she had angered her mentor. She thought she should open the door, welcome him with open arms, and let him have his will of her.

She looked at the jewel-studded watch on her delicate wrist and made the calculation. It would be four-thirty in the morning in Paris. Allowing a half-hour to get through on the telephone, Ned would get the call around five.

She debated for only a moment before she placed the call with the hotel operator. After she hung up to await the arduous process of making an overseas telephone connection in the 1920s, Hanna speculated on Ned's reaction. He would be angry, of course, being awakened so early, but would he be glad to hear from her? How would he react to her request? She had worked herself into a solidly negative frame of mind by the time the phone rang almost forty minutes later.

"I have your Paris party on the line, Madame Mazurka," the hotel operator said. Through the normal static and clicking connection sounds, then dead air, Hanna managed to yell, "Hello."

"Huh?" came the sleepy response.

"Ned?" she said.

"Huh?"

"It's Hanna."

"Oh, it's you," he grumbled. "Jesus Christ, Hanna, what is it, five o'clock in the morning?"

"I miss you," she said.

Silence.

"Ned? Are you there?"

"Really?" He seemed to waken a tad.

"Could you come back?"

"Chicago? Memories not too good."

"Ned?" she pleaded. "To take me home?"

"Home?"

"To Paris," she said, with tears in her voice.

Hanna stood onstage on the white marks Gunther had laid down for her. She was looking out into the dark seats of the opera house, where she imagined her nemesis Ella Jardin was hiding so she could see without being seen. A slight man was bouncing about, training all sorts of lights on her and trying various scrims and gels, ostensibly to flatter her onstage. She wondered briefly if they were all in cahoots to do the opposite — make her appear as dismal as possible. But the boys in the company that liked girls seemed to like her. The boys that liked boys were more attentive to older women like Ella.

"Ready for a run-through of your number?" Gunther asked.

"First," Hanna said, shading her

eyes with her hand, trying to peer over the footlights, "I want to know who's out there."

Gunther was not sure of his duty here. He was saved by Ella calling out:

"I'm here, dear. Have no fear. You won't know the audience for the performance. One houseful of strangers in the dark—one or two rows visible down front. All else is darkness. Get used to it."

Hanna was so unnerved by that "get used to it," that she missed her cue to start singing. The accompanist stopped and Gunther called out from the front row: "Mazurka, that's your cue."

"*Madame* Mazurka, if you please," Hanna demanded, not having any idea why she said that, but suspecting it was a delayed reaction to Ella's treating her like a schoolgirl. The house seemed to go dead. Gunther broke the silence. "What?" he said. "We called Caruso, Caruso, we didn't say Mister. Not good enough for you?"

"I think a little respect would not be too much to ask."

"Respect?" he said. "Well, let's hear you sing, then we'll decide if there is something to respect."

Just something else to make me *more* nervous, Hanna thought. She could feel the icy antipathy toward her. The pianist began again. This time, Hanna took her cue and began to sing— about five notes, when Ella Jardin stopped her.

"*Madame* Mazurka," she said, in gentle mockery, "put some more zest in your voice."

She began again.

"Madame Mazurka, you're still too timid."

Again.

"Madame Mazurka," (two bars later), "you're flat. Can you hear the piano?"

"I hear it. It sounds out of tune to me."

"Well, it's just been tuned, but we won't second-guess that. Your duty is to match the pitch of the musical accompaniment, be it orchestra or piano—out of tune or not. Can you do that?"

Hanna glared into the darkness. "Yes, if you let me sing instead of harassing me every two seconds."

"Then sing it right, and you'll get no interruptions from me."

The music began again. She sang a few bars more.

"Madame Mazurka! The vibrato will not do. It is all over the scale. Gentle vibrato. You sound like a shaking automobile."

Hanna stomped her foot. "I *must* be allowed to sing through this song once. The performance is already Saturday, and I have not been allowed to sing the song through."

"Well, Madame, learn the song correctly, and we will be only too pleased to have you sing it unmolested by me or anyone else who knows a D from a D flat. We have only so much time to devote to rehearsals here and we can't waste it all on you. You must prepare yourself for your solo, don't look to us to carry you. That is not professional."

"Professional? Am I being treated as a professional? Now, will you let me sing my solo without all this carping? I will take suggestions when I am finished."

"You will, will you?" Ella said sardonically. "You think you can tell us what you will and will not do? You are a performer here for reasons that are no secret to this company. You are not the director. Not at *anyone's* sufferance."

There was a silence while Hanna waited for Ella Jardin to calm down and for the music to begin. Then there were muffled, agitated voices from the dark beyond.

"May we start again?" Hanna said, finally.

"I am sorry, your time is up," Ella Jardin said. "Our diva is here and we must rehearse her. Perhaps another day, when you are better prepared."

Madame Mazurka did not leave the stage graciously, but stomped off with huffy leaden footfalls. On her way offstage, she passed the diva, on her way onstage. The diva made a fleeting, but devastating, eye contact with her. There was contempt in both pairs of eyes; Hanna's because the diva's time was considered more important than hers; the diva's because she did not want her performance ruined by this incompetent amateur.

Well, this was a credit Madame Hanna Mazurka was not giving up.

Hanna decided if they tried to replace her at the last moment, she would show up on the stage with her replacement, and they could sing the solo as a duet.

Hanna took a cab directly to her hotel. Under her hotel-suite door lay a telegram and letter. Her mind was too full of the insults she had suffered to open either one of them.

It had been three days since she had not answered Ken Maxwell's knock at her door. What had he expected? A married woman was supposed to admit a married man to her bedroom in the middle of the night?

Did his silence mean he had given up? Men should *not* give up. They are the predators, they surely couldn't expect a young woman to assume that role. Especially not a young *married* woman.

Hanna lay on the bed fully clothed. It seemed she would be dining alone again tonight. It wasn't good for a young woman to be seen alone. People would talk. Speculate. Especially one who had been constantly seen in the company of the city's richest inhabitant.

Several hours of self-pity and self-justification passed before she had the strength to go to the dining room.

She ate lightly, and her spirits were buoyed by the attention of the dining-room staff. It made her feel beautiful all over again. By the time Hanna had returned to her room, she felt she had the strength to open her mail. Perhaps because cables connoted urgency, she opened that first.

ARRIVE FRIDAY 8 AM 20TH CEN-
TURY LIMITED STOP EAGER
TO SEE YOU STOP
NED

She had almost forgotten her husband was coming. He was arriving just in time to see her performance, and she was touched by the gesture. Then she could at last escape the endless insults of this windy city.

She sat on the couch, the unopened letter in her lap. Her head dropped back so she looked at the ceiling. She closed her eyes and thought about her life and the men in it, and how she came to be in Chicago, Illinois, USA, from Brest Litovsk, Poland, via Russia, Switzerland, Paris and New York. She thought again of the man she considered the driving force in her life, the prince. He was last heard from, indirectly, in Paris. So why was she here when she should be in Paris pursuing her lifelong goal? What were the chances she would find the prince in Chicago?

She knew there was nothing like marrying for love. It was not just a young girl's dream — it was the meaning of life itself. She would gladly sacrifice everything, her hoarded wealth in banks, her jewels, her Rolls-Royce, even her career. Her career was only, she told herself, a means to an end. The end was the attention of the prince. She would go back to Paris — right after her performance. Ken was not expressing any interest in her anymore. If he withdrew his financial backing, her career in Chicago would flounder. She'd be just as well off pursuing her career in Paris, where she might run into the prince.

Hanna touched the letter on her lap. She had a premonition it was written notice of the cancellation of her "contract" with the Chicago Opera Company.

Well, if they were letting her go, she wouldn't dignify them with a fight. Someday she would make her name, and then they would be sorry. She mused, with a tight smile, that no one had the courage to fire her in person, they had to resort to a cowardly letter from some attorney, it looked like, now that she focused on the return address.

Before she tore open the envelope, Hanna decided this time in Paris she would hire a private detective to help her find the prince. It was not like Katrina not to answer her letters. Perhaps something was wrong. Maybe they had gotten divorced. Hanna certainly wouldn't want to break up anyone's marriage, but the prince and Katrina — that could offer a temptation. Hanna was so much more suited to the prince — how could either he *or* Katrina be happy? She might be doing them a favor.

Carelessly she tore open the envelope and pulled out a letter, typewritten on the letterhead of Austin, Phillips and Sachs.

Dear Madame Mazurka:

> We represent Mr. Kenneth Maxwell, who has requested we draft an agreement for you both to sign. This agreement is intended to transfer to you the sum of one hundred thousand dollars per year for life.
>
> It will be necessary for us to draw the documents for this transaction, and you and Mr. Maxwell

be required to sign them in my presence.

An agreement such as this requires some participation of the parties in reference to details of the agreement. Please call this office at the above telephone number to indicate times you would be available for such conferences as may be necessary to complete the agreement.

Very truly yours,

Hiram B. Sachs
Partner

When Hanna finished reading, she stared at the letter without seeing anything but a blur of type. Her first conscious thought was, ironically, that this was some conspiracy to derail her career, and, ergo, to keep her from her prince. Why else would there be the verbiage about "participation of the parties in reference to details...”? Obviously there were going to be strings attached. Why else not just start sending the checks?

Then she slid into rationality. One hundred thousand was a lot of money. Hers merely for the asking. Not bad for a poor Polish girl, she told herself. She had seen enough of Ned Sharkey Butterworth to know how erratic he could be, and generous though he was, he could, and would, at anytime cut off all aid to her.

What could it hurt for her to accept the money from Ken Maxwell? He had already told her he had more money than he could spend in a few lifetimes and it would give him pleasure to spend it on her. So, if he didn't want anything in return, why not? But there it was again in her consciousness: the word "details."

Would she be swallowing too much pride to pick up the telephone and call Ken herself? Ordinarily she made no calls to men. They called *her*. But in this case, perhaps an exception was in order. She moved to the desk and called Ken Maxwell at home.

When he answered the phone, she said, "Are you mad at me?"

"No," he said softly. "I was hoping it was you."

"I got the letter from the lawyer."

"Yes?"

"Why would you want to do this after how poorly I treated you?"

"Well," he explained, "I said I would."

"Phew!" she said. "And you are a man of your word. How few of them are in this world! But I must release you from your promise."

"Why?"

"Because I am not deserving. I have done nothing to warrant your generosity."

"But you have. Just being you is enough for me. I would feel well repaid if you just keep on being you. Will you have dinner with me tomorrow night? We can talk more about it if you like."

"Certainly we can."

"Oh, good," he said, "seven-thirty. I'll call for you."

"Fine—oh, and, Ken…"

"Yes?"

"Have you heard from Ella today?"

"No—why?"

"Just wondered."

"Something happen?"

"She was giving me a hard time. Wouldn't let me sing. Kept interrupting me every few seconds. Humiliated me in front of every-body."

"Oh, I'm sorry."

441

"Could you talk to her?" she said. "Find out what's bothering her…or do you know?"

"Well, I hesitate to remind you—but we did talk about it—the last time we were together. She feels you would be better off waiting a while—develop your voice a bit more—but that's no cause to be rude."

"No—well—I hate to bother you with my problems…"

"No bother. I'm flattered to do anything I can for you. You want me to talk to her, I will."

"Oh, I'd appreciate it so much."

"No problem. See you tomorrow night."

It worked like a charm. Next day at rehearsal, Hanna sang her solo start to finish, and no one said a word. Yet, Hanna was uneasy. It was so obvious Ken had inhibited Ella; there was not a *word* after she finished. Not a thank you, not the merest suggestion for improvement. Nothing.

Hanna had been nervous, and she knew her voice wasn't carrying very far—but she had sung, and that was the end of it. The dress rehearsal was tomorrow afternoon—and Ned was due in, in the morning. She would bring him to get his opinion.

That night, sitting across the dinner table, with its fine china and sterling silver, the dainty bowl of flowers between them, Ken looked dreamily into Hanna's eyes. "How did it go today?"

"Now she's gone to the other extreme. They are giving me the silent treatment."

"Well, look, isn't that better than harassing you?"

"Yes…*much*." But there was no conviction in her voice.

"Well, look at it this way," he said. "Tomorrow afternoon is the dress rehearsal. Then the performances, and you're home free. No more conflict, no more aggravation. Just do the best you can— nobody expects any more."

Though he meant that innocently, Hanna managed to take it as a demeaning appraisal of her vocal abilities. "Thank you very much," she pouted.

"What's wrong?"

"Nobody *expects* anything from me, is that it?"

"No, that's not it. Oh, did I say the wrong thing again? Look, would you like me to come to the dress rehearsal to give you moral support?"

"No!" she snapped too suddenly. All she needed was for Ken to run into Ned. How could she tell Ken Ned was coming? "I mean," she explained, "I'm afraid it would make me very nervous if you were there. I would be nervous with every note. I could absolutely not sing, I would be shaking so."

"What about the performance? Am I to be banished from that also?"

"That is different. There will be a houseful of people. Very impersonal. But the dress rehearsal! That means everything to how I sing at the performance." She reached over and laid her hand atop his on the table. "Oh, please, no," she said.

"All right," he said, smiling and putting his other hand on her hand.

During the meal, she made the kind of flirty, eyelash-batting conversation that he adored. No one was better at it than she. "I missed our dinners. I was so alone. Why did you not call?"

"I thought you didn't want me to."

"But nonsense. How could that be?"

"Well, you didn't answer the door when I came after you, perhaps there is someone else—a boyfriend—or even your husband suddenly came to town."

"Oh, you rascal, you," she said, gently poking his arm with her loose fist. "I was there. I was just being stupid. You must forgive us women. We are stupid sometimes. You should have kicked in the door and made love to me. That is what I needed."

His heart pumped wildly as he stared at her, half convinced he had not heard her correctly. "You mean...well...perhaps tonight—without kicking down the door?"

"Well..."

"It has been such a long time," he pleaded pathetically.

"You mean I should just *let* you?"

He nodded.

"Why, you naughty boy! You know I am married," she whispered with throaty sensuality. "That would be *adultery*! It is illegal here, no?"

"It is a law more honored in the breach," he said, smiling tightly.

"Ah, yes—"

"Well?"

"We will see," she said, winking at him. "But what is this business the lawyer wants to discuss?"

"Oh, Hiram," he said, waving a hand to signify the insignificance, "he's an old-fashioned-lawyer type. Of course, he expressed shock at my proposal—offered all kinds of stumbling blocks."

"Well, it is very sweet of you to want to do it, but perhaps it is not practical."

"Practical?"

"If he has stumbling blocks."

"I will get him over those," he said.

"Would you?" she said, excited at the prospect. "I have so much on my mind with my debut coming up, I can't see how I could be of any help in this."

"I do understand," he said, "perfectly."

"Could you take care of it then?"

"Yes, I will."

"If he has any reason to overrule your decision, I could not fight him. Hah! Imagine a poor Polish girl like me against a lawyer!"

"Poor lawyer," he said, and smiled.

She laughed. "Oh, Ken, you are a funny man. It makes me feel so good to laugh at your jokes."

That night, Ken crossed her threshold with Hanna. In light of his promised generosity, making him feel desired was the least she could do.

When she finished working her magic on him, and he was fairly groveling with gratitude, she said, "I have some bad news—"

"What? Bad news? Why? What is it?"

"I got a telegram. My husband is coming."

"Oh, well," he stumbled. "Perhaps that should not be *bad* news. It might make you happy," he said, looking at her on the bed, out of the corner of his eye, and hoping she would disagree. He had never seen a body of such perfect proportions. Never in his wildest fantasies did he ever dream he could get a woman like Hanna Mazurka.

"*You* make me happy," she said, and rolled on top of him and kissed his trembling lips.

Ken Maxwell left Hanna Mazurka's hotel suite, like the good sport he was, at four a.m.—allowing her another three hours' sleep before she took a cab to the train station.

She stood in the cool morning air on the platform only a few minutes, when her husband came bounding toward her with a huge smile of anticipation on his narrow face and a beribboned box in his hands. Hanna's eyes focused on the box—did his smile annoy her as much as his snorting laughter? She tried not to think of it.

They embraced. "Mmm," he said. "You smell so good."

"My poem," she said, into his shoulder.

"What poem?" he asked.

> "Money spent
> on scent
> is money
> well spent."

He laughed, and they separated. "You look just as ravishing…" he said.

"Hardly, I'm a mess," she said. "I have a dress rehearsal and I'm hardly ready."

He handed her the box.

"Oooo, for me?"

"Well," he said, "we don't have a dog."

She laughed, but his raucous laughter covered it.

"Oh, you! Come. I have a cab waiting. Where is your luggage?"

"Being taken to the hotel."

In the cab, Ned said, "Aren't you going to open it?"

"Oh, shall I? Now?"

"Yes — now —"

Hanna toyed with the gold ribbon and peeked at the card. "Oooo, Cartier —"

"Yes," he said. "You weren't buying enough. So, I was afraid they'd go out of business." And he treated her to a few bars of his laugh.

The card said:

> To my dearest wife
> with all my love.
>
> Ned

"How nice," she said. But when she opened the box her eyes got big as moons. "Oh, it's so beautiful!" She extracted the bracelet, with untold rows of diamonds, and brought it to her lips and kissed it. Then she held out her wrist and handed Ned the bracelet. "Put it on, dear," she said, and he obliged. She held up her wrist and stared lovingly at it. "Phew! I guess this could keep them in business for a year!"

"Two!" he said, and roared with laughter.

She admired the dazzling bracelet from every angle, turning her wrist this way and that, catching the light in sparkling hues of the rainbow.

"Like it?" he said.

"I *love* it!" she said.

"There's more where that came from," he said, and he leaned over to kiss her. She kissed him with a quickened interest, then slacked off. "Did you reserve a suite at the hotel?" she asked.

He seemed startled. He looked at the diamond bracelet, then said, "I was hoping to stay with you."

Hanna matched his startled look. The idea of sharing her sleeping bed all night with a man made Hanna cringe. She thought back to that little neighbor intruder in her father's bed, and she tasted bile.

Why would anyone want to be crowded in with another person while she was sleeping? Such sleeping arrangements were strictly for the peasants who couldn't afford two beds and separate quarters. And Madame Hanna Mazurka was *not* a peasant!

"But I must have my beauty sleep—my performance is tomorrow—the dress rehearsal is this afternoon and I look a sight," Hanna said, with a flirtatious pat on his forearm.

"I'd like to *see* the girl more beautiful than you. I'll give you ten grand if you point one out."

"Oh, silly, I'd take you to the poorhouse with that offer."

He snorted.

Good God, she thought. That laugh!

When the cab pulled up in front of the Palmer House, under the elevated train, Ned asked, "May I see you to your room?"

"Well, certainly," she said, turning the diamond bracelet on her wrist with her other hand, "just as soon as you register."

Ned registered like a good boy and felt more than foolish doing so. Hanna said she would meet him in her room after he was settled in his.

He didn't wait for any "settling" but went right to her room. When she opened the door, he saw she had put on a striking negligee.

"Sexy," he murmured, putting his arms around her and

kicking the door closed behind him. "Five thousand miles I came to see my sweetie, and she makes me get my own room first."

"Now, now," she purred, "you're in *my* room now."

They kissed. Ned was careful not to be too overpowering with her. He was not by nature a gentle lover, but he did his best. Still, once on the bed, Hanna felt as if she were the ball in some brute-force athletic contest, but she bit her lip rather than complain. They undressed each other, and he left the bracelet on her arm.

"Oh, I get to keep this," she said, admiring it again. "You certainly are a generous husband."

Ned was so easily, and quickly, pleased. Hanna felt she had done her duty. "Wow," he said, "you really are something! I must be some fool to leave you alone for five minutes. Imagine me thinking I could get that much of a kick out of playing polo! A horse next to my beautiful wife. Not even close!" And he had a merry bout of laughter.

"Ned!" she admonished him. "No girl wants to be compared to a horse."

"Oh, no?" he said. He seemed surprised. "Why not?"

"Oh, don't be silly, lover," she said. "Now it's off to your room with you. I have to rest before my rehearsal or I'll look a sight onstage. Three hours," she said. "Then get us a cab and come for me. Now, out, OUT!" she said.

"What about lunch?"

"I can't eat before a performance. I'll eat after." And she began vocalizing with scales, while he looked at her as though she were some kind of extraterrestrial phenomenon.

On the way to the opera house, in the cab, she put her hand on Ned's knee and said, "Now, you sneak in the back of the theater. Don't let them see you."

"Why not?"

"I don't want them to act different because you are there."

"Why would they?"

"Because these are strange people. Take my word for it. If they ask you who you are, tell them my hairdresser or something."

"Righto," he said, with a snort.

They went in the stage-door entrance and Hanna maneuvered Ned to a seat in the back of the hall.

He was not a great fan of opera, but he was a great fan of *hers*, so he waited with patient anticipation all through the first act. But when she hadn't appeared at the start of the second act, he was beginning to wonder if she ever would. Perhaps she had been too nervous to go on. Ned wouldn't have missed it if they'd cut her part, or if someone else sang it.

Just as he decided that was what had happened, she appeared, at the top of the stairs in center stage. She was wearing a black-velvet, full-length, flowing gown, trimmed in gold. And with all the sparkling jewelry she had adorned it with, it looked to Ned like one of those cloths the jeweler uses to display his gems.

His heart leapt as he saw her descend the stairs with the feminine equivalent of a swagger—with such panache he was proud to be her husband—yes, proud even to be a "stage-door Johnny," the role he had dreaded.

The music swelled dramatically in the orchestra pit, befitting the entrance of the queen of opera, which part, Ned thought, fit his wife like a glove. He held his breath, waiting for her to sing.

Striding down the steps, Hanna had to be careful not to miss a step or step on her gown. While exercising this care, her eye caught a young man in a sloppy suit, sitting in the front row, with a pad and pencil in his hand. Hanna did not recognize him as a member of the company and instantly she had the dreaded thought: he was from a newspaper and was there to crucify her. It was all part of a plot to drive her from the part. For some reason, she could, at that instant, even imagine the headline:

MADAME MAZURKA MAKES IT DOWN THE STAIRS BUT FALLS ON HER FACE SINGING

The steps were successfully descended and the cue from the orchestra sounded. Hanna Mazurka opened her mouth to sing, but nothing came out.

Nothing! She was looking at the young man in the front row—the one in the slovenly suit. The only person she could see in the audience. If she could only see Ned! But no, it had to be this kid with the smirk on his face, beating his pencil against the pad in his lap at a deliberately different pulse than the orchestra. Oh, he seemed to be having a grand old time at her expense.

She wasn't sure, but she thought she heard some gargling sounds coming from somewhere. Was it from her mouth or from the lad in the front row?

Somehow she was able to leave the stage when the music ended, and before the interlude to the next aria. But she left that stage without conscious effort and walked through backstage and out the stage door, into the street, where she summoned all her strength to hail a cab.

Hanna was not far off on her headline prediction.

MADAME MAZURKA WALTZES
DOWN OPERA STAIRCASE
VOICE TAKES A PRATFALL

Well, she told herself, it was that kind of incivility that had driven her out of Chicago. Ned had been a dear, arranging everything. Train to New York—three-day layover and then boarding the *Aquitania*.

Ned had secured cabins next to each other in the first-class section. The proximity was a trifle close for her taste, but she made no complaint, even though his conjugal visits were wearing in their frequency.

At her request, they sat at a table for eight, at dinner, and while Ned found the company boring, Hanna felt it was less boring than when she had been with Ned alone.

She soon settled in his villa outside Paris and found it commodious. It was a large old country house of two and a half stories, with several acres of well-attended garden surrounding it. Rows of tall poplar trees set it off from the villas on either side. There was a swimming pool out back and a barn on the back edge of the property, where three horses were housed. Ned's string of polo ponies were kept farther from town, at the rural polo fields.

Hanna went to several polo matches and enjoyed the challenge of dressing for them, but soon tired of what she thought was the mindlessness of the sport. Opera was still her thing and she reveled in attending every performance, never losing the girlish hope that she would spy the prince at one of them. First, she looked only in the boxes, but then, giving way to the depressing thought that he might have lost his wealth, she began looking for him everywhere—even the upper reaches of the balcony.

He was not to be found. But she didn't give up going to the opera. It gave her something to do and she became a serious fan of the art form—the most all-encompassing art form: drama, music, sets, costumes, lighting. To which she added a copious display of dramatic jewelry.

One of the first things Hanna had done on moving into the villa was to hire a maid and cook. Ned had been making do with a cleaning service and had been taking all his meals out. She asked Ned if he wanted to interview the women, but he waved her off. "Your department," he said.

To save money, she hired a combination maid-cook, in the person of Gilda Trenary. Gilda was a young woman of twenty-two, sorely in need of work, pleasant of face, modest of figure, but not so beautiful Hanna's husband should prefer Gilda.

Next, Madame Mazurka sought out a new voice teacher, well connected to the Paris Opera (he was the chorus coach). The studio of Alen Arvey was the third floor in a walk-up of a narrow building looking across a courtyard to another wall of the same building. The piano was cluttered with music and pictures of the teacher with his celebrated pupils, a desk in the corner was covered with unruly papers.

451

Arvey was a bleary-eyed, fleshy man who suffered from a surfeit of foie gras and an unslakable thirst for *vin*. Though he prided himself on remaining steady, the glow of the alcohol saw him through too much cacophony.

After she unloaded all her pent-up anger at her treatment in Chicago, he said, "Let me hear you sing." He pulled out the music for her Chicago solo, and when she had finished singing it, he nodded. "Well," he said, "what are your expectations?"

"Expect...? I expect you to teach me to become an opera star."

He looked her over for a sign she was pulling his leg. Seeing nothing of the sort, Alen Arvey asked her, "Tell me, why do you want to do this—be an opera star?"

"Well," she sputtered, "I've always wanted to sing opera."

"But you can sing opera without being onstage. Is it important to you to *be* on the opera stage — in public?"

Hanna crinkled her forehead. Was this a question she could answer? She had sought fame so long it had become part of her unquestioned quest. She couldn't tell him about the prince. It would sound too ridiculous. Yet Mr. Arvey was not letting her off easily.

"*Why* is the most difficult question to ask a complex human being," she said. "We can tell you where and how and when much easier than *why*. It is in my soul, that is all I can tell you."

He nodded. "How old are you?"

"Twenty-nine."

"And do you know how long it takes to become an opera diva? And how long a woman can expect to keep her voice up to operatic standards?"

"Whatever it takes, I am willing to do. I am not a lazy person."

"Yes, and you can go far in this world on ambition. But for opera, it takes more than ambition. You must also have the vocal instrument."

"I can develop the vocal instrument," she said.

"Can you?" he asked, not expecting an answer. "How long have you been studying voice?"

"Perhaps twelve, thirteen years," she said.

"Are you a great deal better than you were when you started?"

"Well, I should think so," she said. "Listen, if you feel you cannot teach me, perhaps I should seek someone who could."

Alen Arvey thought it over briefly. Maybe he could help her, he told himself. He would have felt better about himself if he'd had the strength of character to turn her down, but the fact was, he was intrigued by her — by her ambition, so ill-placed in the opera world, her wealth, her celebrity and, not least, her beauty.

"All right," he said. "Let's try it for a while."

Then, to follow the pursuit of her ambition with its sister quest, Hanna made an appointment with a private investigator. Pierre Biet was recommended to her by the nice inspector general of the police department, whom she feared would fall out of his chair in his effort to inspect her legs.

Mr. Biet was a retired policeman who had made his apartment his office, rearranging the furniture to make his living room look like the office of a busy investigator. There were files, a desk and chairs and a central window looking out over the treetops.

At first sight, Hanna thought Pierre Biet was too old to undertake her mission. Too old and too grumpy. He had snow-white hair and lines in his face deep enough to plant grapes.

"Oh," she said, when she sat facing him across his Louis XIV desk, "I had pictured someone…well, younger."

"So had I," he said, without smiling.

"Are you able to…well, to accomplish what I am after?" She was thinking aloud.

"What are you after?"

"Oh, yes—finding some missing people."

"More than one?"

"Well, husband and wife, actually."

"Are you sure they are still together?"

"Well, no. I'm not sure of anything."

"Who are they?"

"Prince Stephanoff of the old Russia and his wife, Katrina."

"Why do you wish to locate them?"

"Why? Is that important?"

"Everything is important."

"Well," she stammered a bit, "Katrina was a dear friend of mine from school. The prince—well, he was also a friend. I saw them in Paris some years ago and now they seem to have vanished." Hanna looked at Pierre's gray head and wished she had more confidence. Yet he had been highly recommended. Perhaps the inspector got a fee-split for the recommendation.

"How much are you willing to spend in this endeavor?"

"How much should it cost?"

"No way of telling. I might find them tomorrow. In that case, you could expect a reasonable bill. On the other hand, it could take a long time. I was merely trying to get an idea of your limits."

"I have no limits," she said.

453

Alen Arvey was a no-nonsense voice teacher, and Hanna found herself looking forward to her lessons. He hammered away at fundamentals and exercises to deepen the resonance of her vocal apparatus. He promised her nothing and let her sing arias only once or twice a week. He was a taskmaster, but he was conscientious and thorough and Hanna, as she'd said, was no slacker.

In her second week, she asked Monsieur Arvey how one went about meeting fellow musicians.

"Give parties," he said. "Musicians love to go to parties."

"Oh, I don't know," she said, "we live rather far out, perhaps at night many people would not come."

"In the daytime then—have a salon."

"What is this salon?"

"A get-together of artists, musicians, what have you. You sit around and chat about the arts. One or two might perform. You could serve them tea and pastries. It is most enjoyable."

"Would you come?"

"Surely."

"Could you bring other musicians?"

"Just tell me when," he said.

A fortnight later, on a Sunday afternoon, Hanna held her first salon at the villa she shared with Ned, outside of Paris. There was an assortment of talents and sexes, as well as sexual preferences, and Hanna was delighted with the attention they all paid her. Ned showed up for twenty minutes after the party hit its stride, but the conversation left him cold. Not a soul there knew anything about polo ponies. He also had less tolerance for blatantly effeminate men than had his wife.

Hanna was dressed to the nines, flaunting excessive jewelry—five bracelets up one arm, three up the other, all her fingers had rings on them, and she wore a necklace which seemed to cover everything from her waist to her shoulders. The dress was simple tightly knit wool, but expensive. Hanna found the more she paid for clothes, the less likely she would see them on someone else. "Simple and expensive," she would explain to Ned. "Simply expensive," he would say, and laugh his aggravating laugh.

"Well, dear," he said, "I must be trundling on." She was standing in a gaggle of admirers, including the young Wilhelm Drang, whom her teacher had introduced as a rising opera conductor. A rather unattractive young man who walked as if he had a permanent knee injury, Wilhelm could not take his eyes off his hostess.

"Oh, dear, must you go so soon?" she asked Ned, in her party-chat mode.

"I'm going to see my ponies—they talk my language." And he patted Hanna on her bottom, causing a blush of embarrassment to rush to her face. Before she could criticize the action, he was gone.

Gilda did a fine job passing the pastries she had made. Hanna poured the tea herself with a flutter and a flourish.

In attendance were a violinist, a Russian pianist, three

vocalists, Alen Arvey, Wilhelm Drang, and Hanna, who tagged herself as an opera singer. The pianist played Chopin, then accompanied a soprano in an aria from *The Magic Flute*. There was a general clamoring for Hanna to sing (save by her teacher), but she said she was too nervous from giving the party.

The day was, she felt, a crowning success. Everyone said so, including her teacher. They all looked forward to her next soirée, in two weeks.

Wilhelm Drang was the last to leave. Hanna had the feeling he was lingering, and she said, "Won't you sit down? Here, let me get you another cup of tea."

"Thank you," he said. "You're very kind." His demeanor was self-effacing. He always seemed to back away from a question before he answered it. Before stating an opinion, he would proffer a deferential bow.

He sat facing her, with the cup of hot tea balanced between his closed knees.

"So," she said, from her ornate chair, which had its roots in French antiquity, "Monsieur Arvey tells me you are a conductor."

"I have been studying, yes. But getting work — that is another matter."

Hanna was comforted to hear that his French was as uncertain as hers. He came from the Palatinate in Germany, he said. He had crossed the border just as the war was ending, so he found himself not too popular in French society.

"You did not have to fight in the war?" she asked.

"My eyesight is too bad for me to be any use as a soldier," he said, hanging his head. "It is a shame I must live with."

"What shame?" she asked, outraged at the idea. "You could do nothing about it!"

"Yes, but one wants to serve one's country."

"Well, perhaps if their cause is just." She was thinking of her first husband, the baron, who hadn't served a just cause. She looked back on that now as though the evasion of duty had been his idea. "Those he-man heroics bore me."

He smiled, showing her his poor teeth for the first time. He was usually guarded about revealing his crooked teeth, but she had for a moment caused him to lose his self-consciousness. He looked deep into her eyes. A slow, longing look. Her gaze was steadily upon his. "Tell me about your singing," he said.

"Well, I'm just back from my debut at the Chicago Opera Company."

"Why, that's wonderful. How did it go?"

"Oh," she waved modestly, "you know. I take the stage with my jewels and my dresses, and I create such a sensation no one cares whether I can sing or not."

He laughed lightly. "I don't believe *that*," he said.

"Well, you're very sweet," she said, and got those crinkles around her eyes, which, when focused on him, made Wilhelm think he was the only man in the world. "Now, tell me about yourself," she said. "What are you working on now?"

"I am a waiter," he blurted. "I must make a living until I can get a position conducting. I sing in Alen's chorus, but that pays very little. I guess I am fortunate to work at a restaurant where they indulge me my performances and rehearsals."

"What is your dream?"

"Oh," he sat up suddenly, almost spilling the tea, "it is to conduct opera. If I want to get carried away with my dream, I would have my own opera company in my own opera house in Paris. Silly, I guess."

"We must have our dreams. If we do not, *nothing* will happen. And if you are going to dream at all, I always say, might as well dream big."

"Hm," he said, murmuring into his raised teacup, "yes, hmmm—but don't bigger dreams make for bigger disappointments?"

"Not if you don't give up. You might die without seeing your dream come true, but at least you've had the dream to hold on to."

"Yeah," he said. "You are a wise young woman."

The simple comment startled Hanna. No one had ever called her wise before. The only comments she ever got from men were about her beauty. She found, to her surprise, this awkward young man endearing. None of her men friends since the prince were close to her own age. It was an eerie feeling for her, but she liked it. She was actually a few years older than Wilhelm, and she was surprised at how good that made her feel.

"What are *your* dreams?" he asked.

She waved at him. "Oh, not much. Just to be the most talented and famous diva in the world."

He nodded solemnly.

She laughed. "Isn't it funny?" she said.

"What?"

"Our dreams are compatible. I would be the diva and you the conductor."

"Oh," he said. "I could only wish to be so lucky."

They spoke easily to each other until the sun began to fall below the western horizon. When they said good-bye, they told each other how much they had enjoyed talking to the other, and how they were looking forward to the next soirée of the group.

Wilhelm went home secure in the knowledge that he had just met the most remarkable woman in the world. He was totally and absolutely smitten with her.

Hanna had strange stirrings herself. Not since the prince...she told herself. But the young man was certainly out of the question for any kind of intimate relationship. He was not handsome, *and* dirt poor. The poor boy could not afford to give her the smallest gemstone in her growing collection.

Next day, to take her mind off the would-be opera conductor, she went shopping for even more jewels. And took some ideas to a new dressmaker she had found who had the talent to make simply stunning creations.

At her lesson, Alen Arvey complimented Hanna on her salon debut. "You are a talented party giver," he said. "There is a demand for people like you who love the arts and can afford to encourage artists. You have such a nice way about you, encouraging, nonthreatening, interested in everyone without being cloying or overbearing. It *is* a talent, and you have it in abundance, and you aren't stingy about sharing it with those less fortunate than you."

"Well, that's very kind of you."

"Because the history of the world is the rich against the poor. When the gap gets too large, the rich must pull back, or the poor will revolt. You have the ability to put your money to good use to lift up the poor, in wealth and in spirit."

"I am already planning the next one," she said.

"Good."

"Tell me, Monsieur Arvey, what do you know about Wilhelm Drang?" she asked, trying to sound nonchalant.

"Not much, really. Sings in my opera chorus. Punctual, conscientious, good sight-reading and music ability. Fair voice."

"He has ambition to be a conductor of opera."

"Yes."

"Do you think it is possible for him to obtain this?"

Arvey sighed. "You know, Hanna, many more people seek stardom than obtain it. It would be nice if talent would always win out, but there are many factors, and being talented is not always high on the list. You must first be lucky, and be where you need to be, when you need to be there. It is politics also. The art of ingratiating yourself to people who can help you. You would seem to be adroit at that. If Mr. Drang has that talent, I have not seen it. That is not to say some great star won't take a shine to him. That is an easy way to the top." He drew a deep breath. "But that is so remote in his circumstances."

"What circumstances?"

"He must work for a living. He is a waiter, I believe. What are the chances of some star eating at his restaurant and, after he serves the dessert, saying to him, 'You look like an opera conductor—I want you to do all my operas'?"

"How does a conductor find work?"

"Many ways." He shrugged. "Some begin leading school orchestras—or even pit orchestras in follies. Others come from the orchestra itself. I don't think Wilhelm plays any instrument that well. Others, I suppose, hang around opera houses, find ways to ingratiate themselves. But it is tough, no mistaking that. For every opera, there are many in the orchestra, many in the chorus and a number of soloists. But there is only *one* conductor." Alen began playing some D-major scales to warm her up and to signal it was time for the lesson to begin. "But why so much interest in Wilhelm?" he asked, truly curious. Drang was, after all, neither good-looking, nor rich, and she was married to perhaps the richest man in captivity.

"I was talking to him yesterday," she said. "He seemed so intense, yet forlorn. He has this big dream." She stopped, then hummed the scale along with her teacher. "I guess maybe I felt sorry for him."

"Well, then," Alen Arvey said, "why don't you buy him an opera house and an opera company and put him to work?"

"Oh, my," she said, throwing back her head and laughing up and down the scale.

Ned came to Hanna's room that night in his robe, which hung open on his naked body, and she asked him politely to postpone his urges.

"Postpone?" he asked with an incredulous inflection that angered Hanna. "You don't postpone lust, you act on it." He crawled into her bed, beside her.

"Oh, do you?" she asked sarcastically, not moving to make room for him, "like the animals?"

"Yeah," he said, pawing her, "that's what we are."

"Speak for yourself."

"Oh, I *am*," he said, and rolled his dead weight over on top of her.

"Please," she shouted so the maid would hear. "Not tonight, Ned!"

"Then make believe it's tomorrow," he said. He began stroking her here, rubbing her there until he was excited beyond his capacity to control himself, and she was just disgusted.

When he had had his way, he rolled off her and said, "Buy another necklace tomorrow. You look good in my diamonds." But it was his snorting, self-satisfied laughter that irked her most. "Filthy animal," she spat at him.

"Yeah," he said, then laughed like a hyena. When she had seen the last of his naked back, she got out of bed, put his robe outside her door, then locked it.

Wilhelm, she told herself, would never treat her like that.

She avoided Ned the next few days, and when he returned to her room several nights later, he found the door locked. He pounded on it in such a frightening fashion that she thought the wood would give way under the fierce strength of his blows. She steeled herself to keep from uttering a sound, and when she finally heard him utter "Bitch!" and step away, she felt she was able to breathe again.

The next morning, when she got up, the house was strangely silent. Usually she could hear the maid downstairs in the kitchen or Ned bustling around upstairs, but she heard nothing.

She made her way quietly down the stairs and found no one in the kitchen. She thought she heard hushed voices in the maid's room, which was on the other side of the kitchen pantry. A casual investigation revealed the maid's door open enough to see her husband in bed with the maid. Hanna's first thought was he wanted her to find them.

"At least you could have the decency to close the door," she said, slamming the door.

From inside, she heard that grating hyena laugh.

Hanna rushed right back to her room to think. Options: move out, make a scene, ignore it. Moving out would be drastic, making a scene would only evoke that dastardly laugh from Ned. And what could she say? He gave her anything she wanted but respect, and she decided he was probably not capable of that. There was no question in her mind that this was the beginning of the end. All that was left was for her to maximize her advantage. Her third option, of ignoring the flagrant infidelity, would seem to serve her purposes best. It would buy her the most time and would probably be the most difficult for Ned to cope with.

Her prime strategy would be accumulation. Buy! she told herself. Ned's greatest asset as a husband was his generosity. She would store up manna against bleaker periods ahead.

She would also write to Ken Maxwell. She considered a telegram, but she didn't want to seem precipitously desperate. So she wrote a simple, chatty letter, hoping he would read between the lines.

My dear Ken:

What a foolish thing it was for me to leave Chicago so suddenly! Now it seems that was not the only foolish thing I have done. I have been a young woman acting sometimes out of desperation rather than good sense.

I often think back on our first meeting. You were such a big, strong, handsome man. So many good times we had since then. But in the case of marriage, I was impetuous. Perhaps it is owing to my childhood, but I am not feeling secure without a man. Undoubtedly you are the finest man who has ever crossed my path. I do think of you often, humbly and contritely—and just the other day I was wondering, could this great man ever forgive me my strong-headedness where he has been concerned? I know it would take a larger spirit than I have to do so.

Do you ever think of our moments together, dare I ask? The closer we come to one another in body, as well as spirit, the more I cherished those moments. Do I dare to hope you still may harbor some pleasant memories of your faithful and obedient servant,

Hanna

Hanna still wrote in her bold, script letters an inch high across the page. Her signature seemed bolder than ever, the outsized letters almost touching the sides of the page.

While eagerly awaiting a response from Ken, Hanna made the rounds of antique shops, art galleries and jewelry stores in her Rolls-Royce. She had calculated the probable time of her letter to get from Paris to Chicago. Of course, the international mail was not an exact science.

In the meantime, Hanna kept out of the path of her lawful husband, and she agonized over how to handle his inevitable conjugal visits. She decided to lock her door, ignore him when he came, and if confronted in the daytime to say she must have been sound asleep.

But he didn't come. It did not take much analytical detective work on her part to figure out Gilda, the maid, was satisfying him. Hanna thought she should perhaps demand the maid be fired, but then thought, what's the point? The maid was deflecting Ned's energies, and that pleased her. She could be sanctimonious about it in the court action. She could wax dramatic about the pain and suffering it caused her. Until then, no sense getting worked up. What she could get worked up about was not hearing from Ken Maxwell. By any calculation, he should have had the letter. Perhaps he had decided to write, rather than cable her.

On Sunday, she would have her third salon for the musical elite of Paris and environs. She had been heartbroken when Wilhelm had not appeared at the second. He had been thoughtful enough to send her a note explaining his opera rehearsals had deprived him of the means of his livelihood so he was having to work. He would make a concerted effort to attend the next one, should he be so fortunate as to be invited.

Fortunately, Ned absented himself Sunday, and Gilda waited on the guests sheepishly. Hanna was secretly amused, but she carried on as though nothing had happened between her husband and the maid.

Hanna was happy to see Wilhelm come in, and she went immediately to him. "How *nice* to *see* you," she enthused.

"Oh, I'm so glad to be here. I've been glum ever since I had to miss the last one."

"Well, we all missed you too."

"Will we be able to talk again afterwards?" he asked.

"I look forward to it," she said.

Attendance had increased at the salon musicale, and of the dozen participants, four played or sang for the others, and there was a spirited discussion of the merits and demerits of the Paris company's performance of *Rigoletto*. Hanna never ventured a negative opinion of any performance, she was always entranced with opera of any stripe.

After the last person had left them alone, Hanna and Wilhelm took up where they had left off, without missing a beat.

"You know, I've been thinking," she said, "of what you said last time, about your dream—you know?"

His eyes were wide open. He was so flattered to have this beautiful, rich woman remember anything he said.

"I am thinking, why not? Your ambition is to conduct, mine to perform. Why not combine our dreams with a company of our own?"

"You mean it?" he said. "Just like that? How would we ever get so much money?"

"I have some money," she purred.

"But so much—and you would risk it for me?"

"It is something to think about," she said. "If nothing else, we can have fun planning it. So what I'd like you to do is give me some ideas. Plan it as though it were going to be a reality. Tell me what would be needed, how much it would cost—where we could find a theater."

Ned had not come home and somehow Hanna and Wilhelm just went on talking, with no concept of the passing time. It was after dark when they parted—Wilhelm a young man high on expectations and Hanna feeling like a diva already.

The next day, Hanna rented a spacious apartment in Paris. It was necessary to furnish it, of course, and that would mean valuable paintings for the walls, as well as antiques, Aubusson rugs and a dozen place settings of fine china and sterling silver. The apartment would not only serve as a repository for her stores, but also as a convenient meeting place for Wilhelm.

Hanna thought the time had come to have a preliminary meeting with a lawyer. She would feel on firmer ground if she had heard from Ken, but she feared waiting so long that Ned would surprise her with some advantage that she could not foresee.

Attorney Darius Monteux was a man considering making the leap to forty.

For he made one think that nothing in his life transpired without due consideration from him—not even the passing of time.

Hanna couldn't explain why she didn't find him handsome. He was tall and solid of body and his facial features by themselves seemed perfectly adequate, attractive even—but there was something about the whole ensemble that she found not entirely pleasing. She thought of Wilhelm and how this Darius was conventionally more attractive—everyone would say so—but Wilhelm appealed to Hanna more.

She had been treated courteously, she had no complaint on that score, and the man seemed to know his trade, and she couldn't complain about that. She was comfortably seated in a dark but expansive office, facing the serious man over his overlarge desk. Perhaps that was what gave her pause—the trappings of his profession seemed oversized for his psyche.

Why was it so important what he was like? she wondered. Because, she realized, it was like being naked before a doctor. You had to feel comfortable baring your most intimate secrets to a perfect stranger. "Everything we say is in confidence?" she asked, just to make sure.

"Certainly," he said. "How may I help you?"

"I do not know exactly how to begin this," she said in her steadily improving, yet thickly accented French. "I am a married woman. My husband is rich but unfaithful to me. I feel I must get a divorce at some time, but I am afraid because he is so rich he can hire a thousand lawyers to beat me to nothing."

"By 'to nothing' do you mean to literally beat you—physically, until you disappear, or until you have no money?"

"Money. Yes. I do not think he would beat me physically—unless—"

"Unless what?"

"Well, I don't know how to say this, I would be *so* embarrassed—"

"You mean he uses force sexually?"

She dropped her eyes and nodded sedately.

"Against your will?" he asked.

"Not in the beginning," she said, "but he has decided to take up with the maid. As a result, I have no more desire for him."

Attorney Monteux made a tent with the fingers of both

hands. The tent reposed against his lips, and he blew gently through it. "If you will forgive my saying so, Madame," he said, "divorce in the best of circumstances can be a messy business. It is not something to enter into cavalierly. Now, if your husband is wealthy and treats you well in every other way, perhaps you should first ask yourself what you want from life and then from him at this juncture."

"Well," she said, adding a dollop of outrage to her tone, "I certainly want a husband who cares enough for me to be faithful."

Mr. Monteux nodded behind his tent-fingers like a man who had heard it all before. "Adultery," he said, "is so common in this country. It is in a way charming to find someone to take it so seriously."

"Well," she said, huffing, "perhaps I am not from this country. I have a strict Catholic upbringing. My husband, he is also not French, but American."

"Catholic?" he said. "Strict Catholic? You are then aware of the Church's position on divorce?"

"Yes," she said, bowing her head modestly again. Darius Monteux decided she had perfected this gesture admirably. "But I am here for advice only. I am not yet asking for divorce."

"Yes, what advice can I give you?"

Hanna was stymied suddenly. She did not know how to ask what she came to ask without seeming a grasping woman. The lawyer seemed so—opinionated! Here he was, telling her adultery was nothing, she should swallow her pride and go home. Well, that was not what she had in mind. Not by a long shot. "This *is* confidential?" she sought to reassure herself. It was one thing to make a fool of yourself to one person, another to have it bandied all about the country.

"I assure you," he said.

"Well, if I...that is, if I decide divorce is my only course, what could...what should I do in the meantime to...well, to make it more likely that I should get a fair settlement?"

"First," he said, "you should make your behavior exemplary. If you wish to use his infidelities against him, it is best not to have any of your own."

She hoped she wasn't blushing. "What about a settlement? How can I...that is, I mean...how might I go about maximizing my settlement advantage?"

"Well, perhaps he will be generous. He may be as eager for the divorce as you and be willing to make a handsome settlement on you. Of course, much depends on his attitude, how you both appeal to the judge, should it get that far. On the one hand you can step up your expenditures to make the case that you were accustomed to a certain lifestyle. But on the other hand, that could look like what it is—a deliberate attempt to pad the record, so to speak—and it could weigh against any wronged-wife act you might want to use."

She stared at him. Why did he have to seem so cold about it all? Hanna longed for some compassion—some sympathy for her plight—she had come to expect at least that from an ally. But Darius Monteux was a cold fish, and she very much feared he saw her the same way.

She thanked him, and asked if he could defer payment of the bill until she filed the divorce action.

He smiled, dropped his tent-fingers and said, "No, the bill is due and payable. If you do file an action, you may, of course, include it in your expenses. My secretary will present you the bill. We would be grateful if you paid it before you left."

They exchanged smiles: his too insightful; hers tight, grudging and disappointed. He understood her. She didn't like that.

At the secretary's desk, she apologized for neglecting to bring her checkbook. "I'll mail it to you when I get home."

Why, Hanna wondered, did the secretary look like she didn't believe that?

469

She didn't get around to writing the check that night, but she decided she'd better tell Ned about her apartment in the city. It would be so much more convenient for her salons, she would tell him.

But when she got home, she was startled to find him there, his shoulders drooping to match his new moustache, waving a cable at her. "Ha!" he said. "Your lover from Chicago is on his way! What good news! Says he's looking forward. Saved a few dollars on words, doesn't say looking forward to what. Better than looking backward, I suppose."

"He is not my lover!" she insisted.

"No? Well, I'm not your lover, so what do you call him then?"

"A friend."

"Friend?" He raised an eyebrow. "The friend you returned to America with? In first class, the two of you, while I was down in second."

"You didn't decide to go until the day before the sailing."

"Yes—since this bozo you called a friend spent the first day of our marriage holed up with you, I thought, whoa! wait just a minute here. Maybe some supervision was called for."

"Don't be silly. He was a married man."

"*Was*, was he? Do I take it from that he no longer exists in that blessed state?"

She glared at him.

"I see," he said. "So, now he's coming to claim his rightful prize. After all, he was responsible for that charade in Chicago. How did you convince him? Hm? Did he ever *hear* you sing? Did anyone—? I didn't, and I was *there*—" And he hit her with another salvo of snorts.

The time, she decided, was not right to tell him about the apartment in town. "Do not talk more to me," she commanded, "until you can treat me as a person instead of a possession."

"A person, eh? Is that what you treat me like? A person?" He threw the cable at her feet and stomped out of the room. She waited until he was gone before she picked it up and read it.

> HANNA
> GOOD NEWS STOP ARRIVE
> WEEK FROM SATURDAY AQUI-
> TANIA STOP LOOKING FOR-
> WARD STOP
> KEN

She locked her door that night, but received no visit from her husband. The next morning, she took the Rolls to her Paris apartment. Then she cabled Ken, care of the ship:

> VERY GOOD NEWS STOP
> WILL BE AT DOCK WITH
> CAR STOP
> HANNA

Hanna continued with her daily voice lessons and practiced with the new piano she'd bought for the apartment. It was a nine-foot Steinway. A good instrument for the salon, it would attract fine pianists.

She placed an ad in the paper for a maid. She was initially afraid Gilda would see it and answer it, and Hanna was relieved to hire the first woman who came for the job—her name was Estelle, and she was Polish. Hanna told her she thought it would be superfluous to interview anyone else, for everyone knew that Polish was synonymous with perfection. Estelle was in her fifties and, Hanna felt, safe from the lustful clutches of Ned—in the unlikely event he discovered her place and came bursting in. Hanna thought it necessary to have some help for the salon and to entertain Mr. Maxwell, not to mention to make her own daily life somewhat easier.

Without mentioning it to Ned, Hanna had cards printed:

> *Madame Hanna Mazurka*
> *has contracted*
> *a town house*
> *at*
> *24 Rue de la Guerre*
> *Telephone 1083*
> *Please direct any*
> *correspondence to*
> *that address*

Then she busily sent them to all her friends, commercial contacts, and other acquaintances. She neglected to send her new address to Attorney Monteux. If he sent a bill to Ned, he would perhaps turn it over to his accountant without looking at it.

On Wednesday, Hanna had reason to marvel at how often things seemed to come in bunches. No sooner had Pierre Biet received her card than he called with news that he was reasonably sure he had located the prince. Her pressing questions availed her naught. "We really must speak in person," he said, and they made an appointment at his apartment for that afternoon.

Hanna was vaguely discomforted seated in the office of Investigator Pierre Biet. She had the feeling, deep inside, that she was doing something shady. Sneaking up on someone without his knowledge.

"The prince was more difficult to find than he might have been," Biet said, "because he did not want to be found."

"Well, where is he?"

He spread his hands. "I will tell you that in good time."

"This is not good time?"

"I have not been paid for my work."

She looked startled. "You will be paid," she said, as though any suspicion on his part was an unfounded insult.

"Yes, I am sure," he said. "Still,

the only guarantee I have is my information."

"But what if I don't like the information?"

"Exactly! Where am I then? I was contracted to find the former Prince Stephanoff and his wife, Katrina. This I have done. I made no guarantees of his condition or anything else beyond my control."

"His condition? What *is* his condition?"

The arms wafted out from his body again. Then he reached for a paper on his desk and with his fingers on top of it like a wigwam, he reversed it so she could read it. "Your bill, Madame."

She looked at it, then up at him. "That's quite a lot."

"It took a lot of time, expertise and money. I have paid out of pocket for informers. I would hope you could understand my wanting to be compensated for my services."

"But why this paranoia about a bill? This is, in my experience, highly irregular."

"Is it? Perhaps if Darius Monteux had asked for his money before he spoke to you, he would have it now."

"Darius Monteux? What has he got to do with this?"

"He just happens to be a friend of mine, and mentioned he had not been paid."

"But...how...how would you know? You aren't speaking of my confidential affairs, are you?"

"Oh, no, Madame. Not a word from either of us about the nature of our contacts. Only the fact that you have evaded paying him. I understand it is your habit not to carry checks with you. That can be convenient if you don't want to pay."

"I've never been so insulted in my life."

"I'm truly sorry about that, Madame," he said. "Do you have a checkbook with you?"

"Well, I...I am certainly good for the money. You know, of course, who my husband is?"

"Yes—"

"And I am a baroness."

"Most impressive, Madame. I am a workingman, Madame. I live on my work. I am most impressed by the rich—but, alas, I cannot afford to be so impressed that I do not ask for payment for my services."

473

"Oh, well," she said, shaking her head tersely, in undisguised anger. "How much is it?" She opened her purse and withdrew a checkbook.

"The amount is on the bill," he said. "It brings you up to today. Should you require anything further, that would be extra…"

"I won't require anything more," she snapped, writing the check.

When she handed it to him, he said, "I also do most discreet divorce work."

She looked at him with the half-closed eye of suspicion. Monteux must have spoken about her affairs. Well, she wasn't going to dignify gossip. Pierre Biet was holding her check in both hands and staring at it.

"It's good," she said. "I assure you."

"Good," he said.

"Now, where is he…they?"

Biet set the check down and interlaced his fingers. "Times," he said, "have not been auspicious for Russian royalty. He and his wife got out of the country with everything they could lay their hands on and carry, which, it turned out, respectable as it was, tided them over for only these ten years or so. Katrina's father helped them for a while, but the prince was very proud and uncomfortable about it." Pierre Biet allowed himself a brief chuckle. "Usually the royals have scant compunctions about taking money from successful commoners and their comely offspring, but that was not the case here. Though his wife was loath to give up all the comforts of home, so to speak, the prince got on this high horse about earning his own way."

"No!"

"Yes—but that was no easy feat for a foreigner in Paris, especially not one the natives might feel had pretensions to royalty. It was just the wrong chemistry, you might say. The question was what could he do? A waiter? Too much animosity; the French can be brutally provincial."

"Don't I know it?" she said.

"The customers would pretend not to understand him. It was the same at the antique store where he worked as a lowly clerk. The owner hired him provisionally because he thought the prince's breeding and familiarity with rare old objects would be a sales asset, but all he got were complaints about how hard it was to understand the bugger."

"How terrible!"

"Yes, but in fairness, he did not seem to have an aptitude for languages, and his French was fractured to the point of being sometimes laughable."

"So where *is* he?"

Pierre Biet looked at her as straight as a laser beam, as if to see if she could take it. In that instant vision, he decided she was a woman who could take *any*thing. "He...and she...are living on the *Joie de Vivre* Farm, some forty miles south of here. They live over the barn. He is a stable hand, he knows horses, you see. She is the cook. They seem to have come to terms with their lot, but they aren't eager to have it talked around. Oh, and he has changed his name to Phillip Driver. His wife is now Katrina Driver."

Hanna stared blankly ahead. Over ten years of searching had not yielded a happy result. Not only was the prince poor, but he was no longer a prince. And he was still married. Hanna could not imagine worse news. She thought she would have been better equipped to cope with news of his death than this.

Pierre Biet took an envelope from his desk drawer and passed it over the desk to Hanna. "Here are all the particulars," he said, "including a map to his farm, as well as a map *of* the farm, marking the stable and other landmarks. Now, if you have any questions...?"

475

She was still staring blankly ahead. She shook her head dumbly.

"Very well, then I shall bid you adieu." And he rose to his feet, but the sickening feeling of poison lead in her stomach kept her from rising.

Pierre Biet was a patient man, and he didn't rush her, but after what seemed half an hour to him (actually five minutes), he thought of leaving on his urgent errand and just letting her sit there. Then he thought better of it, deciding he didn't want her going through his apartment/office.

"Madame!" he said, and it hit her like an explosion in her ears. "I am afraid I have to go. May I see you somewhere?"

"What?" She was startled. "Somewhere? Oh, no...thank you. I have the Rolls."

He helped her up, lifting her by an arm that seemed comatose. He saw her to the car, helped her inside, and left her there, looking like she didn't remember how to drive.

Then Pierre Biet went to Hanna's bank to clear her check before she could stop it.

Somehow Hanna found her way back to her apartment. There she lay on her bed, which bed was said to have been lain on by Josephine and possibly even Napoleon, or someone else who was very close to Josephine. There she reminisced about the gallant and handsome prince who had taken her to the opera and had been so gracious to her, a poor country girl, and who had stolen her heart in the bargain. She permitted herself scant time to remember her dear friend Katrina and their many good times together. Katrina held a strange place in Hanna's memory. Her friend had changed over the years and finally evolved into a turncoat who had stolen from her, blatantly and despicably, the one true love of her life.

Hanna hoarded most of her thoughts for Prince Stephanoff—Phillip. She wanted to *do* something for him. Could she talk to him without his busybody wife interfering? Could she get him to come away with her? She certainly could give him financial help—if he would accept it. But from what Pierre Biet had said, that was unlikely. She could buy him his *own* antique shop. She could do so many things to free him from the tyranny of horse manure. If only he would let her. Perhaps she could help anonymously. But she must see him first.

The streetlights were on when she fell asleep. She was awakened by a knock on her door. Her first thought was she was in her room at the villa, and Ned was knocking for what he considered his conjugal due. Instinctively she did not answer, but a subsequent knock and a whispered, familiar voice, not belonging to her husband, was heard.

"Hanna! Are you there?"

She stumbled out of bed, without thought of her rumpled clothes, and opened the door to Wilhelm.

"Hanna!" he said, looking at her in a fright. "Are you all right?"

Suddenly, Hanna threw her arms around Wilhelm and held him to her. For him it was a dream come true, but he was too startled at first to react, then he reciprocated eagerly.

"I'm sorry," she murmured in his ear, "I'm sleepy, I've had sad news, I'm not myself."

"Tell me about it," he murmured back—and she led him to her bed, where they lay down and folded into each other. "Later," she whispered.

Far into the night they loved as Poe would have it, "With a love that was more than love," this widely, yet shallowly experienced rich Polish beauty who liked to be called Madame, and the awkward, physically plain pauper who had filled his life with fantasies about her that he now experienced with an intensity he could not have heretofore imagined.

Though Madame had given many men such a heady experience, Wilhelm Drang had come to her wholly without experience, and he thought in those moments of ecstasy that he would gladly die there in her arms, a supremely happy man, or live his life as her slave.

And the thing that startled Hanna was that she felt the same unprecedented narcotic effect as Wilhelm.

The next morning, Madame Hanna Mazurka was on the dock to meet the man who aspired to be her fourth husband.

ACT V

THE CAPTAIN OF INDUSTRY

Morales: Look, here comes an old husband with a suspicious eye and a jealous look, he's holding onto his young wife by the arm; no doubt her lover's not far off; he'll pop out of some corner.

—*Carmen*

Madame Hanna Mazurka
remembers:

THE CAPTAIN OF
INDUSTRY
Chicago, Illinois

"Perhaps I could have made Ken
happy, but it would have been to
the prejudice of my own soul's
development, which could
accept only those sacrifices that
pass through the fires of purifica-
tion."

Hanna remembered it as a sunny day, with crisp, cool air that helped keep her awake. Or was it just her happiness that made her think there was sunshine all around?

Her mind and heart were buzzing with the strange, tingling feeling she got from Wilhelm Drang—the residue of her night with him still glowed in her soul.

And yet, she was caught up in the excitement of waiting on the dock for a glimpse of Ken Maxwell, American industrialist par excellence. She scanned the railings on the upper decks, but did not see him. And then her eyes traveled to the gangplank, and there he was, his shiny, round pink face beaming as he descended expectantly, searching the crowd on the dock for a sign of her.

Hanna waved wildly at him, and when he saw her, his beaming broadened into a country-mile smile and he quickened his pace toward her, and she moved toward him. When they met, they embraced. He was such a cuddly bear of a man, she thought. And she couldn't help but feel his admiration for her. She knew he had put up with a lot from her—dashed hopes, sticking his neck out with the Chicago Opera, only to have it cut off when she walked out without notice. Now she would have to tell him about Wilhelm. But not immediately. The time was not right.

"Oh, my girl," he said, "you don't know how good it feels to hold you."

"You're so sweet," she said, even as she was wondering why her men all seemed to be father figures. All except Wilhelm. She must tell him about Wilhelm soon.

"I have been thinking of nothing but you since I got your letter."

"And before that—with my bad behavior—you were thinking *only* of *other* women."

"Oh, no, never."

He took her hand and they walked to her Rolls-Royce.

"Nice car," he said. "Your husband must be very generous."

She wrinkled her nose. "With money, he is," she said. "I hope soon to be *was*." They got in the car, he offered to drive, but she wanted to. She started the car and pulled it into the traffic and said, "I am thinking of divorce."

"I would like to try to make you happy."

"I am always happy with you," she said, then began to sniffle.

"Honey, what's the matter?"

"Oh, it is nothing. I do not wish to bore you with my petty problems. How was your trip?"

"Fine, until I saw you unhappy. Come, what can I do to cheer you up?"

"Oh, you have come all the way to Paris to see me. That is cheering me up already. You are truly a good friend," she said.

He put his hand on her arm. "I hope I can be more than that."

She smiled, and patted his thigh.

"I am sorry to hear you are not happy in your marriage.

Sorry, in a way, of course. I am quite excited that I might be granted another chance with you."

"You are too good to me."

"That is why I am here. Divorce can be a discouraging, depressing, lonely business. I know."

"And expensive," she offered quietly.

"Well, yes. I hope you will let me help with that."

"Oh, my gracious. Why should you do that?"

"Because I love you…"

"Phew! You are so kind—after me walking out in Chicago. I thought you would not speak to me again."

He frowned. "I figured you had your reasons. I guess everyone was pretty hard on you. And then your husband came. He probably wasn't too sympathetic to your opera venture in my hometown."

"Oh, no, you are so *smart!* That was exactly it. He insisted I come home with him, and what could I do? I am dependent on his generosity."

"I wish you would agree to let me show you how generous I can be."

"Oh?" Her question was nondescript. He didn't get the uncertainty in her voice, because she forgot to put it there.

Ken gave the doorman at the Ritz Hotel a whopping tip to take care of the Rolls and Hanna accompanied the industrial baron to the lobby while he checked in. That was as far as she had planned to go.

By the time he had completed checking in and the man in the tails was leading them to his suite, Hanna had decided no harm could come of this impropriety as long as she stayed in the sitting room.

She didn't like the expression on the manager's face. He seemed to have a smirk there.

It seemed like an eternity as the manager explained the services of a hotel they both knew well. When he finally left them alone, Ken Maxwell said, "Sit down, dear, won't you?"

Carefully, she chose the single chair. He noticed with disappointment her choice, but sat himself in the love seat. He smiled, then said, "Tell me, Hanna, do you think when a man sits alone in a love seat it means he is in love with himself?"

She laughed, without answering the question.

"Oh, dear," Ken said, "I almost forgot. When I am in a room alone with your astonishing beauty, I cannot be responsible for logical thought."

"Oh, pooh! You flatterer!"

Ken Maxwell took an envelope from his inside jacket pocket and looked at it longingly before he turned his gaze on her and then handed her the envelope with a tight smile.

She looked with stark curiosity at the envelope, then ran her fingers around the edges in a manner Ken Maxwell thought quite seductive. Then she lifted the unglued flap and took out the contents. Her jaw dropped. Wrapped inside a letter-sized paper with typewriting and a signature was a check made out to Hanna Mazurka for a hundred thousand dollars. Unlike Ned Butterworth's prenuptial check, this one was signed.

"But, my dear Ken, what can this be?"

"Read it," he said.

She kept the check in her hand as she read the note that went with it.

> Trust Fund for
> Hanna Mazurka, Beneficiary
> Ken Maxwell, Trustor

486

> Ken Maxwell, hereafter called Trustor, places in trust sufficient securities to yield Hanna Mazurka an income of one hundred thousand dollars per year for her lifetime.

That was the essence. The rest was boilerplate, until Hanna's eyes fell on the last sentence:

> This trust shall become effective upon the signing of the corresponding agreement by Hanna Mazurka and Ken Maxwell.

She looked up at Ken, who was smiling broadly. He was

pleased to see he could make her so happy. Money, which had been deceptively easy for him to make, seemed to please her inordinately. His wife had come from a family even wealthier than his, and he was unable to have any effect at all on her with his wealth. Hanna, on the other hand, was like a child who had just been given a triple-dip ice-cream cone.

She jumped up and sat beside him on the love seat, then kissed him on the cheek. "Phew!" She looked at the check, then the typewritten page. Then she frowned slightly. "What does this mean—this agreement between you and me?"

He waved off the idea as insignificant. "Oh, that's just the lawyers talking. Want everything in writing. I told them with you it was hardly necessary. I could certainly trust your word."

"My word about what?"

"Well," he said, slightly flustered, "us."

"Us?"

"The lawyers thought our understanding should be in writing," he said. "Every contract in the legal world must have a consideration, according to my legal eagles."

"What consideration?"

"Well, that's what I told them, but, you see, they couldn't believe I would just do this for you with no strings attached. They told me I had to sign some document with you to make this legal on its face. I don't understand these legalisms, that's why I hire all these lawyers."

"Did you ever think we might be better off without lawyers?"

He laughed, a warm and open laugh—so unlike her husband's grating snorts. "All the time," he said.

"So where is our agreement that I must sign?"

Was he really blushing? she wondered. His face certainly had become suddenly red. But, why? "Oh, we can get to that later," he said, putting his arm around her.

She went rigid. "Later?" she said. "Why later? Is not something good? Is something bad in this agreement? Yes?"

He reached into his inside pocket again, then withdrew his hand. "No," he said, "giving you another document to read so soon after we met, after so long apart—it's just too cold. Let me just tell you what it says—what they made me put in it—to protect us both from misunderstanding." He returned the document to his pocket.

She laughed, and tweaked his nose with her fingers. "I agree there should be no misunderstanding. I can't agree on the agreement if I do not know what it says."

"You know," he said, laying his head on her shoulder, "I just love your accent. In fact, I love everything about you."

"You are too sweet," she said, "but you are evading the question. What *is* the agreement?"

"Oh, just that you were in the process of divorcing your husband—"

She started to speak, but he cut her off. "They were afraid if we didn't say that, we could both be sued for alienation of affections. It would look like I was trying to buy your love or something ridiculous like that. So they wanted to get in writing that before you were accepting the money—before I offered it—you were already in the process of divorce—you *are* thinking of divorce, aren't you?"

"Oh, yes—the marriage is over. It has been for months." She sniffled again.

"What's the matter?"

"Oh, nothing."

"You don't anticipate any trouble getting the divorce, do you?"

She shook her head and held a lace handkerchief to her nose, then wiped some imaginary tears.

"You have sufficient grounds?"

"Oh, yes," she sighed. "He is sleeping with the maid."

"No!"

"Yes. And makes no effort to hide it."

"How awful!" He put his arm around her to comfort her.

"Yes."

"You don't know what people expect in divorces. It is usually acrimonious."

"Well, I have plenty acrimony," she said. "I am not a rich woman as your wife. I have lived at the mercy of my husbands. I cannot tell you how sweet you are to take care of me in this way."

"It is my pleasure, believe me. So you won't object to signing the agreement?"

"You give me a hundred thousand dollars a year, I am not

going to quibble. I am getting divorced anyway, if I can afford it. It is very expensive, no?"

"It can be. But usually the husband pays the wife's legal fees."

"So would you take care of that for me too? — oh, I shouldn't ask such a thing. You have done so much already."

He laughed. "You'll have a hundred thousand dollars. That will pay a lot of lawyers' fees."

"Oh," she said. "I thought this was a gift for me."

"Oh, Hanna, you are incorrigible. I'm giving you a hundred thousand dollars a year, and you want me to pay your bills too?"

"It's like a gift," she said, holding the check to her chest, "for presents and things—not for necessities—it would not be as much fun. I want to spend it on clothes and..." she looked at him out of the corner of her eye..."underwear."

He brought her close to him again. This time, their lips met and their primal instincts drew them together, first in a gentle kiss, gradually heating up to passion, then incessant groping, touching, feeling, blending, until somehow they found themselves in the bedroom.

Once again she astonished him in bed. The fusion of bodies; the melding of souls. While it is true there are only certain limited variations on the theme of sexual intimacy, the art is in the enthusiasm, and the couple had that in abundance.

When Hanna finally arrived back at her Paris apartment, she found Wilhelm Drang huddled on the floor by her door.

"What are you doing?" she said.

"Where have you been?" he said at the same time.

"Come inside," she said. "You'll catch your death of cold out here."

He struggled to his feet like one interrupted from a deep sleep. When Hanna had closed the door, she hugged him. But it was not as natural as before. She was holding something back, and so was he. She had left part of herself at the Ritz with Ken Maxwell. Wilhelm was deeply suspicious of her for being out all night. They stood apart.

"I came over after work," he said.

"I thought we had an understanding."

"What understanding?"

"Well, you know—what we had together. Doesn't that mean anything to you?"

"Well, of course it does, what do you think?"

"But you didn't spend the night with me last night."

"Did you tell me you were coming?"

"Coming? I didn't want to leave yesterday morning. You made me, remember?"

"So, you came back to spy on me?"

"No, I came back because I couldn't bear to be without you. Apparently, you did not feel the same."

"Oh, pooh," she said. "Of course I do, but listen to this. Start shopping for a theater."

"What?"

"I've just got the money."

"Last night?"

"This morning. It's in the bank. Oh, Wilhelm, you'll be a famous conductor, and I'll be a famous diva."

Wilhelm was trying to understand what she was saying, but although he heard the words, he couldn't understand their meaning. "You have that much money to spare?"

She nodded. "Just got it."

"From where?"

"Now don't ask too many questions. Start finding us a theater."

"But for how long?"

"How long? Forever."

"No, how long will the money hold out?"

"As long as I live," she laughed, "so you'd better treat me well so I'll live forever."

"Forever?" he said, taking her in his arms. "That's not long enough." And he began kissing her amorously. She was well spent by this time and resisted his efforts to get her to lie down.

"No, Wilhelm, not now."

"So you *did* spend the night with another man?" he asked. "And he gave you all this money. Oh, Hanna, you are a *pro*? Don't tell me that."

"Well, of course not, what do you think?"

"I think you got the money from some man."

"Yes, you don't think my husband would give it to me?"

"What about the maid?"

"Well, I'll have you know he is a very generous man."

"So he gave you money last night so we could go play opera together? Is that what you want me to believe?"

"You must believe what you want to believe. Don't you want to believe we will have an opera company together?"

"Well, yes, sure."

"Then start acting happy and stop worrying and stop asking so many questions. Now, you're going to have to get busy scouting around for a theater to rent."

"Rent? Why not buy one if you have all this money?"

"Buy a theater? Well, I don't know. Do companies *do* that?"

"If they have the money—why not?"

"I don't know. I just never thought..."

"Lots of advantages to owning. Can't put you out, for one. Security, reliability."

"But how much would that cost?"

"I'll find out," he said.

"Good, you do that. I'm going to have to run a few errands. Are you working tonight?"

"I was—but if we have all this money, shouldn't I quit my job?"

"Not yet," she said. "I'll tell you when. I must get a divorce, you know. We shouldn't be taking these chances. Ned will have me followed. I don't want to give him ammunition to use against me."

It took considerable effort for Hanna to convince Wilhelm he must cut back his visits to her. "No surprise visits like this one. Too risky."

She gave him a warm kiss good-bye, warm enough to let him know she was not dismissing him for good. And then she was gone, map to the prince in hand, in her Rolls-Royce.

As she drove out of Paris and through the lush countryside, Hanna began to wonder if she had too many men in her life at the moment. She had a husband who she aspired to put behind her, but not without a handsome settlement. He really needed to be taught a lesson. And she needed the money. Wilhelm Drang affected her like no man had since the prince. He was younger than she and than any of her other men, but he was still poor and funny looking. Her attraction to him was perhaps the strangest of all her relationships. Then there was Ken Maxwell, wanting to give her a hundred thousand dollars a year.

Last, but never least, was her beloved prince—now on hard times. The man who had been the guiding force in her life, her muse, her inspiration, though she had spent only one, chaste but magical, evening with him. Now she would at last see him again. The closer she got to the farm, the more excited she became. But what could she do for him? How could she continue to balance four men on her narrow shoulders? Still, after all this time, she thought the slightest signal from the prince would solve her dilemma—would reduce the field of her men from four to one with the snap of the prince's lovely fingers.

According to the map, the farm was coming up ahead, on the right. She slowed the Rolls and crawled past the large spread, locating the main house, a large château, and, slightly farther on, the barn. There was a low fence around the property, as well as scattered trees between the barn and the road. She pulled the Rolls beyond the barn and parked it on the side of the road, where there were several trees shielding it from the barn.

The fence went as far as she could see both directions. That meant she would have to scale the fence to get to the barn. Hanna wished she had dressed differently for fence-hopping. She was wearing a thin silk dress that emphasized her figure without, she thought, being cheap or provocative. She had drenched herself in jewelry and now, in the barnyard, smelling the manure and urine of uninhibited animals in spite of her heavenly scent, she felt she had overdone it. In the distance, she saw an old man with a pitchfork, moving from one barn door to the next. The smells of the barnyard intensified as she drew closer. She came to a tree with a trunk far fatter than she was and paused behind it. She wondered if she could reach the old man without Prince Stephanoff seeing her. She could get more information about her beloved before springing herself on him.

The old farm hand moved slowly. Other than a mop of gray hair and stooped shoulders, Hanna could not make out his features.

493

She suddenly became self-conscious about trudging across the field, bedecked with silk and jewels. She would startle Stephanoff if she came upon him suddenly. So she moved carefully, from tree to tree, keeping an eye out for some sign of him. But in that time, she saw only the man with the pitchfork, moving with almost stylized slow motions, doing his chores, cleaning out the stables.

When she was within a few yards of the barn door, Hanna straightened her dress and looked down her front, taking stock for the last time. The barn had six outside doors on the side of the building and a large door on the end, which she considered the front. It was there, she reasoned, at the *main* door, she would somehow find the prince.

Faced with the broad door, which she saw moved on a track above, Hanna wondered what barnyard etiquette was. Should she knock, or move the door and enter? Being unable to decide, she returned to the side of the building in search of the farm hand. It would be best, she decided, if she had an intermediary for her meeting with the prince—or Phillip, as he was now apparently called.

Gingerly, she stepped between the manure piles, whenever possible. The old man backed out of one of the center doors, and Hanna caught her breath and said, "Excuse me," to his back. "Can you tell me where I can find Phillip?"

The man turned around. "I'm Phillip," he said.

Hanna gasped as she stared into that decrepit face. Could this be the person she had fallen so inexorably in love with? His eyes were sunken, and his face lined as that of a sixty- to seventy-year-old man. If he recognized her, he did not show it. In that second, she had to decide if she wanted to stay and tell him who she was, or retreat gracefully. The latter action seemed to make the most sense to her, but she couldn't surmount her morbid curiosity.

"I'm Zdenka Oleska," she said.

"How do you do?" he said, nodding politely, but showing no sign of recognition.

She smiled hopefully. "You don't remember me?"

He frowned and shook his head as though he had not given up thinking. "I am sorry, I…my memory is not good."

"We had a date long ago. To an opera."

Still no sign of recognition from him. "Oh, I am afraid I had so many dates," he explained, apologetically. "I was what we called a many-woman man until I married my dear Katrina. I hope I treated you all right," he said. "I didn't always do the best by my women…"

Her face fell, and her spirits with it. So he was not protecting his wife from the memory of Hanna—he really did not remember her. It was inconceivable!

"But, but," she stammered, "I thought…it's just that it seemed…at the time, of course…that we had such a special …well…affinity for one another. I have always held a special place in my heart…for you. I thought…I just can't believe…I mean, I always thought you did too." She smiled with rueful hope.

He stared blankly at her, and she was convinced against her will that there *was* no recognition in those dead eyes. Nor did she seem to inspire any interest in him. She had the eerie feeling he wasn't always present in mind or body.

How different was this meeting to the many times she'd imagined a tearful, passionate rejoining of two souls destined to spend eternity together. Instead of a young, vital, virile lover, eager to rectify the mistake of snubbing her so many years before, she found a hollow shell that put her in mind of someone's grandfather who had suddenly become senile.

Suddenly, with the absence of any encouragement, Hanna flung her arms around Prince Stephanoff and hugged him to her bosom. He yielded as one whose bone structure had been compromised.

495

"Oh, darling," she said, "we're both commoners now!" It was a phrase she had rehearsed, together with the hug, and this kiss she now planted on his startled lips. He stepped back and wiped his mouth with the back of his hand, as though he were a young boy who felt his lips had been dirtied.

"I'm sorry," he said. "I don't know you." And he went back to shoveling manure.

Choking back her tears, Hanna made her way to the house. She went to the back door and knocked. She considered, before the door opened, taking off some of her jewelry, but then she decided she was proud of it and saw no reason to pander to ex-royals with false modesty.

She had no trouble recognizing Katrina when she came to

the door. She was not as plump as she was as a schoolgirl, but she was fleshier than when they met in Paris. Her face was as worn as an old work glove, and perhaps she did look ten years older than Hanna, but everything about her spelled Katrina, from the way she held her head to the way her arms dropped at her sides. And the grin, when she saw Hanna, put the madame in instant mind of their days in the Catholic girls' school. The back door flung open, and the two women embraced. "Oh, Denky," Katrina said. "It's so great to see you. Here," she said, releasing her and standing back, "let me see you. Why, Denky, you are a sight for sore eyes, you are. I swear I never saw so much jewelry in my entire *life!* And that *dress.* Why, Denky, it's absolutely gorgeous." Then she added, in a delighted whisper. "*And* absolutely scandalous."

"Thank you—"

"Come in—come on, don't just stand there—"

"Is it all right? I don't want to keep you from anything."

"Oh, bosh, come *in*, the missis treats me real well. I'm not a slave or anything," she laughed. "But how on earth did you find us?"

"I hired a detective."

"Go on—a detective?"

Hanna nodded, a bit embarrassed. "Well, what was I to do? My best friend disappears from sight. My letters come back, 'No longer at this address.' What's a girl to do? So, I found you, and you are looking wonderful!"

"Oh, my," Katrina said, "you always were one for exaggeration. But you, you truly do look wonderful. I'm so happy for you. I swear, you are so good-looking, I must keep you from Phillip. He would just fall down in a swoon to see someone as glamorous as you. Come," she pointed to a chair at the kitchen table, "sit down—go on, sit—"

The two women sat, not as grown women, but as schoolgirls. They giggled and gossiped and reminisced about old times. "Well, I do swear, Denky, you look better than ever. Life sure agrees with you."

"Oh, pooh," she said. "Save your flattery for someone who believes it."

"Well, it's true, and you know it."

There was a moment of silence as the thoughts of each of

them turned inward.

"Oh, Denky." Katrina looked over at her girlhood friend. "May I share my news with you? I'm so happy—"

Hanna was startled at the notion that Katrina could be happy in her circumstance. "But of course, share," she said.

"We're pregnant."

"Katrina!" Hanna was stung by Katrina's characterization of her condition as *we*.

Katrina nodded. "Going on three months already."

Hanna jumped up to embrace her friend. She somehow felt that action called for. It was awkward for Hanna, hugging her friend who remained seated, befitting her new condition.

"Oh, Katrina, I'm so happy…for you," Hanna said, mechanically, as she was stung with self-pity. What's to be happy about? Hanna wondered. Her friend Katrina had bested her again. Hanna averted her head so Katrina wouldn't see the tears welling in her eyes.

Hanna brought her emotions under control—she had a lifetime of experience at that—and returned to her chair. She was eager to change the subject and, in the process, not above shifting the attention to her own achievements.

"Katrina," Hanna said, softly, "how did this happen?" She gestured with her arms to encompass the house and the barn.

Katrina sighed. "Well, you know what happened in Russia. We were out before all the murders, but he was working for the government when all of a sudden there was no more government. So we were stranded in Paris, with no income. We had to do something in a hurry. Phillip wanted to go back, but he would have been shot. He didn't care at that point, so I had to hold him back. He tried some jobs that didn't work out. Oh, by the way, he changed his name— didn't want any memories, any connection to what he was before— self-preservation, as well as a clean break. He became a Communist, if you can believe it—but I hope I convinced him for all time it was *not* safe to return home—even as a Communist. It's his atonement."

"Oh, dear."

"Yes. He's doing a Tolstoy really. Forsaking all wealth. He won't even take anything from my family."

Hanna's stomach churned. "And you stood by him?"

497

"Well, what could I do, abandon my husband?"

"You have lived the real meaning of 'for better or worse, for rich or for poor.'"

"Yes, but it hasn't been so bad. We love each other—"

"And you can stand to live in a barn after all you were both used to?"

"Oh, yes—"

"You don't mind the…smell?"

"For the first few days, of course. Now we do not even notice it."

"Katrina—would you do me a favor?"

Katrina looked at her old friend, laden with her ostentatious jewels, then down at her own apron, and laughed.

"Do *you* a favor? *Me*? Denky, that is so funny. Of course, anything I can do."

"Let me help you," Hanna said, urgently leaning over and clutching Katrina's forearm on the table. "I have money…"

"He won't take it, Denky."

"Yes, I know. But must he know? I could put it in your bank account."

Katrina laughed again. "We don't have a bank account."

"You don't?" Hanna was shocked.

Katrina shook her head. "What would we do with it? We have no money."

"Then get a bank account—or I could send you cash. *Some*thing to make things a little easier for you."

Katrina looked at her friend. The irony of the turned tables not lost on either of them. "I could not," she said at last, "go against my husband's wishes."

"What?" Hanna was astonished at the thought. "But you are an adult person of your own. You are not his subject or his slave. You have a mind of your own, and you should be controlled by nothing else."

Hanna thought Katrina's silence meant she was looking for a way to take her help. She was, instead, searching for some manner of communicating her thought to her friend who had lived her life at the opposite pole.

"Look, honey," Hanna said, "I've been rich and poor—so

have you, just in a different order. Don't you agree, rich is better?"

Katrina stared deep into her friend's eyes, as though reaching vainly for her soul. A satisfied smile played on her lips. "But you know, Phillip and I have something better than both rich and poor…"

"What's that?"

"Love."

Hanna was seething. Quietly at first, then, in the Rolls, on the way back to Paris, she pounded the steering wheel with her fist. "Damn!" she cursed aloud. Hitting her fist with the fingers full of diamonds caused the rings to cut painfully into her fingers. Was Katrina making innuendo when she said love was better than both rich and poor? Was she casting aspersions at Hanna and her life of wealthy, but unsuccessful, marriages? Well, she had a lot of nerve if she was. A scrubwoman still looking down her nose at a baroness who had more diamonds on her little finger than Katrina had left.

Oooo! Katrina was trying to be *superior!* And on very thin capital indeed! Love? *Love!* Didn't she carry a love in her heart for Katrina's very husband? For a dozen years? Didn't she devote her life to singing so she could please *him?* Certainly there was no greater mistake in this world than Stephanoff marrying Katrina. If only he'd had the sense to marry Hanna! She could guarantee he would not be in the meager straits he was—if he had been Hanna's husband, there would have been no question of his shoveling manure for a living. She would have done it herself before she let a prince sink that low! Love? Katrina didn't know what love *was.* It was not watching your husband demean himself day after day. That you might call tolerance, even understanding, but certainly not *love.* No, Hanna was convinced, Katrina had not the slightest notion how to love a man.

Forgetting her pain, Hanna slammed her fist on the steering wheel again. "Oww!" she wailed.

How crazy it all was. Hanna had shaped her life to fit the mold of a man who didn't even remember her. A young lifetime of voice lessons and daily practicing to capture the attention of a man with no memory! And now he was having a baby with her best friend. A *baby!*

The shock of it was enough to drive the average woman to give up. But Hanna Mazurka was not average. She was, she liked to say, the enemy of the average. She would not give up. She would show Ned Sharkey Butterworth and Ella Jardin, that failed diva, what she was made of. Iron and steel! She would, in the poor prince's memory, take the opera stage by storm. She was in her prime—her voice had never been better—and this new lad, Wilhelm, was doing strange things to her heart. She could not let him down. Would *he* like a baby? she wondered. She could not waste time. The sun would soon set on her baby-making years. But, was having a baby not the essence of being a woman? Katrina was having one, and Hanna was not. Am I a failure? Hanna wondered. But how has life treated me? Not gently, that is for certain. When you start with nothing, life is not a picnic. You are always afraid—afraid if you turn your back on an opportunity you will starve to death.

And it would have been so hard to combine a baby with her striving for an opera career. So Hanna excelled at the rhythm method, not so much by choice as by necessity.

Slowly, for the first time, reality was finding its way to Hanna's heart and mind. These sudden foolish thoughts about a baby are only to compete with Katrina in the eyes of that old stable hand who used to be a prince. It is time I put that foolishness behind me. I don't need to prove I am still young enough to bear a child. I am what I am. With that proclamation, a great burden was lifted from Hanna's shoulders.

So, she thought, it was four men on the way—now it is one down, three to go on the way back. How painful it was for her to let the prince go. But he was certainly no prince now—far from it. One thing she would never believe as long as she lived was that he did not remember her. Impossible! She could never mistake the deep understanding they had—deep in their souls. Perhaps he was too embarrassed of his failure in the face of her obvious success. Well, she was *glad* she'd worn the jewels. She was too poor for him to marry fourteen years ago and now who was too poor to marry whom?

But that was it, she thought. If he really wanted to be a dirty little Communist, he could not acknowledge a successful capitalist from his past. She smiled to herself—perhaps she could hire Katrina as a maid and Stephanoff as a chauffeur. Perhaps not now, but one never knew what life would bring.

She had better put her old friends behind her and go on with her own life. Three men left to cope with. But just imagine if she *had* married the prince. She could not see herself working in the kitchen of the big house and living over the stables with that awful smell. No thank you, she had done her stint as a menial housemaid while Katrina was waited on by her own maids. Now the tables had turned, and Hanna couldn't deny she was pleased with the way things turned out.

What was the name of that Frenchman, she wondered, who said, "It is not enough to succeed, a friend must fail"? She didn't think that, of course, but, all the same, the saying *did* come to mind.

Or was she being too hard on Katrina? Katrina thinks I have not love? Perhaps before I met Wilhelm Drang. Was this, Hanna wondered, an omen—that she should marry Wilhelm Drang instead of Ken Maxwell? Would she have to give the hundred thousand back if she did? There were no strings she knew about. She hadn't seen the second part of the document she was expected to sign, but Ken told her it said she would seek a divorce. Well, the first installment of the money was already in the bank, and she needed it to start the opera company.

Ironical, she thought, her sudden transferring of her operatic ambitions—from the beleaguered price to Wilhem—one man to another. As if she needed the excuse or impetus of a man to act. Hannah didn't care to think about it.

She drove straight to her husband's villa instead of returning to her Paris apartment. She marched inside like a Napoleonic soldier in frenetic battle. There, to her accumulating fortune, she found her husband sprawled on the living room couch, naked from the waist down. Gilda, the maid, was on her knees on the floor, naked from the waist up, and performing on him one of those acts which is disguised by the use of a multisyllabic Latin word.

Ned snorted when he saw her, but bade Gilda continue. Hanna stormed to her room, waiting an interval which, experience told her, would allow things in the living room to be more or less back to normal, then returned to find Ned buckling up and Gilda gone.

"I've had more than I can stand," she spoke carefully. "I am filing for divorce."

"Good," he said. "You never were much of a wife. I suspect your forte is in the realm of the *ex*-wife. Now just get out of my house. I don't want to see any more of you. Look at you, you're nothing but a clotheshorse and a jewelry mannequin. What did you ever do in return? Out—get out of my house."

She cocked an eye at him. "*Your* house? We'll see whose house it is when we go to court." She turned on her heels and marched out with the same martial swagger she had used to enter.

He snorted, and she could still hear that divisive snorting while she was driving the Rolls, miles from the villa.

Back in her apartment less than five minutes, the phone rang. It was Wilhelm. "I've been worried to death about you," he said.

"Worried? Why?"

"You weren't in all day."

"Oh, you. I am a grown woman, and, I must remind you, a married one."

"But not happily. I will make you happy."

"Can you make me money too?" she teased him.

"You don't mean you will stay with that beast for his money?"

"No, I will divorce him for his money."

"I want to come over."

"No, I told you. Now, you behave or there won't be any money for my opera house."

He wished she had said "our" opera house.

"I've got to run, Wilhelm, I'll talk to you tomorrow."

"Tomorrow?! What about tonight?"

"Busy, lover. Working for you and our opera."

Our opera was so much better, he thought. And when she hung up, he was satisfied.

She called the Ritz Hotel and asked to be put through to Ken Maxwell. He picked it up on the first ring. "Hanna?" he said, excitedly.

"Ken—how nice to hear your voice."

"Where have you been? I've been calling you all day."

"Oh, dear Ken, you know how much trouble divorces are. You tell me I must divorce, I waste no time. I am your slave."

"Oh, sure," he said. "May I pick you up for dinner?"

"Well, I hope so," she said. "I've missed our dinners."

"Half-hour?"

She frowned. She could use five hours to recuperate. "That will be fine," she said.

At dinner, in the most expensive restaurant in Paris, Hanna turned the conversation to the word that had preoccupied her since she had left her friend Katrina.

"Ken, what does the word 'love' mean to you?"

He laughed his easy, good-natured laugh.

"When I think of love, I think of you," he said.

"Yes, you're sweet, and I of you. But what does it mean?"

"It means you feel like you can't live without someone. When you are not with him you are empty, nervous, out of sorts until you see him again."

"Do you think you can love more than one person at a time?"

"No, not that kind of love. You can love your relatives, your children—good friends, but you don't get the same kind of craziness when you are away from them."

"Hmm," she said.

"What about you?" he asked. "What is love to you?"

"Yes, it is all those things you said. But it is also a communion of souls, two hearts beating as one, together in one thought."

"Spiritual…"

"Yes, exactly. A deep spiritual understanding, like you know each other's heart without saying anything."

Ken saw in her definition proof that she loved him. A man in love willingly sets aside reason to further his irrational quest.

"There are so many kinds of love," she said. "One person has no right to say his love is better than someone else's."

"Quite true," he agreed.

"Oh, I am so angry!" she said, changing suddenly the tenor of her conversation.

Ken smiled. He liked her shifting moods. It kept life interesting for him, at an age when his interest span was shrinking.

"There are all kinds of love, yes, but…I don't know. I should not tell you this, I will be so embarrassed."

"What?"

"I come in the house today, and there is my husband, naked in the living room, on the couch. The maid, she is on her knees— agh—doing what I can't even say to you. Now, is that love?"

He frowned. The idea itself appealed to him, though he saw no opportunity to express that opinion. "More lust than love," he said judiciously.

"It's disgusting!" she said. "The *maid!*"

"Yes," he said, hoping that would be sufficient to connote agreement.

Hanna had for the moment forgotten she herself started out life on her own as a maid—and now her friend Katrina was a maid. But somehow Gilda, there in the living room of the villa, on her knees, seemed a more lowly maid.

"I don't know what others think," Ken was saying, "but I know I am crazy in love with you. One of my mother's tests of true love was, 'Is this a person you can live without? If you can be away from her and not miss her, you aren't in love.'" He took her hand in both of his. "I love you," he said.

"You're sweet," she said. "Tell me, did you bring along the paper you want me to sign?"

"Oh, you don't want to see it now, while we're eating."

"Why," she said, "do you think I might eat it?"

They both thought that was funny. "Oh, all right," he said, withdrawing the envelope from his prolific inside pocket. He hesitated a moment before he handed it to her; when he did so, he had a sheepish smile on his face.

She looked at him guardedly, then opened the envelope and stripped it of its contents. She unfolded paper and read the terse and impersonal contents with a deep concentration. English was not her native language and it required more study. She moved her eyes laboriously over the part they had discussed last night—about her being in the process of a divorce from her husband, Ned Sharkey Butterworth.

Then her eyes grazed the surprise: "And when said divorce is final, Hanna Mazurka hereby agrees to marry Ken Maxwell." Slowly, Hanna raised her eyes to his face. He was beaming with happiness.

"But you are talking about *buying* my love," she said. "Is not something can be bought." She didn't know how angry she could get away with being, so she didn't overdo it.

"Oh, no," he said. "If I thought you didn't love me I would not be making this proposal."

She stared at him, but could not think of an answer. She thought of Wilhelm. What rotten luck to fall in love with someone so poor! Of course, she realized she was being naive if she thought a man would give her a hundred thousand dollars a year for life not expecting anything in return.

"What's wrong?" he asked. "You did know I wanted to marry you—?"

"Well, I suppose I could have guessed. But isn't this a rather impersonal proposal?"

"What? Oh, the paper. Well, you did goad me into giving it to you."

"I asked," she flashed, "I didn't *goad* you."

"Oh, well, an unfortunate choice of words. Though I felt I did resist, but you persisted."

"I always persist."

"And so you do," he said. "I should have gotten on my knees. Can you forget the contract? Will you marry me? Shall I get on my knees here?"

"Oh, you're sweet to ask," she said. "May I think about it?"

"Well," he frowned. "I suppose," he said, dragging out the word uncertainly. He decided against asking her why he had been summoned to Paris, why she thought he had given her the hundred-thousand-dollar check.

For her part, she thought back to the courting of the baron. She had only her wiles, and though she tried to make it seem otherwise, she had been at his mercy. Now that she had enough material wealth; she didn't need to seem so desperate. And yet, Hanna could not bring herself to the thought that she was secure. Her background conspired against it. Whatever she had, she always seemed to need more. Custom-made dresses, a ton of jewels, a Rolls-Royce, hundreds of thousands in cash. Perhaps the problem was she felt it all could be attributed to her beauty and youth, and at nearing thirty she was beginning to wonder how many more years she could trade on that. A suitable nest egg or financial cushion was called for. Especially now that she'd promised Wilhelm about the opera company. That could eat big money fast.

When Ken took her home, she pleaded for him not to come in. She had an eerie feeling Wilhelm was somewhere, spying on her. Ken was disappointed, but said he looked forward to the time when he wouldn't have to ask.

She put on her pixie grin. "You should *always* have to ask," she said.

The next morning, there was a quiet knock on Hanna's door. She opened it to the forlorn Wilhelm, standing awkwardly, holding a bunch of flowers that drooped as if they had come from the graveyard.

"Oh, how nice," she exclaimed, and took them from him. She rummaged the apartment for a vase and found an antique she had purchased. Wilhelm tried to kiss her, but she was cool. She sat facing him in the living room.

"You should not be here, I told you," she scolded lightly.

"But I could not stay away. I think of nothing but you. When I am delivering the soup or taking the orders, it is you who is on my mind. I am sorry…" He hung his head.

"We will jeopardize the divorce settlement," she said, "we may not be able to afford the opera."

"I don't care," he said. "Even if I am jeopardizing my *life*, I cannot stay away from you," he said. "Now tell me, don't you feel the same?"

She sighed heavily. "I wish I could afford to be so cavalier about my future. It is one thing to care for you, dear boy, and I most

assuredly do, but it is another to be responsible for the money that
would keep us going."

"But I *love* you. Have you *never* been in love like that? Where
nothing else mattered?"

"Oh, my dear boy! What a luxury. '*Nothing else mattered?*'
All well and good if you start out independently wealthy. But I had to
scrounge for every penny of my existence."

"Oh, I don't care. Give it all away. I would love you if we had
nothing. I would be happy to support you working two jobs. We
don't need much money. Enough to eat—a roof over our heads."

"Ah," she said, "to be young and idealistic. I have become
lazy in my comfort. I *do* love you, Wilhelm. But I am a realist by
necessity. I have clawed my way to where I am. It is such a sweet idea
to throw it all over so we could be together in our idyllic love."

"Why can't I come to see you? Where were you last night?"

"Now, Wilhelm, don't make me account for all my moves to
you. Love is spiritual, not actuarial. It involves faith and trust. I am
still married, you know. I am trying to make the transition from the
married state to unmarried. Smoothly. I cannot have the distraction
of you. I can't think clearly. I don't want to be accused of desertion
for another man. Ned will stop at nothing, I am sure, to keep me
from getting what is due me. If he succeeds, you and I have *no*
future. Is that clear to you, my boy?"

"But how can we hide our love under a rug? It's not natural."

"Oh, Wilhelm, please, think of our dream, our opera. That is
worth lying low for six months, is it not?"

"Then we will marry?"

Hanna sighed. Why did her men make her life so complicat-
ed? "Suppose there is a stipulation that I not marry for five years or
something in order to get my settlement?"

"Don't sign it."

"Yes—and perhaps you could get *me* a job as a waitress."

Not seeing her sarcasm, he said, "Yes, I could."

She smiled, but dropped the idea. "I *know* Ned will hire
spies. I know what goes through that pea brain of his, believe me."
She stood up. "Now we must part. I am sorry, but there is no alternative. I do love you, and I too will be thinking always of you. But I
have many decisions to make, and one mistake could cost us
everything."

"I don't care. I want to be with you."

"We will, we will be together, I promise you—just not yet. I can't explain any further. It is very complex. *Trust* me," she pleaded. She kissed him suddenly, hard on his lips, then just as suddenly released him. "Now go!" she commanded. He grabbed her back and began kissing her. She went limp and neither resisted nor assisted. "What's the matter?" he asked.

"Go!"

"No. Let me love you."

"No."

"Why not? I'm here. There is no one under the bed, is there?"

"I want to love you when I am free to—I would be too nervous. I would not be good. Please leave me. My mind is swimming with impossible alternatives," she said. "Now go, and let me work it out."

Dragging his heels, his shoulders stooped, Wilhelm left her apartment—looking back as long as he could see the door, which she had long since closed.

That afternoon, Hanna went shopping to bolster her spirits. There she found that credit from her husband had been cut off. She made a terrible scene in Cartier, but the clerk told her there was nothing he could do. "If Madame would like to pay from her own account, I should be happy to show you anything."

"No, Madame would *not* like to pay from her own account," she said, and stormed out of the store.

She commiserated that night at a dinner with Ken, and he did his best to comfort her.

"The man is simply uncouth. He *told* me I had unlimited credit at Cartier, now he is going back on his word."

"Well, if you want a divorce…"

"I *do!*"

"He is not liable to be so generous."

"But why not? I am *still* his wife. Wouldn't you be embarrassed to call stores all over and tell them you were cutting off your wife's credit?"

"I've never done it—"

"Of course not. You're not that small. Oh, Ken, I am so miserable. This is just getting me down so. I was hoping we could come to an amicable settlement, but now I see we cannot. It shall be a fight to the finish."

"I'm sorry. If there is anything I can do…"

"You are always so sweet. I do believe you'd do anything I asked. That's why I don't dare ask," she giggled. "Maybe I'd be disappointed."

"Try me," he said.

"Well…"

"Go on—"

"Well, of course, I will have living expenses while this goes on. I will not move back to live with that beast—you wouldn't *want* me to do that, would you?"

"Certainly not!"

"So I *can* count on you for some, well, financial assistance in the meantime?"

"I don't see why not."

"Oh, you're wonderful!" she exclaimed, clapping her hands before he had finished his thought. "And I did mention the lawyers, didn't I? Just an advance, of course."

"Yes, you, ah, did."

"Ned will certainly have to pay the lawyers, but…just if they want it in advance."

"Oh, well…" he said.

"Oh, well, what? Oh, well, yes, or oh, well, no?"

"If…"

"If what?"

"If you agree to marry me when you are free."

She looked at him as though he had said something nonsensical. "But, of course," she said.

And she made him a very happy man.

And that night, in his suite at the Ritz, Hanna made Ken a still happier man. She had an uncanny sense of when to use her favors, still considerable, and when to withhold them. She was, it might be said, a genius of timing.

Hanna felt as though a great stone had been lifted from her back. She had settled on the future course of her life. Now all that was left to her was the concentration of her considerable energies to achieve her goal. And she had a reservoir of cunning so deep you would never see the bottom. She was one of the forerunners of the modern press leak, and though her early attempts might be considered crude by modern standards, they were effective. Her singing mishaps had made her the brunt of journalistic jokes, but had earned her currency as a celebrity. The more often they made fun of her, the higher her stock rose, so at this point in her life, Hanna Mazurka had become a household word.

So when she called the largest paper in Paris to hint at marital discord with her third husband, it took less than an hour before a reporter and photographer showed up on her apartment doorstep, the address of which had been inadvertently furnished by the anonymous tipster, who spoke French with a Polish accent. They may have made fun of her, but she was good copy.

When Hanna opened her door, she was faced with a tall, blond, stooped reporter, whose first words were, "Is it true you are filing for divorce?"

"Where did you get that idea?"

"Anonymous tip." He smiled. "I'm Alf, this is Jacques," he said, tossing his head to the man with the camera.

She smiled carefully, not showing any teeth for the short photographer by the reporter's side.

In her early years, the years of romantic attachments and celebrity, all Hanna Mazurka's smiles for photographers were with closed lips. It was not that her teeth were unattractive—they were perfect. It was rather that she thought too much smiling was synonymous with flirting and an inconsequential nature, and she wanted to be taken seriously.

"Goodness," she said, "if you want pictures, you should come in and let us take our time."

Inside her lavishly furnished apartment, the photographer asked permission to take pictures of the room.

"Oh, you insult me," she faux pouted. "Here I am, all dressed in my most startling jewels, with a custom-made dress, and you want to take pictures of *furniture!*"

He ducked his head in apology, and Hanna bade them sit down. "May I get you some tea?" she asked. "I was just making some hot water." She didn't tell them she had made extra, just in case…or that she had given the maid the day off.

She served the tea in one of her many heavy sterling-silver tea services.

She sat as they all savored their tea. "Is it true?" Alf, the reporter, asked. "About the divorce?"

She batted her eyelashes. No one did it better. "Goodness gracious," she said, "the power of the press never ceases to astonish me. I only made that decision *yesterday* and here you are already." She shook her head. "Amazing. Simply amazing."

Alf made a note that Hanna Mazurka was amazed at the efficacy of the Paris press. "How did it come about?" he asked.

She cast down her eyes. "Oh," she said, "I don't know if I can…it is *so* painful, the memory."

"I understand," Alf said, though he didn't look particularly understanding. "What caused it?"

She shook her head, the eyes still casting about the floor as though there might be something there to make things easier for her. She sighed. "I do not believe what I saw with my own eyes. You could certainly not put it in your fine newspaper—it is too terrible."

"I'm sorry…"

"Yes—it was…well, I… I mean, how can I say this without embarrassment? I do not know." She sighed again, the jewels supported on her bare shoulders heaving above her bosom. "I came home from a day in the country, visiting old friends—Prince Stephanoff from Russia and his wife, my dear friend Katrina. They have a lovely place in the country—wonderful house and large barn, with many horses. I have not seen them for long time."

Alf nodded, encouraging her to get on with it. He said, "What happened when you got home?"

"Disaster!" she said. "Debauchery!"

"Oh." Alf was suddenly as interested as any shark at the sight of blood.

She nodded, then seemed to slump in her chair while her eyes searched the floor again. "I ask myself, what did I do to deserve such treatment? Is this a man I married, or an…animal!?" She paused to catch her breath—outrage takes a lot of breath—and to collect her thoughts.

"Yes?" Alf encouraged her.

"There he was, on the couch," she shook her head, "his pantaloons were God knows where—"

"No!"

"And the maid!"

"The maid? Young and attractive, was she?"

"Well," Hanna's head shot up, "she is young; I do not myself find her attractive."

"Was she there on the couch with him?"

Hanna shook her head.

"No?" His shoulders slumped in disappointment.

"No—she was...she was on the floor." Here Hanna indicated by gesture her breasts. "They were uncovered. She was on her knees...on the floor... Oh," she choked, and stopped. "This is just too painful to go on."

"What was she doing?"

"Agh—she was there...and he was—there she had him...it was...I mean, her mouth... And there am I, the wife, seeing this like I was in the middle of the worst nightmare of my life. And then he saw me and he, he...he..." she trailed off.

"Yes? He what?"

"He *laughed!* Oh, it was too terrible. And he...did... not...stop! He just laughed and kept our maid, the girl I had hired, kept her earning her keep, I suppose. Oh, so awful. But you see, you cannot put that in your newspaper. I would *certainly* not want you to."

"Oh, no," Alf said, the soul of understanding.

"May I offer you more tea?"

"Oh, no, thank you. Jacques?"

Jacques was staring at Hanna with his mouth open. She looked so prim and proper with the teacup and saucer balanced so delicately on her lap. "What? Oh, no—thanks—very good though." And he set his empty cup and saucer on the table beside him and took another picture of her in that darling wronged-wife pose. It was the one they would run in the paper.

Alf stood and Jacques followed. "Well, Madame Mazurka, thank you for your time and frankness. If we can ever do anything more to help you..."

"Oh, you are very kind, I am sure. But I don't need help. I am only seeking this divorce and a reasonable settlement because Ned Butterworth must be taught a lesson."

"Yes."

"That he cannot treat women as things."

As soon as the door was closed, the two boys had a good

laugh. Jacques said, "That lusty maid must have sure been giving his thing a treat!"

But they ran the story pretty much as Hanna had hoped they would.

The publicity she sought and delighted in brought with it a downside. The papers decided to get more mileage out of it. They began stationing themselves outside her door and shouting questions at her as she came and went. What began as a clever maneuver on her part soon deteriorated into a real nuisance. If she thought she could use the press, she soon learned it was nothing next to how they could use her. Flashbulbs popped at her wherever she went. Reporters became pushier and ruder. Even her lawyer was besieged for tidbits. He instructed her in no uncertain terms: "Say *nothing*. Talk to *no one!*" And, except in circumstances where she felt she could gain some advantage over her adversary by dropping a bon mot their way, Hanna kept her counsel and explained as nicely as she could that her lawyer just absolutely refused for her to say anything. She herself was just aching to tell them all.

The reporters and photographers became more than a nuisance when she went to see Ken Maxwell. Their insistent questions rattled her.

"Isn't that the American industrialist, Ken Maxwell?"

"Are you planning to marry him?"

"Has he gotten a divorce?"

"Is he paying for your divorce?"

"Have you any financial arrangements with him?"

She tried to smile gravely, and she did break her lawyer's rule to say, "Goodness, I have not divorced one man and already you have me married to another. Mr. Maxwell is an old friend. He goes way back. I love him like a father. He looks out for his little girl. I need help. This is so much a trying time now. He is big and he is strong and he protects me."

When Ken Maxwell read Hanna's words in the newspaper, he marveled at how clever she was in deflecting attention from their relationship. "...an old friend." He chuckled. "I love him like a father." What a performer!

Attorney Darius Monteux was quick to bury his animus for Madame Hanna Mazurka when she finally provided him with a check for his past services and a sweet retainer to institute the divorce against the richest man in Paris. One did not need to be a student of human character to notice the physiological change in Mr. Monteux at the news. The eyes sparkling and intensifying simultaneously, the hands rubbing together, the posture stiffening easily.

And Ned proved a worthy adversary. If anyone thought he would just pay up to be rid of her, the only option granted him was to rethink the matter.

Given her sense of things, Hanna would have rather cut off communication with Ken Maxwell until the divorce sensation blew over. But he would not hear of it, and, as she told a forlorn, frustrated Wilhelm—banished to the wings during the drama—Ken was the one paying the bills.

Hanna had not gotten around to telling Wilhelm of her agreement to marry Ken Maxwell. She thought he would have difficulty understanding.

Hanna kept hoping the newspapers would tire of circling her like a school of barracudas, but whenever things threatened to settle into some dull routine, a juicy new bit of gossip or news of divorce demands surfaced, and the gentlemen of the press (who by this time had thoroughly convinced her they were no gentlemen at all) pounced on it.

There were so many libelous embarrassments to Hanna's person in the press that she was more than once on the brink of compromising her demands. But each time, she steeled herself against the onslaught and fought on. "Ned Sharkey Butterworth must be taught a lesson," she said again and again. "He simply cannot treat women as things and get away with it. He must be made to pay, and pay through the nose, or he will go on preying on poor, defenseless, innocent women for the rest of his life."

"Which one are you?" some reporter would shout at this pronouncement, and the rest of the boys would whoop it up with laughter.

"Go ahead, laugh," she chastised them. "You men will never understand if you stick your heads in the sand like ostrich."

Ned, of course, did not bury his head in the sand, but fought valiantly over everything she wanted. And she wanted *every*thing she had touched or come close to in the marriage. "Not because I care for material things," she said to her pals in the press, "but to teach him a lesson…" But they had heard it so often, they stopped listening.

The list of her demands included (but were certainly not limited to):

THE VILLA OUTSIDE PARIS AND ALL ITS CONTENTS.

Hanna maintained: Ned had given it to her as a wedding gift.

Ned countered: Patently ridiculous. It was *his* home. She had spent very few nights there in the fourteen-month marriage. This was not negotiable.

ALL PERSONAL PROPERTY PURCHASED DURING THE MARRIAGE, INCLUDING (BUT NOT LIMITED TO) CARS, JEWELRY, FURNITURE, PAINTINGS, SCULPTURE, CLOTHING, ARTIFACTS, PERFUME, PIANOS.

(There was no mention of books. Neither of them found time to read books.)

Hanna maintained: He had given her carte blanche to buy whatever she wanted, and had kept money in her checking account (until the final blowup) for her to do so. "Did he mean I was to buy those things for him? Of course not. They were solely for my use and enjoyment."

Ned countered: "Hanna Mazurka never fulfilled her responsibilities as a wife. She refused even to take my name. But she could spend my money like a battalion of nouveau riche girls off the Polish farm like she was. Had she chosen to maintain the marriage, I would have been happy to indulge her every whim, and as you can see, her whims were insatiable. But Hanna chose not only not to take my name, but not to take me either. A rich American is hot on her heels. Has been since *before* we were married. Practically shared our wedding night with us.

"Besides, millions of francs have been spent without my

knowing. She took an apartment in Paris when she knew she was looking for a pretense to divorce me. It was her cold abstinence that forced me into the arms of Gilda. A man can bear only so much."

At that point a reporter snickered. "I heard you bared it all!"

"I only maintain that this money—*millions* of francs—was spent by her opportunistically, with the full knowledge that she had no intention of maintaining the marriage, and therefore was obtained by fraud, and she should have no title to the chattel," he said, working up an uncharacteristic lather. "Why, the only things she didn't ask for were my polo ponies and the yacht."

Hanna replied: "For the yacht, he can keep. I get seasick. And the ponies he shall have so their droppings will remind him what kind of person he is."

The battles raged on, and the newspapers missed none of it. Parisians delighted in choosing sides and debating the relative merits of the arguments. Most men were on Ned's side—the women were divided. Some of them could sympathize with Hanna about the bestiality of men, others thought she might be taking it too far.

In the end, Hanna wore Ned down, and generally prevailed. But as the negotiating and bickering wore on, Hanna thought of other things she must have. It was all well and good to gain possession of material things, and she could perhaps sell them at a fraction of their value, but then how would she live?

Ned countered: "You are already living on that sugar daddy from the States. And for a fourteen-month marriage—your third, my first—I don't owe you a living for the rest of your life." He did offer, through his attorney, to give her a similar allowance for another fourteen months. "It takes a tree to rot as long as it lived," he said. "Hanna rots a lot quicker, but I'll pay until all her limbs are decayed from this insignificant marriage. Fourteen months, not a penny more."

Why did she prevail? Many of her demands *were* outrageous. Unprecedented in the divorce courts.

When a reporter asked her why she was demanding so much more than the average woman divorcing a rich man, she shot back, "Average? I am not average. I am the enemy of the average."

So, finally, her prevailing came down to a matter of stamina. She had more insulation against ridicule in her makeup than her ex-husband. He quickly tired of seeing his name dragged unflatteringly through the papers. She also tired of it, but with her it was a holy cause, and that was just one of the prices she would grudgingly pay.

In the end, Madame Hanna Mazurka was awarded all the possessions she asked for, including his villa in the outskirts of Paris. This had been so important to her because Wilhelm Drang had found a theater for sale in the neighborhood, and they both decided it would be ideal for their opera-company venture.

In addition, Ned gave her two hundred thousand dollars cash, twenty-five thousand dollars a year for life, and an irrevocable grant of three million in his will.

When it was all over, Hanna told the reporters that though she had triumphed and gotten everything she asked for, "This is no victory of material goods. No. This was only to teach him a lesson."

"Do you think you taught him the lesson?" one reporter asked. "After all, you are getting only a minuscule portion of his wealth."

She smiled and said, "Perhaps my small requests were too modest." She was standing beside Ken Maxwell, clutching his arm. "But I have this big, strong man to take care of me now—and I am very happy."

"There were rumors that you might be linked romantically with a gentleman named Wilhelm Drang, an aspiring opera conductor." Madame Hanna Mazurka was startled, but she did her best to hide it. Had the young man himself planted that juicy item in the ears of the press to make trouble with her and Ken?

"Oh, I know so many musicians," she said, "and I am fond of all of them. Perhaps I will work with him someday. Now, gentlemen, we must go on with our lives. I hope you will let us." Both Hanna and Ken were beaming happily.

The press caught Ned at his villa, removing his few remaining belongings.

"What do you think of your divorce settlement?"

He snorted his trademark laughter, then said, "That bitch, I've forgotten her name already."

"Madame Hanna Mazurka," someone supplied.

"Well, whatever she was called, I'd have paid twice as much to be rid of her." And he snorted again.

Wilhelm Drang had been watching the newspapers with an edgy anticipation until news came that a divorce settlement had been reached in the case of *Mazurka* v. *Butterworth*. It is not difficult to imagine his feelings on seeing the settlement announced, accompanied by a picture of Hanna arm in arm with Ken Maxwell—both beaming like a couple of kids.

The maestro had stayed low as long as he could. Hadn't the madame only asked him to stay out of sight until the settlement was reached and then she would come to him? Now it looked as if all this time she had been keeping company with that rich American. How could she explain that?

Wilhelm made a trip to his restaurant to tell them he would not be working that night. Then he went to Hanna's apartment and camped at her door. She found him sleeping there slightly after two in the morning. He was sleeping as if on a bed of nails. She tried to get the door open without waking him, but she didn't succeed. He sat bolt upright, then rubbed the sleep from his eyes.

"Hanna! Why are you trying to creep by me?"

"I didn't want to wake you."

"You don't want to talk to me, do you?" he demanded, getting sleepily to his feet.

"Silly!" she said. "Not while you are asleep."

"Well, I am awake," he said, following her into the apartment. "What time is it?"

"It is too late for you to be sleeping at my door. What do you think the neighbors are thinking?"

"That is not their affair."

"Is it mine?"

"No! Hanna," he pleaded like a child, "where have you been? You are with that man, aren't you? The American."

She sighed and said, "All right, you are here, and I am dead tired, but you sit down and I will tell you the facts of life."

He sat on the love seat, and she sat next to him, taking his hand in hers. Slowly she drew in a sustaining breath. "We must be grown-up about this," she said. "All I am doing and planning is for us, for our opera. To guarantee we would have the money to make guarantees in return."

"What kind of guarantees?"

"Let me finish…"

"Wait—I don't get it. I saw in the paper what you're getting—enough money to live like a queen the rest of your life. So don't start in about needing more from this American."

Hanna was still breathing deeply, as though that was necessary to calm her nerves. "Dear boy," she said. "You are so naive."

"Don't patronize me," he snapped.

"Oooh, we are getting angry, are we? Who should be angry in this opera? Are you questioning my motives, is that it?"

"You're damn right. I'm questioning everything. One day you tell me you love me—we are going to go off and live and love and make opera between us — just as soon as you are financially secure. Well, now you have enough money to make a small country secure, and yet there you are, in the papers, arm in arm with that old American who could be your father. Why?" he pleaded. "Why are you doing this to me? Don't you love me...?"

"Of course I love you," she cut in angrily. "You think I would go through all this for myself? You are right, I have plenty money now. But I did not always, and did not know how well I would succeed with Mr. Butterworth. He said he would fight me to the death. I could have lost everything. The lawyer's fees alone would have driven me to the poorhouse. So I made an...arrangement."

"You mean you sold yourself to that American?" There was no doubt from his tone that Wilhelm Drang held Americans in contempt.

"That isn't a very nice way to put it, Wilhelm. American, yes. He has offered to give me one hundred thousand dollars every year for the rest of my life."

The sum staggered Wilhelm. "One hundred thou..." he gasped.

"And it is in writing. Only, to put it into effect, I must..." She checked Wilhelm's face as if she could predict how he would take it. "Marry him," she whispered.

Wilhelm exploded. He cursed, he railed against the American, against her, against the barbarous cruelties of mankind.

She wanted to tell him to shut up, but instead she let him run down, then nodded sympathetically. "Yes, yes," she said, "I know how you feel. I know you can't believe I am doing this for you — but I am also doing it this way because I must have security. I must know that I will keep up my living standards. This is not automatic, you know. I was once poorer than you are. I too was filled with pride, but I learned soon I could not eat pride. In my life, I have had to take perhaps devious paths — paths I would have not taken if I had been secure — and rich from the start."

"Oh, Hanna — "

"Let me finish! You are a dear boy, the first real love I have experienced. I loved a prince once, but though I thought he returned it, he did not. So that leaves you. I have had three husbands and soon a fourth. Of course, I told myself each time I was in love and it would be the last marriage; I was fooling myself."

"But this is not necessary," he insisted.

"Necessary? What do you know of 'necessary'? You are a man. This is a man's world. We women are nothing if we allow that to happen. I make up my mind young that I can't help being woman, but I will not be nothing! Always I must see the future is taken care of. Mr. Maxwell, he offers to guarantee my future. With Mr. Butterworth, I have to be married to him to be dependent on his whims of generosity. Mr. Maxwell, he will not require a lifetime commitment for a lifetime security. There is our opera, dear boy. It is guaranteed."

"But how do you expect to do opera here if you are in Chicago?"

"I will be in Chicago—only a small time—to meet his mother and marry in her church. I will not live in Chicago."

"Does Maxwell know this?"

"I have explained my career must come first."

"And he accepts that?"

"He must! And you must give me time to ease away from him, back to you."

Wilhelm whistled softly. "You are some woman."

"Yes, if you are looking for the average housewife satisfied to stay home and wash the dishes, that is not me."

"So I notice," he said, shaking his head as if that would help him understand. "So, I am supposed to twiddle my thumbs while you marry again? I am supposed to lease the love of my life to another man?"

She stared at him, trying to make him see the advantages she saw. "I am selling myself, as you so quaintly put it, so we may be together and make opera—and make love." This last she said with a gentle squeeze of his hand. "Now, I must get some sleep," she said. "I am to be married in a matter of hours. I can't look like a sleepy alley cat."

Suddenly Wilhelm began weeping, then sobbing, then lustily crying and gasping for air.

"Oh, now, now," she said, taking him in her arms and rocking him back and forth against her bosom.

Wilhelm was shattered, and Hanna couldn't bear it. She

finally, after interminable rocking didn't quiet him, took him into her bed.

"Now, you know," she said while she undressed him, "you can't stay all night."

He nodded obediently. And though it was now after three in the morning, they loved with a fierce passion—as though they had to make the most of their opportunity—as though it could be their last.

Later that morning, Hanna and Ken Maxwell were married at City Hall in a civil ceremony, in the same room where she had married Ned Sharkey Butterworth.

The couple were followed by photographers and reporters to the train station, where the newlyweds boarded a train for the Salzburg Music Festival.

Like everything else, the honeymoon had been Hanna's idea.

Wilhelm Drang had contemplated attending the marriage ceremony and when asked if anyone knew any reason why they should not be married, he would speak loud and clear and tell them that she loved *him*, not the rich American, whom she was only using for money. But his early-morning postcoital reveries were suffered in such agony, while the wedding ceremony was taking place, Wilhelm Drang was in his bathroom, throwing up.

The rest of the day he spent contemplating suicide.

      𝄞   𝄞   𝄞

Hanna Mazurka was unbelievably happy at the Salzburg Music Festival.

"Isn't it wonderful being in the town of Mozart's birth?" she enthused. "Let's go to his *Geburtshaus*." She was taking Ken absolutely everywhere, not missing an event. He was soon begging for mercy.

As she listened to the many musical performances, her mind was on Wilhelm Drang. Life, she thought, had dealt her a hand of cards that most people wouldn't envy, and she had to play it the best she could. Could anyone fault her for that?

"Hanna," Ken pleaded. "I knew you were interested in

operas, but string quartets? And piano recitals and symphonies and oratorios? How can you *do* it?"

"Oh, I just *love* music," she said.

In her moments of self-candor, she admitted she was trying to see that her new husband got his fill of music so he would not entertain any notion of staying with her in Paris for her opera venture.

At first she couldn't deny him the fulfillment of his amorous excitements, but her mind and heart were elsewhere. He spoke poems to her beauty and what a lucky man he was to be blessed with such a beautiful wife.

And she said, "You're sweet."

The last day of the Salzburg Festival, she said, "Don't you just love music?"

He smiled and said, "Yes, in moderation."

"Oh, I'll teach you yet. Wait till you see my opera-company productions—in Paris."

"Your what?"

"Opera company. I told you about that…didn't I? Of course I did."

"You told me you wanted to have an opera company of your own someday…"

"Oh, well, that day is here. I'm not getting any younger, and if I am going to have my career, I'm going to have to get moving. I came quite by accident upon this theater outside of town which I think will be ideal for starting a company. It's not too big, we won't be competing with Paris, but it's big enough so we'll get noticed. And it won't cost too much to buy…and renovate."

"How much?"

"Oh, I don't know exactly yet. We haven't gone that far."

"And who is we?"

"Well…whoever I get for the company. That won't be difficult. There are always dozens of applicants for every part."

"But why Paris? Why don't you let me buy you something in Chicago?"

"Oh, would you do that too? That's so *sweet!*"

"Too?" he laughed. "*Instead.*"

"Oh, well." She cast her eyes down. "You know I didn't do too well in Chicago, and you were completely right—I wasn't prepared. So I do want to make a career in your country, oh, yes, I do, but I do not want to embarrass you again. This time I come, I come prepared to sing my heart out for you. To make you proud."

"Oh, I'm always proud of you," he said. "But," he frowned, "what is this Paris plan? You are my wife. I want to be with you."

"Well, that is good. Why can't you be with me in Paris?"

"Because I have a job in Chicago."

"But you are bossman. You tell them what to do. They don't tell you."

He laughed and hugged her. "Oh, I love you," he said. "You are so clever. Yes, I am bossman, but I must be there to boss. I have married a very expensive woman and I must keep her in the manner to which she has become accustomed."

"Yes, that is good. So you get me an opera house in Paris and one in Chicago. When I have enough training in Paris, I come to Chicago and make a triumphal American debut."

"You really are something," he said, admiring her.

He said he would think about it. She didn't tell him the property was already in escrow.

When, the next day, they were on the train for Paris, and he said he had decided against the opera in Paris because he wanted to be with her all the time, she argued that they could be together for better quality time—he could visit Paris and she could visit Chicago.

He shook his head. "No. I don't want to be apart from you so much."

She turned stony silent, and pouted.

"Now, now, what's the matter?"

"You said I could have my career."

"And so you can—"

"Not in Chicago. I must *build* my career. Chicago," she shook her head, "set me back for years. Why, I was already a star in Havana. In your Chicago they treat me like dirt. So my husband comes and demands I leave that instant with him, and I did not even have time to see you for a proper goodbye. No, I was *so* humiliated. I cannot take chances in Chicago, for one more failure would cook my goose for good. So if you *are* in sympathy for my career, you know I must rebuild it here. So much mystique in your country for Europe. If they think something is from Europe, it must be special."

If he realized she had inadvertently made a comment on their relationship, he didn't give any indication of it.

"So my plan is to get notices from Paris, that I am the new singing sensation from the Continent. Then I go to America, and it is like I am on a white horse. I will be the toast of the world, and you will get all the credit."

"Oh, no…"

"You deserve it. You have made everything possible. You are such a generous man. You will glory in my success. You don't be jealous like Ned was."

And so, they compromised. She would make the trip to Chicago with him so she could meet his family, who, according to Ken, were dying to meet her. And they would repeat the wedding ceremony in the family's Episcopal church, to appease his mother. Then she could return to Paris, and he would come to visit every six months or more often and she would return the favor.

They were in Paris only a few short days before they sailed to New York on the *Mauretania*, then on to Chicago in his private railroad car.

She wanted to see Wilhelm Drang while she was in Paris, to share the good news, but it was so awkward. Ken did not want to leave her side, and even though they had separate rooms at night, she didn't want to chance going out and getting caught. *That* could hardly do the Paris opera venture any good.

She had to wait until the day of their sailing before she had a chance to call Wilhelm. He was not happy with what she had to say.

"How was your honeymoon?" he asked, sarcastically, getting the conversation off on the wrong foot.

"Oh, please," she said. "No bitterness. I'm doing this for us—"

"Oh, yes, how very altruistic you are."

She was silent for a moment. She waited until he said, "Hanna, are you there?" before she answered.

"Perhaps I am asking too much of you, Wilhelm. Ken wants me to stay in Chicago with him. I have argued I must begin my career in Paris. I may come back in a few weeks. But perhaps you are telling me I should stay in Chicago with him?"

"No, no," he said too quickly. "I can't live without you anymore. Now that I have lived to feel real love, I am good for nothing else. I know there is no one in this world who would love me the way you did—I live for it, Hanna, do you understand?"

"Yes. And I do too. You must understand that I am jeopardizing everything for you. How easy for me to go to Chicago and never come back. I didn't have to call you today. I could have just disappeared from your life."

"Don't do that," he pleaded, and it sounded like the whine of a distraught child. "If that happens, they will find me facedown in the Seine."

"Now, now, be a good boy," she said.

"Bon voyage," he said, and he meant it kindly. It just didn't come out that way.

Chicago was so humid Hanna thought she would suffocate. Her custom-made dresses were clinging to her body, and that delighted her husband.

Hanna's performance with Ken's family was impeccable. In spite of their fears and prejudices, Hanna won them over with her bubbling personality. Ken was bursting with pride in his new wife.

The night after the simple wedding ceremony, Ken visited Hanna in her bedroom. But in spite of several valiant tries, he was physically unable to please himself, which did not displease her. But it made him morose. She patted his shoulder. "Cheer up," she said. "I'm sure it's temporary."

"And will return once you've left?"

"I'm not going away forever, you know."

But it seemed like forever to Ken. After she left for Paris, he sank into a deep depression.

Ken had attained the dream of his fantasies, then abruptly, cruelly, he was unable to consummate that dream. He sought the advice and counsel of a myriad of physicians, some of whom suggested psychiatry, which he was not about to do. To Ken, that was an admission of mental deficiency. Instead, *in extremis*, he began to consult those whose professional reputations were on a lower rung on the medical ladder. The result of his frustration was his agreement to an operation whereby he would receive glands from a monkey, presumably a highly sexed monkey, which would then make him a man with similar capacities.

Somehow, the yellow press got a tip that the rich industrialist was trading glands with a randy monkey, and they were able to create the most juicy stories from it. It made the international wire service and caused Madame Mazurka no small embarrassment in Paris.

There, the opera house had been bought, the company begun and Wilhelm Drang set up housekeeping in Hanna's villa, formerly belonging to Ned Sharkey Butterworth. They had separate rooms, of course, but Wilhelm was a man of youth and vigor and he could do what Mr. Maxwell could not. Perhaps owing to him getting more encouragement from Hanna than she had given Maxwell.

Daily, they worked hard together; nightly, they played just as hard. They were deliriously happy. The realities of Hanna's love smothered Wilhelm's doubts. She told him often she loved him. If he groused about her marriage, she only needed to ask playfully, "Am I in Chicago, or am I in Paris?"

"Paris!" he would shout gleefully and nuzzle her neck.

Over the years, their opera company developed to both their delighted satisfaction. For their first opera, Hanna chose Puccini's *Madame Butterfly*. She and Wilhelm began from scratch, hiring carpenters to renovate the hall and build the sets, scenic artists to paint the sets, dress designers to design Hanna the most spectacular, some said outlandish, costumes imaginable. It was even more fun than Hanna had anticipated. Now she could be the boss and do what she wanted without anyone disdaining her.

Wilhelm busied himself hiring an orchestra, then he began

rehearsing it. Though he had little experience conducting an orchestra—none outside of his university training—he soon discovered the benefits of bravado. The little man who had so lately been a waiter, suddenly flourished into a maestro, and that is what he asked to be called. After the thrill of new work wore off the personnel, and they felt a modicum of security in their positions, and they felt at ease with one another, some snickering about the bosses began. At the Mazurka Opera Company their leaders were called the M&M twins—Maestro and Madame—and the derision grew from those who felt the titles were grossly inflated. "Maestro Toscanini, certainly," they said. "But Maestro Drang? Madame Galli-Curci, yes—but Madame Mazurka?" Here followed a sound made from blowing air through compressed lips—in the vernacular, called the raspberries.

Slowly and subtly at first, then at an accelerating clip, the egos of the maestro and the madame grew by cross-pollination, then by self-fertilization, until they inevitably toppled from overfeeding.

At a rehearsal for their projected (but unscheduled) performance of *Madame Butterfly*, Madame was singing the title role, and the maestro was taking the orchestra through its paces. After the first run-through, Madame asked the maestro, "Could you play softer? You're drowning me out."

"You should sing louder," he said. At first he didn't see her shooting her evil rays down at him in the orchestra pit. When he finally looked up onstage and experienced her displeasure, he shrugged his shoulders, dismissing or denigrating her feelings.

She threw her score on the floor and glared at him. The music began again, as though nothing had happened.

She shouted from the stage to the pit, "STOP!" Wilhelm seemed surprised, but stopped his beat midair. "Don't you *ever* tell me I don't do it right. You don't know the first thing about rehearsal etiquette."

"But you were the one who told me I was too loud."

"Yes, and you *were!* For what do you think I am spending all this money? This is a bottomless hole in the ground. Money and *more* money just goes in and disappears and the hole never fills up. Do I need to remind you whose money that *is* going into that hole?"

"I know…"

"Now when you want to start pouring *your* money down that

hole, you can tell me what to do all you want. Is that clear?"

"But I don't have money," he pleaded.

"*EXACTLY!* And what do they say? She who pays the fiddler calls the tune. You understand that? When I sing I want to be heard. I don't want to be covered up by the orchestra. Understand?"

"Yes, Madame."

That night, they loved with an angry passion that excited them both beyond their experience.

But it was destined to be an uneasy truce.

From Chicago, Ken wrote about his operation "to restore some of the vigor of my youth." The papers, he said, had embarrassed him, and had, as usual, made a muddle of things, but he was beginning to feel early signs of success along the desired lines and he couldn't wait to see results with Hanna, "to be more of a husband to you than I have been."

After he wrote begging her to come home "and meet the new me," she wrote how impossible that would be, much as she would like to, she was enmeshed in rehearsals for a production of her opera company, and she was singing the title role.

She went on to tell him how much she appreciated "your support of my opera venture. It is my whole life (except for you, of course) and I am happy you are a good husband about it."

When he telephoned, suggesting he come to Paris to hear her perform, she said she would feel better about it at a later date. "The way things are going here, all my energies are going into the role, and since it will be my first starring part, I am quite nervous and out of sorts, and am afraid I wouldn't be much of a wife to you. I want you to come when I can devote my full attention to you, like you deserve."

Ken astonished her by saying he was coming anyway. He was, he said, "feeling a very strong longing for you, my darling."

Nor was Wilhelm happy at the news he would have to move out of the house while Hanna's husband visited. "We have separate rooms," he said. "I'll keep out of your way."

"Oh, no," she said. "Not possible." And this time, she did not have to remind the maestro where the money was coming from.

So Wilhelm moved into Hanna's Paris apartment, with the promise she would visit him there for their Sunday music salons. But he did not go without staking his claim with a torrid love scene the night before Ken's arrival.

Madame knew why Ken was coming—to show off his new monkey glands. Wilhelm tried to make fun of the operation, but Hanna turned him off. "Mr. Maxwell provides the funds so we may pursue our passions," she said, leaving no doubt about the *plural* passions. "I will not have him mocked."

"Yes, Madame," Wilhelm said, mocking her.

As soon as Ken Maxwell got off the train, he threw his arms around Hanna and gave her the most passionate kiss. "Let's go to bed," he whispered in her ear.

"Oh, silly!" she said. "You just got here."

"If I could have come any faster, I would have."

"Silly, *silly* boy! I am late to my rehearsal. I told you, is bad time to come—you would not listen to reason."

"Is *good* time," he said, "believe me!" And he squeezed her to his side. "What would happen if you missed a rehearsal? The world end?"

"*Yes*, the world would *certainly* end!"

Ken Maxwell reached out for his wife, pulling her toward him and holding her close while he kissed her so hard she thought she would be unable to breathe. "Feel that?" he said, triumphantly. "It's *back!*"

"I don't understand what you mean."

"Come to bed," he said, "and I'll show you."

"Oh, dear, I am so sorry, but I don't have the energy. I am beat! From the opera. Oh, but I am not a good wife to you. Can you be patient with me, oh, my darling? I am so exhausted from my nervous, but I must go and rehearse."

He stared at her, utterly bewildered.

But opening night he sat proudly in the box Hanna had reserved for him. Ken was excited for her, and a bit nervous himself. He had frankly begun to wonder if someone had replaced him in her affections, thinking the maestro would be the logical contender— they working so closely together.

When Maestro Drang took his place on the podium in the orchestra pit, Ken Maxwell breathed a sigh of relief. The man was homely and he seemed to limp awkwardly when he walked.

No chance, he thought, smiled the smile of contentment, and sat back to experience the opera. *Madame Butterfly* had been abandoned as not quite up to the Mazurka standards, and *The Magic Flute* was being performed in its place.

It had been a two-year journey to this momentous opening and backstage Hanna was proud, but nervous. Bertterflies had taken over her body and she would have given anything to put them to sleep.

The overture was competently played, Ken Maxwell thought. The curtain went up on sumptuous sets and lush costumes. He beamed with pride at his wife's good taste.

And when she strutted onstage, the lights hitting her body full of diamonds so they glittered like a thousand prisms, his heart stopped at her loveliness. And such panache! He saw at last what she meant. She *did* have a commanding stage presence. And the dress she had made for the part was a knockout. Some might consider it over the edge, but not he. She was his wife, and he was proud.

The fabrics, the finest obtainable, were selected not only to suggest the maximum from her figure, but also to highlight the jewels, rocks so large they could be seen in the last rows of the balcony. And her entrance was greeted with heart-stopping applause. Madame Hanna Mazurka was beaming onstage as she watched the maestro for her cue.

Up in his box, Ken Maxwell's smile was as big as all outdoors.

Then Hanna began to sing. Ken thought she must be singing, because the orchestra was playing so softly he could barely hear them and, what had to be proof positive, her mouth was moving.

But nothing seemed to be coming out. Hanna was gesturing with her patented panache, but it was as though she were simply pantomiming the part. The audience was struck dumb at first, then there was a murmur of surprise, which built into inhibited snickers, and on to laughter from some who were trying to suppress it and others who were not.

Somehow the opera continued, with the other roles being competently performed. But each time Hanna came forward to sing, it was the same thing: a lot of pantomimed panache and little or no sound. The audience laughter turned to hooting and catcalls.

Ken's heart went out to her, and he was frustrated that he couldn't do anything to help her. To him, the opera seemed to take three weeks. As it wore on, he sank further down in his seat.

Ken worked his way backstage after the opera finally ground to a halt. He thought the hardest thing to take in his life was the ill-mannered booing of his beloved wife's curtain call. She had smiled and bowed graciously, just as though they had been applauding.

When he could drag his feet no longer, Ken knocked gently on her dressing-room door.

"Come in," she sang out, and it seemed to Ken to have been louder than any singing that had emanated from the stage.

He opened the door to find her seated in front of a large mirror, taking off her makeup.

She turned and smiled and put out her hands to her husband like a gracious diva. "Oh, Ken—I'm so glad you wanted to come. Phew, am I glad that's over!"

"Yes," he said and started to say, "I'm so sorry," but she was rambling on.

"It was a good house, don't you think? Seventy-, eighty-percent full. I was so nervous, but I am glad for the experience. The critics make or break. You think they will be kind?"

"Oh, I hope so," he said.

"I hope so," she said, obviously still "on" and oblivious to his answers. "But," she shrugged, "what can you do? It is so exhausting the way I play a role. My whole body and soul."

"I can see that."

"So, I do my best. What else can I do? I try to give them their money's worth with the costumes and the jewels and everything. Tell me," she said, "do you think they liked me?"

Ken was astonished at the question. She couldn't have heard the booing and asked that question.

"Well, I like you," he said.

"You're so sweet," she said, beaming. "What a good husband. Phew! I am so exhausted I am going to sleep a hundred hours. That is hard work."

"I know it. After you wake from your hundred hours," he asked shyly, "do you think we can do something together? Can we just walk in the park together tomorrow? Have a lunch somewhere?

Maybe go for a boat ride?"

"Oh, I am so exhausted. Ask me after I sleep for a year!" she laughed. "Of course, that is a joke. Tomorrow we begin preparing our next opera." She frowned. "I wonder why the maestro has not been to see me? That is just theater protocol, yet he has not come. I wonder, is something wrong?"

"I expect he will be here. Perhaps if I go, he will come."

"Oh, yes, could you? Perhaps he is shy about meeting you."

Ken chuckled. "What did you *tell* him about me, that I was some ogre or something?"

"No. I tell him you are big man. Important man and good and generous, and it is because of you we have opera. But I must talk to him, so shoo!" She waved her fingers at him as though she were cleaning a path through a coop full of chickens.

"I'll wait for you —"

"Oh, not necessary. I have the Rolls."

"I want to take you home," he said.

"You're sweet, but I could be late. We will probably tear the opera apart, start to finish."

"I'll wait," he said pleasantly, but firmly, and walked out.

By the time she had removed all of her makeup, she was stewing about the maestro. He had ample opportunity to pay her a call, but still no sign of him. Come to think of it, none of the company had stopped by to see her. A serious breach of etiquette toward the star.

Finally, when she had no more patience for the snub, she tore out of her dressing room, looking for the maestro. The stage manager told her he had gone home.

She exploded in curses, and the poor man cowered, with his head bent in suitable obeisance, until she wound down, saying, "You tell him I want to see him first thing in the morning, and I shall not forget his shameful behavior."

"Yes, Madame," he said.

Ken was walking toward her from his waiting station in the front row of the theater. He put his arm around her. "Come," he said. "Let's go home and rest. I'm sure the maestro has a good explanation."

"And the rest?" She was still seething. "All the rest of them too who ignored me? I gave this company my all and then some, and what thanks do I get?"

"Sh," he said gently. "Come on. Sleep your hundred hours. You'll feel better."

As he led her out of the stage door, she leaned against him and said, "You are a dear man."

He kissed her on the forehead.

"Now promise me first thing in the morning to run out and buy all the papers. I can't wait to see the reviews."

Only one paper reviewed the opera.

The review appeared under the heading:

FIASCO IN MAZURKALAND
by Pierre Poulanc

Can money buy happiness? That is a question I cannot answer from experience. But after suffering through the Mazurka Opera Company's performance of *The Magic Flute* I can tell you money cannot buy a voice.

The lady who asks

to be called Madame Hanna Mazurka, whose real name is something Polish, is married to the multimillionaire American industrial magnet Ken Maxwell. She is recently divorced from another American, who resides in France, Ned Sharkey Butterworth. Both gentlemen have been generous in financing "Madame's opera intentions."

They have done music no favors, I can assure you. The madame struts in what must be ten million francs' worth of eye-popping jewels and costumes custom made to her provocative body. She smiles like the morning sun, but when she opens her pretty mouth to sing, it is sundown in that department, and nothing comes out. This in spite of the fact that the orchestra wind players are turning blue from trying to play so softly you could hear a mouse sneeze. I have a suspicion we were secretly blessed that nothing came from her.

The audience responded with catcalls and boos which seem to have been rude. But my sympathies were with the audience.

Maestro Drang, in his debut as music director/conductor, at times coaxed some real music from his troupe. The company should regroup under his leadership and retire the madame to the role she is most suited for—that of patroness. Opera is expensive. She loves opera. There is no reason she has to pretend to sing. She can afford to buy us a real singer.

A word of advice: If the name Madame Hanna Mazurka appears on any opera program, and you want to support opera as the worthy enterprise it most certainly is, go to the theater and buy a couple of tickets.

Just don't go inside.

As soon as Hanna awoke, she called from her bed, "Ken, do you have the reviews?"

Ken sighed, picked up the paper and went to her door and

539

knocked one sharp knock. "Come in," she said.

"Ah, you've brought the papers. What a good husband you are." She was smiling in eager anticipation as any good child on Christmas morning.

"Hanna," he said with a serious demeanor. "Have breakfast first."

"Nonsense." She held out her hand. "Let me read it—"

"—some coffee anyway."

"Oh, come now, they can't be that bad," she said. "Come, give them here."

Finally, he handed her the paper. "There is only one," he said, softly. "Promise not to be too upset."

She opened the paper and began paging. "Oh, here it is." She frowned when she saw the headline. Then the lines deepened and increased as she read on to the end. Without lifting her eyes from the page, she said, "Why, the man's a savage!"

Ken nodded.

"The attacks are personal! He is obsessed with money!" She bunched up the paper suddenly and tried to fling it across the room, but it only went a few yards before it fell ignominiously to the floor. "He is insanely jealous of my wealth!"

"It is but one man's opinion," Ken said in a conciliatory tone.

"I devote my whole life to this, and in five minutes he dismisses me because I am rich!"

"Now, now, Hanna, go easy on yourself. It isn't worth it to get so worked up."

"Fifteen to twenty years I sing, sing, sing—practice every single day until I get in my face blue. Money I spend like a drunk sailor to bring my art to the people. The people love me. The critics, they can go to hell!" She sank back down into her pillows and began to sob. It tugged at Ken's heart. He went over to comfort her. He sat on the edge of the bed and reached for her hand.

"Oh," she said, turning her head as if to avoid an unwanted kiss. "And that's another thing," she said. "Where is my music director? Surely he has read this disgrace to me. And yet this viper said only good about the maestro. Well, let us see him do it without me!"

Ken found her hand. He took it in his with no resistance now. "Hanna," he said with his gentle kindness, "let us think about your career."

"I *will* have my career!" she insisted. "Don't you try to talk me out of it."

"But can't you love music without being on the stage?"

"What?" She was startled.

"You have everything you need and want in this world—"

"I don't have praise as a singer."

"So maybe you don't have a big and booming theater voice. You could always sing in smaller settings."

"Yes, the theater is too big. Perhaps I should buy a smaller one."

He smiled. "I was thinking of small rooms—singing in your living room perhaps—for friends—for people who would not tear you apart because you weren't loud enough."

"But…but my career is the opera stage."

"Why?"

"Why—why?" she sputtered, as though he were asking an impossibly audacious question. "Because that is what I want."

"Why do you want it?"

She looked at him as though anyone should know the answer. She frowned. "I want to please others," she said. "Entertain them."

"But why? Do you think there is a shortage of entertainers in this world?"

"Ah, but I have a special quality. When I come onstage, I bring excitement, I have *panache!*" And she gestured with her free arm to demonstrate it. "Singing is my life."

"And if you work twenty more years—what will you have that you don't have now?"

"Well," she huffed, "twenty more years I should be twice as good."

He thought to himself, ruefully, twice nothing is still nothing, but that was a mathematical concept he thought probably beyond her ken.

"Perhaps," he said, "it is time for a clean break. Come back to Chicago with your husband. We'll find a nice, intimate theater there. Get you some good notices in a house where we can hear your lovely voice."

She seemed to consider the proposal briefly.

"Where *is* that maestro?" she asked, agitated.

"He's not here," Ken said, taking her in his arms—"*I* am."

Ken was a considerate, tender lover. Was he too considerate for her? he wondered.

Hanna told Ken she wanted to enjoy these moments of tenderness, but she was distracted. She was late already for her theater. "The new show is already starting."

"Oh, Hanna—do you want to put yourself through all that again?"

She winced. "I will see. But I must go now, my dear. I will come back for dinner."

Today she decided her chauffeur would be in order—to emphasize where the money was coming from. When they arrived at the theater, she told Carlos to wait.

When she came in the door, resplendent in her daytime jewels, a little heavier on the bosom than usual, she heard sounds of the orchestra rehearsing. Funny, she thought, they weren't scheduled for a rehearsal so early in the new-opera schedule.

She made her way closer to the pit to see what was going on. She heard the familiar rap of the baton on the music stand and heard the voice of her beloved maestro—the voice she had missed so desperately since the performance.

"Very good," he said. as though preening his voice, "But if a certain reviewer saw fit to single out my work, I guess you don't need any reminder from me of how fine my orchestra is."

Hanna stopped short behind the curtain. Someone was asking the maestro a question. Hanna heard only a few words, as the interrogator was blocked by the stage. The voice was female. "Alone," Hanna heard, and "without her." There was a unison chuckle from the pit.

"Sh!" he said, rapping the baton again on the music stand. "I will tell you confidentially I am working on that. But as she has not kept a secret from anyone, and as the reviewer so clearly points out, she has been the money behind the enterprise."

There was a low, rustling groan from the orchestra.

"But our reviewer has pointed out certain things that perhaps needed to be said. It is no secret that Madame's voice is…" Here he paused, as though searching for tact. "Perhaps not a large voice. We did our best to have her heard, but as you know, our efforts did not...were not sufficient. So I think...yes...I am working toward the time when, yes, we can do something on our own—"

There was another inaudible question from the pit.

"Well...yes...we can try to do that...but you know to have people your caliber is expensive. And money...it is not easy to come by so much... But, yes, I think the review could help put things in perspective for her, and I would hope she would continue with our work without perhaps requiring such a highly...ah, visible role for herself."

There was a smattering of applause from the orchestra pit.

Hanna was burning from her head to her feet. A small voice told her she should not make another scene, but her louder outrage drowned it out. She stepped dramatically in front of the side wall curtain, holding it in her hand as though she were making an understated curtain call—perhaps when the applause was dying out, and there was no time to reach center stage. She made a sound with her throat. "Ahemm!" And the maestro looked into the eyes of the madame, and in that moment a century of crimes against humanity passed between them.

She spoke first. "The rehearsal," she said as imperially as she could, "is over!" Her gaze never severed from the maestro, whose mouth opened, she wasn't sure if in astonishment or protest. The orchestra members looked to him for liberation from this shadowy tyrant (most of them couldn't see her because the stage over their heads blocked their view).

"I cannot work under these conditions!" the maestro said, trying to sound just as important as Madame. But his voice faltered and cracked on "conditions."

"Perhaps you would like to *pay* the orchestra," she said, with her eyes at the angle of disbelief. "It is a pretty penny, but I expect with your new fame you will be rich."

"No, Madame, I am not rich. It is *you* who are rich from the fortuitous set of husbands you have had. But no matter. If you dismiss the orchestra, I am going with them."

They held each other's gaze for another uncomfortable moment. The orchestra sat without seeming to breathe, waiting for the first one to blink.

"That is your decision. Now, orchestra, out of here. We will call you back if we are to continue—with your services."

Slowly, the musicians packed away their instruments, while Hanna continued to glare at her lover. A few of the orchestra members muttered words to Maestro Drang, unintelligible to Hanna.

When the last one left, he said, "Satisfied?"

"Satisfied?" she said. "Satisfied about what? Satisfied that you are telling my musicians you will perform without me? Satisfied that after my performance you did not deign to come to see me? You left without even saying goodbye. And you call the orchestra in to gloat!"

"I did not!"

"Well, what are they doing here on the day after the performance? You cannot treat this company as your plaything and just go on as though I did not exist."

"That's not—"

"Don't interrupt me. You ignore me, but you can't interrupt me. I can see what a swelled head you got from that miserable review. But I don't expect you to treat it as a positive occurrence just because that awful man did not savage you like the rest of us. Is he a friend of yours?"

"No!"

"*Don't interrupt!* He's a friend or not, I don't care. His review was rude and uncouth and here you are, like the *worst* prima donna peacock, strutting your feathers in front of your band that I am paying—and it is not only without my permission, but also without my knowledge!"

Wilhelm Drang started to walk out of the orchestra pit.

"Where are you going?" she demanded with a sharp snap of her words.

"I told you if you fired the orchestra I was going too."

"Oh, yes! High-and-mighty maestro. Well, get your waiter's suit out of the mothballs, you're going to need it, because you are *finished* here!"

Hanna stalked out and didn't turn to watch Wilhelm recede in the distance.

"Have a nice rehearsal, Madame?" her driver asked when she crawled into the backseat of the Rolls.

"Very nice, thank you, Carlos."

As the car drifted from the curb, Hanna's thoughts were roiling in her head. She was on the very edge of distraction. She was not ready to go home. She was afraid if she had to face Ken she would burst into uncontrollable tears. So she asked her driver, Carlos, to follow a different route over the French countryside. She gave the directions from her memory of the single trip she had taken at the wheel of her Rolls-Royce.

Now, in the backseat, she watched the verdant land drift past her as though the world were spinning at her will.

It took some time to reach Hanna's destination, but time was not a consideration. Her mind was not on science. It was on her art and the art of her life.

Epiphany time she called it to herself. Her mind was reeling in tempo with the passing scenery. Her emotions were of devastation and betrayal. Was she, she wondered, fighting, in spite of her single-mindedness, a losing battle?

Hanna had Carlos stop the car behind some roadside poplars. The sky was clouding over, shrinking the distance between the big house and the barn, and she realized in that moment that her friend Katrina was inseparable from her husband, the stooped, graying figure, the shadow of a man Hanna knew so briefly so many years before. The man was more a phantom than a man—and she had let him shape her life, and it was that ephemeral shape she was here to question.

545

She got out of the car, without a word to Carlos, but the communication was there and Carlos understood. He would wait all night if he had to, and gladly. Madame had always been kind to him, even as he perceived she was being temperamental with her peers.

Hanna floated without conscious thought to her movements, though it is worth noting her drift took her closer to the barn than to the house. She found a tree whose trunk was of sufficient girth to shield her from view, but she noticed no person there to view her.

Suddenly she was a child again in her own barnyard in Poland. It was raining in her memory of Poland, and Poppa was underfoot in the house and he and Momma were fighting. Little Zdenka Oleska was going to teach them a lesson. She would kill herself for the glory of all mankind. She would be a martyr to the cause of peace on earth. But she merely got a slice mark that she carried on her wrist to this day. She looked at it now, the inch-long scar that gathered her flesh in that permanent shiny line across her wrist.

Her life was not free of silliness, she realized. The songbird she pretended to be in the saloon; the intransigent fight she waged against her poor poppa's new bride; giving her first husband TB in order to save him from greater harm, only to see him suffer the greater harm. Now she had the luxury of reflection; then she acted viscerally to get what she thought she needed to survive. She was always, it seemed now, escaping one predicament for another. She told herself she was pursuing pure art in the form of an opera career, but it always seemed tied up with accumulating wealth and prestige, though she realized to someone who didn't know her well, it could seem like avarice and greed. But those are big words for those of humble origins who are more used to words like necessity and survival. She had survived as best she could, and she wasn't ashamed of it. She hadn't meant to harm anyone, but she knew it had happened. Oh, if we were given a picture of the end of our lives at the beginning, we might live them better, she mused. But the mystery caused the mastery or the miss, depending on so many circumstances, not the least of which was the character of the person living the life.

Where had it led her? To today's blowup with the unlikely man she loved the most of all her men, save the phantom prince. Vanity, all was vanity, they said. Why was it so? Perhaps what she needed was to be a humble wife to someone—some poor, struggling man who had only his wits to get him by. Wilhelm was such a man, but they had clashed perhaps beyond repair.

Then she heard the scraping sound of a barn door opening, and Hanna looked up to see the stooped gray figure come out behind a wheelbarrow piled high with manure.

She watched him roll that excrement across the barnyard to its resting place, where he unceremoniously dumped it, then wiped his brow of the perspiration and the light rain that was beginning to fall.

Hanna was profoundly saddened by the change in her prince. But life was change, and it was too bad he had changed for the worse. It was now time for Hanna to change for the better.

The former prince, the man now called Phillip, disappeared

back into the barn as suddenly as he had appeared. His life was prescribed by the digestive process of barnyard animals, whereas he had been one of the richest men in Russia. Hanna, on the other hand, had begun life in a barnyard and was now rich beyond her finest fantasies, and money was still rolling in from the men who had been so generous to her through the goodness of their hearts or by court fiat. Not everything she had done made her proud. But neither did it make her ashamed. Shame, she felt, should be reserved for those born to advantage.

Change. Yes, she would change, and for the better. It would not be a sudden or precipitous change. She would rather change so few would perceive she was changing.

So deep were her thoughts, she hadn't realized the rain had begun to fall in earnest and she was getting soaked through her dress.

She was grateful Carlos had not disturbed her with the proffer of an umbrella or a supplication for her to return to the car. Carlos was a sensitive driver, and he instinctively understood when he should leave her alone.

Now, back in the owner's seat of her Rolls, she said softly, "Thank you, Carlos."

He understood.

"Let's go home," she said.

It was on the long ride to the villa she won in her divorce from Ned Sharkey Butterworth that she formulated her plan.

Ken Maxwell was ecstatic when Hanna told him her news. So ecstatic, he readily agreed to finance a concert tour for her in the States and to arrange for some positive reviews.

The time had come for her to consider retiring her ambitions for diva-hood, but she couldn't imagine just giving it up cold turkey. "I want to go out in a blaze of glory," she told her husband.

And though he thought that would take some doing, it was not an ambition he wished to discourage.

There were many plans to make, there was the opera company to put in mothballs, the advance publicity. This time there would be hyperpublicity to pave the way. Advertisements in music magazines, carefully laid out to look like laudatory reviews of Hanna's European performance. Her tour would begin in the famed Carnegie Hall in New York. Her mind was on fire with ideas, and Ken gratefully chipped in with friends of his who could help.

This time nothing would be left to chance. It would all be choreographed with the precision of a priceless timepiece.

The publicity machine hummed exemplarily. The new photographic profiles of the madame were simply beautiful and beautifully simple. The dress she had made for her first recital was electrifying. She continued to shop the best jewelry stores for the most dramatic gems in the most unique settings, befitting a beautiful woman who had startling, eclectic taste, and the wherewithal to bring it all off with show-stopping panache.

And so it was at Carnegie Hall. She was a vision of loveliness when she came onstage with her custom-made, silver satin dress with silver coins woven into the fabric. The coins jingled when she moved, but the tinkling sound was not unpleasant.

Several newspaper and magazine critics were approached by one Fred Underwood, a short, jaunty fellow with a flair for wearing a derby hat. He slid onto the barstool next to his prey and got to the heart of the matter.

"So, Sam, how are you boys paid for your work?"

"Not bloody well," Sam lamented in an effort to make some fun of the British, whom he did not, if truth were told, hold in very high regard.

549

"That's too bad," Fred intoned seriously, "for good music criticism is a great service."

"To the intelligentsia, yes," he said.

"Buy you another?"

"Wouldn't mind."

The speakeasy was a crowded, dark and musty place and it smelled heartily of stale beer and a recent mishap with the sewerage system, but it was close to the paper, and the proprietor didn't charge an arm and a leg for a bucket o' suds.

Fred was careful not to broach any touchy subjects until he saw some sign of inebriation in his mark.

"Thank you for your kindness, sir."

"My pleasure...sir. Now, Sam, the boys in your profession

ever have any opportunities to turn an extra dollar or two?"

Sam shook his head. "Nah," he said. "Oh, I won't say the occasional bloke who can write like a house afire couldn't pick up some extra change house painting or something. One or two stars in the firmament might try their hand at a book and, if they're lucky, pick up a few weeks' pay, but nothing substantial, no."

"Would I be out of line to wonder then," Fred said, in a manner that bespoke consummate skill at his task, "to suppose a man such as yourself might not be adverse to feathering his nest with a few extra quid?"

"Aye, my mate, that I would not." There was a silence between them as they both toyed with their drinks. "Had something in mind, did you?"

"Oh, that, well, perhaps. See, I don't know all the ins and outs of your profession, so I hope you will forgive me if I, in any way, step out of line. But I represent a rather wealthy party who finds it in his interest to promote the career of a, shall we say, certain close friend of his who has a concert coming up in this neck of the woods." Fred paused for signs of protest, but Sam was just staring straight ahead. So Fred was emboldened to continue. "The only reason I tell you this man is wealthy is to give you an idea of what he has in him that might come out in the right circumstances. Now, my guess, and I hope I don't insult you with this speculation, is a man in your position might be hauling down somewhere in the neighborhood of two, three grand the annum."

A short laugh shot from the mouth of Sam.

"Surely, you don't mean it is less?"

"Ah, me man, I am sad to report it is indeed less."

"Is there no justice in the world?" Fred said, hot under the collar.

Sam merely shrugged.

"I don't suppose you'd be pleased to tell me what it is you take home from the sweatshop so that I might be in a position to make a recommendation to my principal that he might see his way clear to making that a more respectable stipend?"

"That is a generous notion, sir," said Sam, "but why would you consider such largesse?"

"Well, as I said, he has a certain interest in a singer…"

"Ah, yes, that."

"And I am persuaded to believe, in reading your considerable body of work, that you are a man who has a way with words, and the desired result might be achieved by you with your eyes in the down position."

Sam savored the compliment. He didn't get many. "My miserable stipend is thirty dollars a week."

"No!" Fred was aghast. "That is indeed shocking, sir. A man of your caliber…" Fred shook his head. "What would you say to an offer to double your take for a year…?"

"Say?" Sam seemed to awake from a dreamy stupor. "I'm not into murdering anybody."

Fred laughed. "No, no, what he wants is the opposite."

"Opposite?"

"Yes, you might say he wants you to save this young woman's life."

"Her life? How?"

"Simply by writing a few nice words about her."

"And for that I'm in for $1,560—is that what you're saying? A few kind words?"

"That's it—in a concert review, of course."

"Concert? Where's the concert, at some Baptist church?"

"Carnegie Hall."

"Go on—"

"No—truth."

Sam was licking his lips. "Who's the broad?"

"Madame Hanna Mazurka," Fred said, slowly.

"Oh, Jesus, Joseph and Mary, she is some piece of work, isn't she?"

"Yes."

"Oh, my Lord in heaven, there is one woman I would *not* kick out of bed."

"Yeah, me neither."

"Jesus, Joseph and Mary—man, I could write paeans of praise to that beauty for the rest of my life for nothing and rest easy in my grave."

"Ah, yes, so could we all. But the particular notion her principal has in mind is the, ah, how shall I say, praising of her voice."

551

"Her voice?"

Fred nodded.

"I hear she hasn't much of one."

"Well, I don't know about that myself. But I'd be glad to find a few nice things to say about it for a lot less than fifteen hundred."

"Oh. Her *voice*. Yeah, I get it. A music critic. A critic has only his integrity, you know."

"I know that," Fred said. "That's why you aren't being offered peanuts. Criticism is only a matter of opinion, after all—is it not?"

Sam nodded. "Yeah." He licked his lips again and the details of the deal were gone over to both parties' satisfaction, and the deal was struck. One half down, one half on the appearance of the review in Sam's paper.

They weren't all that easy. The man at the *Times* cut Fred short. "I know what you're getting at, and you can save your breath, we don't sell out at the *Times*. My God, man, if she is so bad she needs to *buy* reviews, no one is going to believe it anyway. Our credibility would be shot."

But with little effort, he bought two others, and Ken Maxwell was pleased to do it to please his wife. Perhaps then she would please him. The decision was then made (it was rumored, by the madame herself) that there should be no free ticket for the *Times*. If they were predisposed to badmouth her talent, let them pay for it. Hanna's secret hope, of course, was that the *Times* would be so affronted, they would not cover the concert.

Madame Hanna Mazurka was not lazy about the study of voice and she found a new teacher, who, by the night of the Carnegie Hall concert, had achieved a major coup in getting Hanna's voice heard across the footlights. However, those who heard it did not necessarily consider that a blessing. It did not take a seasoned musician to realize there was something awry with her pitch. At the intermission, one defender, smitten by her beauty, offered this dubious defense: "Perhaps the piano is out of tune and Madame Hanna has perfect pitch."

To fill the audience, Madame and her husband had resorted to the practice known as "papering the house." Tickets (with a handsome price tag) were given to members of the public who were chosen mainly because of some perceived lack of sophistication in the

552

vocal arts. People who might enjoy the spectacle portion of Madame's show, which she had honed to a fine art, but who, at the same time, were not in a position to criticize her voice.

The denouement did not work out exactly as planned. Sam was the only concert reviewer who kept his part of the bargain:

MAZURKA MAKES
CARNEGIE SPARKLE

It has been many moons since this hard-bitten scribe has been so smitten by a vocal concert as he was last night at Carnegie Hall. There resplendent in a silver-satin creation which was, I understand, a creation of the same creative force behind the unique voice, I heard Madame Hanna Mazurka for the first time, and I certainly hope it won't be the last. To those who stay away from vocal recitals because they find women's voices overbearing, harsh or shrill, Madame Hanna Mazurka is your answer. She is a person who takes over a room by being in it. She makes it sparkle! Her voice has a modest loveliness that will soon enthrall you. And the manner in which she "sells" a song is nothing short of enchanting.

553

Sam went on to find something in several of her pieces to praise. There were kudos for the pianist and a passing mention of Hanna's copious jewels, that sparkled as she did.

Sam was cheerfully and promptly paid the balance of his contract. After the check was safely banked, Sam calculated that not only was that his highest paid work, but he was paid more for each word than the average critic earned in a day of toil.

The *Times* reviewer unfortunately found a free ticket (there were so many offered, so many places, strict control of the recipients became impossible). He had some very choice words for Madame. Words like: "embarrassment," "painful," "no sense of pitch."

> This émigré from Poland has nothing if not a trainload of chutzpah. The house was reputed to be heavily papered with complimentary tickets and Madame Hanna Mazurka—it is her idea of the respect due her that she should be called Madame—gave them their money's worth. And after hearing her sing, if there *is* some reason to call her "Madame," it is not related to her singing voice.
>
> I actually felt sorry for the pianist, who had to employ a supremely elastic rubato to keep up with Madame's erratic rhythms, and, of course, either she was deaf to the pitch of the piano accompaniment, or she has no sense of pitch whatever.

Fortunately, Ken Maxwell had covered this eventuality with the purchase of the two other reviewers, so the final score should have been three to one. Unfortunately, one of those two claimed to have had an attack of conscience and left the concert at intermission, as did two-thirds of the audience. He returned his first payment with a note saying:

> I am truly sorry I have been unable to stretch my conscience to the limit required to puff your princess. Sure is a good-looker though, but that voice should not be inflicted on the public. I am returning your advance herewith.

The fourth critic was more difficult. He did write a review, and it could have been considered favorable except he forgot to praise her voice as agreed. Instead, he spoke of her as:

> A vision of loveliness who gorgeously displayed an array of jewelry and sartorial finery unseen in this land heretofore. Most women would be content to look half that good, without insisting on a vocal career. But Madame Hanna Mazurka is not your average woman and she insists on singing, and sing she did. Not only did she sing arias from Puccini, Mozart and Verdi, but art songs and folk songs as well. She is quite a woman, as was apparent in her every move—

On reading this review, Hanna insisted they not pay his final installment, and that they get the man to return the payment he had already taken.

"This is an insult to my intelligence," she said. "I am an *artist*, and all he can talk about is how good I *look*. Jewels, clothes, he treats me like a brainless model in a fashion show. Get the money back."

It was a command her husband and Fred agreed should be ignored. But Hanna didn't forget. She persisted in sending Fred back to see the ingrate.

"So keep the second payment," he said.

"But Madame says you did not fulfill your bargain and you should return the money already paid to you."

"Sue me," he said, and walked off like a gunslinger after a perfectly placed shot.

She could say she had mixed reviews, but she decided big cities were too hard on her. She was convinced the people loved her, but the critics were too persnickety. They were grizzled, jaded veterans of one too many concerts, who had their favorites and wouldn't let anyone else break the barriers to stardom.

A concert tour, with attendant advance publicity, was arranged to smaller venues: Spartanburg, South Carolina; Allentown, Pennsylvania; Youngstown, Ohio. She was so excited to be treated like royalty in these places when she came to town. It was so much friendlier, more personal than that cold and bloodless New York.

Welcoming committees came out to greet her train. She was feted by the pillars of the communities, hosted at laudatory lunches and post-concert parties—given the key to each city, for which she would always beam and say in her charming broken English, "And to you I give the key to my heart!"

And they loved her. She was a celebrity. Written up in papers the world over. Even Will Rogers talked about her. And the small town could usually be counted on to turn up a newspaper reporter who would not speak unfavorably of her performance.

Ken Maxwell came to the final concert of his wife's tour, in Peoria, Illinois. He had not told her he was coming, he wanted to surprise her and not give her cause for nervousness.

He took a seat far back in the small auditorium provided by Bradley University, in the hope she would not be able to see him. But the audience was so sparse, he got up and walked to the rear of the room, where he could see the entire audience without being seen. Moments before Hanna was to come onstage, a battalion of college students, all male, filed into the auditorium and took seats in a body. Ken's first thought was relief that more of the seats would be occupied—but when Hanna came onstage in a particularly unique dress that suggested much but showed little, the boys began to whistle and hoot their approval.

Hanna reacted to the raucous sounds as though she was being complimented, and when she curtsied to the audience, the boys broke into loud applause. Hanna couldn't see the young men and assumed she was facing a normal audience appreciative of her talents. She smiled broadly.

When she moved to rest her hand on the piano to begin singing, the boys miraculously hushed. Hanna nodded to her accompanist to begin. The introduction to Schubert's "Who is Sylvia?" crept into the silence, the music taking the auditorium space for its own.

Hanna sang perhaps four bars before the snickering began. It is not certain the soloist heard it right away, because she continued to sing and gesture as though nothing was amiss. Then, as she proceeded to gesture and her small voice produced sounds at variance with the piano, the boys got the giggles. They seemed to be making an attempt to suppress the inappropriate sounds, but to no avail. One minute, they were all fighting giggles; the next, they all surrendered to them simultaneously, and their laughter drowned out the music.

"Shh!" Ken said from the back shadows, but he couldn't be heard. His heart went out to his wife, whose small voice was no match for these baboons.

One by one—stretching the length of the song and into the scant applause after it—the boys beat their retreat. They did not seem aware of the stern, disapproving glare from the performer's husband as they passed him on their way out to fresh air.

"Oh, man," one of them said, "she's something else!"

"Phew, oh, my God, get me out of here," from another.

"Did you see those bazooms?"

A smattering of spectators left with the few remaining boys who waited to leave until "Who is Sylvia?" wound down.

After each number, a few more escaped, and by the intermission, Ken was overcome with sadness for his wife, who seemed not to notice the desertions, but continued her battle with the music valiantly. After the intermission, there were only a few hardy, or curious, souls left in the seats. But Hanna did not throw in the sponge. She was not a quitter—and during the last half of the program, her husband took a seat, hoping to appear like one more body in the house.

By the time the program was over, Ken was the only one applauding. The two women who remained, a few rows in front of him, seemed to be asleep.

When he went to her dressing room afterwards, he was surprised at her reaction. She was so delighted to see him. "Why, Ken, how awfully nice of you to come to my recital. How did you like it?"

"I just love you," he said, taking her in his arms so she couldn't see the tears in his eyes.

"Oh, thank you, I thought it went well too," she said. "But, gosh, I'm exhausted. What a tour! Takes a lot out of an old girl."

557

"How was the rest of your tour?"

"Oh, I was so well received," she said. "People were *so* complimentary up and down the country."

"Well, that's nice," he said. "So are you ready for a rest?"

"Well," she said, "a few days perhaps, but there is no rest for the weary. I expect I'll be working on even bigger improvements before long. Another tour perhaps…"

"Oh, Hanna," he said, standing back to look at her. "Can't we have some time together?"

She seemed to take in his beaming countenance for the first time. "Why, Ken, why are you crying?"

"I'm just so happy to see you," he said.

Hanna put so much of herself into her performances that the aftermath was a letdown. She had become restless and ill at ease in the company of her older husband.

She continued to speak of her career, while deep in her heart she knew it was over. Secretly she was plotting an escape from boring Chicago and her staid, if attentive, husband.

Ken sensed her unrest and did everything in his power to dissuade his wife from leaving him again for France. He even bought her a theater in Chicago, simply because she said she had to return to her Paris theater—"It is my *life*."

More and more her mind returned to Wilhelm Drang, in Paris. She had not forgotten their passionate fights, but the loving was just as passionate. Ken was an old man to her—and she felt no passion for him. The longer she lived with him, the more she saw him as a father figure. She soon convinced herself that is why she married him—her own father had let her down by choosing that bland girl over her.

To keep her interested in Chicago, Ken arranged for another flurry of portrait sittings, even a bust of her sculpted for the new opera house, as well as ads in music magazines. It was as if he and Hanna both knew her beauty was a temporal thing that had to be captured before it was too late. He even hired a well-known music critic to come to the house to praise her singing.

Ken had completed the purchase of the opera house and put the title in her name, as she requested. "I get more respect," she said, "if the ownership is mine."

But the property languished and Hanna's spirits sank. Her inability to improve her voice was not her only frustration. She was married to a sex-crazed man, she thought, and she did not share those feelings. He tried to talk about it numerous times, but she was not receptive. She began to put on weight. Was it to make herself unattractive to her husband? Or was it her body's natural reaction to the doldrums of her spirit? Perhaps it was both. But if Hanna's extra weight affected Ken's ardor, it was not noticeable.

On this night, a full moon shining in the window, Ken sat on the edge of her bed, touching her, without reciprocation, and begging her to allow him under the covers. She could not admit that when she thought of men that way, she only thought of Wilhelm. And she had been apart from him for more than a year, but she had not gotten him out of her system.

"Hanna," Ken pleaded, as he so often had, "I love you so much."

"That is very nice," she said, holding the covers in place with her stiff elbows.

"I just want to hold you…"

"You want *more* than that—"

"But we are husband and wife. Married people make love… Don't you love me anymore?"

"Of course," she said, "I always love you. It is a spiritual love. We are too old for babies, and that is all the physical is for."

"Now, Hanna—you don't mean you want to have a child."

"Not now," she said. "I am too old."

"And your other three husbands? Did you want children then?"

"That is personal question."

"You are my wife. Personal questions are permitted."

"No—not about past husbands."

"Well, about *you* then. Did you try to have children?"

"Then I was too young," she said with a cavalier wave of a hand, without releasing the pressure on the covers with her elbows. "Now I am too old."

"Please, Hanna—it won't hurt you. It's very nice. You used to say so yourself."

"But why does a man like you persist? The Lord has blessed you with five children; why is it necessary to go through those same motions forever? You have fulfilled your purpose on this earth in this life. If it is carnality that interests you, it must be for a future life."

"Hanna—"

"No, think about it! God fulfilled you, you fulfilled His purpose for you. It was against nature you went to get those expensive treatments so you could be a sex machine as long as you could breathe. Is not natural."

"It *is* natural!" Anger was building in Ken. "Abstinence is *un*natural."

"I don't know. My mind, it is on some…thing else."

"What?"

"The spiritual side of life. Nature has done for us, so we must do back."

"How does that affect you and me? How does your loving me interfere with nature?"

"It is frivolous activity. Selfish. To no purpose."

"And what is not frivolous?"

"All things of the spirit. Like music." Her eyes drifted off in a gaze. Ken didn't know it, but she had cast her mind to Paris and a certain person to whom she felt a strong spiritual attachment.

Ken left her with a kiss on the forehead. He remembered hearing somewhere that in life there were those who loved and those who consented to being loved. But Hanna wasn't even consenting.

It was that night that he finally admitted to himself this marriage had been a mistake. He had not given it enough thought—

perhaps not *any* thought, so smitten was he to think a young woman—perhaps the most beautiful woman in the world—would really lust for him personally. His money, certainly, but without the money, he realized, she would have been nowhere in sight. Why didn't he see the pattern in her former marriages? A wealthy Russian royal, a wealthy, socially prominent New York doctor, the wealthiest bachelor in the world, and now one of America's richest men. He was a fool to think she cared for him. How could she? The calluses on her heart must be as thick as planks. With each marriage, she got richer. With all he had done for her, he didn't know what more could be done. What was left? Apparently nothing, or she would have asked for it. She was so distant, she seemed not to be in the same room with him. Well, he wasn't going to fight it any longer.

As Ken's thoughts were of Hanna that night, Hanna's were of Wilhelm and Paris. She longed to see him. Wondered what he was doing. What if he found another woman? Well, I must just then take him back. The spiritual love of her earlier professions had turned quickly to corporal images as she felt the force of his young body against hers. She knew Ken wanted with her what she wanted with Wilhelm. But she also knew she felt nothing for him and she didn't see how she could force herself to love him physically when she felt as she did. It wouldn't be honest.

By the end of the week, Madame Hanna Mazurka was on her way back to Paris.

She had asked to use Ken's private railroad car and he was on the verge of granting the request, as he would have in the past, without giving it a second thought, but this time he caught himself. "I'm afraid that won't be possible," he said, with a benign, eyebrow-raised smile.

"Oh?" She was startled, like a schoolteacher being thwarted by her most docile student. "And why not?"

"Because I have decided that I will no longer cooperate in your ventures to ignore me."

"But how do you expect me to travel? By coach?"

"My dear, I have given you enough money in my time to buy you the railroad. The matter is entirely up to you."

"Well, that is not very friendly," she huffed.

"Perhaps more friendly than your repeated desertions."

"But you agreed that I could have my career. From the

beginning, I said I must have my career. I *will* have my career."

"Hanna," he said, shaking his head, "your 'career,' as you call it, is all in your head. You have a small, sweet voice—it is no opera voice, and it never will be. You are almost forty years old. I cannot believe you are actually so naive to believe you will still one day be a big opera star."

"We will see about that," she said.

"By going back to Paris?" He shook his head again with a weariness born of this tardy dawning of reality. "When you are in Paris, you want Chicago; when you are in Chicago, you want Paris. Your voice will not improve by traveling across the ocean a hundred times. Think about it. I want to give you another chance to be a wife to me. Like those corny wedding vows say about 'to have and to hold, to love and to cherish.' But I guess you have heard the vows so often you stopped paying attention when we went through them."

She glared at him. "What an ugly thing you say! You are treating me worse than dirt."

"Oh, really?" He raised a calm eyebrow. "One hundred thousand a year for life. Dirt? A lot of people would like to be…treated like that kind of dirt—"

"The spiritual being is not touched by your money."

"No, apparently your love and loyalty were not touched by it either. What a fool I was to think I could buy your affection. I realize now my promising you all that money for life only makes you independent of me. You have no more motive to even stay by my side. I had dreams we would grow old together—I some years before you, of course—but I was such a fool. Once you got the money, you only went through the barest motions with me personally. So go to Paris if you must. I will consider it desertion."

"Oh? I am not deserting. You may come too."

"For what? To be the only one applauding in your Paris audience?"

"Ken!" she shouted. "You are being so cruel."

"Deserting me is not cruel?"

"I *will* have my career," she reiterated, then turned on her heels and marched out of the room.

Ken watched her go for a moment, a bemused smile on his face. Then he brought his flat hand to his lips and blew her a kiss.

Going to New York first class on the train was not the same as having a private railroad car with servants. Hanna was confined to her own tiny compartment, and the staff on the train was nice enough, but there was not that extra edge of civility, or servility, Madame had become accustomed to.

Her thoughts as she gazed out of the window at the countryside clicking behind her were jumbled. She would never return to Chicago. The opera house was in her name, but she would rent it or sell it through lawyers. She expected Ken would divorce her, and then she would be free to marry Wilhelm. It would be her first love match, she thought.

Perhaps marriage to Ken Maxwell

had been a mistake. The financial arrangements were to her liking, of course, but the man just never lit any fires in her. Was she wrong to encourage him? Was she the opportunist many accused her of being?

One thing she knew was unless you began life poor, you had no right to make those judgments. What did the rich know of economic distress? The agony of not knowing how you could go on living?—a woman alone in the world must make the most of any opportunity that comes her way. It isn't opportunism, Hanna thought, it is *necessity*.

Here in mid-life, Hanna realized she had done the best she could. It was natural for women to want to be cared for, and how much better that caregiver were a captain of industry than a bartender.

The press could make fun of her excesses—her dresses, her jewels, her extravagances—but they gave no thought to the alternative life she could have led as a farm wife in a tiny house in the Polish countryside. Would any one of her critics have opted for poverty?

She couldn't put her finger on what it was exactly, but she was experiencing doubt for the first time. It was not only doubt about the present state of her larger body or smaller voice, but doubt as well about the future.

She had gone to all the musical trouble in the first place to attract the attention of the prince. Well, she had seen the poor *ex*-prince, and he didn't even remember her. She had been sure she could have overcome that onstage with an electrifying performance; he would have been so smitten with her voice and person he would swoop her up in his arms and carry her off to paradise.

But now—*now* he couldn't even afford the price of a standing-room ticket, let alone get to the theater.

So who would I impress if I were the greatest diva in the world? she thought. Not the prince, not my ex-husbands, living *or* dead. She smiled to herself and wondered about that. Could she get in touch with the dead? Would they notice what she was doing? Understand what she had done? There were so many mysteries to life and she longed to explore them all. I am a person who feels very deeply, she thought.

While she was in New York, awaiting her ship for the ocean crossing, she wandered into a bookstore and gravitated to the philosophy and religion sections. She browsed through numerous books and rejected some as too costly, others as too turgid, and still others as not touching her soul (not understandable).

She collected an armful of books, and the next day took them on the ship with the rest of her trunkloads of luggage. With three steamer trunks and assorted smaller luggage (which, laid on its side, was taller than she was), she barely had space for the minimum of three outfits she needed each day.

Madame Hanna Mazurka read with fascination the books on religion and philosophy. Some of the latter were difficult for her to understand—the religious books were more simply written. Of all the religions she explored on her ocean voyage, Buddhism struck the most resonant chord. The four holy truths—the awareness and affirmation of the unsatisfactoriness of the world, the perpetual thirst of the human soul to be consuming (especially experiences and ideas), the cessation of desire (cooled from the heat of passions), and the path to the pure state of being.

That path was paved with morality, meditation and wisdom. All life is *anicca* or impermanence—*nothing* remains the same. And so Hanna's life was continuing to evolve.

There were so many religions for her to read about, and she took to them as she did everything else in her life; avidly, voraciously. She was on a new path, Buddhist or not: a search for *meaning*. When she put her life on the table to examine it, what did she learn? What was the meaning?

"Achievement!" she said aloud. Then she thought about how far she had come—from virtually nothing but her wits to crossing the ocean first class on the *Île de France*. She realized she would never need to worry about money again. So she could achieve the cessation of desire, and she felt herself on the path to that pure state of being.

But while she was able to subsume her desire for more money, she was not as fortunate in sublimating her desire for Wilhelm Drang. It was all she could do to keep from sending him a cablegram announcing her arrival. She *would* have liked him to meet the ship, but she also wanted to surprise him.

Hanna spent more time in her cabin lazily reading than she had on previous crossings. She was still the toast of the oldsters aboard, and at mealtime they vied for her attention, but somehow the limelight was less important to her. Her snares were not out, she was on her way to the love of her life and felt secure in her skin for perhaps the first time. She was on her way to *nirvana*.

She had cabled ahead to her household staff, which she kept employed in her absence while Ken was paying the bills. Now, with his announced intention to let her fend for herself, Hanna would have to reevaluate that situation. For now, she was pleased to have the chauffeur meet the ship and take care of all her luggage.

She asked him to drive by her apartment, then by the last known abode of Wilhelm Drang. She looked up at his windows expectantly, but saw nothing. Then she went to his restaurant. The chauffeur was dispatched within to inquire if Monsieur Drang was still employed there. He came back with the news that he was not, but was rather residing in a fashionable arrondissement on the Right Bank.

Pursuing that address yielded only a sense that Monsieur was not destitute and had perhaps had good fortune in her absence. It was not in itself news unwelcome to Hanna, though she would rather have had him needy and more susceptibly dependent.

Her perfervid mind tumbled in speculation about Wilhelm Drang. Some financial fortune had befallen him.

The chauffeur parked the Rolls. It was an overcast day and the neighborhood streets were lined with cars. She marched with her head high up to the postwar brick building she reminded herself no waiter could afford.

It took a moment before Hanna could summon the courage to knock on the door. It was not long before the door opened and a pretty young woman smiled and cocked her head questioningly. "Yes?"

Hanna realized too late she was staring dumbly at the young woman. Hanna's first thought was the girl was Wilhelm's daughter. "Wilhelm Drang?" Hanna said, uncertainly.

"I'm sorry, he's not here," she said. "Who shall I tell him asked for him?" She was not prodding, merely friendly.

"What? Oh, I'm an old friend," Hanna said.

The pretty face was studying her elder. "Do you have a name?"

"Name? Oh, yes, well, of course," Hanna laughed, a tinkling, musical sound. "Madame Hanna Mazurka," she said.

"Oh, the famous!" the girl said. "I'm Nicole Lavallé, I've heard so much about you I feel I know you. Could you come in?"

"Well…I wouldn't want to impose."

"Oh, no imposition. Come in then," she said, and led Madame into her tastefully (and expensively) furnished living room. They sat facing each other in delicately woven fabric chairs. Hanna frowned, trying to understand her surroundings. "Well, how is Wilhelm?" she asked.

"Oh, he's fine," Nicole said. "And you've been abroad?"

"Ah, abroad. Yes. Well, tell me—you are such a pretty girl—how old are you?"

"Oh, I'm twenty-three, and how old are you?"

Hanna laughed. It was not a question she answered in good grace usually. "I'm nearly forty," she said.

"Wow, you don't look it."

"That's very sweet of you. But tell me," she asked, looking around the room, "you are so young to have inherited…do you have a large trust fund?"

The girl giggled. "Oh, my, no."

"Do you work then?"

"Oh, no. I wait on Wilhelm mostly."

"Wait on him?"

"Yes, you know, keep house, cook—domestic things."

Hanna raised an eyebrow. "Really?"

Nicole's nod was full of all the vim and vigor of her youth. Too much vitality for Hanna's taste.

"And what does Wilhelm do?"

"Do? I thought you knew him—"

"I did."

"Then you know he's a musician. A conductor."

"And he has work?"

"Not just at the moment, no."

"But then, if you will forgive me for asking, just how do you pay for this apartment? This furniture?"

Nicole looked genuinely perplexed. "You don't know?"

"No."

"Sure you do. You should know anyway—it came from you!"

"From me?" Hanna said, trying to imagine how the salary she paid him, generous to be sure, was enough to stretch over his layoff so he could still afford to live like the upper crust.

"Yes, he always used to talk about your generosity and all. He was very fond of you."

"Yes…it was mutual," Hanna said, still trying to understand it all. "Where did you meet Wilhelm?"

"Oh, I was a dancer. The follies. He was out for a night on the town. You had just left, I believe. He was down, but I consoled him."

"You mean he came backstage to find you?"

She nodded enthusiastically, her eyes wide open, then giggled. "Said I was the prettiest thing he'd *ever* seen."

"And you are," Hanna said. Oh, the irony, she thought. Hanna had wanted to be discovered on the stage, but Wilhelm discovered someone else. "Are you…married?"

"Oh, no," Nicole giggled.

"Do you want to marry him?"

"Sure, I guess."

"Why aren't you married then?"

She frowned. "I don't know exactly." She shrugged. "He hasn't asked me, I guess."

"Then why are you living with him?"

"Oh, dear, I couldn't afford to live this nice on my own."

"There is an old saying among men of his type, my dear," Hanna said. "It would do you well to heed it. It goes, 'Why buy the cow when the milk is free?'"

"Oh, I get it. I'm the cow."

"Well, you know what else they say."

"I don't want to know," Nicole said.

"If the shoe fits, wear it." Hanna got to her feet. "You were awfully nice to ask me in. I must go now."

"Oh, why?"

"I have to begin my singing lessons."

The girl tittered behind the back of her hand.

"What is funny?"

"Oh, nothing."

"No—what?" Hanna insisted on an answer.

"Well, I was just thinking. Wilhelm told me about your opera. I guess it was something of a disaster."

"Did *he* say that?"

She shrugged again. "Well…I guess so."

"Of all the ungrateful… Well, tell him I was here to see him, and I will expect him at my villa at ten tomorrow morning. He knows where it is."

The girl was watching Madame Hanna Mazurka with wide-eyed fascination. She didn't get up to see her out, but stared until Hanna had closed the door behind her.

Then Nicole Lavallé, former follies dancer, said, "Moo!"

Hanna found herself surprisingly (and irritatingly) nervous about meeting her former lover. Here she was, after all, suddenly in competition with a girl almost half her age.

She spent some time choosing her wardrobe. Interesting, even fascinating if she could manage it, but not provocative. Definitely not provocative. She didn't need to do that. She was still attractive, wasn't she? She verified it in the mirror. There *was* some slight wrinkling of the skin, she admitted. And perhaps there was some thickening in her flesh; she could take that in hand. Her hair seemed to have a little less shine also. She smiled broadly at the glass and decided she had an engaging smile and it might be advisable to use it from now on.

The teeth were as good as could be; it was time to start showing them.

She worked with her jewelry for forty minutes after she had finally decided on the simple black (slimming) skirt and a white open-necked blouse with an expensive, but understated, string of small diamonds set in an exquisite gold chain.

By the time Wilhelm arrived, the maid had set out the tea service of heavy silver, polished to gleaming perfection, and some small, fresh-baked cakes. Let's see that little snip of a twenty-three-year-old do *anything* this gracious, Hanna said to herself.

She greeted Wilhelm with outstretched arms and her new, warmer and more open, smile. "Darling!" she said, and embraced him thoroughly. She stood back. He seemed ill at ease. He too had added some pounds, but on him they helpfully softened some of his unattractive sharp angles and made him look cuddly.

"Well, Wilhelm, it's so good to see you."

"You too."

"Gosh, it's been too long, has it not?"

"Too long," he agreed automatically, without any noticeable expenditure of feeling. He was trying not to fidget, but he was uncomfortable with his older lover.

"Sit down, please," she said, gesturing the love seat. "Let me pour you some tea—"

He sat, she poured. "Now," she said, after serving them both—and sitting next to him, "you must bring me up to date on your life since I left."

He shrugged. "Not much," he said. "I met Nicole, as you know—"

"Yes—a dancer. Tell me, did she dance with her clothes on?"

"Some of them," he said, blushing.

"Yes, I can see your attraction. She is a pretty little thing." There could be no questioning that she meant that derogatorily. "But, tell me, what do you talk about?"

"Oh, Hanna, you don't want to criticize her."

"I don't? Of course not. But must I infer from your evasive answer that you don't have that chicken around for conversation."

There was a remorse on his lips that Hanna found strangely touching. "Well," he said, "you and I never had any trouble talking to each other. It just got so loud at the end."

"What? You are afraid of a small fight now and then—?"

"They weren't so small," he said, "and a little oftener than you seem to remember."

She waved her hand at the air. "That is past. I am back now. When can you move back in here?"

"Move? Back? Why would I?"

"Why—you find me too old suddenly? Next to that baby I am…mature, I am sure."

"To each his own." He raised a shoulder for a moment, then let it drop.

"Oh? Then tell me, how are you living so high on the hog?"

"You paid me very well, remember?"

"How could I forget?"

"And I lived here, then in the apartment. I didn't have any expenses to speak of."

She nodded her head mechanically. "You think I am stupid?"

"No." He blushed. "Why?"

"You know why. If you saved every penny that I paid you, you wouldn't have enough to live like that for one year. Where did you get the rest of the money?"

"Well," he faltered, "I've had some work. Nicole worked."

Hanna nodded that I-don't-believe-you nod. "I am beginning to see," she said. "I should have watched the expenses more for the opera. I never even looked at your accounts."

Wilhelm fidgeted in his seat next to her.

"I see, I see. Now I see," she said, awakened by the revelation. "You would do that to me?" She shook her head. "If you can't trust your lover, who *can* you trust? So…that was it! You *stole* from me."

"I didn't steal."

"No? What do you call it then?"

"Nothing."

"You call it nothing, I call it stealing. Do you want to tell me about it or must I hire an accountant to go over everything? Trace every penny? I expect an accountant could figure it out, don't you?"

Wilhelm Drang offered a few more weak protests, then he

blurted, "We were like husband and wife. I saw the opera account as our account."

"And that included a lifelong pension for you?"

"Call it what you like," he muttered.

"Shall I go to the police?" she asked.

His eyes bounced wide open as he stared at her, as though the thought had never occurred to him. "The *police*?"

"Is what you do when you have thief."

"Hanna!"

"How much?"

"What?"

"How much did you steal from me?"

His face dropped, he bowed his head to stare at his hands twisting in his lap.

"A million francs? Five, ten million?" she prodded him. "Tell me, or I get accountant."

He tightened his lips. "I don't know exactly."

"How did you get it?"

"Padded some bills. Made up some others."

She stared at him. He didn't stare back. There was an excruciating silence.

"So," she said. "How are you going to pay back?"

"Pay back?" he stammered. "Where would I find so much money?"

"I don't know," she said. "Certainly not in jail."

"Jail? You wouldn't!"

"So…then… When can you move back in here?"

"Back? I…"

"I think this afternoon would be fine."

"This after…but that's im…poss…"

"Not so impossible," she said. "The little chicken can stay where she is until the rent is up."

Now Wilhelm was staring straight ahead into the void his life was falling into. Wilhelm's mouth was twisting as though he were in agony. At last he broke the silence. "Nicole's pregnant," he said.

"What? You didn't!" Hanna simmered. "Well," she said at last, "there are cures for that."

Wilhelm shook his head. "She won't."

"What do you mean, won't?"

"She's religious," he offered in apology.

"I will pay," Hanna said, as though that settled it.

Wilhelm shook his head again.

"But...but," she sputtered, "I will not give a penny to care for the child. How will you do it?"

"That, Hanna, is not your affair."

Hanna exploded. "Not my...how dare you? It is my money you stole, that is my affair." Her glare burned him to the pit of his stomach. "You are in no position to call the tune of this opera," she said. "You do as I say or I will go to the police. Perhaps Nicole can have the little bastard in the prison hospital."

Wilhelm's glare sunk to the core of Hanna's being. The hate in that look made Hanna tremble. Hanna had gone too far and in that one indiscretion had turned the tables.

"No," Wilhelm said, through his angry, clenched teeth, "you won't go to the police."

"Oh?"

"And I'll tell you why you won't. A young man like me—an old woman like you." He paused to gesture.

"I am not *old!*" Hanna protested.

"Oh, yes you are. Look at you next to Nicole. You could be her *mother!*"

"Wilhelm!" Hanna was apoplexy-red in the face.

"The police would laugh you out of the station house. It will be so obvious what happened. An old woman buying affection from a young man. He gets a younger woman, and the old lady wants her money back? Hah! You got your money's worth and you know it. When you think of it, Hanna, it's no different than what you have been doing to all those rich men over the years. Love 'em and leave 'em and get as rich as you can in the process."

Though his words stung her, Hanna reached out to Wilhelm. "Wilhelm," she pleaded, "my lover, do not talk like this to your love who has come halfway around the world to be with you."

"No," he said, "not to be with me, but to get away from your husband. Number *four*, is he? You have always run away from your husbands. Desertion is as natural to you as breathing."

"The police..." she reiterated, weakly.

"Oh, go to the police," he spat at her. "Tell your story. I'll tell mine gladly. You want the kind of publicity that will get you?"

"No!"

"I don't think so. There will be a thousand photographers to take your picture, and look at you—you've gotten *fat!*"

Wilhelm Drang didn't so much leave Hanna's house that day; he fled her life.

Hanna cried off and on for three days. She always referred to it as her three-day midlife crisis. That was all she would allow herself. "Self-pity is an indulgence," she told herself, "I have not time for. It is the purview of average people. I am not average. Nicole, Wilhelm's chicken, is average. Wilhelm is average. Their bastard will be average. I am not average, and I must not let this insignificant person defeat me." But how can I do better with all these jackals baying at my heels? Yet, why must I let this bother me? The prince is poor, but I am rich. I should never want for anything material. I have had my pick of rich men—men devoted to me—men adored me. This pipsqueak and his chicken must not be allowed to ruffle my feathers. Perhaps those feathers are not as bright as they once were, but I am content. Yes, I am *content!*

Then, some weeks later, she got a cable from her husband, Ken Maxwell.

EXTENDING YOU ONE MORE
OPPORTUNITY TO RETURN TO
CHICAGO AND LIVE AS MY
WIFE STOP

She could not deceive herself. She was very pleased Ken wanted her back. And she considered his offer, she really did. It *would* extricate her from this impossible situation. It would ameliorate this stigma she felt at being, after all these years, a woman alone. Then she began to wonder, on rereading the cable, if there were some hidden meaning in the phrase, "Extending you one more opportunity"—was that a threat? Was it something a lawyer told him to do to skimp on a divorce settlement? "One more opportunity." Well, if he thought he could take advantage of her like that, he could think again.

Hanna spent days stewing about the cable from her husband. Why didn't he telephone? They could have discussed the matter rationally.

Then she received a letter from a solicitor, telling her that Ned Sharkey Butterworth had died. She was to inherit three million dollars from him. The news stiffened her backbone, and she settled down in earnest to consider Ken's offer. Hanna sat down and began to draft the conditions of her acceptance. After she felt she had asked for every advantage she could think of, she got a letter from a Chicago law firm.

Ken Maxwell was filing for divorce on grounds of desertion.

Hanna was stunned. Then she turned furious. How dare he?

She telephoned her New York attorney, Felix Barton, and was told he had retired from practice. With tireless cajoling in repeated calls, she was given permission to call him at home. She told him what she wanted.

"Pay? This man is already giving you a hundred thousand a year for life. How much more do you think would be appropriate?"

"Are you being sarcastic with me? Is that what you are doing? Because I won't stand for it. I am not one of these women you can step on anytime you like. I know you men—always trying to take advantage of the weaker sex. Well, I resent it, and he is going to pay if he wants a divorce from me."

"All right, Hanna, just calm down a minute, will you?" he said. "You have to consider what a judge is going to think—in case the parties can't reach a settlement. So why don't you tell me what you want, and I will speak to Mr. Maxwell's attorney. Maybe we can avoid a court fight."

"I want ten million dollars," she said without pause.

"Ten million?" He was astonished. "Madame, I do you a disservice if I do not acquaint you with what their thinking is liable to be and what a slim chance you have to prevail."

"Ten million!" she said.

"I will call his attorneys," he muttered. "When I get a feel for their thinking, I will call you back."

Her lawyer took his time about calling back. It was days later and Hanna gave him a piece of her mind.

"It takes time," he said. "A lot of people involved: you, me,

Mr. Maxwell, his personal attorney, his divorce lawyer. Here is what they will claim: In a nine-year marriage, you spent less than a year in common domicile with your husband. In that time, he bought you a theater in Chicago, a theater in France, countless personal items and paid all your expenses until you left him the second time. In addition, you were given nine hundred thousand dollars cash in that period, which they calculate would be enough to feed and house twenty to twenty-five families of six in the United States. More in Europe."

"Is that supposed to be funny?" she snapped.

"I'm just relaying to you what they say. They further state that you abandoned him, not the other way around. And finally, they claim, and I have no contrary facts with which to argue, that the average settlement for the average divorce, for an average marriage, where the couple *lived together*, is far less than the hundred thousand per year you have already locked in."

"Average!" she spat the word out like it was repugnant to her soul. "I am the enemy of the average."

"Madame," he said calmly into the crackling phone, "are you aware of the state of the American economy?"

"What has that to do with it?"

"Quite a bit. Mr. Maxwell is on hard times. His stock plummeted in the stock market crash in twenty-nine. There has been a severe depression in America since. If your demands are perceived here to be unreasonable, and in this economic climate anything over subsistence is perceived as not only unreasonable, but impossible, then your case will be surely hurt."

"You ask nothing, you get nothing. I want ten million," she said. "Get it!" And she hung up the phone. Did he think she had nothing better to do than do his work for him?

These were not happy days for Madame Hanna Mazurka. She drifted through them, waiting for that insufferable attorney to call her with the news Ken Maxwell had capitulated. Oh, why can't I be at peace with myself? she wondered. God knows I am trying. I had my epiphany with the prince, but sometimes the provocation is just too great for any mortal to bear.

Next time, she promised herself, she would do better. But next time there was always something else to get her goat. Inner peace and contentment and the vanquishing of conflict seemed to be a losing battle.

When the phone finally rang from New York, the news was not good. "His attorney says he is adamant. You may have your theaters and the hundred thousand a year for life if you do not contest the divorce. If you decide to hold out for more, they will go to court and request not only the divorce on grounds of desertion, but also they ask to keep the theaters *and* cut off your hundred thousand yearly allowance."

"But that is preposterous! Nine years of marriage and he would cut me off without a *sou!* You can't let them get away with that."

"I can't? Madame, there is nothing I can do. If you don't sign the agreement, they will go to court."

"Oooo! You!—you…are…incompetent!"

"Please understand, Madame, any efforts you might make to replace me as your attorney would not meet with resistance from me."

"Oh—so you don't *want* to be my solicitor?"

"Do you wish my resignation, Madame?"

"Don't you dictate what I will or won't do. I will let you know."

"I shall wait to hear…" But, she had hung up on him.

Hanna had half a mind to let it go to court. Let the chips fall where they may. How could he renege on an offer agreed upon in writing? And hadn't she kept her part of the bargain? She divorced Ned Sharkey Butterworth *and* she married Ken Maxwell. Nothing else was required of her. It was ironclad. It had to be.

But just to be certain, she visited Darius Monteux, her Paris attorney. He had gotten fat since she had seen him last. Rich food provided by my rich fee, she thought.

Attorney Monteux told her that her American attorney's position was eminently reasonable. He could not prevent the other side from going to court, and once there, there could be no guarantees what a judge might decide.

"Look at it this way," Monteux said, seated at his desk, blowing air through the tent he made with his fingers, "as of now, you are married to one of Chicago's leading citizens; the divorce court will be in Chicago. Who is the man who has been so generous to all the arts in Chicago? Your husband. Now, you will not get a judge who does not know him, if not personally, by reputation. And all the judges are men. Men, in divorce cases, are sympathetic to men. Unless there was cruelty or some other obvious fault of the man.

"You were his second wife, he your fourth husband. You have him two to one in the realm of experience. I don't see what kind of a defense you can make on the desertion charge. You *are* in Paris and have been for most of the marriage."

"He could come *here*," she said. "In the beginning, we talk of my career. He agrees I should have career. I do not desert. I am pursuing my career."

Darius Monteux nodded. "You may certainly make that case in court. It will be unpleasant and very expensive. If you lose, it would not surprise me if one of those Chicago judges doesn't slap you with all the expenses—yours *and* his."

"You lawyers are all alike. Everything is 'Don't do!'"

He dropped his tent-fingers to the desk, as though it were necessary to hold himself in place. "Madame, I will leave you with but one thought. I don't know anyone who earns a hundred thousand a year in these times who thinks it is not enough. And the judge in Chicago will feel the same. He himself earns a fraction of that. It is not too great a stretch of the imagination to realize how your case will appear to him. No," he shook his head, "these days, greed is out of fashion. The newspapers would make a circus of you, as they did before. But this time, you would come out the monkey."

"But I am Madame Hanna Mazurka." Her back stiffened, her face drew taut around her mouth. "You do not treat me like that."

"If that ever cut any ice, I'm afraid those days are over, as are your days of snaring rich husbands. I'll venture to predict if you marry again, it will not be to a rich man salivating on your trail. Those birds will be following younger worms!"

"Mr. Monteux, you are disgusting," she said, and stormed out.

He smiled. "Perhaps," he muttered aloud, "but accurate. And, I would never have collected for my time anyway."

Hanna didn't give up. On Sunday, she polled her music

salon, which had become quite the ticket in Paris. She was disappointed in the results. While a few of her bigger boosters sympathized, as you would expect of a friend, not one of them thought it would be worth her while to make a court case. "Those lawyers can make hamburger of the King of England," one of her British friends said. And so, reluctantly, she called Mr. Barton in New York.

"Well," she said when he came on the phone, "everyone is telling me it isn't worth the fight. Even though I am right, they might make goulash of the whole sad mess."

"I think you've made a wise decision," he said, gently.

Well, she decided, her life was changing. Women had to face certain realities as they got older. Just as that horrible Darius Monteux had so indelicately put it.

ACT VI

THE ALSO-RANS

THE INVENTOR

Susanna: I seek for happiness that is not in me, I know not who possesses it; I sigh, lament without desire; my heart does beat, I know not why. I find no peace by night nor day, yet I am pleased to languish thus.

—*The Marriage of Figaro*

Madame Hanna Mazurka
remembers:

THE INVENTOR
London, England

"Everything about him was negative. He looked older than his age. He seemed haggard. Quite blind in one eye, his other saw but little. His hands trembled so hard he could hardly lift his glass of vermouth to his lips, from which a cigarette eternally dangled.

"Must I be as little as a wife in order to become bigger?"

So Madame Hanna Mazurka went about adjusting to her new single status. In a way, she missed the attention of the gossipmongers, audiences, rich men and her fans. In another way, she was tired of all the attention. She always considered herself a loner and a deeply spiritual being, and her new life put those assessments to the test.

For five years after her divorce from Maxwell was final, Madame Mazurka retired from her former life. She kept up her music salons and never missed an opera performance. She always got first-row seats, where she would encamp at the last minute so the entire audience could see her creative outfits and ever-changing, show-stopping jewels. When the music began she would close her eyes and seem to be in a swoon as she moved to the music (to the dismay of those around her). She was considered by some to be somewhat eccentric.

While still living outside Paris, she received a letter from her half brother, whom she had never met. It was a long, rambling, chatty letter bringing her up to date on the family—news she was not interested in hearing. She had left that behind her and did not relish being reminded of what she thought was a sorry state of affairs. The idea that she should be presented in this fashion with a half brother from the loins of that child who married her father was not short of disgusting. To make matters worse, the letter ended with a naked plea for a handout, times being so tough for them all (including her old father), and what with her being so "well-off."

She did not answer the letter. But the young man would not take the hint. Instead, he showed up at her door, making the most pathetic supplication for a handout. The maid, after consulting Madame, within the villa, returned to tell the young man Madame didn't know him; and though the maid did not put it so broadly, she left the young man with the unmistakable impression that she had no desire to know him.

When Madame got restless, she considered several projects to keep her occupied. She actually began a perfume business called The Madame Hanna Mazurka Perfume. She was photographed for advertisements, holding the bottle between her hands and upstretched forefingers. She was all in black, with a tall hat from which an embroidered veil cascaded down her shoulders. A simple strand of pearls (real) hung around her neck and disappeared behind the large bottle, the size of which seemed more suited to toilet water than perfume.

She was still beautiful, though the picture was retouched to smooth out some wrinkles that had begun to appear. She limited the rings on her fingers to two—one on each hand—one with a large single pearl, the other with two smaller ones. Her earrings were pearl pendants that almost touched her shoulders. The whole outfit had a gypsylike flavor to it, but that was soon overcome when she commandeered the Rolls-Royce for a parade through the main streets of Paris, promoting the perfume. In spite of these efforts and a generous print and radio advertising budget, Madame Hanna Mazurka perfume sank out of sight when the demands for cash infusions to the enterprise far outstripped the promise of return.

Next she thought a string of beauty salons bearing her name would be a gold mine. But initial investigations into the possibility discouraged her, and though she had elaborate plans, the beauty business never got off the ground.

Then came the rumblings of a man curiously named Schicklgruber, who simplified his name to Hitler, that made all of Europe mighty uncomfortable. The direct threats to France frightened Madame Hanna Mazurka, and she moved to London until it would all blow over.

There, while attending the opera at Covent Garden, she met John Queen, an inventor who was working on secret weapons, and the intrigue excited Hanna as she had not been for some time. He was a poor man, living by his wits in the lengthening time between payoffs on his inventions. But he struck her as so romantic—doing all this for the war effort when he certainly could have gotten a steady job and a regular paycheck *some*where.

Secretly she wanted to do *her* bit for the war and she thought this could be it. She could underwrite his efforts. She never told him that in so many words, but she was most encouraging, and he liked that.

She visited him on weekends and took great pains not to seem to want to interfere with his important work. Three months and five visits after they met, they were engaged. Hanna had never experienced long courtships. She was impatient for quick results. Two months after the engagement was announced:

BARONESS TO
WED INVENTOR

they were married.

The union proved disastrous from the start. It was as though as soon as the vows were exchanged, the plug was pulled on civility. They both dimly understood, if did not acknowledge, that everyone was on his best behavior during courtship. But the extremes of behavior were experienced hot, heavy and early. Madame complained he was drinking himself to death. And his incessant smoking

591

was sure to ruin her singing voice.

Mr. John Queen, for his part, said she was a spoiled-rotten Polish peasant, with pretensions way beyond her breeding, ability or intelligence.

The war, she told her friends, was driving her back to America. She left early one morning, without saying goodbye.

After his death, a few years later, the executor of the John Queen estate sent a plea to his estranged former wife for fifty pounds sterling to cover the inventor's funeral expenses.

Hanna's first thought was to tell the solicitor to consult the prenuptial agreement. But, in time, she softened. What was fifty pounds to her, after all? A cheap enough price to close the chapter on that creep anyway.

Besides, it would make her appear generous. So she sent the fifty pounds with a brief note of condolence to which she added this postscript:

> No requests for further payments will be honored, per the prenuptial agreement.

THE WHITE LAMA

Madame Hanna Mazurka
remembers:

THE WHITE LAMA

Santa Barbara, California

"The divorce lawyers simply couldn't believe I was never in love with Dr. Theodore Xavier. They looked at this intimate, extremely subtle drama of two old souls as any common case of a rich and mature woman marrying a young and poor man who professed to be a writer, but who was actually living on women's credulity and their money, in exchange for some dubious yoga's exercises such as standing on the head, per example."

Back in New York, Hanna moved into her old suite at the Pierre Hotel, and renewed her earnest study of Eastern religions.

Madame Hanna Mazurka was finally at the stage in her life where she could take her spiritual pursuits seriously. And she did, almost to the exclusion of everything else in her life. She realized her pursuits of fame, glory and money were all behind her, by biological necessity if nothing else. She spent most of the war years in search of spiritual awakening, in the course of which she attended many lectures and seminars throughout the city.

One such lecture series was held in her own Pierre Hotel. She arrived early, and, as was her signature at lectures and operas, she sat in the front row.

When Theodore Xavier came in and took his place at the speaker's podium, he took her breath away. He was the most handsome man she had ever laid eyes on.

He was not yet thirty years old. She was climbing upon fifty. And, much to Hanna's delight and amazement, the young gentleman did not seem to be able to take his eyes off her.

After the second session, Hanna garnered the nerve to ask Mr. Xavier questions about his religion (Buddhism), then a few about himself.

He was a California boy, he said, had gone to law school and practiced briefly before throwing it all over and going to Tibet to become a monk. He wound up being the first white lama, a distinction, she thought, of which he was justifiably proud.

Then he stared down at her, with those penetrating blue eyes, and said, "Will you marry me?"

Her reaction was to laugh. But something within told her not to slam the door by saying anything untoward, like "But I'm old enough to be your mother." Could it really be that this young, godlike man found her attractive?

She was sure she was blushing when she said something she couldn't remember minutes after she said it, but they did find themselves having lunch together after the class.

They sat in the Russian Tea Room, across from Carnegie Hall, at a table resplendent with all the accouterments that made Hanna feel successful: white-linen tablecloth, heavy silver and obsequious waiters.

Best of all, Theodore Xavier was making Hanna feel loved. He looked at her like a man enraptured. It made her feel giddy—and young.

She was talking excitedly about Confucius, the Taoists, Motze and the personal God, heaven, hell, religion under the Han dynasty. She had read widely and she was using it all on Theodore. He was impressed.

Then she spoke of Mohammed and his marriage to Khadija, who was much older than he was. But she was rich, and the marriage was happy. Hanna paused to frame her question—"Do you think that could happen? An older woman could make a younger man happy?"

"I'm sure of it!" he said. "It worked for Mohammed."

"Yes," she said, "but we know nothing of his childhood. Or that of Jesus, for that matter. How much is myth and legend?" she asked. "Is religion only the opiate of the masses, like Karl Marx said?"

"Whoa!" he said. "That's a lot of questions. How much time do you have?"

"I have a lot of time," she said, smiling and batting her eyelashes as she had done so successfully in years gone by.

"Perhaps the opiate of the masses, but not *only* that. You can argue that everyone wants a dad to make decisions for him, to protect him, make him feel secure. And people want meaning. They want to believe they are part of something that has some logic to it."

"Are we?"

"Well, I hope so. You know, there are so many stories connected with religion. Some quite scandalous, like Krishna's adolescence. All that dallying with milkmaids—erotic adventures. That could be to keep up the interest of the masses."

"You didn't grow up in a Buddhist family, did you?"

"No," he laughed. "We were half-baked Christians. I always had trouble wrapping my mind around the dogmas, you know—virgin birth, resurrection. I was only interested in those aspects which dealt with being a better person. And that is essentially Buddhism—a discipline—a way of life—the eternal truth. We aren't tied to a single personage. There have been a lot of Buddhas. We don't have to encumber them with miracles and the supernatural.

"Gautama the Buddha, for instance, wondered why men are born, only to get sick and die. Don't we *all* wonder about meaning?"

"I certainly do. With the life I've had, how could I not?"

He smiled. "Once you get caught up with Buddhism, your past will be irrelevant."

She liked the sound of that.

They had many more lunches, then dinners, and every time he would say "I am serious, I want to marry you," she would just laugh.

But when she was alone, she spent a lot of time thinking about it. She adored his mind. It was all full of her current interests. And he was so darned good-looking. Once or twice she thought he

597

might be interested in her money, but she was unaccustomed to that dynamic with men she was about to marry, so she had trouble grasping the thought. Wilhelm Drang, she thought in retrospect, certainly had more than an idle thought about her money. But it made her think perhaps she should bring it up.

When she did, in the dining room of the Plaza Hotel, where she had been courted by Ken Maxwell and Dr. Weidner, and experienced the one-nighter with Royce Saxon, she casually mentioned that any woman her age, in her financial situation, would have to be wary of any young man's attention lest he take advantage of her to enrich himself.

"Money?" he laughed. "Did I ever mention it?"

"Nooo."

"When you understand Buddhism better, you will see it is a spiritual endeavor. We are interested in the soul. The material things of this world are of no moment to us. Money is not only unimportant, it is nothing. No, my dearest Madame, my interest is in your inner being, not your external trappings. It is your soul that glows."

What woman nearing fifty could resist that? And she did believe him, with all her heart. How could she not have wanted to?

The war was overheating Europe, and she feared for her property there. She called Darius Monteux and asked him to dispose of it for her. He marveled that she must have forgotten their last conversation, where she was so insulted. But the nice thing about selling property was he could take his fee off the top. But with France under the boot of the Germans, he warned her it would not be an easy sale.

As Theodore Xavier and Madame Hanna Mazurka grew closer, they were freer about relating their hopes and aspirations. Theodore wanted to get a Ph.D. from Columbia and had advanced to the point where much study was required to result in his doctoral dissertation. And he thought the best place for him to do that would be the West Coast, the locale of his birth.

Hanna knew little of California, but he was so enthusiastic, she agreed to go with him for a visit.

They went on the train and experienced the benefits of marriage, without the requisite documents. He was the first man who made her feel good about her body, she said. He was a uniquely skilled lover and Hanna was convinced it was a natural communion of two simpatico souls reaching out for one another in validation of their own beings.

Theodore couldn't have agreed more.

While in California, Hanna used her wealth to buy gas coupons on the black market. She hired a car and chauffeur and drove with Theodore from Los Angeles to San Diego and La Jolla, then back up the coast, through Santa Barbara to Carmel and San Francisco.

At the end of the trip, Theodore asked Hanna, "If you were fantasizing about the best place to live in California, where would it be?"

"Oh, I liked something about each place," she said.

"So why don't you get a house in each?"

She laughed. "Because I don't want the headaches of another house to keep."

"So what would be your first choice?"

"If I must choose, I choose Santa Barbara. Is beautiful and warm. The ocean is right there. Very nice."

He clapped his hands. "My favorite too," he said. "Shall I look for a place?"

She shook her head, laughing. "No," she said. "I don't want more headaches! I live close to the Metropolitan Opera in New York—opera, you know, is my life. California has no real opera and is long way from New York."

He wrinkled his nose. "Think of living in California! You can be outside all year, it is never too hot at night to sleep; the noise and traffic and the temperature in New York can be insufferable."

"My goodness, you are *some* salesman!"

"If that is a compliment," he said, smiling his devastating, youthful smile, "thank you."

That night, in a hotel room in San Francisco with a view of the city and bay, he made her feel particularly good about her body. In appreciation, she said she wanted to do something to make him happy.

"Oh, you already do," he said.

"No, I want to buy you something," she said. "Would you like a new watch?"

"Oh, no thanks," he said, "my study is all that is important to me."

599

"Well, then, a book or something?"

"Hmm." He thought a moment. "You know what would be paradise for me?"

"Paradise? No."

"To have a place to go to for my fellow monks. A retreat where we could go and study, meditate, improve our inner lives."

"A place like...wait," she said, "I want to guess... Like Santa Barbara?"

He kissed her. "Hanna!" he exclaimed. "You are a mind reader—but how could you be so generous? I'll start looking tomorrow. If I'm going to be looking for property, perhaps I should get us a car. If you move here, you'll need a car."

He was so bubbly with enthusiasm, she didn't have the heart to squelch it. But she had to return to New York. The opera season was about to begin and she didn't want to miss a performance. She left him to his house hunting and took the train back across the country.

By the time she got to New York, she already had three telegrams from him, enthusing over various properties and telling her, after a thorough investigation of the automobile industry, a new Cadillac seemed the best bet.

Theodore had found one a dealer was holding back from the last batch made before converting the factory to the war effort. For a premium price, he would be persuaded to let it go.

What a dear boy, she said to herself—to give an old woman so much attention. If the Cadillac makes him happy, why not oblige him?

After he bought the car, Theodore began bombarding her with estates for sale. One especially caught his fancy. It was almost forty acres, with a large house and adjoining guest cottage, as well as another house on the property.

"Forty acres!" she exclaimed into the telephone. "What am I going to do with forty acres? You must be crazy."

"No, you must see it. It would be perfect for my retreat. You could do good in the world, advance the cause of Buddhism, and have the loveliest place to live you can imagine."

"I can imagine," she said.

What she couldn't imagine was the persistence of Theodore

Xavier. He did not give up. And since that was a trait of her own she took pride in, she had also to admire it in him.

But she did not give in right away. He told her how wonderful she was, how much he loved her, and how the glow of her spirit ignited his own, numerous times over a period of several months before she, with professed reluctance ("I must have head examined"), capitulated.

They decided to call the property Lamaland, after his religious historicism.

But before they were married, a year and a half after they met, she had arranged with a Santa Barbara attorney for a prenuptial agreement that stated, simply, that in the event of dissolution of the marriage, each party would be entitled to nothing from the other. Since the Buddhist monk's net worth was close to the clothes on his back, he would be unable to profit from the marriage.

"No problem," Theodore Xavier said when asked to sign the document, "I'm not interested in money."

Corporal Schicklgruber, the peacetime paperhanger, took the easy way out. When his game was up, he poisoned himself in his underground bunker. He died like a mole, which many thought was a higher station than he had achieved in his lifetime.

Quick to disown Adolf Hitler with his razor-cut hair and his funny little moustache, the Germans turned their efforts to the manufacture and sales of expensive automobiles, electric razors and kitchen appliances.

The Japanese bowed their way to surrender on an aircraft carrier in the Pacific Ocean, a body of water they had had designs on dominating. Two astonishing blasts of atomic fission, and the threat of more, brought the Nipponese to their knees. Douglas MacArthur, their conqueror, became their savior. Not so quick to disown their emperor, they turned their efforts to making inexpensive cars, television sets and electronic equipment.

After the war, Madame experienced hot flashes, and she did not like to consider their portent. She always said to anyone who would listen that age was a state of mind. But in her heart of hearts she felt it was something more. It was no small factor in her marrying a younger man, though her official story was he simply wore her down with his persistence.

For her sixth marriage, Hanna realized the tide had shifted somewhat. She was the wealthy partner, as she had been in number five, but she was also twenty-one years older than her bridegroom. And there was no more career pursuit to inhibit her from being a regular "wife." She took her new position as a challenge. Theodore had even made her feel so good about her body that she relaxed her rule about having separate bedrooms. So she was more than a little surprised and chagrined to hear her new husband announce he would not be sharing a bedroom because it would distract him from his meditations and interfere with his spiritual journey on his path to Enlightenment.

And the young man (boy really, Hanna thought) took charge of the marriage. Hanna realized she had not been firm enough with him, but how else was she to experience being the wife? She must humble herself, she thought. And so she served his breakfast on a silver tray and felt honored when he allowed her to take hers with him.

She soon thought him rather demanding. They didn't dare run out of his favorite strawberry jam; and he paced the floor if the newspaper wasn't there on the dot of eight.

She was often discouraged by new revelations of his personality. Things he did and said grated on her, but she instructed herself, in those moments, not to give up.

Hanna did not make friends easily. Especially with women, who were bound to be jealous of the many men in her life. Her having a husband so handsome and so much younger caused a great many raised eyebrows that she thought inappropriate. It made her sufficiently self-conscious to stay at home most of the time.

They were not married a year when the huge house seemed crowded with the two of them in residence. Hanna couldn't wait for the opera season to begin in New York so she had an excuse to escape Theodore's company.

When the season was over, and Hanna could find no excuse not to return to her handsome young husband, she cringed. But she was not a quitter, and she took the train for no other reason than it took longer.

Theodore met her at the train and embraced her enthusiastically. She was encouraged. He drove her home in the Cadillac she had bought him. He seemed happy.

"I have a surprise for you," he said.

"Oh?"

"Yes. You always say you want me to be happy—"

"Yesss—within reason."

"This won't cost you anything."

"Hmm—what could it be?"

"When we get home, I'll…show you."

She was not looking forward to the discovery.

He drove the Cadillac slowly down the long driveway to the house. There, standing on the stoop to greet them, was a gentleman, perhaps five or ten years older than Hanna herself. She frowned. Theodore popped eagerly out of the car and opened the door for her.

"Hanna," he said, "I'd like you to meet Victor Overton. He's been staying here in the blue house, to kind of watch over things. We had some vandalism and Victor takes walks at night, and we haven't had an incident since he came."

Hanna forced a smile and took his hand. "Well," she said, "well…"

Victor bowed low and said, "Madame Mazurka, I am honored to meet you."

She forced another smile, then looked quizzically at her husband.

"Is it all right if he stays? We can really use a caretaker."

"Well, I don't know what to say, Theo. Perhaps tonight, then we will talk."

Once inside the house, with Victor out of sight, Theodore took Hanna in his arms and they had a lusty and joyous homecoming. Hanna felt young again.

"Well," she said when she caught her breath, "bring me up to date. What is happening around here?"

"You mean Victor?"

"Is he the only news? Where did he come from?"

"He's an old friend of the family," he said, with tightly knit eyebrows.

"Yes—and how many more friends would you bring to live here?"

He chuckled. "Oh, Hanna, just Victor. He's down on his luck, and it's a charity."

"Is he a Buddhist?"

"Oh, no. He's a Christian. What do you say?"

"I say no," she said. "But he is already here. You did not ask me first, you just move in here a stranger."

"But he's no stranger. I've known him all my life."

"He is a stranger to me," she said. "I do not like strangers living with me."

"He's in the blue house. It's a block away from here."

"Does not matter. Is my property. Tomorrow, he goes."

But tomorrow was not convenient for Victor to go. Nor was the day after, or the day after that. The married couple fought about Victor, but getting him to leave was not in the cards. Hanna did not want to give the point up, but she didn't want to call the police either, so she just became exasperated.

Theo offered her a proposition after Victor had lived with them three weeks. "I've been thinking," he said. "My meditations are not as comfortable as they should be. Not as successful. I couldn't understand why. Now I think I know."

"Oh?"

"Yes, it's the altitude."

"The altitude?"

"Yes, I am too low to get in touch with the gods."

"Oh—too low?"

"Yes, I need to be closer to the heavens."

"Really?"

"Yes, something higher up."

She looked at him through half-closed eyes. "Oh, Theo, I can't sell this house to buy one higher up."

"No, no, I don't want you to sell it. I just want a place to

605

study and meditate."

She nodded. "Closer to the gods," she said.

"Yes. And I can take Victor with me. I'm so sorry you don't like him. I shouldn't have invited him, but he seemed so…so needy. I didn't have the heart to turn him away."

"Oh," she said, shaking her head, "I don't have the strength to look for more houses. We have three on this property, but it isn't high in the sky enough for you."

"No. You won't have to shop. I've found the perfect place."

"Oh?"

"It's just up the mountain a few miles. It's like a penthouse of the gods."

"Really?"

"Yes."

"And Victor could move there?"

"Yes. I'm sure he'd love it. I would come back at night, of course. It would only be for study and meditation."

"And Victor would stay there, day and night?"

"Yes."

So she bought the place, and Victor moved up the hill—for one night.

"Thanks so much for buying me my penthouse," Theodore said, throwing his arms around her and planting a loud, wet kiss on her startled lips. "My meditation, umm, perfection," he said, blowing a kiss to the air.

"And Victor is all settled?"

He frowned. "I hope so," he said.

"*Hope* so? That was the bargain."

"Yes, yes, I know. Well, he's up there. I hope he doesn't get lonely."

"Lonely? What do you mean? There is no lonely about it. He is out! If he doesn't like it, he moves somewhere else, not here."

"Okay."

But the next day, Victor was back. "It's creepy up there," he said. "That's definitely not for me."

"Then you go," she said.

"Where?"

"I don't care where. I am not your keeper. You have sponged

off my good nature long enough," she said.

"I am sorry, Madame, I am not as rich as you. I have been on hard times lately. I have never before asked a favor of my son."

"Your son? Well, where is he? You can certainly ask a favor of your son if you can ask it of me."

"Where is my son?" Victor seemed surprised at the question. "Why, he is right here, of course."

Hanna looked around the room. "Where? Don't you tell me you have moved your son in here also."

Victor laughed. Hanna didn't like the teeth she saw. "Theo is my son."

Her mouth was open, but no sound came out.

When Hanna confronted Theo with that shock, he said offhandedly, "Oh, I didn't want to prejudice you."

"For or against?" she asked.

"Either way."

"But his name is different than yours."

"Yes. He had some difficult times. He changed his name. The poor man has nowhere to turn. We can't put him out."

"We can't? You can't perhaps, but I can. I've been tricked, lied to, deceived. I want nothing more to do with him."

"Has he been a bother? He stays out of your way pretty much."

"Oh? How would you know? You're in your penthouse of the gods all day. I am down on the flatlands with Vic...your *father!*"

Hanna had never felt so powerless in her life. Theodore and Victor just seemed to ignore her pleas for him to move. The longer he stayed there, the more helpless and contrary he became. Hanna thought she had to do something, but just didn't know what. She threw a tantrum, but it had no effect. She told Theodore it was her money and she had to be in charge. He soft-soaped her with talk of the transcendence of the soul. There was a lecture about how we were all children of God, and every soul was important to God and anything we did for another soul was a star in our crown in the eyes of the gods. But Hanna was becoming leery of the religious aura which had attracted her to him in the first place.

She finally garnered the courage to say, "He *goes*, or you both go!" An eternity later, Victor packed his meager belongings and left.

A few days later, Hanna received a letter from him—humble and contrite and grateful. She couldn't believe the same man had written it.

Life settled down for a while. The lama went daily to his penthouse to meditate and Madame pursued musical endeavors, never missing a concert or musical. She also began to take more interest in the vast gardens on the property, that took a staff of three to maintain. She was alone every day and she enjoyed walking in the forty-acre garden. She found she had no trouble meditating at the lower altitude.

When it was time for the opera season, she was torn about uprooting herself from California again, but her demanding husband, who she thought must have been a terribly spoiled child, was so demeaning in his orders and expectations that she fled Lamaland to preserve her sanity.

When it was time to return, Theodore called her daily to check her plans. "I want to meet the plane," he said.

"Oh, that's not necessary. It's so far to Los Angeles, and George can come for me."

"No, I want to," he said. "Just tell me when. I haven't seen you in so long. It's the least I can do."

Hanna dared to hope things would be better between them. He seemed so solicitous. "I just don't know when I can get a plane. So many people are traveling."

"Well, you just tell me. I don't need any notice really. Just call me when you are about to board the plane. I'll be there."

So she called him. It was a lovely day for flying, on both ends of the trip. He thanked her for calling. "I'm looking forward to seeing you," he said.

"Oh, I hope so," she said. "We must make it work."

He agreed.

Hanna was definitely encouraged that Theo wanted to have an extra two hours with her though George was perfectly capable of driving her. It was like how he begged her to buy Lamaland and his meditation penthouse. He was always so childishly eager. Well, perhaps she should try harder. Fifty-one-year-old women were a drug on the market. Her New York friends couldn't believe their ears when she told them about her handsome, young husband. And when she showed them pictures of him in only a loincloth, in some stupendous yoga position, their eyes wanted to pop out of their heads.

In the air, high above the clouds, Hanna thought of all the good times she and Theo had together. Certainly if she would dwell on the bright side of things, and could overlook his obvious weaknesses (everyone has them, after all), they just might make a go of it.

By the time the plane landed, she had built herself almost to a fever pitch with excitement over seeing him.

But in the Burbank Terminal, he was nowhere to be seen. She looked all over, even going to the curb to see if his car was there. Nothing.

A seedy-looking man in a shiny suit, with floppy, dirty, blond hair, came up to her. "Madame Hanna Mazurka?" he said, and her first thought was he was going to ask for an autograph. Then she thought he was an emissary from her husband.

"Where is he?" she asked. "Is something wrong?"

"You *are* Madame Mazurka?"

"Yes," she said, "but I don't see Theodore."

Suddenly the man thrust a handful of papers at her. Startled, she took them. "What's this?" she asked, looking at the man, not the papers.

"Read it for yourself," he said. "Divorce papers." And he disappeared as suddenly as he had appeared.

It was her most acrimonious divorce. Theodore Xavier had the nerve to ask for money after they had both signed crystal-clear and ironclad prenuptial agreements. Theodore claimed she had spoiled him, and he was now accustomed to a life of wealth and ease, the sacrifice of which would cause him extreme hardship, suffering and pain.

When Hanna got over her shock on the sidewalk in front of the airport terminal building, she was obliged to hire a taxi. She thought the ninety-mile trip would cost as much as her flight, but she had retained the presence of mind to bargain with the driver for a cheaper fare.

Her first action on returning home was to remove the sign that said "Lamaland" out front. She would think of a new name later.

She found that her anguish was relieved by long walks on her property. She was cognizant of the plants for the first time, taking note of their broad differences. The flora diverted her mind from her troubles. She told herself she was glad Theodore had instituted the divorce, so she didn't have to. If she had, it would have been a sign of surrender.

The proceedings dragged on, and the attorneys got richer by the minute. The newspapers got into the act again, but the coverage was neither as sensational as it had been before, nor as deep. It was as though they were dredging for news about an old curiosity that no longer mattered. One Hollywood wag put it this way:

> After getting free of her sixth mistake, will she go on for seven or eight? She is only in her fifties. Many women have bagged a number of men after that age. They may not be titled or rich or young or handsome like those in Madame Hanna Mazurka's stable to date, but one should never give up hope. I am willing to put my dough on the old girl for at least two more — maybe four. Ten would be a notable collection. But I must make a confession, I am losing interest in her mates. Though they were all colorful in their day in their way, the color is draining out of the dear madame herself. And from here on it is liable to be a collection of has-beens and wannabes, and that becomes tedious.

Hanna was "highly incensed" by that article in the Los Angeles newspaper that she said made its disgusting circulation numbers by *being* disgusting. Her own Santa Barbara paper was much more gentle. But the facts themselves called for a certain kind of amusement and Hanna was feeling self-conscious about it.

So, instead of standing firm to the bitter end, she allowed her lawyers to talk her into a compromise to "get the rotter behind me." This in spite of the discovery by detectives that Mr. Theodore Xavier had a wife, that he had neglected to divorce, and children roaming around somewhere. Hanna reluctantly agreed to deed him the penthouse of the gods and pay his lawyers' fees, with the understanding he would leave the country and she would never have to see him again.

Theodore kept his part of the bargain. He sold his "penthouse" and took the proceeds and headed back to Nepal with a new wife his own age. There he could meditate at the highest altitudes available on earth. And there he disappeared from the earth as we know it, baffling (and, of course, saddening) his new wife.

On hearing the news, Hanna speculated that Theodore had gotten *too* close to God, and the Great One did not like what he saw and simply vaporized the lama. "Is what you call having too much of a good thing," she said, smiling wryly.

Now Hanna was truly alone in the world. Not only technically, as she always said she was. Not long after Theodore Xavier vanished, she received word that Ken Maxwell had died. All six of her husbands were in the ground. All she had left were her memories, which she promptly sugarcoated. And, of course, the money. But that could be a nuisance. People were always after your money, she thought. I can hide here on my forty acres and be a recluse. "I don't need nobody," she said aloud, her English still not at the level of sophistication to recognize the double negative.

Hanna wrote a book about her husbands and her spiritual quests. She had very little nice to say about any of her husbands, and the more recent the memories, the greater the acrimony.

It was a rambling, disjointed effort, privately published and gently reviewed in some leading journals. But it was a book that pushed stream-of-consciousness writing to its extreme.

In it she spoke of how each of her husbands let her down, how their vast wealth couldn't touch her soul, how the love she had for Maxwell was purer than carnal love, but he was unable to be satisfied with this feeling from a higher plane. How numbers one and five were drunks. She even remembered to complain of the aggravation number two's coughing fits caused her.

The work was brazenly self-serving, which might be forgiven a poor Polish girl who, in her way, had taken the world by storm.

One surprising revelation was that she finally admitted she could not sing.

"Then how can I live?" she asked. "I must have work. I must have accomplishment."

She wanted no more husbands, and she knew the chance of a successful opera career was gone forever, but she needed to work, or die. There had to always be a goal to occupy her time. Some grandiloquent project—some legacy to leave the world.

Madame Hanna Mazurka stiffened her back. She was not going to sink with defeat. Life may have handed her a bunch of lemons, but, by God, it was time to make lemonade. This she thought one day while wandering in her garden. The sun was bright and cheerful. It was so conducive to reveries and clear thought. Perhaps if Theodore Xavier had been able to meditate here and hadn't insisted on higher and higher altitudes, he would be alive today.

But perhaps… Why not?… The garden. It was a natural. She had the money. She would make her legacy the garden. Madame Mazurka's Garden! It would be famous the world over. And everyone would know it was *her* creation. Not some husband's. Not some hanger-on musician's or white lama's, but her own. Madame Hanna Mazurka! *Extraordinaire!*

So she called her three gardeners together and told them she wanted to make her garden the greatest in the world. How should she go about it?

The man nominally in charge of the crew, Harry Azuma, muttered that it would cost a fortune in money. Hanna waved her hand. "I have money," she said, dismissing the notion as petty.

The forty acres had been kept more or less on a subsistence level to date, but the three men had been kept busy watering, trimming and weeding. A lot of the acreage was in its natural form. About a quarter of it was planted with nonnatural vegetation. There was almost an acre of grass; three ponds made up another acre.

613

Madame had reduced her household staff to her secretary—
a woman she hired on her first interview—a woman who was to stay
with her for thirty-five years—a woman who bore the brunt of her
many tantrums, but who also enjoyed better times and the associa-
tion with a legend.

George, her faithful chauffeur, had an easier time of it.
Madame was always easier on the men in her life. She liked to
protest that she never flirted, wouldn't know how. But there were
many men who crossed her path in those later years who would contradict that notion.

Madame began buying new plants in earnest. And she went
about it as she went about everything else—with an avaricious lust.
She didn't buy one or two of each plant that caught her fancy, she
bought hundreds and then massed them together in various sections
of her vast garden. The planted acreage grew from ten to fifteen,
then twenty and twenty-five. The three gardeners increased to six,
then nine.

She found she took to the work, and it gave her the feeling of
accomplishment she had sought all her life. She loved to watch the
changes taking place under her direction. She hired all the best people she could to design and build her creation. She had finally found
a worthy outlet for her enormous wealth, which was growing daily, at
a rate faster than she was able to spend it.

She planted a vast rose garden, but her efforts were not all
roses. She was still the headstrong, combative woman of her youth.
The old dog did not learn new tricks, she merely refocused the old
ones.

Hanna had started with cacti. They were plants foreign to
her. Cacti didn't grow in her Poland, Russia, Paris, London, Chicago
or New York. Here, in California, they would grow, and she bought
them by the thousands, planting entire fields of the same columnar
cacti. Then agaves and aloes, also only viable in her new home.
Ferns, bromeliads, eucalyptuses, bamboos, palms and, finally,
cycads. These last were the rarest and most expensive plants money
could buy. And she bought with a vengeance.

A Los Angeles cycad grower, Larry Wellcomb, had two of an
extinct cycad species of *Encephalartos*. Madame Hanna Mazurka
paid him a visit with her head gardener. She asked to buy one of the

plants. Larry Wellcomb told her he didn't want to sell them.

She said, "Why? You have two. Why not sell me one?"

"Because there are no more like them," he said. "I want them for my own collection."

But the madame badgered him—making him feel selfish for not sharing. The grower realized she didn't know one cycad from another and was only nagging him because of the scarcity. She wanted to stand out in the crowd—and that rare cycad would help.

"I wouldn't know what to ask for it," he said, showing a sign of weakening.

"I give you a thousand dollars," she said.

"Oh, no," he said. "It is worth much more than that."

"Two thousand!"

He finally sold it for twenty-five hundred. A very good price for a cycad in the 1960s, but she got a priceless plant.

As soon as the deal was made, she changed her mind. She wanted the plant he had in the ground, instead of the one in the wood box, which he had said he would sell her.

"But the boxed one is the better plant," he said. "And I don't want to dig the other up. You never know what will happen when you dig. Cycads are hardy, but I don't want to take any chances with these."

"No, no, no!" she said, stomping her foot like a child. "That is the one I want."

He must have already spent the money in his mind, because he capitulated. They could not have been back in Santa Barbara more than an hour when Madame's head gardener called and said, "Guess what?"

"She wants the other one instead."

"Close. She wants them both."

And she *got* them both.

Another time, she drove with George, her chauffeur, past a house with a yard full of tall *Dracaena draco*, commonly called dragon trees. She bid George to stop and sent him into the house to inquire if they would sell them.

"No," the man said. "I plan to stay here till I die. Those are my landscape and I've become fond of those strange-looking things."

She began offering a lot of money. He shook his head. Every

time she went higher, his head shook with less resolution, until she reached the point where he knew he could relandscape, and fatten his bank account at the same time.

Now, at last, she was able to put it all behind her—the combativeness, the naked ambition, the thirst for fame, the hunger for financial security. There was not only beauty in plants, there was peace. An inner calm she derived from watching things grow—plants that would outlive her and carry her touch to future generations—finally fulfilling her quest for immortality.

There were no conflicts with her plants—conflicts were for people. She might cross swords with a gardener now and then, or a nurseryman she thought was robbing her blind, but never with a plant. A plant's sole function, in her eyes, was to offer beauty. She had offered beauty in her own way in her lifetime, but she was never wholly comfortable with it. She always wanted more—she wanted to be admired for her talent, not her beauty. With her plants, she was satisfied that they provided beauty. And she could admire them for their beauty content in the knowledge that her plants would not resent it.

And so she built one of the most astonishing gardens of her time. It was truly an opera of gardens—"Opera," the plural of opus, mean works. In opera, you have music, drama, art, singing, lighting and acting. In Madame Mazurka's opera, she had cacti and aloes, palms and cycads, ferns and bromeliads, aquatic plants, and even a Japanese garden to remind her of *Madame Butterfly*, her favorite opera. The one she had most costumes made for, for the role she never sang in public.

She opened her garden twice a year for worthy causes, and endowed its continuation in her will, which she changed seventeen times in the last years of her life.

She went through numerous personnel. Many of them simply could not stand her erratic treatment of them. They were geniuses one day and fools the next. She often gave irrational commands and demanded they be obeyed. She lived in fear that people were taking advantage of her and laughing at her behind her back.

They did both, but much less than she imagined. She had finally arrived at a place in life where her age and accomplishment warranted the appellation "Madame." And as soon as she had, it seemed less important to her. And when she arranged in her will for a foundation to run her beloved garden after she was gone, she decided she wanted her garden to be called

Hanna Mazurka
Nirvana

She put her name over the title, like she would have liked to have seen it on some opera marquee. That was past, and past is prelude. But she decided against

Madame Hanna Mazurka
Nirvana

because she was beginning to think in the state of California in the U.S.A. the only people who called themselves Madame were fortunetellers.

During her early years, she had found it desirable to fudge her age, this way and that, so when anyone asked her age, she claimed not to remember. She was far into her nineties when she died. The sentimentalists said she was a hundred, but she was really a few years short.

Near the end, she had to use two canes to get around her garden, which grew more magnificent with each passing day. As the garden grew, the trees created more shadows to remind her of her humble beginnings in Brest Litovsk, Poland. She often thought of those times and her love of the cooling shadows she sought in the heat of summer. She refused to be helped into the shadows now. She would rather be bedridden than admit to the weakness of not being able to navigate on her own. She had no regrets. She refused to speak of the past. "That is no more," she would say if anyone asked about her history. She even claimed to not remember how many marriages she had had.

Perhaps she could have seen her beloved garden for three or four months more before she died had she allowed her garden staff to help her. But that was not the way of Hanna Mazurka. Toward the end, the garden became overgrown, not because of neglect so much as Hanna's confused state and the erratic orders she gave.

And when she died, they found the house full of mounds of trash interspersed with millions of dollars' worth of diamonds, gold, silver and other precious gems. Only her faithful, beleaguered secretary was by her side when Hanna died. Madame Hanna Mazurka wanted to be alone. "You were born alone, you should die alone," she said, and she did.

Of course, average people collect loved ones around them at the end. But that was *average* people. Hanna Mazurka was, as she always said, "The enemy of the average."

ATTRIBUTIONS

EPIGRAPH

La Bohème
Act II
Music by Giacomo Puccini
Libretto by Giuseppe Giacosa and Luigi Illica
1896

OVERTURE

Pelléas et Mélisande
Act IV, Scene 1
Music by Claude Debussy
Libretto by Maurice Maeterlinck
1902

ACT I

Louise
Act II, Scene 1
Music and Libretto by Gustave Charpentier
1900

ACT II

Der Rosenkavalier
Act I
Music by Richard Strauss
Libretto by Hugo von Hofmannsthal
1911

ACT III

> *Otello*
> Act III, Scene 5
> Music by Giuseppe Verdi
> Libretto by Arrigo Boito
> based on Shakespeare's tragedy
> 1887

ACT IV

> *Boris Godunov*
> Act III, Scene 1
> Music and Libretto by
> Modest Petrovich Mussorgsky
> 1874

ACT V

> *Carmen*
> Act I
> Music by Georges Bizet
> Libretto by Henri Meilhac and Ludovic Halévy
> 1875

ACT VI

> *The Marriage of Figaro*
> Act II, Scene 2
> Music by Wolfgang Amadeus Mozart
> Libretto by Lorenzo da Ponte
> 1786

Enemy of the Average

was set in Electra Old Style Face,
based on the font by W.A. Dwiggins, issued in 1935.
Distinguished by its clarity, readability and debt to
Neoclassical form and designed in the U.S.A. for the Linotype
machine, Electra has remained a staple face of the
American book trade since its initial release.

Printed on 60-pound Booktext natural acid-free paper
3-piece case bound with Roxite B and Kivar 9 cloth, Smyth sewn.

ABOUT THE AUTHOR

Margaret Nicol is an opera buff and an avid gardener. She has limited herself to one husband. They live in the hills of Santa Barbara, California in an empty nest.

Select titles also available from Allen A. Knoll, Publishers of books for intelligent people who read for fun

THE PAPER DYNASTY by Theodore Roosevelt Gardner II

The true and explosive story of the most remarkable family in America inspired *The Paper Dynasty*. Here is a can't-put-it-down account that is far more fascinating than Citizen Kane.

This spellbinding family saga spans five generations. The feisty founder of a Los Angeles newspaper empire arrives in a dusty cow town and builds a four-page rag into a mighty media conglomerate.

"Gardner's robust saga provides crackling entertainment." (Publishers Weekly)

ISBN: 0-9627297-0-1; 600 PAGES; $23.45

THE REAL SLEEPER

The Real Sleeper is the story of Edgar Wellington, a book editor pushing sixty and afraid love has passed him by forever. Then Kelly O'Leary, beautiful, sensuous, tenderhearted, steps into his life. An enchanting story that will captivate your imagination as it reaches deep into your soul.

"His skillful use of dialogue, his well-rounded characters and plot development make for a contemporary novel that is both well written and interesting to read." (The Allentown Morning Call)

ISBN: 0-9627297-8-7; 229 PAGES; $14.95

SOMETHING NICE TO SEE; illustrated by Peter Hamlin

This delightful story of tolerance is set during the creation of the awe-inspiring Watts Towers. Some 30 years in the making, the Watts Towers are this country's most spectacular and enduring folk-art monuments. Illustrator Peter Hamlin has captured their unique whimsy with magical full-color drawings.

This is the story of Barry, a lad who arouses resentment in his classmates because he can do something they cannot. He can read! Fatherless, he finds inspiration from the gentle folk wisdom of an Italian immigrant, Sam Rodia, creator of the astonishing Watts Towers.

"Lovely and charming...right-minded, and so good for the children." (Marvin Bileck, Caldecott Medalist for *Rain Makes Applesauce*)

ISBN: 0-9627297-6-0; UNPAGED, FULL COLOR; $15.95

LOTUSLAND: A PHOTOGRAPHIC ODYSSEY

Lotusland is one of the most unique gardens in the world. This spectacular book eloquently chronicles the gardens and the life story of the eccentric Madame Ganna Walska, the legendary woman who spent more than forty years and untold millions developing these gardens. This hauntingly beautiful book contains more than 280 photographs, 233 in color, taken over a period of 100 years.

> *"Containing by far the most breathtaking photography of any book this season,* Lotusland *is an exquisitely executed work of art."* (San Diego Union-Tribune)
>
> ISBN: 0-9627297-5-2; 144 PAGES; $65.00

CALIFORNIA GARDENS: By Winifred Starr Dobyns

This long-awaited reprint of *California Gardens* is significant to lovers of fine gardens and landscape historians everywhere. Better than any other source book, *California Gardens* beautifully documents the garden images that Californians selected for themselves in the first two decades of this century.

> *"My favorite [garden book of the season] is* California Gardens: *in refreshing black and white, it shows gardens from the Golden Age of California estates that will send many landscape architects back to the drawing board and bring on hopeless fantasies in gardeners like me with our 50-by-150-foot lots."* (Los Angeles Times)
>
> ISBN: 1-888310-88-X; 231 PAGES; $55.00

SOUTHERN CALIFORNIA GARDENS: AN ILLUSTRATED HISTORY
By Victoria Padilla

Originally published by University of California Press (1961), *Southern California Gardens* is the prime source book for horticulture historians and landscape preservationists. The only work of its kind, it is a comprehensive and engaging overview of more than two centuries of horticulture—and the plants, people, nurseries, parks and gardens that contributed to the greening of a mild-climate coastal desert.

> *"Though written nearly 40 years ago, this gardening classic is anything but dry or dusty...a real page turner."* (Sunset magazine)
>
> ISBN: 0-9627297-1-X; 384 PAGES; $39.95

Allen A. Knoll, Publishers books are available through your favorite bookstore or library, or directly from the publisher. To order, please call (800) 777-7623, or send a check for the titles desired, plus $3.00 shipping to:

Allen A. Knoll, Publishers
777 Silver Spur Road, Suite 116
Rolling Hills Estates, CA 90274

For a free catalog of Knoll Publishers complete titles, please call or write to the above.